JAYIDA

Natacha Pavlov

I am the way and the truth and the life. No one comes to the Father except
through me.
—Jesus (John 14:6)

CONTENTS

CHAPTER ONE

JAYIDA

SPRING 533 AD – BANU SA'D, NORTHWEST HIJAZ

"Is it true that what is not remembered is lost?"

Crouching with her fists overflowing with purslane, Jayida lifted her inquisitive frown to her parents foraging with her nearby. Their grey mare Kamila stood close, while their calm flocks of camels, fat-tailed Awassi sheep, and long-eared black Hijazi goats grazed all around, protectively encircling them in the blessed pastures of the lush Wadi Al-Wafra.

"That's a very good question," said her father Zahir, his dark contemplative gaze radiating with pride.

"That's what some say, but I hope not," said her mother Zoraya with a solemn air. Her mother's undyed cream dress sprawled around her slim form, making a perfect—fertile—moonlike pool around her.

Pinching her lips together, Jayida looked away, and shoved the leafy *rejleh* purslane stems in her Bag of Treasures draped across her torso as she held back angry, frustrated tears. That had to be wrong, too, Jayida thought as she tried to cheerfully focus on selecting more plants for their collection. Evading the thorns of the *arak* branches that doubled as mouth-cleaning chewing sticks, she gathered small, fragrant flowers helpful for digestion, and clusters of juicy red fruits, a pungent treat whether fresh or dried.

After all, she knew some things, when she'd lived through eight springs and was now old enough to spend more time with her father, as most boys did around that age, and began practicing the prime manly virtues of *muruwa*. Bravery being foremost, her father encouraged her to be bold and say what she thought. And even as she had much more to learn, she at least knew that the *kahina* had been wrong to tell her half Taghlib-half Tayyi mother that *al-'ayn* was on her, that evil eye barring her mother's monthly feminine flow—and longed-for descendants.

Even Moharib, her father's older brother, had tried to add to that darkness with his vile words that had echoed doubt in her mother's abilities. That was more than enough for many a *badawi* to shed blood over threats at their prized bloodline.

But instead of going by the ancient and common code of an eye for an eye, her father had marked his limit by choosing to leave his tribe the Banu Zubayd—residing at the famed Tayma—for the Banu Sa'd, led by his beloved friend *sayyid* Aziz. She'd never forget that it was also the first time her father had felt he could relate to some of Shanfara's verses, that rebellious *su'luk* bandit poet whose blade-sharp rhymes chose loyalty to the desert over his tribe who'd rejected him.

Jayida derives from "the knowing one." But for your protection, you'll be Jonder to the world; your true name and person hidden, protecting you from the effect of al-'ayn, her father's words echoed.

And as your brave, respected deeds grow, weakening al-'ayn and restoring the balance in your favor, you'll know the right time to reveal your secret true name, said her mother with her usual loving, trusting glow. It was reassuring to imagine her parents—her father from a northwestern tribe and her mother from an northeastern one—as an eternal pillar of one love that defeated any obstacle in their way.

Jayida took some precious golden frankincense tears from her pouch. The chalky film covered her fingers as she rubbed, smelled, and looked them over. Each time, it humbled her to have these far-traveled treasures from the south to offer as tokens of appeasing thanks for the day's plant findings. Then, with a hint of lingering conflict, she dropped them into scattered cracks and openings.

Though her father never spoke of it nor said a bad word about Moharib, Jayida wondered if she was failing in her test when she sometimes felt so angry at him; the mangled, shadowy sight of his *jinni* in her night visions worse than all the shattering screams...

But some of it also had to be the other *jinn* of the ancient volcanic land they dwelled on, whose boundaries ran north-south and extended east to the nearby oasis of Khaybar. Oddly, lately she'd been worrying more about the mysterious hills that hid potential dormant eruptions.

"Having those bad dreams again?" said her father.

Jayida nodded. "*Na'am*, on and off."

It was strangely familiar by now: seeing those Najranite, Rûm, Aksumite, and Fars priests, and the wailing faces of men, women, and children. These followers of the crucified Yassu—who'd been massacred by the Israelite Dhu Nuwas far south in Zafar, San'a, and Najran shortly before she was born—had come to feel like shadowy companions. From ever since she could remember, it was often as if she'd been there herself, witnessing all its violence in horrifyingly vivid night visions. To shake off the dread, she tried each time to think of *Negus* Kaleb's counter expedition sailing across the Red Sea that soon followed, right around the time of her birth.

With Yassu's help, Negus Kaleb sailed from Adulis with over 100,000 men and seventy vessels, but not even Dhu Nuwas's trade blockades and iron chain to prevent landing could stop him from triumphantly entering—she'd soothe herself with the miraculous tale.

"It must be your guardian angel guiding your *qareen* and helping to refine your *noos*, especially if you take after your gifted grandmother Rania—may she be at peace—and your *Umm* Jarida before her," said her mother.

Jayida's frown deepened.

"What is it?" said her mother, worry creeping into her doe eyes.

"Is it true that some people are destined for good fortune while others are ill-fated? Even with our *qareen* as constant companion?" said Jayida.

"That's also what some *badawi* say. But we don't want you taking to that dramatic, fatalistic talk that'll wear down your spirit," said her father, his slightly rising strong shoulders barely hiding his mounting concern.

"But if *al-ilah* knows everything, then he must know what happens?" said Jayida.

"*Sah*, that's what makes him God," said her mother.

"So he wanted for Moharib to say what he did, and for me to be like this, constantly watched by his lurking *'ayn*. But what if I suffer divine judgment for the lie? An ordeal by fire—like the martyrs?" Jayida stopped, swallowed back a surging sob.

"Oh no, my heart! Come here," her mother whispered tearfully with open arms. Jayida went and dropped before her parents, their arms wrapping tightly around her as they'd first done in a nearby cave eight winters before. Her father's strong, large hand laid protectively on her head as they embraced.

"Don't even think it, my lion eyes!" he said, keeping his tone low. "I don't know about any ordeal by fire, or about this great authority some give to martyrs. But I know he had no right to say what he did, and while we're not that revengeful kind, *he's* the one who should be concerned for the consequence of his misled ways!"

"And I for one am glad that in these eight springs he hasn't dared shown his face here, although we still wouldn't reject him," her mother said, rubbing her arms as she reigned in her own storm. "So now, let us say it again together as one."

"The *kahina* was wrong."

The resonating whisper wrapped them like another secret warm blanket as they repeated it three times. For a moment they wallowed in the emotion, the wave of relief washing over her reflected in their own strengthening smiles.

"*Aywa*; let's finish up," said her mother.

"*Yallah*, let's go! Sabah, Katifa—Hania! *Yallah*, Hania! Don't make me come get you!" called her father to their respective mounts who liked to lead the proud caravan, and whose kin back at camp totaled nearly three thousand camels.

Jayida beamed as her beloved Hania finally emerged, her own grin proclaiming she knew to vanish and reappear right on time. Hania had proven a perfectly quick learner, when not long before Jayida had to gently but firmly put her in place, lest she become too clingy and constantly invade her space, as many a young camel might do unless disciplined. In the cases when the flock bickered with each other, Jayida was all too glad to let them be and rarely intervened, letting them resolve their rank issues that eased their rearing.

As they led Kamila and the rest of the flocks, Jayida glanced up towards a stretch of massive hills, searching out the hidden cave where she'd been born. As he'd so often recited to her, she imagined her father holding her and looking into the storming valley waving its veils of rain, as he cooed a verse from the holy *injil* of the Israelites and Yassu followers: *You are my son, today I have become your father.*

By the time they'd returned to camp, the valley was drenched and promising vegetation within days, the seeds that had sat for so long, faithfully waiting for the abundant pouring, finally ready to burst in perfect timing. So was newborn Jonder presented and celebrated amidst the flourishing grounds—perhaps not unlike the Garden of Eden the Israelites and Yassu-loving *Masihi* spoke of, said her parents—as the celebratory feast went on for days.

That had to be why she felt safe speaking of uneasy things there, in the heart of the blessed Wadi Al-Wafra that took care of all its guests. In respect to the privacy and sacred nature of birth, no one would dare ask—nor most parents reveal—exactly where their child had been born. So while the valley already soothed both nearby desert-dwelling and passing *badawi* with its faithful filling up of precious seasonal rains and plants, it had the additional magic of sharing in her secret.

Thus Jayida dared to think that the valley took pride in feeding their Zahir camels, so named after her beloved father, as much for his generosity as for his breeding of easy, strong milkers of liquid gold milk, and lean racing choice beasts. Naturally, the consecrated, unridden ones to be given as sacrifice were also perfect and blemish-free. Soon, they would shed their woolen coats to face the summer heat, and replenish themselves and their owners' garment collection in time for the colder seasons.

They returned to camp, filled their clay jars with camel milk, and had a quick meal of flatbread and some of her favorite sour buttermilk. Jayida relished the tangy taste of the *makhid allaban*, letting it strengthen her bones like Shamshun's, the strongest of Israelites beloved by *al-ilah*.

She finished, and with her father's encouraging nod, she disappeared to their sleeping quarters and returned with her short bow and quiver draped around her. She straightened her robes and headdress, hoping she looked more confident than she felt.

"Have fun, and remember: you're getting better each day," said her mother with a kiss to her forehead. "Meanwhile I'll proudly replenish our stock with your findings."

With a nod, they left and rejoined the *sayyid*'s son Nasr, and his cousins Sufyan and young Shams, who stood next to his older brother holding his bow a bit too proudly. Jayida met Nasr's piercing smirk and suspected their shared thought. Though Nasr was three years older than her, it reassured her that it had been happening more often between them.

"My bold Shams insisted, so he'll be our cheerful patron," shrugged Sufyan, although she guessed that their mother had been just as commanding. Samira would surely take advantage of any little time that Sufyan was around. At seventeen, he spent increasingly less time at camp and secretly told Nasr—who then confided to her—that he might leave and marry outside of the tribe. Though it was usually women who left their tribe to be with their husbands, all kinds of arrangements existed. Shams, about two springs younger than her, already seemed unlike his brother, and as energetic as the sun deity he was named after.

"*Maniha*, good," said her father with a smile.

They headed to their designated area at the southwestern edge of camp, marked by a thin tent for shade, scattered sandbags, and straw-stuffed forms propped up on red acacia poles. Jayida wasn't sure what to think when *sayyid* Aziz would tease and say that this species of acacia were once possessed by *jinn*. Wouldn't it have been best to choose another kind instead? But thrill lit up his eyes, as if empowered to own their previous homes without fear of their possible revenge.

"You know the routine: focus on the target and shoot. Shams and I will be right here, cheering for you and ready with blessed water," grinned her father.

He settled under the low tent and Shams reluctantly sat beside him, frowning in lingering envious curiosity.

"Don't pout, little brother; your time will come soon enough," said Sufyan as they walked off closer to the targets ten paces away. "So young and already so eager to please his mother, like he doesn't have his whole life ahead of him," he mumbled.

"And remember, Jonder," her father's deep tone drifted to her.

"*Sah*: relax, rest, and release," she said, trying to stifle her lurking frustration.

They stopped, each faced a target, and let a momentary silence engulf them. Sufyan took aim without a word and hit the center of the target as though it was the easiest thing in the world. He continued and Nasr followed, releasing his shot with the knotty rope bracelet tied around his wrist to ward off the evil eye.

Nasr had recently fallen sick again, draining his strength, as it had several times in the past. Once again, the panic spread like wildfire, and though no one dared say it, it had crossed all their minds: the work of *al-'ayn*. Once more, his mother Warda despaired and *sayyid* Aziz had shaved his head in humble penitent offering for his son's health, though he did it so often that one could almost think him as naturally bald. Yet each time they had also sent for *mubassir* Ayyub, and he'd come all the way from Jabiyah in Al-Sham, full of stories of the Ghassanids, the market, swords, wines, and the Bosra Cathedral—built in the time of the true Rûm believer *Qaysar* Anastasius—with its majestic pointed dome glorifying the Al-Sham region. With faithful Ghassanid soldiers at his side, he'd come to recite sacred scripture from the *injil* on Yassu, and *memre* homilies and poetry dedicated to Yassu by Saint Ephrem and Mar Jacob of Serugh. And every time the missionary's faith in the blessed *al-Masih*, son of Maryam, fended off the lurking, malicious *jinn*, the proof seen in each triumphant recovery over these tests of Fate. Jayida marveled at Nasr's enduring strength, and wanted to feel and be as relaxed and confident as he and his cousin seemed.

Shaking off her sweeping tension radiating from her core, she lightly tugged back at the string, considering the bow's flexibility and strength—thankfully easier to use than the longer, clumsier bows. She reached behind her for an arrow, placed it above her middle finger, and rested it above her opposite hand. Keeping her thumb down, her little finger yielded to the three main fingers. Her thumb pulled back to rest against her cheekbone, and she tentatively pulled the string back several times, each time hoping that her hand wouldn't ball up in a knuckle instead of staying flat. Holding in a grunt, she finally released, her hand locking in on itself as the arrow flew off straight into the ground.

"Not all arrows are meant to strike, just remember to open," said her father, his large fingers encouragingly flying up in guidance.

If they were not all meant to strike, then why did they exist? For reluctant, stiff hands like hers that struggled against her will! With a sigh Jayida reached for another arrow, forcing herself to remember that this was not just practice, but early practice. She loosened her shoulders and arms with a shake as Nasr passed her an understanding grin. Would they still be as supportive if they knew that she was a girl, or given up hope long ago? But she wanted to push and know too, and though Shams was still young, his yearning and frustration were at times uncomfortable reminders of her own internal struggle.

She caught herself stiffening again, and it dawned on her that easing that might be the hardest. She reloaded, loosely, letting the tension drift to her elbow. With her fingers hooked around the string and hand somehow staying flat, she fixed on the target and released, her fingers straightening open after the arrow. Thin as a strip of leather, it flew swiftly into the side of the target, surprising her with its lightning speed.

"Jonder ibn Zahir!" thundered Sufyan approvingly, referring to her in the traditional patronymic.

"Well done, Jonder! Soon, you'll outdo us all," said Nasr, as an echo of praising shouts rang out.

"I don't know about that, but at least I'm not breaking the string or punching myself anymore," Jayida laughed. Being around his calm, supporting manner made her feel safe, not unlike his father who'd welcomed her parents to the tribe.

"Whoever says they haven't done that is lying," Nasr chuckled, and launched another that hit dead center.

"May *al-ilah* keep my eager brother from being among them," chuckled Sufyan in a low tone. Tall and ruggedly handsome in his way, he had a playful, but sometimes too easy approach that surprisingly contrasted Shams's seriousness. "If that's the way Fate wants it, perhaps *he'll* make our mother happy," Sufyan mumbled again, and she had the uncomfortable impression that they shouldn't be hearing this. Selfishly, she'd never longed for a sibling, wanting it to remain as they were, and in such moments she was even more grateful not to expect any.

She looked to her father waving a cloth as a cheerful banner and Shams clapping, and returned a wave in thanks. It did feel good to make her first strike, and if she could do it once, she could do it again. Despite her constant fear of failing, her father was right that practice made perfect. Though tiring and painful by the end of each session, starting her bow training this early for a while each day would change her muscle shape, thicken her right shoulder, and make her right forearm stronger. It was all in the proper process of discipline that would pay off in time.

"So, our future *sha'ir*, what will you recite us today?" said Sufyan, launching one into a massive sandbag.

"I haven't planned anything," shrugged Nasr as he released, his arrow intentionally flying off wildly.

"We are but your humble audience," yelled her sharp-eared father, raising a waterskin towards them then taking a swig.

"*Sah*, oh spiritual kin to Imru Al-Qays; we trust your mysterious tongue's gift," said Sufyan, and flicked his tongue at him.

"The tongue is just one tool, not the source," chuckled Nasr.

Named after the eagle deity, Nasr's wisdom often made him sound older than his eleven years. No wonder he was the next *sha'ir*, keeper of the tribe's history, even if his father was *sayyid* Aziz. His sister Yazida was a spring younger than her and already a doe-eyed beauty, like a smaller, girl version of him.

"But since it *is* always good to practice, I'll dedicate this to Imru Al-Qays, the Kindite poet-prince who inspires us all, and whose family has greatly suffered in the events I'll now recall."

While most poets took inspiration from Imru, whose two-part form often served as a model for other *'arabi*-speaking *badawi* poets, Nasr didn't hesitate to reverse the order and themes, and add or even repeat segments to create his odes. Instead of the *nasib* opening section, Nasr began with the second rhyming *rahil* boasting segment, praising his Banu Sa'd tribe, starting with his birth. He raised his bow and, following his lead, together they took aim and released an arrow after each recital, indicating both a pause and a transition.

Her jaw clenched when he took a deep breath, then began the descriptive second intense *rahil* segment, speaking of their fathers' shared march northeast to Kutha a few years before her birth. Along with tribesmen of Tha'laba, Mudar, and other tribes, they'd answered the call of the southern Yassu-loving ruler Ma'dikarib Ya'fur of Himyar. As vassal to *Negus* Kaleb of Aksum, it'd been his fervent Christian display of his kingdom's shifting loyalty to the Rûm Empire as opposed to the Fars, and an opportunity to assist *badawi* revolting against the infernal Lakhmid ruler Al-Mundhir, then vassal of the Fars *Shah* Kavadh. All the better if their incursion helped the Kindite King Al-Harith in securing the throne of Al-Hira, and ousting Al-Mundhir in the process.

Though it'd been a moment of great pride for her father, the rare times he spoke of it it was as though he still felt like he'd foolishly missed his opportunity. From the moment he'd finally laid eyes on Al-Mundhir, who'd been endowed with great authority over the northeastern *badawi* tribes, her father knew at last that the horrible stories about him were true. At first Zahir had been impressed by the mix of foreign troops and fire-loving Magian cataphracts, the fighters and horses' heavy silver armor glinting across the burning desert. But when the frowning *ghul* emerged on his horse, his hooked nose and hard, stone-like features as if disgusted at what lay before him, Zahir knew he was unworthy of their service—from local *badawi* to Indians who'd moved to the area, as much for fighting as for backbreaking work in the nearby copper and silver mines.

From her father's memory she could feel the icy reach of Al-Mundhir's dead eyes, heavier than all the combined quality steel armor adorning the fighters. Then, with a screeching rallying cry Al-Mundhir had charged off like a rabid beast, swinging his sword as if competing with everyone else on the number of slain men.

And then, what Zahir had both dreaded and yearned for at last came: in the midst of battle he caught the Nasrid zeroing in on him, reeking of rage as he raced at full speed. Would he, Zahir son of Gayas, have the honor of slaying him, clashing so fervently he'd cast him off his horse and down, deep into the hungry earth where he belonged? It was like something about Al-Mundhir brought out the worst impulsive *jahl* in him, but as *muruwa* required, he would stand his ground while maintaining his *hilm*, monitoring his patient self-restraint just enough to ensure his primeval survival.

Staring back at the beast, Zahir had braced himself to meet his blow and face him in single-hand combat... when at the last moment his metallic horse flew past him, the belligerent demon striking instead at a man next to him with such wrath he feared the man was done for. Unrelenting, Zahir had jumped to his help, his fearlessness taking over at the dawning fact that Al-Mundhir, by a strange turn of fate, hadn't actually attacked him. But Zahir was far from the only one wanting to fight the Nasrid of Lakhm—and possibly gain the honor of taking him down—and soon Al-Mundhir retreated—surprisingly, it was agreed—as his friend Samaw'al, the gifted poet of Tayma, and throngs of others closed in on the enemy. Such had been her father's fateful meeting of *sayyid* Aziz, who'd been struck instead of him, and whose gratitude and *sayyid* status added weight to his nearly endless praise of him, transforming them into three nearly inseparable friends.

And *al-ilah* had kept being on his side—something Jayida was sure Moharib hated—when the experience also yielded the meeting of her mother as they made their way back and were hosted by the Banu Taghlib. Shortly after, Ma'dikarib

Ya'fur had honored their march with an inscription, but when he died, persecution of Yassu believers swept through the south.

Stifling the already wrongful secret that eventually caused her parents' relocation, her core muscles tightened at the later massacre of Najran. It was soon after, on the year of her birth, that *Negus* Kaleb from Aksum invaded Himyar to overthrow Dhu Nuwas, and restored the destroyed Zafar Cathedral, built centuries before by Theophilos.

Weaving simple, yet vividly effective rhyme after rhyme, Nasr laid out events she'd been too young to remember, but made up some of his earliest memories. The rhythmic flow and fluctuating emotional tones lulled them each into their own reveries through sad and joyful elegies. Though it would take time before Nasr composed his final long and rhyming *qasidah*, he'd clearly already been organizing his poetic subjects and images for the honorable task. There was a playfulness to his rejection of form and rules, as though he could do anything in the moment and still win his audience's approval. Something about his friendly, confident defiance made her proud to have him as a helper and friend.

They launched arrows and Nasr went on about the new Rûm *Qaysar* Justinian, who'd nearly fled his throne in the recent Nika riots, then pacified some agitators with gold, and had his generals Belisarius and Mundus end the affair by indiscriminately massacring remaining rebels. Taking after his uncle and predecessor *Qaysar* Justin who'd favored *Negus* Kaleb's intervention in Himyar, *Qaysar* Justinian had also sent embassies to *Negus* Kaleb at Aksum to strengthen their Yassu-loving alliance against the Fars and their Lakhmid allies. Nasr also sent well-wishes to the headstrong general-turned-King Abraha in Himyar, who'd rebelled and overthrown *Negus* Kaleb's chosen leader for Himyar and appointed himself as king in his place. If nothing else, its success proved Abraha was able to earn men's loyalty.

Amidst all the changes of ancient empires around them, Nasr's shifting, plaintive tone echoed her disgust of the unrelenting *ghul* that was Al-Mundhir. While her father's experience was enough to make her despise Al-Mundhir, he'd only kept adding to his reputation as a bloodthirsty entity. Her heart pounding amidst Nasr's verses, she tried to calm herself by flicking her arrow's feathers, but horror shook her with his long list of despicable acts.

Nasr aimed to the sky this time, and they each let it fly, and with an emotional sigh he continued into the *rithā'* lamenting segment on the poet Imru's family. A few years after her birth, Al-Mundhir had finally been expelled from the capital of Al-Hira by the Kindite King Al-Harith. In that time, the Kindite Al-Harith ruled over Banu Taghlib and Banu Bakr, and even gave his daughter Hind in marriage to Al-Mundhir, surely in hopes of placating his prior enemy by becoming family.

But it was short-lived, when undeterred Al-Mundhir eventually regained the city and killed the Kindite Al-Harith, along with fifty other member of the Kindah royal family. Jayida could just imagine Al-Mundhir's glee, devastating Kindah's power while killing the famed poet Imru's grandfather in the process. Tribes were split up, and Imru's father Hujr had since been granted rule of the Banu Asad and Banu Ghatafan.

They took aim again, and she imagined with all her might that it was Al-Mundhir who stood before them. Her arrow flew into the neck, no satisfaction that in the midst of this he'd kidnapped a large group of *Masihi* nuns and sacrificed them to the goddess Al-Uzza. Innocent, helpless girls and women, ripped from their homes to die such a horrible death. What if that had been her? What would she have done in such a terrifying situation? It was certain: if there was one man she hated, it was Al-Mundhir, and she couldn't wait for his Fate to turn—be it from *al-ilah*, Manat, Al-Lat, another deity, or from none other than Imru himself, to avenge his grandfather's and their kin's murders, and free his aunt Hind from his twisted grip.

"But as Fate wanted it, something unexpected happened, and his name was Al-Harith ibn Jabalah, from the Jafnid royal house of Ghassan," perked up Nasr, kicking off the final boasting *rahil* segment to close the chaotic ride.

About four springs back, Julian Ben Sabar, a Samaritan messianic leader in the Holy Land, had declared himself king of Israel. With his Samaritan army he'd launched a war to create their own independent state, murderously ravaging through the land from Scythopolis down to Bethlehem. The ruthless violence shook her like those of Najran, with accounts of destroyed churches, and *Masihi* priests and believers hacked to death, then burned with relics of beloved saints.

In response, *Qaysar* Justinian had called on the Ghassanids as *foederati*, and with the Jafnid Al-Harith's help the revolt was finally put down two springs ago, leaving thousands dead or enslaved. For his brave victory, the Jafnid Al-Harith was bestowed the greatest honor ever granted to any non-Rûm client in their service. He was made *malik* of the vast region of Al-Sham by *Qaysar* Justinian, set on securing the empire's eastern borders from invasions by the Fars *Shah* Khosrow and his ally Al-Mundhir.

Supplanting the Tanukh and Salih *foederati* tribes who'd served the Rûm in past generations, the new title granted *malik* Al-Harith great authority over all the northern tribes on Rûm territory, along with a *salaria* to ensure military protection against Al-Mundhir's greedy raids. A follower of Yassu with a heart as kind as it was proud of his ancestors' ancient origins, *malik* Al-Harith even made agreements with tribes far beyond their Ghassanid boundaries like the Tayyi, and their kin the Aws and Khazraj at Yathrib. Accounts praised the increased security of the trade routes, thanks to his Ghassanid troops strategically posted to protect caravans and collect taxes.

Malik Al-Harith's brother *malik* Abu Karib had also been granted authority over the province their father Jabalah had ruled, from the southern Holy Land to parts of the northern Hijaz. All this imperial favor, yielding marvelous construction of buildings, weapon factories, and vast dedicated *hima* territories full of camels and glorious war horse reserves, inspired as much admiration as jealousy from some envious of this strong, united brotherly duo.

They aimed their last arrow and hit the central target as one. Jayida wished people could find a way to live alongside each other without bloodshed, but the violence from these events shook her too much to be indifferent to the plight of the Yassu believers. The more she heard stories the more it seemed that they were the most persecuted, starting with Yassu's gruesome death. It was as if something about them made everyone want to turn on them, and she both wanted and dreaded to know why. Like her father's stories, hearing about *malik* Al-Harith's brave achievements that brought security filled her with a mix of relief and wondrous fascination.

"Someday you should go to their court at Jabiyah and recite your poetry there," Jayida said as they gathered their arrows.

"And we'll gladly come with you and roam those glorious hills of the Golan, on their war horses, of course," winked Sufyan.

"Maybe, but the tribe does fine as my court, too," said Nasr, his humility touching her.

They headed back to camp, her aching muscles reminding that she was doing well and growing in her skill each day. In the late afternoon, they gathered around the visiting *mubassir* Ayyub.

"How it gladdens my heart to see this flock congregated around me," he said, his deep voice radiating with sincerity each time.

The learned elder, with shaggy grey hair and a long beard that rested on his dark robes, was wrapped in a mysteriously welcoming air of authority. His deep piercing gaze lit up when he spoke of the *injil* on Yassu, passionate and zealous like he'd lived those events himself and had no doubt of their truth. That he, a man who lived the life of angels with other monks, depriving himself of comforts while not only surrounded by, but fed like daily bread by reading the holy texts, had made the long journey to them was a privilege they were all aware of and could not pass up.

"Let us begin with passages about my namesake, the holy book of Ayyub, which are among the favorites of *malik* Al-Harith." He took out his small book from his robes, a worn leather cover wrapped around velvety, cream-colored double leaves of parchment pages made for years of usage. "There was a man in the land of Uz," he said, the verses of the *injil* flowing from him as he closed his eyes. From time to time, his eyes opened, glancing at the page with the written word of *al-ilah*. He did not need the book to remember, for he'd memorized it, and as his words spilled freely, it was clear that the few pages couldn't contain the full story, just bits and pieces. Even so, he held it with such care that anyone would guess, and be curious of, its important contents. "So Ayyub died, being old and full of days," he said, the story leaving them once more as shaken as inspired by the tale of the man whose faith, though sorely tested, ultimately triumphed.

While each time this Bringer of Good News had been summoned by *sayyid* Aziz and Warda to attend to Nasr, his care was such that he often spent his whole days talking to everyone and trying to convince them of the importance of hearing and learning more about the *injil*. Jayida was already grateful for his constant help when Nasr's health weakened, and when he sat with them to share the memorized holy passages, he seemed almost untouchable, as if he'd appeared to them from another time and place.

"Our church may have many enemies, even *Qaysar* Justinian himself. And yet, in His perfectly mysterious ways, the Lord has given us the Believing Queen in none other than his wife, the blessed Empress Theodora," said *mubassir* Ayyub, scanning to catch every eye. "Like her, be bold of heart, as Saint Ephrem and Mar Jacob of Serugh also praised of the Canaanite woman in their homilies. Though she sensed her unworthiness, she insisted for the crumbs of a dog, entreating Yassu's unfailingly generous nature."

Was this what her parents meant, when they said her secret would be forgiven—their bold measure a test of their faith, like Nasr with his health? She knew that her situation was different, even with some of the *mubassir*'s strange tales of Pelagia the Penitent of Antioch, Marina the Monk, and Matrona of Perge; all women who'd escaped their fates by dressing as men and living out their simple, self-sacrificing humble days in monasteries and caves in far-off deserts. Upon noticing their reluctant yet amused demeanors, the Yassu-loving missionary always insisted that they were true and beloved popular tales, especially among the Rûm.

It was a great sacrifice and challenge, especially for a woman to make, *mubassir* Ayyub said. While Jayida agreed with that part, she concluded that it was their unusual rarity that made them popular, and maybe inspired other versions, confusing her as much as others what was true or false. More importantly, that her father thought differently enough from Moharib—and others like him—to make such a decision for her often felt like a kind of triumph in a way she couldn't explain. And like the Canaanite woman, it was comforting to think that things could be asked of *al-ilah*, and sometimes even granted.

"Much toil in this world is a curse, as the account of Adam and Hawa and the Book of Steps remind us, but we should never forget or stop looking for Him. Flee from the many heresies, especially that of Nestorius, who says Yassu has two natures when he has only One, undivided divine *and* human nature! Flee also that of Mani, that false, self-proclaimed prophet who claimed to be the heir of Buddha, Zoroaster, and Yassu! But Yassu himself warned about the many false prophets that would come. And likewise remember wise Ibrahim, and do not put your trust in lifeless idols. As I come to you as a balm to your wounds, believe the *injil* told in our blessed Syriac language that is the oldest in the world—and which I faithfully translate to you in your *'arabi*," he beamed.

Jayida often struggled with what he said, some of which didn't make sense. It seemed cruel for an angel to touch the mouth of a man with a hot coal, even if it was consuming, fiery medicine to remove his guilt, as the book of Isha'yah said, and Saint Ephrem recited about in his poem on the Eucharist. And how to tell things apart when men were easily misled? In her longing curiosity she'd once wondered if she should tell him about her night visions of her striking Aksumite princess guardian angel, as much to share the happy sight of her beauty as to try to understand it better.

Seeing her was always a breathtaking sight: her piercing warm gaze, glowing, coppery skin, adorned in a glistening robe covered in bright pearls, rubies, and emeralds. She wore layers of gold necklaces and bracelets, complementing the massive dazzling crown on her head. In her hand rested a radiating golden disc with a carved cross, like a pulsating sun. But Jayida's selfish wish to keep it to herself, along with her parents' concern that the missionary might dislike it, confirmed her in saying nothing.

Just as it was a listener's task to decipher the meaning of a poem, when she didn't understand she shrugged it off, preferring to return to Nuh's arc filled with all the pairs of animals, Musa leading his people across the Red Sea, and Danyal saved by *al-ilah* from the lions' den. Sometimes she would whisper to her mother to ask him to recite about them again, and along with Yassu, her favorites of Shamshun and Mikha'il, who kicked *shaytan* and his demons out of Paradise.

Pleased at the requests, he'd cite verses from the eulogy by Abba Severus the Great, praising the angel Mikha'il. *Mubassir* Ayyub always proudly reminded that despite his exile in Egypt, Abba Severus remained the Patriarch of Antioch, the ancient city where the followers of Yassu were first called *Masihi*. *Al-ilah*'s divine favor was clearly with Abba Severus when he'd refused to leave his faith for the belief of *Qaysar* Justin, who then ordered him arrested and his tongue cut off. But the Believing Queen Theodora, even before her marriage to his nephew Justinian, discovered the plans and warned him, allowing his safe escape to Egypt.

"Mikha'il gives strength to the living in their time of need, and for the departed he prays to God to show mercy on them," the *mubassir* summed up Abba Severus's teaching. "And as for our one and only God, remember: There are two sides to the Only-begotten, one concealed and the other revealed. The revealed side is not to be veiled, and the concealed is not to be searched out. *Shaytan*, who is craftier than all, took us from the revealed side, and by the concealed side he choked us, that we might not be revived by the revealed one. Yet all is not lost! For concealed is His concealed side, so that not even Angels know the manner of it. And not only is it so with that Majesty incomprehensible, but all creatures each have two sides, so that one side is revealed and the other side is concealed. Such a mystery! And therefore, who would compare natures which are not like one another in their births: for from all of them is the Nature of Him who created all, different," *mubassir* Ayyub finished with Rhythms on the Faith from Saint Ephrem.

Was everything already planned for her, and everyone else? It would be cruel to be destined a hard life and maybe even death, without any chance at resolution. But their prosperity so far, with Zahir camels blessing—at the very least—the Taghlib and Ghatafan, and roaming at Tayma, Wadi Al-Qura, Khaybar, and Yathrib had to be a good sign. Even the fierce Basus War that had raged for forty winters between the Taghlib and their cousins the Bakr—all because of a Bakri camel who'd been slain for wandering onto Taghlib land—had finally recently been settled at Dhu Al-Majaz near 'Ukaz. Jayida smiled as she imagined them drawing their bows, one on top of the other, and shooting the arrows together as one, the alliance trading their common anger for joy.

So if it was right to dare for more—like her parents, *mubassir* Ayyub, *malik* Al-Harith, *Negus* Kaleb, and King Abraha believed—then what did she have to fear, when time and her guardian were on her side? The thrill of boldness swept through her: she'd be even stronger than Shamshun by wisely guarding her secret until, and only until, she was sure.

CHAPTER TWO

AYYAM AL-ZALAM

SPRING 536 AD

Surrender! There's no escape!

The towering, monstrous leering mountain commanded, its smoky flaring nostrils suffocating the air, paralyzing. The consuming stare sought Jayida's, the sneering doom relishing her helplessness. Dread snaked through her blood at the sweeping realization that she wasn't strong enough to hold it off and ease its eternal, tortuous grip on her.

Somehow, she looked away, the deafening wailing screams of burning bodies piercing through her bones, calling forth endless shattered souls. What had she done to end up there? How to get out? Restraining her pounding heart, she fought creeping tears, hating the familiar desperate fear.

With a start, Jayida awoke and sat up in the darkness, her chest damp and heart racing under her long *qamis* robe. She glanced west to the tied, thick blanket separators that blocked the entrance leading to the other quarters. Her father protectively slept closest to it should anyone dare to enter, and kept his sword and shield he'd used at Kutha nearby for added protection. Next to it to the east, the separator marked their bathing area ahead—containing multiple jars of water that some said were spirit conduits—yet seemed equally undisturbed.

Still as a betyl, she waited. There was only their breathing and their sleeping animals' in their own quarters beyond. In the lingering silence, she glimpsed the shape of her father, with her mother in the middle sleeping as soundly. She looked away to the opposite tent wall at her side. Even in the darkness she could make out her collection of smooth white and dove blue stones, and her audience of figurines that made up her small shrine.

The onlooking gathering consisted of Shamshun's lion, carved by her father from alum rock salt from Tayma. Using the same rock, he'd made her a camel, horse, ibex, a feminine figure of the Tanukhid Queen Mawiyya, and a Hand-Up Woman with raised arms, their bodies as translucent as the lion's. There was also a human form of Yassu as a shepherd that her father made out of obsidian from Himyar, and a carved wooden cross passed down from her *Umm* Jarida to her mother, from when she lived with the Taghlib. That her mother also kept the jar of her afterbirth, safely stashed away in a dug pit, was another reassuring precious link to her life before crossing into the world. Jayida raised a hand out to her audience, invisibly touching them at a distance, and thanked them for their presence.

Her gaze drifted next to them, where rested the glorious metal pile of a boy's chainmail shirt. It was one of the two her parents had placed her in as a baby, making a silver cradle. When men would give nearly all that they possessed—or be ready to pillage—to have a protective adult coat of mail, her father had been granted two, proof of her grandfather's boundless generosity. Jayida couldn't wait to be older and strong enough to finally wear this precious armor, gifted to Zahir on his twelfth year by *siddi* Gayas. To think that metalsmiths in Bosra had toiled, creating and assembling each link by link until it gathered as one glorious metal sheet of riveted rings filled her with awe and respect. The persistent longing seized her, promising that she would be safe once she was in it.

Jayida took a deep breath.

"I am brave, and maintain my *hilm*, that most admirable patient self-restraint, as the prime manly virtues of *muruwa* require. The opposite of *majnun badawi* who are *jinn*-possessed and full of untamed impulsive *jahl*, I also demonstrate *sabr*, patience and strength in the face of attack. I'm hospitable, respectful of women and honor, and protective of the weak and orphans." She whispered the honor code to herself, trying to banish her doubt with the image of the perfect, self-controlled *badawi*.

Seized by a strange pull, a moment later she bolted through their sleeping quarters and the women's, then stopped before the entrance in the public area. She untied the central and lower straps, her frown deepening as she went.

Jayida peeked out into the usual obscurity dotted with scattered tents, twilight veering on early morning. Or at least that's what she hoped her constant *qareen* was saying, and not a mischievous, deceiving *jinni*. Her nostrils flared, taking in the unseasonal thick, dry air. Something was there, hovering, and a knot in her stomach tightened at the realization that her recurring nightmare had woken her up again.

No escape!

The terrorizing chaotic images reflooded her soul, shaking her worse than before. Something with a far-off blazing explosion, past the farthest edge of the world, surrounded by water. That nauseating, consuming scent of burning, creeping over skin, demanding to be let in...

Jayida sat cross-legged and waited, watching in the chilly silence, the sky barely lightening up enough to confirm her suspicion. A thick fog blanketed over the land, and while its source was far away, it flaunted its strength by looming over them like a bad omen. When she finally rushed back in and informed her parents, their instantly roused concern echoed her growing fear.

"Let's see what Aziz advises," said her father, and promptly dressed.

Her mother's darkened gaze fixed on her. "I almost don't want to ask, but were you awoken again by certain dark visions?" said Zoraya.

Jayida nodded. "I think something happened, like an explosion," she frowned.

"I'll be back as soon as I can," said Zahir sternly, and left.

Jayida joined her mother in sitting pensively in the women's quarters, and shared a single flatbread and some buttermilk when her father soon reappeared. He lowered himself next to them, a hand on each knee and deep gaze darting back and forth between them.

"A few days ago, *sayyid* Aziz heard reports of clouds of smoke sweeping far beyond the Rûm Empire. They didn't know what to make of it and assumed it would pass, so they kept quiet, preferring not to worry everyone. But with this, and with Jayida's visions that alerted us, I thought it was the right time to tell him about your visions. He already seemed convinced when Nasr surprised us all by suggesting what we've already suspected, which is that you may be *kahin*."

Jayida froze. "Me, a seer? But he's the gifted *sha'ir*, led by his *qareen* to create honorable poetry. Has he seen anything? Do you think he knows—"

"No; no one has, and I couldn't tell if he was more proud or relieved about your possible case," smiled her father. "With all that, Aziz requested to keep it between us, at least for the moment, and thinks it's best we take no chances and move to Khaybar, hopefully only for a short while."

"We'll start packing then," nodded her mother, and reached out to firmly grip her hand.

Jayida tensed, at once relieved and disturbed at the curious sense of confirmation of what she'd dreamt. If her night visions weren't a premonition of this, she couldn't explain it. A rattling radiated from deep in her core at this uncontrollable shift. Before, her night visions had been of events that had already happened, like the massacre of Najran and the Ben Sabar revolt. Her throat clamped at the dreadful dawning thought of eventually being pestered with questions. But she forced herself to shake it off: if it came to that, she would simply say what she saw.

"Praise Yassu for your guardian and *qareen* helping to sharpen your *noos*, as uncomfortable as it must be," said her mother, reading her thoughts.

"But she wasn't there," shrugged Jayida.

"Their ways are mysterious. May your army of protectors grow and always show up on time," said her father. Jayida pinched a longing smile, hoping it wouldn't be too long until she saw her Aksumite princess guardian again.

They finished eating and packed woven bags with clothing, blankets, weapons, trinkets, and foods. They covered their camels' hump in woolen blankets, placed cushions to the front and back of it, then saddled them, leaving the clay jars for the strongest mounts.

Jayida saved her bedding and figurines for last, letting her attachment to the Wadi Al-Hamd valley area just west of camp fill her up like a poet ready to recite his *nasib* opening mourning segment. But it was no time to lament: if the *wadi*, already beginning to dry up, filled up with too many people, it was only a matter of time before conflict erupted among competing, and often violently impulsive *badawi*. The impending shortage would likely require seeking water for their flocks even further away, and maybe even involve losing some, or several of them. Their resources and connections at Khaybar would offer more security, and as *sayyid* Aziz said, it was best to take precautions.

With a sigh she gathered her figurines into their designated woven bag, joined it to her bundle of frankincense tears, and secured it on Hania's saddle. Hania stretched her long neck and blew in her face, and Jayida returned her affection with amused petting. She tied her bow on the other side, somewhat reassured that she could better use it if necessary. They dug up their tent spikes, gathered their acacia poles and fabrics, and scattered the weight of these amidst their large flock.

Then, wrapped in the melancholy haze, the tribe faced west and waited in silence. With a solemn look on his bearded face, the stout *sayyid* Aziz rubbed his gold Hand of Miriam amulet hanging around his neck. With his brother Hubala—who was as slim as Aziz was robust—and Nasr at each side of him, he said some grateful words of parting to the empty campsite, and to the beloved Wadi Al-Hamd to the west and Wadi Al-Wafra to the northeast. He finished with gratitude for the peaceful Wadi Al-Raha to the southeast where his parents and kin rested, promising they'd return as soon as possible.

Then he let Nasr recite a shortened *za'n* passage that made a touching caravan departure scene, the odd, thick veil hovering all around calling forth a range of conflicted frowns. At fourteen, Nasr had grown taller and more handsome, a slim version of his father's friendly and wise bearing combined with his mother's gentle beauty. Her parents agreed that he was handsomest between his cousins Sufyan and Shams, and others in the tribe. Jayida secretly thanked her friend for having faith in her and for strengthening them with his verses, no matter their subject. At last, with long sighs and lingering glances, they mounted and headed east to Khaybar.

As usual, *sayyid* Aziz trekked in front, with Nasr at his side and Hubala, Sufyan and Shams close behind. *Sayyida* Warda and ten-year old Yazida, as well as Samira and other women, reclined in their respective *hawdaj*, their riding litter shielding the bizarre, gloomy weather and any unwanted gazes. At the center coursed the large flocks branded with their owners' *wasm*, watched by fellow tribesmen at all sides while she and her parents did the same, keeping a measured distance from the rest of the tribe.

Jayida tried not to see herself and everyone as mere shadows drifting in a faceless land, focusing instead on their secure destination. There echoed a series of high-pitched and deeper cries between Shams and Sufyan, and she welcomed the urge to smile.

"Now even in this mysterious fog, there's no chance of anyone getting lost," winked her father. Their grey mare Kamila, tied alongside her father's mount, snorted, as if sharing their amusement.

The area's flat steppe terrain soon made way to the coal black lava fields of Khaybar. The dark, thick carpets of hardened lava merged with the grey-white sky, at times giving the impression of traveling through a timeless cloud. In the distance lay other, milky-colored volcanoes surrounded by white sands and blue-gray rock, transforming the view with peculiar variety.

They trekked along areas of thick, misshapen rock, some tall, jagged forms looking like they'd been squeezed up and out of the ground like dough. Others gathered into thin clay rows, like rope bundles or strings of spun wool. Further ahead to the east rose Jabal Abyad, the tallest volcano whose shoulders and peak were draped in white volcanic ash, with its matching smaller sister Jabal Bayda rising nearby.

The curious, overwhelming sight reminded Jayida of the tales of the earth before man's creation, the persisting triumph of the all-watching, unseen powers mysteriously suspended everywhere in endless contorted forms. Only they knew when they would burst alive like fire-breathing snakes, and cover the earth with new layers of ash, smoke, and lava, burying and replacing the land and all who dwelt on it.

She shifted in her seat at the thought of the stories from Al-Sham to the north; of bandits who dwelled in the volcanic area of Harrat Al-Harrah, lying in wait for travelers to rob—and worse. Goosebumps prickled through her skin despite the stifling air. Though the scenery appeared vacant, there were always places for looters to hide. Not to forget the floors caving open, swallowing victims into the tunneling grounds below. Just as frightening as the wildlife dwelling underground—even human, if it could still be called that—might be the absence of any help when needed. In this secluded place, with the Banu Murra and Ghatafan out to the west and south of the lava fields, it seemed one way to disappear without a trace.

"Oh Jonder, do I detect some unkind *jinn* bothering you with unpleasant thoughts?" said her father winking at her mother, their cheerful perceptiveness always somehow catching her at the right time.

"Oh; I was just thinking of the ground opening up, falling in. Being taken away to a hyena's lair, my skull left behind as proof of my passage... or lurking bandits in the ancient Khaybar caves, and at Harrat Al-Harrah and all the others," said Jayida.

"*Sah.* Thankfully, it's a rare thing for that to happen, and if anyone were to fall in, we've got enough long ropes to ward off any of Fate's passing spirits of death."

"My lion-eyed one," cooed her mother through her thick woolen scarf. "As for Harrat Al-Harrah, it's nothing the great *malik* Al-Harith can't handle, amidst everything else. *Al-ilah* knows he's had constant trials, and handles them admirably."

"And that he's a worthy match for Al-Mundhir makes me glad, too. May Yassu protect him," Jayida said, her chest swelling with heartfelt respect. Amidst their unexpected changed circumstances, thinking about them added lightness to their journey. "Someday I'd like to see their church dedicated to saints Sergios and Bakchos at Sergiopolis," she sighed, trying to think of happier prospects.

"Me, too," said Zahir. "It seems there's something powerful about these two Rûm soldiers martyred by their own that draws *badawi Masihi* from all over."

"They say it's the most important pilgrimage center after Jerusalem," said Zoraya. "And while we're at it, we'll also make pilgrimage to the pillar of Saint Sim'an the Stylite."

Jayida smiled at the name, confused yet fascinated by the ascetic who spent much of his life atop a pillar near Aleppo, amidst *malik* Al-Harith's territory. The presence of the revered pillar had to be another source of the Ghassanids' protection.

"Will I ever have some of their famous endurance? How do they so fearlessly march into battle, covered in glorious armor and wielding banners with unwavering resolve?" said Jayida.

"As my child, you already have bravery in you," chuckled her father. "And noble and strong Kamila would surely agree that we all have it in us."

"And the *Masihi* believe what makes the *injil* stories different from others is the resurrection of Yassu?" asked Jayida to their confirmation.

Though she loved many stories from the *injil*, her favorites were Shamshun and Yassu, a gripping resistance always seizing her at their violent, but also heartbreakingly inspirational deaths. Maybe it was wrong for her to even think it, but she wanted even a small bit of that strength for herself.

At least they interested her more than stories of fickle, elusive, and cold gods who seemed more eager to grant revengeful pain than happiness. She'd once wondered if the gods some worshipped all over were just copies of the Rûm, Fars, and other pantheons, or entirely different entities, and had surprised herself in soon realizing that she didn't really care to find out either way.

"*Sah.* As for the others, remember: despite what you hear in the poems, or from followers of Mani, or the legend of Gilgamesh, the Iskandar Romance, and other epics, boastful as they are and often meant to glorify and inspire fear, the goal—"

"Should always be to preserve life; *na'am*, I know, *yaba*," Jayida nodded.

"*Sah*, and not for any reward, but because it's the right thing to do. And I'm sure that *malik* Al-Harith, that proud supporter and host of the poets, knows this, too. A man in his respected high position often has to negotiate well and he's known for returning captives. I wouldn't be surprised if he captures them just to prove his point to more stubborn minds, of which there's no shortage," laughed her father, shaking his head. "*Aywa*, my child: enemies are everywhere. But so are friends, so life is to be treasured."

She wished more people felt like her father, because there were always those who preferred death over defeat.

"What about the monks and nuns living at the monasteries? If their peaceful ways prevent them from using weapons, do they just trust that they'll be protected, then?" said Jayida.

"Seems so; they likely take it as a test of their faith, too. They *could* also have weapons stored away, just in case. They may live the life of angels, but Mikha'il has a sword, and some monasteries have arrowslit windows to accommodate archers," her father smiled. "All the same, they're supported by their rulers and communities, so they're hardly alone. That's why everywhere, community and alliances are so important."

"Like the *kahinat* guardians at the shrines at Nakhla and Mina, and other places," said Jayida.

"Exactly."

They picked up pace, ushered the flocks along, and gradually the dark mounds of ground receded, revealing flatter, lighter terrain. Ahead, the surrounding Khaybar wall came into view, and beyond it, the towering date palms stood out like giants in the mist, marking the way. Jayida followed her parents in moving up front to the *sayyid*'s side, who squinted pensively as he scanned the surroundings.

"Praise *al-ilah* we're early," said *sayyid* Aziz, somewhere between concern and relief.

Her past visit coupled with the new situation gave the impression of seeing the place for the first time. The area was blessed by the ancient Nabatean Qusaybah Dam to the south, and remained an age-old stop on the trade route. To the north were stretches of ancient tombs in moon-shaped rocky mounds, and caves full of rock drawings that drew visitors and added to the constant bustling air of activity.

Beyond the Khaybar wall before them, several fortresses, each occupied by a clan, strategically looked down on them from the surrounding hills. The prosperous Israelite tribes dwelled in mudbrick buildings, with multiple storehouses, stables, wells, and irrigation channels ensuring the date-growing residents' prosperity, along with their handicrafts and metalsmithing.

They reached the massive wall with a menorah drawn into the archway and its heavy double wooden doors drawn back. Guarding it was a group of young armed guards in frocked garments and sidelocks at each side of their face, gathered around a seated older man whom she recognized as Harun. *Sayyid* Aziz dismounted while they lingered close as he spoke to them. As *sayyid* Aziz explained his concern over the curious situation, Harun glanced over at them. His etched gold menorah amulet glinted under his beard, his serious demeanor commanding more respect than intimidation.

"We've come to humbly request *nasi* Musa's protection. As you can see, we bring much that we trust will be of use to you and your residents, too."

Harun's wide chest rose in contemplation. "*Aywa*, your urge may be right. It's said that it's a volcano that exploded far north or west, unlike any ever seen. So we've begun preparing for crowds—the Banu Murra or even Rabi'a may barge in at any moment, boisterous as some of them are—but I'm grateful to see you first," he said with the flash of a smirk. "Give me a moment."

Harun disappeared behind the wall, and returned moments later with another familiar grey-bearded man. With his warm demeanor, wide waistline wrapped in indigo robes striped in white, and his similar golden menorah amulet, he inspired as much comfort as their *sayyid*.

"*Nasi* Musa, may *al-ilah* grant you thousand blessings always," said *sayyid* Aziz, exchanging a kiss on each cheek.

"May He reward you with the same," said *nasi* Musa, without a trace of Hebrew or Aramaic accent. "Peculiar situation or not, you're welcome to camp in the southeast plot I've allocated for you. You'll see your date palms from there, and when you wish we can gather what's available of your plots, all thanks to the Lord always," he sighed.

Nasi Musa instructed Harun to record their passage, which he promptly obeyed by dipping his ostrich feather into a pot of ink, and writing their tribe's name on a piece of parchment. To her relief, the sight of it being the very first on the page was somehow reassuring.

"I'll let you settle, and once you're ready, come and join me," said *nasi* Musa.

They clustered through the gateway and veered southeast towards the palms as instructed, meeting both curious and smiling resident gazes. Though the grounds were vast and pleasant as ever, Jayida was suddenly concerned by how quickly it could fill up—with people and noise—depending on the number of tribes that arrived.

As much to conserve space as from a defensive urge to huddle, the whole of Sa'd set up their tents closer together, with Hubala and her father's tents at each side of the *sayyid*'s. They toiled solemnly on building their waterproof houses of hair, the flocks sensing the tension and reluctance to unpack all their belongings and be fully at ease like they were at Wadi Al-Hamd. Even Kamila's quarters were smaller and closer to their area, and she sensed they both wanted it that way.

It was only temporary after all, but to know they were protected amidst the oasis brought its own comfort in this unsettling shift. Jayida lined her figurines along the head of her bedding, then found a few cracks in the desert floor and dropped a few frankincense tears inside as a gift for their stay.

"Have you found Wafira?" said Zahir, nodding east to the date groves. She looked up and settled on a row of dark, rough trunks and leafy pinnate crowns intertwined in mist, and nodded.

"Surely Wafira saw us coming first," Jayida smirked. A collective chuckle erupted, her attempt at humor thankfully helping to lighten the mood.

As her name intended, Wafira bountifully provided dates multiple times a year, thanks to the agreed-upon exchange of the twelve camels Zahir had given *nasi* Musa winters ago. Should Jayida ever get disoriented in the vast premises, she only had to get closer and look for the seven trees extending right next to it to the east, decorated with straps upon straps of leather, red and cream tassels woven by Warda, and gathered armies of eagle offerings at its base carved by *sayyid* Aziz as proud father to Nasr.

A haunting, shattering echo resonated, chilling her to the bone. She'd etch her father's advice on her skin, if needed: to plan ahead and always try to have multiple sources of food. Though their sheep and goats foaled at least once a year, and their camels birthed at least one calf every two years, everyone feared how droughts and floods could quickly and drastically change conditions. She had to be as resourceful as him, and this arrangement he had with *nasi* Musa, as did other *badawi* according to their own means, was another way of helping to soften the hard times, along with the priceless friendship.

Leaving the women to rest or do some cooking, Jayida went with her father and joined *sayyid* Aziz and Nasr to find *nasi* Musa. They headed towards the mudbrick homes, the draped woven carpets and blankets propped upon acacia poles outside the dwellings providing often needed additional shade. Soon *nasi* Musa emerged in the distance, and met them halfway.

"Ah; like arrows in the hands of a warrior are the children of one's youth, says the one hundredth twenty-seventh Psalm," said *nasi* Musa, and led them towards the date groves. "I know that as future *sha'ir*, you may be ready to embellish stories," he glanced at Nasr, "But may you also have good memories of your time here."

"We already do *nasi* Musa, starting with your generous protection," said Nasr with a light bow.

They strolled on, surrounded by pools of liquid silver created by the system of stone water tunnels that kept the prized date palms' roots well hydrated, along with the volcanic earth's rich nutrients that fed them. Jayida perked up at the sight of crops of wheat, barley, sorghum, grapes, pomegranates, and olives. They brought as much security as the coveted silk garment stocks arrived from afar on the caravans, and local metal workers who transformed the rough metals into prized jewelry and weapons.

Cattle, Awassi sheep, and black Hijazi goats grazed freely in the unusually ashen greenery; their unhurried manner making her wonder at such a life where most necessities were nearby. Her gaze drifted further to a *hima* sanctuary of horses, with some surely acquired from nearby Ghatafan and Dhubyan breeders, then on to another vast area of roaming camels.

"And there's our flock's relatives!" Jayida exclaimed, meeting her father's grin.

"*Sah*, they are," laughed *nasi* Musa. "Their superior breeding have been nothing but a blessing. May He keep his hand over them, for despite their undivided hooves, they are still His creation," he smirked.

"We're honored that they can serve you," said Zahir, and cast her a knowing smile. Like him, she loved the idea of their camels dwelling in different parts of the land, and to know that the creatures would likely recognize them no matter how much time passed extended the bond despite the separation.

A weighty silence fell over them as they entered the shadowy date groves. Though the sight of their sheer size easily left visitors speechless, they'd never quite looked like this, both majestic and threatened in the foreign, enrobing veil. For a moment they all just lingered, their gazes darting in the peacefully enclosed space, as if revelations might come as movements, whispers, or even letters writing themselves on the bark. In that instant Jayida was sure that no statue, pillar, or monument could ever compare to the blessed living trees, and that the *woquf* tradition of standing before the divinity at various shrines had to be inspired by such life-giving giants. In the stillness she thought she heard a rustling; surely a sand cat, gerbil, or a sandgrouse.

"I suspect I know the answer, but I'll ask anyway. Humility does come before honor, says the fifteenth Proverb," said *nasi* Musa, his deep, serious tone echoing their thoughts. "May I count on you, if and when the time comes?"

"A *sayyid*'s cloak is wide, full of his tribe's demands. I share your concern, so we are your servants, and our sons are honored to be here," said *sayyid* Aziz.

Nasi Musa sighed and nodded, his features a mixture of relief and nagging contemplation. "With *al-ilah* and these unshakable towers as my witness, I'm glad you are here. Now come, let us pray it is all just precaution, and share our first meal of your stay here."

Jayida caught Nasr's glance as they turned around, each asking what was the meaning of this? A sinking feeling of impending uncertainty and danger rattled her, but Khaybar was a renown fortified place full of skilled fighters. And now they were in it, and at least old enough to be of some help if needed, even if limited.

The first night she was woken up by the screams of massacred Najranites. Her heart racing, she tried to calm down by focusing and asking the right questions. Could they really trust who was around them? What if some Israelites of Khaybar turned on them, and each other, during their stay? But that couldn't be, when *nasi* Musa had shown his gratitude at the date groves, and her father and *sayyid* Aziz had sound judgment in their loyal friends. It was a blessing to be among *nasi* Musa and his kin, whose tribe the Banu Nadir descended from the priestly

Harun, the brother of his namesake. Even if the rumors were true that Dhu Nuwas had been paid with gold from rabbis in Tabariyya, it couldn't be that everyone agreed with him, especially when many northern Israelites didn't consider those in the south to be of true faith; that theirs was a heretical form at best. So they could hardly approve of their fanatic murdering ways, or the Samaritans'.

Resolved, she recited the code of *muruwa* to herself, and finished with her father's reminders to always be prepared, and that despite the danger, true friendships were there, too. It occurred to her that she might begin to understand what her father meant when he said there could be a fine line between precaution and paranoia that guided him to tread carefully.

Days passed, and the dense, dry fog did not vanish, but brought a chill and turned the sky into variants of odd, unnatural shades. At times it was a grey-white, others a dusty yellow that made everything look sick, and difficult to tell the time of day. While like many others she had little concern for exactly which month they were in, they were now largely deprived of the different tones and rhythms usually common to each day. Thankfully, while many *badawi* relied on the twelve-month calendar to track their special pilgrimage and market season, their camels followed their own natural breeding call. There was also always opportunity to trade camels in all seasons, especially if doing so from bustling Khaybar or north at Wadi Al-Qura.

So the effort of time-keeping hardly seemed worth it, when not only were there multiple names for each month used by different tribes, but sometimes a thirteenth leap month was intercalated to maintain the special months in place, or to accommodate some other emergency situation. With all the changes bound to happen, it was a wonder anyone could manage to track and remember it all. If she really wanted to know, they could just as easily find out from someone else, and best of all, from *nasi* Musa while they remained there.

In this ambiguous air, the alternating thick and cool atmosphere seemed to suck up all their breaths and force them into deceitful clouds suspended over them, with no chance of purifying rain in exchange. When most started wearing their woolen coats—as much for protection from the cold as from other unseen and potentially harmful elements—she thought of *mubassir* Ayyub's mention of Yassu's miraculous robe the soldiers had cast lots for, said to bring rain in times of drought.

In the evenings the gatherings around the fire were lean, without the need for cooling mint tea, and soon empty, in favor of retreating inside, as the lit-up Khaybar towers offered hope to wanderers in the dark. Mostly, Jayida awoke unpleasantly from dreamless nights, as blank as the bleak skies blotting out the sun and stars.

Not for the first time, Samira's fretting spread to some other women, making her mother Zoraya even more reluctant to visit Warda's and others' tents to socialize. Though many had taken to smearing their lids in *kohl* to fend off *al-'ayn*, lurking flies, and disease, Samira had so much of it that it only enlarged her beetle eyes.

"I know all of this is troubling, but why insist on making it worse with drama and gossip?" said her mother. "Warda must be as frustrated, but at least she has Yazida. In the times when Samira also tries to lure Yazida out to grow her audience, the girl has cleverly taken to saying her pigeons are nervous and refuses to leave them alone. She's even taught her favorite to take food from her mouth," chuckled Zoraya.

"Oh? I want to see," pouted Jayida. Though she had a good friend in her brother Nasr, as the growing, maturing Jonder, she knew not to ever expect to spend much time with Yazida, or other girls of the tribe.

"Surely you will in time," said her mother.

Unsurprisingly, Samira's husband Hubala and oldest son Sufyan tried to keep away by doing useful things. Though he was still young, Jayida wondered how Shams put up with all the nagging in a situation no one had the power to change. *Sayyid* Aziz did his best by encouraging the worried women to stay in their tent, safe in their world of weaving, cooking, and storytelling, for surely it would pass. Even Nasr shared cheerful lines of poetry, trying to convince of its temporary nature, for if the Basus War could end after forty years, surely this wouldn't be as long. Most importantly, their husbands and the tribe would ensure their safety, as it always had—*sayyid* Aziz pointedly reminded—but even Jayida wondered how he could promise such a thing. As her father reluctantly noted as they plucked their dates off the bunches and packed them in straw baskets for storage, it had never lasted this long.

When they weren't out watering the flocks, exercising Kamila, or taking a pleasant quiet walk, they lingered inside their incense-scented tent. They tried to add cheerful life by decorating with her mother's bright woven rugs in blended shades of crimson and saffron with cream motifs. Along the walls were the folded loom, the churn, and the grinding stones, constantly questioning if they should do more or less given the circumstances. Jayida tended to the sprouting *rejleh* purslane pots and picked their smooth leaves for stews, and watched other new tiny sprouts, willing their magenta-muddy hue to turn green. She nestled against Kamila as she spoke with her and her figurines, and soon grew tired of playing knucklebones, preferring the dancing images of stories that took her away to happier places.

Her mother's recitals offered their own dreamy atmosphere she never wanted to leave. Amidst the bulk of their blankets and decorations expertly made by Zoraya, Jayida glanced at the faded saffron and crimson blanket woven by her *sitti* Rania of Taghlib, hoping she looked in on them from beyond. With bales of handspun dyed yarn sprawled out around them, they braided colorful *wasm* bracelets, necklaces, and ornaments, and mended camel halters and weaning straps. As her mother made use of her toes like another set of hands for tensioning the wool, her fingers flickered above her legs as she looped the alternating different colored threads to make an eight-strand, black-and-white braid.

Dazzled, Jayida drifted as her mother repeated the tale of how she and her father met: how he'd arrived with *sayyid* Aziz and the poet Samaw'al, full of inspirational stories from their march to Kutha. Through all the praise her mother saw Zahir's genuine kindness and had instantly felt drawn to him, but was afraid he wouldn't want a woman who might be barren. After all, the *kahina* had warned her as much when *sitti* Rania had died giving birth to her. As if it wasn't enough for her to be descended from her strong Taghlib grandfather named Amir, and her father Ghanam who'd bravely fought—and in Ghanam's case, even died—alongside their *sayyid* Al-Muhalhil, leaving Zoraya in the care of her grandparents. Their *sayyid* had been duty-bound, when it was his brother Kulayb who'd been killed in revenge for impulsively slaying Al-Basus's camel that had wandered into his land, sparking the long Basus War.

Jayida tensed at the thought of *sayyid* Al-Mulhalil, who'd also had his own bouts of wrathful impulsiveness. Though Al-Muhalhil was grateful to her family for their loyalty, and was a gifted *sha'ir* who mourned his slain brother and Ghanam with honorable verses, Zoraya had also quickly learned to keep her distance from him. It was his daughter Layla who'd tearfully told Zoraya that when she'd been born, he'd ordered her mother Zaynab to leave her out and exposed; demanding warrior sons rather than useless daughters. But Zaynab couldn't bring herself to do it, and had given Layla to the care of a slave to be hidden away, until seasons passed and Zaynab softened Al-Muhalhil to the fact that his beautiful daughter was alive and well, and would make him proud someday. Thankfully, he'd had a tearful change of mind and welcomed her back, but other similar cases didn't turn out that way.

Jayida tried to enhance that memory with her mother's brave decision to share only the truth of her uncertain life with this new honorable man she met, free of deceit or expectation. Yet to Zoraya's everlasting joy Zahir had been immediately accepting. He'd settled on thousands of his camels as dowry, shrinking his flocks without second thought or regret to the Taghlib's lasting awed praise. And so her father had returned to Tayma, flush with battle and amorous pride, topped with Samaw'al's honorable verses to mark the occasion—which she also imagined Moharib must've hated.

"In spring we marched to Kutha,
Proud tribes to the Euphrates led by Yassu-loving Ma'dikarib—
Bravely we fought the *ghul* Al-Mundhir,
And returned with the glorious boon of friends, testimonies,
And a pearl of Taghlib," said Jayida proudly, loving her father's summary of those days. A while after they'd left the Zubayd, and her mother had revealed her pregnancy to her father on the night they camped at Hijr, right next to the largest unfinished Nabataean tomb on their southernmost settlement.

On they went, recalling the ancient *injil* tales of *mubassir* Ayyub; of Nuh's Ark marking out its path on the water in the shape of a cross before resting on Mount Ararat. Generations later, Shem and Melchisedek retrieved the body of Adam from Nuh's Ark and, guided by an angel, the earth once more opened up in the shape of a cross when they placed it into its final burial place at Golgotha. Each time *mubassir* Ayyub's eyes glistened as he shared these details, proudly reminding that he memorized them from Saint Ephrem's Book of the Cave of Treasures.

Then they glided to the Euphrates her mother had seen during her younger years with the Taghlib, then met Gilgamesh on his quest to immortality, and Iskandar the Great conquering the eastern lands all the way to India. It was said he'd even considered venturing into their own dwelling, but died before he got to it. They paused in memory of the victims of the recent earthquakes at Antioch, founded by one of Iskandar's generals. Their braids' saffron dye brought to mind King Sulayman's copper mines in Timna, and the milky hue the rock salt of Tayma, where the Babylonian King Nabonidus had conquered and stayed for a time. Later, his successor Cyrus the Great's name would be commemorated in the *injil*, calling up the Israelite's ancient connection to the Fars land, beginning with Ibrahim.

And so, their roaming continued across time, the Samaritans' defeat by *malik* Al-Harith as if quashing their hope for a return to the Promised Land once and for all. But how could they lose hope or feel alone as *al-ilah*'s chosen people? Wasn't it enough that they'd witnessed such miracles from their God, who rained on them bread from Heaven and parted the Red Sea for them to flee Egypt into safety? Yet the *Masihi* believed their long-awaited savior, *al-Masih*, had come as

Yassu. Since the Israelites did not believe, what more signs did they need, and how would they know when it was finally him? Unbelievably wild and real, the stories gathered and whirled in her thoughts, enchanting and unsettling in turn.

Jayida wondered what others in other places were doing, like in Hispania and China at the far edges of the world, or at the southern island of Soqotra said to have the strangest plants. At least the headstrong King Abraha in Himyar seemed strong as ever, when in addition to defying *Negus* Kaleb and making himself king, he'd also since defeated the force that *Negus* Kaleb had sent to oust him from power.

Cautiously, she offered a thought to Moharib, and tried to think of the happiest memory her father had of him. As children, *siddi* Gayas had taken them to Hijr, where they'd played hide-and-find among the scattered tombs. Somehow, they'd both ended up accidently picking the same place of the largest, unfinished Nabataean tomb, and as the others called to them, they'd stayed in, nestled within the small space together. At first Zahir had been unsure about being there, not wanting to unintentionally disrespect the place. But Moharib had insisted, saying they were paying homage and could always make it up with offerings to Dhu Shara, Al-Lat, and Manat, who'd been worshipped there. And so they'd remained, giggling and whispering, like they'd shared a secret brotherly mission in that special, magical place.

It was long before they were found, and though *siddi* Gayas's serious calls sounded ripe with punishment, they vanished when he found them and realized they'd been together all along. Though Zahir could never say what exactly had caused Moharib to turn harsher than he'd already been, it had gotten worse after *siddi* Gayas's passing. With a sigh Jayida added a thought to Khaled's safety, wondering but doubting that he was as pleasant as Nasr. All the better that her mother had later added another pleasant memory to Hijr by announcing her pregnancy to her father when they'd camped there on the way to the Banu Sa'd. Though the Zubayd was her father's tribe, Jayida noted again that she had little interest in going to Tayma except to pay respects at the grandparents' graves, and see the poet Samaw'al and his Qasr Al-Ablaq dwelling.

"My better blood, I hate to disrupt your happy musings, but here's one story you won't like," shared her father at the end of the week of their arrival. He took a moment before continuing. "A drought in the north has gotten worse, and crowds have gathered at Al-Mundhir's. Not only has he refused to help and turned them away, but he's taken advantage of the chaos to invade into the Ghassanid territories deep along the western Euphrates. As usual, he's taking any opportunity to go against the already fragile Eternal Peace agreement made with the Rûm and the Ghassanids," said Zahir, shaking his head in disgust.

Her stomach clenched, as it did at each mention of the *ghul*'s name. Conflict and carnage: that's what he fed on.

"*Nasi* Musa already suspected it, but now he's almost certain many will be flocking here. He wants us prepared and ready, because unfortunately not everyone works in harmony, especially in such troubled times," said her father.

Pleasant rest eluded her like it did many others, and a few days later, it was no night vision when she heard the resounding wailing and complaining. Quickly they dressed and rushed out to the gates to the sight of the Khaybar walls surrounded by crowds, begging to be let in.

"*Ayyam al-Zalam* are upon us! The Days of Darkness are here!" cried men and women in varied, yet similar voices. "Let us in and be blessed, and let Al-Mundhir be punished for his unkindness!"

Compassion and sadness filled Jayida at the suffering, especially that of the screaming, frazzled children. Some gladly offered all they had in exchange for staying together, while others handed over their children as slaves, as if relieved to be rid of the burden. The shock hit her like a punch to the gut, and she swallowed back angry surging tears, hating that some could so easily dismiss their own kin and expose them to the greed and mistreatment of others. Even if slaves weren't a costly symbol of wealth, they deemed it unnecessary, and her mother prided herself in creating a nurturing private space for them free of intrusive prying eyes.

Inside and out, Khaybar's armed tribesmen stood ready, as *nasi* Musa gave directions for properly examining those most in need, recording names and allocating watering times, and gradually letting people into designated areas. As she'd suspected, the camps filled up quickly, creating a constant chaotic hubbub unlike the festive one she'd recalled.

Jayida left her father with *sayyid* Aziz and *nasi* Musa, and followed her mother back to the tent to bake more bread, both to find some solace in and pass the troubled time with useful work. While her mother peeled flatbread after flatbread off the hot stones, creating beloved warm towers of fresh bread, Jayida made more flour. Kneeling before the grinding stones placed in a larger woven straw basket, Jayida tipped a bowl of barley seeds into the hole in the middle of the two circular grinding stones. She took a firm hold of the wooden handle at its outer edge and turned the top millstone in circles, each new round crushing the sacrificial seeds into finer powder. She repeated the process until all the seeds were gone, surrounding the stones in dunes of nutty-scented barley flour.

"Can we also make more *wasm* and give them as gifts? We have so much wool," said Jayida, looking at her mother.

"I love your kind idea," Zoraya smiled.

They finished up with the bread, brought out their bundles of wool, and worked in the quiet, letting their movements whisper to them of hope and sun and rain, yielding woolen braids and rope bracelets.

"Will we be here very long? Or will we scatter into the wind like the Thamud and countless others?" said Jayida with a half-smile. It dawned on her that she'd never been around so many people and noise all at once, and though she missed the peaceful walks, she'd rather not run into anyone, even if she was with Nasr. A discomforting feeling seized her that their stay might be longer than any of them expected.

"Maybe a bit of both?" chuckled her mother. "But hopefully it won't be too long. No one has ever seen something like this. Not only do they say the wine in Al-Sham has gone sour, but that the darkness has spread to the whole world. At least we know that in the meantime, we can manage here," said her mother cautiously.

"I don't mean to complain; we're lucky to be here and for all that we have. I just don't like the *feeling*, like it's all gathered in one place," Jayida frowned.

"I know what you mean. At least we're together and we're safe. I hope that will help ease your night visions."

"I haven't seen anything since we arrived," Jayida shrugged. Her mother sighed, mirroring her doubt on if it was a good sign.

But it couldn't go on like this forever—something had to happen to make it change; it always did. At least that's what some *badawi* said.

They didn't see her father until evening, who plopped down next to them in exhaustion.

"Kind *nasi* Musa had to finally force himself and the rest away for the night. He ordered the gates closed, and doubled the guarding shifts and rotations," he said, rubbing his face and eye sockets. "But it's more than anyone could've anticipated, and the grounds are fast reaching capacity. He has to be sure there will be enough."

"Who can blame him? He's doing all he can," said Zoraya with a hint of frustration. "I wouldn't be surprised if Moharib is sending others away as easily as Al-Mundhir."

"Or he would take them in, but only for the joy of boasting," Jayida blurted. Her parents stared at her a moment, then nodded in shared agreement.

"May he and all the tribe be blessed," said her father, leading them into quiet contemplation.

On a whim, the next morning Jayida rose early and slipped out silently, her incense pouch and short blade wrapped tightly at her waist. Walking with her back straight and arms stiff, her hand grazed near it just in case, as she took in the rare moments of quiet before the camp bustled with noise again. It was not out of defiance to her parents, especially since she wanted to be back before they rose, but she felt a pull to be alone and explore, and all the better if it reassured her of their safety amidst the walls. If she couldn't take an early morning walk in blessed Khaybar, where could she?

Jayida drifted east to the palm groves, the soft chirping of birds and cooing of doves adding melancholic cheerfulness to the misty scene. The gentle buzzing of wildlife had an alluring peacefulness and she wished she could drift in its protective arms all day. Perhaps it wouldn't be so bad being there if she could still have these peaceful, uninterrupted moments to herself.

She strolled amidst the wise fruitful giants, the early fog curling around their trunks and leaves like milky silken scarves. The branches were all stripped of their date fruits, distributed to their owners and surely rationed to last as long as possible. Her core tightened, fearing for their next crops given the diminished life-giving sunlight. She caught a rustling and turned an ear in its eastern direction, smiling at the vast, vacant space concealing some other early-risen, exploring creature.

Jayida reached in her incense pouch and buried a frankincense tear sporadically into the ground as she went. At the sight of Wafira and *sayyid* Aziz's palms she beamed and patted their thick trunks of rough, plate-like layers, thanking them quietly for their presence and service.

"Holy tears for fruitful trees," she chuckled to herself. She circled the trees and buried more incense bits, humming and happily forgetting herself in the activity.

Satisfied, she straightened up again, and in instant she froze at the sight of a low, peeking eye staring at her from behind one of *sayyid* Aziz's trees. Her dominant hand instinctively fell on her short blade while the other made a fist, but held still as she saw one of his hands extend out slowly, thin and almost limp.

"Who are you? Come out of there," said Jayida, aware she sounded harsher than she meant.

"I—no harm, I mean no harm," whispered the man as he held up his hands and crept out in a hunched manner.

He was so frazzled, his dark, shaggy hair and beard greyed from dust, wearing the thinnest, torn *qamis* robe and flimsiest sandals made of worn palm fibers that she frowned in shocked pity. She instantly had the strongest urge to cry and sniffled violently to hold it back, which she was sure only made her look even angrier. Thankfully he kept his gaze lowered and averted, and she took that time to gather herself.

"What are you doing here? You must be cold," said Jayida, her serious tone softening.

"It's—it's my favorite place. Usually there's no one here this early," he said, his low tone now hinting of amusement.

"What is your name?" she said, wondering if he'd just snuck in without *nasi* Musa's knowledge. But surely that couldn't be. He seemed to rock slightly as he wrung his hands and looked away, and her vision once more threatened to blur. It was her turn to look away too, and it took much force for her not to sigh roughly, lest he took it the wrong way. Something about him seemed so fragile and sensitive. "I'm Jonder, son of Zahir, friend of *nasi* Musa who blessedly manages this oasis. This is our Wafira, and these seven yield fruit for our *sayyid* Aziz of Banu Sa'd," she said gently.

"And you take good care of them, *sah*," he said, looking at her feet. She had the impression that unlike some others, his disheveled appearance was disarming rather than off-putting, wrapped in a faint scent of salty tears and dry earth.

"Surely not as good as *nasi* Musa. We're staying here for a while now, and I just wanted to go for a walk, in the quiet," she pinched a smile and searched his gaze. She thought of offering him a pair of her father's boots but for some reason, didn't. He slowly looked up and something in his reddened dark eyes almost broke her heart.

"I, too, like the quiet," he nodded vigorously, wringing his hands. "No trouble there." He looked so tormented that it reminded her of the tales of holy men who'd fled family and society to live alone, chained in caves to fight their torturing demons.

"You don't have to be nervous; it's safe here. But you can't stay like this, you'll get sick," she said.

He turned to her and frowned, the first burst of energy flashing out of him. "I can!" he said in a louder voice, more thoughtful than aggressive.

She smirked. "As you may have noticed, there's more people here now. Seems we may both need to find new places to wallow in. Unless we both agree that we can roam and sit here quietly, without meaning to bother or harm each other."

He looked away into the trees, and nodded after a moment. "Truly? You don't chase or mock me?"

"Why do such things?" she said, trying not to break. She untied the incense pouch from her belt and handed it to him. "May you take this gift as protection and reminder of our first meeting."

His sunken face cautiously glimpsed, then shook. "I can't. I can't."

"*Aywa*, you can. But I won't force you to take them, so I will leave them here, and you can take them if and when you'd like," she said, her throat pinching. "Now I must get back, so until next time." She gave a light bow and left him, huddled like a child nodding after her in contemplative wonder.

She hurried back to the tent and slipped into the women's quarters to the sight of her sitting father, smirking at her. He seemed almost twice the size of her mother, and without his headwrap, his thick, wavy unbraided locks cascaded past his shoulders, longer than the dark beard that hung below his chin. If her father's reputation didn't already precede him, his direct gaze added to his imposing bearing, countered by his observant, poised demeanor that hinted at an inner, nearly unshakeable calmness.

"Had a pleasant walk, my roaming cub?" he said, patting the seat next to him. She joined him and accepted the flatbread he handed over.

"*Na'am, yaba*. I just wanted a moment of quiet, to see if—"

"It was still like before?"

"*Sah*, I guess." Jayida frowned and took a small bite.

"And?"

"It wasn't."

"People have a way of changing things," he chuckled.

She nodded. "There was a man, at the palm groves, right by our trees."

Her father stilled and fixed her darkly. "Who? And where is he now?" His whole body tensed, ready to bolt out after him.

"No, no; not to worry," she said, and gently squeezed his arm. "He was harmless, so worn... and sad. I asked his name but he didn't say. I gave him the rest of the incense I had. I don't mean to waste, but at the moment that's what I thought of doing. I think I may see him again, on the condition that we share the space peacefully, since we both seem to enjoy it."

His shoulders relaxed. "Don't worry about the incense; you know that we trust you. In such tough times, he must appreciate their value, too. Now, I can't wait to hear what *nasi* Musa has to say about this," he said, echoing her thoughts.

That evening he filled them in with *nasi* Musa's knowledge. He began with *nasi* Musa's surprise that the man, who called himself Attab the Shadow, had shown himself to Jonder, as he made a point not to be seen and avoid human contact. But—since *sayyid* Aziz had since discreetly informed him on Jonder's curious visions—he'd quickly ascribed it to the *kahin* in young Jonder that drew the hermit out, just as the visions had inspired *sayyid* Aziz to lead them to the safety of the oasis. She smiled at that, both pleased and humbled that he would take it that way.

Attab had been at Khaybar for a few seasons already, and demanded nothing of *nasi* Musa except to be allowed to dwell there, nearly invisibly, and to be given just the bare minimum food he needed to survive. *Nasi* Musa hardly agreed and constantly insisted and tried giving him more, starting with new clothing and boots, but Attab refused. *Nasi* Musa tried to learn more about the mysterious reclusive man, and all he could gather was that his family had been killed. As heartbreaking as that was, *nasi* Musa suspected he must have remaining kin, who also worried about him and would surely take him in. But he didn't know them, and even if so, he didn't have the heart to refuse him when all he wanted was to be there, and especially near the blessed palm groves.

"The poor man. And yet I'm glad that he can be safe here, at least," said her mother.

"May he find peace. But I still want you to be careful. There's no telling how people can be in the midst of grief, too," said her father.

"*Na'am, yaba*. But I think it explains why I felt so sad around him. He seemed so helpless, almost like a child, and I just wanted to cry," she said, and her mother drew her into her embrace.

With her parents' permission, Jayida saw him again the next morning, glad to see that her gifts were gone, suggesting he'd likely taken them. She greeted him by his name, and he nodded shyly, as if surprised by what *nasi* Musa had revealed.

As days passed, she did not pry or force anything out of him, and preferred to let him speak first, which he rarely did. She quickly found that his presence was not a disturbance to her own roaming. Rather, she often had the impression that they forgot each other as much as themselves, as they basked in their revelries and peacefulness of the sacred, shaded trees.

One early afternoon, her father took her and Nasr along and made the rounds of camps across the districts to get an idea of its members.

"Be aware, although you'll likely guess as much yourselves, oh our wise children, that there may be bandits in the guise of soldiers and merchants in our midst. Why some northerners would venture all the way here could look suspicious—especially when *malik* Al-Harith is taking in many into his territory. That would certainly be closer and more convenient, as might Tayma," her father paused. "All the same, *nasi* Musa is as generous as he is no fool. No matter who they are, they may well be in need. So as long as they abide as peaceful, and maybe even helpful visitors, then he will assist as he sees fit."

"No wonder it's been feeling more and more like a hostile seasonal *aswaq*, or what I imagine of the market, anyway," said Jayida.

"So as usual, even here we'll do well to continue being on our guard," said Nasr with a hint of annoyance.

"*Sah*, such can be the risk of doing right. But anyone who would turn on his generous benefactor—of all the times—would have to face payment to his offended kin, along with his own judgment in Time," reminded her father, his tone not as convincing as she'd hoped. She wasn't sure whether to feel better or worse by their shared concerns.

"Now, come. I'm willing to bet this next part will be among your favorite memories from all this."

Her father took them up to one of the closest fortresses, where throngs of soldiers armed with longbows and arrows solemnly patrolled the grounds and filled the towers, adding to its withdrawn, yet powerful ever-watchful authority. There were narrowslit openings carved along the walls, narrow on the outside and wider on the inside, allowing archers to shoot at the enemy from various angles with little chance of being hit themselves.

They climbed the stairs to the top, where the sweeping hazy view overlooked the vast grounds. She looked west and imagined that on a clear day they might be able to see traces of Wadi Al-Hamd in the distance. But now, along the thick Khaybar walls were scattered camps, with some perhaps still hoping to get in, or praying they were safer just by closer association.

Nasr raised a hand, then stopped himself. "I wonder who would see me if I waved," he said pensively, staring in the distance. Jayida held back her surprise. Surely many a young girl would notice the handsome young man in the clouded tower, with a self-controlled strength that made her feel safe.

"Little matter when your verses would surely travel on swift wings and uplift their souls much like all these blessed resources," said her father. "As for the questionable neighbors, you can see that if anyone got any ideas about storming in, *nasi* Musa has teams of archers ready to do their part, along with the other six forts," he added, reading her mind. "Speaking of which. How about trying a different archer's bow? In the other direction, of course," smirked her father as Nasr perked up.

Zahir left them for a moment and returned with a tribesman about Sufyan's age with sidelocks at each side of his familiar bearded face. They exchanged greetings with Dawud, son of *nasi* Musa, who was more than happy to offer his bow for the experience.

Dawud called out to a guard down below patrolling within the inner court, and alerted him to their plan, as much to avoid injury as to gather the arrows. They each took turns struggling with the longbow that was bigger than them, and clumsily but resolutely launched arrows that flew off and disappeared down below. Nasr took naturally to it, and she concluded that he would excel at it if he kept it up. As much as she enjoyed it, she still preferred her short bow, but hoped they ultimately would not have to use any of them, or other weapons, to quell violence.

After a while they came down the fortress and noted *sayyid* Aziz hurrying their way as they headed back to camp.

"My beloved ones, you won't believe who's here," said *sayyid* Aziz with a teasing smirk. From her father's sudden alert gaze she knew they shared a similar flash of discomfort.

"Now you know I wouldn't be smiling if it was anyone unpleasant," chuckled *sayyid* Aziz. "Samaw'al has come, checking in on his kin and of course, asking about you, too. He's awaiting us at *nasi* Musa's."

Her father's tight jaw eased into a grateful smile. "Happy news, and good time for our sons to meet him, too," he nodded.

They strode on together to *nasi* Musa's mudbrick home. The entrance was decorated with a stone mezuzah scroll on the east side, protecting against evil. Motioned inside by *nasi* Musa, they entered the cool, spacious room where stood the swarthy handsome man about her father's age whom she'd heard much about. Behind him was a wooden table with a stack of leatherbound books, one lying open and propped up on a wooden folding bookstand with decorative carvings. Surely they were made of precious acacia from their Holy Land, like their Tabernacle and Holy Ark. Inscribed on velvety, cream-colored parchment, the sacred Tanakh scripture radiated out protectively over the space and into all the other rooms with a mezuzah at each doorway. Jayida mused that they also had buried magic bowls at different corners underground for added protection.

"How good it is to see you again," said *sayyid* Aziz. He stepped open-armed to Samaw'al and exchanged a kiss on each cheek, then playfully grabbed his chin.

"Getting handsomer by the day," said her father, making Samaw'al laugh while they embraced in turn. They paused and held each other for a moment, wallowing in the emotion of the unspoken time gap since her father had left Tayma without telling him. That the poet seemed to show up in times of trouble instantly made her like him even more. *Tribesmen hit and get hit together*, went the saying that added to her reassurance.

"And here is my eleven-year old Jonder," said her father, gesturing to her.

"And what could you not pierce into with those eyes," smiled Samaw'al, and drew her in. "You're the same age as my Hassan. Blessings to you, Jonder ibn Zahir." He pressed his face firmly but gently against hers, the pleasant trace of incense wading out of his dark cloak.

"And to you and your family," she said with a humble bow.

"And here is my Nasr," said *sayyid* Aziz. "As our future *sha'ir*, while you're here perhaps you can give him some of your blessed poet's guidance."

"*Na'am*; may we teach each other, blessed *sha'ir* Nasr ibn Aziz," grinned Samaw'al, as Nasr bowed in acceptance.

They reclined on the carpet where rested an earthen jug, cups, and a basket of copper-red cakes.

"Enjoy the fresh ashishot," said *nasi* Musa, as he poured them each some goat milk. Samaw'al's gaze passed over her and Nasr, and drifted back to their fathers in a dreamy smirk.

"I wish it was under different circumstances, but I'm happy to see you both again. It's a long time since our march to Kutha, but I think of it often," said Samaw'al.

The pleasant weight of their past shared experience seemed to hang over them, drawing out a playful solidarity even as it spoke of serious matters. Like Nasr, she tried to observe him without intrusive staring, taking in all his words and manners. Unlike some other Israelites, he had no sidelocks at each side of his strong, sun-kissed appealing face, but wore the required fringed cloak, its tassels the reminders of *al-ilah*'s commandments. His thick gold chain hung down his chest, with one matching medallion with a menorah to honor his Israelite father, and one with a cross to honor his Ghassanid mother.

Jayida stiffened for a moment, wondering if *nasi* Musa and others would curse and banish her for wearing boy's clothes, forbidden in their sacred scripture. But as her parents faithfully reminded her, she had an honorable reason to protect herself from harm, and someday the truth would be revealed. That something told her that Samaw'al wouldn't be angry, and might even like the stories of women dressing as men in service to *al-ilah* and their community, also secretly made her smile.

"Not so fast, friend, you'll give me tears," chuckled *sayyid* Aziz as they took turns reaching into the basket of cakes.

"As you've given me plenty," said Samaw'al, and she guessed that he was partially aiming that at her father.

Jayida carefully bit into her fragile cake, and savored the cinnamon-spiced red lentils sweetened with honey. For a moment they ate silently, letting old and new emotions surface.

"If there's one thing we can appreciate amidst the tough times, it's knowing who you can count on," said *nasi* Musa. "Be blessed for coming, Samaw'al, even if by *al-ilah* blessings, we are doing fine."

"There's no telling how long this will last," Samaw'al nodded darkly. "And while I understand the fearful and concerned measures, no amount of prayers, chanting, liturgies, fasting, almsgiving, votive gifts, *kahinat* prophesying, palm reading, star reading, entrail reading, or other offerings and sacrifices will tell us, either. So like our ancestors, we take it a day at a time. And so far Tayma is fine, too, but then again, Moharib is not as generous as my blessed father 'Adiya, and you. It's near impossible dealing with harsh minds."

Jayida caught the mix of annoyance and mockery in his tone, and made a point to keep chewing with gaze averted, as if she'd hardly heard the name, while ignoring Nasr's side glance on her.

"May *al-ilah* reward you and your kin's generosity," nodded *sayyid* Aziz.

Zahir gently smiled. "Blessings to all Tayma. We pray you keep being safe, and of course the same for Moharib, *sha'ir* Hakim, and all the Banu Zubayd, along with our Tayyi kin, down to the whole of the land. Now that I think of it, Khaled is Nasr's age now. May they be blessed always," said her father with his best light air.

"They are," smirked Samaw'al with a tilt of his head. "Khaled is especially curious about you and his cousin. I've often had to repeat to him all that happened at Kutha. It's like he can't get enough."

"*Esh?* What? Truly?" chuckled her father.

This surprised her, too, but after eleven years without contact from Moharib, and with this new troubling situation, none of them could be fooled into forgetting that he could've already searched them out and welcomed them back home if he'd wanted to.

"Can't blame him. And with the way you tell it, it must be something to hear," smiled *sayyid* Aziz.

"Let us count our blessings," nodded *nasi* Musa thoughtfully. "At least we still have light—unlike the pitch darkness of the Egyptians amidst the ninth plague—and even if it is unlike anything our generation has ever seen."

They slipped into a momentary silence as they drank their milk, the cool saltiness a pleasant contrast from the rich treats.

"We are honored to be here and to do all we can to assist you," said *sayyid* Aziz solemnly.

"It is my honor to do the same. Perhaps we should have a first *maysir* game to help lift the spirits?" said her father.

It made her proud, and sometimes a little worried, to have such a giving father. What if these news of Zahir camels and quality camel meat being handed out traveled fast and far and made even more people come? How could she ever be that selfless, instead of thinking of herself first? But even if some might try to take advantage of his giving heart, she had to be like him, stand firm and trust that they would have enough. After all, as they often gratefully reflected on in the privacy of their own tent, they had plenty and had never gone wanting so far.

"That's a very good idea," perked up *nasi* Musa. "Just name the day and host it as you'd like."

CHAPTER THREE

REPLENISH

In the persistent grey-white atmosphere, they went through their flock of conse-crated, unridden she-camels and a few days later, her father had selected several unblemished she-camels as choice sacrifice options.

"So what's the plan?" said her mother with a teasing raised eyebrow. "I know you won't leave us nearly empty-handed like Hatim of Tayyi, but just checking."

"Surely they're too harsh on him," said her father. "And as Saint Ephrem says, the fool makes more of his beasts than of himself, for he cares for his possessions rather than for his soul."

"My blessed husband, deflecting his own genuine generosity to another, even if it is a saint," smirked Zoraya.

"Hardly," chuckled Zahir. "It'll be one she-camel for now, of course. But there's so many people that there's bound to be more demand. Plus some outside the walls will beg for some."

"*Sah.* So we'll say our goodbyes, then," said her mother.

It was their bittersweet ritual to take time to prepare those chosen on their last remaining days. They fed and pet them, bushed their coats, played and cud-dled—creating a few more moments of joy before they offered them to the needy hungry. It was always emotional for Jayida and, feeling like a child, she would only shed her tears while alone with them, whispering and singing into their thick woolen bodies words they not only understood, but accepted.

Like the eternal seasons, we were made for this, and always will be.

The humming resonated in her soul, and though it made her tears hotter for a moment, there was mysterious relief in them, too.

She informed Attab the Shadow one morning of the *maysir* to be held, and invited him to come and participate, even if only as a spectator.

He shook his head dejectedly. "I don't deserve anything. I lost them." He hid his face by looking away, and though he made not a sound, she knew that hot tears painfully flooded him.

"And yet you are here," she said, restraining her own tears. "And though they accept your tears, will they not take your smile, too?"

"It's all I have. Each time I think there's no more, it starts all over," he murmured.

Jayida had the impression of hearing a confession she shouldn't, of witnessing an embarrassment of overwhelming emotion. How could she, still a child, be of any help? But if she was too young to know and understand, then how did it move her so? It was beyond explanation, but filled her with a sense that even in silence and tears, there could be consolation.

"All the same, if you change your mind," she nodded with a pinched smile.

The chosen day came and, to respect the Israelite scripture law, *sayyid* Aziz chose a space outside the Khaybar walls for the sacrifice. Jayida held back and let the crowds gather around the *sayyid* as he prepared to slay their beloved chosen animal. He sharpened his blade as Nasr gently secured a leather muzzle over her mouth, then tied the rope around her neck to a peg on the ground. Her heart pounding, Jayida took a cautious glance, emotion seizing her that the camel and Nasr seemed so natural around each other it was as if he'd raised her himself. Still, it was no time to risk being hurt or even killed from her strength or sudden anger. So Nasr reached for one of her front legs, folded and tied its lower part backwards, leaving her to balance and hobble uncomfortably on three legs. The sob caught in Jayida's throat when Nasr reached up to the she-camel, and caressed and whispered her into calmness with secret *sha'ir* words Jayida wished to know.

Don't be afraid, we honor your gift, she imagined him saying, certain that the creature believed him.

A throng of men formed a wide circle and began circumambulating around the prized animal, the procession steadily growing in size as new participants joined in. A steady rumbling rose, some reciting words to their chosen deity, others humming, and still others looked on silently, lost in thought. A hush swept over them as *sayyid* Aziz exchanged places with Nasr, who stood aside.

"May *al-ilah* replenish," said sayyid Aziz, and gently passed his hand over the she-camel's face.

After a pause, *sayyid* Aziz plunged his knife deep in the hollow of the sternum, and sliced across just above the neck. The thick blood gushed out like a fountain, the bright red large pool fast spreading over the desert floor. Men and women hurried over and threw fistfuls of dust to cover up the blood, eager to sweep it away and limit the bloody mess—and any potential *jinn*'s revenge.

The she-camel's initial confusion yielded to protesting muffled groans, her body gyrating in defiant show of her strength. Her ability to balance eventually waning, her front leg gave way, and she lowered her chest as if in prostration, as her hind legs momentarily tried to keep their upright position. Her last jerking attempt made her fall to her side, her neck flailing and legs kicking around. After a few moments, her movements slowed, and then finally stopped.

In the deafening enrobing shouts, Jayida pinched a tearful smile. Like her parents, she wasn't sure if she could ever fully release her bittersweet attachment after years of rearing. And yet, just as mysterious was the undeniable relief of the ultimate sacrifice of their life to sustain theirs. Her last silent goodbyes to the beloved creature drifted like the fast spreading word to the non-Israelite *badawi* of the *maysir* game that might allot them some camel flesh.

The hardest part done, Jayida rejoined her mother gathered with Warda and Yazida, who smiled at her. Nearby, Hubala stood with arms folded like his son Sufyan, as his wife Samira cast frowning glances at Shams, who seemed deeply engaged in all that Nasr explained to him. The flesh was to be split into ten portions, and four players most in need were chosen from different tribes. They were Hubays of Banu Judham, Wassam of Murra, Raza of Numayr, and Zurara of Dhubyan.

Knowing *sayyid* Aziz's constant generosity, she couldn't imagine him favoring either of them, even if Raza and Zurara were members of kin tribes as descendants of Mudar. It was in such moments of need that they should all unite as one clan and help each other.

Sayyid Aziz handed the *ribaba* to her father, who opened the pouch to verify its contents. He counted the ten untipped and unfeathered arrows: the seven *al-ansiba* arrows with their value marked in notches counting from one to seven, and the three *al-aghfal* arrows without value left unmarked. Satisfied, her father returned them in the *ribaba* and retightened the rope around it.

"Now select your number of choice," said *sayyid* Aziz.

"Two," said Raza.

"Three is mine," said Hubays, holding up three fingers as if to call forth his luck.

"Four always brings me fortune," said Wassam.

"Six works for me," said Zurara.

"So that leaves one, five, or seven for our *baram* to pick," nodded *sayyid* Aziz.

"I'll be *baram*, if you'll allow it," said Attab the Shadow, who suddenly stepped forth in the engulfing hush.

She caught Nasr's approving grin at the appearance of her elusive friend. Deep stares turned to him, making it the first time most saw Attab or heard him speak, to some of their envious disappointment. For the little he consumed and rare times he asked for anything, it was only fitting that the role of *baram* should earn him some meat free of risk, even if his number wasn't cast in time.

"Of course I'll allow it," smiled *sayyid* Aziz. "Your number?"

"Seven," said Attab with lowered gaze.

"*Sah*. So one and five are unclaimed, along with the three unmarked *al-ansiba* arrows," said *sayyid* Aziz.

"I'll be *raqib*," Sufyan volunteered as watcher, though if one thing was certain, it was that Attab would never cheat. Sufyan took the blindfold handed by their *sayyid* and secured it over Attab's eyes and, once ready, handed him the *ribaba*.

Sayyid Aziz clapped his hands. "To remind of our rules: the first claimed number gets three portions and the second gets two, if both are cast within seven rounds. The third and fourth get two portions, but only if cast within three, and two respective rounds. Lastly, the fifth gets one portion if cast in one round. If not, the next claimed number that is cast takes any unclaimed meat, and ends the affair. Zahir will help me keep track of the portions."

With Sufyan's supervision and the crowd's focused attention, Attab shook the *ribaba* several times, making the arrows bounce and rotate inside. With a swift motion he tilted and thrust, allowing only one arrow shaft to emerge.

"One, unclaimed," said Sufyan, and picked it up and replaced it in the pouch to repeat the cycle. Attab rattled the *ribaba*, then spit out another contender.

"An *al-ansiba*," Sufyan said, picking up the unmarked arrow.

"Are spirits teasing?" chuckled *sayyid* Aziz.

"Seven!" yelled Sufyan, as Attab's lips made a circle under his blindfold.

"Name your three portions, Attab," grinned *sayyid* Aziz. "Go on," he said, sensing his hesitation.

"The hump, loins, and the left front leg," Attab stammered, clearly shocked by his bountiful luck.

Even if he'd only gotten the hump, he would've had the best part of the animal. As the first draw, he had his pick of large choice cuts, and Jayida guessed that it'd been a long time since he'd played the game, and deserved it.

"Noted. That leaves seven portions left," said Zahir, while Attab once again shook the pouch and cast.

"Six!" said Sufyan, to a resounding stir.

Sayyid Aziz nodded. "Name your two portions, Zurara."

"I'll take the ribs and right front leg," Zurara said, looking relieved.

"*Sah*. Five portions left," said Zahir.

The tension rose as bodies shifted, frowns appeared, and arms crossed, considering the higher stakes. The unclaimed five was drawn, then an *al-ansiba*. The next would either win or lose.

"Two!" exclaimed Sufyan, as Raza clapped gratefully, catching his prize just in time.

"Your two portions?" said *sayyid* Aziz.

"I'll have the two hind legs," smiled Raza.

"Noted. Three portions left," said Zahir, winking at Jayida. So far everyone had won something and she hoped it would keep going that way.

Attab jiggled the *ribaba* and thrust again. An *al-ansiba*, then another followed, leaving disappointed Hubays scratching his forehead and mumbling to himself.

"The arrows have skipped your three, so it now moves on to Wassam. If his number four is picked next, he gets all the remaining meat," said *sayyid* Aziz.

All eyes glued on the pouch when it released an *al-ansiba,* causing a collective groan.

"*Ya Allah*, how could you pass your faithful servant? I would be fine with just one piece!" cried Wassam. There was such desperation in his entreaty to the deity some believed to be the highest, and so contorted the leathery features of his face that Jayida frowned to stifle her own emotion.

"It may change yet," said *sayyid* Aziz tentatively.

But another *al-ansiba* came, then unclaimed five, then unclaimed one, that she marveled at none possibly claiming the meat after all.

"Seven!" shouted Sufyan, his surprise filling her to the core. He took the blindfold off Attab's face and hugged him, congratulating him repeatedly.

Then it was *sayyid* Aziz's turn to overtake the winner. "Your *qareen* decreed today as your day. May you be blessed and enjoy it," said *sayyid* Aziz, and gripped Attab's shoulders. An echoing rush of praise engulfed them, but not enough to dissipate the lingering disappointment.

"If I may, I'd like to say something, please," said Attab, trying to raise his voice above the noise. *Sayyid* Aziz called on the gathering to quieten down and hear what Attab had to say, and was promptly obeyed. "I want to offer my portions, all of them," Attab said.

"All? Are you sure?" said *sayyid* Aziz. His share was enough to last him a month or two, even without his second round of winnings.

"*Na'am*. So please give Hubays and Wassam their shares, and take mine," said Attab.

Sayyid Aziz frowned for a moment. "In that case, we shall cook your portion tonight and feast, with you included, of course. How does that sound?"

"As you wish," nodded Attab, with the first hint of a smile she'd ever seen from him.

"*Aywa!* If you needed more proof of this man's selflessness, now you have it!" said *sayyid* Aziz, who embraced him again and kissed each of his dusty cheeks.

The men dispersed to carve, hand off, and begin cooking the meat, as cheerfulness swept over the camp. Soon the wisps of incense and sweet aloes merged with the elevated spirits. Jayida helped her mother pass out extra bread they'd made, along with their stash of woven tassels that could be worn as bracelets or necklaces, or added to a belt as decoration to ward off bad spirits.

Amidst the rush of preparations outside the Khaybar walls, Attab had vanished almost as swiftly as he'd appeared, and Jayida searched the quieter places until she found him pacing through the Khaybar palms.

"I'm so happy that you decided to come. But may I ask why you played, if you were going to give it all away?" she said.

He seemed so absorbed elsewhere that she thought he hadn't heard her, or wouldn't answer. Then he turned to look at her.

"Oh, Jonder, it wasn't about the meat. For some reason, today I thought I'd take a chance. And now I know that luck is still on my side sometimes, even though we're in the *Ayyam al-Zalam* and it's selfish to ask. But I dared, and I'm grateful," he said, his eyes brighter than she'd ever seen.

Her throat clamped. "So you're happy, then?" she said, emotion filling her up, too.

"*Na'am*, I am," he nodded.

"*Aywa*, I'm glad to hear it. So join us later, when it's all ready," she said, and left him to his musings.

Jayida sniffled a happy tear away as she walked off. Her father had been right again, to use this chance to add some joy to their worried hearts. Though her father had requested not to mention it, word soon spread that it was one of his she-camels that had been offered. A funny thought came to her that Samaw'al had something to do with that, filling her with amused gratitude.

In the chilly evening they gathered around the scattered fires, with *nasi* Musa, Samaw'al, and other Israelites joining them and bringing some of their own generous permitted breads and pastries. Attab huddled nearby, nearly swaddled in a woolen blanket that her mother insisted on him wearing, and often made a playful point to check he still had it.

With her parents at one side, and Nasr, Yazida, Sufyan, and Shams at the other, she clung to Samaw'al's words for the little time they had him among them. He wove striking panegyric tapestries of poetry, praising his father's Alrayan tribe which, though once mocked for being smaller, eventually became powerful rulers of Najran and other parts of Himyar. In that time, his father 'Adiya had been young and like others, converted to the Israelite faith, and later moved north to Tayma with his family, where he built his castle Al-Ablaq and where Samaw'al was born.

The poet drifted into the enduring history of Tayma, and his foray to Kutha with her father and *sayyid* Aziz. Marveled gazes stole glances at her father, amazed at his heroic fighting of Al-Mundhir. It was the only time Jayida liked to imagine herself there with him, fighting that greedy, destructive *ghul*.

After accepting their praises, Samaw'al suggested Nasr to recite his tribe's history, from whom the day's blessed abundance had come. Though her friend humbly warned that he was no match for the poet's own skill, Nasr accepted and thanked the invitation to join in.

With his back straight and arms stretched taut at each side of him, Nasr released older and new verses, beginning with his father's birth. Jayida happily caught the places here and there where he'd already enhanced the passage with more vivid imagery. He improvised a *rahil* part praising the generosity of *nasi* Musa, and lampooned Al-Mundhir with a fitting biting *hija'* for turning away those in need. His plaintive high pitch dripped such tormented sadness that it drew tears, and if he could already command such emotional reaction, she marveled that one day some may gladly travel and pay to hear him.

"*Aywa*; may we both someday meet at the glorious marble reciting hall of *malik* Al-Harith, where our verses will echo into eternity," beamed Samaw'al when Nasr finished. It touched her that he would praise her friend's skill and invite him to the courtly residence of his mother's powerful kin.

The day ended in a long night huddled around Samaw'al sharing stories, until the crowd finally dispersed. Attab kept the blanket and eventually slipped away, too, leaving only her and her parents with Samaw'al and *sayyid* Aziz. Even Nasr had fought his sleep as much as he could before ceding, promising to rise early to see him off in the morning. For the first time since their arrival, she forgot that they weren't at Wadi Al-Hamd and that the sky would still be grey in the morning.

"See; we're the last ones standing," whispered *sayyid* Aziz with a grin. His rosy cheeks bloomed from his fair share of Khaybar wine—and sometimes the

Al-Andarin, Adhri'at, or Wadi Jadar varieties from Al-Sham—unlike his brother Hubala and nephew Sufyan who'd dozed off. Her parents chuckled lightly, sharing a warm cup of Al-Andarin wine that they passed on to her at times. She took small cautious sips, savoring the rich sweetness and amusing scene. Their *sayyid* was like a big, playful child when he got like this, and she only wished everyone would be the same under the influence.

"I'll remind you these reserves are meant to last a while," chuckled her father. "There's always pomegranate juice."

"*Sah*, but if this isn't the time to enjoy them, then when? Praise Nuh of the Ark for being the first winemaker to lighten our dark times," said *sayyid* Aziz.

"Ah, my friends. While I've enjoyed seeing you, I hope it won't be so long until I see you again," said Samaw'al tentatively.

"So then come visit us, we aren't hard to find," blurted *sayyid* Aziz a bit too loudly to their collective amusement.

"True, and I'd say the same but I suspect a certain person has something to do with it," said Samaw'al, his smirk fading into the fire. "It's not my place to pry, but I know that whatever made you leave had to have been a good reason. I'd like to tell you that if you'd ever want to come back, you're welcome to. If I didn't say so sooner, it's because I assumed you knew, after all we've been through."

Zahir smiled pensively. "A thousand blessings to your kind soul, but I'm grateful to feel that somehow we're right where we need to be."

It was true, and though she had her own curiosity about Tayma, she couldn't imagine going to live there now, and trading her current life along with Nasr, and even over-zealous Shams for Khaled, and others, as companions.

"Perhaps when Jonder's a bit older, we'll come visit and he can meet your family and son Hassan, and see Al-Ablaq," said her mother.

"I hope for it, even if, like so many others, it's on your way to other northern travels. I do enjoy hosting passing pilgrims; just like the Biblical days," said Samaw'al with a subdued air.

In the morning they blessed his travels as they chatted from tent to tent, then tent to mount, then followed by foot alongside his mount, until finally they released the poet to the desert and watched his shape diminish in the thick haze. For the first time, Jayida looked in that direction with an excitement of future possibilities. At least Khaled was curious about Jonder, even if she didn't exactly share his enthusiasm.

Day after day passed, similar and redundant as the next, yet pleasantly fulfilling in her morning routine of strolling through the date groves before helping her parents with all the day's work. She watered, fed, sheared and groomed the flocks, and collected the camels' patches of molting fur that always amused her with their temporary wild, rugged appearance.

"Every spring, Hania renews her clothing," chuckled Jayida, grateful at the sight of their humps that kept their full shape despite the uncertainty. They washed, spun and wove the wool, cleaned and dusted, and told stories as they made lentil and *rejleh* stews and constant batches of fresh bread.

Though the news stirred by the *maysir* had since brought Attab the Shadow to wider attention, he still kept his distance, and everyone knew that Jonder was second only to *nasi* Musa in finding him. It wasn't that they expected or demanded him to come out, but rather that there was henceforth a common confirmed knowledge of his benevolent *qareen*-like presence, who might watch over them without their knowledge.

When Jayida did see him, it soothed her heart that he at least was a bit better than before. In a way, he seemed untouched by the lingering uncertainty, though it came at the cost of already having lost those he loved most.

One day she brought Kamila with her, both as exercise for their mare and to introduce them to each other.

"Truly a noble, fine mare," said Attab, who happily brushed her smooth grey coat and fed her bits of dates.

"*Aywa*. And to think, some would've so easily given up on her," said Jayida as Attab looked on, sadness and fear flashing in his gaze.

She shared the story of her father who'd acquired Kamila in his seventeenth year. While grazing his flocks northwest of Tayma, he'd come upon Wabara, a lone, struggling tribesman of Ghatafan who was ready to slaughter her for food. Wabara had ventured far from camp in search of worthy pastures, and one by one, he'd had to trade his other mares to avoid starving, until at last only Kamila remained. He tried everything to avoid ending her life. He traded off all he had and desperately resorted to slicing carefully into a vein at her neck for some of her blood to fend off hunger, until he was left with few choices: either slaughter the mare and spare her more pain, and feed himself in the process, or watch her waste away a bit more each day. By then she'd since gotten so thin that no one had wanted to risk taking her. The little food he gathered he did his best to share with her, but didn't stop nature from taking its course. Kamila became weaker and he often made her sit to preserve the little strength she had left.

"I've shamed my tribe," lamented Wabara. "How can I go back with her? We breed the best horses and I'll be the laughingstock for having come to this," Wabara said, his wrinkles as deep as his anguish.

"Can a man control the elements? Yet you've come this far, and here we are. I propose this: you'll stay and eat with me tonight, and in the morning I'll give you seven camels for her," said her father Zahir, while Mubara just stared at him.

"*Sayyid*, with all my respect, but is this a trap?" said the man.

"No trap. I confess that I like the thought of the camels I bred spread all throughout the land," Zahir smiled.

"But how can I repay you?" Wabara shook his head.

"By accepting."

"Your generosity is a balm to my soul. I must know who you are," pleaded Wabara.

And they'd done just as her father had offered: they went back to Tayma, with Kamila seated on a woolen tent pulled by his headstrong mount Sabah. They ate and talked around the fire well into the night, and in the morning Wabara left with seven camels in tow, but not before professing his eternal gratitude, to him and *siddi* Gayas for having raised such a generous son.

Jayida didn't tell him the part about her father having to ignore Moharib's mumbling contempt—*Seven camels for a horse who'd surely die!* Instead, dedicated to the task, her father spent long days feeding her small amounts of barley and dried grasses throughout the day, cleaning up her diarrhea messes, and fighting the urge to overfeed her to make up for lost time. Then, within two full moons, she began regaining her health, her thickening flesh bringing out her beauty as much as his father's pride and tribe's praise.

Some called it miracle, and others a happy gamble, but it'd never occurred to her father that it wouldn't succeed. The way he saw it, there was never any losing, so long as he tried, and if and when it was her time to go, she would—such was *al-ilah's* law. As anyone could see, Kamila's playful, energetic gait revealed nothing of her past struggles. Some might not even believe it, but they knew the truth.

"Like my father, I like to imagine that she's grown stronger from it; like a close brush with death that makes the survivor almost immune to it," said Jayida. Moharib may not have approved, but it had strengthened young Zahir's confidence in his own judgment, as well as *siddi* Gayas's.

For a moment, Attab stilled, in awe of the living pillar that stood before him, proof of the mysterious endurance of life.

"Your father has a good son who tells nice stories," said Attab. Slowly he rested his hands on Kamila, as if her stone-colored body might impart some of her strength to him. "Do you have more? I used to know some verses, and some of

the *injil* and the Tanakh, but I can't—If I could just remember, then maybe—"
She caught his nose shriveling as he looked away.

"I do know others," she said, hoping it would cheer him up. Her heart sank at his torturing *jinn* that seemed to find any way to stress him even more.

Jayida shared the stories she knew of the *injil* and he listened so attentively that she momentarily grew embarrassed and thought of stopping, when such sacred stories should be told to him by a *mubassir*. But who would come in these uncertain times? She couldn't refuse him this little solace, and she tried to reassure him that with repetition it might help his memory. But in any case he shouldn't be so hard on himself, for who could say they remembered everything all the time? Most importantly, his *qareen* watched over him no matter what, as each person had at least one guardian. Attab nodded as he listened, his demeanor perking up as if relieved to be confirmed in his few happy wishful thoughts.

From then on, each time they met she repeated the stories, and he gradually began feeling bold enough to share what he remembered of them, too.

"May you take and keep these *wasm*, in memory of your loved ones," she said one day, handing him a handful of white and saffron woven bracelets. "It might also help you to connect different stories to different motifs, if you'd like to try."

Attab remained immobile for a moment. "In a way—You remind me of someone. Maybe it's a sign," he said and opened his dusty, rough palm in acceptance. She bit her lower lip, wondering if he spoke of a lost son or daughter—or even both—and didn't dare ask. He closed his palm over them, squeezed it tight and let it rest against his bearded lips. "You know, at least in sadness you can find release in tears, even when you think you no longer have any. But in anger, there's no rest; it always wants more torture. It's too exhausting, and I'm thankful that I don't have it," he said, his watery gaze staring into something far away.

She wasn't sure what he meant, when something about sadness also had to be tiring. But then again she had never been—and hated to think it—but hoped never to be in his place. At least, like the incense, she prayed they brought him some much needed comfort and rest.

Her own chilly, uneasy nights were still mostly vision-less, and the few times she had them, it was not of her Aksumite princess guardian. As *nasi* Musa said, she tried to count her blessings, and being with her parents and near the palms made her feel safe, in a different and yet similar way to her sightings of her guardian.

But why was that so, when she could use her guardian's reassurance then most of all? Had Jayida done something wrong that kept her, and maybe others, at bay? The questions repeatedly caught her off guard, like flying arrows marked for her. How long would the sun remain so veiled? Her father had already offered six hundred camels—causing as much shock as delight—and though they had much more, she couldn't shake the fear of no end in sight.

Soon after, Sufyan shared news of the Banu Sulaym—a kin tribe to the Sa'd—seeking workers for their gold mines south of Yathrib. With his older age, restlessness, and wish to get away from his nagging mother, she could understand his desire to leave wrapped in a wishful sense of adventure. Still, if she had to choose, the extent of her own interest was limited to meeting the tribe and seeing rather than working the mines.

"Just the thought of mining is harsh enough," said Nasr. "Is it really worth it to go so far?"

"For gold, I'd say so," chuckled Sufyan as Nasr rolled his eyes. "And maybe for a wife, too."

Now it was Nasr's turn to laugh. "You'd be in for surprises. Wadi Al-Qura and Tayma might do, too. Maybe even the mines of Al-Sham."

"That's an idea, and given their famed steel factories you might bring us all back some nice weapons," grinned Jayida.

"*Sah.* But I'll probably wait; make sure everything's fine first," sighed Sufyan, referring to his worried mother. "It's just—some days it feels like life is just going on all the same, and without us. And others I wonder what's the point to doing anything, especially if it might all end at any moment and I should enjoy my last earthly moments," he added with his dark humor.

She shared his frustration, though she told only her parents that sometimes she thought things would never be the same again. Whatever had happened to darken the sun for so long could not so easily pass without lingering effects, and the worst was that they could do nothing other than face and bear whatever unpredictable things came their way. As she'd told Attab, and as *muruwa* required, she had to believe that they'd come out more patient and stronger for it.

The erratic dread straggled, abated only during cooking that would inevitably come to an end, once they ran out once more, and her father would provide again. Hubala and Sufyan kept away from grumbling Samira, and often ended the night drinking with *sayyid* Aziz. At least they were blessed to enjoy delicious Khaybar wine, while others still swore the sour wine from the north was the worst they'd ever known—and feared for the future of their crops.

Jayida kept silent their own similar concerns—as if that might help keep them at bay—and while the trickling stories of the displaced were heartbreaking, so far they didn't have to worry about drought and food shortages.

Feuds between clans camped at Khaybar erupted—over supposedly stolen items, or watering privileges—and *nasi* Musa found himself increasingly frustrated, even considering forcibly removing some of the troublesome tribes if they didn't promptly—and peaceably—work out their problems.

"Ingratitude is the worst thing," *nasi* Musa discreetly seethed around the fire one night. "Some are eternally grateful, like Attab, while others will pounce on your kindness for ways to snatch more. As if you owe it to them. Proverbs thirty-seven says to refrain from anger and turn from wrath, but some of them need an iron hand. So I pray *al-ilah* gives me strength and patience," he said, raising a palm to the sky.

"A *sayyid*'s cloak is wide," sighed *sayyid* Aziz, and she read in her parents' eyes complete, concerned agreement.

More news spread—the short, flowing, and at times rhyming *risalah* form used for easier recalling and faster spreading sounding somewhere between factual news and dramatic poems. It was said that some members of the Banu 'Abs from central Najd had barged in on the Sulaym south of Yathrib, bent on claiming a share of the gold mines for their own, and custody of the idol Al-Uzza at the kabah further south at Mina. Though some had escaped, the Sulaym took most as slaves, pending negotiations and resolution. It sounded so extreme and unexpected that opinions were split between the 'Abs being as dishonorable as foolish, while others dreaded the bold move as but a glimpse of worse intentions—setting everyone even more on edge. Her stomach lurched at the name of Al-Uzza, to whom Al-Mundhir had sacrificed Yassu-serving nuns. Sufyan had been right to decide to wait, and she hated to imagine him possibly caught up in such dangerous conflict.

"Cowards betting on intimidation tactics, *sah*? I'll have no lazy thieves as my kin, no matter how distant or close our common ancestor," sneered *sayyid* Aziz.

"They should be ashamed of their scheming instead of discussing like honest men," echoed her father.

Jayida shared in their disgust that in hard times, when *badawi* should be coming together, some thought only of themselves and taking advantage.

For safety, they decided to remain at Khaybar at least until after winter, to which *nasi* Musa repeated they were welcomed to stay permanently if they wanted. Their camel flock had already lost hundreds more of its members—reducing their nearly three thousand camels by half—and though the fear always lingered at never returning to their previous numbers, she took comfort in seeing the genuine respect it generated. Though her father might be among the rare tribesmen on the land not to expect anything in return, it was reassuring to see public offers of alliance pouring in—offers which it would shame any *badawi* to make and then retract upon his word, should he be called on to fulfill it and yet be unwilling to do so.

So while Zahir declined anything material at this time, he accepted the honor of being trusted and recognized. His contemplative smile lingered, as if the comforting knowledge that he had a long list of offerings was enough to free him from those exact needs. At night they whispered of it between themselves, memorizing all the favors, if only to make clever rhymes.

"Enough seed for Zahir to feed his family into eternity," giggled her mother.

"Just imagine if I showed up at Banu Judham, Murra, Numayr, Dhubyan, and all the others I gifted camels to, and demanded an offspring of my gifted camels? My, I'd be all set once again," smirked her father. But it was not from mockery or vanity, when he knew all too well the deep embarrassment of need that could fall on anyone. Just like a treasure stashed away for harsh times, his joy was in being able to give and help restore the spirit of one who needed it. That Samaw'al alone could help meet his needs, both from ability and generous friendship, was an added balm.

Gradually the veil began slowly lifting, and as caravans arrived from the south, with less but significant enough quantities of weapons, silks, and spices, and news that despite the lingering uncertain conditions movement was taking up again, several began leaving the oasis. Whatever their reasons, it inspired others, and *nasi* Musa breathed a bit easier to see his lands return to their ideal conditions.

One early spring morning Jayida awoke, so cozy under her blanket that for a moment she forgot where she was. She drifted in the space between dreams and reality—a lingering softness wrapping her up in its jeweled embrace—then slowly squinted her eyes open.

"Finally! I saw her; I saw my Aksumite princess guardian!" she said, turning to her parents.

"You did!" said her mother who came to her side. "And now just in time for this, too. *Nasi* Musa wanted you to have this Mikha'il amulet for protection."

Jayida glanced at the winged gold angel with sword in hand. "Oh! It's beautiful!" she said, clutching it with both hands.

"As for more good news: we wanted to surprise you and tell you that we're heading back to Wadi Al-Hamd today," said Zoraya, and planted a soft kiss on her forehead.

Chapter Four

DARING

Summer 537 AD - Banu Sa'd

Fss, fss, fss.

Hunched down in the darkness, Jayida froze in the center of their tent's public area, the faint scratching at the entrance unsettling her. Her throat clamped, suppressing a rising nausea. She glanced at the dormant fire pit at her side, its imaginary hot coals crackling to echoes of faint, yet distinct horrifying cries, drenching her brow.

Fss, fss, fss.

She looked over her shoulder through the darkness, the lingering stillness confirming no one else had awakened or stirred. With a stifled, frustrated grunt she straightened up, and tugged at the front and sides of her undyed linen cloak, rechecking that the leather belt held tightly secured around her waist, containing short knives at each side and all her layers of clothing beneath it. She reached up to her face and tugged at the layers of her matching headdress, loosening the snake coiled around her neck.

Jayida closed her eyes, took a deep breath and forced her mind to flood with the facts. She was no lion-slaying Shamshun, having already tasted wine and trimmed her hair a few times, but she had to implore his strength as beloved of *al-ilah*. She shifted uncomfortably, the heaviness on her chest and arms making her second-guess this outing. But she reached for that glimmer of truth, that lone shining star in the pitch dark: it was already getting easier than it used to be. She would face her fears; this day was as good as any to prove it, and put all the taunting voices to rest.

She crept near the entrance and lifted her Bag of Treasures and spear. Her fingers ached under the fingerless patches of leather tied around her palms, protesting from long afternoons of polishing blades. With a last resolved sigh, she pushed aside the tent's entrance curtain and slipped out.

The biting cold pierced her like a thousand flying arrows.

"Finally! I was starting to wonder if I'd have to go in there and drag you out myself," Shams gritted through his teeth as he sprung to her side. His woolen blanket draped around him like a cape as they rushed to Nasr. She walked on silently, having long ceded to his habit of acting like he was the one in charge. It was all part of his learning, and perhaps a fair trade-off for her closeness to Nasr.

In the sooty early morning darkness, her hurried breathing made small white wisps, and for once she tried to take his usual eager enthusiasm as a good omen. They reached their seated saddled camels as mounted Nasr watched them with noble, quiet amusement. She secured her bag on the saddle and, summoning her strength, straddled Hania and adjusted her weight by slightly leaning back as Hania rose, excitement and fear battling through her.

With Nasr towering over them at the center, they rode west towards the somber hills in silence, until the tents disappeared behind the bend as they ventured deeper into the vast Wadi Al-Hamd.

Jayida raised her scarf up to her nose, fending off the lingering chill. Though it seemed the worst of *Ayyam al-Zalam* was behind them, its dark traces still lingered like a bad spell cast over the whole world. Worry filled her, for if their camels had thankfully been spared shrinking humps, it had not been the case for everyone else's. If the air cruelly thickened and darkened again—and she feared that it might—her father would either have to start saying no to others, or they could stand to lose their main provision.

"Beware! Whoever lurks is not ready for us!" yelled Shams, like Gilgamesh who, on his quest for immortality, had walked alongside the sun and across the Waters of Death.

She smirked, thankful that his tone was more comedic than challenging. Like his namesake he was a ball of fire, full of longing and plans, as if making up for lost time cooped up during the *Ayyam al-Zalam*—and including this great idea to sneak out while everyone still slept. But even she hadn't told her parents, and this breaking of the rule was a push, a confirmation that there was no going back for her now.

Once you prove yourself with respected deeds, al-'ayn will weaken and you'll have lasting security, her father's words echoed. The earliest tests were always the hardest, they said, and even if she feared the unseen danger of *al-'ayn* that constantly lurked, especially in her father's absence, she also wasn't alone. She wasn't sure what it meant, but there was also another part of her that was curious, who wasn't so cautious, and wanted to see things, test them and find out if they were even as she'd imagined.

"So, fiery fearless one: naturally you didn't mention a word of this to your parents or to your brother?" said Nasr, glancing sideways at Shams. "They might not be pleased with you avoiding your duties and leaving the bulk of the work to Sufyan."

"But I've *been* doing the boring pasturing with them every day for moons! I want something new: adventure, poetry, battle, the royal courts!" pouted Shams.

"*Aywa*, yet *hilm*, that most admirable patient self-restraint, is required by *muruwa* to make the perfect man. Now, I've yet to hear of one who's only eleven winters old doing all these things. Your perfect Time will come," laughed Nasr, whose calm manner never offended.

"*Sah, sah*; I know you both still get bored, even if you won't admit it," shrugged Shams.

"Pasturing may not be the most exciting, but without it we don't eat. I love seeing our flocks healthy and grazing," said Jayida, hoping she sounded as light as she intended. "And for the rest, if you think about it long enough, it's almost as if you're there. Maybe verses would even come to you."

Shams shook his head. "I try, but nothing happens. It's like the *jinn* only love Nasr and give him all the verses," he said, enviously peering at his cousin.

Nasr grimaced unlike she'd ever seen before. "Certainly not. Just keep at it, and if you use your quiet time wisely while pasturing, you'll hear your *qareen* amidst the misleading *jinn*, and that faithful companion will fill and guide you." Shams's pout cautiously retreated as Nasr passed them both a reassuring glance.

Though Jayida understood his frustration, this mouth habit of his made him look childish. Surely he would soon realize that, and stop it, and preferably before he set eyes on a chosen girl. As for his longing, echoed by many others his age, it often sounded more like jealous whining than honest yearning. Boredom seemed a vain luxury, and worse, a sign of misdirected attention when there were always things to do. Aside from keeping the required look out, it was a time to sharpen tools, forage for useful rocks, branches, and herbs, and any other potential treasures. And for some like Nasr, there was the poetry, too.

She glanced at Nasr's sculpted profile, marveling at his mysterious ability to create spellbinding verses. Though she'd known him her whole life, there were things she was still discovering, like that motherly protectiveness that both fascinated and confused her. What was it that called his *qareen* so often to him? Was it his aquiline nose, not unlike the glorious eagle deity he was named after? Or his gentle, dark eyes? Or surely it was his deep voice that commanded attention, subduing even his *qareen*? He swore there was no secret method to doing it, that everyone had their own way, and the answer was to discover it. Then, gradually, you'd grasp it and begin a dance whose steps never quite repeated the same way.

Jayida smiled at the playful thought, wondering if she might ever be able to recite something, more out of curiosity than necessity. But sometimes she concluded that a life spent with their flocks was all she needed to be happy; it was a blessing of its own to have large flocks to care for. *Aywa*, she could be happy that way—and once she had proven herself and earned the tribe's respect.

Pierced with the sun's emerging white glow, the dusty sky yielded to a lighter blue amidst the chill. They reached a diverging point of Wadi Al-Hamd, and came to a momentary stop.

"Lead the way," smirked Nasr.

"Onwards!" blurted Shams.

They forged southwest to the valleys of Wadi Tirah, and veered away from the northern branch of Wadi Al-Jizil. Jayida breathed hungrily the pleasant moisture in the air thanks to the curvy streams flowing all the way from Yathrib. The surrounding rolling hills towered over a wide, silvery stretch of water adorned with thorny *arak* shrubs along its path. Just as pleasantly, the wooly hamd plants the surrounding area was named after beckoned their mounts with their beloved knotty clusters of short, salty leaves.

A familiar echo of ghostly whispers gathered, swirling somewhere behind her. Jayida's chest tightened under her layers, restraining the memories of stories of winter night storms and deadly flash floods which, while possible anywhere, were more common in this area.

"*Shway*, slowly," Nasr teased his mount. With his spear and bag he hopped off as his mount headed straight for the water's edge.

Jayida cued Hania to stop, and armed with her own Bag of Treasures and spear, she let her rejoin the others in drinking and feasting on the plants. Shams made funny faces, imitating their loud manners with bottom jaw swinging left then right in repetitive chewing.

Like every summer, the valley was quickly drying up, with their flocks, along with other wildlife visitors, seeking out the best quality edibles it offered before it diminished. Jayida sent silent thanks that amidst the early morning, aside from them and their noisy mounts, the valley appeared free of other human life. Even if this time it had to be luck, since this outing wasn't her choice, they weren't babies and knew to heed the stories of children enticed and carried away by bandits with gifts of fruits. With Nasr's protection, their weapons, and alert attention, they were safe, and they could enjoy the faint buzzing of wildlife retreated deep underground to seek precious shade during the blistering days.

"What are you smiling at, Jonder?" said Shams.

"I was just remembering a time before the *Ayyam al-Zalam* when *yaba* brought me north to Wadi al-Jizil. It was an early spring morning, and the valley was lush and green, humming with life. There were oryx and gazelles drinking and lounging in the shade, and other *badawi* camped nearby with their flocks. Captured by every detail, I looked everywhere to absorb it all. Then it got quiet and when I turned, suddenly I saw a cloud of white butterflies hovering, and swarming up to surround me. Their creamy, silken wings fluttered so gently yet vigorously that I wanted to touch them. So light, so gentle, that you wouldn't even feel them if they landed on you. At first I didn't dare, but then I stretched out my hand, and slowly, with my fingertips, touched several. They seemed endlessly streaming out of a bush, before lifting higher and flying off in the distance. I've never seen anything like it again," she said with nostalgia.

"The blessed encounters with animals run in your family," said Shams, his lip threatening to protrude again.

"We all have them," she smiled, pitying his silliness. Some days it was easier than others to try to be patient, until she reminded herself that she didn't have a mother like his.

"*Sah*, Shams, you have your whole life ahead of you," said Nasr. "Now, since you wanted to explore, we'll go for a walk while our friends happily feast."

Using their spears as walking sticks, they hiked southwest along the *wadi*. The vacant long valley made it easy to spot anyone approaching while keeping an eye on their mounts. Shams trotted off, then ran up and down the hills, his thundering step and lashing spear surely banishing potential venomous horned vipers and scorpions.

"How patient you are with him, with us both," said Jayida, basking in the surrounding abundance. She liked those moments when it was just them two, the comfortable silence between them contrasting Shams's erratic, and sometimes restless, spirit. Perhaps when he got older he would calm down. Her mother often joked, saying that she would end up marrying Nasr, and though Jayida couldn't really imagine it, the thought wasn't unpleasant either, and especially when compared to other boys in the tribe. The more she thought of it, Nasr was the only one who might interest her.

"Do I have a choice?" chuckled Nasr in a lower tone. "We both know how lonely he gets; Sufyan is lost in his own affairs. So I want to be there for Shams and Yazida. And you, too."

"We're lucky to have you watch over us." She pinched a smile.

He nodded, his smiling eyes generously flashing like his father's. Would he have seen through her secret already if she had his sister's girlish beauty and doe eyes? With her boyish clothes and manners, she could never compare to Yazida, but she was relieved that she'd at least managed to keep it up so far. Sometimes she still wondered if Nasr, and even Shams, would be disappointed if they knew she was really a girl. But at least it would be a while before that was revealed.

"It's strange, Jonder."

"What is?" she said, a squeeze gripping her stomach.

"It's just—I've sometimes thought that I want to get away." He let out a long sigh, his gaze fixed in the distance.

"Where? Have you made plans?"

She tried not to frown at the reminder of his marriageable age of fifteen. Some *badawi* even betrothed their children at birth, in hopes that it might add some sense of security in an uncertain future. And though his father, and her own, were nowhere near so strict, it was an important matter to start considering at his age. His fearless and skilled hunting of gazelle had recently earned him his own tent, and she wanted the same thing for herself. His marriage would change things between them, but if that was to be expected, she hoped it wouldn't end their friendship. Nasr shook his head, his mouth tensing as frustrated contemplation drifted over his face.

"I am Shams, named after the great sun goddess! Hear my call and bless us with your bounty!"

They turned to the source and found Shams up on a hill, one arm pointing his spear up to the sky, the other waving in imploration to the gleaming disk.

"*Aywa*, now *all* the land knows! And while you're at it, don't forget to call on your consort, Almaqah!" Nasr shouted back, hearty with laughter.

"Ha! The great Shams needs no consort!" he shot back.

Cocking her head, Jayida stared at Nasr expectantly, trying to take his resurging light manner as reassurance. She had the recurring impression that he wasn't as easy to read as others.

"Whatever you're up to, I suppose we'll know soon enough, then?" she said cautiously, not wanting to push.

Nasr fixed her. "Oh, Jonder of the piercing lion eyes. Do I dare tell a budding *kahin* not to worry?" His gaze lingered in such a way that she didn't dare to protest his faith in her—her friend who'd first called her *kahin*—even as it dawned on her that he might expect Jonder to see into him. But what could she do for this handsome, generous and self-controlled *sha'ir* who'd already done much for her?

If only it'd been in her power to help heal his bouts of sickness, she would've gladly done so. "It must be that new bizarre summer heat. Sometimes I'm just tired; I'm sure you know what I mean. Come on," he nudged his head, and went on to the beckoning terrain.

She joined him in scavenging the land, ignoring her upper muscles' protests as she bent in eager foraging for their families. After all these years, she'd never had a reason not to believe or trust him; in fact it was the opposite. She hoped he wasn't having another bout of sickness coming on but resolved to make him a few more knotty bracelets that doubled as decoration, just in case. Amidst her searching she glanced at him, thankful that there was nothing to physically reveal the health struggles he'd already overcome.

She stuffed a woven storage bag with *hamd* leaves and another with *arak* branches, when Nasr's crunching steps approached then came to a crouching stop before her. "And here's one for you and another for Shams," he said, placing a large and perfectly smooth, cream-colored Zubaidi truffle in her gloved palm.

"Blessed Nasr! Is that your *qareen*, too? I've been looking for these," she said.

"What if it's yours who told me," grinned Nasr, walking off in direction of Shams.

"I might say it's unfair, though it spares me having to examine the endless cracks the land has to offer," she smirked and followed him.

"It pays to persist," Nasr laughed.

They met up with Shams, who happily added the truffle to his own bags of riches, then turned back to rejoin their camels, adding branches and leaves for fire fuel to their finds along the way. They refilled empty leatherskins with the *wadi*'s cold water, and after a while longer of browsing and spotting gerbils, rock hyraxes, and dark-nosed desert hedgehogs resting amongst rocks, they decided they'd done well for the day. Nasr and Shams mounted while she lingered to walk alongside Hania with her spear.

On the way back, they coursed through another stretch of hills that ran parallel to the way they'd come. Despite the familiar scenery of towering, bare hills contrasting the flat land with sporadic shrubs lying below, some places felt different in a way she couldn't, and often didn't even want to explain. An echo of muffled whispers seized her, tingling her spine. So long as her *qareen* protected her from any *jinn* waiting to play mind tricks on those passing through, she saw no harm in it.

Shrugging off the phantom wails, her leather boots pressed on the dry gravel floor, crunching beneath her weight, her dragging spear leaving a faint trace.

"I see something!" exclaimed Shams, who slipped off his camel and bolted past them, spear in hand.

"Shams, wait!" yelled Nasr, quickly dismounting. Her grip tightened on her spear as she scanned the floor for any animal or human tracks, and finding nothing, read similar confusion in Nasr's expression. They hurried after Shams, already an impressive distance away, and finally reached him, standing and staring into a space surrounded by low shrubs. For a moment they gaped in equal surprise into the shallow pit scratched into the earth.

"*Aywa*; blessed find, Shams!" said Nasr, glancing back and forth between them.

"Finally! It shall be said that I found a big nest of ostrich eggs!" beamed Shams.

"*Sah*, but first—"

"*Na'am*, cousin, I'm as surprised as you! But we would've spotted their huge dark feathery parents from atop our mounts," said Shams, his irritated yet keen observation for once making him sound older and wiser. Even if the discovery of over a dozen unsupervised eggs was rare, it was no mirage.

"By the bountiful Shams, talk about careless parenting! All the more for us," laughed Shams. "There are fifteen, so I offer three to each of you."

"We humbly accept your generosity," nodded Nasr.

Satisfied, Shams dashed off and lured their camels over, retrieved several large leather satchels, and slipped in his share of the large, heavy eggs. They followed suit and helped each other secure the prizes on their mounts, still hardly believing their luck.

"Let's see how proud *yama* is of these!" said Shams, every part of him ready to fly home.

"Indeed," said Nasr, trotting off behind Shams.

Her limbs aching, Jayida paused to gather herself as Hania walked on ahead after her friends. She dropped her spear, arched her back, and stretched out her arms. After a moment Jayida was ready to catch up when Hania's ears thrust forward and her large body scattered back, her open jaws releasing a defiant grunt. An icy rush shot up Jayida's spine and she instantly reached in her robes and turned around, just as a violent weight fell upon her, sending her back flat to the ground with a clinking thud.

Jayida crossed and locked her arms above her face, the small space in between revealing light green eyes and yellow spotted fur reeking of pungent butter mixed with blood and earth. Pinning her down, the massive leopard's guttural groan rattled through her like an evil *jinni* trying to get in, his hot breath spurting out in short bursts. His jaws widened and in the rush of wailing cries, begging for help, her left arm pushed up with all her might, twisting a fistful of the beast's furry throat, while her dominant hand stabbed away repeatedly at its jugular.

The thick warm blood covered her fist and dripped onto her face and clothing, as sharp claws struck at her, pressing, crushing her down with such force that she feared she might suffocate. His nostrils flaring, the beast snarled in pained shock each time he tried to bite down on her arms, but met resistance in its dying attempts.

Wincing, Jayida squeezed ever tighter around the throat, and kept stabbing into his neck until the weakened brute spasmed, and with a kick she cast him off of her. In a flash she was up, grabbed her spear and thrust it into the corpse, ending his life once and for all.

Panting, she folded over, gripping her knees to catch her breath, trying to keep her balance. She retrieved her blade off the ground, wiped it on her cloak and looked up—to the sight of Shams staring open-mouthed and Nasr proudly smirking, his ready spear now relenting.

"Brave Jonder! Are you hurt?" said Nasr, hurrying to her as if he already knew the answer.

"Just some scratches," said Jayida in a smiling daze. She could hardly believe what had happened: if it wasn't for them being there and the blood covering her, she wasn't sure she'd believe it herself.

"Blessed Shams, but how? He repeatedly tried to bite you!" shrieked Shams.

"*Aywa*, he tried," she said, and she lifted up a sleeve to reveal the coat of mail secured underneath. The long days of heavy weight and sweaty discomfort: it had all been worth it.

"Amazing," said Shams, captured by the riveted metal rings made to fit a young boy.

"By *al-ilah*! That devil had it coming! What a day for great rewards and stories," exclaimed Nasr, gripping her by the shoulders. He picked up the corpse and set it upon Hania who, though none too pleased at the scent of the slain predator, settled down when Jayida soothed her.

They hurried home, the realization dawning on her that the beast had long stalked then killed the elusive ostrich parents. But what mattered was that they were the real victors, with much to show for it. Relief engulfed her, considering how it'd all happened so fast that she'd had no time to think. She could only act and defend herself, expecting the worst and fighting with every bit of strength she had. But why had she been the one attacked? Too vulnerable? Animals knew, and could sense fear—had it picked her because she was the lesser threat? For a moment the worrying thought upset her, but then her pride took over: where had that gotten him! She showed him! It was frightening, almost paralyzing; seeing his claws, sharp teeth and piercing eyes aiming straight for her soul—the searching, latching evil eye—and yet she'd done it.

Satisfaction filled her, for as much as she'd feared that first kill, it hadn't been as hard as she'd imagined it'd be. Though she loved animals and often didn't like the idea of hurting them, there would be times when it was necessary—only now did she truly understand her parents' reminder. She'd been attacked, and now she knew that any moment of hesitation could be fatal. For so long she'd feared that she couldn't do it, or might be too sensitive. But now she knew better.

She was Jayida, known as Jonder, son of Zahir. And she liked the way everyone believed her, because it was real. She had two names: one known by the world and her other, true name known only by her and her beloved parents. It was her protection, the warding off of Fate and *al-'ayn*, as her parents said. And just like evil *jinn, ghilan*, and *'afarit*—spirits, ghouls, and demons—who couldn't be conquered unless their true names were known, they couldn't have power over her. She kept on her guard and now she'd proven that she could do it.

A new, intoxicating sense of achievement swept through her. Was that the feeling that warriors and poets spoke of? With the still warm corpse draped across her, she gazed at her drenched leather-covered fists and sticky fingers, the red clay-paste of blood like another layer of skin.

A peculiar delight flooded her, suggesting anew that she might one day learn to soften harshness with verses—reaching deep into the endless darkness to retrieve the conquering beauty amidst the violence.

Chapter Five

TIMELY VISITOR

"Shams ibn Hubala!"

Samira's angry shout struck even at a distance, her finger-waving ample shape referring to him as her husband's son, as every frustrated mother did. "*Ya Allah*; you hurry back here now!" she said, the entreaty to the deity and desire for hurried fulfillment so often connected.

"Oh my beloved *yama*, you'll have nothing left to be mad about once we arrive," said Shams, waving a hand poetically in her direction. "Yah, yah!" he ordered, lashing his *bakurah* stick side to side, the stinging leather strap forcing his mount into a run. "Charge onwards, to my well-earned praise!"

They bolted off after him, and for the first time Shams's manner of returning home as if charging into battle had a playful lightness she supported. Amidst her own troubles, she'd forgotten that if he'd often felt like this before, perhaps he might at least feel it less this day.

They'd hardly arrived to camp when Jayida glimpsed her mother's lovely bare-headed form rushing over. Her seven long ebony braids, which Jayida had helped make, curled on her shoulders like vines reaching for Shamshun. Her angelic face contorted in motherly wide-eyed shock, her dusty hands struggling not to grip the old linen skirt-covering tied around her waist.

"Praised, beloved mothers, we are fine," said Shams, sliding off his camel with such a nonchalant air that Jayida half wondered if he'd rehearsed for this very moment. "You shall hear all about the fine adventure we had today," he said, flapping open his leather bags and proudly presenting its contents like a merchant his fine wares.

"And you think this frees you for sneaking out before dawn?" Samira's beetle eyes flashed. She gripped her wide hips expectantly and Jayida had the impression that she was purposefully avoiding looking at her and Nasr. Her saffron and crimson headdress made a thick, high crown on her head, as the remaining fabric made a long cape set on extending its commanding shadow. She was a lifelike menacing mountain, and Jayida had the resurging idea that the combination could use some softening, starting with humbler, undyed clothing.

"No, *yama*, but at least you may enjoy these for a while, yet." Shams grinned ever wider, even as he let a worried frown overcome his features in a pleading, tentative manner. Samira crossed her arms with a sigh, her creeping grin adding to her dramatic art.

"*Aywa*; that's an honorable find, indeed," Samira nodded.

Zoraya stepped forth, peering at Jayida, and from her darting eyes all over her body, Jayida guessed she was doing her best to control her conflicted emotions.

"As for Jonder, he was attacked by a leopard, but the beast was no match for him, as you can see," smiled Nasr, just as her towering father swooped in at her mother's side. Clad in undyed clothing with his hair pulled back, his concerned deep frown yielded to a bearded smirk of relief that instantly transferred to her mother.

"Praise *al-ilah* you're all safe, as is always the case when they're with you," said Zahir, nodding gratefully to Nasr.

"It's my happy duty; there will be much to recite," said Nasr, humbly lowering his chin. He passed Jayida another approving glance, and she avoided the weight of Samira's as they each dispersed to their tents.

"What a fine first trophy that makes," said her father. He led Hania away by the reigns, grinning back and forth between her and the pale yellow coat patterned with black rosettes and gore.

"*Sah*, it is. But oh, how I worried; even if we knew this day was coming," whispered her mother with lingering concern. "Now, after all that excitement you must be hungry. But first, a change into unsoiled clothing," Zoraya added quickly, as if trying to assess the chaos without fully looking.

"Later *yama*; first I want to help *yaba*. And anyway, I don't mind it," Jayida smiled.

Her mother chuckled, shaking her head in acceptance. In twelve summers growing up as Jonder, it was easy for Jayida to forget herself, but her mother, in her gentle and discreet way, tried to tame her boyish ways. Unlike other mothers it was not overbearing, and if it should ever be, Jayida could hardly blame her mother, given her unique situation. Despite their occasional distance required by hunting, grazing, and exploring, she was lucky to have two loving parents who fiercely protected her and their secret. It had taken this long, but finally she could boast of one glorious deed that would someday soon reach the ears of Moharib—even if she'd yet to meet him.

Her mother helped her scrub her hands clean with a rough fiber brush, scraping and massaging into and under her fingernails to remove any polluting traces of the slain attacker's blood.

"There; the first round of many. Thankfully another benefit of all your layers is less contact with such elements," said Zoraya, giving her side glances.

It was custom to avoid much contact with blood, and while some feared that shedding too much would call forth the slain's revenge, Jayida realized with satisfaction that she hadn't thought of it and, even more surprisingly, didn't feel afraid. Her hands still pulsed happily as she helped her mother carry inside the heavy bag of eggs and her Bag of Treasures to the women's quarters.

Then she retrieved a large bag of alum salt and rejoined her father in the cloth-covered, shaded space next to the sheep and goat pens. She placed the salt next to large, water-filled clay basins kept on hand, and knelt across from him on the handwoven straw mat. He had already begun skinning the leopard: his short, sharp blade moving skillfully from leg up to torso, cutting off excess membrane tissue, flesh, and fat.

"See; all that fat needs to come off this spotted cat," he smirked. Gripping one of her blades, Jayida leaned forward and began slicing off thick milky-colored, smooth chunks as he continued to peel back the skin from the flesh. "*Aywa*; don't worry, you're doing great. We remove the fat otherwise it gets absorbed in the skin, and the last thing you want is a greasy skin whose hair comes off."

"Not after all our hard work," laughed Jayida.

The focused silence drew out the deep, bloody slashes she'd inflicted, marking out her self-defense that had kicked in in ways she could hardly believe. But the proof was there, and now everyone would know it.

They continued until they had the whole hide peeled back, hovering away from the flesh like a cape, connected only by the head. They set about carefully on the face by carving around the eyes, and continued to peel back along the upper jaw and lifting up and away at the wide nose.

Once completely peeled off, they turned the skin over with the soft interior side facing up, and her father scraped the hide again with his large curved sword, removing any last remnants of tissues. Then they plunged the skin in a water basin, rinsed off any traces of blood and dirt, and lightly wrung it. Jayida filled a taller and narrower water basin liberally with salt, and they transferred the folded up skin in there, fully soaking it.

"*Maniha*. Now we'll leave it in there overnight, then we'll cure him some more with alum salt. I'll finish up here, and now, the little lion of Sa'd secretly clad in mail should go eat and clean up," her father winked.

She left him and joined her mother in the public area, a spread of fresh bread and goat cheese beckoning. With her mother's doe-eyes following her, Jayida wrapped a piece of cheese into bread and took small bites, chewing slowly.

"Delicious, like always" said Jayida, the food somehow tasting different, richer this time.

Zoraya nodded and looked away, but not fast enough for Jayida to miss the twitching corners of her full lips. A moment later her father appeared and swiftly settled among them.

"We might have to say the look suits you, all that red," he grinned. Her mother gently swat his arm, and when he caught her hand and kissed it, her cheeks were also red.

"Oh, Jayida. You know how proud you make us," said her mother, gathering herself. "But now take your time to eat, then you'll get cleaned up and tell us all about it. After all, as your parents it's our privilege to hear it *first*." Zoraya smirked and retreated to finish tidying up.

A steady swishing approached just outside the tent, and she met her father's gaze in equal anticipation of *sayyid* Aziz. Her father rose and lifted the curtain just in time for their friend. The *sayyid* wore his locust bean-dyed faded headdress and matching cloak and robes, colored like laughing doves, along with a curious expression.

"Seems a fine day for you all to have a visitor," said *sayyid* Aziz. Leaning in, he peeked his salt-and-pepper bearded face inside, his gold Hand of Miriam amulet gently swinging as he chuckled in approval upon seeing her.

"A visitor?" said her father, the coat of mail weighing on her again.

"*Na'am. Sha'ir* Hakim awaits you in the guest tent. I assume he'll be here at least a day or two." His hand grazed his forehead along the headdress that concealed his usually shaved head, confirming he was just as aware and on alert to this most unexpected visit. Amidst her discomfort, his concern reassured her of the bond that he always communicated: that he stood by her father no matter what.

"We'll be right there, then," said her father, glancing at her.

"What a day for new stories," said *sayyid* Aziz, patting his shoulder and winking at her on his way out.

"*Sha'ir* Hakim? Do you *want* to see him?" scoffed her mother, flinging aside the separator.

"Time sure is a curious thing," mused her father. He crossed an arm over the other, one hand stroking his dark beard in contemplation. "I think it's worth enquiring; he did come all this way."

"Oh! Certainly wouldn't want to miss the generous thought that took twelve summers to come," said Zoraya with a wave of the hand. "And you, our fierce little lion?" Her mother came to her side and cupped her face, wiping off some of the dried blood on her cheeks with her skirt-covering. "Does it upset you? You don't have to go if you don't want to."

Jayida frowned defiantly, her mounting resistance fueling the impulse to flee from seeing this man who surely came to do Moharib's bidding. Why hadn't Moharib come himself, and with his own son Khaled to pay his respects, even if in the guise of showing him off, too? Why now? Without realizing it her hands had balled into tight fists. *Sah*: it was a day for new stories.

"No, it's fine. And I certainly won't wash up just yet. I want him to see me like this, and all the better if he talks about it," said Jayida, reading glowing approval in her parents.

"As you wish, my love. With that fierce gaze and blood that proves your bravery, you're one memorable sight. As for me, if I'm not here when you return, you may find me with Warda, singing your praises," said her mother, and planted a kiss on each cheek. Jayida smirked and followed her father out of the tent.

Already the buzz swept through camp as they walked east to the guest tent, the approving nods and excited murmurs fast spreading the news of their morning's adventure.

A thrill radiated through her. While the possibility of an unexpected visit was always in the back of her mind—*Always be on your guard*, as her father said—after all these seasons she'd almost doubted it would happen. But as much as she might not want to see this man, at least he'd picked the right day to arrive. If the initial shock had momentarily unsettled her, she gradually saw that she had no reason to be. At last Jonder would show himself, let his young yet noteworthy bearing speak for itself, and get some answers in silent observation while her father guided the long-overdue conversation.

They approached the tent, and with its fastened curtains pulled back at each side like welcoming wings, she made out a tall, slim man inside. His dark shadow paced in a slow circle, his wooden staff dabbing the ground at intervals. Her father slowed his pace and she had the impression that he might be as cautious as *sha'ir* Hakim on how to begin the interaction. They passed each other a final quick nod and entered.

"*Sha'ir* Hakim, I trust you had a safe journey," said Zahir, stepping towards him and extending his arms out in greeting. Their gazes locked and lingered for a while, as if silently measuring the effects of time and space. A smile slowly took shape amidst *sha'ir* Hakim's long grey beard and, nodding, he walked into her father's embrace.

"I did, praise *al-ilah*," said *sha'ir* Hakim, his deep rough tone indicating his late age. Gripping each other's arms as they exchanged a kiss on each cheek, the elder took side glances at her.

She stood still, her stiff bearing and raised chin rendering her as proud as an eternal sculpture. His deep gaze sparkled with an amused—maybe even pleased—curiosity she hadn't expected. His long cream *qamis* robe made a bright strip amidst his new ebony cloak, and if his wise bearing shrouded in its matching draping headdress and cloak was supposed to intimidate her, it failed. She let her eyebrow and jaw muscles slightly relax, letting the vivid, drying blood do its work.

"My son Jonder," said her father, his hand on her shoulder inviting her forward. *Sha'ir* Hakim approached and leaned down to her. "Jonder, son of Zahir, son of Gayas. It's my honor to meet the lion-eyed warrior on his day of victory," he said with a lingering friendliness. They exchanged the customary kiss on each cheek, his large bony hands and layers giving off the smoky odor of incense mingled with musky sweat.

"Welcome, *sha'ir* Hakim. I pray to add to my father's honor for as long as I can," she said with a hint of defiance.

Her father invitingly motioned him onto the low stool in front of the large earthen bowl of water and pile of clean cloths. *Sha'ir* Hakim accepted with a nod, and they reclined on the carpeted floor with a pitcher of goat milk, cups, and a woven straw basket of date-filled *maamoul* pastries. Her father reached for the elder's short wide boots, drawing a playful chuckle from the *sha'ir*.

"Oh, Zahir, you haven't changed," said *sha'ir* Hakim.

"I'm sure I have," said Zahir, setting the dusty leather pair aside. *Sha'ir* Hakim gave an appreciative nod and slipped his feet in, his eyes momentarily closing to wallow in the pleasant cooling effect. Her father filled their guest's cup first, and the *sha'ir* took his first big gulp of milk in weighty silence.

Keeping her back straight, Jayida sat cross-legged, an elbow resting on each knee with hands clasped. After a moment she reached for the bowl of pastries, and held it up to *sha'ir* Hakim in offering. With a nod he accepted and retrieved one.

"We'd love to hear about your journey," said her father lightly.

"Oh, you know. Business, as usual," said *sha'ir* Hakim between bites. "I went along with a caravan down to Himyar. As ageless as I seem, I assure you, I won't always be here," he laughed, gazing into the water.

Discreet not to bring the caravan with him. There just might be hope for him.

"Did you see the capital of Zafar and the restored church?" said Jayida, keeping an even tone.

"I did. I admit, that was one of my reasons for going," said the elder solemnly.

"Is it as big as the Bosra Cathedral?" said Jayida.

"No, and while that jewel of the north deserves all its praise, Zafar's is just as special in its own way, especially with its martyr relics," *sha'ir* Hakim sighed as if in silent prayer. After a moment he reached for a cloth, dried his feet, and with a grunt, shifted off the stool and onto the carpeted floor.

She pinched a smile, filled with the bittersweet longing to see the structure restored by *Negus* Kaleb after the massacres of *Masihi* that happened there, at San'a, and Najran. Curiously, it also reminded her of her elusive, yet loving Aksumite princess guardian.

"Surely it's only a matter of time before King Abraha builds his own, and won't accept only the Israelites, Fars, and idol worshippers in his midst showing off all *their* spiritual power," said her father. Not only had King Abraha defied *Negus* Kaleb by making himself king, but he'd also since defeated not one, but two forces that *Negus* Kaleb had sent to oust him from power, proving once more that he had popular support.

"*Na'am*, and hopefully reconcile with *Negus* Kaleb, too. They are brothers in Yassu-loving faith, after all, despite their different views and approaches," said *sha'ir* Hakim.

"*Sah*, as always: when convenient, they *might* graciously put up with the differences," Zahir smirked and sipped some milk, catching the elder's barely veiled reference to Moharib.

Sha'ir Hakim's demeanor softened. "*Sah*, and like many pleasant things the trip had to end, and as usual, on the way back we stopped at 'Ukaz. We had the pleasure of seeing Imru Al-Qays, although if he was more drunk on wine or verses, I could not say. But I am almost certain his father wants him around, even if he disapproves of his obsession with poetry," he sighed. "We continued to Ta'if and Yathrib, and finally I sent the caravan ahead so that I could come in search of you." *Sha'ir* Hakim glanced at her father and back at her. "Twelve winters is a long time, oh piercing lion-eyed leopard slayer."

"I'll admit, we thought we might see you much sooner than now," said her father soberly.

Sha'ir Hakim peered into his cup. "There was no invitation."

Jayida fought to keep herself stiff as her core muscles tightened, lest she give away signs of her annoyance. From what she could tell he appeared sincere, carefully treading, but many a *badawi* was skilled at pretending, too. Some said that was part of being and reciting as *sha'ir*. And though he already wasn't as bad as she'd expected, he wouldn't fool them either. Why should they be the ones to invite Moharib, when he'd been the reason for her parents' decision to leave? Surely he'd love that; as much for the boast as the potential of making her father appear guilty of wrongdoing, reflected in an invite that could be wrongly taken as an initial attempted apology. When the vile words had been all his doing!

A whiplashing rush burst through her, gathering like a smoky cloud, and in an instant she understood why *sha'ir* Hakim had come, now of all times. Whatever urge she'd had to soften towards Moharib vanished. Moharib was in the wrong, and they would stand their ground. Unshaken, their *hilm* would win, their self-control conquering the rising whirlwind of emotions.

Look at me; you came all this way, so look at me and don't forget! Her *qareen* screamed at both of them, and for an instant she thought she might explode—anger, sadness, and fear battling as he kept his eyes averted, put down his cup and stared at his knees. Every long, encased breath pulsated and scraped like a fine blade under her coat of mail. She didn't know how or when, but someday Moharib would admit how wrong he was—this was just the beginning.

"Since when would he need an invitation to go where he wants? Does this territory, or any other, belong to me?" Zahir frowned.

Sha'ir Hakim gave a lonely smile. "Isn't brotherhood stronger than any feud? Wouldn't Gayas and Rumayma, may they rest in peace, want their sons reunited?"

Her father chuckled darkly. "One's beliefs are shown through their actions, of which I was the recipient. Our beloved parents know the reasons, so may they be at their deserved peace."

The elder's eyes narrowed and fixed her father with a odd look of shocked anger. But he remained silent, contemplating.

"Come, Hakim. I think we both know where this is going. If he's been worried about me struggling without his generosity, great though it is, I trust you can now reassure him," her father added with a curt laugh that only he could make sound inoffensively dismissive. "What's important is that you're all well."

That was her *yaba*: humility without self-pity, and effortlessly sweeping away the tension. She wondered if Moharib had ever done a similar gesture in thoughts of her father, and almost swore she heard a faint voice from somewhere saying *no*.

"*Aywa*, your brother would say his affairs have especially prospered," said *sha'ir* Hakim.

Jayida reeled in her resurging annoyance. Of course they were; it was Moharib! She already saw all the vainglory in her mind's eye. Surely he had nothing to fear when he'd hoarded his substantial provisions during the *Ayyam al-Zalam*, unscathed and remorseless while the fearful chaos raged. Perhaps he'd even made an alliance with the *ghul* Al-Mundhir over trade and territorial matters, as men of like minds knew to seek and selfishly bolster each other at the proper time. Jayida looked down, sure that her gaze would give all her anger away.

"Thousand blessings to you all. And between us, if he might joke that my departure is the reason for his prosperity, all the same; another thousand blessings to him," said Zahir, as surprise invaded the elder. But if he knew her father at all, even after all these years apart, *sha'ir* Hakim should know as well as she that his own words were of heartfelt congratulations, even if they were one-sided. "And what of Khaled? Strapping young man, surely," continued her father, and she almost wished he would stop being so sincerely kind.

"*Aywa*; he's making us all proud. Handsome and strong, he's slayed and earned more hyena and wolf pelts than he knows what to do with."

"Impressive, and what a blessing for it to run in the family," Zahir beamed. "My Jonder hasn't even started full weapon training yet."

"Natural-born fighter. I will consider it a good omen to have met you on this day," said *sha'ir* Hakim, and she had the renewed impression that he was sincere. "By *al-ilah*, how fast Time flies. Moharib is already starting to consider potential marriage partners for Khaled. He's hardly happy about it; seems more like a joking matter to him," chuckled *sha'ir* Hakim.

"Blessed as he is, he'll have no shortage of choices," said her father and bit into a pastry.

"*Aywa*; you know your brother; eagle-eyed and intent that if there's a fine potential in our midst, it's for us to claim her first."

"*Sah*, and yet, life can have its surprises, too," smirked her father.

Jayida reached for a pastry and bit into it, chewing slowly to savor the sweet sticky richness of the Khaybar dates. Khaled's deeds may be many, but all they had to go off of so far were words. Still, this disinterest in marriage was one thing they had in common.

She could hardly imagine it, even as her mother often said she would change her mind when she got older. The teasing had already begun, wondering who Jonder might marry, but she'd noted long ago that there was no one in the Banu Sa'd that quite moved her the way the poets often recited. Nasr was caring, handsome, and poetic and she enjoyed his company, but she could hardly even imagine kissing him and doing the other private things that people did. The thought almost made her laugh in playful disgust: it might be like kissing her brother, if she had one.

Why did she have to get married if she could take care of herself? What if she just stayed as she was? Love, love, love—the stories and poets raved, but sometimes it all just seemed exaggerated. The verses bled with heartbreak, so what was there to want from this? It all sounded like a tormenting disease that made everything dramatic and complicated, and distracted from peace and self-restraint.

"May he be blessed with a fine match, he deserves nothing less," said her father, and she caught his gaze on her that confirmed it pertained as much to Khaled as to herself.

"And same to Jonder," *sha'ir* Hakim nodded and rose.

The afternoon elapsed, and amidst her respectful distance, she pleasantly confirmed that he wasn't unlikeable either. They took him around for a tour and to everyone's surprise, he declined staying for what was set to be a bountiful meal, but she was also glad that her father didn't insist after a few honest attempts.

It was selfish, but part of her wanted to revel in the day's glory without him around. Still, she delighted at *sha'ir* Hakim's gift of some frankincense, and her father in turn offered him an ostrich egg, which he accepted only after much coaxing. That was only a gain, when such a treasure could serve as a marker of the day *sha'ir* Hakim had visited Zahir and met his son Jonder, the leopard slayer. Besides, if the past was any indication, and though their encounter had been cordial, there was no telling when they'd see him or anyone from the Banu Zubayd the Great again.

At last the elder bid them goodbye, wearing a contemplative seriousness that gave him a melancholic air.

"Until we meet again soon," said *sha'ir* Hakim, his tone hinting of solicitation.

"May *al-ilah* hear you," said Zahir. *Sha'ir* Hakim gave a final lingering nod, then turned away on his mount and headed north.

"See, that wasn't so bad," chuckled her father as they made their way back to the tent.

"*Sah*. If anything, it was a success," she contemplated with relief.

"Now that I recall; since you've started wearing the small coat of mail, was there a coin stored with it?"

"No."

"Hmm. I thought I might've kept them together."

"When did you last see it?"

"Uff, long, long ago, before we came here. I'm afraid it may be lost." His shrug countered his frown.

"I didn't know to look for it, so I could've missed it. I'll check again," she said, her curiosity now piqued and hoping she may have overlooked it.

"*Aywa*. Now go add to your mother's happiness by washing off all this blood," he said, leaving her to slip inside the tent.

CHAPTER SIX

KAHIN

Zoraya cocked an eyebrow at the sight of Jayida. "Let me guess: napping until the feast?"

Jayida shook her head. "No; just a perfect introduction, and even better: he's already gone."

Her mother mirrored her grin. "Something tells me neither of us minds that brevity. Even if I've always liked the man, he has another to answer to. *Aywa*; a day full of pleasant surprises! And now, little lion, your bath," she said, waving her to the back. "I'll be right there."

Jayida skipped through the women's quarters and entered their dark, cool private quarters, across from their sleeping area. A few sunrays protruded narrowly from on high, the roof covering rolled up just under the roof to allow air to circulate. On the ground was a raised clay basin used for bathing and washing, woven bags filled with bathing supplies, and a few wooden buckets of water covered with sackcloth nets to keep out flies and insects.

It was her second favorite place, after the sleeping area, nestled safely within the tent with its two layers of somber fabrics to seal off potential prying eyes, and the precious clear water from their camp's well. She smiled at Kamila's soft rustling coming from her quarters just next door, confirming the mare had both heard and smelled her.

With a defiant moan, Jayida pulled off her stained headwrap, untied her belt, and cast off her bloody cloak. She shed the two layers of linen *qamis* longshirts that covered the chainmail, adding to the pile. Her back spasmed with soreness as she snaked her arms and torso out of the chainmail shirt, and let it fall to the ground with a grunt. The final tunic layer underneath pressed on her sweaty limbs like smooth Hudhayl honey. She peeled off and tossed the drenched garment aside, her clammy warm skin and seven disheveled braids begging for refreshing water.

Her mother's delicate, sure step resurged, and a moment later she reappeared with a large bucket of water in each hand. Zoraya emptied them into the basin and Jayida climbed in and lowered herself on her knees, her teeth delightfully clenching at the blessed coolness of fresh well water.

"Oh, my heart," cooed her mother, settling at her side with the bathing supplies.

"And to think, as a baby your bundled form slept peacefully nestled in the coat of mail like a silver cradle. You won't fit in there much longer." Zoraya leaned into her and soaked a cloth, then made a waterfall over Jayida's face. "What a day. I was so afraid and yet here I am, a proud mother. Praise Yassu!" she said, her eyes sparkling.

"Such doe eyes you have, *yama*. This poetic image could've only come from seeing yours," said Jayida, reading in her beautiful mother as much concern as relief.

"And such honeyed, lion ones *you* have." Gently stroking her cheeks in repetitive motions, her mother appeared in such contemplation that Jayida hoped she wouldn't cry from sadness.

"*Yama*," said Jayida, wanting to reassure but her tone involuntarily sounding more questioning. "The first is the hardest," she said, reminding them both.

"Mmm." Her mother sniffled, cupped her chin and covered her cheeks, eyes, and forehead in kisses. "Oh, how much I've wanted you and prayed for you! If anything were to happen—Oh, forgive me! Today you showed them: you conquered!" Her mother hugged her tightly, smothering her with her frenzy of consuming love. Though it saddened her to see her mother worry, Jayida tried to replace her own shared concerns with the day's hint that she was on track to ultimate security.

Jayida settled back in the water, and as usual she yielded to her mother's expert scrubbing, relaxed by the massaging motions of the rough cloth and fragranced paste of *'ujrum* ashes, green *ushnan* powder, and alum rock from Tayma. Then her mother loosened her ebony braids and covered her hair in the earthy clay paste, repeatedly dipping into the watery muddy mixture to soak her locks.

"At least, it's not much longer that I'll be seeing you like this," smirked her mother, reaching into her armpit.

"Like what?"

"Like a handsome boy," Zoraya laughed, pinching her side. "Soon, your breasts will sprout, your hips will widen, and I'll be the proudest of mothers fending off the constant suitors eager for your true beauty that I've always known."

"*Sah, sah*, just not *that* soon," shrugged Jayida, whose limbs were swiftly splashed with reprimanding streams of rinsing water.

Jayida hoped she looked like a boy: her body hadn't yet started showing the signs of growth that erupted in Nasr and other boys, and she sometimes feared her face might make her look too sensitive, like a fragile girl. Thankfully, her thick dark, and often furrowing eyebrows added to her intense gaze, which was exactly what she wanted. It's not that she truly wanted to look mean or angry, and was usually unaware of it, but if it helped her look serious, or even in the midst of contemplation, then she didn't mind it. Like her mother she had a long nose and full lips, while sharing her father's strong brows and direct gaze, along with his bearing she aspired to emulate. Her mother's graceful beauty was accentuated by such a fine, feminine figure with ample breasts and a medium waist that she doubted she would ever match it.

"Oh, just you wait and see; one day you'll be singing a different tune. And remember—"

"Hair is a woman's glory. Just like Shamshun's strength," grinned Jayida, and shook her head to cause a light rain.

"You're your father's son," said Zoraya, playfully coaxing her out of the basin and onto an adjacent mat.

Zoraya draped a long linen sheet on Jayida's shoulders, the afternoon heat hardly requiring any drying off, and retrieved a small glass vial of scented oil. She dabbed a few drops of the spicy-sweet cinnamon-tinged concoction into Jayida's hair, under her earlobes, armpits, and wrists. After changing into a clean set of bottoms, a long-sleeved robe, and cloak, her mother completed the ritual routine by passing the ivory comb through her damp hair, rebraided it into Shamshun's seven braids, then loosely crowned her with her head scarf.

"Oh, it's nice to be light again, but I shouldn't get used to it," Jayida chuckled, glancing at her coat of mail.

"It's wise of you to practice wearing it so soon, but I think that's enough for the day."

Refreshed, Jayida slipped to the adjacent room, and found Kamila reclining near her trough of hay in her cozy quarters. At the sight of her the mare's head lightly shook up and down. Did she know? Did she already see her differently?

"*Aywa*, I slayed a leopard," Jayida said, unleashing the delightfully strange words out loud. She knelt at her side, stretched out her arms around her dove-grey neck, pretending she could grasp her fullness all at once. Her hands traced along her wide cheeks, and rubbed her neck and withers, her soothing liquid eyes closing under her touch. In these intimate, quiet moments, there was no doubt the mare understood her, and was proud of her, too.

In the evening, armed with supplies and full straw baskets, they rejoined *sayyid* Aziz's campfire just as the sun set. They set down the piles of fresh bread and cooking supplies, oiled their large red clay pan and set it above the logs. Zahir withdrew his blade and, tilting it at an angle, he struck the ostrich eggshell hard repeatedly, sending small bits of shell flying off. He continued until finally a thick piece of shell came off, exposing the sturdy membrane.

"We'll try to keep the yolk intact," he said. He proceeded to remove almost half the shell, his fingers maneuvering to keep as many of the shell pieces as large as possible, and pierced the lining with the sharp point of his blade.

With a careful tilt, he poured out the egg into the pan, its orange yoke alone as wide as his hand. Zoraya seasoned it with some salt and pepper from Aksum by way of Himyar, as she gathered the intact shells and supplies into a basket and promptly brought them back to their tent. She returned to the sight of *sayyid* Aziz and everyone cheerfully gathering to join in expanding the celebratory meal.

As usual, Jayida sat with her parents at one side and Nasr and his family at the other.

"How proud is this *sayyid*, to have our children follow in our footsteps. And praise to our blameless father and mother, for watching over us all," said *sayyid* Aziz. He paused and looked away, before showing them each his glittering, sentimental eyes. "Let the *Ayyam al-Zalam*, those Days of Darkness, be behind us, with this bounty they've founf and brought us!"

Jayida smiled, touched that he openly showed his honest emotions, and was seen as no less a strong leader for doing so. Even after several winters of his mother's passing, he often called both his parents to memory during communal meals. *Sayyid* Aziz joined his brother Hubala in breaking Nasr's three and Shams's four gifted eggs, their seemingly unrelated appearances countered by their playful interacting.

While Yazida helped her mother Warda pass out bread, Sufyan and Shams rejoined their mother Samira, who still seemed to evade her gaze.

"Soon we'll be able to trust them alone with the camp," said Sufyan. "So for once I won't complain his ditching of duties, and praise my younger brother for this bountiful meal," he said, wrapping a long arm around the proudly grinning Shams.

After a moment, Sufyan sprung up, gathered some of the pans and distributed them to other tribesmen, spreading the tale of his brother's achievement along the way.

"Today, our Shams's burning fire has paid off," nodded Samira to her husband Hubala, who chuckled in agreement. For a moment Jayida thought Shams looked uncomfortable.

"With many more to come. And praise *al-ilah* that my maternal fear is eased, knowing that our Nasr, like his noble eagle namesake, watches over you all," said Warda. She shot a playful look that bounced from Zoraya to Nasr.

While gossip was the specialty of women's tents, by now everyone guessed that it was usually Shams who had the daring ideas, so that if anyone were to blame, it would likely be him. But their code of loyalty to each other also meant they wouldn't give each other away, if it ever came to that.

My brother and I against our cousin, our cousin and I against the stranger—so went the ancient *badawi* code. And even though Jayida was not Nasr's brother, that they were close enough to upset Samira and Shams was not something she did on purpose or could control. She'd even expected Nasr to distance himself or say something about it, in his gentle way, and that he hadn't only confirmed that she shouldn't do anything different. He was the only friend with whom she felt truly comfortable, and hoped to enjoy his friendship for as long as she could. In any case, it was their task to overcome and prove their own growing ability to provide and survive.

Thankfully, her mother's closeness to the *sayyid*'s wife Warda, and her general good relations with the rest of the tribe only helped solidify Jonder's position. Her heart always swelled at the difficult, yet wise decision her parents had made to live among them. That such happiness had gradually eluded them at the Banu Zubayd was a constant frustrating reminder of the ways even blood ties could change, and may not be resolved for years to come.

As such, Jayida had no wish to come between Nasr and his cousin Shams, and hoped that he would soon see that their friendship didn't need to be a threat. She tried to see it as another test of her patient *sabr* and *hilm*, and though often annoying to dismiss, whatever little jealousies emerged was overridden by their tribal code of loyalty. They would protect and fight side by side, and if that didn't count for something, nothing would.

The eggs crackled in readiness and were drawn closer to reach, their distinct rich scent making her stomach growl. The long time since they'd last tasted ostrich eggs added to the anticipation. Finally gathered around, more fresh bread circulated and, thus armed, they eagerly dipped in. The soft, white-translucent egg had a rich buttery flavor that for a while kept everyone nearly silent, except for their lively chewing.

After the feast came the praising, her parents retreating to the background as younger children and adults alike swarmed to congratulate her on the leopard slaying. A pinched smile dominated her face, holding back her touched emotion at the sight of the children's amazement, their shared wish to someday do the same humbling her with their fast-trusting praise.

"If I can do it, you can," said Jayida, happy and overwhelmed in a new way. Thankfully, after this morning, the thought of training was somewhat less frightening.

The sky shifted to pale blue shades and amidst the hubbub, a hush swept over them as her father reappeared among them, gripping the skinned leopard carcass upside down by each pair of legs. He stood near the fire, with her mother at his side holding the smoking *bakhur* incense holder, both looking at her trustingly.

"What would you like to say, Jonder?" said Zahir.

"Thousand blessings to my parents and to the Banu Sa'd, to all their kin, and friends," said Jayida without a second thought.

"*Aywa*, Jonder ibn Zahir!" shouted *sayyid* Aziz in approval. He glanced at her father and with a final nod, Zahir tossed the creature in the pit, the flames lapping around the flesh to resounding cries of praise and whistling. Her smile turned to a playful frown as her father lingered in place, still commanding all attention.

Zahir reached into his folds, retrieved and unfolded a small linen bundle, revealing four leopard fangs that he'd spent all afternoon extracting.

"Fine trinkets to fend off *al-'ayn*!" clapped *sayyid* Aziz to echoes of agreement. Zoraya waved the frankincense *bakhur* smoke over it, and after a few moments her father rebundled the contents.

Touched, Jayida nearly said something to change the subject, when with a brisk movement, his arm reached in his robes again and came out with a fine, straight-bladed steel sword. "Straight from the Bosra armories," her father grinned. Awestruck, Jayida could only stare as her mother repeated the *bakhur* smudging over the prized blade.

"*Aywa*, give it a try," Zahir chuckled, handing it to her.

The thick handle fell heavily on her palm, filling her tight grip. The pristine straight blade glistened like melted coppery gold in the fiery glow, confirming why the quality steel struck in Ghassanid factories were renown and praised by all. She imagined the royal swords adorned with engravings and precious stones, and even without them, it was no less impressive.

A delightful confusion seized Jayida. She loved everything about it: its reflective surface like liquid silver, its flat edges contrasting the Indian curved blades more effective for slicing than the thrust required to pierce armor. There was another piece of beautiful metal to protect her, just like the coat of mail that was already becoming like a second skin. Yet, with some reluctance, she yearned to keep it unblemished, like a holy relic display commanding such awe it deterred violence. Dare she say it: she had no wish to bury the blade into anyone.

But then there was the leopard, who'd called forth her instincts at the right moment. Respect and fascination filled her at the bearing of this powerful weapon, whose use and purpose was no mere children's games. Resolved, she straightened, took a discreet deep breath, and glanced at her loving parents and their *sayyid*.

"I am Jonder ibn Zahir, and I vow to make myself worthy of wielding such a prize. It will be known as Al-Wasiyah, the guardian," she said to resounding cheer. It thrilled her to soon learn and be worthy of properly wielding it.

"And so you'll be each other's guardian once you begin practicing," said her father.

"*Na'am*. And so, blessed *yaba*, please do us the honor of reciting again how you earned your first sword," beamed Jayida, and rested hers across her lap.

Her parents sat down and the voices settled again, all communal attention locked on him. He looked around for a moment, clearly amused.

"I was a bit older than you. We went out on a hunt northwest of Tayma, slayed gazelles and later passed by some caves. It seemed empty, quiet—too quiet—until a ferocious lioness appeared. Her small mane almost made her look like a young male, and from her mean roars as frightening as her size, it was clear she had cubs nearby. She attacked a Zubaidi tribesman, closed in on his leg and began luring him away. He screamed, pleading for his life, when I went in and struck into her with my spears. There was no time to think: when a mother protects her young, it's either you or them. As a reward for my bravery and saving his life, your blessed grandfather Gayas gifted me the beauty that you know. And ever since then, it's been Al-Hamiyah, the protector."

The warm stream of praises lingered as they continued reciting stories, and amidst the happy bustle she noticed Yazida glancing at her. Her smiling eyes shone with a curiosity she'd never seen before, like she might want to stay up all night around the fire and hear Jonder's whole story. With some regret, Jayida wished she could talk to Yazida as a girl, and though that day would likely come in the future, all she could do for now was smile back in grateful acknowledgement. Shams appeared rather boldly chatty with Yazida, but at least the *sayyid*'s daughter would be hearing more about their adventures from both him and her brother Nasr.

In the gradual, enveloping stillness reassurance filled her, and she turned to Nasr at her side, his noble bearing commanding all attention as only a skilled and handsome *sha'ir* could.

"This is the tale of the earliest great feats of Shams and Jonder of the Banu Sa'd, shortly after the *Ayyam al-Zalam*," he began, his tone slowing to draw out his poetic images.

Nasr weaved a detailed opening *nasib* passage describing their leaving camp before dawn, and smoothly transitioned into the *rahil* stage of their camel-borne journey in search of adventure. Amidst his gifted rendering, he also brought in elements of poetry from the *badawi* dwelling further west in the mountainous Hijaz. He replaced the honorable, and often preferred, sword weapon with their simple spears and daggers, and the glorious warhorse mounts, like those of the Jafnid royal princes, in favor of she-camels. Jayida's heart started pounding when he got to the part of her humbly walking by foot—just as she'd done right before she'd been thrust to the ground. The poetic language made it sound dreamy, enticing even, but for once it was true and not a heroic embellishment.

Though *mubassir* Ayyub said that Syriac was the king of all languages, from which all others came, she was moved by their own *'arabi* language's effect. Evocative and melodious, he lulled them with his magical rhyming tone, casting a powerful spell they couldn't get enough of. Hearing him reminded why some warned that it could be dangerous from the wrong people, and was best left to *kahinat* serving the deities. His eyes closed at intervals, his handsome features contorting in such a way that he appeared like another person, lost in another world.

"And all along, Jonder uttered not a single fearful cry, like a true born fighter who'd awaited just that very fateful moment," said Nasr, his observation and the tribe's attention on her sealing up her throat.

Not only had he noticed, but only now did she realize that indeed she hadn't screamed out or even said a word. In the chaos her body had gathered its strength deep into itself like a fortress, concentrated into her eyes, arms, and hands—to face it, seize it, and make it end.

Nasr finished with the *fakhr* closing segment, with Shams and Jonder praising their beloved tribe they heroically returned to, their hearts as full as their bountiful bags of treasures. This well-rounded form drew even more emotional outpouring and gratitude from the tribe than she'd ever dared imagine. Floating in the enrobing glow, her tugging heart wondered that she could learn to love him someday, if they were to marry.

"Oh, my Nasr, blessed *sha'ir* of Sa'd! Surely this *nasib-rahil-fakhr* form is the one that will become most popular," said his mother Warda, on the verge of tears with beaming pride, leaving them all aglow for the rest of the night.

The temperature had dropped to a chill when they finally retreated to their tents, and as eventful as the day had been, a part of her still buzzed wildly. With Al-Wasiyah at her hip and an oil lamp in hand, she followed her parents in ensuring the tent curtains were securely tied shut, and the small fire at the center of their tent safely put out, and settled in their sleeping area.

Jayida bundled Al-Wasiyah in a clean, fumigated linen cloth and set it down before her statues like a votive offering. With a playful, careless motion she cast off her headdress, pulled off her leather boots, and finally reclined on her bedding, her moist toes wiggling in delightful freedom.

With one hand lightly on Al-Wasiyah, she turned a cheek to her shrine along the tent wall, smiling at her little silent audience. She fixed on the translucent Hand-Up Woman, carved in Tayma alum rock salt by her father after seeing her from cave drawings. After all these years of looking upon her, her arms raised up to the sky with two strands of hair extending out at each side, the questions still lingered. Who had drawn her? Had she drawn herself? Did she live there? What did it mean?

For the first time, somewhat unsettling yet amusing, it occurred to Jayida that maybe they were a bit alike. What would those hearing her story—Jonder and Jayida—in the future say about her? But even with all the confusion, the praising woman had outlived to fascinate anyone who saw her. With defiant satisfaction Jayida accepted that someday she might make a similar effect—and there was something pleasing about allowing herself a moment of vanity after the day's events.

She turned to her mother kneeling behind her seated father, passing an ivory comb through his long locks. Propped up on an elbow, Jayida observed them with fascinated amusement. How proud she was that two such handsome beings should be her parents, who passed her their own traits in yet another mysterious mix! In such moments she also often had the impression that they were like children in larger bodies.

"So, this being a big day for you, would you like to end it with your own recital?" said her father.

"But you already know what I'm going say." Jayida bit her lower lip as one fist formed.

"Practice makes perfect. Only if you want, of course," he said.

"Oh, my heart. It doesn't matter if what you say is the same, because the moment never is. So whatever you'd like to say, we are but your humble, yet loving audience," cooed her mother, putting aside the comb after briefly sweeping it through her own loosened ebony silken waves.

Jayida sat up, drew Al-Wasiyah closer to her side, straightened her shoulders and spine, and made a wide bowl with her arms. This time, she wouldn't worry if she rhymed or even how it sounded: she would just try, allow it and see what happened. She closed her eyes and took a deep breath, elevating her chin as though to draw her *qareen* into filling her with inspiration.

"Twelve winters ago, Zahir, son of Gayas and Rumayma of the Banu Zubayd the Great, proud member of Banu Tayyi, became a father. His son Jonder was born during the winter *rabi* rains, in the year of *Negus* Kaleb, the great king of Aksum who avenged the Yassu-loving slain of Najran. With such blessed rain, it was followed by one of the region's best harvest seen in ages, yielding lush green pastures, bountiful barley and wheat harvests, and flocks that multiplied in abundance," said Jayida, her large-sleeves sweeping across at intervals for emphasis. "In honor of the son's birth among the generous Banu Sa'd, the celebration lasted several days, with feasting, singing, and poetry. However, not even these happy news drew Moharib," she paused, her brow crinkling. For a moment she wondered if she'd gone too far this time, but read amused approval of her improvising in her parents' attentive gazes.

"For twelve winters, they heard not a word from them, except from hearsay here and there. Now, unknown to Moharib and to fend off his offending words and *al-'ayn*, Jonder had another name, known only to her and her parents, the secret name protecting and sheltering her like a tent its grateful resident. So the days passed and Jayida-Jonder grew among the Banu Sa'd and, one glorious summer day, she slayed her first wild attacker. Without a moment's notice, Jayida turned around and, amidst the suffocating smoke, the rush of desperate tears and deafening, wailing screams, she saw the evil pair of eyes staring, smiling, pushing down with his weight, demanding surrender. Harder and harder he pushed into the ground, but Jayida, wrapped in her metal coat, was stronger. Like flashing lightning, she stabbed, over and over, the blood calling out for mercy, until at last, the deceiving beast lay lifeless at her feet."

She paused, staring into space, the sob welling up in her throat threatening to quicken her breathing. Her mother's hand flew to her twitching mouth, restraining her own emotion as much as her motherly urge to shield her child in her protective arms. Jayida swallowed hard and took another deep breath.

"Now, on that same fateful magical day, a visitor came to the Banu Sa'd. It was none other than Hakim, *sha'ir* to the Banu Zubayd the Great, and who, witnessing Jonder's glory, could not deny his achievement. Moharib found that not only would Zahir not crawl back to him to touch his tent ropes like a beggar, but had indeed survived the *Ayyam al-Zalam*. And that was just the beginning, for if Jonder had only twelve winters behind him, how much more glory stood before him?" said Jayida with a final nod, proud yet relieved that it was done.

In the stillness, her frown merged with her parents' angered surprise, and after a moment she bowed her chin in thanks for listening. How lucky she was, to have a father who not only listened but encouraged her to share her thoughts, even if that was part of what boys were expected to do.

Once again, her parents were right: practice made perfect, and she never really knew what might emerge during those moments of reciting, even if they were often similar to what she'd said before. Though she was no poet, all the same, her constant *qareen* wouldn't fail her.

"Let him think as he will, as if he could control us," said Zahir, with something harsher in his tone than ever before. "*Aywa*, perfect timing; *sha'ir* Hakim will tell him."

"Come here," cooed her mother. Jayida went to her and was instantly engulfed in her loving embrace. "So that was what you saw when it happened?"

"*Na'am*. But I'd also had more night visions last night. I was so worried this morning that I almost thought of not going," said Jayida, sitting up. "But I'm glad I went. I couldn't always avoid it; we knew the day would come."

Her father looked away, but not enough to conceal his emotion wracking his jaw. "Wise of you. And as you said, it's only the beginning. Still, I hardly need remind you that if anything happened to you or your mother—"

"I know, *yaba*," said Jayida, and he reached over and squeezed her foot, fighting away his emotion with his frowning, pinched smile.

"So I'll take it as perfect timing with Hakim," said her mother.

"I was thinking the same," said her father, clearing his throat.

"I hope so," Jayida smiled.

Her mother's squeeze tightened around her. "We love you, our treasure. You've made us so proud today. Always remember that," she said, caressing her face.

"And one day, when time is right, everyone will know just who you are," said her father, and leaned over and planted a gentle kiss on her forehead. For a moment they wallowed in a soothing silence, the kind they often shared, filled with more meaning than they could ever say. Content with their shared understanding, Jayida crept back to her own bed, and kept Al-Wasiyah protectively next to her.

"May you rest and dream of more happy adventures," said her father, the crook of his arm waiting for his wife.

"And may Yassu, his angels, and his Aksumite princess guardian he sent you surround you as you sleep," said Zoraya. "And dream of those lovely ostrich egg earrings, like Mawiyya's." She reached over and covered the oil lamp with an earthen lid pierced with holes, dimming the light, and rolled back into Zahir's arm.

Jayida passed one more glance towards her figurines and bid them goodnight, wondering if she should make a form of the Aksumite princess and add it to the others.

In the dark she reached out to the bundled Al-Wasiyah and flinched, goosebumps emerging. Everything had all been so fast, and with the day's events she'd hardly had a moment to think about it alone. Now, the consuming darkness faced her. Would she forever see his yellow-green eyes, boring into hers; his hot breath like fire, claws scratching, greedily groaning for her flesh? How scared she'd been with his warm blood pouring down on her as she fought, so hard and fast she thought her arm would fall off.

But it hadn't fallen off: she had won. This ferocious creature, attacker of life, would now serve her, and spread Jonder's victory—Al-Wasiyah would see to it. She smirked darkly: she might almost thank the beast, for showing her and others just what she was capable of, on this of all days. Triumph filled her, casting her doubts away.

Happily drifting, she imagined Mawiyya, the Tanukhid *badawi* warrior queen, who became a believer of Yassu, and led her armies into Phoenicia and the Holy Land, as far as the frontiers of Egypt. Jayida could just see the intimidation overtaking the Rûm, so much so that at last they agreed to her truce, on her condition that she be appointed the bishop of her choice. Just like that: a powerful widow, supported by her people, refusing to take foreign orders. But as a true leader, later Mawiyya even assisted the Rûm by sending her cavalry when they were being attacked by the Goths to the north, and gave her daughter in marriage to a Rûm official, uniting the bloodlines.

And then there was the Aksumite princess, powerful and unpredictable as only angels were. A warm, loving presence, that seemed to say she was protected even as she drifted in the realm of endless spirits.

CHAPTER SEVEN

KHALED

BANU ZUBAYD - TAYMA

Khaled sat motionless with his eyes closed and back straight, relishing the early morning silence in his tent. Focused on his breath, the heaviness of his sore limbs wrapped in faded indigo linen robes drifted away. The spicy-sweet scent of fresh incense enveloped him, airy spirits alternating between strong and faint.

If only it could always be this way: easily forgetting himself, simply being, without the demanding expectations, as he basked in the relaxing peace in his well-earned own tent, his thoughts trailing elsewhere.

Where! The echo unfailingly barked, the thought betrayal enough.

Anywhere but there; riding off into any and every place with Majid, his one and only best friend. *Aywa*; it didn't matter where they went, so long as they were together, inseparable like the Yassu-loving Rûm soldiers Sergios and Bakchos—but obviously always gloriously evading the painful-death-for-their-faith part. Though Khaled would've loved the role of older brother, his mother was blameless for not giving him any siblings, she who doted on husband and son with every drop of her gentle, caring soul. The lone wolf to the dove and the greedy lion.

His strong shoulders drew back, his chest rising and falling in deep breaths. After a moment he glanced at his display of fox and wolf hides draped along the tent wall, hovering like defeated yet eternally greedy *ghilan* above his weapons. Silk tapestries and piles of precious woolen blankets woven by his mother lay neatly folded in a distant corner, untainted by the requisite savagely decorative animal corpses.

Reluctantly his gaze fell on the pointy-eared, grey and black striped hyena. Frowning, Khaled followed its erectile mane down its back, and ended at its thick, topaz-like spiked claws. His jaw tightened at the faint snicker, the salivating *ghul* always lurking in the shadows.

So young, so alone—and if it was all for the best, why did it feel so wrong? Why couldn't he have just stayed, hidden somewhere, just in case?

Cruelty.

Khaled hadn't yet known the meaning of the word then, but as he'd later pondered he'd realized that's what it was, and its essence had latched onto him ever since.

That had to be what the poets dealt with, when they had all these overbearing feelings, visions, and impressions, and had to narrow them into compact terms for their metered poems. By now Khaled knew his own bravery, if that's what it'd been, but he had no urge to boast of these conquests, even as he hoped someday that would change. Thrust into the darkness, he would recognize it anywhere now, at least. But the worst was that he couldn't escape it. Not yet.

His legs swung under him and he rose, and with careful, wide motions of his contorting arms and legs, he took his time stretching his tall frame and aching limbs. Like any young fighting *badawi* knew, it was all part of building his *sabr* and *hilm*; tests of patience and self-control. Though he cared little for his father's wealth that he would one day inherit, he was proud of his deepening fighting skill, spent alongside Majid in the fighting tents. What else did he need, when he knew he could survive off his skills?

While it humbled Khaled that his fellow tribesmen didn't hesitate to remind him how proud his father and they were, he'd secretly grown to increasingly dislike his father's talking of his achievements, as if starving for insatiable praises. Like none of it could be his son's own achievement, but only about himself, and the ways Khaled could always benefit Moharib. The offspring: a mere piece of branded livestock to be reared and shown off at will, to the glory of its owner. Was he Ishaq to let himself be slain at the altar, as commanded by *al-ilah*? But his father, shameful as it was to say, was no Ibrahim. Part of him sometimes wondered what if he hadn't slain the hyena? What other kind of twisted pleasure would that have brought, if the hyena had killed him instead? At least death would've offered an escape from his father's domineering ways. But Khaled had lived, and his father had gifted him a sword after it, as if to compensate for the cruelty and cold harshness. Khaled had named it Al-Fatih, the conqueror, but the bittersweet memories seemed hammered and struck into the very steel.

Khaled pulled his torso forward, curved his back, and grunted pleasantly at the release. With a conflicting mixture of submission and defiance, a smirk stretched his lips. What if he ever left and went his own way? There was a whole world to see, and not even his father could stop him from exploring. Let him worry about the salt, copper, silver, and gold mines, the trading and caravans, endless scheming, talking, and agreements.

It's for the best, as he had said.

Nor was his return guaranteed; it was an inconvenient truth every *badawi* knew. Even with blood ties, kin alliances were broken and made all the time. Every man had to make his own decisions. Though his father never spoke of it, it reminded Khaled of his elusive uncle Zahir, who'd left thirteen springs before when he was nearly three and too young to remember. He'd thought his father might finally go to them during the *Ayyam al-Zalam*, but even that didn't make him bring them back.

Instead, Samaw'al had discreetly told him about their meeting at Khaybar when Khaled had wandered to his castle Al-Ablaq for a visit. All along, his father had been too busy making other beneficial alliances that he in turn so stuffed his ears with that Khaled thought he'd either go mad or deaf, maybe even both. While he understood Moharib's concern and need to show his power to other greedy *badawi*—of which there were plenty—Khaled hated that sometimes he'd been unnecessarily harsh. Part of him had wondered if the thick air would sink into him and soften him, but if it had, the unbending Moharib had never shown, let alone shared it. His father certainly offered much needed protection, but he also tallied up all his gestures and everything that he could count on in return, so that Khaled often wondered how many had come to Tayma out of desperation rather than genuine desire.

Was his uncle Zahir as tough, which ultimately pushed him to leave? Still, that Sadiqa, his beloved mount, was one of the forty camels left behind by his *amo* Zahir always made him nostalgic somehow, and yearning to know more of him. Everyone knew of his march east with Ma'dikarib Ya'fur, and members of Banu Thalaba and Mudar, and though Samaw'al often obliged him with their thrilling war stories, he longed someday to ask his uncle about it in person.

He lunged forward, and one leg stretched back while the other made a bridge holding him up. He grimaced as the muscles pulled, and with a curt breath, he glanced into the shaded corner, his trio of dusty idols looking blankly back at him. He reached for the bronze incense burner and set it below them, the coiling smoke giving them life. His collection might not be as large as others' but as far as he was concerned, he had the essentials.

There was his father's dull red, man-like form of Al-Fals, revered by some among their glorious kin, the confederate of Tayyi, for looking over their flocks who grazed near the mountain range of Jabal Aja. Located a few days' ride southeast, he'd yet to visit the shrine in the highlands of Jabal Aja, one of whose outcrops of reddish granite they said was shaped in the form of a man. Next to it was the form of the Israelite shepherd Ibrahim, gifted to him by Majid, and another shepherd representing Yassu. It was one of the first forms he'd ever made as a young boy to commemorate a Tayyi victory, who largely professed their faith in the son of revered Maryam.

Let his father be dismayed by his indifference to engage in one or several of the cults, let alone hurry to pilgrimage south to Jabal Arafat, near Mina and Muzdalifah. Tayma's dedicated tent-sanctuary was there for anyone, local or foreign, to pay their respects to deities as they wished. That was good enough, especially when neither Banu Tayyi, nor Kalb, among others allied to the Ghassanid powers, recognized the other cults, as per Yassu-loving *malik* Al-Harith's suggestion. With some amusement Khaled envisioned his father steering clear of Mina just to avoid being surrounded by big-mouthed oracles who read faces and futures, and might have things to say about their lack of resemblance. As if either of them could entirely control their appearance. Still, Khaled was not indifferent to the deities, though they often sounded more like children's stories than true accounts that could benefit him.

Perhaps one day he'd tell his children of Suwa, goddess of the night, who granted beauty and youth, and the moon god Hilal, provider of beloved dew in the evenings, unlike the fiery Shams who set everything ablaze with her sunrays. Not to forget Manat, goddess of Fate, destiny and death, and Al-Lat, goddess of fertility and war. However, like Majid, he had an aversion to Al-Uzza, worshipped as the morning and evening star and a deity the wild Al-Mundhir had sacrificed humans to. Some honored Allah as the supreme deity, and was invoked by many *badawi* in times of great stress—but he secretly doubted it made any difference. But that he knew and sometimes thought of these, among a nearly endless plethora, had to at least count for something. Even if he was inclined to, he could hardly be expected to remember them all, let alone offer sacrifices. That was the work of *kahinat*, after all, not warriors. He added some passing thoughts to Ahura Mazda, worshipped by the Fars in the northeast, just in case.

With a final, satisfied long breath, he slowly rose again, carrying the one thing about his father that he didn't mind: his inherited tall, strong frame, which had only grown more quickly in recent seasons and with continued intensive training. Everyone was already praising him for it—his blossoming shape surely an early sign of more to come. He draped his indigo headwrap over his head and messy horse tail, when he caught the approaching sound of crunched gravel.

"*Sayyid* Khaled, your father is asking for you," said Ayida with her frail, accented southern voice.

His whole body tensed. Of course his father would send the slave girl instead of coming himself. Once more, he told himself it wasn't her fault, still striving never to show her his frustration. But something about her made him increasingly uncomfortable; from the moments when she appeared on the verge of endless tears, to those when she fixed him with a strange mix of pleading and accusation.

He'd tried a few times to go graze the flocks with her, but she'd appeared so panicked that he relented. Ever since, he hardly spoke to the girl, and if he averted his gaze from her, it was not from dislike of her dark skin, as some did, but out of respect for her, as well as other girls. Didn't she know this? Or was she like all the others, who said one thing but meant another? It was one of the many silly, girl-related things he and Majid gladly dismissed in favor of more important manly matters.

The stillness lingered, tugging at him like a nagging child.

"*Aywa*, I'll be there," said Khaled, and she slowly shuffled away. Frowning, he shook his head in annoyance. Even her retreating steps dripped with an air of dejection.

He straightened himself and with a swift motion, swung one end of his headwrap around his neck and let the other hang down the side of his smooth face. With his strong, sculpted body he didn't need a beard to look even older than fifteen years, but he didn't mind playing with his appearance, often to his father's dismay. While his controlled shaggy look wasn't one he thought of changing, something about the refined courtly noble warrior intrigued him—that raw masculine strength decorated with beautifying fineries of heavenly-scented oiled skin and hair, and jewelry and embroidered clothing befitting the manly form that existed before woman's.

Khaled chuckled. As a boy he'd sometimes amused himself by playing the pampered noble warrior; donning his mother's rings, necklaces, and silks, as she recited stories and poetry verses, the magic propelling and suspending them elsewhere like pleasant mirages. And even when his father cut his hair and short beard and gave them as offerings to Al-Fals or some other deity, his father complained—not oiled enough, not the right length, something always missing. Soon Khaled knew that it didn't matter what he did; there would always be something to find fault with. Couldn't he enjoy his youth a bit more, before life aged and wrinkled him with all the stress their life would inevitably bring? He slipped on his indigo cloak and short leather boots and quickly visited his mounts' quarters. He greeted his fine pigeon-blue Ghassanid mare Aminah—facilitated by

Samaw'al's connections—and his beloved Zahir mount Sadiqa, then reluctantly stepped out.

Khaled headed east, pacing briskly to his parents' tent a short distance across from him, grateful that even that little space offered a taste of freedom. Amidst the mounting morning bustle, he glanced northeast to the hosting tents, imagining that Majid was surely preparing or already there, ready to teach and learn from any visiting warriors.

He reached his parents' tent and stepped through the public area's welcoming entrance, the sight of *sha'ir* Hakim making him smile.

"*Sha'ir* Hakim, welcome back from your travels," said Khaled. He leaned down to meet the rising elder, greeting him with a kiss to each cheek, before catching his father's whiplashing, hawkish gaze reprimanding his tardiness. Perhaps if there was more variation to his father's perpetual air of frustration, he might give it more special attention.

"Ah Khaled, you may need to veil soon, lest *al-'ayn* jealously target your beauty," said *sha'ir* Hakim in his hoarse tone, as they both lowered to the carpeted floor upon which rested a silver tray with milk and moist Tayma dates.

"I've thought about it," grinned Khaled, and glimpsed his mother Khamra quietly mending garments behind a thin curtain, the modest gesture more to please her husband than herself. Clad in her milk-colored robe and loose head-wrap, her smooth dark hair glowed as much as her radiant smile.

"So, anything interesting?" said Moharib, his back straight and hands resting on each knee. Oddly, his intensity seemed even stronger than usual.

"Most things you already know," *sha'ir* Hakim began. "He's with the Banu Sa'd, breeding his flocks, and teaching his son Jonder."

Khaled's eyes widened. He hadn't known that the elder would be bringing back news of his *amo* and cousin. He reached for a cup of goat milk, relishing the sweet taste amidst the *sha'ir*'s pause.

"*Na'am*, and what of him?" came his father's tone, struggling to feign indifference.

Moharib was always agitated, but why should he still be so upset about it, when they'd been the ones to leave without reason? Even *sha'ir* Hakim's skilled pauses seemed longer than usual, but as an elder *sha'ir*, no one knew better than him how to guide the conversation.

"He made a most memorable impression," said *sha'ir* Hakim. Khaled set down his milk and leaned forward, perking up with a curiosity which his father's glare did not in the least diminish.

Moharib grunted and reached for some milk as if for distraction. The *sha'ir* slowly chewed a date, and the silence hung over them long enough that he thought his father would have to break down and ask the elder to elaborate.

"Jonder was covered in fresh blood. It was fated that I arrive on a most favorable day for him, as such a sight is not easily forgotten."

Khaled smiled, suspecting that his father was getting as annoyed by the details as he was excited to hear them.

"He'd just returned from an outing during which he'd slain his first leopard that attacked him. And there he appeared, alongside Zahir, his lion eyes as striking as the bright crimson drenching him," said *sha'ir* Hakim.

Was it his imagination or was the *sha'ir* also enjoying this recital, as displeased as his father was?

"By *al-ilah*. Did he dedicate it to any deity?" said Khaled.

"No."

Khaled felt a welcomed satisfaction. Jonder was either as indifferent to the deities as he was, or mistrusting of sharing his most private leanings.

"Their boon included ostrich eggs, one of which Zahir gifted you," said *sha'ir* Hakim, and drew his satchel over to reveal the massive unblemished egg.

"It's nothing my great Khaled here can't do," said Moharib, ignoring the gift as he let out one of his coughs that he always shrugged off.

"I don't know about leopards," said Khaled lightly, impressed.

"No leopard *yet*," came the curt reply.

Khaled suppressed a snort: another item for the long list. Why did his father have to dismiss Jonder's achievement? Why fuel this sense of competition? One's achievement didn't take away from another's, as each fighter had their own strengths and challenges. Despite *amo* Zahir's departure, they were still cousins and should be friends and getting to know each other instead. Was it really too much to try to mend past feuds and strengthen their alliance once more? Even after fifteen years, they were still given an honorable gift.

His father's vacant glance pierced him—an eerily familiar smirk surfacing. *Fight, fight, fight,* his father said, and Khaled appreciated the way his abilities unfolded, but not the way his father tried to push and force everything. Like any other young man his age, he wanted nothing more than to be a skilled warrior, but he wanted to do it on his terms, not just be a replica of his father or even necessarily do things like him. Each man had to make his own path, even when learning from his family and ancestors.

"So, what's Jonder like? He has lion eyes, you say? I don't recall *siddi* Gayas or *sitti* Rumayma having such eyes," said Khaled.

"They certainly didn't. No one in the family did," Moharib snorted, his tone dripping with mockery. Khaled clasped his hands, struggling to hold back. Now his father had to insinuate that Zoraya could've been unfaithful, or, even if agreed to by Zahir in their quest for parenthood, their son ultimately sired by another man. And even if that was the case, what did that have to change? It was not that unusual, especially for those who desperately wanted children.

"He's still rather small, especially compared to you," said *sha'ir* Hakim gently.

"Everyone's small compared to Khaled," laughed Moharib as the elder nodded in agreement.

"That makes the leopard slaying even more shocking then, both for his age and form. I wish I could've seen and asked him myself," said Khaled. "Now that we have these good news, we know that we may always call on them if this new and latest northern border dispute gets worse between the Lakhmids and Ghassanids. Even if by now everyone knows that it was Al-Mundhir who started it," said Khaled, feigning innocence.

"Surely they've got their hands full as it is," blurted Moharib.

And there it was again—his father's cough that he swore was getting increasingly pronounced. Before Khaled could move to assist, his mother rushed over with the pot of Hudhayl honey and offered him the coated honey stick to taste. He leaned forward and waved it away, his hand pressing down on his rattling chest. Khamra knelt at his side, distraught and equally perplexed. For some minutes, the only sound was the throaty, persistent racking that seemed to render helpless his father's massive frame.

"I'm fine, woman, don't fuss," sneered Moharib, his cough at last relenting. Pinching her lips together and looking away, his mother took the jar and silently retreated. Khaled's heart tugged, boiling his blood, hating the way his father was severe with her when she was only trying to help, always only trying to help. "Nothing I can't overcome," grumbled his father, like he'd never had another's help.

Sha'ir Hakim nodded in silent reassurance, the elder's renown poise and patience inspiring him. Khaled had suspected it before, but now he knew without a doubt that his father would do anything to deflect from acknowledging a moment of vulnerability—even in front of their loyal *sha'ir* who preceded them all.

With resurfacing shame it dawned on Khaled that the narrative repulsed him, that of his own father whom he should be emulating. *Moharib the Invincible*: that perfect image of him, ultimately overcome by unnatural, persistent coughing. Was this exemplary life? One in which being a leader meant never showing weakness, one's true human self? How far should one go to preserve that image?

"Just a small stone on the path to greatness, that's all it is. But you must be aware of those around you, Khaled; it could be those closest to you who could be most ungrateful for all you've done for them," sneered his father.

Khaled kept his gaze averted, the tension ensnaring them enough. There was so much he wanted to say; how maybe that shouldn't even matter, that as the older brother he could set the better example to forgive, and go to him. And that if they'd left of their own will, there had to be a reason, even if they'd kept it to themselves. He wanted to say that a true honorable man of their kind was generous—one of the *badawi*'s most prized values as part of *muruwa*—giving without boasting. Others could speak of it, perhaps even recite poetry on it to survive the ages—*generous as Hatim*, as the saying went in honor of their famous poet kinsman of Tayyi. It was its own reward, and holding onto grudges was not honor, although many confused and used it as such. But the truth was that his father was a hard, proud man; he and his mother knew this better than anyone.

"*Na'am, yaba*; I know this well, as I'm learning from the best," said Khaled, and it disturbed him that in some ways he was caring less each day whether his father understood his true meaning. So once more, he yielded, the loyal part of him wanting to obey, and not anger him more, calling on his self-control for the patience to someday better understand his hard ways. With a side glance he caught the hopeful glint of encouragement in *sha'ir* Hakim's gaze.

"In passing, did you hear anything from Zoraya?" said Khamra, gently peeking from behind the curtain.

"I did not. But Zahir did ask about you all, and sends thousand blessings," said *sha'ir* Hakim, his news clearly at an end.

"Praise Allah you made it back safely," said Moharib, waving his hand with a hint of finality.

"As always, *sayyid*, it is my pleasure to be of service," said *sha'ir* Hakim. He rose and, glancing at them both, there was a hint of lingering conflict in his crinkled brow. But the respected elder instantly resumed his dignified air, and strode out of the tent, tapping the ground with his cane.

"That'll be some fun news to share with the *shabab*," said Khaled, bolting up at the thought of his companions.

"Not just yet; the fighters and fighting tents aren't going anywhere," smirked his father. "I'll want to hear you recite one of these days, since you have all the workings to be *sha'ir* someday."

"You have so much faith in me, *yaba*. But I think we can all agree that *sha'ir* Hakim will outlive us all," said Khaled in his best comical yet humble tone. He refrained from saying that he often thought Majid would be ideal for it, and already enjoyed creating verses.

"*Aywa*, and a man should always be prepared. And for that other important matter. I'm sure it hasn't escaped either of you the way that Layali and Nuha have been increasingly lurking around you, my son. There are many others, as we all know, but these two are the most beautiful. If you had to pick one, who would it be?" said Moharib, clearly reanimated.

"Oh *yaba*, marriage, again?" said Khaled, throwing his hands in the air.

"He's young still," cooed Khamra in her understanding way.

"Has any of them asked for me?" said Khaled, his parents exchanging glances.

"*Ya Allah!* Have you lost your mind? Surely you know they all want you, that's not the issue!" shot his father.

How could they want Khaled, and he them, without really knowing either, aside from all the potential material benefits that came from marriage? He was grateful for their bountiful blessings and considered himself to have all he needed. But his father would say that a man could never have too much, not in a world where things could change so fast. His father's boasts echoed in his night visions sometimes, self-praising his iron fist that had ensured they hardly felt the hardships of the previous year's *Ayyam al-Zalam*. But others didn't have nearly as much, and somehow they'd also managed, and hopefully without adding even more bitterness to the experience.

"Who's the better cook?" Khaled chuckled, and for once the silence hinted at the ignorance. "And what if I married someone from another tribe?" So long as his father pushed, he'd defy it with light humor, one of the few things he'd learned that could make awkward, undesirable situations tolerable.

"Which one? And certainly not a matriarchal one, to squander my envied inheritance," said the paternal raised eyebrow.

"I hear the Yassu-loving women of 'Udhrah are the definition of chaste," said Khaled, and caught his mother's subtle amusement.

"So they say, but there's no shortage of honorable matches here. It's not for nothing they also say that marrying a stranger is like drinking water from an earthen jug—"

"While marrying within your tribe is like drinking from a cup: you can see what you're drinking," finished Khaled, trying not to roll his eyes.

"Oh come; won't you even take a pick? Don't pretend you haven't seen them!"

From the little Khaled had noticed of his best friend's sister, Nuha seemed quieter, reclusive, and he therefore couldn't tell much about her personality, but assumed she would be an accommodating kind of girl. As for Layali, he'd noted for years her fiery streak, something that intrigued as much as repulsed him; like a dormant volcano whose eruption could occur at any moment.

"*Tayyib* then, Nuha?" shrugged Khaled.

"Ha! How did I know you'd pick the opposite of me!" his father clapped loudly, and rose to pat him on the back. Khaled didn't like the way his father acted as though it'd been a real answer, his far-off look already lost in potential preparations he hadn't agreed to. He glanced at his beautiful mother, whose gentle, constant smile indicated she was on his side, as she'd been all his life, ready to lovingly coax her husband in his favor. While he had his father's stature, he was thankful to share a closer physical resemblance with her, that would get passed on to his own line—a mysterious, yet perfectly balanced gift of Fate.

Khaled drifted to the exit, ready to end this conversation and finally rejoin his friends.

"Don't worry, father. Timely Fate will help me find the right woman, even if it's one who already has multiple husbands streaming in and out of her tent," he said, folding at the waist in a light bow.

"And doubt your own offspring? *Hadha*; enough of this. If only my son acted like a serious *sha'ir* rather than a child," his father crossed his arms.

"Perhaps this oracle here will help us all," said Khaled, and took the satchel with the egg.

"You know he's just playing with us," his mother's words gently drifted as Khaled slipped out.

Shaking his head in stifled disgust, Khaled, hurried to his tent and set the ostrich egg next to his statues, nearly certain it was among the trinkets he was happiest to own. If his father had no care for it, he would gladly accept it, and hopefully soon quash the pang of not having extended their own generosity since they'd left.

In a dreamy daze and eager to communicate, he went southeast and hurried to the stone carved with ancient inscriptions. It was said to be dedicated to Salm, introducing the new deity to be worshipped henceforth, from the time when the Babylonian King Nabonidus stayed at the Tayma oasis. Even the Rûm had more recently called this far-off station home, along with nearby Hijr, Wadi Al-Qura, and Dumat Al-Jandal, filling him with a delightful sense of connection. Before he could stop his child-like wonder, he placed his hand on the writing-covered limestone and offered thanks to his *amo*'s family—as much for the egg as for the camels he'd left them as a parting gift and that still blessed them. Likewise, Khaled gave thanks for their ancient Haddaj well at the center of camp that faithfully provided for them and their flocks.

Satisfied, he rounded his walk northeast to the fighting tents, famously hosted by *sayyid* Moharib and known throughout the land, as were Khaled and Majid's names fast catching up—or so he could imagine. Let his father fuss over marriage, along with everything else, in an endless turning, grinding wheel of mutual disappointment.

While all that that was fodder for jokes around the campfire, he couldn't understand the big deal around marriage. He was young, with so much yet for him to accomplish, and though he knew one day he'd marry, it seemed like something so far into the future and presently the last thing on his mind. He was a fighter, and his love was for adventure and trekking alongside his friends, and protecting and providing for his tribe. If his father didn't like it, he had only himself to thank.

He was just a ten-year old boy when he'd left him alone in the Shadow Lands, amidst graveyard tombs marked by stacked stones west of camp, in the pitch, freezing night. He'd pleaded the *jinn* and *afarit*, but especially the female *ghuleh* not to lure him away to be eaten, swearing he did not mean to impede on their territory.

Nor was there solace in sleep, when he was just as afraid of asking questions and getting answers from any potential incubational dream the poets spoke of. Yet, somehow sleep eventually overtook him, and he'd imagined a boy named Salim saying he'd protect him...

Then he'd woken up, startled and wrapped in thick fog—and with something lurking around him. In the greyness emerged a hyena, its mane erect in threat, pacing around him. Nearly frozen stiff, he'd reached for his spears and wrapped his palms so tightly around them he thought they'd break and meld into his flesh. When he finally stood the beast had been about his size—until something in his sad eyes made him remember his mother. He could not leave her alone, and though he'd realized right then how wrong it was to think it, he could not leave her with *him*.

Waving his spears Khaled yelled at the top of his lungs, hoping the *ghul* would scuttle away and leave him alone. But it remained, trotting back and forth like it was just waiting for him to tire and surrender, so that in the end it had all done itself. With a cry Khaled thrust the first spear in the belly, spurting bright blood into the cold, hard earth, and the second in the neck, the impaled seeping corpse satisfyingly shrieking into silence. He had no choice but to conquer this menace, roaming alone, who could annihilate most trace of him by digesting his bones and dragging his skull away to its lair. Somehow, he thought he'd heard his mother's deadly anguish at such an outcome, and had answered without a second thought. His heart pounding he'd watched the blood spread over the ground, hoping it would satisfy the *ghul* and free him from their wrath.

Hurrying, as if the monster might spring back to life, he'd even skinned the beast himself, fascinated and repulsed by the odd skin folds around its genitals. Vaguely he'd remembered the jokes saying they looked like women's private parts between its own sex organs, and he still shook off his disgust that some men might use its sex organ as an amulet to ensure their fertility. Even then he'd known that he would never resort to it, or any other such help. And if his lineage should suffer for it, who was he to go against Fate?

Khaled restrained a smile amidst the echo of praising tribeswomen he passed by, each pleading or teasing not to forget their daughter, who'd make him happiest. Something about their need both lured and repulsed him; the way life seemed simpler for them.

What would people say? I had to be sure you were ready to join our world, or if you needed more time with your mother.

But Khaled wasn't sure if it was so much men's world, as *Moharib's* world, for though his father was a powerful, feared *sayyid*, not everyone was like him. *Siddi* Gayas hadn't pushed them that young, so where did it come from? Did his father think himself better than his elders? Moharib might keep up appearances, as many a *badawi* did, but if his father thought he was being the perfect tribesman demanded by their honor code of *muruwa*, then he had to disagree. And Khaled was old enough to know that others did, too.

Khaled was supposed to be proud—the envied heir of Banu Zubayd the Great, who traced their roots all the way down to Himyar's western coastal plain of Zabid from which they took their name. And while in some ways he was, he'd also never felt so alone. So he tried to focus on the triumph: he'd passed the test, had conquered, and would always keep his gaze ahead.

One day he'd continue the ancestral exploring to the north, and pay visit to the court of the Jafnid royal branch of Ghassan at Jabiyah, in the hills of the Golan. He might even venture to the court of the Nasrid royal branch of Lakhm at Al-Hira, though hopefully by then Al-Mundhir would be replaced by someone else. There was a satisfaction to both royal houses vying for the desert-dwelling Banu Tayyi's loyalty as they maneuvered their client relations. The circulating stories of these luxurious palaces full of poetry, wine, and arts captured his curious mind, and though he could only claim to know fighting and horses, he wanted to experience and enjoy them all.

But first they would make amends with their family.

At last his large steps brought him to the fighting tents, emitting the boisterous fun that he imagined Jonder would enjoy as much as himself. A rush filled him, because he'd already resolved that someday soon he would get to the bottom of it, no matter how—and perhaps especially if—his father continued to refuse to reunite them, if only to finally meet and acknowledge their familial bonds.

It was only a matter of time.

Chapter Eight

PROGRESS

Banu Sa'd

The thick desert engulfed Jayida, her short breaths merging with the collective panting around her. Heavy, crunching steps added to the muttering sounds, the thirst for victory stronger than any bodily weaknesses. Dust rose, coiling and drifting like misty wisps at every turn.

There was nothing to fear. It was just another test of *sabr*, pushing her patience with a blazing firestorm, stalking her, creeping to nibble on her skin layer by layer. She had done it so often before, and would keep trudging through this torturous, burning land of endless *jinn*, *afarit*, and *ghilan* that insatiably roasted victims for failing to properly pay with honorable sacrifices.

Groaning, she shifted her heavy leather bag to another shoulder, and lowered her chin into her hard chest.

Let them come and make clear demands, then!

Why did the deities have to be so fleeting and elusive? Men rushed to holy shrines and sanctuaries, often giving little of what they had, and all for a possibility, at best. Nothing ever guaranteed, except Fate—and that fiery disk that revealed all its life-consuming glory; challenging, always demanding her to overcome, over and over again. It was always there: a blazing, grotesque nightmarish grin—Dhu Nuwas, Moharib, and Al-Mundhir into one—tempting her to give up, accusing that she was just pretending. Just a little *badawi* girl playing at a losing game.

But then, how had she slain the leopard? His cured hide now hung proudly on their tent wall for anyone to gasp at. But even as her father's words prevailed—practice made perfect—quashing the doubts, they kept persisting. But so would she: her proud *hilm* faithfully guiding her self-control.

A snort-like noise drifted from the side and she glanced at Shams, whose pained expression and protruding mouth threatened to unleash complaints. As if stating their frustration would make a difference. They all dreaded and yet wanted to be there, but there were few glories without struggle—her father the eternal wise man.

"Finally!" blurted Shams, his playfulness echoing their own as they came to a stop at the designated area at the southwest edge of camp.

"Gather everything here," chuckled *sayyid* Aziz as he rounded the camels. With relief she dropped the satchel and stepped aside with Shams, as the other, younger small band of boys streamed along, their excited curiosity contained by intimidation.

Jayida squinted to counter the flash of brightness and met the blank faces of practice targets. All around, their straw-stuffed bodies propped up on red acacia poles and stick arms spread wide like belligerent thieves. Their clothes of old leather hides, ragged linen sheets, or tattered woolen robes made them life-like. On the desert floor, scattered sandbags and stacked saddles laid everywhere as additional practice points.

Her father led Kamila and Al-Nabith, *sayyid* Aziz's ebony stallion, into a mock tent made of draped pieces of undyed fabric, and rejoined the *sayyid*'s side. A hand resting on each hip, *sayyid* Aziz passed a satisfied smirk to the young boys.

"All praises to your generosity, young fighters, for bravely carrying all the supplies we need. For now, you'll begin by practicing carrying the spears, but I urge you to observe and serve Jonder and Shams as your own commanders."

Zahir reached into a satchel, withdrew two scabbard steel Mashrafiya swords, and handed one to each of them. Jayida wrapped it tightly around her waist and slowly unsheathed it. Its straight blade and simple, sturdy handles beamed at her, the fine weapons come all the way from Mu'tah, north of the ancient Wadi Musa in Al-Sham.

"We'll start slow, get you used to the weight. And keep your wrist aligned with your arm, otherwise it'll strain," said her father, brandishing his own Al-Hamiyah.

The young eyes set on them as Shams faced *sayyid* Aziz, and Jayida positioned herself, legs apart and hips forward, across her father. Slowly she swung side to side and forward, her father gradually building up momentum in crossing their blades. Focused, she met and avoided his sword even as she kept an eye on her surroundings.

"Now, who will begin to tell us about *muruwa*?" said *sayyid* Aziz, addressing the young audience as he began playfully taunting Shams.

"They're the prime virtues of a warrior!" yelled one.

"*Aywa*; continue!" said the *sayyid*, lunging at Shams who met him with equal enthusiasm.

"They are hospitality, respect for women and honor, protection of the weak and the orphan, and bravery in war," said another, more serious boy.

"*Sah!*" said the *sayyid*.

"What are the three most important weapons?" said Zahir, his calculated lunges blocked by the body of her blade. In the excitement she forgot her screaming muscles, squirming under the weight of the coat of mail.

"Spear, bow, and sword," said another young boy.

"Which is the most honorable?" said *sayyid* Aziz.

"The sword!" yelled the first.

"Ah!" said *sayyid* Aziz, coming to a full stop and stepping away with palms up, offering them a pause. "And why the sword?"

"It takes the most skill, since it requires closeness to your target," said the serious one.

"So they say, and it is honorable indeed. But I add that the most honorable is the one you use best, and the one that will keep you alive," nodded *sayyid* Aziz with a warning hand. "Now, for your weapon."

Zahir joined him in handing short javelins to the band of boys, the sight of a few struggling to balance the length and weight reminding her of themselves at their age.

"Begin there, and then switch to the heavier spears," said the *sayyid*.

"Thankfully that already seems long ago for us," said Shams, his chuckle joined by hers. "Now, after you, Jonder ibn Zahir." He gave a slight challenging bow, and faced her in readiness.

"No, after *you*, Shams ibn Hubala," she grinned, returning the patronymic address.

They took their places opposite each other, and carefully drew closer, mostly avoiding each other's strikes, swerving, ducking, and rolling to devise ways of counter-attack. At first his jumpy, eager lunges made Jayida nervous until, fired up, she dropped her cautious guard and strengthened her own attacks. Her grip and sword handle made one, holding strong against the onslaught, like timeless stone outcrops that stood the ages. More importantly, he wouldn't strike that hard, and even if so, he couldn't—wouldn't—pierce through her coat of mail. Not with blades that were purposefully not finely pointed enough. In the whirl of clashing metal, it dawned on her that maybe that was what pushed him even further, a mixture of curiosity and envy testing its limits. But despite the tiring efforts, she was reassured by her quick learning and self-defense. Like the coat of mail, the beginning would be hardest, with each day getting easier so that soon she'd be used to it, too.

"I think I hear *jinn* trapped in the sandbags calling for some attention, if only to release the fullness of your youthful wrath," *sayyid* Aziz chuckled at them, maneuvering with Zahir amidst the young boys and their thin javelins.

Swords in hand, Jayida raced off with Shams to the lifeless sandbags, came upon them at the same time and, panting, took a moment to catch their breaths. An air of solemnity radiated between them as they each faced a bulging mound made of scraps of old leather patched together, packed with sand.

With a grunting yell Shams struck out first, the point barely getting through but enough to undo a few seams and drip some sand. He seemed to wait for her with a side glance and, her fingers squeezing the handle even tighter, she took a deep breath and struck out at hers, again and again. The seams peeled apart like dried leaves, the spurting cream-colored grains thankfully so tame compared to the leopard's thick blood and sharp buttery scent.

They continued to other sandbags, Shams always more eager than herself to cause carnage. Maybe if she stilled herself and kept it all in, it would come out later when she really needed it. How could she go back now, knowing the difference?

A gentle understanding washed over her. It was fitting practice to begin with, and though it hadn't been her choice, now she knew they couldn't compare. A strange reassurance filled her with this, and she wished Shams's persistent thrusts and frustrated groans sounded less plaintively envious of her experience.

Her father came upon them, waterskins draped across his back.

"*Aywa!* What a glorious mess you've made and what fun you'll have mending them!" he beamed and handed them each a skin. They sheathed their sword, gulped eagerly and followed him to the propped forms and the pair of short bows and quivers awaiting them.

Jayida exchanged the waterskin for a quiver she draped around her shoulders, and picked up a bow. It was predicitably different from her own, but as the training intended, she was learning to be less intimidated by new things.

"When you're ready, let them fly," cheered her father.

They stepped up about ten paces away from a target, took aim and released. Her arrow flew straight into the lower stomach, while Shams's missed. Frowning, his lower lip protruded angrily and he immediately set off another string of fruitful arrows, as if unsure to keep being angry for his missed first attempt, or to rejoice at doing better in the next tries. She wished he didn't get so annoyed, but wondered if his anger was a drawback or a benefit to his performance.

At her father's guidance, they repeated the process, alternating the distance and angles, marveling at the way each slight change made a difference. Though less intimidating than the sword, she'd have to get familiar with the longer distances to hit her desired targets. But it was precisely what made her prefer it over the others, this ability to ideally remove any threat before it even reached her. Over and over she retrieved the scattered arrows and launched them, her drenched body and new aches following all her movements.

"Switch!" called Zahir, as *sayyid* Aziz and the band approached. They moved to the next station of scattered sandbags, short and long spears, and javelins.

"*Aywa*, now for the oldest weapons used by our ancestors, and commemorated onto cave drawings everywhere," said Jayida, picking up a short javelin about her height, with a steel double-edged point.

To her surprise, Shams picked up a large javelin and bolted off into the distance, keeping it hovering near his head. A moment later he looked like a soaring bird flapping his wings as his back arched and he threw it hard, burying straight into a target.

"What speed and arm, Shams!" said *sayyid* Aziz, the boys fast swarming around.

"Well done!" said Jayida, and ran after him.

They alternated between javelins and spears, delighted that it was, in some ways, the easiest. Using the spears they lightly engaged in sword play, maneuvering their length and weight with slow, angled forward strikes and blocking each other. It may have been the simplest, but its effectiveness made it clear why it'd remained in use across time. Her arms soon ached and they took a break, when they noted *sayyid* Aziz and her father approaching astride their camels and guiding their horses to them, the young infantry running alongside them with their chosen spears.

"Now, time for you to get off the floor," smirked *sayyid* Aziz. He drew along his stallion Al-Nabith, his ebony coat shining like a beloved dark pool of wine that earned him his name. Her father, astride Sabah, handed her Kamila, whom she fondly petted and embraced.

Ready, Jayida held the rein and saddle horn in her left hand, stood slightly back, and with a strong, swift motion, swung her body up, her right leg hooking over and securely landing her onto her mount. She caught the pride in her father's gaze, both recalling how they'd practiced to perfect the graceful mount. Keeping hold of the reins, Jayida leaned back to balance the weight of her torso with her legs. The safety strap at center brushed her fingertips for convenient quick reach.

Her free feet swaying gently against Kamila's ribs, the mare rocked lightly under her, reassuring her they were both at ease.

Beaming, her father secured a javelin to her saddle. "Remember, keep a firm seat and good posture and your javelin may do well, though it takes many seasons to perfect it."

"Yah, yah!" yelled Shams, dashing off into the distance, his stiff body bouncing so wildly he nearly fell off. Jayida sighed in relief when he quickly caught himself and slowed down, the echo of the stampeding cheering boys easing the tension. "Catch me if you can!" he said, brandishing his sword her way.

"Come back here and face me!" Jayida laughed, waving hers in the air as she flew after him.

At length they met up and, each pulling and steering their mounts, they made a dance of sidestepping and backstepping without touching. The band of infantry stood safely at a distance, cheerleading and playing. Her body contorted as their controlled, nonaggressive weapons swung, missed, and clashed. Once agreed, they switched to the javelins, struggling to keep their balance and laughing at their clumsiness to properly maneuver them. Jayida followed his cue when Shams raced off again to a stash of sandbags, their enthusiasm carrying them further than their harmless fallen javelins.

"*Yallah*, Sa'd! *Yallah*, Sa'd!" echoed the shouts, as the young boys announced the arrival of *sayyid* Aziz and Zahir on their she-camels.

"That's not fair! You're towering over us on them!" she laughed as her father lured Sabah closer, waving his spear.

"As it should be," chuckled Zahir, swinging side to side. "All in good practice. Soon you'll be able to defeat anyone coming your way, no matter who he is or what he's riding." In an instant he poked her rib with the edge of his spear, then her leg. Frowning, she thrust her spear forward and clumsily barely scraped the edge of his robe. A quick sideglance revealed Shams was having equal problems reaching his uncle.

"Soon, soon, my brave nephew," laughed *sayyid* Aziz, lightly tapping him on the head with his own quick spear.

The afternoon elapsed in a hot blur, leaving her exhausted by the time they returned to their tent.

"My whole body is aching in places I didn't even know I had," moaned Jayida. "I confess I have renewed respect for fighters," she said, dropping down onto her bed.

Her mother helped her change her clothes and soak her feet, and blessedly massaged them. Her expert fingers dug and worked in all the right places, kneading all the pain away. "Oh, that is so nice, *yama*," Jayida sighed.

Her father chuckled. "Don't be hard on yourself, little lion; it's only the first day. Before you know it, it will be like second nature to you."

"*Sah*, our brave one. How could we forget that it was you who took it upon yourself to secretly start wearing the coat of mail, and finally venture out alone with your friends," said Zoraya with a tender reassuring smile.

"Speaking of; still no sign of that coin?" said Zahir.

"No."

"No matter; perhaps the desert claimed it for itself. So, then. Do you know your favorite, or shall I say what everyone says?" smirked her father, reclining on a mat with a cup of sour *makhid allaban*.

"The bow. I know it's everyone's dream to master the sword—it has easy control, requires close combat, and is the most resilient and versatile of all—but I like the distance and performance with the bow."

"I don't mind it myself," said her mother, sitting next to her and vigorously drying her feet with a cloth. Jayida pinched her lips together and grew quiet.

"What is it?" Zahir frowned.

"Is it possible that I could live without ever killing someone? I really wouldn't want to," said Jayida. "Maybe that's why—at least with the bow, it might be from afar; maybe they could even survive the wound." She thought of Nasr with his quieter and humble nature, so at home when he held the bow, skillfully keeping the approaching mock attackers at bay with his keen eye and perfect angle shot to stop them in their tracks. "Maybe that's a weakness I already have."

"No, my pure heart. That makes you a kind, feeling, honorable soul who values life," said her mother, kissing her forehead hard. "May Yassu and his servants always protect us all."

"I wish for nothing more than that you can live and never have to take a life, and no one offends yours," said her father, his demeanor serious.

"*Sah*. Life is to be treasured," whispered Jayida pensively.

Her father drew closer and gripped her shoulders with his strong hands, their combined presence a protective wall around her.

"Jayida, this is why I tell you: I'm teaching you so that you may defend yourself, and live. Always remember to lean to restrained *hilm* and not the wild folly of *jahl*, for killing is a serious matter," he said, his sad air unsettling her. "There's no going back from it, once you've done it. It changes you, and I wouldn't want you to ever have to do it. If I could, I would protect you from it forever." He looked away for a moment before looking up again. "I want you to live, but also, whenever possible, I want you to leave your opponents alive. In the end, it could be the more difficult one," he said, and slowly released his grip. "If it doesn't make sense now, in time it will."

Jayida frowned, a curious mix of confusion and relief sweeping through her.

"It's harder to stay alive," she nodded pensively.

"*Na'am*," said her father. "Unfortunately, we can't know how we'll react; as you've seen, you don't always have time to stop. You make us so proud, as you've already shown us all how gifted you are with your self-command, and being in control of your emotions. *Hilm*: that's what should come first in *muruwa*, reminding us to restrain ourselves and clarifying when to hold back and when to act. If a man can't control himself, he's a slave to everything else, worse than a wild beast. That's the hardest of all, and is no small achievement."

They were silent for a moment, as her mother rubbed her back and their glowing affection soothed her despite the weight of the conversation.

"At some point, I'll have to practice alone, too."

"*Aywa*, after your grazing duties, and after more training with *sayyid* Aziz and Nasr, too," said Zahir.

From then on, her days filled with helping her parents, grazing, and training, her fast developing skill emboldening her more each passing moment. One day blended happily into the next, her constant *qareen* and Aksumite princess guardian whispering she was worthy of her place, and right on track with her learning.

On a bright, late summer she accompanied her father, *sayyid* Aziz, and Nasr to Khaybar, exciting her as much to check on their dates and Attab the Shadow, as to have her prized leopard fangs made into pendants. In the vast blue morning brightness hovering around them, her father's melancholic silence stood out.

"What are you thinking of?" she said in a low tone as *sayyid* Aziz and Nasr steered their camels ahead. "It shouldn't be as tense as the *Ayyam al-Zalam*."

His gaze morphed into an averted frown, searching in the distance.

"Oh, it's just—I wish it was different. I don't know; I'm thankful for this life, I've seen some nice places, and yet still, I've often felt this longing for something else. Like a void that needs filling."

"You sound like Nasr," said Jayida, and looked away in a wave of sadness that inadvertently seized her to the core. Did no one want to be where they were? Yet even she longed for that day when her true name would be known, *al-'ayn* weakened, and her security assured.

"No, don't misunderstand: it's not you or your mother; you're all I could ever want," he said, drawing closer and wrapping his large hand around her arm. "I suppose everyone must feel this at some point. Everyone speaks of it: poets, believers of different faiths, soothsayers—about this great yearning for something *bigger*. But I'm grateful. Don't forget how important it is to be grateful. Oh Moharib, no matter what you're doing, I send you all my best wishes," said Zahir, kissing the tips of his fingers and offering the blessings to the invisible air.

No wonder he felt sad thinking of Moharib, and it both touched and annoyed her in a way.

At sunny, bustling Khaybar her father, *sayyid Aziz,* and Nasr enthusiastically informed *nasi* Musa of Jonder's leopard slaying and impressive ongoing training. *Nasi* Musa listened intently, and chuckled at the sight of her three leopard fangs. *Nasi* Musa handed them to a blacksmith and happily reminded them that they were always welcomed among them, for any length of time, given all the work there was to do.

"As for your fruits," added *nasi* Musa, "You'll have a mixture of ripened and nearly ripened dates."

"With everything that's happened, we're grateful for the good that endures," said *sayyid* Aziz.

The low hum of chants grew louder as they reached the beloved date palms, a sight she'd longed to see during the *Ayyam al-Zalam.* Workers hovered above, usually strapped in leather harnesses high up into the palms, calling out before hacking down massive clusters of dates to be caught by harvesters below. Some recited poetry and sang as they toiled in the blistering summer heat, the melodies reverberating high and low. Some were dressed nearly in rags, while a few even climbed the trees harness-free, partly to show-off their strength and balance, reminding that a number of them were there mostly out of necessity of work than anything else.

"I'd never go up without a harness, I don't care how strong the branches are," said Nasr. "May the angels of the air keep everyone safe," he added.

Jayida helped pack their crates of dates, and went off to find Attab the Shadow in the nearby area where *nasi* Musa had indicated. She found him moving about in a new, long *qamis* robe and dusty boots, gathering leaves and making a pile, as he hummed to himself. In his daydreaming he looked up at her, smiled and lowered his chin, while happy emotion gripped her to see him looking even better.

"Blessings Attab. We've come to collect our dates, and I have something for you," she said, slowly approaching him. Jayida reached for her pouch and handed it to him, full of frankincense tears and the fourth leopard fang. "It's from the leopard that attacked me, but I slayed him. May it protect you."

"Oh, Jonder. Blessings to your safety for always thinking of me," he said, looking away. His hands fumbled at his side and reemerged. "I've made you this, for when I saw you again. I hope you like it." He handed her a black and white, four-stranded braid that must've taken him a while.

"It's a perfect *wasm*," she smiled, and tied its hook at the side of her woven belt until she added the gift to dwell in her shrine. "I'm happy to see you well," she said, and helped him gather a few more treasures for his pile. After a while she left him, each in their own speechless happiness.

Jayida left the groves and found her kin, gathered around *nasi* Musa.

"Your trinkets are ready, as is your wine," said *nasi* Musa.

"Wine?" she said, wide-eyed.

"*Nasi* Musa has generously gifted you three wineskins from Al-Andarin, Adhri'at, and Wadi Jadar," beamed her father.

"*Nasi* Musa, that's too much," she said, shaking her head.

"Not at all; to the first of many brave feats," chuckled *nasi* Musa, and vigorously gripped her chin. "And we'll be sure to fill in Attab on all the details that you humbly didn't share," he winked.

Nasr proudly pat her shoulder and they drifted home in a happiness she could hardly express, and didn't try to. Sunrises and sunsets followed in eternal cycle, and for the first time, the arrival of fall and winter deepened her confidence. The uncertainty and stillness in the cold air somehow soothed, despite the lingering unspoken mystery of the *Ayyam al-Zalam*.

When her father and *sayyid* Aziz were away grazing the flocks, Nasr patiently, yet sternly taught her and Shams. He pushed them to hold their bows at full draw, training her to better aim and shoot despite her shaking arms. He taught them to make and shoot their slingshots, challenged them to catch by rope, and to two-on-one sword fighting. He instructed them to run carrying bags of sand, made them crawl across the dusty hard floor with sandbags tied to their ankles, and ordered their constant racing to test their speed and jump lengths. Always he monitored their posture when riding and shooting bows in a nearly endless stream of exercises.

Her muscles strengthened, proudly burning with satisfying exhaustion as she recited each night to her parents all that had happened. Kept safely concealed in her layers during the day, her gold Mikha'il amulet and leopard fang pendant protected as they witnessed her mounting force. Her parents each wore the remaining leopard fangs in shared satisfaction.

"As for us, you may not believe what we heard today," her father paused, teasing her by drawing it out. Jayida let a friendly sleepy smile linger on her face, waiting.

"*Qaysar* Justinian has finished rebuilding his church of Hagia Sophia that was destroyed during the Nika riots. It is now a marvel named in honor of *al-ilah*'s holy wisdom," said her mother dreamily.

"To represent the whole empire, he decreed that all territories under his rule should send pieces for its construction," continued Zahir. "He even had marble used for the floor and ceiling imported from the north of Al-Sham, and columns imported from Egypt. It's a masterpiece with a huge dome, with supporting arches covered with mosaics of six winged angels. The walls have mosaics made of gold, silver, glass, terra cotta and colorful tesserae showing scenes from the *injil* of Yassu. They say it is the largest building in the whole world."

"How I wish we could see it someday—and the one dedicated to Saints Sergios and Bakchos," said Jayida in playful echo with her mother.

"*Aywa*; it's right near it," said Zahir.

"He sure doesn't hold back, this *Qaysar*," Zoraya grinned approvingly. "Sergiopolis must look even better now with the new garrison to protect the city from those provoking, terrorizing Lakhmid bandits in service to Al-Mundhir and *Shah* Khosrow. They say the fortress's arches are made of white stone sitting on columns, shimmering like crystals in the sun."

Jayida saw them in jaw-dropping glory in her night-visions, streaming like endless stories recited by her guardian the Aksumite princess, or by other friendly faces from near and far. The evil eye fixed its darkness on the world, but the eternal sunlight was pushing it back again.

⊱•─────❀─────•⊰

"I think we're ready for warfare. And Yazida will join us, too," Nasr announced on the following first budding spring day. Shams's eyes widened as she grinned. "That should challenge everyone to be especially careful. But anyway, she's tougher than some of the young boys and I know you'll take great care of her."

On an early morning, *sayyid* Aziz, her father, Hubala, and Nasr—half their faces covered and weapons in tow—led the tribe's younger children to the training grounds. The elders rode their faithful she-camels while their offspring sat proudly on the family mares or stallions. Yazida, astride her brother's white stallion Bariq, appeared as amused as Jayida felt.

"What shall it be today?" said *sayyid* Aziz.

"Iskandar conquering the Parthians!" yelled Shams.

"Good place to start. Their descendants the Fars still cast a greedy eye on these parts," nodded *sayyid* Aziz. "The tribe is the shield of war, brave ones. Show us what burns in you!" he thundered.

The gathering was split into opposing camps, made of *zahf*, the large army, and the *katibah* as the mounted cavalry, creating the *dhar al-sarh*, or dawn raid. As mounted cavalry, Shams and Jayida led the Macedonians as Nasr and Yazida led the Parthians.

"*Yallah,* Iskandar!" Jayida yelled through her headwrap, mounted on Kamila and pointing her sword ahead.

And with that cue, they unleashed their tame, yet energetic raids on each other, a boisterous mix of happy roaring screams and clumsy, eager complaining enveloping them along with the rising dust. Thick spears dominated their surroundings, bodies at times knocked off their mounts as much by accident as by exaggerated mock defeat. Others raced off, hurling long noosed ropes at bands of fighters and taking them away to their camp. Jayida raced off after Yazida, who evaded her, spirited away by Bariq who zigzagged like a gazelle through the crowd.

"You won't get away next time!" yelled Jayida with a laugh.

Shams bounced forcefully ahead, trying his own attempt, to no avail. Their gazes met and together they set forth after Nasr, whose mount fled before them like smoke. Frowning, Shams paused then set off again, and finally managed to corner Nasr and clash their swords. Yazida reappeared, distracting them just enough to allow Nasr to get away.

"That's not fair; if she can do this without even training," pouted Shams.

"All the better for us!" laughed Jayida, grateful that Yazida, younger though she was, was doing much better than several of the boys. That Nasr and her father must've been teaching her made Jayida's heart soar.

"Not *now*!" cried a boy at his she-camel nearby who, unfazed, dropped into a seated position in the middle of the fray. "Please! I'll give you all the bitter *hamd* leaves you want!" he pleaded. Another young boy promptly took advantage of the scene by casting his net over them in playful capture.

"Fearsome you all are!" shouted *sayyid* Aziz, and roared in shared laughter as Hubala and Zahir waved at them playfully in the distance.

Though the battles were not fought for real victory and often ended up as a draw, Jayida counted herself victorious just for enduring to the end like others, and unlike those who proclaimed defeat just from sheer exhaustion. They'd all heard of the famous chariot races and feuding between the Greens and Blues at far-off Constantinople, who'd temporarily joined forces against *Qaysar* Justinian to protest the high taxes to fund his wars. Thankfully, his wife the Believing Empress Theodora had refused to flee, and the violent riots were quashed by the generals Belisarius and Narses. Shaking off the dread of bloodshed, Jayida took inspiration to stand her ground, even as she prayed that neither their playful games nor the tribe's business matters would ever reach such violence.

Each day, each new season, the fun scenarios were as familiar as they were varied: the Taghlib against their cousins the Bakr, the Ghassanids against the Lakhmids, the Himyarites against the Lakhmids, the Ghassanids against the Samaritans. Or it was blessed prophet Musa against the Pharaoh and his men, or Shamshun and the Philistines, and other nearly endless combination of feuds they could imagine.

Their playful cries resounded like clashing cymbals, echoes to Nasr's poetic verses that he chanted in the rush to inspire and add to the festive storm. His compositions grew as much in length as in variation, and Jayida almost swore no one was more impressed than she was. She was touched that he confessed to her that he didn't want others to predict what he was going to say, and so preferred to improvise each time instead of keeping to a certain meter or length.

"As our young *kahin*, I think you understand," smiled Nasr, flattering and confusing her at once. "It's like a rush of voices, filled with endless subjects demanding their moment of attention. Who knows if I'll praise the glories of the royal princely houses of Kindah or Jafna of Ghassan—and obviously not that Nasrid Al-Mundhir of Lakhm—or the desperations and triumphs of our desert lives? There's something freeing about letting your *qareen* flow uncontrolled, surprising the audience and myself in the process."

"You know we'll be your honored, eager audience either way," said Jayida, fascinated by his mysterious, semi-familar *qareen*.

One day, when a certain indifference over what to do seemed to hang over many of them, they were roused with curiosity by the news of an approaching passing caravan to the east of them. It was sent by King Abraha to *malik* Al-Harith, containing some holy relics of their slain kin at Najran. The gift was a sign of alliance between the Yassu-loving rulers, and to bless the church at Sergiopolis in Al-Sham, which had recently had reinforcements. They eagerly rode out to spot it, and soon, the echo of a solemn chanting reached them, the riders waving incense burners and nodding at them quietly in sign of peace—but also stern defensiveness if necessary. There were so many armed Ghassanid guards protecting the relics shrouded in a veiled *hawdaj* that they could only look on in emotional awe at the heavenly-scented procession.

One evening, Jayida and her mother were making a banner out of a linen cloth when her father shared *sayyid* Aziz's news. It spoke of trouble between the Banu 'Abs with Banu Ghatafan and Hawazin, all kin to the Banu Sa'd as fellow descendants of Mudar. The thought of her father marching off to Kutha alongside some of Mudar and Thalaba always made her feel proud.

"Let's hope it's the usual petty squabbling, but it's caught Aziz's attention yet again," said Zahir.

"I'm starting to think that maybe the failed gold mine stint during the *Ayyam al-Zalam* wasn't the isolated work of some of their rogue members," said Zoraya. She loosened some linen with a bone needle to create frayed edges, then passed Jayida the cloth along with a small cup of wine.

"Yassu, his servants, and the whole might of Banu Sa'd will protect us, as represented by Nasr, the victorious eagle," said Jayida. With an approving nod from her parents, she dipped her finger in the dark liquid and drew an outline of the creature, wings spread wide apart. She repeated the motion until she was satisfied and finished with her father by securing it atop a smooth, sturdy red acacia pole.

With pride Jayida carried it off to mock battles and dutifully, but sometimes reluctantly, ceded the honor to others. For added fun they merged different time periods and made up new scenarios: with Yazida playing the Tanukhid Queen Mawiyya marching against the Rûm, or with the Rûm against the Goths, or in turn the Fars marching against her and the Ghassanids, always eager to antagonize the Rûm and its neighbors. No matter the scene, they always ended with proud echoes of "*Yallah* Sa'd! *Yallah* Sa'd!" in honor of their tribe.

While Jayida could never bring herself to play on the Lakhmid side, she often blissfully forgot herself and relished her growing abilities. She might have little wish to fight but if she needed to, she could skillfully defend herself and others. While this was all the reassurance she needed, she tried to meet her mother's rising concern with playful banter.

"Are you sure it hasn't come yet? No cramps, no red blood stains in your private garment?" her mother frowned. "Maybe we'll get you an amulet of the Annunciation, and I'll make you a mixture of birthwort leaves with myrrh and pepper..."

"No, *yama*, I'm not taking any strange-magical potions! And what use is my Mikha'il amulet if it needs help? Just as well; what if as a *kahin*, I'm dwelling with the angels and have little concern for earthly time?" chuckled Jayida. Neither would she remain fourteen years old, and if it hadn't come yet, there had to be a good reason.

Amidst those long days with her friends, Jayida grew more patient and amused at their antics, the sense of belonging and deepening bonds reassuring her. She couldn't ignore the extent of Nasr's skill with all weapons as much as his playfulness with kids, and marveled again at his praiseworthy traits that made him more endearing. As for Yazida, Jayida was proud of her and tried to compliment and encourage her, while all the boys predictably vied to catch her and be her rescuer from her kidnappers. Now and then, Jayida glimpsed Shams intent on this goal with a fierceness unlike she'd ever seen before.

Would Nasr react in a similar way if it was for her, if he knew? So far he'd still never mentioned interest in any particular girl as potential bride. Which other tribe did he have in mind? Amidst the boisterous play, he taught them a much lighter form of weapon-free pankration, once practiced by Heracles to fight the Nemean lion, and later also used by the great Iskandar. Glowing with his kind demeanor that favored friendship and unity over competition, their gazes often met, filled with a mutually hearty, stomach-clenching laughter she wanted to keep forever. But somehow, something also seemed different. Nasr was still that caring, handsome young man, but with an added strength, even an unexpected dark edge that she liked. With some shyness she dared to think that someday she might learn more secret things about him.

Overcome with gratitude, Jayida burnt more incense than she'd ever done, giving thanks for the blessing of having caring parents, and also being taught by the kind-hearted man who'd generously welcomed her parents with open arms. Though their flocks had decreased by half during the *Ayyam al-Zalam*, the blessed pregnancies and calving, lambing, and kidding suggested their continued prosperity.

It struck Jayida to think that, perhaps had things been different, she would've been learning from Moharib... But then caught herself, because if they'd stayed there, she would've been just another, maybe even pampered girl. She would know Khaled in place of Nasr. But just the thought of calling him "cousin" felt wrong: he was a stranger to her, and any *badawi* knew that kinship was not strictly determined by blood, when in fact it was often the opposite.

Her father was right, as always: the weapons became less intimidating, new sacred objects endowed with power to assist her at will. Though she still had much to learn, she was proving herself more each day, often to her own surprise. Each day there was less to fear, so long as she kept going and doing her part among a great tribe, full of loyal members.

And someday, *sha'ir* Nasr would succeed his honorable father as *sayyid*, and a burden lifted to realize that she would be ready to reveal herself to him and be trusted and accepted as Jayida, as he'd always been of Jonder.

CHAPTER NINE

'ANTARAH

SUMMER 539 AD - BANU 'ABS, CENTRAL NAJD DESERT

Antares, enemy of Ares—the bright red scorpion's heart written in the stars.

'Antarah.

If you had been a girl it would've been Atarah, my Iyasus-loving crown—his mother's words like milk and honey from Aksum, starting with his name, meant to protect him.

But to what extent, when Yassu was flogged and hung up on the cross-shaped tree by his own people? If he, the Israelite *al-Masih*, fulfiller of scripture—proudly worshipped and proclaimed by *Negus* Kaleb and King Abraha who shared his own dark skin—couldn't escape it, what hope did 'Antarah have?

'Antarah almost hugged his mother a bit tighter that morning before leaving camp, but then decided against it. He didn't have the heart to tell his beloved *ema*, that sometimes he wondered if Yassu and all the other *injil* and Israelite stories she told were even real. It's not that he was against it or didn't want to believe. But he didn't know what was crazier: that holy Henok was, then a moment later was no more, or that Yassu, *al-ilah* in the flesh, had to cruelly die on a cross. How had He not hated humans more after taking their form? How could any human love like this; forgiving, maybe even *wanting* such constant savagery, if only as a selfish test to surpass it? Timely Fate had crushed *al-Masih*'s bones and blood in the stonemill, just as it kept doing to the whole land, and in the people's drunken, wishful wailing misery they'd imagined seeing Him returned from the dead. Still, there was something oddly satisfying in that.

For all his own mysterious, inhuman patient *sabr*, even 'Antarah couldn't deny that it was there—that creeping hunger, that insatiable thirst to push further, defend the life his blameless, beautiful slave mother Zabiba had given him. Best of all, he had an idea what she might say if he'd told her his doubts.

"Never forget that so soon after being freed from Egypt, fed manna from Heaven and given a safe path through the Red Sea, the Israelites were grumbling, wishing for their slave days, and worshipping a golden calf while Musa was on Mount Sinai obediently waiting for the Ten Commandments. Don't *ever* be these fickle, ungrateful *yahudi. Mawai temawe meskal*: victory through the cross, so cling to the one and only Iyasus!"

His mother often said this in her distinctly gentle yet direct way, her accented tone made of its unique blend of Aksumite-*badawi* influences. And somehow her fiery faith pushed him on, and in his wild fantasies he imagined meeting King Abraha at his court, asking him questions about his rule—maybe even about how he'd defied *Negus* Kaleb—and seeing the Zafar Cathedral restored by *Negus* Kaleb, and the ancient Marib Dam.

On this cloudless, burning morning like countless others, his frowning dark brown eyes hovered amidst the folds of his old, undyed linen robes. Leading his master Shaddad's Awassi sheep flocks, he roamed the vast valley of Mutathallam north of the red sand mountains of Dahna, a spear in each hand tracing snake-like forms, scattering harm. 'Antarah glanced to the northeast towards Wadi Al-Rummah and Wadi Al-Batin, leading all the way to Basrah, near the Fars territory. A deep sigh made him flinch, wincing as his shoulders and back stiffened into straight position.

He might be a lowly sheep herder, forced to pitch their tent with his mother and brother at the outskirts of camp, just a step ahead of Israelite drained-and-burnt sin offerings, but at least he wasn't suffocating and being hacked up in the hellish mines. Just the thought of the pitch darkness made him shudder, as it called and lured him deeper into its gateway, ready to swallow him whole without a trace. But just in case he ever ran out of other options, there were the Jabal Al-Shizm copper mines to the west. Or better yet, Mahd adh-Dhahab, that cradle of gold between Yathrib and Mina run by their distant kin the Banu Sulaym. As a mere slave, he hadn't been allowed to be among the 'Abs who'd marched to seize it during the *Ayyam al-Zalam*—if he'd even wanted to. And yet, if he had no other choice but to toil there, at least his possible death by precious gold-encrusted stones might offer him safe, bountiful passage into the beyond.

Thankfully, he had his prized clothing to crown and protect him, and which he kept nearly spotless. It was the least he could do to honor his mother's toiling under the sun at the *wadi*, her diligent washing and scrubbing off of dirt, and sometimes his own blood, tiring her strong, callused hands.

His throat tightened, and amidst the blistering buzzing, he cued his hearing for any sound that wasn't that of the fat-tailed sheep's chewing and soft rustling hooves sweeping the dry earth, foraging for *raghal* and other saltbush and shrubs.

Once more, he let it unfurl, the visions speaking of life and death—a last justification, no matter how wanting.

Fatherlesss, savage, impulsive herder of beasts—lacking the smallest drop of *hilm.*

Though the insults had been hurled at him so many times, 'Antarah still couldn't resolve himself to it. Beasts had to go by instinct to survive, so how could that be wrong? That he was there, alone, waiting, proved his own self-control—at last they would finally see. With a spear he waved some invisible flies away, along with the rising echo that those who didn't want to see, wouldn't. Unless he made them.

How could he be savage and so wounded by words that were rarely just words, but followed by action? He wished that's all it ever was, so he could've ignored it—or tried—as wrong as it still was. Didn't they hear themselves; the lies they repeated that others fed on in rotting feasts for their own selfish benefit? Instead he turned the words inside and out, searching out hidden meaning in their expressed sounds, a *kahin* glimpsing into his own Fate.

'Antarah was no beast, just a dark skinned raven who'd endured seventeen bitter winters, aimlessly flying back and forth in search of a true home like the one Nuh had sent off after the Great Flood. He, inheritor of his mother's slave title, as if he'd had a choice in that. The edge of his full lips curved up: sometimes he liked to think that he did, his eyes burning with grateful tears that, though he'd spent long days considering it, he felt not a drop of shame for his appearance. Try as they did to hide it, he'd even caught those whispers of his handsomeness, which curiously had only humbled him. The realization that he didn't need them to confirm what he already knew to be true was still his best reward. Death didn't seem so bad, if he could die remembering that. Maybe it helped to face it, but either way there was no escaping his Fate—every *badawi*'s torment. And now, his moment was at hand.

His chest swelled under his thin linen *qamis* robe, because despite his low rank, he was not alone, though he'd yet to show it. He'd discovered this as a mere boy, that his *qareen* had gifted him with images and ways of saying things others wouldn't see or understand. It was not something he had to make himself do; it just happened and filled him with a joy he couldn't express, almost like it was enough to just exist for the living poetry to flow through him. His mother wasn't sure which would most offend and stir jealousy—his skill or subtle happiness, and notice they would—and advised to keep it to himself, at least until time was right.

And what if that day never came? He would've lost his chance of using his gift, of letting the blissful words fly out of him, and that devastating thought, only second to that of harm to his family, as much hurt as inspired him. But instead, just another brutal day skinning him a bit more, of the slave who should be grateful to be owned by Shaddad of the Banu 'Abs. An animal-man in their midst, they said.

They branded him with names, so he might as well have two names for himself, as much to reflect their dissatisfaction as for him to counter their word. He was Man of Peace in times of war, and Man of War in times of peace, at the call of his trusted lance. They had things to say about him, and so did he of them—his poetry demanded it, even if he kept it only for his family or to himself.

He might not know much, but he knew no animal-man could do what he could: take those lying curses and reshape them, weaving tapestries whose unique patterns only he could make. Who was he to question or reject that ability that some others struggled with? True; he was no Najdi armored warrior-poet astride his noble mare praising the Jafnid, Nasrid, and Kindite royal houses in hopes of getting favors. Or even a walking, beekeeping Hijazi poet with his *nasib* opening *za'n* caravan departure scene amidst the *harif* rainy season. But he was 'Antarah the raven, and unlike others, he didn't need to pay any poets to create verses for him, romanticizing his suffering—deciding on his tragic or triumphant end! No: he would be the one to do it, and would've rather died than lie about something like that. It was enough that it sent his soul soaring, and often when he least expected it. Even if he resisted it, it was stronger than him, and he had to do it justice.

Intoxicating, like rich and inky Adhri'at or Al-Andarin wine—so he imagined—knowing he could stop them in their tracks with another kind of weapon: his verses, poured on them like silken Hudhayl honey, turning them into transfixed idols, awaiting—wanting—more from his divinely blessed slave tongue. Lord of Heaven! How he longed to see their faces then! With pounding heart he restrained a sob: if only he could unleash it, just once, before it all ended. But were they worthy of it, of hearing, let alone being praised by his gift?

But to know the blessing was to know its pattern; how temporary conviction could be. How could something so strong, so real, feel so uncertain? That familiar, dreadful sadness wrapped him like a perpetual mourning veil. And what if they were right and he, in his rough, unrefined ways, was blind to the truth? What if he, despite everything, wasn't so different from them?

Doubt.

That's what tortured, and made it worse than knowing.

He will not stop, so we must stop him.

A painful tightening gripped his chest, threatening to unleash a roaring cry. He was not trying to be that way! Everyday he submitted and obeyed, followed the orders put to him by their severe master Shaddad, and went on his way. Without complaint he led the herds to far-off pastures roamed by the Banu 'Abs—north to Hazn, south to Samman, or west to Shaqiq and Qassim—his *qareen*, and maybe also *jinn*, and who knew what else, pointing the way.

He'd even thought of going as far west as the camps of the Banu Hawazin and Ghatafan, near Khaybar and Yathrib—both tribes their *sayyid* Zoheir longed to dominate. That they were kin should help facilitate it, along with any rich gold mines attached to them. *Sayyid* Zoheir might freeze his eyes to steel, feigning indifference, but his envious words betrayed him all the same. The volcano was just lying dormant, waiting to reach and claim his own cradle of gold. What reward was in it for him, if he'd ever dared?

Dutifully, each day 'Antarah brought the flocks back, well-nourished and not a single one stolen or lost. Always he dared hope that they'd notice, and finally trust him with the prized camels, maybe even give him some arms training to go with it, but to no avail.

In fits of anger 'Antarah had thought of joining raiding parties, like the *su'luk* poet Shanfara had done, his verses spewing with defiance. But that was always short-lived. Even as his mother eased his turmoil with her rapturous smile, her selfless love swearing she'd go anywhere he went, he would not risk her safety during such forays.

And yet, there was another possibility, as extreme as tempting.

Would he dare go to the northern courts and reveal his talents, his skill finally earning him renown and enough to care for his mother as she deserved? He only had to follow the eastern path of Wadi Al-Rummah leading to Basrah, then course north until he reached the Lakhmid court at Al-Hira. But what was he thinking? *Shah* Khosrow often provoked feuds with the Rûm Empire through his restless vassal Al-Mundhir, sworn enemy of *malik* Al-Harith. His fancies always brought him back to the same paralyzing place: what chance did a mere slave like him have? His heart clenched at the cruelty of such fantasies, but the *qareen* in him always propelled him to new heights, relishing and fanning the wild flames.

It was no use lying: he'd already decided he'd go someday, whether living or dead; a roaming ghost until he'd unleashed all his verses—if it even knew an end.

At last, there was no more holding back.

'Antarah closed his eyes and mentally called for help in his quest: if his *qareen* or *jinni*, or whoever else was there listening, brought him a life, he would offer it in sacrifice. They, more than anyone, had to know how ready he was, that he could offer the sacrifice in mutual exchange; that he would not ask without delivering. And if he was just wishfully speaking, they'd get his own life for it.

His head tilted back up to the bright blank sky. Perhaps if he knew who his father was, it would help to explain some things.

Longing. Yearning. Agitated. A piece of him missing.

Especially that very urge in him, simmering, eager to defend, take life if needed—like any warrior did. And as he'd already done, unintentional though it may have been.

"Your true father is the Lord of Heaven," said his mother, when he tried to learn more. Her strong gaze was as direct as it was unreachable, commanding his obedient respect.

Enrobed in her simple white linen robe and headdress, her smooth bronze complexion hosted gentle doe eyes, perfectly sculpted nose and lips, and a near ageless form—more than a match for Makeda, or Bilqis, as the *badawi* called her. No wonder she was the jealous envy of other women; she of perpetual youth without even trying. That a mere slave could command such attention was beyond what many a bitter tribeswoman could take.

His jaw tensed, his pride struggling to stifle his simmering anger. The price of that had been many a *badawi* yearning for her: capturing her, taking her by force, yielding her first son and his brother Shaybub, up until Shaddad's own kidnapping and taking of her, right around the time of his birth.

Despite their different natures, Shaybub made life seem sweeter, like anything was possible. His brotherhood and friendship was the only one 'Antarah had and couldn't imagine being without it. Together they could face anything; forget their low rank and create their own priceless moments of happiness. He pinched a pained smile, his brother's first absence marking him. But it had to be this way, and though Shaybub had initially protested his lone venture, he'd eventually yielded.

A shudder snaked down his spine, rattling him.

Let it not be the last time, let me make them proud.

But even Shaybub's absence still protected him, when that brotherhood is what enabled him to be there, alone yet confident with the flocks, the fruit of season after season of secret practicing with weapons, riding off in the early morning darkness, undetected.

Distraught, sore with overwork, limbs screaming for rest, their self-imposed push thankfully felt different, a welcomed distraction. Testing themselves to the brink, Shaybub had long since become a fast runner and expert archer, while 'Antarah had mastered horse riding and the lance. That Shaybub was more resolved to such momentary joys made him wonder if he was wrong for longing for more—the unspoken song unrelenting from deep within. Let it sing, then, as if he could stop it.

A hard glance at some of the sheep, ears dangling like heavy obelisk earrings, revealed them digging in the tall *sam'a* grasses, its green leaves turned yellow from wilting.

His coiled tension built up, swirling out of his core, and he invisibly seized it, trapping it in place.

Wait. He would keep waiting—until he didn't.

A stillness emerged with the rising heat and, grimacing, he bent down to the desert floor, a spear at each side of him. Reclining on one side, he propped himself on one arm, commanding his back muscle's tearing pain into submission, nearly concealing himself amongst the creatures. With a deep breath he closed his eyes, listening, as his mother guided him to, ever since he'd been a child.

"Seek the quiet, and it will strengthen you," said Zabiba, gratifying him that he was beginning to understand the meaning of it more each day.

Like magic: how the elements all seemed to slow down, the sky and sun fixed in place like eternal cave drawings. Sweat burned down the side of his face, and he kept still, concentrating.

A shock invaded him, for finally, he heard it: scuffling, approaching steps creeping from somewhere in the west.

Not one, but several beasts.

And this time, they were men. Didn't they know they should keep quiet? Their reprimanding whisperings gave them away. He might've chuckled but for breaking his concentration, and maybe even give away his position. He would not make it so easy on them.

'Antarah shifted and laid flatly on his back, biting away his pain. Would he ever get used to this, and was he blaspheming for even asking if he had to? His limbs spread over the earth, vanishing in plain sight—and now he wasn't sure if it was them or he who wanted it most.

"Please, let it come. I'm right *here*, I'm *ready*," 'Antarah begged in whispers, the sun blazing upon him, transforming him into a fiery torch.

He will not stop, so we must stop him.

Could they? And could he let them, and submit himself to that extent? Shrug it off; not personal, not *his* master's idea, because Shaddad had to know he had purpose, little as it seemed. He was still his beloved slave Zabiba's offspring, guardian of the flocks and camp outpost. His heart raced, violent tears threatening to cloud his vision.

There it was again, that same rustling of this band of conniving men, none other than his own tribesmen—come to kill him by order of Shaddad. *He will not stop, so we must stop him.*

Fate, that perfectly punishing element.

The war raged inside: casting off sadness for thankfulness to have overheard the words the night before, when without their knowledge, he'd approached the tent. Flinching, his throat constricted with confused emotion. Maybe he deserved it; the stern man always seemed disappointed with him. His back still protested, smoldering with the recent marks of his insatiable whip.

Maybe it was time to let it end and march off with death, his life's only promise. But first he would show the others, show them some more of what he had. And if Shaddad really wanted him dead, then why didn't he do it himself, when he was his property, with which to do as he wanted? Something was holding him back—and he would show him how right he was!

"I'm right here," 'Antarah repeated, summoning all the force of his soul. "By *al-ilah*, come, get me."

His head spun in the burning fire, the dead, silent stillness for a moment making him think it was all over. It couldn't be—not so quietly!

Then he stiffened, his heart nearly bursting with joy when finally, he caught it. The slightest tremor in the dry bush, the hesitating hairy paws. The lowering massive head, sniffing, approaching. The flocked scattering of Shaddad's Awassi, lingering nearby like they knew they had little to fear.

Someone heard him!

In his erratic shock 'Antarah bit a smile, thrilled that the men's whisperings grew louder still, dripping with fear... then stopped. Afraid, they were so afraid that he almost pitied them, they who outnumbered him! His heart raced, recalling Shaybub's words to maintain his *hilm*.

A hot, musty scent of shaggy, dusty fur wafted over, as the earth vibrated under the creature's weight. Each hand wrapped tightly around a spear, his rough, dry palms enhancing his grip.

A pause. Silence.

Now!

'Antarah jolted up on his feet, the largest wolf he'd ever seen now in full display before him. The wolf gnarled at him, his glistening white fangs fit to be turned into protective charms. With blazing eyes his legs bent in readiness.

"*Yallah*, go on, 'Antarah!" yelled 'Antarah, and the creature pounced, answering his call. Reaching into the air, his spear thrust into the wolf's throat, releasing his seeping blood. He speared the shrieking creature to the ground, his snapping jaw still trying to bite his large hands closing in on his throat, suffocating as his legs kicked wildly, in vain. The corpse stilled but 'Antarah maintained his grip, the greedy exposed fangs still laughing, taunting.

He will not stop, so we must stop him.

His bloody palms gripped the lower jaw, burying over the thick canines, and pulled down, so hard until finally it gave way, cracked and dangled down his neck.

"You're just a dog, but I'm a lion by rage and force," 'Antarah winced.

He stared at it, grotesque, listening for confirmation that it was accepted and spirited away, freeing him from the beast's revenge.

There was no telling how long it was until 'Antarah got up and became aware of a hurrying, receding sound of steps. Always so fast, the unfurling chaos, its bittersweet result hopefully outlasting it. He would know soon enough.

In a daze 'Antarah returned to camp, the clustered Awassi following his bloody form dragging his trophy like a rag sweeping the desert floor. In the distance were shapes like mirages, and before he knew it there was a whirring, an echo of deafening, agitated voices, engulfing his head. Strangely he could've sworn tribesmen stood aside as he approached, as if respectfully making way. In the background he caught the tall, approving figure of *sayyid* Zoheir, with a stone-faced man at one side and a smirking one at the other. Just his *qareen* trying to comfort him again; let him enjoy his last moments before Shaddad demanded his death, this time face-to-face and in front of the whole Banu 'Abs.

For his part, he'd shown something else that he could do, had fulfilled his bargain with the benevolent *jinni*. A melancholic gratitude filled him: at least he'd been heard, his sacrifice paying his way forward, and the creature's hide could be used and worn—a second life in place of his, if that's the way it had to be.

Confused, 'Antarah frowned at the commotion all around him, as significant as his own internal turmoil. Grimacing, shouting faces, some with concerned, even understanding demeanors; whispering onlookers, all with varying degrees of surprise in their manner. Other slaves, cowering before him, eyes pleading. Deafening tension like banging metal pans—talking, shouting. Saying what? Things he couldn't hear, didn't want to hear. He already knew its dreary refrain: their constant disapproval of his untamed ways.

Reckless, shameless beast, they said, when that drab, sunless day of the *Ayyam al-Zalam*, poor widowed Mulaika, respected and loved for her noble age, as usual approached to graze her few sheep at the Jifar waterhole in Qassim. But Daji, that vain, favorite slave to the future *sha'ir* Ahmar, son of their *sayyid* Zoheir, blocked access to all in favor of his own flocks. Humble and helpless, Mulaika pleaded, but it only seemed to encourage Ahmar's cruel mocking of her. Moved at the sight, 'Antarah had stepped in to her assistance, citing the generosity of their kin to placate Daji, who mocked his dark skin and told him to remember his place. Taunting, Daji and his entourage cackled like hyenas, making circles around them.

But when the brute dared to shove Mulaika hard enough to make her fall, their laughter redoubling at her exposed flesh, it was all 'Antarah could take. Without a second thought 'Antarah had flown to Daji, and struck him so hard that he fell back onto a rock, his cracked head yielding a snaking pool of crimson. It'd been unintentional and yet he could hardly pity the corpse. He couldn't stand by and watch the blameless woman be so disrespected, and by a slave at that, even that of their *sayyid*'s son.

Back at camp, Hashem, Ahmar's younger brother, had flown to his defense, his robe protectively stretched over 'Antarah as he praised his selflessness. Even if it was just for show, 'Antarah hadn't expected that, and could only keep his chin lowered out of rattling confusion and anger. But all the same, Shaddad had unleashed his wrath on him, whipping him in a rage for his rashness that would cost him at least a handful of camels as blood price and stir troubles among the tribe. But it'd hurt most to see his suffering, tearful mother pleading that it was an accident and he wouldn't do it again. He wished he could've said so himself, quash away all the doubts, but as the blameless one she should never have to pay for his actions.

Though 'Antarah didn't dare utter that it was worth it, Shaddad had stopped, his angry panting carrying on his violence. It was only after the story circulated, and it was clear that not only would there be no retaliation from Ahmar, but that *sayyid* Zoheir approved and forgave, backed by his youngest son Hashem, that Shaddad dropped his angry stare. The slaveowner's fears had been stilled: that his property might not only cost him dearly, but also make him look bad.

He won't stop so we must stop him; what if next time he kills noble sons of sayyidun, and not just their slave?

As if he couldn't already have done it, if that's what he'd wanted.

'Antarah had slain before then: animals of smaller size, followed by the same refrain: reckless beast. But indeed, this time it had been a man, if he could be called that. Sometimes he wondered if it'd been the *Ayyam al-Zalam* commanding his participation, and though he wasn't proud of it, neither did he have any regrets. They might protest his lack of *hilm*, but they'd seen that his wrathful *jahl*—also important to *muruwa*—might do its part if needed. And no amount of gold could express his satisfaction that they'd remember it henceforth.

While Ahmar demanded no reparation, even appeared indifferent—too proud to admit he'd suffered a loss, though as budding *sha'ir* 'Antarah suspected he was plotting some revengeful verses—'Antarah knew the enmity was sown. He tried to take some comfort in knowing that he had the support of *sayyid* Zoheir and Hashem, so that his decision was not without reward.

All the same, his help had been needed, and that's what he'd do, and would keep doing, no matter the cost. At least he'd leave knowing he'd done something worthy. Thankfully, some of his doubts had been quelled by the gratitude confessed by the tribeswomen, who now felt safe with him and deemed him a worthy protector. That it had not been in vain was all the reward he could want.

A hush fell over the crowd as Shaddad's tall and dark-clad form approached, his curved Indian sword at the hip proudly commanding attention. Fixated tribesmen followed at his side like shadows, some clearly displeased, others disappointed, almost sad. Folding his arms, Shaddad stood before him, observing him with a curious contemplating air he'd never seen before. 'Antarah lifted the wolf corpse and Shaddad glanced it over, let out a rough laugh and handed it off, grinning as it drifted from hand to hand. With his strong bearing and features, 'Antarah once more thought the man could inspire admiration, if only it wasn't so often diminished by his coldness.

"*Ya Allah*, 'Antarah. With your mounting achievements, these men have just tried to claim you as their own, falsely claiming your mother was already pregnant with you when I took her into my home. Now, after this most revealing assembly meeting, everyone knows how proud I am that it was not the case," said Shaddad, his sharp gaze glistening with a hint of self-satisfied amusement.

"But that's not all the good news. After all our troubles, today our great *sayyid* Zoheir has proclaimed his dominion over the Banu Fazara, who now submits to our rule. I'll admit: I hardly expected them to cede so easily, but Fate has done its work. That's something else for Ahmar to compose verses on; a welcomed change from the praises to the royal houses in favor of our own great 'Abs lineage," he chuckled. "By the power of fateful Time and the great Allah, everything is falling right into its proper place."

'Antarah lowered his chin in a nod, a pile of stones dropping in his core. To finally know his father's identity, this fickle man whom he'd called master, who hadn't recognized him in seventeen winters, was little consolation for the fact that just the day before, he'd ordered his own son's death.

For being his 'Antarah, his enemy of war—deflecting yet guilty, even in survival.

Chapter Ten

SPRING PICNIC
Spring 540 AD - Banu 'Abs

Smirking, 'Antarah glimpsed the last halos of the setting spring sun ahead, the camels silently following him, his mother, and Shaybub back to camp. Since their winter relocation to Jiwa, further inland west of Mutathallam, he wallowed in the emerging sense of serenity. He let it enrobe him like the nearby mountain range behind them, their roaming grounds now between Tawi and Qarah. Their camp rested safely north of the forking *wadi*, between Sharabbah and Qaww in central Najd. It might be his imagination, but the flow of life sounded different in this pulsating heartland, the silent rush quieting and disturbing him incessantly. The change was slow, subtle, but—he dared to think—tinged with something like solace.

Like every evening and morning, at camp they retrieved the clay bowls and gathered the lactating females and their calf, and let them headbutt and nibble on their ticklish udders and teats. After a few minutes they joined them in squeezing the teats, until finally the fresh, warm milk was let down. They set the bowls aside to cool in the evening chill, while they returned the she-camels to Shaddad's securely fenced grounds.

Once ready, they each took a bowl of the lightly salted liquid gold, and he smiled as Shaybub followed their mother into his *aba*'s tent—relieved that he paused less often at the thought of the still new fatherly title. They entered unannounced, and there was satisfaction in that, too.

The call of duty still pulsing in his blood, his own guided steps took him to his uncle Mutaz's tent, his father's brother for whom he sometimes also did favors, and slipped in after announcing himself.

In the dimness lit by scattered oil lamps, for a moment 'Antarah was struck and froze, unsure if he'd stepped into a dream. There sat Suhayyah, Mutaz's wife, loosening their daughter 'Ablah's braids. Her long, ebony locks cascaded down her shoulders and across her back like a fountain. Just as striking, her naked pearly arms out of her cream sleeveless robe glowed like moonlit pillars amidst the sea of hair.

Everything seemed to still until, caught by his presence, 'Ablah bolted in an instant, her wavy locks now a flowing river behind her, her mother trailing after. Out of respect 'Antarah looked away and set the blessed drink down before Mutaz and his son Waiz, and stepped back. 'Antarah stood along the tent wall, taming his raging blood into stone, waiting until they finished as time around him slowed. At some point the empty bowls came down, and he collected them without looking up at them, and with a final deep nod, departed the tent.

He laid awake that night in their tent now moved next to his father's, grateful for the silence to wallow in his sleeplessness. He tossed and turned, the welts on his back less painful than moons before.

Of all the moments, of all the sightings. But who was he to question it, if Fate wanted it that way? Who was she, where had she come from? 'Ablah, his beloved lance, drawing blood at his command. But also 'Ablah, his uncle's adopted daughter, Suhayyah's fruit from another man.

'Antarah must've—had!—noticed her before, but hadn't seen the same thing, had seen something else, entirely. He dug deep, calling forth every moment he'd spent with the girl, outlining all the fleeting moments.

Her bored indifference, smug smirk, teasingly cruel at times—her mother's daughter. There was also her gentle kindness, hidden warm smile and laughter under her veil: the perfectly restrained, well-mannered princess. But they were just children then; even he had changed since.

Her manner, her shapely form—at fourteen, she would not be unmarried much longer, especially with that kind of rare beauty. No wonder Mutaz hid her well out of sight.

But not out of his.

Conflict seized him, gratitude and rightful yearning battling. Let them think he was an unfeeling boy incapable of real manly passion, if it kept him closer to her to protect and serve her—because he already knew that's all he wanted to do. What he felt—and didn't—was for him to know, when no one outside of his mother and brother had ever asked before. 'Ablah's honor was his own, but even he couldn't reject the blessing of seeing her perfect beauty.

In the cloak of pitch night that was her silken hair, he walked back into the perfect dream he hadn't dared imagine. It had to be, when he could never be the same again. But Fate wanted it, dared him to stake his claim, and no matter what happened, he would always be Fate's servant. He bit down a conflicted smile in the dark, pleasure warming him like undiluted wine.

His father's words, drifting, in the privacy of men's coveted spaces, away from the ears of his wife Shemia. His father, who still enjoyed his ageless mother, as recently as the previous night. When it once had him recoiling in shame—pressing down on his ears to stifle Shaddad's muffled groans in the night, moaning out to *his queen*—the sting had since gone. He saw it differently now, how it was part of him, too: her secret Aksumite carnal power—boasted of by Egyptians, *badawi*, and others—that his father desired, contributing to his present existence.

By *al-ilah*, his father had wanted it, even him, whether he admitted it or not! And if no one else knew it but them, the secret had latched onto his father, stronger than him. The secret was that his father wanted to be put into place. Only now did 'Antarah understand his mother's unshaken confidence, slapping his father hard, over and over, in the throes of twisted pleasure, searching, asking his unborn wandering soul to help her in keeping him in place—and there he was. Their painful life had called him forth, and pride swelled in his chest to know there was more yet to show.

In the whirl of consuming visions his *qareen* appeared, merging with his breath, as it always did.

I saw a white girl whose hair falls to the ground, pitch like the night.

Under her shadowy braids like prayer rope bracelets, she's like the dawn rising from darkness. She's so beautiful that everyone admires and hurries to serve her. And I'll hide my love deep in my heart until Fate also makes me her servant.

The hard searching eyes lingered, inspecting, as they had from the day he'd first opened them.

"Don't let me down, 'Antarah. The tribe exists only for war, and while I'm away assisting *sayyid* Zoheir in subjugating the resistant Banu Ka'b, I now put it in your hands. If you fail," Shaddad said, raising a thick finger in his lowered face. "Praise Allah that thankfully for us, no one need remember you."

"*Na'am, aba*," said 'Antarah with a bow. Though his belt seemed to constrict, he suppressed a grin as his short blade dug into his waist. Through his father's curt nod, he glimpsed an evasive smirk spread over his features like a mask—invisible but just enough for him to catch. Sometimes, a son could read his father, despite the distance. With a final glance to their sleeping quarters, his father disappeared briskly out of their tent.

"May the Lord of Heaven and his Anointed One protect us through you," said Zabiba, emerging behind the tent divider. Adjusting her cream headwrap, her loose sleeves swept across her form like doves' wings. She was a heavenly, loving gentleness that often stunned him, but in his perpetual turmoil, was slowly beginning to make sense. "And while this is a blessed day of this fifth month of Dhu-Mabkaran to prove yourself, as you bravely keep doing, please be careful with 'Ablah." Zabiba tilted her head up and her winged hand grazed his cheek, and something in her small smile almost broke his heart.

Undaunted, this selfless woman—secret keeper of the Himyarite calendar, land restored to Yassu by *Negus* Kaleb—would always be the first woman he'd answer to. An eternal timekeeper, she guided their steps, confirming their place in time and space. That she and Shaybub instantly sensed the change in him was proof of their bond. How blessed they were, for such a caring heart for a mother, free of common nagging and manipulation, who only always tried to protect them, wanting the best for them. He might've inherited his tallness and physical strength from his *aba*, but he had her to thank for his ungraspable endurance that constantly pushed him on.

Like Shaybub, she was more cautious than reluctant of 'Ablah, if only because of the little anyone knew of her. The last thing his mother wanted was a spoiled young beauty manipulating him to her whim, in addition to all those around her who might do so for their own advantage. 'Antarah needed no reminder that 'Ablah would not be an easy prize for anyone, and though she'd yet to show her interest, that could change once he proved himself—and first earned his freedom.

"I know it might seem hopeless, and Shaybub thinks I'm *majnun*. I don't mean to add to your troubles, *ema*, but it just is," said 'Antarah.

"My love, you're not crazy and you trouble yourself most," chuckled his mother, surprising him. "There's Shaybub, and there's you; each man walks his own path. I think you're beginning to see that love is not always logical, and often not the way we want it to be. I'll always pray for my two guardian angels, and in the meantime, always do your best to put it in the Anointed One's hands."

Yassu's oozing, nailed hands.

Already 'Ablah showed him the extent to which yearning and love pushed him. Even if he'd wanted to be, how could he be angry at his mother for not telling him about his father? She'd been hurt and sworn to silence, and she was right that his knowledge would've influenced his behavior and their interactions. Such was his mother's patient wisdom, and her knowledge whose surface he barely scratched humbled him to service and unquestioned obedience. He had so much more to learn and that she trusted him and demanded no explanation was a healing balm to his troubled soul.

Their gazes turned to the entrance where Shaybub emerged, his broad form weighed down with concern.

"Shemia has ordered preparations to make day camp and feast at the river. *Sha'ir* Qasama and the others will stay behind," said Shaybub. "Looks like she could hardly wait for Shaddad, Mutaz and the rest to ride off to say it," he shrugged.

"They'll say it's the spring fever, surely," Zabiba smirked.

'Antarah's lips thinned. He almost protested the wisdom of that idea, but part of him couldn't resist the thought of a playful light day, and of nearly having the sight of 'Ablah all to himself. Perhaps it was a spring gift. He had to take what he could get, and anyway it wasn't his place to question what Shemia wanted.

With Shaybub he loaded the camels with the tent materials, bow and spear weapons, then helped their mother pack woven straw baskets full of cooking utensils, dates, clarified butter, spices, and barley flour. Last but not least were the bulging wineskins and cups, and the selection of young Awassi lamb to bring along to be slaughtered.

He informed *sha'ir* Qasama of their departure and whereabouts, reassured that as the remaining elders they were less likely to be targeted, and at least had the most experience. He and Shaybub had more to risk, and the weight of 'Ablah's life in his hands sent a thrill through him unlike any he'd ever felt.

They gathered and brought over the mounts of Shemia, Suhayyah, and 'Ablah, and made them sit, as the other slaves did the same for their *sayyida* coming along. Ready with his spear in hand as a walking stick, he approached his father and Shemia's tent and stood before the closed thick curtains, his proud bearing concealing his thumping heart.

"*Sayyida* Shemia, everything is ready. We await your orders," said 'Antarah. Through the lingering stillness erupted laughter.

A shuffle followed and Shemia emerged, clad in a blood-red dyed robe embroidered with gold. Her matching thick headdress towered like a crown, its draped silken fabric hovering just above the ground.

From respectful habit 'Antarah lowered his gaze, and caught her robe's gold hemline grazing her sandaled feet colored in *za'faran*. Decorated with henna, saffron floral designs of stems, leaves, and flowers danced on her skin, to the sound of her ankles' tinkling silver bangles with every step. Humming, she swung a small leather bag from her wrist with an air of amusement. Everything about her manner commanded so much childishly vain, greedy attention that any blind man would easily find her.

'Antarah struggled not to stare when Suhayyah and other tribeswomen emerged from the tent, smirking with evading, haughty airs. Though Suhayyah was also a beauty, and one greater than Shemia's, it paled in comparison to her daughter 'Ablah's, but he thanked all the deities and spirits in existence for being part of making her. When he caught 'Ablah's form, his throat parched like a *wadi* in drought. Kohl traced her dark eyes, and with her pearl silk veil and wine-colored Tyrian purple robe outlining her waist with an amber woven belt, she looked like a princess amidst her royal court.

'Ablah avoided his gaze, confirming that she was aware of it. He restrained a smile, for along with her unmatched beauty, they had to envy her garments that looked so close to the real purple from the Tyre coast in glorious Al-Sham. Most could only dream of obtaining a close fake, when often only the imperial courts could afford the price of killing the countless required sea snails for their dye. If anyone should ever have such robes, it was her, and a pang of remorse seized his core that only a miracle would allow him to offer her such garments as part of his bride price and wedding gift.

"*Aywa*, 'Antarah, since you've been instructed to care for us fragile women, lead the way," snickered Shemia, hardly looking at any of them. She mounted her camel and urged her up, smirking as her friends followed her suit, giggling and continuing their gossip amongst themselves.

"*Na'am, sayyida*," said 'Antarah, taking discreet note of 'Ablah's position further behind.

With a hard step he rejoined his mother and Shaybub, whose bow and arrows hung on his back, and the other slaves marching in the front of the group, and led the way south to the nearby Zat Al-Arsat pond area of the *wadi*.

In the perfectly pleasant weather the sacrificial fat-tailed, curious lamb stepped innocently by the grasses, wooly *hamd* plants, and prickly *arak* shrubs in their path. Soon, a faint honeyed milk scent greeted them at the pond, radiating from the blossoming white and rose *diflah* laurels, the oleander plant leaves resembling olive tree branches. All around, lush *sam'a* grass waved like horses' manes, and scattered *adanah* desert roses emerged out of their short, swollen trunks, adding to the desert garden variety.

"Make camp here," said Shemia, pointing to a vast vacant space across the stream whose surrounding foliage thankfully provided some secluded privacy.

She halted her mount and dismounted, and after filling a cup of wine, she went around the premises, lightly sprinkling the liquid on the ground.

"Oh, *muluk al-ard*, accept this offering for allowing us to camp here for the day," she repeated, calling to the spirits of the land with a self-satisfied air, her friends flocking around her and echoing her words.

'Antarah instructed the others to settle the camels protectively around them, and with Shaybub he pitched them an open tent, where the lively women immediately reclined to enjoy date pies and milk laid out by their mother and the others as they awaited the feast.

He followed Shaybub and the Awassi lamb to the water's edge, and after a moment of weighty silence petting it, Shaybub slaughtered it with a quick hard thrust to its neck. He let the blood drain away into the stream, and audibly implored the water spirit Athtar to accept it, for their tribeswomen who were keen to it. With a knowing glance, 'Antarah met his lowered breath in calling on Yassu to bless the offering for themselves. They carved and cleaned the tender flesh and let its wool dry in the sun, for later use as an offering or for clothing, while their mother and other slaves foraged for shrubs and *ghada* wood and made a fire.

Soon, the designated smooth stones, rinsed clean with water and fired up by the sun, were covered in round mounds of barley flatbread, their pleasant, fresh softness contrasting their cracker-like texture in half a day. After seasoning the meat with some spices and pepper from Aksum via Himyar, they strapped chunks of flesh to thin metal rods to roast above the fire.

Gathered with the other slaves around the fire, with the stream to the east and the tent to the west, 'Antarah had full view of everything around him as he tended to the meat. He caught his mother's cautious smile and as always, returned it. While there were thankfully no signs of fresh fire pits or camel dung to hint at recent visitors, water holes were always attractive spots for all types of *badawi*. He met Shaybub's intent glance, reassured that they were of one mind in keeping aware of their surroundings.

"'Antarah! Serve us some wine while we await this meal," called Shemia.

"Already?" whispered Shaybub, causing a discreet shared smirk. 'Antarah rose obediently, knowing that Shaybub would've followed him if he'd only told him to. Let her taunt him; he couldn't mind so long as he was able to be near his beautiful, elusive one. 'Antarah unpacked the wineskins and cups, filled them up and handed them a drink, beginning with Shemia and Suhayyah, their smirking side glances following him. 'Ablah flatly took hers without a glance, her emotionless expression searing his heart as he continued serving the others.

In the mounting heat, Shemia rose and wandered off to the stream, thronged by her following. Their ankles jiggling and wrists swinging their small leather pouches, they passed a wineskin along between them as 'Ablah's floating, evasive shape made a shadow among them. She held back as they rushed in, giggling and shrieking at the cool water piercing through their leather sandals. An excited rush seemed to seize them as they revealed their preferred idols from their pouches, held them up to the sun, then sprinkled them with freshwater and wine, their rising singing praises echoing like ancient Nabataean nymphs.

'Antarah watched this shortened customary display of the spring season with renewed interest only for what he might glean of 'Ablah. Her back to him, his gaze bore into her like an invisible javelin, willing his mind to nudge hers. She stepped in and waded deeper, not bothering to lift up her dress as it darkened to black-purple, an angel dwelling in between worlds. He both hoped and dreaded her going further in, fighting every urge to join her and merge with the elements. 'Ablah stilled for a few moments, the side of her face shrouded by her translucent silk veil turned to him, her invisible ear listening, then stepped back, his pounding heart slowing. Then she rejoined the others and dallied, the wine flowing as Shemia grew louder and playful. His core fluttered. At this rate, it might not be long before he could talk with 'Ablah alone.

By the time the skewered meat was ready, tender and mildly flavored, they had finished a wineskin, barely touched by 'Ablah. The women returned to the tent and reclined, while the slaves offered them trays full of meat, clarified butter, and flatbread. 'Antarah had never so relished his own authority, little as it was, to know that it was understood that serving 'Ablah was left only to him. With a calm demeanor he served 'Ablah her portion and turned away, lest she think him too demanding. It was also a painful necessary change, if only to prove his self-command. Only after making sure they had plenty did the slaves have their share. Not that he had much appetite when he could only think of how and when to approach her.

The women leisurely ate their meal and Shemia opened and passed around a second wineskin. As he and Shaybub weaved in and out, cleaning up, Suhayyah unleashed a tune on her flute and, rosy-cheeked and inspired, Shemia took the invitation, her singing and dancing calling her friends around her in a circle. Shoulders shimmied and arms waved to the festive chanting, causing the silver anklets, bracelets, and ornaments suspended from coral necklaces from Himyar to glisten like shining coins and short blades.

Like a stroke of lightning, 'Ablah emerged at the center of them, laughing and singing, her teeth strung like pearls between her reddened lips. She held up the sides of her clear veil, twirling, gazing, looking everywhere but at him. It was the most perfect sight of his life, not just because she smiled openly, searching, seeking things the others couldn't see, but because he knew then that she was just as out of place as him. Nameless: that elusive thing that made her stand apart, yet just distinct enough to catch. Like him, she was reaching for something else, maybe even without her knowledge.

In a swift motion Shemia pulled off her own headdress and let it fall with a defiant grin. A moment later she reached over to tug off 'Ablah's, her long braids bouncing like whips as she kept dancing with selective gaze.

Suppressing his shock, 'Antarah cautiously drew near, scooped up the prized veils and carefully put them in the tent, trying his best to focus and get back to cleaning up. He caught Shaybub's approving wink and his mother's caring gaze that told him it was all taken care of.

At last happily exhausted, the women settled into the tent, fanning themselves with palm-leaf shaped fans made of straw.

"Such a perfect day for this," sighed Shemia. "Unfortunate that the only thing missing is the most honorable art of poetry. I'll pass on *sha'ir* Qasama's, though I'll never admit it if you tell him," she said, her laughter echoed by the others. "I could use a bloody epic on *Shah* Khosrow's daring breaking of the Peace Treaty with the Rûm with his sacking of Antioch. They say he carried off thousands of slaves and treasures, and even bathed in the Mediterranean Sea before returning to his empire," she said with a dreamy air.

A crushing weight stilled 'Antarah, locking his jaw. Every part of him wanted to unleash it, reduce them to stupor with unheard verses, proving his undeniable talent that they and anyone who heard it would both envy and praise. But he would not just offer it on the spot, and to the woman who often scorned their mother, too. He and Shaybub were one thing, but a woman's jealousy for another was another cruel matter. But something in him caved again. Maybe he shouldn't be so tough on her, when she only had an older daughter Waha—even if well-married off to a Tamimi—and therefore couldn't know the blessing of having two sons always there as her faithful guards.

Still, though his poetry was his own, verses on 'Ablah had been dancing all the more in his soul. 'Antarah glanced around, feigning his stolen looks at her, wishing she'd command it out of him, or give the smallest sign, she who was part of its holy source. But there was only the sound of rhythmic fans, swirling the air *jinn* around.

"A beautiful virgin pierced my heart with the arrows of her gaze, whose wounds never heal. She passed at the feast, among the young girls with rounded necks, like gazelles whose gazes are javelins. She walked, and I said: *It's the jasmine branch waving in the wind.* She looked and I said, *It's a startled gazelle, taken by surprise by the dangers in the middle of the desert.* She smiled, and I saw pearls shining between her lips that hide the cure of lovesick lovers."

In his trance-like elation, it wasn't until the silence returned that he realized this time it was different. Without warning, his *qareen* had decided for him: his lovelorn thoughts had crossed over into this world, now heard by others, and most of all by his beloved. He wanted to keep going, into eternity, feeding on the life-giving flowing words that brought them back to the Garden of Eden, as perfect Man and Woman of No Conflict. In the reigning stillness he lifted his chin, stole a glance at motionless 'Ablah, and looked down again.

Frowning, Shemia slowly sat up and turned to him. "Whose verses are these that you've taken? Where could you have gone to hear them?"

"They're mine, 'Antarah's, son of the great Shaddad and Zabiba," he said, his heart beginning to race.

"*Sah*, yours!" scoffed Shemia. "Poor 'Antarah. You'll do anything, even lie, just to impress us."

"I have no need to lie," he said, his jaw clenching.

"By Allah! And they just came to you, out of thin air?"

"Sometimes they do."

An echo of laughter erupted, and he swore he'd take the scorn over the pity any day.

"In that case, you could only be praising one person. You forget your place, to cast hopes on my daughter. At least we have plenty of other simpler options," sneered Shemia.

"*Al-ilah* decides who I love and serve, and none other," said 'Antarah with a rush of satisfaction. "Did I give myself this gift? It's exactly my place to speak the truth, and speak it well."

Wide-eyed and speechless, Shemia looked him up and down, searching for the secret signs that she might've missed in the eighteen springs of his life. "If that's so, then do it again." Her devilish smirk challenged.

A shock blasted through him, rebelling at the thought of his verses being for anyone other than 'Ablah, and worse, commanded by his mother's rival.

"Ha! I knew it, it was all just a passing *jinni*, never to be repeated again," laughed Shemia, reclining again. "Explains why he never said a thing."

'Antarah didn't stop himself, because if he had, he would've receded. He already knew: not the exact order that the words would flow, but just that they would, the images flashing in his soul like bright guiding stars. His *qareen* had spoken, so he might as well keep going.

His back straight and head raised, 'Antarah unleashed a stream of verses that did each woman justice, even as he tasted its bitterness for the first time. He'd never tell them that he wouldn't have thought it possible for him to so easily recite verses that he didn't want, just to indulge them. But always he turned back to 'Ablah, hoping that she knew he wasn't so much freely saying the same lovely things to them, as he was showing what he could do with his poetic talent. If he had a choice, he would do that forever, if only to recite the endless scenarios of them two in each other's presence. And if nothing else, she at least had to know he cared about women's safety and could protect, just as when he'd flown to Mulaika's help.

And while none compared to what he'd uttered of 'Ablah, especially not when he'd taken days to perfect it, they each seemed satisfied to be spoken of in his unusual, elegantly rhyming style. Some instantly began repeating the verses, eager to etch them into their memory, to be recalled and recited as proof that someone had once seen them that way, if necessary.

To his pleasant surprise, a weight lifted all around, replaced by curious amusement and strolls along the water, the continued flow of food, wine, and short verses transforming time. The spring sky turned a pale, sandy saffron, and each time he thought to bring the matter to Shemia, he relented, postponing. They were enjoying themselves and if this poetic revelation might inspire Shemia to soften a bit towards them, he called on his patience for 'Ablah to reveal her feelings amidst her constant avoidance.

She was not like the others; she was not just unique, but precious, so how could he expect to win her so easily? He'd only just begun and already he was becoming lazy, demanding. Yet the mirage of a flag waved in the distance as his guiding post: if 'Ablah was his beloved lance, his *qareen, hilm,* and fiery *jahl* were his other weapons.

The day lazily coming to an end, he rejoined the others in packing up, intoxicated with a love that filled him with sharp clarity. But even then, the light dimmed, when the undeniable rumble rattled through him before he met Shaybub's gaze, the mirror image passing the weight onto him.

"*Ya Allah*, Numayr! *Ya Allah*, Numayr!" the shouts echoed, clouds of dust fast approaching from the south.

"Quickly, cover yourselves and stay together!" said Zabiba, leading the rattled, panicking women to the tent. With their cheeks as red as their robes, they made a frightfully confused flock, their senses slowed and numbed by wine.

But not him. In an instant, he was more alive than he'd felt himself in a long time. He would kill them all if necessary to spare 'Ablah the humiliation of being kidnapped, and worse, violated.

'Antarah gripped his spears and with Shaybub, his bow and arrows ready, they sprinted ahead, his brother fast returning the falling arrows flying at them from the enemy horde. His true arrows fell into their chests, arms, legs, knocking three off their mounts.

Flying on his own wings, 'Antarah grinned at the sight of the rest of the six charging Numayr bandits, with several horses in tow, relishing that he and his brother could take them. Just the thought of any harm coming to 'Ablah was enough to transform him into that fearless, protective beast who'd back down at nothing.

Marking out the few remaining attackers, 'Antarah focused on the nearest and hurled his spear with all the strength he'd suppressed all his life. The true spear struck straight into the enemy shoulder, knocking him off his horse, just in time for 'Antarah to catch up and seize his enemy's sword.

'Antarah hurried to Shaybub who, pinned down, finally got the upper hand and hurled his attacker off of him, and wrestled away his sword for himself. Just then, from the corner of his eye, 'Antarah caught one of the bandits blasting towards the women on his raven horse. Snorting with rage, 'Antarah bolted after him, the creature outpacing him as he maintained his aim.

"No, let me go!" shrieked 'Ablah, his blood boiling at the sight of the rider hoisting her fidgeting form onto the saddle. Like lightning 'Antarah was upon him, his iron grip on his leg and arm hurling him off the mount with all his might, as 'Ablah slipped and squirmed off the opposite way. Grimacing, the Numayr *ghul* brandished a short blade that 'Antarah swiftly kicked off, and punched the bandit on each side of his face into dazed submission.

His mind whirling and heart racing, 'Antarah rushed to the huddled form of 'Ablah, trying to crawl away. Horror frozen on her face, he reached down to her arm to help her up, when her shaking form abruptly avoided his grip, and ran back to the tent.

Fear. She was just afraid, and how he longed to take that away.

His rage renewed, 'Antarah mounted the horse and joined Shaybub in racing after the remaining scampering wounded who tried to retreat with their stolen bounty of horses.

"By Allah and the Lord of Heaven, you'll leave us these horses or we'll send you to your new hell on the other side," said 'Antarah, fixing the one who appeared to be the leader. Panting, Shaybub stood at his side, his bow loaded with two arrows, one for each of them. "Pathetic sons of Numayr: your *sayyidun* may slay undesireable baby girls, but that might explain your shortage of brave warriors," he said. Shaybub chuckled, the frazzled attackers looking away in shameful rage—anything, even death, rather than being lampooned with such words, now unleashed to travel on tireless wings. "Don't you know that real men fight proper opponents? You may prey on the defenseless, but as for us ravens, you'll remember that we're not easily defeated."

"We know it now," said the leader with lowered gaze. For a moment 'Antarah thought one would at least try some mockery over some of the 'Abs's failed stint at the gold mines, but he saw only fear. "Tell us your name, that we may remember it?"

For a split moment, 'Antarah hesitated. He had to stop doing that.

"Who's this little boy back there?" said 'Antarah, gesturing to the wretch who'd dared to seize 'Ablah.

"Eyad, son of Assam. His first foray," said the leader, surprisingly apologetic.

"Could've been his last," sneered 'Antarah. "But I am 'Antarah ibn Shaddad, the raven of the Banu 'Abs. Now, we have the kindness of leaving you your camels, so make like mist and evaporate, before I change my mind," he said, waving them off with a grimace.

With averted glances they nodded, released the four horses, and hurriedly gathered their wounded. With an eye on the bandits, he and Shaybub cooed to the creatures in admiring introduction, awed at the white, brown, black, and grey Arabian mares, too glorious and unworthy of their thieves. At last the ruffians scuffled off with their camels as fast as they could without looking back.

With their flock, the mares and two swords in tow, they silently returned back to camp at sunset, the sobered, shaken up women contrasting their blessed mother always managing to be the calm in the storm.

"I command you all: say nothing of this to Shaddad or anyone else, you hear?" said Shemia just before reaching camp. Amidst the communal nods, he thought he glimpsed in 'Ablah's furrowed brow a still shaken, yet softened air.

The next few days elapsed in unbearable tension, wondering if they should inform *sha'ir* Qasama and maybe even other nearby tribes, like Banu Tayyi just north, before members of Banu Numayr returned, this time charging from the south with a larger group. 'Antarah hated to think that the bandits had lurked like *al-'ayn*, maybe even awaited the departure of their *sayyid* to test their opportunity. Yet he stood ready to return the mares on the condition that they confessed that they'd been the ones to attack, placing the responsibility on them.

No one came.

Maybe the *diflah*'s poison laced on the arrowtips, slithering in the blood within moments to over a day had helped, one way or the other.

He and Shaybub concealed the weapons and merged the mares with their glorious purebred Arabians bred by their cousin tribe Banu Dhubyan, and kept constant watch by taking turns patrolling the area.

"I'll just say I stole them," 'Antarah contemplated, his brother's disapproval palpable from the corner of his eye.

"You should say what really happened. She's not more important than him; you're his *son*," said Shaybub.

"So are you."

"By generosity, not by blood. You know it matters, even if he pretends it doesn't."

But he'd already given his word, and he would not go back on it, and in a way, he *had* stolen them.

The constant shadows resurfaced, returned from the southwest, with *sayyid* Zoheir flanked by Shaddad and Mutaz in a sea of smug, relentless 'Absians.

"We've shown those Kaabi! They are falling in line, as will the Sulaym, Hawazin, and Ghatafan, and whoever else, all in due time," said *sayyid* Zoheir. His biting tone betrayed his lingering dissatisfaction, as 'Antarah hid any emotion at the name of Banu Ka'b closely linked to Numayr.

It wasn't enough that the captured bounty of camels and horses rejoiced the people, another glorious proof of the might of the Banu 'Abs. It had to be more, always more—complete nonresistance and submission to their rule. The familiar conflict always returned: wondering if he'd ever get to be among them and experience it, but also somehow pleased that he wasn't part of it. But Fate avoided no one, so he could only keep serving and hopefully soon be put in a better place.

"Never underestimate Fate, 'Antarah," said his father. "It knows just what to do. Hujr, that Kindite father to Imru Al-Qays who roams from land to land with his poetry, was just slain by Banu Asad, who turned on him! It was meant to be," laughed Shaddad.

A shock bolted through 'Antarah as he stood motionless, sad and conflicted. The ancient Kindite house of Ma'add, keepers of the *badawi* calendar, was dismantling all around them, and Banu 'Abs, like other tribes, ready to pounce and take their chances.

"So, tell me how tedious the women were while we were away," smirked Shaddad. He motioned for him to join him, as Shemia reclined nearby, feigning indifference while she fanned herself with her straw fan.

"Everything was fine," 'Antarah shrugged with a shy smile.

"Come, you're being too easy on them. Not even one thing? It'll stay between us."

'Antarah shook his head, discomfort creeping again.

With a grunt, the lightness in Shaddad's face disappeared and morphed into a vacant idol's image.

"In that case, it's set and I can just let *you* take over, *sah*? Did you think I wouldn't notice?" Shaddad's controlled manner—one he'd never seen before. "Where did they come from?" Ice cold tone like a frozen blade in the dead of night.

"I was pasturing the flocks near Qarah when I found them who'd gone astray, so I took them," said 'Antarah, lost in the hypnotizing rhythm of the fan.

"You miserable, unrepentant liar! These are no wild mares left to themselves; you could only have gotten these fine ones by killing and robbing their owners!" said Shaddad, hitting him so hard on the back of his head that 'Antarah fell forward and curled up on his knees. The angry 'Absian jerked up above him, ripped off his leather whip from his belt and pulled 'Antarah's robe up over bare head, exposing his naked, scarred back.

By habit 'Antarah braced his jaw and the whip slashed wildly into his skin, slicing deeper and burning more ferociously with each strike. He flinched painfully as tears flooded his sight, his hot short breaths struggling to lessen the pain.

Innocent. He was not innocent—he couldn't lie before Yassu when He had to know how much he wanted her so much. Isn't that why all of this had happened? The risk he wanted to take, just for the forbidden chance of seeing and being around her.

"When will you learn?" The unrelenting father shouted again, unfurling his wrath.

Wincing, a cry burst out of capture, his pounding head as if barraged with hurled stones. Slowly 'Antarah turned his face to him from under his folds, and saw his blood splattered on his father's hand, clothing, and enraged face. Shemia's hennaed feet, toes curled in—attempted ornaments that could never help reach 'Ablah's pure beauty. He would not look up further and give her the satisfaction of seeing her. Any other *badawi* might come, seeking protection, slicing his palm and smearing it on the tent rope and be granted mercy, while he was there, his life slashed away to greedy, delighted stares. He thought he would've gotten used to it by now, but it was a new, gut-wrenching, uglier pain.

Just as the wounds had slowly started to heal, they were opened again. But the all-consuming fire raged, and he would not let them be the last image of his miserable, guilty life. He bit down on his snotty, salty full lips, his fountain of tears slowing, and summoned his *qareen* with all his strained breath.

"A beautiful—virgin—pierced my heart—with the arrows of her gaze—whose wounds never heal." 'Antarah cried out, a sting so profoundly sharp that he envisioned his muscles pulled apart like the hacked flesh of Yassu-serving martyrs. But he reached, the pain somehow receding as he concentrated on the words floating in boundless space.

"What did you say?" panted Shaddad, his thousand mad *jinn* suddenly hesitating.

"She smiled—and I saw pearls shining between her lips that—hide the cure—of lovesick—lovers."

Out of breath, his eyes closed, panting, the swirling visions of 'Ablah writhing before him. At least he'd taken the risk and told her the full short poem before he left. But there was so much more to say, and now his time had run out. The crushing sadness enveloped him, worse than ever before. His *qareen* had known: that's why it had insisted. Somewhere in his imagination, the whip had stilled, a sense of uncertainty lingering.

"Stop! My 'Antarah!" shrieked his eternal mother, sweeping over him like an angel. He wanted to tell her not to worry, but though he could feel and hear, he could not move. "What have you *done*! You want your son's blood, is that it? By Iyasus, if you want his, then you'll have mine too!" Such defiant, raging strength in her tone that it lifted him up like his verses.

Slowly, he opened his eyes, saw her knees fold next to his, her soft naked arms fussing to expose her own brown shoulders and back. Was that how it'd been at Najran, avenged by *Negus* Kaleb and ruled by King Abraha whom he could only meet in his playful visions? His arm twitched, trying to lift a hand to her, the thought of her suffering worse than any punishment he had to take. Even then he knew Shaddad's fears about him were not completely wrong. There was no stopping 'Antarah, because if Shaddad dared to hurt his mother, it would only start the cycle all over again, until it finally ended. If only Shaybub were there, at least it would be all three of them.

For him to love was to bring conflict, although he'd done less than that to earn that name. 'Ablah's Man and Man of Discord merging into one to serve those he loved.

In the dazed mirage came the sound of a breaking voice he'd never heard before, tinged with feminine remorse.

"Shaddad, my beloved Shaddad. I have to tell you something," Shemia sniffled.

CHAPTER ELEVEN

PRINCE OF KINDAH

SPRING 541 AD - BANU SA'D

Still as a stone, Jayida laid flat on the mat sprawled out on the cool desert floor, Al-Wasiyah strapped faithfully at her hip. Blindfolded with one side of her face pressed down, she listened for sounds above and below, her arms and long legs spread out in embrace of the buzzing earth. Her leather boots at her side, her naked feet laid on the perfectly warm dusty ground that was neither burning lava or frozen rock. Soon, the ground would scorch any exposed skin that touched it.

She strained at the scratching sound of a rustle nearby: a small creature, possibly a sandgrouse. A moment later something soft, then gently vibrating under her palm, disappeared somewhere underground—reptilian; perhaps an elusive sand-fish or harmless sand boa. Jayida chuckled, satisfied that her continued training constantly sharpened her senses. When she'd once worried to limit one of her senses, she'd since experienced the magic ways her *qareen* made the others kick in. In a nearly silent move, she rolled over, dampness already dangerously close to tickling her neck.

Jayida could swear that she sweat more recently, urging her to fumigate her clothes more often with *bakhur* incense of aloe wood, and sometimes even frank-incense. But that was one thing she would not give up for as long as she could. She would spare all except the essentials, and would count and ration every tiniest stone of precious frankincense tears for the blessing of musky robes. It was part of her *noos* refining, as her mother said, and the protective heavenly-scented veil that kept the malicious *jinni, ifreet, ghul,* and evil eye away were a necessary luxury.

After a moment she lifted her blindfold and raised her palm, bathing it in the sun's gentle, light glow. The waves of her skin made crisscrossed paths of merging *wadis*, coursing in all directions. Staring, she brought her hand closer, her slow rotating wrist catching the light at various angles. Amidst the scattered, flashing sparkles across the surface, she noticed paler shades of green, rose, and pearl—translucent like a fly's wings. Her throat pinched, strangely moved by her own mysteries she hadn't paid attention to before.

Jayida dropped her hand and remained still, an intense overwhelming joy nearly bringing her to tears. She chuckled it off, slightly unsettled yet humbled by this new impression. Something about it made her feel small, like *mubassir* Ayyub's *injil* stories. Yassu had made himself small too, when he'd entered Jerusalem on a peaceful donkey instead of a glorious, war-waging Arabian mare or stallion.

She slipped her boots on, amused as she tried to make out each pair of towering camel legs roaming around her amidst Wadi Al-Hamd. To the northwest was her father's determined step, foraging for plants and other potential happy finds. Something told her that Hania, along with the rest of their flocks, approved of their ancestors' participation at Yassu's birth, carrying the three Magi kings bearing gifts from the east.

It was so unlike the recent sack of Antioch provoked by *Shah* Khosrow, though surely Al-Mundhir had something to do with fueling its fire. She frowned and replaced it with a sigh, wishing *malik* Al-Harith all the continued strength necessary to keep his Al-Sham borders and territory safe.

She wouldn't mind it staying like this: roaming the vast gardens with no hurry, no fear of passing time or not enough food, with nothing to worry about and nothing else to do but to praise *al-ilah* with his angels, as *mubassir* Ayyub quoted from the Book of the Cave of Treasures. What a marvel that this perfect place must've been real, even if so long ago it now seemed impossible, when everyday she had a sense of peace while accompanying the flocks' grazing.

At least not all changes were unpleasant. Pressing her knees together she rose, the weight of the concealed adult coat of mail nearly forgotten. She dusted off her robes and straightened her sword, proud that now in her sixteenth year, she had sprouted up for all to see, making her nearly as tall as her father. She might not be as strong as Shamshun, but she didn't have a violent streak nor a lusty, wandering eye. Smirking with her back straight and a hand on Al-Wasiyah, she feigned a princely air and leisurely swaggered to her Bag of Treasures, pleased at her long, protective shadow.

Under her secret layers, her narrow waist contrasted her widened hips and her breasts, smaller and yet distinct, blossomed as curiously as the hair in different parts of her body. Conveniently, the layers of lose clothing added girth to all the right places, contributing to a strong bearing that had the desired effect. Though the blade kept hair off her face—so she might say to any tentative inquiries—her naturally thick, dark brows complimented her intense eyes and long nose all the more. It added to her amusement that, should an unwanted hair appear, it was another excuse to ignore it.

Still, in moments of self-reflection, Jayida sometimes felt like an outsider looking in at herself. While her mother was all the reassurance she needed, she imagined sharing it all with Yazida, if only for curious comparison. Surely Yazida already had her monthly flow, which she'd yet to begin, much to her mother's mounting distress.

But where was the need, so long as she was Jonder, selfless brave protector of the tribe? *Mubassir* Ayyub often spoke of the blessed Bnat Qyama, those holy Daughters of the Covenant devoted to *al-ilah* who had no need for their earthly functions, and often even shed them—surely if he knew about her he would see it as a sign of favor.

Her own concern was fleeting: even that wasn't worth what she had, with the skills and strength she'd acquired and the freedom to move around. Even if she couldn't just leave without alerting her family, she didn't envy Yazida and other girls her age, prime young women now increasingly kept in seclusion to ensure their safety, as much from the jealous *al-'ayn* as from lustful gazes.

Jayida retrieved her quiver, adjusted it on her back and picked up her bow. Purposefully making herself rush, she aimed at a nearby sandbag and released, the arrow landing straight in its center.

A woman's beauty seemed a double-edged sword of safety and danger, which had to be closely guarded from those wanting to profit from it. She shook off the shuddering thought that called forth her distrust of nearly all outside the Banu Sa'd.

"I don't understand this madness," Jayida confessed to her parents. "And it's in those times that I'm most grateful for the decision you both made for me."

"May Yassu and his angels protect you always, and though as a mother I do worry, I thank Him too for your clear signs of growth, and not least your beauty," said her mother. As always her father nodded quietly in those moments, reigning in to himself their shared weighty contemplation.

Jayida took aim again and the arrow fell just next to its target. She would not worry and assume the worst, after all her progress. There was something both amusing and frustrating that her parents should be more worried about it than herself. Surely her Aksumite princess guiding spirit was on her side, even if nothing seemed to happen.

Smirking, she pulled up her veil, fully covering her face. In her mind's eye she recalled and calculated where she'd earlier dropped a sandbag northeast, and took large cautious steps in its assumed direction. After a moment she stopped, raised the bow and aimed, sending the arrow buzzing off in the distance. She lowered her blindfold and saw that the arrow had fallen near it, missing its mark.

She hadn't expected it to hit, but it hit much closer than she'd estimated. Drawing closer to the target, she repositioned herself, aimed and released, imagining the arrow flying like a lightning bolt. For a moment her breath swelled her veil like a hot cloud until she lowered it. Jayida blinked fast, lest she saw wrong. The arrow struck the target!

Her heart soared: finally after all these seasons, it had worked! She didn't care how *majnun* or pointless it seemed to practice this way; it was at least another exercise. Some even suggested she use live creatures strapped with bags for the purpose, resorting to their moving sounds as target reference, but she wouldn't risk putting them in harm's way, even if animals were there to serve their masters.

Life is to be treasured—her father's words echoed in her soul in verbal, binding law. It was cruel and unnecessary.

In disgusted, sad anger, she shook off the stories of some who killed a creature at any opportunity to add strength to their wishes. At least the Israelite *shechita* methods made death as quick and painless as possible when sacrifice was necessary. That some didn't see the creatures' pain, or worse, didn't care about it, set her blood boiling. Was it for show, or vanity, or both? Because worst of all, sacrifices surely didn't work all the time. If so, wouldn't everyone always get what they wanted? She had much more to learn, but even she knew that wasn't possible.

Jayida laid down her bow and gathered the arrows, target, and sandbags in a pile for later packing. Her father waved at her in the distance, surrounded by some of the newest calves born since the *Ayyam al-Zalam*. She sniffled and returned the gesture with happy tears, then set about doing some stretches with side lunges. Her father had joked a few times that if they had been back home at the Banu Zubayd, her and Khaled would surely be betrothed. That was the only time that he ever made her mad, and thankfully he didn't say it often. He might mean well, but she couldn't deny her lingering dislike of the proud Moharib, whose son wouldn't be the only one to follow in his father's ways more each day.

Even so, as her mother had said, it was true that her own feelings were changing. When asked about Nasr, she admitted that her feelings had deepened. But she struggled to express what was surely her girlish silliness: that there was something missing, that it didn't feel quite as expected. Zoraya reminded her that it wasn't necessarily a bad sign, that the bond would deepen in time. Still Jayida wondered about the painful verses sung by poets, their hearts aching with passion. It confused her that as much as she cared for kind, handsome Nasr, admired by the tribe as provider and *sha'ir*, she could hardly envision feeling that tormented way for him, to that passionately longing extent.

To add to her confusion, even that didn't lessen her joy of the intimacy they shared on the days when Shams was away, leaving them two alone. But even that was surely innocent, brotherly love for him, when he was ignorant of her situation. Though nineteen, he still hadn't announced his betrothal. Was it possible that, like her, he didn't really *want* to get married? With his angelic beauty and brooding nature, he sometimes seemed above such earthly things. Curiously, it added to her confidence that she, his closest friend in disguise, might have a chance with him. Surely, like her, he was waiting for the right time.

But it was hard to say. Jayida bent down her heavy torso and her gold-capped leopard fang and gold Mikha'il amulet fell out, dangling across her lips, as the bundled metallic weight of the concealed coat of mail pulled down on her limbs. There was something more about him, that though occasional was no less a part of him, and which she took as another trait of his evolving strength, and continued mastering of his *hilm*.

Some days he seemed taken by a sadness that she couldn't reach, but didn't want to press him until he willingly shared. An unpleasant remnant from past sickness—the collective hushed whisper suspected but dared not say, lest it be triggered again. But Nasr always came back stronger, and she hated that sometimes it still felt like it wasn't enough to conquer the doubt. There were also days of deep intensity, when he seemed so engaged elsewhere, his bottomless ebony eyes as if filled with anger and hatred at what he'd contemplated.

Jayida came up and winced as a back muscle pulled, forcing her to stop and catch her breath. Before she could stop it, she recalled the discomfort of that one day, and though she dismissed it as a one-time event, it lingered like a bizarre tale that seeps and creeps into the skin.

"*Yallah*, Jonder, you're being too soft on me," Nasr had said, taunting her to come to him at full force with Al-Wasiyah. She pounced on him, their blades clashing, heavy steps pacing, eyes locked on each other to get the upper hand. Their standoff had lasted so long that she was almost sure they'd have to call it even, until suddenly, he lunged at her with such force that she fell down on her back to avoid the unexpected violence of his oncoming blow.

"Come *on*," he'd said, pacing around her menacingly as she scuttled back, speechless and alert.

She'd never seen him like this before. His sickly shadowy gaze grinned with a taunting triumphant air. It wasn't his beloved good natured air, but something else, even—she hesitated to say—intending harm. And for the first time she'd had the instinct to protect herself from him.

"Don't hold back, Jonder. I know it's *there*, yearning to be let out," Nasr sneered, his sweeping eagle—or was it vulture-like?—sleeves urging her to continue.

She jumped up, palm squeezing the sword handle, considering where to strike him with a blow of similar force. It tore at her that she didn't *want* to but felt she *had* to, if only to protect herself. They'd all knocked each other down before, that's what training was for, so why did this feel anything but playful? It was like a real, blood-shedding challenge, and one she realized she'd never expected from him of all people. But if he'd started it, demanded it, she would answer it. Her brows gathered firmly as her jaw tensed and, resolved to it, she went towards him.

Their swords were just about to clash when he straightened his posture, stepped back and lowered his palms, his sword flicking away at his side.

"*Aywa*, Jonder, you passed the test; just as I thought," said Nasr with his glowing smile, and like that, he seemed his warm self again. Was this a hard lesson he'd postponed amidst their usual fun? If so, this new tactic of intimidation was definitely effective, if off-putting. They'd all heard of stories of fighters being so into the throes of action that it was as if they became someone else, just as those who slayed lions and ate too much of their meat were said to become like wild beasts.

As her father would say, it was another reminder to always be prepared, and though she knew its importance, it had the bittersweet effect of now making her aware that it could even come from her closest friend. Thankfully it'd never happened again, and his lack of reference to it made her wonder if he regretted it enough not to mention it.

Jayida rejoined her father in gathering some salty *hamd* leaves and thorny *arak* branches, then packed up and gathered the flocks to head home.

"*Shway*, slowly, Hania," Jayida chuckled in warning to her beloved mount.

As the oldest among the youngest, Hania sometimes took advantage of this by gently asserting her dominance when necessary. Still, Jayida was taught to rarely intervene in favor of letting them resolve their rank issues themselves. She laughed as Hania nudged a young one, reminding her of Hania invading her own space and having to be put in place when they'd both been younger. There was something at once concerning and comically reassuring about growing camels unaware of their own strength.

Cooing their flock to motion, they headed back east to camp, gratitude filling her that their flocks had kept prospering even after the worrying days of *Ayyam al-Zalam* that had decreased their count by half. Each time they passed through this area, so near her triumph over the leopard attack, Jayida vowed that she would grow braver and do the right thing as part of the tribe. That they had never come upon ostriches or their nests in this area again, nor any leopards, made the incident even more unique in the tribe's eyes, so that they sometimes spoke of it as if it'd been divinely appointed only for Jonder.

"Now what's the matter with him?" said Zahir, and she looked east to the sight of Shams hurrying to them on his mount. The closer he got the more his agitation confused them. "Are you alright?" said her father when Shams finally reached them.

"Glorious morning! I've been looking—I couldn't—I had—" Shams panted, as if it hadn't been another creature's legs doing the work. His body had grown after fourteen springs, but it still had to contend with his boundless fire.

"*Shway*, slowly; you're scaring us," said Jayida in her lightest tone.

"You'll never guess who—" said Shams with a dreamy smile.

She shot a glance at her father. "Who?"

"Won't you even guess?" said Shams, appalled. "It's an honor, unheard of—"

"Surely not *mubassir* Ayyub again," said Zahir cautiously, and relaxed a bit when Shams shook his head.

"Oh, come! Stay—and—" Shams waved his hand expectantly.

"Weep with me?" laughed her father incredulously.

"You're joking!" Jayida's jaw dropped.

"By the glory of Shams I am telling the truth!" he nodded. "The one and only Kindite prince Imru Al-Qays, of the most ancient house of Kindah, is approaching from the northeast. We all know how he's been roaming from tribe to tribe, after having avenged his slain father Hujr—may his tribe increase. And now he's heading this way!"

She gladly chuckled at his shift from serious poetic tone to excited, child-like burst, guessing that he'd probably practiced reciting this very bit.

"Bless you for the news, Shams. We'll hurry right along," said her father, picking up pace.

"*Sah*, let's. Everyone is piling inside *sayyid* Aziz's tent just to get a look at him," Shams said, and raced off.

Even Yazida, our tribe's greatest young beauty, Jayida almost joked, but in her kindness didn't. Everyone knew the rumors though, how Imru seduced his way everywhere he went, making some reconsider their instant hospitality. She hoped that it didn't have something to do with him losing his alliance with the Banu Taghlib and Bakr in the time he was with them.

But then again, *Today's guest is tomorrow's host* was its own kind of incentive, and even a dispossessed poet-prince remained a poet-prince. Just as important, nothing was easier to spread than stories and lies. To think that now they might actually hear him recite his famous beloved *qasidah* ode, whose superior style so many tried to replicate, left her nearly speechless. She imagined Nasr, humbly honored to also add this event to his own growing trove of *sha'ir* verses.

"So what do you think? Do we need to shut away our women and surround him only with men?" said Jayida, hurrying the flocks along with her father.

"Not sure we could, even if we wanted to, and I like to think our women can hold their own, along with our protection, of course. But what I know is if he ever dared try anything with your mother, I'd squeeze all the poetry left out of him," snickered Zahir.

"And then Nasr would happily recite of it, too," Jayida laughed, and suddenly wondered if Nasr would be also be lovingly jealous of her, if they both knew her as Jayida rather than Jonder.

At camp her mother rushed to them, radiating with playfulness.

"I had Shams hurry off to inform you; thought you'd like the news," said Zoraya.

"Have you met him already?" said her father a bit too briskly.

"Of course not. That's for you to do, and later report back to me," her mother said. She pat her husband's arm teasingly and led the camels away, looking over her shoulder with a seductive smile.

They walked on and from a distance noted the crowd flowing out of *sayyid* Aziz's tent, whose entrance drapes had been raised and tied up to allow more people to gather and see the poet. Jayida glanced the shadowy, dark-clad visitor at center, with an older man and a younger one at one side, and *sayyid* Aziz and Nasr on the other. Next to him were Hubala, Sufyan, and Shams, who looked flushed as much from his rushed return as from his own contained animation. She slowed with her father as they approached the crowd, keeping to the outer side to find a place to sit just as the *sayyid* fixed them and waved them over.

"Ah; as I was telling you, prince Imru," said *sayyid* Aziz as he rose. "Here is one of my most trusted friends and advisors Zahir, and his son Jonder, likewise close friend to my Nasr."

Imru Al-Qays rose leisurely and pinched a calm smile at Zahir, his curious lingering smolder mixed with a vacant kind of sadness. Tilting his head, he lifted his ebony winged arms and her father went to him.

"Prince Imru: may your father Hujr be at peace and you be watched over. How you honor us with your presence," said Zahir, exchanging a slow, solemn kiss on each cheek.

"May my father, the bravest of Ma'add, hear you," said Imru in a deep, serious tone, and invited them to settle. He had just the hint of an accent that she couldn't pinpoint—central or southern, maybe a unique mix of both—and wondered if he was even slightly doing it on purpose.

Younger than their fathers yet older than Sufyan, Imru had an unhurried easiness about him that had to be the result of his pampered, princely life. With his thick lips, deep, kohl-smeared eyes, and robes dark as ink, embroidered with gold designs and belt in mourning for his father, he made a curious mix of distinct, yet diminished presence wrapped in a veil of cold indifference. His gold circular amulet etched with a face, and a few rings encrusted with precious ruby stones added to his royal bearing, but with some disappointment Jayida saw that he was not what she'd call handsome.

"We could hardly dream of such a gift as your visit," said Jayida, lightly bowing as he turned to her.

"*Aywa*, nice to hear from a *kahin*, as your loyal friend Nasr says of you," Imru smirked at her. They embraced, her cheeks grazing his shaggy but lightly oiled beard. "Tell me: can you see in the dark with those eyes?"

"When there's something worth seeing," she said, to the tribe's resounding chuckle.

His gripping gaze lingered, and it thrilled her that by his flickering brow and emerging smirk he hadn't expected that.

"Now *that's* a poet's answer, and I've often thought that there isn't much difference between a true *kahin* and a poet," Imru nodded.

They took their place next to *sayyid* Aziz and Nasr, and from the hypnotizing pull of his presence, hardly anyone took notice of the inviting cups of milk and baskets of dates. Jayida mused that the women were likely fast at work baking and cooking, in playful rivalry against each other and perhaps in hopes of catching the princely poet's attention.

"We were just talking about the never-ending work *malik* Al-Harith has to keep his borders free of rampaging Al-Mundhir, and his Fars patron *Shah* Khosrow," said *sayyid* Aziz.

"It's good to be among men who share and understand my dislike for the *ghul*, aside from my faithful Asheer and Atiyah," said Imru, turning his profile to his two nodding companions. With their simple robes and grave demeanors, and one elderly and another about Sufyan's age, they were as different from the princely poet as they were clearly devoted. "Though plenty out east may say they agree and revile Al-Mundhir, many will not utter a word for one fear or another," Imru sneered. "I'd heard of you having served at Kutha, and I'm grateful for it," he added with a deep nod.

"*Al-ilah* knows we fought in hopes your grandfather Al-Harith would be reinstated. May Al-Mundhir pay for slaying your *sitti* and the rest of your kin," said *sayyid* Aziz, grasping Imru's arm like a binding decree. "Our stories and poems are no match for yours, but such memories are not easily forgotten, even after twenty springs."

Jayida caught Nasr's darkened expression, immersed in unpleasant thoughts of how close they both came to losing their fathers in that war.

Imru sighed. "*Aywa,* bless my *sitti*'s good name Al-Harith, who ruled the eastern half of the land from Al-Hira down to 'Uman. How perfect that it should also be the name of the current *malik* from the royal Jafnid house of Ghassan, who despises Al-Mundhir as we do. Surely it is time I seek more helpful horizons. Perhaps *malik* Al-Harith will help me get my poor, Yassu-loving aunt Hind out of his grip? And we may spare talks of the sacred bonds of marriage in this case, especially since he hasn't changed his ways, much less converted." Imru rolled his eyes, more to lighten the mood than to disrespect his aunt's virtue. "At least, I would like to meet this *malik*; he must possess a rare *hilm* that I should learn from. And while there, perhaps I'll also meet with my Kindah kin in the Holy Land, all thanks to *Qaysar* Justinian's help, before my fickle tormenting Time in this life finally runs out."

A shared melancholy settled over them in solidarity. In his conflicted tone, the controlled praise reminded her of the tales of his strained relationship with his own father Hujr.

Following in the steps of his Kindite father Al-Harith, whose ancestors had come from Himyar and became its vassals once they'd moved north of its boundaries, Hujr of Kindah had been a great fighter. The Israelite-*Masihi* wars and *Negus* Kaleb's expedition into Himyar—around the time of her birth—followed by his father Al-Harith's murder by Al-Mundhir had called Hujr to march further north. After going around the Rub' al-Khali and northeast towards Haliban and Jabal Uraynibat, west of Jabal Tuwayq, he met his quarrelsome brothers, and soon assumed supremacy over multiple central tribes of the confederate of Ma'add.

As a father of many sons, of which Imru was the youngest, Hujr disapproved of Imru's inappropriate poetry and drinking, seeing it unfit for the son of a royal *sayyid* who should care most about fighting and avenging his slain royal kin. That, along with his lack of care for his responsibilities—especially in the midst of *Ayyam al-Zalam*—set Hujr off in a rage that eventually pushed Imru to run away. Some accounts even said that Hujr never wanted to see him again, but then repented of his anger.

When tempers cooled, Hujr sent for Imru and he returned to his father's court. However, insistent Hujr soon had to admit his son's stubborn, unrepentant ways. Imru was banished, marking the start of his errant journey.

The stories told that Imru went south in exile to Dammun in Himyar and was in the midst of a wild gathering, full of backgammon games, wine, and women, when he got word of his father's assassination by a rebellion of the Banu Asad who'd turned on him about a spring ago. Imru drank for several days, reveling, until he sobered up and—amidst his siblings' reluctance to avenge their father—swore off anointing himself with oil, along with wine, meat, and women until he'd marched on the Banu Asad and avenged his father.

With weapons and a band of rebellious wanderers from various tribes, including some Bakr and Taghlib, he marched on the Banu Asad. On the way he sought the counsel of the Dhu'l-Khalasa oracle in Tabala, worshipped as a powerful idol in the form of a white stone. The shrine's *kahina* cast her three arrows—inscribed *Do*, *Don't*, and *Wait*—and three times the answer came as *Don't*. Furious, Imru grabbed the arrows, broke them and threw them at the idol, exclaiming: *Shameful stone! If it'd been your murdered father you'd have a different answer!* And with that he continued on his thunderous way, rallied allies, and exacted his due revenge on the treacherous Banu Asad.

But fickleness and selfishness soon shrank their flock. Restlessness along with one feud after another led to his losing allies, and to make things worse, tribesmen still bitter at his father's rule had long been trying to get help from Al-Mundhir against him. Thus Imru had become the fugitive Wandering Prince, seeking protection from one tribe after another with what surely felt like only temporary security.

There was as much to sympathize with as there was to criticize in this story, and though Jayida concluded that there was no simple answer, she couldn't be the only one glad that he'd come to them. In addition to fighting at Kutha, surely *sayyid* Aziz's reputable generosity had something to do with it, and she wished that Imru would find genuine help and resolution to his troubles soon.

"*Sah*, your meeting with *malik* Al-Harith must surely happen," said *sayyid* Aziz. "Your fellow soul-kin in poetry Samaw'al at Tayma will happily help you meet him. The Jafnid king helps those in need, and as another of noble blood, he'd welcome yet another poetic prince to fill his marble halls with verses. Although; you'll remember to keep them virtuous and free of lusty references," he smirked, holding up a warning finger.

"And I'd be honored to offer you some of my camels as security along for your journey," said Zahir, just as she'd expected.

Imru pinched an averted, nodding smile and the *sayyid* gripped his shoulder affectionately. "You bless us with your presence. So now we leave you briefly to get some rest, and tonight we shall feast in your honor as we share your sorrows and call forth your justice," said *sayyid* Aziz.

In a happy hubbub they dispersed to make preparations, and the afternoon flew by in the joyful hustle and bustle of cooking and, for many women, donning their best garments and cosmetics. In the late afternoon heat, the rich aromas gathered and blended, unleashing streams of fresh breads, sweet pie pastries, curdled cheese, and tender camel meat, spiced with turmeric, cardamom, and saffron. Jayida helped as much as she could—or was allowed to—her mother teasing her not to worry and go enjoy the poet's presence while it lasted, so that she could report details later with her father.

When all was ready, *sayyid* Aziz gathered in his tent with his poetic guest and his two companions, and reclined around a long and wide space of clay, copper, and silver dishes filled with foods of all kinds. From their roaming stunned expression, Jayida guessed that their guests were as confused as herself on where to start.

There was goat meat, camel meat, lentil soups, and multiple *tharida* soups of sopped bread and meat. Not to forget *sawiq* gruels flavored with butter or fat from sheeps' tails, *hays* sweet meatballs, pigeon pies, *ka'k* pounded biscuits, and even a few truffle dishes. In addition to fresh and sour milk, there were date wines and other variants of sweetened drinks, though Imru unsurprisingly went for wine.

For desserts were all kinds of pastries sweetened with quality, costly local and Hudhayl honey rather than the cheap date syrup substitute, and raisins, and pomegranates. But most plentiful was the *halawa min at-tamar*, the thick date puree favored by many as much as the *maamoul* cookies.

Jayida dug into some lentil soup and *hays* meatballs, while some women at their husband's and children's side looked on, trying to gage favor of their creations from different expressions. Others humbly hung back, rejoicing mostly for the chance of having used special ingredients for the worthy occasion. Jayida beamed proudly to be part of a tribe that expressed their affection and welcome through their best food, even, and maybe especially, when some of its members didn't have much of it for themselves. As she ate with her parents and Nasr at her side, immersed in the abundance around them and the presence of the youngest member of the ancient Kindite clan, she savored the rarity of the scene. Who knew when it would happen again, but in this moment, she dared to think that it was enough to last them a lifetime.

Imru had barely stopped, taking a pause by reclining, when Samira, dressed in a freshly steamed crimson dress, rushed over with Sufyan and Shams at her side. Clearly she'd made sure to be first to present Imru with a large basket of *maamoul* date-filled cookies and other snacks straight from her red-tipped hennaed fingers. With her predictable insistent grin Samira swore that Imru would enjoy them, and that her brave sons had helped her make them. Jayida felt a slight nudge, and discreetly turned to catch her mother's light smirk that radiated to Warda. It pleased Jayida that like her mother, Yazida hadn't gone out of the usual way to impress the visitor, and looked all the more sincere for it.

Cued by Samira's leading example, woman after woman clad in some of their nicest robes streamed after her, laying out their offerings they swore they'd pre-pared just for him. Some even teased, saying they would divorce their husbands if he refused to accept in the face of his fast mounting bounty. Jayida tried not to roll her eyes at this extreme expression that could be as comical as dangerous in the wrong situation, should the person have to carry out their oath. But with a surprisingly humble demeanor, Imru accepted it all, and soon he had so much food transferred to his visiting tent that it confirmed he was set with his companions for quite some time.

In the mounting festive mood, *sayyid* Aziz offered them all wine, which Nasr and Yazida happily helped pass out, filling cup after cup from fresh wineskins. Jayida sipped lightly in between bites of date puree, the rich tangy wine merging well with the sweetness.

"In the midst of all this roaming, I commend your strength in being away from your wife and family," said *sayyid* Aziz.

"I saw my Unayza recently, and while I'm always glad for it, she may not feel the same," sighed Imru. "But as the only one who stole my heart by solving my riddle, she will always have part of my thoughts."

"Which riddle was that?" said Nasr, sweeping over the poet's shoulder and refilling his cup.

Imru chuckled and his features took a nostalgic air.

"I had sworn that I would only marry the woman who could solve my question. It was: what is eight, four, and two?" Imru said, looking around him.

"Fourteen," echoed several responses.

"That's what they all said, but no," said Imru. "Then one obscure night, I met a man guiding a very young woman, beautifully bright like the full moon. She smiled at me. So I asked her, and a few moments later she answered: eight is the number of dog's breasts, four is that of the camel, and two is that of the woman. For the first time, without thinking twice, I asked for her hand in marriage."

Jayida joined in the resounding laughter. She couldn't decide what was worse: the silliness of the story or that it might be real. Could something so simple really have made him fall for her, or was it something else; a need to stay true to his oath? She imagined it was a combination of both, along with other unexplainable things, and that supposed spontaneous poetic lure of love among them.

"May she be blessed, and your kin increase," said *sayyid* Aziz, and took another swig of his drink.

"*Aywa*, may she and her people the Banu Tamim be at peace, though she makes my tears flow like dried and bitter colocynth seeds," said Imru. "If I didn't make her happy after the wedding, at least I did offer her a fine dowry. In addition to her desired dowry of jewelry, silk robes, and wine, I sent her one thousand camels, ten servants and three horses, not to forget the best quality honey, butter, and a fine striped coat from Najran. On top of that, she has my daughter Hind, or as she would say, *her* daughter. She's about ten now." Imru tightened his lips and scrunched his nose, his emotion about his daughter touching Jayida, even as she wondered about the other children he may or may not know about. Perhaps he thought of that too, his tormented soul seeking to keep it all at bay under a controlled distant air.

"Still, as one of the Proverbs says, I would rather be alone in the desert than with a nagging woman," he added, trying to cheer himself.

"Does it really say that or is that one of your verses?" said Shams.

"*Na'am*, it surely does; at least one reason to heed the Israelite's ancient wisdom," chuckled Imru.

"And how is your mother? We pray she is well," said Zoraya affectionately.

"I try my best to stay informed. Last I heard, she is safe among the Kindah. After all the trouble I've given her, at least she has my brothers to care for her. Surely *they* don't mind my absence," said Imru with a hint of bitterness.

"May the woman who birthed you be blessed. Let us drink to her health—try this," said *sayyid* Aziz, and handed him a cup of a different wineskin.

"Oh, it is divine." Imru's eyes narrowed. "Al-Andarin region," he nodded.

"The finest palate in the land; indeed it is! Via Khaybar, thanks to the good *nasi* Musa, whom you'll have to visit on your way to Tayma, too," said *sayyid* Aziz.

"It is such wine that could make me forget that my name isn't Imru, but rather Hunduj ibn Hujr. I shall begin at the beginning," crooned Imru, his lyrical tone announcing his daring gift.

"First there was *al-ilah*, then angels and *jinn*, and animals of all kinds, and last and worst of all, men. There was *sayyid* Al-Harith, then *sayyid* Hujr. They say twenty-nine springs ago, the youngest of Hujr's sons was born. His name was Hunduj, after the soft, clear sand that covers so much of this land. But he soon made himself another name, whispered by his constant *qareen*-friend: Imru Al-Qays. The man of Qays, who lived in the time of Rûm *Qaysar* Constantine, and whose name eternally survives, inscribed on the Namara inscription northeast of Daraa. You'll find it near *Qaysar* Diocletian's Road, now a fortified road and fort in Al-Sham." Imru paused, drank up their eager stares. "Do not fear that you can't read the rectangular basalt stone inscribed in an older *'arabi* tongue! The ancient Nabataean Aramaic script will whisper to you of his achievements—subduing the Asad and Ma'add—and dwell in the memory of all those who look upon it."

In rhyming, descriptive verses he flowed through bits of the story of Imru Al-Qays ibn Amr, whose name had inspired him. It'd also been the time of the Fars *Shah* Shapur II, who'd compiled the Avesta and persecuted *Masihi* in reaction to *Qaysar* Constantine's and his empire's new faith in Yassu. Though it'd been generations before, Imru might've nearly been speaking of current events, when it often seemed like little had changed since.

Imru drifted into his own life story, and there was an aching melancholy to his emotional reciting; his vulnerability emboldened and strengthened by his unspoken plea for forgiveness in exchange for verses. At times Asheer and Attiyah averted their gazes, like a pair of wounded guardians who carried some of his pain for him.

"He tortures me yet our shared blood binds my duty," said Imru. "Wretched as I am, I took a chance to prove myself. But the grief follows—that shadow as loyal as Fateful Time—and only with true company can the torment be kept at bay."

Sayyid Aziz sniffled and held his shoulder. Encouraged, Imru continued with praise for the Taghlib, Bakr, Tamim, Tayyi, 'Udhrah, Ghatafan, Hawazin, and Sulaym who'd taken him in, many of them kin to the Banu Sa'd with their common ancestor of Mudar. He thanked his two companions Asheer and Atiyah for remaining with him—the elder who'd always believed in his poetry when his father didn't, and the younger who was wiser than him—and finished the tribal list by praising *sayyid* Aziz and the whole of the Banu Sa'd, to resounding cheers.

His pained spirit temporarily eased from the sad burden, he lulled them on to seemingly endless stories; of ancient tales of bygone days, of tribes in the southwest claiming Greek ancestry, of bandits hiding treasures, of great battles and brave heroes, of life-giving love and heartbreaking loss.

He commanded conflicted language in such a powerful way that it could win hearts, even make others do his will if he wanted. Who knew if the stories were real, exaggerated, or untrue? They blended in an immeasurable way, and Jayida realized that perhaps most stories always would. It was only with the help of memory and *qareen*, dwelling and working in their own sacred, vast and mysterious realm, that she could hang on to them, and possibly recall differences if she ever heard them.

Clearly Imru had been gifted to do so, his *qareen* drifting back and forth, and he'd become an expert at letting it flow through him and shower it on his yearning audience—one that so rarely included his own father. Just as when she listened to Nasr, longing filled her to one day be able to weave and share her own trove of stories with her family, the words conquering even dreaded time.

He told them an old tale of the Edessa-dwelling Euphemia and the Goth soldier in the Rûm army, who deceitfully married her when he already had a Gothic wife. Though her mother Sophia had taken the Goth to the local shrine of the Confessors and made him promise to protect her daughter, he treated Euphemia as a slave. When Euphemia gave birth, the Gothic wife jealously poisoned the child, only for Euphemia to poison her back with the leftover poison used to kill her child. Euphemia was shut up in the Gothic wife's tomb, meant to kill her, and in her desperation she prayed to the Confessors, and found herself miraculously back at the shrine and with her mother. When the Goth returned, they testified against him and with the intervention of the Bishop of Edessa, the Goth was beheaded.

Did Imru see himself in the Goth? Or Euphemia? Maybe even both? Yet Jayida hoped he'd simply shared it as both entertainment and a reflection of his vast knowledge. And though the story, supposedly passed on by a shrine guardian, was meant to inspire faith in it, she had little desire to go see it.

To contrast the odd mood, Imru then told them of King Abraha's new Al-Qalis Church and his relocation of the capital of Zafar to San'a.

"It has a marble staircase, leading up to a copper door, and the walls are of white, yellow, green, and black stone that King Abraha used from one of Marib's older castles. The inside is decorated with carved woods and ivory, with more precious stones and gold panel decorations. There are two beams, one named Ku'ayb and the other Ku'ayb's Wife, from which some seek good fortune. To add to that, two of its three sections are decorated with mosaics with gold floral patterns, and crosses on the walls and ceilings that shine in silver and gold. They say *Qaysar* Justinian dispatched an envoy to him specifically for that," said Imru.

Then he made them laugh with his version of the tale of the Seven Sleepers, saying that the youths sealed up in the cave had surely fallen asleep not from the passing of time but from drinking wine, whose bottles may even be found in the caves as evidence. As a renown skilled poet, it was only natural for him to make up his own version, when even the earliest sources disagreed on some details. The Israelites and *Masihi* of Najran said there were three brothers, while those in the Lakhmid territory said five. Others yet in the northwest and elsewhere said seven or eight. But even *mubassir* Ayyub's explanation of Yassu's protective power wasn't enough to take away its mystery. What did it mean?

The consistent part of the curious story was a group of youths who hid inside a cave outside the city of Ephesus, to escape persecution for their faith in Yassu during the reign of *Qaysar* Decius. Sealed inside by enemies seeking their end, they fell asleep. When they awoke, a landowner who'd opened up the cave was before them, assuring them that they hadn't slept just a day or even a few, but centuries. They were soon shocked to find that the city was now full of *Masihi* churches, and their ancient coins caused as much confusion from the townspeople. After telling the bishop their miraculous story, they died praising Yassu.

Was Imru himself looking for his cave all over this land, even as his restlessness *jinni*—or was it *qareen*—kept calling him out of it? And was she herself doing her own version of it; "hiding out"—even if in plain sight—until the time came and things would be magically different?

"I like such tales of resurrection," sighed Imru. "Oh, great Origen of Alexandria! Was it the ancient Egyptian beliefs or Yassu that made you believe in reincarnation?" His lifted gaze searched an invisible presence in the ebony sky. He closed his eyes, took a deep breath, and opened them again. "Maybe both. In my mind, I see him at the majestic city of Bosra in Al-Sham, debating Bishop Beryllus to convert him to his faith. I think I would've, if he'd preached to me. May his soul be at peace, clothed in the purple of Tyre where he died after years of unjust torture. Speaking of that same era: some even say that the first secretely *Masihi Qaysar* was actually Marcus Julius Philippus, before *Qaysar* Constantine. With those constantly conquering Rûm, could we be surprised? First they persecute you for your faith, then claim it and say they're *al-ilah*'s best heirs," he shook his head. "But as for me, what shall I come back as, you think?" Imru looked at them, though a glint in his eyes beckoned him elsewhere.

"What do *you* want to come back as?" said *sayyid* Aziz.

"As an angel, like my Asheer and Atiyah here," said Imru.

"You're sure you want to come back at all?" said Nasr.

"Where else would you go?" frowned Shams.

"Surely Heaven is the best place," said her father, and winked at her.

"Ah, my good generous hosts, perhaps you are all right, in a sense," chuckled Imru, for the first time his hearty laughter brightening his demeanor.

A cozy lethargy began to settle when Samira announced she and some other tribeswomen would offer a short performance. "To give thanks for your visit, and that you may remember the Banu Sa'd, though we are no Kindite court," grinned Samira.

"I could want nothing more," said Imru and lowered his chin in a deep, accepting nod.

A moment later Yazida emerged at Samira's side, and Jayida wasn't sure if she, Shams, or Nasr, with his controlled clenched jaw, was more surprised to see her there, easily the most beautiful and glowing beauty of the bunch. *Sayyid* Aziz must've agreed to Samira's planned scheme, although everyone knew how pushy she could be in her incessant nagging to get her way.

The women with instruments spread out slightly behind Samira and Yazida, who each gripped their own tambourine. Samira broke out into song, chanting of a wandering prince-poet who'd lost his place in the kingdom but regained it to greater splendor, her crooning voice decent but not particularly impressive. It might've been the familiarity that made Jayida hear the latent whining in it, but thankfully it was helped by the echoes of flute, tambourines, and clapping.

Yazida began dancing, her dainty feet darting up lightly, and after a moment she took over a passage and belted out her verses in her striking singing voice, nearly making Jayida's jaw drop. So this was part of what she'd been missing out on all along: Yazida fast becoming a skilled dancing and singing girl! For an instant she was annoyed that they had to wait for visiting poets—even a princely one—to be granted such a pleasant display. But Jayida beamed at the sight of her delicately swirling and bouncing form, an angel whose robes and arms flapped like graceful wings at every movement. No wonder Nasr was both proud and protective of his sister's talent.

Shams crossed his arms and at times reluctantly glanced away to avoid staring at Yazida, while Imru's gaze often darted to Samira. Jayida found her somewhat silly, like an overgrown child trying too hard. Even if her husband didn't mind—and nothing showed he did—at least someone was enjoying Samira's overbearing antics.

"What talent you all have," said Imru, clapping heartily when their piece came to an end.

Samira beamed as if the compliment had been only for her, and she took her time cleaning and passing out woolen blankets, so that she was the last one to retreat and finally let them have the evening with their visitor. An intimacy drew them all closer to their guest, and *sayyid* Aziz affectionately laughed as he drew up the blanket over his brother Hubala, who laid next to him, rosy and drowsy from wine.

"At least he won't offend you by yawning or sneezing," chuckled *sayyid* Aziz. "I wouldn't want you seeing any bad omens here."

"Kind of you, even if I'm not sure of their nature either. But they do work as poetic devices, and all the same, superstitions are plenty," smiled Imru.

"Like those who disagree for my daughter to go about unveiled when her gifts are evident anyway. I hope she may one day know your Hind, and perhaps may even sing together in your honor," said *sayyid* Aziz with flushed cheeks.

"May it be as you say. I both want and dread to know when I'll see her again, because having to leave her is just as hard," said Imru, and gulped his wine. "Until then: There was a boy who was not made for his father's weapons, though it only enraged him more."

These moody outbursts, darker than the ones earlier, seemed more for himself than others. That they should be there, hearing his whirlwind fanned by anger and wine, was a priceless gift many wouldn't trade for anything.

"The boy tried to tell him he had another weapon of his own: his verses, but they were rejected. Even in his death, the father had to summon him to bloodshed. I often lament not knowing the Orders of the Unknown, but I know that for some, nothing has permanence except discontent and wrath, but my poetry will outlast all that, and defy Time itself," said Imru.

"*Aywa, aywa,*" echoed Asheer and Atiyah, with even more certainty than him.

"Surely time is on your side. Though the Kinana now keep the calendar, none can forget that it was your kin who kept it before," sighed *sayyid* Aziz.

"Amidst all my laments, perhaps that's one I can't mourn as much. I wouldn't have been a good fit for it; all this discussing with other tribes and tracking of intercalating months. As if I needed another reminder of the looming Judgment Day," Imru chuckled darkly.

Jayida smiled in her own kind of agreement. If even a prince from the royal house of Kindah wasn't versed, or maybe even worse, interested in the confusing and stressful art of calendar-keeping, she could hardly be blamed for her reluctance.

"So, is it true?" said Shams, and Jayida turned to the grotesque grin on his face aimed at their guest.

"Is what true? When you ask a question, it's only right to be clear," said Imru.

"Just that, eh, the stories. Of you and Fatima of the chaste Banu 'Udhrah," said Shams.

"Stories?" said Imru.

For the first time in her life, Shams stifled a frustrated sigh. Instead, he took a big breath, and fixed the poet directly. With a hint of challenge, he recited Imru's verses boasting of evading guards and slipping in a young, untouched beauty's tent, to their mutual satisfaction. Jayida wasn't sure what surprised her most: that Shams had memorized—surely with Sufyan's help—the passage from his long *qasidah* ode, or that he'd picked such an improper line to ask him about. All eyes pierced Imru at once, a mix of shock, aversion, and envy in their glazed eyes, especially Sufyan's.

"There are many Fatimas in the world, just like there are Himyarites who don't circumcise their women and eat locusts," Imru smirked.

"Did you really dare with her while you were there?" said Shams. "They say their men create the most romantically chaste poetry and would rather die than go against their oaths of chastity. How did you escape?"

"Perhaps there wasn't much to escape, since I'm still here," winked Imru, and threw back his wine in a way she didn't like. Did he have no respect? And what was Shams trying to prove by asking, even if it was at his brother's coaxing? Unsurprisingly, Nasr's darkened, unamused air reflected her own.

Imru shrugged. "I would tell you a secret, but a tribe such as yours, filled with generous hearts, already know this: not all verses are true. As for whatever honor I have left: nothing ever happened anywhere that wasn't wanted. All the same, I will be judged, just like everyone else."

"Perhaps you are too hard on yourself," said *sayyid* Aziz with a wave of the hand. He picked up a wineskin and refilled their cups in a firm but wobbly manner that Nasr affectionately monitored.

"What's also sure is that a brave man can always use more generous friends," said Zahir, lightly shifting the conversation. "Surely on your way to Samaw'al at Tayma, you should stop by Khaybar, then once more to our kin the Tayyi, which Hatim would love. Some say he's fast becoming known as the most generous man in *all* the land, not just the tribe," said Zahir, as proud of his kin as he was humble of his own generosity.

"That I would believe. Oh, it's been too many years since I first met him and his honorable father Abdallah. I think I will follow your advice," nodded Imru. Her father smiled brightly, and she glowed to think that some of their Zahir camels would join him along on his journeys.

The night dwindled into more pleasantries around the fire, sweetened with wine, pastries, and friendship. Her heart pinched for him, a lost prince whose torments barely relented. That his *sitti* and father had both been assassinated were not only heartbreaking, but to his poetic imaginings, maybe even a worrisome omen looming on the horizon. As with other less pleasant aspects of his poems, she hoped it was just lower, weaker *jinn* trying to influence him however they could.

Not that he was innocent either, when he'd often put his own desires before anything else, and some would say, had always been part of the problem, before his father conquered tribes of Ma'add. Jayida shuddered to think of all the lives he'd taken—and now this man, loved and reviled, was a welcomed guest among them.

By tribal law even if he attempted, by some madness, to do them harm, many a *badawi* would not retaliate under the oath of hospitality. It had to be part of the reason he was even still alive, roaming the land and now sharing his stories with them. But whatever hesitation she felt receded as his cold voice pierced her soul, saying:

"They killed my father while he slept in his tent. Even with all the troubles between us, I cannot think of a more cowardly death," said Imru. "They had to know what was coming, and if they didn't, actions often have consequences, even as many don't. And Fate, for once, was on my side," he continued, his grimacing features now frighteningly animated. "When at 'Ukaz, on our way north, we met none other than Abid ibn Al-Abras, that vile Asad poet who'd been involved in my father's murder. Oh, sublime restraint I hardly knew! He had lots to say, so I let him, and each time I asked myself: is that it? Was that the best he could do? When he stopped I unleashed lampoon after lampoon against the Asad, and even before they quickly shrank in embarrassing hate of themselves and their cowardly tribe, I knew then—as I've known since I was a child—that the victory was *mine*! It was everywhere: in widened eyes, in praising cries, and writhing flames; my perfectly woven verses relished by others who clung to them, repeating, memorizing, some even scribbling their quills drenched with metallic ink on parchment—each eating it all up in their own, greedy way! Did he foolishly think my father's murder would take away my gift?" Imru scoffed, his wild air consuming him. "Instead, it's Abid's shameful fate that was instantly sealed! *Aywa*; a miracle happened in the midst of that market, forbidding bloodshed, for the thought came to me then. Why taint myself and any other surface with his blood when I sent his mediocre *qareen* away? He'd have his whole life to be reminded of it, and all the better now as the servants of the Banu 'Abs!" he chuckled.

Imru went on about how, since his father's death, the Banu 'Abs had overtaken the Banu Ka'b, Numayr, and Asad, who now paid tribute to them. And while that was certainly a blow to the Asad, Imru had to be concerned that Abid could keep spreading lies among them, too, while the 'Abs may in turn boast of having subdued the tribe who'd killed Hujr of Kindah in an enduring cycle of competing conquests and losses. Amidst the turmoil between these tribes residing east in the Najd, Jayida hoped the 'Abs had given up their earlier sights on the Sulaym mines.

Not a muscle stirred at the end of his speech, the intensity coiled around them like chains. Had Imru ruined his fate by disobeying the oracle, when her answer had thrice been "Don't"? Was that why he looked anything but satisfied, with little working out, his allies vanishing down to a lean, nearly ghostly trio? Almost like her and her parents, in different form.

Jayida stifled a deep groan, knowing that she would have to disobey her father's warning to reign in her chaotic *jahl* and not to take life if her parents were ever taken from her that way. If a part of her might hesitate to act, it seemed just as wrong not to do anything. In her creeping torment she looked away in the darkness outside the fire's range, aware of how easy it was to pass judgment and think she knew better when she hadn't been in his situation.

But Samaw'al and *malik* Al-Harith would help him straighten his path, and one day the tribes would see him return as a new man with a loyal army. And the glorious verses would flow: from himself, Nasr, Samaw'al, Hatim, and other poets she didn't yet know.

He'd suffered constant struggles, and while no one was spared them, now they could do their part in offering him some comfort, and though not a requirement, they might even be remembered in his verses someday.

CHAPTER TWELVE

POETIC GAMES

"I saw my Aksumite princess guardian again; she must approve of Imru's visit," Jayida beamed to her parents the next morning.

"I wonder who is his, aside from his *qareen*," said her mother, as her father frowned.

"Surely a woman, or several," her father chuckled, then cleared his throat. "We're taking our guests along Wadi Al-Wafra; might help change the brooding spirits a bit."

After eating, Jayida packed her bow, quiver, and spears, and they rejoined the *sayyid* and Nasr, who appeared before their tent astride their mounts. To her pleasant surprise, there was Yazida, veiled up to her eyes on her own mount.

"It's not every day that she could ride with Imru as our guest, so I allowed it," grinned *sayyid* Aziz. Her brother may have been another boost, when it was his idea to teach her some use of the weapons, too. Jayida almost wondered if Samira was coming too, but seeing only Sufyan and Shams approaching at each side of the guests, she sighed in relief.

"We'll keep her safely tucked in among us," said Zahir, and winked at Yazida whose smile lit up her eyes.

They merged with their guests, who thankfully looked a bit more cheerful than the previous day. With Yazida at the center, they led their mounts north to the place of her birth, her father making a point to steer clear of the western area that was so special to them. Though they couldn't always avoid the beautiful location that might suggest deeper importance or meaning, even she felt protective of it and wanted to keep stomping feet and prying eyes away.

They slowed as they entered the valley that stretched out before them like a blossoming garden. It may not have been the southern lush, tropical gardens as

Imru knew them, nor should they be, but it pleased her all the more to see Imru's features brighten as he took in their own version of it.

"Oh, though I've passed ample time in sweet presence of the fair, yet none was so sweet as that spent by the neighboring pools of the Sa'd," said Imru with a dreamy air.

This time the melancholy in his verses were no match for the glow enveloping him. Had his *qareen* showed him a glimpse of what she'd seen all these years ago, that sense of silent magic in the air, bursting with white butterflies that vanished she knew not where? Maybe he was right and the little *kahina* she was shared some things with a poet.

In front of them, Sufyan stopped and held up his hand.

"Blessed oryx ahead," said Sufyan in a near whisper. A few sat in shallow holes they'd dug to counter the rising heat.

"Shall we then?" said Sufyan, his eagerness matched by Shams's. Despite their different personalities, they'd grown closer as brothers, surely bonding in part over their shared frustration with their mother Samira.

"I'll pass on hunting today, but if you will," said *sayyid* Aziz, waving ahead.

"I'll pass too," said Nasr, lingering close to his sister.

"The bounty is yours," said Zahir, echoing her thoughts.

"*Aywa*. In your honor, Imru, Asheer, and Atiyah: will you join us?" said Sufyan.

Asheer and Atiyah agreed, even as she caught an air of restraint in Imru, who followed behind.

"Now let's see about those rumors," said Nasr to his sister, in a tone Jayida hadn't ever heard before. It was a mix of curiosity and sarcasm that echoed the tribe's, though they might never say it aloud.

They held back as the hunters rode off ahead towards the grazing, straight-horned oryx, and she frowned at Imru's showy manner that made him look swaggering even atop his mount. Did he always have others do his hunting for him? Even for those honored to serve him, with his shrinking friendships and his past pampered life it could be a matter of survival to successfully hunt.

Sufyan crept ahead, keeping a measured space and his bow and arrows drawn, with Shams at his side like a smaller shadow. The oryx looked up, alerted to their approach, and the hunters waited, immobile, so that soon the oryx returned to grazing. After a moment, Asheer and Atiyah moved ahead silently and, bows drawn, launched their arrows into the flock. Two arrows struck an oryx, sending the others scattering. The rush sent the hunters bolting and shooting in all directions, and to her diminishing surprise, she noted the way Imru hung back, adding to his air of helplessness.

In a flash, she had the impression of gazing at him with his father's constant critical eye. Was this enough for him? Or had he given up too long ago to want to try again? Was poetry enough of a gift if it had to be recognized by others in order to eat and live? Or did he know something she didn't, like how to whisper his verses to the desert to bring him what he needed?

She glanced at Yazida and read her troubled concern. So caring, like her parents and sibling. Jayida tried to soften towards the wandering poet, who had to be at least a bit embarrassed to be seen in such a light, by both other men and women—including an unknown one who could hunt better than him, Jayida could now proudly say. But he was their guest and had accepted the invitation, and its consequences.

The eager hunters scuffled, pouncing to and fro after the wounded oryx who wobbled away. Sufyan and Shams aimed, and Sufyan's arrow went straight into the tough creature's shoulder. Then another shot by Asheer buried into the oryx, who at last dropped to the ground.

"*Aywa*! Praise to Imru's name!" *sayyid* Aziz called out, and Yazida followed with a lovely ululation.

Asheer and Atiyah offered to set the massive white-bodied, dark-legged animal on Imru's mount, but stopped when he waved it away with a laugh. Atiyah helped Asheer set it on his mount, and they continued on their path, rounding west through Wadi Al-Hamd on their way back to camp.

"It is a blessed place here," said Imru. "I can see why you'd quietly dwell here, and all the better to preserve it like a secret treasure," he smirked.

"It's for anyone who shares our view of life. No unnecessary fussing, quiet, harmonious living, troubles and feuds promptly and reasonably resolved. That shouldn't be so complicated," said *sayyid* Aziz.

"How I envy you," said Imru, and they all knew that he meant it only with kindness.

They refilled their waterskins at a nearby stream, and dismounted to stretch their legs as they continued their leisure trek back home. Even with Yazida trying not to draw attention to herself by keeping close to her kin, Jayida noted that Atiyah was not indifferent to her presence.

"What will you do with the rest of the oryx's body?" said Nasr.

"Keep the horns as prized memory of my passage here, of which I already have many," sighed Imru.

Jayida spotted the corpse of a falcon, his body eaten up and soon to be made unrecognizable by the heat, and gestured to her father to lure Imru away. He read her mind and did so, neither of them wanting him to take this as a potential bad omen. Maybe they were overdoing it, but she wanted to spare him another sight of death when he'd seen so much of it.

As they drew away from the *wadi*, Nasr went on to tell him about Shams's finding of the ostrich eggs, and Jonder's slaying of the leopard, whose fang necklace she tugged from her neck as happy proof. She guessed that instead of such trinkets he had prized heirloom jewelry, as much as they came with their own conflicted memories.

While Imru and his companions drifted off to chat with *sayyid* Aziz and her father, Sufyan drew them closely together.

"*Aywa*, you'll be ready then?" said Sufyan, eyeing Shams, Nasr, and Yazida.

"So long as you call it," said Nasr, and smiled at his sister.

"And what are we talking about here?" frowned Jayida.

"A mock attack, with Yazida as the prize," said Nasr.

"Great idea, Shams," nodded Jayida.

"No, it was mine," smirked Sufyan.

"*Sah*; same thing then," Jayida grinned. "And to think that Yazida agreed to this scheming." She glanced playfully at the target.

"I did," Yazida smiled.

"It's all in good fun. Plus I saw the way Imru was looking at our *yama*. I'd be insulted, but I'll go with flattered instead. At least this should be more exciting than the hunt," Sufyan winked.

When the camp came into view, Sufyan informed Imru and his companions of his mischievous idea. They were all to be the boisterous invaders, catching the camp unaware, with Yazida on foot as the highest prize. Imru nodded as blankly as his companions' expressions lit up, and to hear Sufyan tell it, teasingly naming which tent belonged to whom, she imagined that not a few women of their tribes would secretly wish to be taken away by the restless poet. His whole visit might surely figure among their favorite memories, and something to boast of to others.

Let me tell you how we welcomed him, and how he bravely caught all our hearts!—They'd laugh and say to each other, the dreaded shame and humiliation of real kidnapping replaced by creeping desire.

Let them romanticize it. If Imru could certainly use some well-meaning cheering up, Jayida simply could not fawn over him the way others did, and found it rather amusing.

At last Sufyan raced to the front, his arm raised and waving his *bakurah* stick, and they pulled up their scarf over their nose and followed at his heels.

"*Yallah,* Sa'd, *Yallah,* Sa'd! The brave Imru is upon you, charging upon you to seize your women! What *will* you do?" called Sufyan.

"Come and get me, warriors!" yelled Yazida. Waving a crimson flag, her flashing smile made it impossible to gage to whom it was intended. She rushed past them, and once at camp slipped off her mount, laughing as she repeated the call.

"Imru is coming to catch us; help protect me!" cried Yazida, and rattled the tent drapes to communal amusement. Yazida bounced from place to place like a gazelle as they thundered upon the camp, and in perfect timing mostly women flooded out, their cries more like melodic ululations of laughter, as men tried to exchange their grinning amusement for dumbfounded and helpless airs.

"Oh no! What shall we do!" yelled some women, running daintily in Imru's path, as others coiled around Asheer and Atiyah, who did the poet's bidding.

"Imru has found us!" cried others, waving bright handkerchiefs in the air to be better seen through the rising clouds of dust.

In the rush of the race, a mounting competitive jealousy seized Jayida. None of these men had particularly proven they deserved her, and there was a shocking satisfaction to that thought. By now Shams assumed he was the natural contender for Yazida. But Nasr had yet to express either approval or disagreement, just as he'd yet to say anything about his own situation. At least Jayida wasn't the only one postponing—or was it evading—this complicated decision.

"Here I am!" yelled Yazida, just as Jayida came upon her darting side to side around tents like a *jinniyeh*. In an instant, women crowded around Yazida, and her mother Warda protectively came forth, nearly distracting Hania with some treats. But with graceful maneuvering from long days of training, Jayida pulled her back and rode out of reach, grazing past tents like a gentle breeze without toppling any. Amidst the veil of dust she made out Nasr, Sufyan, and Imru at opposite ends, the yelling Shams easily betraying his location somewhere behind her.

Jayida took advantage and forged ahead, and reached back to her quiver for an arrow she then locked in her veiled mouth.

"What men are you, that you can't even catch us?" echoed feminine voices, somewhere in the invisible space, scattering it across the campgrounds.

Without a second thought Jayida clucked her tongue and Hania galloped ahead, and the further she rode, the dust dissipated, revealing Yazida racing in the distance, not bothering to look behind her even as she kept waving the taunting crimson flag.

Like lightning, Imru was at Jayida's west side, brandishing his spear in Yazida's direction. A flicker of worry seized Jayida: with only two spears, perhaps he was confident of his shots. Jayida's muscles long poised to the metallic weight of her coat of mail, she freed the arrow from her lips and aimed her bow. Before she could release, Imru launched his spear with careful aim, missing Yazida's dress by just a few paces.

With a proud yell Shams emerged from the other east side, placing Jayida in the middle of them. Jayida waited as Shams aimed his bow and released arrow after arrow, each missing the mark of Yazida's robe. Yazida kept zigzagging, and Jayida had the impression that she seemed even more enthusiastic than she'd been the night before.

Never losing her pace, Yazida made several twirling turns, then one of her winged arm rose to her head and pulled off her headdress. Her hair unfurled like a silken ebony flag, whipping and streaking like ink writing across her face and the dusty sky. Whoever was this elusive, unusually playful version of Yazida, Jayida instantly liked her.

Imru's second spear flew at Yazida and landed right past her, his mount receding behind Shams's, as Jayida fell behind. Her nostrils flaring, Jayida finally aimed, her gaze following Yazida's curving path. Jayida released and sent the arrow flying into the hem of Yazida's dress, securing her into place and marking the target as her own.

Monitoring her racing breath, Jayida slipped off Hania and rushed over to Yazida, then carefully pulled out the arrow from her garment.

"Now you'll have to mend my dress," Yazida grinned through her perfectly flushed panting.

"It shall be done," smiled Jayida with a slight bow.

"It appears the winner is Jonder," said Nasr with a knowing smirk, while Shams tried to contain his frown. But for once it hadn't been Shams she'd wanted to test, but rather the princely poet and his companions. That she won pleased her as much as it added to her disappointment of their famous guest. Jayida glanced at Imru and met his resigned, surrendering smile, echoed by Asheer and Atiyah congratulating Jonder for his true aim.

Jayida looked back at Yazida, whose glowing gratitude reflected her handsome brother's, and stirred a strange rising turmoil in her. Why should she feel guilty at her victory? She was Jonder, son of Zahir, *kahin* of the Banu Sa'd, and now even the best poet of them all, Imru Al-Qays, not only knew it, but would remember it. If she hadn't ever dreamt of such a thing before, she now glimpsed the dormant power in it.

The Banu Sa'd clustered excitedly around, praising and thanking the brave Imru and his companions for the light fun, and to each compliment they offered to Jonder and the other participants, the happy riders nodded and bowed lightly in humble acceptance.

The evening passed in celebration and feasting on the succulent oryx, her wine cup kept full by Yazida who glided amongst them and, Jayida almost swore, closest to her own person than she'd ever done before.

"Imru chirps long before daybreak, when given generous wine as guest of the Banu Sa'd," Imru cooed in a tipsy melancholy, his sight lost in the dark liquid.

"May it lift your spirits," chuckled *sayyid* Aziz. "Oh, how we shall miss you when you leave, *if* you leave," he said, affectionately elbowing the poet.

"All things must end, which is why we must seize any moment of happiness," sighed Imru. His tone had such despair that Jayida wondered if that was the closest he'd come to voicing his earlier embarrassment. But at least she knew as well as everyone that no one in the tribe would speak ill of him. In just two days they'd already grown fond of him, the men praising his fine lineage and endurance, and the women doting on him like a caring gazelle an orphaned calf.

"Blessed poet. We know the gifts you're capable of. Won't you treat us to your *qasidah*, and rejoice both your spirits and ours?" said *sayyid* Aziz.

Imru gulped the rest of his wine, and nodded. "Now I'm ready," he said, to resounding laughter. He released a sigh and began.

"Stay, and weep with me at the
Memory of one beloved
At the sight of the location
Where her tent was raised
By the edge of the bending sands
Between Al-Dakhul and Hawmal,
Tudah and Mikrah, whose trace
Was not fully erased
Though the south and north
Winds wove the twisted sand..."

The tribe huddled, transported on the breath of Imru's words that unfolded his bittersweet memories. He began with his long *nasib* segment of rhyming descriptions of the ruined abode, mourning his beloved who once lived there.

Jayida braced herself as he went into his erotic escapades, when he'd taken a group of bathing women's clothing and refused to give it back to them unless they came out to him fully naked. The day passed and after they were forced to come out, they berated him for leaving them hungry, at which point he offered to slay his mount for them.

She tried not to grimace as he continued into his most shocking amorous stint with a mother while she bottle-fed her amuleted baby, and caught a hint of criticism in his tone. What if it hadn't been him who'd wanted that, but the woman herself, and in refusing, she would've been insulted—more than enough to start another war?

But Imru might have his spicy fun, or transform it in his verses, twisting the event into something else, as the woman and others did of him. He was the creator of his verses, but Jayida had the shocking realization that even he himself couldn't completely control its final form and reception. His *qareen* could only help him with images to express his visions, and even though he knew his true meaning and intent, it could take a life of its own through different listeners' interpretations.

Much to her surprise, there was something reassuring about him saying these verses she hadn't thought she'd want to hear. At least it had the effect that he wasn't trying to be obscene or vulgar, but instead showed a glimpse of his defiant *qareen* and hinted at his comfort and sense of acceptance among them.

He continued into his night of inner turmoil that spoke to them all, taking them to endless varieties of fearful sufferings in the ruthless desert. But then, as it always did, dawn came, announcing the *fakhr* boasting segment, whose heroic poet on his strong mount went into an oryx hunt, his journey ending with a wild desert storm. The ending result was the lasting effect any skilled poet should make: it left her a little flushed, thoroughly moved, and most of all, forgiving and understanding of the poet despite his faults.

Tearful praise resounded, followed by more food, wine, and songs, wrapping them up warmly deep into the icy night. It was the middle of the night when she finally stumbled back to the tent.

"There's the lion, crawling back to his lair," whispered her father to her mother's sleepy giggle.

Her cheeks pleasantly flushed and too lazy to change her clothing, Jayida fell back upon her bedding, her soul dancing into some hazy paradise.

CHAPTER THIRTEEN

FACES

Jayida awoke with a start, her brow sweaty and throat parched, with the unsettling sensation of a nearby presence, staring at her. Frowning, she sat up, her vision trying to adjust to the dark amidst the faint unpleasant spinning rising up her spine.

Her father's loud snore shook through her, confirming she wasn't dreaming. In the midst of their motionless deep sleep, she made out Nasr kneeling at her side, his serious expression so fixed that for a moment it startled her. It reminded her of that odd training episode she hated, and often tried not to remember.

"What is it?" she whispered. That she still had her day clothing on was little consolation for not having heard him enter. Careless. She could never be careless.

"Let's go." Nasr shot up and turned.

"*Esh?* What? Where?" And how could he sound like a spirit who chose who heard him?

Stiff as a stone, he turned to her so slowly that she almost wondered if he might be night walking. She realized she wasn't sure how much he'd had to drink, and it unsettled her that he seemed to look through her as if she wasn't there.

"Imru is missing. So is Yazida."

From deep in the recess of his dark eyes was a command, not a request.

Jayida grabbed a spear and followed him northeast in silence with his mount between them, the only sound in the desert stillness their steps upon the dry earth. An uncomfortable heat still wrapping her limbs, she hardly noticed the deep chill, and swallowed the queasy feeling seizing her stomach. The moonlight was so bright that she lowered her scarf over her face and wanted nothing more than to crawl back into her dark den and sleep it all away. She reached for the gourd hanging down the saddle, and forced herself to slowly sip, hoping to offset the effects of the wine.

She wanted to ask where they were going, but Nasr's unshaken intensity—as if he already knew everything—deterred her from it. Surely they were having similar thoughts: that Imru had deceived them, committed the worst disrespect by luring his sister, the welcoming *sayyid*'s daughter, away. Jayida mimicked his search for tracks, the lack of human ones as if only more strongly beckoning him.

They veered east of Wadi Al-Wafra, and came upon another valley with a small stream stretching along them to the east. Nasr stopped and ordered his mount to stay there, then cued her along with a jerk of his head. They crept ahead deeper into the valley, the moon a large shining pearl in the glistening water. There was no denying it: the scene was so preciously romantic that she felt a pang of envy at not having known of it herself. Would Nasr have taken her there under different, and lawful, circumstances?

Nasr walked on hunched over, the manner nearly confusing her until they approached the water, and she noted the hill dipping below out of view. If Yazida had been the one to pick this place, which she assumed she did the more time passed, she certainly knew what she was doing. Nasr stopped and held up a finger to his lips.

Silence.

Then a rustling, coming from below out of view. A muffled giggle—and Nasr didn't wait for more of it to rush down the hill. Jayida ran after him, who in an instant grabbed Imru and pushed him off his sister. Yazida sat up, pulling her robe back over her shoulders, her open-mouthed shock as telling as Imru's avoiding, guilty expression.

"What shall we do with you, fine prince, eh?" said Nasr, kicking him right in the ribs, sending Imru doubling over in pain. "That's how you treat a generous people who welcome you?"

"Nasr, please! It's my fault. Please don't hurt him," said Yazida, shifting to her knees and tugging down on his arm in beggary.

"You!" said Nasr. He raised his hand and looked at her with such disgusted anger that Jayida thought he would slap her.

Disentangling himself from his sister's grip, Nasr turned to Imru, and kicked him once more, sending him rolling over on his other side.

"*Yallah!* Come on! Aren't you going to fight? If she's a *stolen* prize, isn't she at least worth that much?" challenged Nasr. That Imru looked so helpless was far from endearing, but it was not lost on her that even defending himself, wrong as he was, would likely only deepen Nasr's anger.

Panting, Imru seemed so distraught that Jayida was at a loss what to do. She could hardly believe what was happening, or what Nasr was bent on doing. She'd never seen him so angry, but then again, this had never happened before. As Yazida shook, pleading over this man she hardly knew, Jayida had the impression of hardly knowing her at all.

Nasr lowered himself, crouched, and stared. "Do I really need to remind you, of all people, that others would kill for much, much less reason?" Nasr's tone had a mix of aversion and amused mockery that turned her blood cold.

"You're right. Please forgive me. It's not her fault; it's mine," coughed Imru, looking up at him with raised helpless hands to brace himself.

"Of course it's your fault. That's your whole life story, isn't it?" said Nasr, and got up and stood back, as if regretting he'd come so close. Something in Jayida's heart broke, seeing Imru's pained grimace at this statement that struck deeper than any blow.

Nasr yanked Yazida up by the arm, and she trudged along him like a child towards the camel and back to camp. Jayida hung back with Imru, who stumbled pitifully along. What was she to make of all this? Imru and Yazida were both guilty in this, they had to be. And as much as Imru clearly had had a chaotic, difficult life tinged with moments of pleasure, it certainly didn't excuse his behavior.

But she hated the now rising, crushing doubt of his personality, a mere act he'd come to master, part of his poetic identity that he used to his advantage. He may well have been also interested in Samira, but now she and Nasr both knew that it had served in deflecting at least part of his intention. The thought that he'd played so many roles that even he himself no longer knew where one began and the other ended sent a shudder down her spine. Jayida, at least, knew herself, and hadn't tainted herself with dubious and carnal pleasures.

But there was no making sense of Yazida. Did she really like him, or was it some kind of bored girls' games? If Jayida could've expected this from him, being older than them and more experienced, what could she say of Yazida? But like her budding singing and dancing skills, Jayida realized again that she'd only had her idea of Yazida—as Yazida only knew Jonder.

A short distance from camp, Nasr stopped and turned to them.

"Now, pay close attention. There will be no word of this to anyone. Sometime in the morning, you will pack and announce your rushed need to leave; we all know you have pressing business up north anyway. You'll be provided whatever you need, and we'll make as if nothing happened. As for Yazida, things will be discussed with her privately. And let me be clear: if you ever boast of this in your poetry, and in such a way that it's recognizable to inspire even the slightest suspicion, I swear on my honorable father's life that I will come for you," said Nasr.

Yazida's shock reflected her own: such a decree was akin to prophecy. Imru opened his mouth as if in protest, but Nasr had turned back so quickly that he probably didn't see it, nor cared either way.

Jayida slipped back into the tent, relieved and somehow slightly embarrassed that her father sat in the dim men's quarters, quietly waiting. She told him everything, and soon read his disappointment in their famously notorious guest.

"Poor Samira. Or does he also like her and wants to take her off Hubala's hands for a while?" frowned Zahir in conflicted humor.

Jayida laid flat on her back, a lingering wave of queasiness washing over her. "After what I've seen these past days, I feel like not even people closest to us can be trusted. I can't believe that Nasr snuck in without my knowledge! Praise *al-ilah* I hadn't undressed," she said, her hands squeezing her face.

"That might've had its own interesting developments," her father gave a suggestive smirk. "Thanks to both of your far-seeing *qareen*, because I'm not sure I want it to be Imru's spell over us all," her father shook his head.

"It won't happen again," she frowned. "But has Yazida said anything about Shams for marriage?"

"Not that we know of. But then again: it would be worse if she had and then did this," Zahir said with raised eyebrow. "I'll lure them away one last time to Wadi Al-Hamd in the morning, while you settle matters with Yazida," he added, patting her knee.

In the morning as soon as they left, Jayida rushed to Nasr's tent. Though less intense than the previous night, he was no less authoritatively poised, especially in the private space of his own abode. He'd modestly decorated with beautiful colorful rugs, mats, and blankets woven by Warda, with a shrine full of knotted bracelet *wasm*, and even his wolf and oryx hides seemed not so much menacing as subdued and pensive. With admiration Jayida could understand why he rarely had anyone in his space, and of the great self-controlled *sayyid* he'd make someday.

Still wrapped in her guilt, Yazida met her gaze timidly, her sunken eyes hinting she'd spent a troubled night. A palpable silence hung over them.

"Explain yourself, then. What were you thinking? You know that if Samira finds out about this, she'd love for Shams to recite poetry, or worse, hire poets to make verses and spread them far and wide. We can only speculate with *yaba*, but I can almost guarantee he won't be easier than me," said Nasr. He paused, and fixed Yazida who only stared at the saffron-red woven carpet. "So who was it?"

Yazida pinched her lips together, and Jayida pitied her loneliness in her conflict. "Him."

"*Yallah al-ilah.* And you defended him so far as to take the blame! Why?" said Nasr, his gesticulating arms falling hard at his sides.

"He's a cultured prince!" retorted Yazida. "He's not this vile man you think."

"*Aywa*, since you miraculously know him so well then!" sneered Nasr, echoing Jayida's thoughts. "Why don't we ask his wife, or shall we say wives? Who knows how many there are, not counting the endless flings, of which *you* wanted to be one," scowled Nasr.

"I know how it looks, but it wasn't like that," said Yazida sadly. Was that regret in her voice?

"I hate to say it, beloved sister, but you know as well as I that if he wanted you, he had only to speak to *yaba* on the matter, the right way. And yet, he didn't. Unless, of course, it was a secretive *mot'a* matter on which we've yet to hear a thing from either of you. Was it?" said Nasr.

Yazida shook her head. "No. I mean; he didn't say *suitor*."

"By *al-ilah*, I wonder why," said Nasr.

Yazida lifted her chin, mirroring his frown. "He said he's dejected and embarrassed. Wants to marry me, but after he comes back with more to show for it."

"And you believe him. And for what? What can he give except verses, drama, and longing? Can he protect you?"

"A child is still worth all that," Yazida's voice nearly cracked. All this time she'd thought of that while Jayida hoped to delay it for herself as long as possible.

Nasr's face darkened. "If there is even one! How could you be so selfish? If we hadn't arrived on time and he'd gotten you with child without *yaba*'s knowledge of your intent, who knows what he would've done for your disrespect! After everything he does for you! The deception would've still hurt, even if he'd likely relent in his constant kindness. And if children are what you so suddenly want, there's no shortage of choices here!"

"He's not like others, and you know it!" Yazida frowned.

"How true that is. I'll remind you that, despite what dreamy images he can conjure, you're still flesh and blood and need food to survive. It remains that what you both did is wrong, but since I can happily wish, too, perhaps he'll come back having properly asked our *yaba* for you," said Nasr. He rose and walked off, shaking his head. "I'm making another round," he said, and slipped out of the tent to make sure no one caught them unaware.

"Jonder, I know you might look at me differently now. But as the sister of your closest friend, please believe me. Tell him, convince him that I'm telling the truth. I didn't mean to disrespect or dishonor anyone," said Yazida.

"I don't think it's you he doubts as much as Imru. But as your brother wisely pointed out, and with you looking so sad, I can hardly understand your draw to him," said Jayida.

Yazida looked away. "Uff! You don't know what it's like to always be caged up, never able to go anywhere. I've noticed Shams's interest in me but I don't know that I feel the same. I just wanted a moment with Imru, even if no one else approved. I can't explain it, and *na'am*: even with the consequences."

Jayida rolled her eyes. "Clearly he's gotten to your head because you're not making any sense."

"It's easy for you to say. You don't ever feel anything!"

"*Esh?* What did you say, Yazida? I don't feel anything? What do you know about what I feel!" Fire pulsed through Jayida as Yazida's vanity rushed at her like a torrent.

"Nothing, because you don't show it," pouted Yazida.

"And that's the same as not feeling, then! Tell me more about myself and my feelings, that you know as well as your perfect Imru's!" sneered Jayida.

"I mean it's easy to misunderstand—"

"Precisely, as your brother rightly said!" shot Jayida, struggling to watch her tone. "Perhaps it hasn't occurred to you that maybe it's not your task to understand in the middle of chaos, but to obey! We often don't have time to show feelings; we're too busy thinking of solutions to survive, so that you can live, and try to manipulate others by showing *your* feelings while you dwell in your trouble-free castle-tent!"

"I'm sorry, Jonder. I didn't mean to upset you all. You're right, I do live in my thoughts. But don't we all?" said Yazida.

"In a sense, but your childish gullible ways blind you to danger. You don't realize how dangerous that was. What if there were wild animals or bandits roaming about? Or both, since I hardly need remind you some bandits make such beasts their pets! Even your prince had years of experience to get to you." Jayida frowned, recalling how Nasr had slipped into their tent and caught her unaware that same night.

"I—wasn't going to say it, but I had a knife with me," blurted Yazida.

"Oh? And you would've used it on him?" Jayida raised her brow.

"On whoever required it. It's better than nothing," said Yazida.

"*Sah*. I'm glad you thought of that at least," said Jayida with a smirk. Still, she had to ask. "Did he force in any way?"

"No, he didn't." Yazida looked away and Jayida fixed on her, crossed her arms, awaiting the rest.

"If any of my traits displease you, tear off my clothes from yours and let us make a new skin. Such tormented words! I wanted to know what it's like to kiss the lips of one who imagines such things," said Yazida with shaking voice.

"And was it as magical as you expected?" said Jayida after a brief pause, trying to sound playful rather than mocking. She'd hardly remembered the line of his *qasidah*, and hadn't really thought about who Yazida might be interested in, but didn't think he'd look like Imru.

"For a moment, I thought it was. I knew I might never have the chance again. But it's not just that. There's something so sad about him."

"So he's shown us all, though if it was genuine—" Jayida shook her head. No matter how she turned it, it seemed the closest she could get to the truth was that none of them truly knew him, or each glimpsed different parts that she could only hope had been honest. "And yet, was he worthy of being saved from his misery by you, I wonder. Was it worth it for you?"

"*Na'am*. What is life if not to give another soul a moment of love, no matter how brief it might be," said Yazida, lost in space.

Jayida stared, touched at this first display of deep affection from her friend's sister whom she only saw at intervals. Was Yazida already in love, as little as each of them knew of it? But something about its rushed impulsivity—the opposite of self-control—seemed childish, and therefore misleading. That Yazida would selflessly give her affection was both endearing and a little repulsive, fueling her reluctance.

They heard a rush of determined steps, indicating Nasr's return.

"So, do you believe me?" said Yazida.

"*Na'am*," nodded Jayida, and smiled as the wave of relief came over Yazida.

The steps outside came to a stop, and Nasr appeared.

"Clearly I have a gift for catching people right on time," he said. "They're just now heading back, with Imru's slayed gazelle as a timely parting gift, although if there's more news to add, we'll see," added Nasr, with a side glance to his sister. "Remember that if we're tough with you, it's to protect you. There's much darkness you don't know about, and though you may not like it sometimes, that's what we're trying to keep you from. Maybe my giving you freedom to practice-fight with us is misleading you; not many other brothers would do as much. If you ever want to roam at night, you have us to ask for that! You don't just wander off without consent, even if it's some prince whisking you away on his verses," said Nasr in his serious, yet lighter air.

"*Na'am*, brother. Please forgive me," cooed Yazida, and they knew by Nasr's tone that his anger had dissipated and considered it a closed matter.

The situation had been contained, even if Jayida suspected that Yazida might think of Imru a while yet. But to evade suspicion, any emotion Yazida had about him would have to be concealed, like a dream she might often revisit. But that she at least had her own brother in on the secret was a gift in itself. Still, Jayida dared to think that Imru might keep his word, and come back in the future. Of all the things, she hoped he'd been truthful when he'd said as much to Yazida.

Together they emerged out of the tent, and Yazida rushed back to her mother to announce the news of Imru's departure. Jayida smirked, pleased that her mother, cued in on the events, had done her part in keeping Warda engaged during their interrogation. The news of the departure now spreading, the women lingered behind as the men all gathered closer to the returning poet and his companions.

"Imru's dawn hunt was blessed, and he's honoring us with these two gazelles as a parting gift," said *sayyid* Aziz, patting the poet's shoulders. Her father appeared, luring the three camels he'd chosen to gift to Imru and his companions. Zahir pet and cooed at them and Jayida swallowed back emotion as they affectionately blew in his face in imminent goodbye.

"You're leaving us?" said Nasr, feigning surprise.

"*Na'am*. I cannot thank you enough for your hospitality, but I must make my way north, get things in order sooner rather than later," said Imru. "It may be selfish of me, but I hope that part of you will follow me like my own faithful shadow." It might've been her wishful thinking, but Jayida hoped she was right in thinking he sounded sincere.

"If you ask, then you may count on it," said Nasr, amusing her with the double meaning of the words that recalled his nightly decree that he'd come after the poet if necessary.

"I hope you'll accept my thanks. It's been so tiring to leave on bad terms, but I wish you to know that I treasure the time I spent here. With all the places I've been it's still rare that I can say this," said Imru.

Even now as he frowned, she was sure it was to control his emotion, rather than from manipulation. But even if he was being dishonest, she knew the true blessing of being among the Banu Sa'd, of all tribes. She could only marvel how different things might be if he was staying longer.

"May they help you on your path," said her father, handing him the camels' reigns. His jaw tightening, Imru accepted with a light bow, while Asheer and Atiyah nodded gratefully.

"May you have blessed travels, and we hope to see you again," said *sayyid* Aziz. "Stay, and weep with me at the memory of one beloved—" the *sayyid* crooned the opening of Imru's poem, and kissed the poet on each cheek. Imru frowned, bit his thick lips, and in the lingering silence she froze, reading his hesitating features for signs of something more to say.

But he only nodded, blinking fast, and without another word, Imru and his companions mounted on their camels loaded with the Banu Sa'd's culinary love packed into varied, colorfully dyed bundles. Jayida suspected he'd made a point to know which were from Yazida and her mother Warda, and surely included pigeon pies made from her flock. Imru gave a last wave and turned away, averting his gaze that surely would've revealed more emotion than any of them could take.

Gradually, the conflicted poet and his two friends shrank on the horizon. But if they'd both agreed to a *mot'a* marriage, where Yazida would've kept the offspring, then why didn't Imru just say it? How hard had it been to say *suitor*, for her to reply *I wed* and accomplish the marriage without witnesses when he'd had so many conquests?

Seduced by the poet's reputation and skill, some would've been all too boastful of having their women chased, and even better, impregnated by the princely poet himself. *More warrior poets for the tribe!*—assuming sons came of it. That Nasr was as kind as his father was evident in his reaction, for clearly, to approach a man with interest regarding his daughter and to sneak off with her were two very different things. Imru's brooding line about seizing any happiness resurfaced in her mind in a different light, and was certainly no excuse for what he'd done.

Still, Jayida wanted to believe that this time it was different for Imru, with Yazida inspiring him to something more permanent, and helped ease some of the bittersweet parting.

"Let's get these prepared," said *sayyid* Aziz after a moment, and Nasr glanced at her, then followed him with the gazelles in hand.

Her father drew to her side, each heavy with contemplation. "May his story change for the better," he said.

"*Aywa*. And even if the circumstances for his departure were similar to others, I'd be willing to bet that this was his nicest-hardest one yet," sighed Jayida.

CHAPTER FOURTEEN

BANU TAYYI

EARLY SUMMER 541 – JABAL TAYYI

Chants of praise filled the space, pleasing Khaled as much as his warrior attire adorning his massive body. With pride he glanced at Majid and their fellow tribesmen. The metal breastplates strapped under their thick cloaks, and swords from Bosra at their waists only added to their already large frames and commanding airs. Time was on his side, adding to his prideful glory, starting with his expanding body.

Clouds of frankincense hovered, drifting closer with each person. At each stop it lingered, engulfing the receiver in spiraling sweet, musky fragrance that coiled around their innermost, whispered desires.

At last Khaled held it, the bronze burner with a decorative ibex emerging from the top sitting heavy in his hands. He lifted one side of his headscarf, stretching it like a small tent, and drew it closer to his face, the rich smoke washing over him, inundating him with a pleasant dizziness.

He closed his eyes.

What did he want? Battle? Glory? Riches? Poetry? Women? All of them? But even as the affirmative answer formed, he wondered what his punishment would be for this incomplete answer. What if the answer was no, or something else he didn't yet know? He almost laughed at the poet part: he was no smooth-talking *sha'ir*, at least not yet, and from the way he'd seen it emerge painlessly in others, he wasn't sure he would ever be.

Glory to Banu Zubayd!, echoed the songs, challenging him. But it was just fear talking, it had to be. Conflict raged again, as it always did, sending the Rûm and Fars clashing, each through their own allied clients of *badawi*. And there were

188

some tribesmen of Zubayd, he among them, reconvening with their mighty kin the Tayyi, ready to show support and assist in any way.

In time they would see real battle, Majid reminded him, and Khaled felt pride to be able to fight alongside such a fighter, one he deemed even better than himself, and who so loyally said the same about him. The more time passed, the more he treasured this friendship whose hints of competition were all camaraderie rather than malice.

The frankincense tears fizzled, and warm, tangy sweetness filled his lungs, as a determined hand slithered over him.

Were you just going to leave without a word? Layali moaned into his ear, pulling herself up onto him.

We shall make you proud, he mumbled, caught off guard.

I expect nothing less than glory, said Layali. Her thigh lifted up around his hips, her exposed smooth skin sliding out from under her skirt. Her cheek grazing his, her hot breath closed in on him, biting his lips and kissing him so hard he thought she'd swallow the life out of him. She took his hand and slipped it under her untied tunic, exposing the bulging upper mound of her full breasts. With gusto, her fingers knead into his hand, inviting him to mold her fiery flesh.

For inspiration, hissed Layali, her words rattling through him. The rush set his body on fire, tormenting him. Did he want, or did he not? With difficulty, his hands gripped her gyrating waist and firmly pushed her away, breaking the burning spell.

Grunting, Khaled took a moment to gather himself from the familiar dream. Striking though she was, there was something draining about Layali, like a beautiful *kahina* who consumed her target's life force to fuel her own insatiable need. If he was to accomplish great things, he needed all the energy he could get to focus and grow in strength. That Majid not only understood it, but shared his wish to concentrate on fighting only confirmed his decision. Some teased others for such exaggerated, so-called 'Udhrah or Ghassanid-like chaste restraint, justifying it as part of their natural needs. But if that piety helped the Ghassanids reach their powerful military status and endurance, then there had to be truth to it. He imagined that Nuha, his friend's sister and the other potential wifely contender, would understand that, too, and something about that thought warmed him.

Khaled rose and quickly dressed, relishing the cool dawn mountain air that contrasted the Banu Zubayd camp's climate further northeast. He greeted his mare Aminah and his Zahir mount Sadiqa, promising he'd soon return. Without a glance to his sword Al-Fatih, he grabbed a bag of his mother's *maamoul* pastries and left his tent, a sharp glance at the dark grey vast camp indicating most were still asleep.

The Tayyi's summer gathering—and in case of any greedy move by Al-Mundhir—was more than he'd needed to finally come. With the Tayyi's multiple alliances, everyday new visitors arrived, swelling what was already a large confederate of tribes. The Shammar Mountains were so full of Tayyi, spread along the red-orange Jabal Aja and the grey-black Jabal Salma mountain ranges, that they were more simply called Jabal Tayyi after them.

As Khaled had every morning since he'd arrived, he let the relief of his father's absence wash over him, promising another rewarding day of cavorting these vast, varied plains with Majid and other tribesmen, both proud kin and non-kin alike. He and Majid had gladly pitched their tents with the Al-Ghawth branch of the Tayyi and, like guests before them, were treated to a generous welcome from *sayyid* Abdallah and his son Hatim, whose own extremely selfless nature was already fast becoming legend. It added to his pride to be allowed to train his eleven-year-old son Adiyy in the honorable fighting arts.

Khaled arrived to Majid's tent, its overhangs already pinned back in invitation.

"Look who's up," said Majid. He draped his mantle over his wide shoulders, and lifted out his messy bun of long ebony waves. "Long night?"

"You would know; you were there," winked Khaled. His friend's tent was as bare as his own, a happy reminder they were away from home.

"Some of the best memories," sighed Majid, casting him amused side glances.

"My strong friend, whom nothing can disturb. Someday it'll be my turn to tease you about women," said Khaled, rubbing his face.

"I doubt it, but until then, I don't mind postponing it and leaving it to you," said Majid, and kissed his golden amulet of Mikha'il at his neck.

"Careful my self-assured friend; they say the most controlled ones are the most tormented."

"We'll see, then," smirked Majid, making them both laugh. "You could also just marry my sister and be done with it."

"Your dear Nuha is surely too good for me," said Khaled. The opposite of Layali in nature, Nuha was no less a beauty. But her gentleness and reserve was such that he sensed the gap between them too wide, and that he'd have to mind his manners so much that he might not be himself around her at all. With conflicted reluctance he had to agree when his father said that just because Majid was his best friend didn't mean he had to marry his sister.

"*Sah*, but you're allowed to dream," Majid grinned and pat his shoulder.

Quietly they left the tent and walked to the beckoning As-Samra peak, the wisps of smoke swirling from the mountaintop visible from a distance. The arduous climb, dotted with shrubs amidst the gritty clay-infused sand, made great exercise, and Khaled noted with satisfaction that he was already getting used to it. He reached the top, happily panting and absorbing the majestic view.

Directly north lay a patch of dark hills, flanked to the northwest by a large stretch of red-stoned mountains surrounding the Jabal Aja peak. On cool early mornings that promised fair days ahead, clouds hovered above its slopes, blanketing the green palm trees and colocynth viny plants in dew. He'd yet to join some of his kinsmen in the evenings to its sanctuary and shrine of the deity Al-Fals, located on the site, but assured himself that he had plenty of time.

Just beyond it lay Jubbah, its large sandstone outcrops and inscriptions emerging from the Nefud sand covering the ancient lake bed. Further to the east dwelled the Banu Tamim and Banu Rabia, beyond which lay the Lakhmid-Nasrid court at Al-Hira.

Behind him to the south, the Jabal Salma Mountains to the southeast completed the stretch of the Shammar Mountains. Stories danced before him, reciting of the ancient residents of Jabal Salma, and Fayd east of it, who carved into its native grey-black basalt stone for structures, inscriptions, and graffiti. Khaled searched the horizon, bringing forth the Harrat Hutaymah lava field that lay out of sight further southeast. He recalled the tales of the volcanic area's cones and vents, gushing forth with fiery smoke and lava so long ago, before men even roamed the land. Rings still dotted the landscape, the nonhuman traces testifying to the land's movements.

A frown curbed his brow. Further south still, past the Unayzatan Mountains and towards the mountains of Al-Jiwa, were the Banu 'Abs. It might be another rare thing on which he agreed with his father: that the boisterous 'Abs led by *sayyid* Zoheir was one tribe to keep an eye on. A defiant resolve filled Khaled, grateful to be among his brave and numerous kinsmen who roamed this delightfully strange wild place, and were as welcoming as they were protective of their own dwelling.

"Ah, my first guests of the day," said Hatim, appearing a few paces away in his wide-opened tent. Beaming like a wise man in his cream robes, Hatim gestured for them to join him around the fire. Khaled had taken an instant liking to the bright-eyed poet, who though almost twice his age, looked younger. Crowned with his unhurried, poised manner, Khaled decided that it was his generous spirit that made him think of little else than helping and giving to others. In some it might be a well-played ruse to deter the evil eye, but as the most relaxed person Khaled had ever met, Hatim's sincerity prevented him from pretending.

"Perhaps the only guests?" smirked Khaled in playful selfishness, and offered him the bag of *maamoul* cookies.

"*Aywa*, noble Hatim. And what if no one came? Would you stay here and wait?" said Majid.

Hatim chuckled. "There are always guests," he said, and his features took on a dreamy air as he carefully arranged the *maamoul* into a straw basket like some imaginary mosaic. "We must always be ready to help those in need, or even passing angels in disguise, as Yassu *al-Masih* says." He patted his chest, upon which rested a golden amulet etched with a cross.

Khaled at once admired and envied his faith that gave him an air of conviction, an ease of moving through life that he often feared he lacked and struggled with.

"So Majid, tell me the reason for your friend's troubles," grinned Hatim, handing them bread and milk.

"What else could it be? A woman is invading his night visions," said Majid.

"Ah, love. The source of all torment and happiness," nodded Hatim with a humbled air.

"That's just it. He's not sure it's love, or even a woman at all," Majid smirked.

"How did *you* know when she was the one?" said Khaled.

"There are endless variations, and yet, the difference is there. And it calls to you, so you will know. My Mawiyah inspired me, made me feel things I'd never felt before. All love stories are like this. Even so, nothing is easy, not even marriage. Sometimes she gets so upset with my ways that, fearing for our future, she threatens she'll leave me. I don't know what would break my heart most: for the tent to be turned away or empty, so I pray for neither and for her to grow patient in understanding," said Hatim.

"Are women never satisfied? Is love not enough?" said Khaled.

"It must be, if all life is love—different forms of love. But there comes a time when man must ask himself which love he wants to dedicate himself to most. She knew about my giving nature when we married, and she swore that it was what she loved most about me. With all this, she will not take our son if she wishes to leave. I pray Yassu keeps blessing my father Abdallah, whose generosity spreads over the whole tribe. If I am to take up after him as *sayyid* someday, and our son Adiyy after me, I wish to honor his name and the tribe's," said Hatim firmly.

"Surely Yassu will hear your prayers, and by then we'll visit with our families too," nodded Khaled, glancing at the quietly contemplating Majid.

"*Aywa*, how nice that would be," said Hatim.

"You are too good for this world, dear Hatim," said Majid.

Khaled was tempted to add that the loss would be hers, but refrained out of respect. Talking with Hatim had a way of reassuring him even as it laid out life's complications. The absurdity of women's displeasure and fickleness came to mind, considering that if some easily criticized a man's stinginess, generosity was no less spared. If Hatim chose to ignore the natural balance of giving and taking, choosing instead to do as Yassu did and giving more than his fair share away, at least he had been honest from the beginning about his faithful ways.

Curiously, even as Hatim made him feel like he'd never reach his level of giving, there was no condemnation in it. Each man walked his path and set his own limits. Khaled was well aware, and unashamed of his own attachments, and if and when he wanted to give some of it away, he would. As Hatim said, he would know when the time came, and until then he would try to enjoy his life as he could.

Hatim's gaze fell behind them towards the bend of the hill, followed by his widening smile. "Someone's coming!" Hatim squealed.

The sound of crunched gravel grew louder, and a thick-lipped, dark-clad man emerged. His open mouth seemed on the verge of words when he bent at the waist and knelt forward with hands on his knees.

"You wild Tayyi—perching—atop your mountains like eagles," panted the frowning newcomer, waving in annoyance as if to call breath into his lungs.

"Praise Yassu! Imru Al-Qays has returned!" Hatim darted to him and Majid mirrored Khaled's open-mouthed surprise.

"Generous, *sah*; with pain too, making me climb up here," mumbled Imru, straightening up. His use of a southern accent that Khaled nearly strained to understand added a comical effect.

"That's what happens when you spend too much time amidst stone castles and parties, instead of here with me," laughed Hatim. His wide sleeves stretched over in embrace, then grabbed his friend's face and kissed him on each cheek. Khaled and Majid perked up at the sight of the two men, one brooding in dark clothing and the other as bright as the sun, both of them married poets around the same age from tribes whose ancient roots stretched far.

With a pang Khaled noticed that all that remained of Imru's princely lineage adorned his body, from his fine attire, his sword at his waist, and some jeweled rings on his hands. As the stories spread of Imru's revenge on the Asad for his father Hujr's killing, his loyal retinue had long since thinned and scattered across the land. The disloyalty disgusted Khaled, and despite his own troubles with his father, he dreaded to think of the kind of person Hujr had been. But at least Imru still had Hatim to count as a friend, a worthy balm amidst his struggles.

"Come, come," said Hatim, waving them over to the poet-prince. "Surely Asheer and Atiyah—"

"Are with your blessed father," said Imru. "My good friend, forgive me that I cannot be long. Seeing as I don't wish to draw attention—*aywa*; a miracle—you'll later find my reason for coming awaiting you with him."

"And yet since you are here, you want to be held at least a little bit," smiled Hatim. "So come and meet these brave young men."

Imru reclined next to them and nodded at each, his piercing dark gaze a mix of pain and intense alertness.

"Here is Khaled, son of Moharib of the Banu Zubayd, and Majid, son of Abjar, also of the Zubayd," said Hatim. He offered Imru milk and bread, which Imru accepted, as Khaled and Majid exchanged mutual greetings and blessings with the famous princely poet. "So, my wayward friend, where have you been?" smirked Hatim.

"We just came from Khaybar, where the comforts of that beautiful oasis and *nasi* Musa made it easy to linger a while," said Imru. Recovered from the hike, he now spoke evenly in their dialect, a smoldering poetic bearing gradually return- ing. "That had been by recommendation of *sayyid* Aziz of the Banu Sa'd, where we were before then. That tribe lavished us in food, and the *sayyid*'s friend Zahir kindly gifted us three camels, one of which is yours," said Imru.

Khaled perked up. "The Banu Sa'd? So you met Zahir and his son Jonder?"

Imru fixed on him. Was that a flickering tremor that shot through the poet?

"I did." His dark eyes flickered to Hatim. "The thought might've even occurred to me that Zahir might rival you in generosity," chuckled Imru, and gulped his milk.

"Praise Yassu that our kind thrives," beamed Hatim.

Khaled met Majid's surprise, and turned back on the visiting poet. "That's great news. What were they like?"

Imru smirked. "You seem as approving as you are surprised. How is that?"

"It so happens that Zahir is my *amo* and Jonder my cousin. But I've never met them, as they've been with the Banu Sa'd since I was a child. So you can imagine my curiosity," said Khaled.

Imru nodded, and Khaled sensed that he understood the unspoken complexity of family ties when he himself had struggled so much with his own closest kin.

"They were very welcoming, and your lion-eyed cousin is a budding *kahin*, too. I've been to many tribes in recent moons, and that's one of the few where I felt truly welcomed as a person; and not just for what I might bring or for the Kindah royal line I represent," said Imru with a nostalgic air.

Caught by his words, a pang of jealous longing struck Khaled, imagining what it would've been like if he'd been there too, alongside his *amo* and cousin, audience to the finest, if at times controversial and troublesome, poet in all the land. With Jonder also a *kahin*, the urge to visit only burned in him even more.

"If you ever do visit, I think it'll be worth it," said Imru, reading his mind. Khaled wanted to ask, or even joke, why he'd left at all, but decided against it.

"And where are you headed?" said Hatim, gesturing invitingly to the *maamoul.*

"I've been advised to meet with Samaw'al ibn Adiya, who through his kin-ties could arrange a meeting with *malik* Al-Harith at Bosra," said Imru. He bit into half the *maamoul* and with eyebrow raised, finished it with a second bite in nodding approval.

"Khaled's mother Khamra will be so honored to hear that you enjoyed her pastries," said Majid, as Khaled offered him another that Imru accepted.

"*Aywa*, a sound plan. If any man can help, it would be *malik* Al-Harith," said Hatim. "He's often sent us his envoys to settle peaceful agreements, which many among us love to boast of. And you'll surely love his marble recital hall at their capital city of Jabiyah, adorned in mosaics, as they say. But remember: keep your poetry chaste. They're even more Yassu-loving than I am," chuckled Hatim.

"Is that possible? But there's no fear of me forgetting when the warning follows me everywhere," laughed Imru.

Khaled leaned in. "Please send my greeting to Samaw'al and his son Hassan. While my father Moharib is certainly there to assist you if needed, I imagine that poets naturally gravitate to each other," said Khaled, nearly certain that Imru grasped his meaning. His own father might be easier than Hujr, but with their distinct types of harsh discipline, he mused that Moharib at least partially agreed with Hujr's strict methods.

"I shall," said Imru, and with averted gaze he rubbed his hands, then braced them on his knees and propped himself up. "As always, my dear Hatim, words will fail me with you, but I must be going—"

"To the memory of one beloved?" said Hatim. "We will see you off then."

"My good friend; whose drawn-out goodbyes I welcome as much as their sincerity," said Imru, and locked an arm around Hatim's.

Khaled and Majid followed the poets down into the valley and the gradually stirring camp, the sight of the camels outside of *sayyid* Abdallah's tent pleasing Khaled. With their cheerful demeanors, thick healthy humps, and *wasm* on their back right leg, he nearly swore he'd recognize them anywhere. With a renewed pinch of conflicted envy, he guessed that the addition of the half moon-shaped bow to the disk and spear *wasm* had to be for Jonder.

Aside from his mother, no one knew better than Majid how much he longed to visit the Banu Sa'd, and this seemed yet another sign to do it. Khaled wondered what his father would say of this chance encounter, even as a part of him considered he might delay sharing it, or maybe not even say anything at all.

At *sayyid* Abdallah's tent, the greetings of Hatim's companions, the elderly Asheer and the youthful Atiyah, gradually transformed as their hosts reluctantly embraced them all in warm goodbye.

"What do you think? If our wives evade us, perhaps Yassu will one day reunite them at their Banu Tamim," said Hatim, eyeing Imru.

"At least they would be together, even if in complaints. As for me, I'll keep reminding of the wise Proverb that says it's best to be alone in the desert than with a nagging wife," Imru shook his head. He turned to Khaled and Majid. "As for you, young men, may we meet again someday in better circumstances."

"We'll be praying for it," said Khaled.

"May your travels be safe," said Majid.

"Remember Yassu sometimes, prince of Kindah," said Hatim.

"Hmm," sighed Imru. "In every place is Your mysterious Presence, *al-ilah*, and from every place You are withdrawn. Though Your mysterious Presence be in the height, yet it feels not that You are what You are."

Hatim nodded. "Though Your mysterious Presence be in the sea, from the sea You are concealed: though Your mysterious Presence be in the dry land, it knows not that You are He. Blessed be the glorious hidden One, since even Your little mystery is a fountain of mysteries!" Hatim smiled. "I'm glad to see that Saint Ephrem's *qareen* will also accompany you on your journey."

They exchanged a final nod, and Hatim's pinched smile followed their retreating forms as he waved them off. After a few moments, Imru turned his mount around to them and exclaimed: "Oh, how I shall weep thinking of blessed Tayyi!"

His eyes watering, Hatim chuckled and waved as Imru turned back to his friends, his clear emotion touching Khaled. Leaving Hatim to his thoughts, Khaled and Majid made off to retrieve some weapons and join the fighting tents that lay on the other, eastern side of camp, the rising sun following their movements.

"My warrior friend, already lost in his plans," smirked Majid.

"I'll take their visit as a good omen; I know you do, too," said Khaled, and playfully shoved his friend.

So what if they both had to restrain their urge to talk of the elusive poet they'd just met, laden with choice camels from his uncle and cousin? At least it was between them, if only for the time being, and with bittersweet feeling Khaled concluded that not everything had to be shared with the world to be enjoyed. Thankfully, as brief as their encounter had been, there was a kind of solace in the connection and sympathy he felt for the poet, whom he hoped they'd see again. Khaled wavered, wanting to honor his own father for not ever banishing him and giving him all he needed, while knowing that the dark coldness in him had always been, and would always be, present.

The morning elapsed in a series of jousts, with boys and men routinely lining up to fight him and Majid. As usual they kept it firm yet playful, instructing on wrong moves here, and demonstrating better tactics there. Perhaps it had been his own early training, but Khaled sometimes felt like it was too easy—and was often somewhat sad and disappointed that others, especially older than him, didn't already know what they did.

In the reeking, sweaty heat, contorted grimaces of blowing nostrils, swollen reddened cheeks, and altered limbs caught in chokeholds and twisted forms, Khaled saw little competition, but a field of learning, where each man could come out stronger. With a satisfying defiance he wondered what his father would say, if he knew that his son didn't want to defeat anyone in the traditional way, but wanted everyone to learn and grow together. It was not a competition to be on the elusive top, but skill enough to avoid the deadly blow to survive and go on to the next challenge. And all the better if he made friends rather than enemies along the way.

But for all his imagined goodness and selflessness—if that's even what it was, though he hoped part of it was—Khaled couldn't deny that he loved the pride that came from showing his skill and earning the respect of the fighters. It had only added to his stature and to the spread of his name among the Tayyi, and while he and Majid took turns letting themselves be defeated, he kept waiting for that undefinable, crushing challenge that had yet to come.

At midday they called for a break, and Khaled left the fighting tent for his own space. Amidst his pleasant stroll, he glimpsed a bustling gathering around a tribesman's tent. He was just going to pass it by when the sight of a camel outside it made him wonder if he'd taken a harder hit than he'd thought. Adorned in a long, woven ornament around the neck attached to the riding litter, the striking woolen cloth made varied shapes of pyramids and cubes in saffron, crimson, and cream—his mother's favorite.

The good times are never long enough, he lamented, repressing a deep coiling snarl.

Khaled hadn't even entered the tent when he heard his father's booming voice, his tone as commanding as inflexible. Of course his father had likely come with only a few submissive companions, leaving *sha'ir* Hakim and Ajbar to watch the Banu Zubayd. Even if the elder wasn't getting on in age, Khaled couldn't imagine why the *sha'ir* would want to travel with his father. His jaw tense, Khaled slipped into the tent.

"You tricked me! The real dye does not fade, and the crimson-black glows red-purple in the sun. Is this how you do business, giving honest men cheap, fake garments?" spat the stranger with a northern accent. Though a full head shorter than Moharib, he made up for it in passion and Khaled instantly guessed that he would not back down.

His poised father showed not a hint of annoyance. "My *badawi* brother, I share your frustration. But the rules of *mulamasa* trade are clear: once you touch the bundled item, you've bought it," said Moharib. "We have both been deceived, when I've only just acquired it and didn't even think to inspect it myself. I'm no less a victim than you!"

The man shook his head. "This will not do. My three fat-tailed Awassi are worth far more than this cloth. I demand compensation," scowled the man longingly at the sheeps gathered behind Moharib.

"The deal has been made. You know the rules," said Moharib with a wave of the hand. Just then Khaled met his father's piercing glance, silently accusing *Where have you been!*

Without thinking twice, Khaled stepped forward between them.

"Kind man, allow me to introduce myself. I'm Khaled, honorable *sayyid* Moharib's son," he said with a humble bow. "Please don't be upset. This is unfortunate, and yet, as per the rules, we know that he maintains the right to keep the creatures. However, if you will allow, I offer myself at your service to recuperate your loss by hunting, so that you shall not leave empty-handed," said Khaled, his father next to him as solid as a stone.

The stranger's eyes narrowed, glancing at them back and forth. After a moment, his shoulders relaxed, and he nodded in agreement. A gust of approving voices surrounded them, the witnesses whispering among themselves.

"I accept, young Khaled. I am Imran of the Kalb. You shall find my tent camped west of *sayyid* Abdallah's."

"I would find you at all costs," said Khaled, relieved by the man's firm yet friendly nod, then retreated in the crowd.

Khaled casually glanced at his father, hoping that his light smile looked as humble as he intended it to be. But his father's demeanor remained blank as ever; the blameless righteous man who had no reason for remorse. With a familiar pang Khaled realized that even after all this time, it still stung that his father hardly ever showed any emotion, least of all approval.

Khaled wasn't sure which was worse: to be denied that basic paternal support or to know that he would make up for his father's deceitfulness, and this time among an even a larger group of witnesses than the Banu Zubayd. Because he knew that his father was lying, but he'd never betray him, at least not in public.

Disappointed frustration filled him, that the man he was meant to look up to often deceived men in trade, using the desperation and lax laws as justification. Khaled had always been expected to side with his father in all things, but as he got older it was getting harder for him to remain indifferent when every man struggled for his living. With all the abundance his father had amassed, why wasn't it enough?

Khaled imagined the eternal wheel of fear turning in his soul; demanding he gather as much for himself, in exchange for safety—at least until the Fateful day when he finally had to pay for all he'd done to others. But who knew when that would be—and who better than the deities to know and understand his own righteous needs? So he was justified to rule with an iron fist that stretched his cloak over many tribesmen. That had to be rewarded, too—Khaled already heard his defensive refrain.

From the first time Khaled had witnessed his father's deceitful dealing with traders passing through Tayma, he'd decided he'd never be that man. Even if his Moharib had his reasons, time was only showing how different they were as men. But even such a resolution couldn't lessen his guilt at such a feeling towards his father, so he held back from judgment, looked the other way. He would defend him and stand by him, and maybe even make him proud, although with self-deprecating humor he counted less and less on that. Nevertheless, he had given his word, and would stand by it.

Khaled left and alerted Majid, who immediately agreed to join him on the hunt, as he always did. They rested a bit and ate, then packed their weapons and set off on their mounts in the late afternoon. They rode off into the western hills covered in shrubs, and came upon the *wadi* whose red earth and stones emerged along the banks and through the water.

In silence they continued, and after a while they came upon a flock of drinking oryx, their cream bodies standing out among the dark rocky and saffron surroundings. They looked up and glanced at them with a mix of curiosity and alertness. With gratitude it came to Khaled that even they weren't strictly innocent creatures, with their pointy striated horns strong enough to kill lions. Majid signaled he was riding ahead and away from their sight.

Khaled gripped his spear and gently guided Sadiqa onwards, whispering to her in soothing coaxing. He approached and waited patiently, lingering to get them acquainted to his presence. After a while they seemed resolved to him and strolled on, while some rested in shallow holes.

Caught between guilt and duty, Khaled kicked Sadiqa in the flanks, and with a sudden burst, the flock scattered as he fell upon a large male with short, thick horns. With his focused aim and eagle-gaze on the front leg, he launched his spear and struck straight into the oryx's shoulder, and repeated the hit a few more times for safety's sake. He slipped off Sadiqa, covered the shed blood with dirt to deter any *jinn*, and with a grunt, lifted and draped the warm beast on his mount. He turned to the rumble ahead, and saw Majid lampooning his own oryx, a smaller female with longer and skinnier horns.

He followed his friend riding back to him with a grin. While he saw through his father's forced nonchalance, Majid's natural easiness was enviable.

"Here, add this one to your spoils," said Majid back at his side, handing him the female.

"I can get my own female!" spat Khaled with feigned revulsion, barely recognizing himself.

"*Sah*, you can. But this one is a gift, to go along with your own today. He can boast of having been gifted a pair of oryx; no small reward, especially with the horns," said Majid.

"And who am I to argue with your wisdom," smirked Khaled. He mounted Sadiqa and together rode back to camp.

With a hint of conflict Khaled wondered how much his friend suspected about his father. It wasn't from lack of trust that he'd yet to tell him about it, and part of him suspected that he knew, and respected the difficult situation by refraining from mentioning it. Everyone knew Moharib's hard nature, so not everything could be surprising.

With some envy Khaled thought of Majid's father Abjar, who was trusted by Moharib enough to be left behind, along with *sha'ir* Hakim. Though surely Moharib was reluctant of Abjar, as he was of everyone, and especially other skilled men, what was certain was that Abjar was no man to be taken lightly. Khaled may not say it aloud, but if his father had any potential adversary, it was Abjar, and he could hardly fault the good man for it. At times he even thought Abjar would make a better *sayyid* than his father, or at least a much kinder one. But even Khaled had to stop himself there, when the Zubayd were no betraying Asad, waiting to cowardly slay a *sayyid* in his sleep like they'd done to Imru's father. Despite Moharib's faults, the Zubayd's loyalty had never failed, and Khaled prided himself that it never would.

Back at camp they made directly for Imran's tent, and Majid waited as Khaled presented the slain beasts to the seated trader, surrounded by his fellow Kalb tribesmen.

"Kind Imran, do these please you?" said Khaled with a light bow.

"By Yassu, they do," said Imran, and stroked their strong bodies in gratitude.

A wave of grateful relief washed over Khaled that while some men were stubborn and perpetually displeased, there were others who were easily forgiving.

"It warms my heart, and I pray your visit among the Tayyi fills with more pleasant memories," said Khaled, hoping he wasn't asking for too much.

"If everyone were as eager as you to please, few would hold grudges," chuckled Imran. He stood up and embraced Khaled, and planted a kiss on each cheek. "Your father has a good son," said Imran. The ultimate compliment touched Khaled as much as the surrounding approval around him.

Khaled gave a final nod and departed, and with Majid beaming at him like an older brother, they spent the rest of the day cavorting in the tents, letting any happy gossip spread without them. While he wasn't exactly glad that his father had come, the problem had been resolved, and likewise Imru wouldn't run into Moharib during his visit to Samaw'al.

How curious that even amidst the long summers of simple sameness and repetition, there could be days full of happenings and revelations, like unexpected blessed water springs gifted by kind spirits. With satisfaction Khaled relished his deepening awareness of his successful role in deterring aggression, and that it was not always so arbitrary. The day elapsed happily in such revelries that it wasn't until evening that he made back for his tent.

Sadiqa, reclined by his tent, turned her face to him as he neared, and a short distance away was his father's caravan and pitched tent. At the sound of his crunching steps his father stuck his head out, and gave a quick head tilt, indicating his wish to speak to him in his tent. Khaled slipped into the dim space lit by an oil lamp, hot stuffiness engulfing him in the vacant space.

"Been having fun all this time?" said his father. He stood with only a mat and a bowl on the floor, as if he'd been holding audience with himself all day.

"Our blessed kin are most generous; praise to you for allowing me to come and spend time with them," said Khaled, hating the unnecessarily intense manner. He suddenly wanted nothing more than to fall into deep, invigorating sleep.

"Hmm," Moharib nodded. "Khaled, the son of *sayyid* Moharib. Slaying two oryx for the man who insults his father. Now is that really honorable?"

"Who would dare insult you? *Yaba*, it's over. He's satisfied with what I brought him."

"*Sah*; so now it's Khaled who passes final judgment," shot his father.

Khaled's jaw dropped. "*Yaba*, what more do you want me to do? Whatever it was, it's over. He can say nothing about you: as you rightly said, everyone knows the rules." He heard the echo of his own voice, wondering why it was louder than he wanted it to be, like someone else inside him wanted to speak—or scream.

His father lunged at him, his angry eyes boring into him in a way he'd never seen before. "Shame on you! That a doted son can watch his father be so insulted in public, while you so easily shrug it off? Is this all I get for all I've given?" his father shouted, his breath hot on his averted face. "I've never been so humiliated, and by a pitiful Ghassanid-serving little Kalb slave at that!"

Khaled stared, wondering if his father genuinely knew anything about Imran or was just assuming out of spite. And worst of all, as if he had been innocent in the transaction himself.

"There's only one way to fix this. I don't care how you do it, but you're going to do it."

"*Esh?* What exactly am I going to do, *yaba*?" said Khaled, half wondering if he was dreaming.

"You want to prove yourself? Prove that you won't accept such an insult, and to your father least of all. You're going to finish him; it's an order," said Moharib.

There it was.

What Khaled had feared most of all had come: that he would have to unleash it too, no longer hold back from the man who sired him, and who, after all these eighteen summers, felt more and more like a stranger to him. His heart pounded, rattling his bones.

"*Order* me to kill him? No, I will not. I don't stand for anyone insulting you, which is why I've always stood by your side, and want to keep doing so. Even today I was there, when we both know the truth of it," said Khaled without regret.

In a blur, Khaled's hand flew too late to his face as he fell to the floor. A painful throb spread over his cheek from the force of his father's blow, but his mistrustful alertness revealed the lingering glare on him.

Enraged—Moharib was enraged at the whole thing, and now, perhaps even enraged that he'd missed striking the proper blow.

Even if his father had meant it as a mere warning, there was no more space for pretending, for friendship, let alone the approval he'd longed for all his life. Panting, Khaled bolted up and stepped back, keeping his distance.

"Stood by my side? All thanks to the great Khaled! Ha! More like overcompensating! No; it's for yourself, to build your name, which you can only hope will even reach the slightest hint of *my* fierceness!" yelled Moharib.

His crimson face contorted his features in such a grotesque way that Khaled wondered if he was *majnun*, and some *ghul* carved in the red Jabal Aja stone had invaded him. Khaled could hardly believe what was happening; how it had all spiraled out of control, and out of something that had been resolved, though his father still refused to admit his own guilt. Khaled realized that deep down he had always feared that this might happen, but had shrugged it off as fear, that his father had his reasons, and though tough, was a good, fair man at heart.

All his past conflicting thoughts on his father rushed at him like a thundering storm, and now he couldn't deny that his father had intended him real physical harm. Even when leaving him at the graveyard alone at ten to face the hyena, he could've said it was part of his training and not personal; that the beast only followed its nature if it had attacked him.

But this was different. Curiously, there was something freeing about this ugly situation.

"What if I don't want to be fierce like you? And if you want other sons, what's stopping you?" smirked Khaled, relieved at his own easy declaration.

He expected more venomous words, but instead Moharib's eyes widened, and he at once looked so helpless that Khaled almost pitied him. The change was complete, the *jinni* vanished, yet lurking to strike again unannounced.

"It's sad when a man doesn't recognize real loyalty when it's in front of him," said Khaled, and left him.

CHAPTER FIFTEEN

STRUCK

Khaled spent a horrible sleepless night tossing, turning, and brooding over the dire situation with his father. It seemed impossible that there would be any going back from this. Time had only shown that his manners were getting worse, and he hated to wonder how much worse it'd get if he hadn't protested.

Ironically, their relation wouldn't be very different from before, at least not based on appearance. Khaled would maintain all outward loyalty to his father and display no animosity, but now marked with a distance and even less time spent around him. Mostly, he would never drop his guard from him, or anyone else. Henceforth, there were only two people he decided he could fully trust: his blessed mother Khamra and Majid. Zahir and Jonder came to his mind again: had his father pushed Zahir away in a similar way?

With bittersweet resolve, Khaled told his friend all about it early the next morning. He'd kept it from Majid long enough, and their loyal friendship required he confide in him these important developments. A man only had one father, and also had to be aware exactly who he could call his allies. Majid's serious air only deepened upon hearing the recent outcome.

"Is it so shocking?" said Khaled.

Majid sighed. "No, which in some ways makes it worse."

"Why did he have to come? He could've just stayed away, busy with other things as he always is! And now, this. Am I the worst son ever?"

"No, but you certainly are a patient one, and blessed as your mother," said Majid.

A weight lifted off Khaled to find that his friend had suspected aspects of it all along, without bearing judgment and instead offering his constant friendship and support. It eased the need for explanation, and the real solace was in knowing that his friend expected none, trusting in their bond to reveal in time what needed to be known. His own father Abjar knew enough of Moharib from their dealings, and that their own closeness now transferred to himself in a unique way touched him more than he could say.

"So then you don't completely hate me?" said Khaled.

"Just the usual, as brothers do," smirked Majid, and drew him into a hearty patting embrace.

His confidence renewed, Khaled threw himself fully into giving his all, hunting for the tribe and giving nearly all his spoils away to whoever needed it, his selfless bravery quickly catching the attention of all who witnessed it. When he called out his praising shouts of glory, "Glory to Moharib of Banu Zubayd!" omitting his own name, it was taken as another instance of his selflessness. It was not his intention, and yet he would hardly argue with them when only a few knew the real reason behind it.

At the fighting tents he sought even more to form friendships, or at least connections, no matter how fleeting, yearning to contrast the draining, sickening insatiable competition that too many fed on. Still, in the midst of teaching, even he knew that a warrior should never give away all his secrets.

Khaled and Majid drew so much attention that several tribeswomen soon lavished their praises and unleashed their daughters, some veiled, some not, off on errands in hopes of sparking a conversation. There were beauties, to be sure, but what more could he say? They were fleeting gazelles gazing as curiously at him as he was at them; a stream of alluring mirages that he could never fully grasp, and whose loveliness might fade—or worse, entirely vanish—if he looked too long. It was that sense of fickleness, lamented by the poets, that put him off.

And yet, his curiosity was again revived to see some of them at camel and horse races, openly cheering him on, and secretly making him wish some would join along. But rare were the tribesmen who allowed their daughters such freedom, and so far he'd yet to meet one of them. He indulged in their attention, and took pride in dazzling them by winning many races upon his beloved Sadiqa and his pigeon-blue Ghassanid mare Aminah.

A few days later, word spread that Imran was found dead, his crushed, dusty body apparently trampled to death. The tribe gathered like a fortress, and with no witnesses and none of his belongings stolen, there seemed little explanation other than it was an accident, although by which angered animal was anyone's guess. Hatim, in his renown generosity, instantly offered mourning *rithā'* verses that had listeners in tears. After the passing deluge that brought a subdued relief, *sayyid* Abdallah offered several camels and ample goods for his kin's northern journey home. At last they bid farewell to the Kalb tribesmen, who sang of burying the body in their beloved dwelling of Dumat Al-Jandal, near the ancient Marid castle and Wadi Sirhan.

Evading Majid's gaze on him, Khaled felt like he'd been punched in the stomach. Was his father content now? He hated to wonder if he had anything to do with it, although it was nearly miraculous in itself that despite the throngs of people, there had been no witnesses—or at least none that said a word. Had his father, for once, realized his mistake and let it go? Had Imran made other enemies, even among his own, during his stay? Or was it simply an accident, as common as the other scenarios?

With the time Khaled had spent away he'd begun doing the same thing again; trying to understand and downplay his father's harshness. But this event only confirmed the volatile behaviors, the veils that some learned to wear to evade suspicion. He could not deny that he himself had witnessed his father in his worst light yet, but that did not make him guilty of this death. *Badawi*, especially those with untamed *jahl* from lack of training, often reacted too impulsively when angry. So how could he, or anyone, judge without evidence? Even *kahinat* could make mistakes, so who was he to say? There was no right way to say it, but he could only hope that Imran's death had been an unfortunate accident, even as some said there was no such thing in light of unescapable Fate.

Amidst the melancholy that Hatim wore like a cloak, and lingered over the tribe for days after, Khaled prayed that his father's anger had relented.

Please let that never happen again; let him calm down, know that at least I'm not after him, Khaled entreated himself, Yassu, Al-Fals, the *jinn*, the angels, and any good spirits who might listen and help make it so.

Khaled and Majid's successes only continued, bringing so much abundance and harmony around him that he wondered if it was a happy sign from Imran from the beyond. His passing seemed all but forgotten, slipped away like Nefud sand dunes. Hatim even sang verses about their generosity, making Khaled sometimes joke that perhaps Majid and himself would linger with the poet on his mountain for a while, like Yassu-loving *mubassir* hiding away from the world.

Though grateful for the tribe's admiration, a lingering restlessness cruelly clung to him. Push, push: he would keep pushing, if only to keep his father at bay, make it clear to him that he was not against him, but would defend himself if he had to, as any man should.

Serenity often met them on evenings around the fire, the savory, precious sips of wine easing at least some sharp edges. Khaled searched for hints of softness in his father: the slightest smirk, the affectionate gaze, the proud whisperings of his son's achivements, but in vain. If they were there, it's as if they'd been buried so deep that even their owner didn't know how to retrieve them. Khaled took comfort in thinking that at least Imru was with the doting Samaw'al, or might even already be on his way to meet the brave *malik* Al-Harith. Movement: that's what helped lessen the pain.

A late summer day, Khaled rode off southeast with Majid and a band of a dozen friends. They came upon a valley and dismounted along the water, noting at each side of them a distance away the other small groups of tribesmen, resting by the long river. They settled with some fresh bread and *maamoul*, refilled their gourds, and bathed their feet in the cooling water while their mounts gulped down as much of the river as they could.

From Majid's darting glances that drifted behind him, Khaled eventually knew that someone was coming their way. Discreetly, Khaled turned over to an older, short man in dark, dirty clothes with a hard smirk, revealing missing teeth. He had a long scar running across his face that only worsened his already unpleasant features.

"Young men, where are you headed? We may be on the same path," said the man with a strained accent, gazing at them and their food.

"We're just roaming, exploring the land," said Majid, spreading his thick arms with firm yet easy nonchalance. Khaled tried not to smirk at his friend's skill for easily dismissing questionable attention. Not only was the stranger offputting, but he seemed to think they were blind and deaf.

"*Aywa.* We're of the Banu Taghlib," grinned the man.

"Ah, a most honorable tribe. You've called to mind my blessed relatives, although, they don't sound like you," frowned Khaled in mock confusion.

The stranger's face hardened. "How dare you insult me!"

"How dare you insult us! What do you mean by this charade with your fake accent? It's you who's come to us with your wandering *al-'ayn* and lies," said Khaled, his muscles tensing. Their raised voices drew the attention of the stranger's companions who approached from behind, and Khaled and his own rose in response, ready to fight. That the strangers were older and outnumbered could be as much a relief as a threat.

The man turned a cheek to his companions and dismissed them with a wave of the hand, then looked back at them with a cruel smirk.

"*Yallah al-ilah*, go on then," said Majid, thrusting his chin in dismissal.

"That's unfortunate," said Khaled. "One could think you're the ashamed rejects of your tribe and looking for trouble by bringing another innocent name into it."

"A free Asadi is never ashamed!" the man scowled.

"Is that so? Are you up here hiding out from your treacherous own tribe, or your new masters the 'Abs?" sneered Majid. Just the thought that one of theirs had killed Imru's father Hujr in his sleep reeked of cowardice.

"From no one; Time always runs its course!" spat the stranger.

Twisted hate darkened the stranger's face with an evil smirk, and Khaled wavered, caught between wanting to fight and just letting it go. But something about the stranger pulled him to violent action, and he once more struggled to admit how difficult it could be to resist it.

"Enough; let's go," Khaled finally said. With his companions he turned away and noted yet another band of tribesmen who seemed to be approaching from the opposite way, led by a young man.

An instant later, a sharp weight struck into Khaled's right shoulder from behind. With a piercing cry deeper than any he'd ever made, his elbow struck up to block and pull it out, unleashing his own wincing wrath. Khaled caught the disfigured attacker's wrist, forcing the blade to drop, while his other hand closed around the enemy's throat.

"Khaled!" cried Majid, rushing to his side.

"What shall I do with him?" grimaced Khaled. "I wouldn't mind watching the sorry life slip out of him."

"I say drop him and let the desert do what it will to him and the rest of them," said Majid. The stranger's distorted face, marked with provoked strife, made such a vile impression on him that he was shocked by his own revulsion. Just like that, it was easy to choose *jahl* over *hilm*, that praised self-control that could easily become a double-edged sword. There was no light in that man's eyes, and though for a moment Khaled wasn't sure if he'd regret it, Majid was right.

Khaled released the man, gurgling under his grasp, and watched him thump to the ground like a sandbag. Even with his usual wisdom and restraint, Majid couldn't resist kicking him several times, then shuffled in his small satchel for something to bind the wound.

"What's happened, how can we help?" cried the young man in cream robes who now came upon them from the other tribe. Was Khaled hallucinating or had he caught his northeastern Taghlib accent?

"Steer clear of this vile Asadi and his cowardly band; he pretended to be Taghlib while he was assessing us, surely to kill and rob us," said Majid, wrapping a long strip of cloth around Khaled's bleeding shoulder.

"Vile *ghul* indeed! At last, we found you," said the boy, and followed it by his own hard kicks to the unconscious mass on the floor. After a moment he straightened himself, dusting his arms and tugging down on his waisted mantle adorned with a sword, perfectly poised. "I am Amr son of Kulthum of the Banu Taghlib," he said with a hand over his heart. "I am honored to be *sha'ir* of our great tribe. Word traveled to us of bandits passing off as ours, so I wasted no time in bringing men to investigate. It's been days, and with your help, today we know who it is," said Amr. His manner of speaking made him look older than his age, which Khaled guessed couldn't be more than thirteen or fourteen. "I should've known it would be some treacherous Asadi, and look, his companions are already scuffling off! Shameful!" he sneered, and spat on the scarred man.

"Kind Amr, you're quite a way from home," winced Khaled. "Blessings to you and your tribe, and my kin Amir and Jarida."

"By Yassu; tell me!" beamed Amr, leaning into him.

"I'm Khaled, son of Moharib of the Banu Zubayd. My *amo* Zahir married Zoraya, grand-daughter to Jarida. Please pass them our kind greetings," said Khaled.

"It shall be done. But might you want to join us and say so yourself?" said Amr with a hopeful air.

"Bless your generosity, but I must decline. We must be getting back to Tayyi, though I hope we'll meet again soon," said Khaled.

"I shall pray for it! And if we can ever be of assistance, remember to call on Amr ibn Kulthum," said Amr. Khaled pinched a smile, hoping that as *sha'ir* he wouldn't make embarrassing reference to this event. And yet, his gladness to have run into him at the right time surpassed even that.

Amr helped them pack up and wouldn't let him leave until he accepted a skin of his wine.

"It's my favorite, from Al-Andarin. It will help you heal," nodded Amr, and Khaled suspected he might be speaking from experience. Amr waved them off with blessings, and in trying to ignore his pain, Khaled half imagined that Jonder might be as serious and matter-of-fact as him.

They galloped as fast as they could and when soon the Tayyi camp came into view, they slowed down at a distance by Khaled's cue.

"No need to draw attention to this. Let's keep it quiet unless we have reason to break it," he said, grateful for the group's silent agreement. He hated that what tormented him most was what his father would say about all this—when he should just as sadly be used to it by now.

"*Sah*, so perk up for a moment more and follow me, then," said Majid.

Khaled followed him to his tent, and laid on the floor, the tent folds tied shut in privacy. Trying to ignore his pain, he watched his friend move like a warrior who'd done it all his life. He offered Majid some wine that he declined, then downed nearly all the strong, undiluted Al-Andarin wine, treasuring the crimson liquid all the way from Al-Sham. Majid cleaned his wound, lathered it with a leafy, pungent unguent, and stitched him up while he winced through his teeth.

Soon the wine began kicking in, and the scent of Hudhayl honey, coating his wound, soothed him like his mother's milk.

"How could I have been so careless," said Khaled with half closed eyes, the self-pity the worst pain of all. "Even now it has to torment me over what my father would say; that maybe I deserved it."

"It will pass. What matters now is that you rest," said Majid, and tucked his gold angel Mikha'il amulet into one of the bandage folds.

It went dark.

With the wound less severe than he'd thought, and his friend's caring hand, Khaled recovered faster than he expected. In the meantime, their cavorting slowed down in favor of conveniently sneaking off to Hatim's mountain, the peacefulness strengthening him in a way he could hardly express. They confided in Hatim, who was the only other person non-present that day who knew of the event, and Khaled appreciated the poet's constant concern for him.

"Those lawless Asadi," sighed Hatim. "Attackers bent on bloodshed always gets what's coming to them; Yassu says so. May this mere scratch be part of pushing you to greater things and to keep meeting true friends along the way," said Hatim, placing his hand gently upon the bandaged shoulder.

"Oh Hatim. How could I ever spare your caring decrees now," said Khaled.

The changed, slowed pace made Khaled contemplate. It'd already been six moons since he'd arrived to the Tayyi in early spring, and though he'd grown so fond of it to consider it his second home, he also sensed the end had come. The resurging restless longing called him to roam again, somewhere far away, and all the better if it was too far out of his father's way. Majid, and others, would follow him anywhere if he asked, and the options beckoned to him.

He might go east to Al-Hira and visit those famous taverns and maybe even take up Amr's offer to visit further north to the fierce Banu Taghlib, and greet Jonder's Taghlib family in passing. That could be something to bring back to his *amo* Zahir, when he finally got to the Banu Sa'd. But with his father's reluctance, it would be just another source of argument, and even worse if he tried to send him as a business ambassador to Al-Mundhir. The obvious option was to head northwest, where *malik* Al-Harith dwelled near their kin, the Banu Zubayd the Small, and to which Majid immediately agreed. Perhaps they might even run into Imru on the way.

A warm evening he approached his father's tent and announced himself. A thunder of coughs resounded through which he was allowed in.

"Greetings, father. May you be well," said Khaled, keeping a distance as much from the man as from the *khat* leaves he liked to chew in the evenings. As usual, in their time apart Moharib had kept busy, meeting daily in long councils for endless petty squabbles that Khaled despised as much as his father enjoyed. Majid had even mentioned the whispers of people's shock at Moharib's softened attitude. After all this time, was it really, finally happening? No one was getting younger, after all.

"What's on your mind," said his father without looking at him, and buried a leaf in his inner cheek. If others saw Moharib differently, so far everything seemed the same to him.

Khaled locked his hands. "I recently rode out with the *shabab* southeast. There was a scuffle and I was wounded, but I healed fast, thanks to Majid."

"*Esh?*" His father fixed him. "Why didn't—"

For a moment his face froze in confusion, his red eyes flickering with something Khaled dared to think was concern. In the pause Khaled wondered if he was looking for the right words.

"*Hadha*, I know why: because you insist on protecting more worthless slaves! What if gossip spreads?" said Moharib, his features back to their constant scowl.

"I handled it, and the right people know the truth of what happened," said Khaled, grateful again that Amr of Taghlib had also been there.

At first Khaled had feared telling his father, but then realized he shouldn't hide it as if he was ashamed. If his father deemed him weak for it, then so be it. Maybe he already did anyways, with his perpetual dissatisfaction. But as a young man Khaled had shown once again that he'd stand up for himself, and if nothing else, after this encounter he knew that even he, too, could take a life if he had to. That he hadn't proved his own restrained *hilm*, and this successful self-control in trying times reassured him amidst his conflict.

"What I wanted to say is that I've thought about it, and I want to see my kin."

"Your kin?" slurred Moharib, sucking on the *khat* while his alert, reddened eyes speared into him.

"*Na'am.* I'll be back, of course. Majid and I will just be a while—now you know."

Pride emboldened him, for after all this time among the Tayyi and all his heroic feats, his reputation now secured him many friends and allowed him passage nearly anywhere he wanted. Moharib had his hardness that caused tension, and Khaled had his flexible friendship that reassured, and which he was glad to extend when fitting. Though it had all happened so fast, he was honored that his deeds pleased others, not as much from vanity as from a genuine, grateful sense of purpose. If he'd wanted to run away, he could've done it long before, and wouldn't be there respectfully announcing his plan.

"I haven't given you permission to go," said his father.

Khaled's jaw tensed. Was the man not hearing him? He wasn't asking for his permission. Each time he thought he could ease up on him, the man did something else to push him further away. Would it never end?

"I'm going. I just came to inform you, that's all." Khaled drifted to the exit.

"I said no," said Moharib, his eyes widening. His chest swelled, and he unleashed a fit of relentless coughs that threatened to persist.

"Perhaps it's time you see a healer for this," said Khaled. "If I find anything for it up north, I'll be sure to bring it back."

"North?" His father's body rattled, but finally settled after a few moments.

"*Sah*, north. I'm looking forward to visiting the Zubayd Al-Sughra, who surely call themselves small in humility."

Moharib nodded and waved a hand in vague approval, and Khaled almost wanted to confirm what he meant, but decided against it. If he had something to say, he should say it. After all he'd never been the type to hold back. With a last glance and bow, Khaled left, relieved to have the matter done.

With bittersweet happiness he made his last rounds of the vast camp with Majid. They bid goodbye to the tribe and finished with *sayyid* Abdallah and Hatim who offered them plenty for the journey.

"And may this protect you," said Hatim, and handed him a gold amulet with a cross on it, similar to his.

"How can I ever thank you," said Khaled, and lowered his head as Hatim slipped it around his neck.

"By remembering Him," smiled the generous poet.

So much had happened here, none of which Khaled would forget.

In the late night he walked to his tent, taking in the last night's crisp air. Through the crunching of his steps, a whispering rumble filled his ear, whispering:

There is a dark man of Zubayd,
who will not tolerate a bad word said about him.

Oh! But a stone is like fresh dough in comparison!
Truly, trapped in the wheel of Fate
is the man who refuses to make better change
For he will keep adding to his own chains.

Khaled stopped, scanned around him, a high pitched cackling echoing from somewhere in the dark distance. He waited, listened for another lurking hyena—or something else.

Stillness reigned.

He reached his tent, bid Sadiqa and Aminah goodnight, and it wasn't until he heard it again when he dropped into bed, and closed his eyes in sad agreement that the visiting ghost left him.

CHAPTER SIXTEEN

NASR

LATE SUMMER 541 AD - BANU SA'D

When will it come?

Sitting in the darkness, Jayida seethed at the question that was starting to concern her as much as her mother. She ran a searching hand across her dress and bedsheets, still dry and bloodless.

Jayida glared at the form of the Praising Woman whose arms raised into the shadows, then rose and took wide steps into the bathing area. With expert soundless motions, she slipped into her usual second skin of at least three layers amidst her coat of mail.

Well into her sixteenth summer, her monthly flow should've started by now, so where was it? Try as she might to ignore it, she still wanted to know, even if she had no interest in being a mother anytime soon, and thought with some added defiance that she may never want to be one at all. Even then, she still didn't care if it made her sound unwilling, but she would not wear more amulets against *al-'ayn*, drink wine, do less or more exercise, make sacrifices to Al-Lat or look at any animals' entrails for answers, among other nearly endless suggestions.

How nice it would be for a woman to simply not have her flow until she met a man to stir these emotions in her enough to want to get married in the first place! And if not, it would just take care of that problem. Jayida certainly couldn't force her body to make blood flow, and if she could, she could just as well stop it.

A shiver ran down her spine. What if she *was* doing it, even without her awareness? *Kahinat* were said to have strong mental powers, hence their keen foresight that others sought out, either within their own tribes or in service of deities at their far-flung shrines. Was her reluctance blocking it? Was her life as

Jonder confusing her *qareen*, and in turn, confusing her about who she truly was, making her neither a girl nor a boy?

For the first time, Jayida felt the weight of the gnawing horrible question: was something *wrong* with her? Yazida not only already had hers, but already considered who would sire her children, while she'd yet to shed even one drop of blood. When *mubassir* Ayyub spoke of those holy women who proudly didn't bleed, it was often along with emaciating themselves by rejecting the other earthly needs of nourishment. Yet she did no such thing, and was strong and healthy by any and all appearances. Each day it was becoming more difficult to suppress her wavering doubt.

Just as bad were her unanswered pleas to Yassu and her guardian. Why couldn't the Aksumite princess, often present in her beaming, loving glow, just say or even give a hint on when it would come? But what about all those stories! One thing that seemed eternal were stories of women, with and without monthly flows, begging for children, who in the right time were granted them. Her own worries had made her see why the *injil* had so many tales of them, reminding its followers to have faith in the Israelite *al-ilah*. What if at least some of these women were *kahina*, too? It had to be why Shamshun's barren mother had an angel appear to her—twice!—and why she understood before her husband that the angel wasn't there to harm them, but to instruct them on how to raise their blessed future son.

Jayida grabbed a spear and Bag of Treasures, swollen with her bow and quiver, and slipped out into the cold dawn. She loaded her belongings on Hania and mounted, and met with approaching Nasr and Shams.

The pigeon-grey skies, suggesting the looming rainy season, reminded of the *Ayyam al-Zalam*. Perhaps with them she could try to forget some of her feminine worries, even if they were promptly replaced by others. She pushed through her fear, remembering how lucky she was to be with brave *sha'ir* Nasr, and even fiery Shams had grown stronger and more self-controlled.

"I want to take you to a place we haven't been to together before," said Nasr, and they trotted off north. It's not that he couldn't go other places without them, and obviously had, but something about it added to her frustration.

As they trailed north leisurely, parallel to Wadi Al-Hamd, the sky gradually cleared to bright blue, burning away the clouds like a passing memory. The flat expanse was soon dotted with rolling hills and mountains in the distance, bringing to mind her parents' journey to the Banu Sa'd. Someday soon she would be the one to plan their trip further north to Wadi Al-Qura and Hijr, and relive all her parents' memories with them and her friends.

They arrived at the juncture of Wadi Al-Hamd and, leaving the path coursing north, followed Nasr as he veered west. He appeared so thoughtfully absorbed that Jayida decided he'd made the journey often, perhaps even wanted to savor this stretch of the way.

The *wadi* narrowed as they paced west, changing into a different place. With new, awed curiosity she noted the rocky valley covered in large boulders scattered throughout, that surely had housed many travelers. She pinched her lips together under her scarf, touched that despite the often repetitive sceneries, there were still hidden gems to discover, and perhaps always would be.

"So is this where you steal away to at times, to hide away from the world?" said Jayida. The enrobing stillness made her think of similar places where lone *mubassir* and monks might retreat to as they sought Yassu and divine interaction.

"*Na'am*, in a sense. It could be yours, too, if you ever need one," said Nasr.

"And here I thought you'd wanted it for yourself," said Shams, almost offended.

Nasr gave a small smile. "What's the fun in showing everything all at once, especially when you like surprises," he said, urging them along with a tilt of his head.

They coursed parallel to the nearly dry lakebed, scattering white-grey clouds of dirt in their wake. At some distant rumble they all stopped and glanced at each other knowingly, waiting until it revealed a small departing group, riding north out of view.

"Who could that be," said Shams, extending his neck in case he might, like the sun, see that far ahead.

"Anyone's guess. They seem to be leaving, but as usual, eyes peeled," said Nasr. They rode on a bit further and following Nasr's example, they dismounted and prepared themselves.

With his quiet bearing and sword at his waist, Nasr would've looked like the natural leader even if they'd also brought their own. Like Shams, she had her bow and quiver on her back and, spear in hand, they led their camels by the reins.

They followed Nash along a dirt path that led up a hill, and pushed forward in such an unusual, secluded area that she suspected Nasr had been the one to forge it. Her brow tickled in the mounting strain, and at first she thought the effort was mainly for a nice view. Then, the consistent climb gradually revealed closely packed, jagged formations that made for conveniently concealed caves, easily missed or mistaken from view down below. Only those who had ventured up would've been able to see what was there. With a pang of jealousy she wondered if Yazida already knew of this place, too.

Finally Nasr slowed, his drawn sword and free hand gesturing for them to standby at the ready as he cautiously explored the entrance to ensure its vacancy. With his spear drawn, Shams followed close behind him, while she faced out into the valley with her bow, covering them from potential danger at all sides.

For a moment, all around them was pure, absolute silence. An undisturbed stillness, empty of threat. Then Hania voluntarily folded her legs, and dropped into a seated position in fitting reward for the uphill hike.

"To echo Hania's thought, it's all clear," chuckled Nasr. He sheathed his sword and with a head tilt he invited them in to gather around a sooty set of stones, surrounded by a circle of dark stones.

"And all this time, this has been your second home," said Shams, shaking his head and dropping his belongings.

"I'm glad you like it," smirked Nasr.

They helped Shams unroll a long mat and laid it down for them to recline on, with their weapons gathered close. Nasr shuffled in his bag and passed around some fresh bread. "Everyone needs at least one other place they can go to. And now I'll know we've shared it."

Jayida caught his dreamy air and wondered if he'd ever brought a girl there, his own chosen special space that his sister also had had with Imru, as brief as it'd been. Did Jayida share this emptiness with Shams, or was she the only one who hadn't yet found such a place for herself?

Nasr glanced back and forth between them, amusement spreading across his face while Shams inquisitively shrugged. Nasr reached down and turned some of the dark stones upside down, revealing a range of carvings.

"Nice collection you made," said Shams. Somehow he still looked tense even when giving a compliment.

"They're not mine. I found them here, scattered all over the place. They seemed forgotten, left behind, so I gathered them here, to remain present, yet out of sight," said Nasr.

"Not yours?" said Shams, startled. "I won't ask how much *bakhur* you burned to turn away the *jinn*'s wrath." He leaned back stiffly.

"Plenty enough," said Nasr. "But don't worry; if any shows up, I'll protect you."

Jayida fixed the *sha'ir*. Of course he would, when it was in his protective nature. But why that odd veiled threat, like he knew something they didn't? It reminded her of the day he'd pushed her during training.

"You shouldn't joke about this," said Shams.

"Easy, Shams. How could they be harmful when thinking about these stones has made me happy? I wanted to share that with you, and I want to hear what you think of one in particular. It'll be a good story," said Nasr.

Shams's face softened with a long sigh, and they leaned in together.

"That one's a camel for sure," pointed Shams.

"And a horse and ostrich," said Jayida, amused at the simple drawings that even a child could make. She had to agree with Nasr that she couldn't see or feel anything threatening in them. And anyway, he'd left them peacefully in place where he'd found them—even as others often took things they found during their travels.

"And what of that one?" said Nasr, his hovering wrist with its knotted bracelet a fitting barrier between them. "I want to hear as many ideas as possible."

Cautiously, they leaned forward to scrutinize the crude outlined sketch. It was a rectangular body with two strands drawn out above one side of the head, with one short stick arm and three fingers sticking up. Under the figure were also drawn two upward curved lines, as though on some flying carpet.

"Could be a goddess, but which?" said Shams.

"It almost reminds me of the Praising Woman from Tayma that *yaba* carved for me, but with one arm up," said Jayida.

"Or a dancing-girl; with her loose hair swirling above her head," said Shams.

"Or maybe a cheering tribeswoman; her raised arm drawing them out into the open and enticing them to victory against the enemy," said Jayida.

"I've *got* it!" said Shams. "It's a date palm, with its roots and palms! And to think I almost missed it," he beamed.

"A date palm? I've never thought of that one," laughed Nasr.

Jayida felt a strain in her neck and tilted her head side to side to stretch. Fixed on the drawing, she frowned at the new emerging angle.

"But then—if you rotate it like this, it could also be an oryx," said Jayida, as they all erupted in laughter.

"My smart companions; that's two new ones I'd never thought of," nodded Nasr, although she wasn't entirely sure she believed him.

"The longer I look at it, the less it makes sense. What if that was—part of its spell?" said Shams.

"Then perhaps its meaning is lost with the one who made it, when we can hardly reach a final answer," chuckled Nasr. "Most importantly, never forget that part of a spell's—or any other evil eye's—power is in your fear you give it."

His wisdom earned through his health struggles left them in contemplation for a moment, visible and mysterious like the drawings before them.

"If anyone can interpret it how they want, how to know which is right?" shrugged Shams. "It's enough to wonder if these were made by the same person; why some are obvious and others not?"

"*Sah*; so if you don't know, how can that be your fault, and why should you fear any punishment?" said Nasr.

"You know how fickle the spirits are," said Shams.

"*Aywa* and yet, here we are. It's a miracle, no? That with how many angry *jinn*, *afarit*, and *ghilan* surrounding us, along with flesh and blood people, we've made it this far," said Nasr, but this time there was only his joyful, boldly trusting manner she loved so much.

"At least one thing is certain. Since there isn't any writing, none of them say anything like: *Curse whoever removes this stone from this place*," said Jayida, trying to lighten the mood. "Of all the things to leave behind, why that? Requests to grant security, gifts, or even goods, I might understand, but I'd never want to leave a curse. It's too cruel, even if, like us, others might not be able to read it." She wasn't sure she would trust its meaning even after tracking down multiple readers, to compare and confirm that they weren't each just making things up and lying.

"My dear friends," sighed Nasr. "We all know by now how lonely and dreary grazing flocks can be. I wouldn't be surprised if it was done by a young man much like us, who made his way up here, one day, long ago, but perhaps unlike us, didn't have as pleasant company."

His sincere, affectionate tone drew their loyal attention, and gratitude filled her that she'd never tire of these bonding moments with them. It had to be for the best that he hadn't yet spoken of a potential wife, when she awaited her feminine flow that would then allow her to express her fruitful wish for him.

"We will give thanks with a poem," said Nasr, and she wondered how long he'd practiced alone before getting their input. Shams got his flute from his satchel, and as Nasr began reciting, the melody fueled the reflective mood.

To consecrate the place with their first shared visit, Nasr chanted of the three companions of Banu Sa'd; the wolf-slaying *sha'ir*, and his two ostrich egg-catching, and oryx and leopard-slaying friends who roamed along Wadi Al-Hamd. He revealed their bravery during the gloomy *Ayyam al-Zalam*, their training and refining weapon skills, and of the most famous Imru Al-Qays who'd stayed among them. As if discreet proof of his forgiveness, Nasr praised Imru's mission to visit the Ghassanid-Jafnid *malik* Al-Harith, who'd surely help him set his affairs straight and return, gloriously honoring his tribe of Kindah—and maybe even his own sister Yazida.

Jayida wondered if Shams would change his mind about Yazida if he knew what had really happened with Imru, but with his stubbornness, assumed he wouldn't. Still, it was bittersweet to consider that Imru had to hurry back if he was serious about Yazida—and for her friend's sake she hoped he was.

Nasr closed with a passage on the stones, gathered in his secret cave and fueling their stories about their origins, so moving and flowing that no *jinni* could refuse his praise. She was not trying to compare and yet she preferred his recitals full of solace from anything else she'd heard. Imru had forged his own path, for a long time chosing poetry over duty, while Nasr naturally created from it, drawing from the one and same source.

With their moods lifted, they packed up and ventured back down into the valley. At the foot of the hill she mounted Hania, and looked up at the surrounding hills, delighted by the concealed caves secretly bidding them goodbye, not so unlike her own birthplace of Wadi Al-Wafra. Nasr was right and they'd have to come back, just as others had passed through and either made or brought the drawings with them.

Then it hit her. What if Nasr's poetry were to be written someday? The daring thought struck her with its complexity. The first impulse was to dismiss it, when a *badawi*'s word was more important than any paper or document, for who was to say if it was genuine or forged? Surely vast worlds of endless images could not just be taken captive, given form and put on a surface, without losing meaning along the way. How could it be that simple, and the same thing as being there during a recital breathed into life by its author?

And yet, it had to be a kind of magic in action to see the airy words take physical shape on a surface, capturing closely the essence of what the author meant. No wonder it seemed akin to immortality, when this granted instant access, or at least to those who could decipher it. But what if even that wasn't most important, and it was enough for it to exist? Like her collection of statues, at least some images made a pleasant impression; a visual reminder of someone who'd been there and spoken to the viewer through physical materials and letters.

Still, from what she recalled, the process of writing and creating books was tedious and costly. First, she'd have to find a scribe who spoke her nonwritten *'arabi* dialect, and then decide on the intended audience, so that he could translate it for them to read. That could be Syriac or Greek for the north, Aramaic for the Israelites, or Himyaritic in the south—or even a multilingual combination of them, as some inscriptions had. Only after deciding that would she finally reach into her memory and dictate to the scribe the content of Nasr's lavish poetry, some of which she'd been part of. Creating one copy by hand would be no small feat, and she envisioned several piled on top of each other with a mix of glee and discomfort.

Though it was hardly encouraging in this form, she hoped that at least it helped the text and book-making empires of the Rûm, Fars, Himyarites, and Aksumites to better remember the stories they were meant to preserve. Her brow flinched to think that, worst of all, it may make people lazier by relying too much on these books instead of their own memories. Jayida shook it off instantly, grateful that she and her kin would keep doing what *badawi* did, and hold fast onto their memories to be passed on swift spoken words across generations.

"You know, sometimes I wonder about those great, learned writers; like what they'll write about this place," said Jayida, breaking through her reverie.

"Great things, of course. Why wouldn't they, when we dwell in this marvelous, mysterious place few can endure except us valiant warriors!" said Shams, brandishing his spear to the sky.

"I share the thought," said Nasr. "They could be truthful, or misleading. Maybe a bit of both; like with those drawings that we can't be sure about. Or warring tribes painting themselves in the best light."

"Can we never escape it? And what would those stories be called?" said Shams, his eyes narrowing in contemplation.

"A Thousand And One Nights!" blurted Jayida, and grimaced.

"*Esh?* A thousand *and one*? Why on Shams's green earth—the idiom is a thousand; a thousand will do," frowned Shams, as if to himself.

"Or, it might be *Arabian Nights* for short," sneered Jayida with a force that even she hadn't expected, as they turned to her in surprise.

"*Esh* Arabian? Like those who speak *'arabi*? And which kind of *'arabi*?" said Shams.

"Wish I could say, but it sounds *majnun* to me, too! But you know what's crazier? That I have this strange, gnawing idea that they'll write those stories, spread them all over the world, and none of them, *none* will even be set here! They'll be in the Fars territory, in Al-Sham, and the Holy Land guarded by warriors in service to *malik* Al-Harith and his brother *malik* Abu Karib, with some stories set in Egypt, and even India and China—but none here, and least of all in the Najd or Himyar!" said Jayida, her stiff hand swatting air in emphasis.

"Jonder! I daresay I've never seen you so agitated!" chuckled Nasr.

"But—can you just imagine?" said Jayida, incredulous.

"Oh, why must our *jinni* torment us so; me with my restlessness and you with this—" said Shams, as confused as she on what to name it.

"Because they're testing you!" laughed Nasr. "*Aywa*; so long as they honor our generosity, that's the most important of all. At this rate, I conclude that Hatim Al-Tayyi will be in it, and a fitting symbol for our good parents, too," said Nasr, nodding to their approval.

"Speaking of Tayyi; Sufyan has been considering a woman from there. He's also heard that Khaled of the Banu Zubayd has been making a name for himself. Your cousin, right?" said Shams, as she stared ahead.

Jayida tried not to think that his lingering jealousy of her and Nasr's friendship reared its head again with this detail.

"To this as yet unknown cousin, may *al-ilah* keep watching over him," smirked Jayida, catching Nasr's knowing gaze that caught its double meaning. If that included keeping them away as they'd done so far, she was hardly disappointed.

That Nasr hardly mentioned him was another confirmation of their closeness, when she neither wanted to talk about him nor had anything to say. She wished Khaled no ill will, but until she met him and saw for herself the kind of person he was, she wasn't particularly interested in whatever he was doing.

"Just as well; there'll be no shortage of brave heroes to write about," said Nasr, with his renown air that diffused as much calm wisdom as it did authority.

After a while, they came upon the juncture that split north and south, and Nasr glanced behind him and all around.

"We may be followed, so let's gently pick up pace," he said, his tone urging obedience.

"Are they the ones we glimpsed earlier?" said Jayida, hoping that identifying already took away half its threat. How could she have missed it? She stiffened herself against Hania's bouncing and discretely looked behind her for signs of anyone, and saw nothing. The only sounds were their camels' crunching steps on the gravel, and the occasional fluttering of creatures seeking shelter from the burning heat. After some time they turned east and exited the *wadi*, and she turned again.

There, in the bright light of day, were four shadowy figures following them.

"They're closer behind us now. What are your orders?" she asked Nasr, and reached for her bow and quiver and draped them over her torso. Better prepared than not.

"Might they be needing some hospitality? But why haven't they announced themselves?" said Shams. His features darkened as he grabbed his bow and quiver, his usual boisterous self struggling to recede to poised concentration.

"Ride fast, *yallah al-ilah*!" said Nasr, swatting his *bakurah* stick and kicking into his mount's sides.

In the racing rush she looked behind again, and saw a cloud of dust swelling around their pursuers. Her blood froze, hoping she was seeing wrong—but she had to be patient and wouldn't, couldn't strike first.

"Who are you?" Shams turned and thundered, trying in his way to deflect the lurking danger.

"Don't—" shouted Nasr, then grimaced, as his back arched and an arm flailed up, revealing the impact of the enemy arrow sticking out of his lower left side. Groaning, Nasr leaned forward, and she pulled on her reins to draw closer to his mount, the blood fast soaking through his layers. Everything was horrifyingly surreal, and though part of her wanted to cry out, she could only focus on what needed to be done.

"Hang on," yelled Jayida. She reached over and grabbed him and with a grunt, pulled him stomach down onto her lap. Wincing, his bloody hand tried to reach and press down on the arrow.

"Yah, yah!" Jayida commanded, the alarmed Hania groaning under the added weight even as she obeyed.

"By the great Nasr of Banu Sa'd!" yelled Shams. His face contorted in angered shock, he aimed and launched an arrow at the attackers.

The whirlwind exploding in her, she followed suit and twisted her torso as far as she could, then aimed and released. She sneered as her arrow landed in a leg and caused the rider to tumble in his companion's way.

Meeting her rhythm, Shams shot some more arrows to fuel their mounting confusion.

"I'll race ahead and warn the tribe," shouted Shams, and grabbed the reins of Nasr's mount. Just like the day she'd slain the leopard, her coat of mail was an emboldening invisible protector. Already Shams was paces away, rousing the Banu Sa'd to their help.

"We're almost there, Nasr," said Jayida, resisting the urge to pull out the arrow herself. Nasr groaned, his eyes drooping in a stupor, helpless for the first time in her life. Her jaw clenched, fighting back enraged tears. Fools, the lot of them; because if their goal had been merely plunder, wounding the *sayyid*'s son would yield dire consequences. Their beloved camp's tents came into view, along with rows of gathered tribesmen. That the lawless beasts may have lurked around at the *wadi*, awaiting them like shameless thieves set her blood boiling.

With some relief she reached the approaching first line of gathered warriors, led by Hubala and Sufyan. They made a space to let her through, and rapidly reclosed it to rush into and surround the attackers. The others, with Sufyan among them, clustered protectively around, eager to see the outnumbered fools who'd dare challenge the innocent Banu Sa'd. Everywhere, faces dripped with communal disgust.

Her father and Shams appeared at her side, and each taking an arm or a leg, they carried Nasr to his parents' tent as their nearly unconscious friend mumbled in his daze.

"*Allah al-ilah!*" shrieked Warda and Yazida, bolting up at the alarming sight of them. Meanwhile Jayida's own worried mother Zoraya dutifully gathered strips of linen, bowls of water, and ointment.

They carefully set Nasr down, and Warda fell at his side in horror. "My son! My pure, innocent son!" she wailed, every sob rattling through them.

Struggling to contain his own emotion, *sayyid* Aziz reached into a pot of camel fat, anointed the arrow, and with one swift motion, removed it. Nasr moaned as his father rose, clutching the arrow, his features caught between pain and cold indifference.

There was a shuffle at the entrance and Samira appeared, glancing in sneering disgust, and Jayida hated that it didn't look so different from her usual way. She of all people would see some potential benefit to this, if only for Shams to take Nasr's place—if only it horribly came to this.

"*Al-ilah*, please protect your servant Nasr," said *sayyid* Aziz, and swallowing back a sob, he bolted out.

With her father and Shams, Jayida followed in silence, and by the time they rejoined the rest of the tribe, the brigands were surrounded, clustered at the center like trapped prey. Intensity stifled the air, with the palpable chance of erupting violence. Trying to stay a step ahead of what might happen, her senses sharpened and rose as if somewhere outside herself, marking the fine line between peace and chaos.

There, before them, was a source of evil: six of them, lean and mean-looking beasts with rogue-ish airs. Tribe deserters, surely. Men without loyalty to anyone but themselves; or possibly each other, when temporarily convenient, and who survived by plundering others, at the cost of life.

The leader in front was as disheveled as his faded dark robes and was marked by a large scar running across his eye. That he looked like he hadn't washed in several moons added to his unpleasant air. They weren't worthy of the fine horses they rode, and even less if stolen from the nearby Banu Ghatafan or Dhubyan breeders.

The coiling excitement of the challenge burst within her, and she restrained her urge to laugh. These were madmen; a mere six of them marching against an honorable tribe that outnumbered them with skilled warriors! Even if they were good fighters, there was no way they'd overcome the Banu Sa'd. Jayida fixed her hard gaze on them and their evasion had the desired effect.

"What do you think, my kinsmen; is he afraid, are they all afraid, to dismount and face us, like real men?" said *sayyid* Aziz.

The leader chuckled. "We like the view from up here."

"Ha! Sounds to me like some tribeless rejects; no loss on their end, then," said *sayyid* Aziz, turning to his kin who echoed his sneer. "Our *sha'ir* and poets would love to commemorate your cowardice in verse, to circulate your vileness all through the land!" he yelled, pointing the greased arrow to the leader. The leader grinned and from the *sayyid*'s flaring nostrils, her heart pinched at his recognition of the one who'd struck his son. "Imagine that: no hiding," said *sayyid* Aziz, his tone now clearly defiant.

"Oh, to see such fatherly emotion for a son," laughed the leader. "I'm not familiar with it. Still, the arrow simply went where the air took it; nothing a real man can't handle."

"How *dare* you! He did you *no* harm!" *sayyid* Aziz stepped to him. "Why don't you come off that horse? Or shall I throw you off myself? Can you handle that, eh? Me throwing you off, your head possibly, accidentally, bashing against the hardened floor! It would be no one's fault then, would it!"

The leader's ebony horse backed up a bit, an air of concern flashing over the rider's face. Even if he didn't believe in the wrath of any deity or *jinn*, he'd been the one to start the violence.

"Perhaps, but you're known for your generosity, so you will not refuse," grinned the leader.

Jayida's soul raged, that such a vile man should use the *sayyid*'s honorable traits in such a repulsive way, and be so indifferent to harming life just to risk benefitting from it.

"So they say," *sayyid* Aziz paused and looked away, struggling not to break. Was this all his generosity led to? The stakes had never been so high before, and any man would be reluctant to confess what looked like weakness to another, especially one as unfeeling as this demon. "But whatever your demands, you'll dismount and ask me, face to face, with your feet standing on the same earth. Choose quickly," said *sayyid* Aziz.

With a glance at his companions, the leader reluctantly dismounted, and slowly approached the *sayyid*, whose hand rested on his sword handle. Jayida held her breath, half thinking their *sayyid* might brandish it and pierce it through him, or hack his head off—and knew the whole tribe was thinking it.

"Ten camels," said the leader.

Jayida heard what sounded like a single disgusted collective gasp.

"As greedy as vile," said *sayyid* Aziz. "Now; you'll camp here, where all eyes will be on you at all times. And whatever higher power you believe in—assuming you're capable of it—beg to them, because if my son dies, I swear by *al-ilah* and all the deities that I will do all that's in my power to tear you to shreds and scatter all your bits everywhere, so that you'll never rest," he said, pointing the arrow at him again to send him back his wrath.

In near indifference the leader retreated with his companions to an area on the western outskirts of camp, along with Hubala and Sufyan among two dozen armed men chosen by *sayyid* Aziz to guard them.

The day elapsed in tense slowness, her anxiety gnawing her over Nasr's recovery. She was in and out of the tent, hopeful that he was responding to the ointments and herbal tisanes. He slept soundly on his back, his handsome angelic face surpassing the beauty of any carved statue.

"The ointment blessed by *mubassir* Ayyub will heal him, as it always has. He looks better already," said Warda, with a tentative smile that she tried to share. Jayida squeezed Warda's arm, hoping she was right and it would have the same power, even if this time it was for a deep wound close to his vital organs.

Amidst the constant stream of rotating visitors, Yazida remained by his side, tending to him, and Jayida was moved to witness the closeness that siblings, even of different genders, could have. At times the tent emptied, except for the three of them, filling the air with their potent intimacy.

Sitting with her legs folded under her, Yazida repeated her routine: rinsed her cloth in a clay pot, then gently dabbed it on her brother's head, taking side glances at her from time to time. They hadn't been alone since that whole Imru affair, and given their secret, she wondered how often Yazida thought of the poet since then. Jayida mused that Nasr might know, but then surprised herself that he might not.

"He kept the skins of the gazelles Imru slayed, as a memory to me of his passage, he said," said Yazida tearfully.

Jayida nodded, hoping that wherever he was, Imru thought of Yazida, too. Despite Shams making his attention to her clearer, Yazida seemed grateful but restrained. What if it wasn't so unlike herself with Nasr? But she almost laughed out loud: it was different, not to be compared.

In the pleasant stillness, undisturbed by words, so like the kind she shared with Nasr, a knot tightened in her core. What if—she hated to even think it—it came to the worst and Nasr stated his final choice of Jonder as partner for his sister; what would she do then? Would Yazida be the first to whom she'd reveal her secret, forever changing their relationship? But it was just fear talking, and in this peaceful space, with Yazida and Warda's doting care, she could easily dismiss it.

"He's lucky to have a sister like you," said Jayida.

"As he is to have a friend like you. You should get some rest, too," sighed Yazida.

Jayida nodded and exited the tent, and exchanged a knowing glance with approaching Shams.

Back at their tent, her mother instantly offered her food, and though she hadn't eaten since they'd left the cave that early morning, she had no appetite. She went to their shaded sleeping area, fell flat on her bedding and buried her face in the cushions, exhaustion eventually overcoming racing thoughts.

CHAPTER SEVENTEEN

FLIGHT

The gentle shake rattled Jayida awake.

"They want you," said her father. Even in her disorientation, the tension hinted that something was wrong. She glanced at her parents, whose pained expressions mirrored her own confusion.

Jayida rushed to the *sayyid*'s tent in the pre-dawn dark and bitter cold, and met Warda, whose reddened eyes and cheeks revealed her own torment.

"He's been asking for you," said Warda, gripping her hands. "Oh, Jonder I don't know! We've tried everything: the ointment blessed by *mubassir* Ayyub, the birthwort ointment, all the herbs we had, the amulets, the idols, the prayers of *mubassir* Ayyub! He seemed better, and now..."

"*Yama*," said Nasr with a surprising tone of command.

Warda sighed. "He wants to see you, alone," said Warda, with an air of wounded confusion. "I'm just afraid it might be the last—" Her vision flooded, her raised hand stopping the flow of words from her lips.

"He wouldn't—" Jayida frowned, speechless yet hoping to pass some of her strength by wrapping Warda's hands in hers.

"I'll leave you to it," said Warda. Her hold reluctantly released, and she left them.

Cued by Nasr's outstretched arm, Jayida went and knelt by his side. Earlier he'd been in a deep, restful sleep, but now sweat covered his brow, caught between forcing his eyes closed or wallowing in an intense state of alertness. She struggled to keep her balanced expression to conceal her own shock at his raging battle. Her hand covered his, and his other moved on top of hers.

"There you are, Nasr," she said.

"Jonder, Jonder," he groaned, his eyes nearly closed. "I remember how *yama* used to say that I was so excited to be around you when you were born. What a time we had." His clammy hold released her hand, but there was strength in his voice. Her throat clamped, not wanting to believe what was happening.

"Nasr, you're a fighter; you've always been. You'll get through this," said Jayida.

"No, Jonder. Not this time. It's—it's always been there, and I can't—" He closed his eyes. Jayida's chin dropped, her hands rubbing her face awake. Was he losing his mind?

"Jayida!" said a deep raspy voice, and she immediately turned to the entrance, half expecting her father. But it couldn't be: he wouldn't have used that name, but worst of all, it hadn't sounded like Zahir at all. Not like Nasr either.

A shudder shot through her, freezing her blood as she looked around the tent for another presence. It wasn't just that her real name was uttered, but the challenging tone it had, like it wanted to tell her it knew all her secrets and fears—and always would.

She looked back at Nasr, and his dark eyes were now wide open, staring at her, and he seemed more alert than even his usual self. A deep, twisted knowing air fired through his eyes, with an unsettling smirk she'd seen before—that day of training when he'd pushed her, his rough manner so different she'd avoided thinking of it ever since. Like lightning he grabbed her hand and hung on with unearthly force.

"Na'am; he told me your secret," chuckled Nasr. His wiggly fingers oddly dabbed her hand, almost like a child curious at what he was looking at, and despite her hesitation she kept it there. Her inner primal fear yielded to her defiance, urging her to stand her ground.

"Who? Who told you?" She gritted through her teeth, in case anyone else appeared.

"He watches, always. And he'll come for you, too!" said Nasr, his sudden strong pull on her arm drawing her face to him. She stared deep into his wild pained eyes, and though she saw that disturbing darkness, there was also a raging flame—faint, like fluttering ghostly wings but its glow distinctly present. Convulsing, his grip loosened, and he once more took on his frail manner, the energy draining out of him.

"I was right about you: you'll do great things," Nasr whispered in his normal self again, and tears suddenly flooded her, unleashing sadness and urgency. "Please, hurry! Call them in with Shams, *now*," he said, nearly out of breath, and she fled in obedience.

Moments later Jayida returned with his sister and parents, her own, and Shams, all speechlessly gathered around the diminished form of the *sha'ir* of Banu Sa'd.

Warda and Yazida fell at each side of him, bathing his hands in tears.

"I am Nasr, son of the noble *sayyid* Aziz of the Banu Sa'd. No one is to avenge me: not my father, not Jonder, not Shams," he commanded.

"My son, my beloved; you are exhausted, I know, but it must be done," said his father, wrecked with emotion.

"*No one* is to avenge me!" Nasr yelled, his grating voice startling as much for its strength as for his bodily fragility. For a moment his strained breathing made the only sound. "Give them what they want, and send them away; that will be the end of it." Nasr fixed his father, who shook his head in tormented disbelief and confusion. "As before, Jonder is to be listened to and trusted," Nasr continued. "His *kahin* sight is true and I hold him as my beloved friend, as I have all my life."

At those words Jayida could no longer hold back the stream of tears, cascading down her cheeks as she stared at him.

"As for whom Yazida should marry, I recommend Shams. And off the eagle goes, by the light of day," Nasr said, and Yazida hid her shaking sobs in his palm. His gaze drifted up, lingered at something beyond the tent roof, and with a last deep breath, his eyes closed.

"No, no! Nasr, wake up! My son, my Nasr!" Warda screamed, and shook him awake relentlessly. She gripped him so forcefully that *sayyid* Aziz flew to her and engulfed her in his arms. "This can't be, this can't!" Warda groaned in his neck. "Let me see him, *let me see him*!" she raged, trying to shake free from his grip and rush out of the tent. But they all knew exactly where she was bent on, and as much as they understood, and wanted to themselves, it could not be allowed. *Sayyid* Aziz held her and rocked her in his arms, crying together through their shock and dismay, until she calmed down a bit.

"Shams, get ten camels with eagle *wasm* and tell the others to gather. I want them gone fast, before I change my mind," said *sayyid* Aziz. From Shams's pause Jayida thought he might protest, but the *sayyid*'s glare reinforced his command. Stroking her brother's face, Yazida looked like a young girl again and Jayida's tears redoubled at the sight of their shared pain.

Yazida pulled the sheet over him, and they solemnly left him there. In the brightening light promising another day that she'd never again share with Nasr, Jayida seethed like a pacing lion, demanding revenge on those responsible for it. Hardly a day before she was marching off with him, and now he was gone. Though every part of her wanted to believe it was a bad night vision, that she'd seen it all with her own eyes added to the cruelty of its quick unfolding. How abruptly his life was taken in a senseless way.

They rejoined the tribe and Shams with the flock of camels gathered at the brigands' camp, the whole Banu Sa'd at once on edge and dejected at the news Shams had given them. A tangible hate, sharp as a fresh blade, coursed through them, ready to seize weapons and pounce on them to water the earth with their blood in sanctioned revenge.

"*Aywa*, a fast recovery," grinned the leader, gawking at the camels. *Sayyid* Aziz's face contorted so violently that Jayida thought the brigand had finally gone too far and reached his own end once and for all.

"You *ghul*! Your evil eye will turn back on you and make you pay for this!" said Warda, and spit at him so hard it landed on his arm. The leader frowned in a mix of confusion and offense, then perked up as something like shocked understanding washed over him.

"Truly, my son is better than me," said *sayyid* Aziz. "But before I release you only by his wish, you'll answer my question: why didn't you just ask?"

The leader's eyes narrowed. "Better death than asking, like a beggar."

Sayyid Aziz huffed. "My blameless son's life for your cursed, lazy pride." He turned away, his hands on his hips as if holding himself together.

"It worked, didn't it," chuckled the leader.

In an instant, *sayyid* Aziz whirled around, clawed the leader's side and threw him to the ground in a loud thud. Like magic his blade appeared in his hand, and hovered above the leader's face, his companions making to jump to his aid yet prevented by the outnumbering clustered tribe and drawn weapons.

"Did it?" said *sayyid* Aziz. "Because now everyone knows that you could hardly reach the heel of a beggar." In a swift, hard motion, he swiped his blade across the leader's scarless eye and cheek, the gash opening up a red, straight mark. "That's to keep my decree fresh in your memory: by *al-ilah* on whom I call upon, you've doubled the weight of my promise on you now. And if a man's words are his life, then so is a dying man's. It was my son's wish, and his wish only, to spare you. So remember this moment, forever, and stay far, far away, because if I ever see you again, I will fulfill my promise with twice the power."

Sayyid Aziz spit on him and shoved him off, and wiped his bloody blade across his cloak. The leader struggled up, stifling a groan as he gripped his face and mounted, a shadow betraying his lurking fear of the binding decree. *Sayyid* Aziz dismissed them with a disgusted wave, and the tribe retreated just enough to let them ride off unimpeded.

Her jaw locked, Jayida's nostrils flared in conflicted satisfaction. At least the leader and his companions had two reminders of Nasr's lingering presence: the new cut on his face and the camels branded with Nasr's eagle *wasm*.

Maintaining the alert, the tribe remained still for a while, caught between settled closure and impending reaction. Samira drew close to Shams, the pushy mother ready to send off her offspring to work yet again. A few times Jayida caught one of the bandits turning around to them, lingering behind his band.

"No, this can't be," sniffled Warda. "We shall go after them the way they came after our innocent children!" she said, reaching for her husband's sword.

"My love, you must not," said *sayyid* Aziz, closing her hands with his.

"Must *not*? How—how can you say this? You *must*!" she broke off in desperation. "I thought I could do it, let them leave like this, but it's our *law*," she cried, her fists pounding into his chest. "How can he ever have peace if we don't do it? Your son's blood is crying out; avenge it!" cried Warda, her tortured tears streaming, rendering her face almost unrecognizable that it took Jayida all her strength to restrain her own conflicted grief.

"Do you wish to disobey his precious last words? I cannot do it, even as every bone in my body is reviling against it!" *sayyid* Aziz said.

"I can't let it! Jonder? Shams?" said Warda, then looked back to her husband. "If you won't do it, then I will!" She aimed again for his sword, but he instantly crossed her arms on themselves. "No, let me, *let me*!" she shrieked in his arms, her knees buckling in defeat as she sank to the ground.

Sayyid Aziz led her back to the tent with Yazida, followed by most of the tribe while Jayida hung back after them, if only to make sure Samira didn't send Shams off after the brigands. He might be Yazida's future husband but Jonder was still to be listened to, and like their *sayyid*, as much as she hated the feeling of rewarding such an evil deed, Nasr's last wish deserved to be respected. She was not fooled that even if Shams did go off after them, it may be less to avenge Nasr than for Samira to boast even more of her son. It was hardly the time for it, and she could at least take some pride in Nasr's choice of Shams for Yazida.

They returned to camp, changed into dark robes, and joined the solemn procession of *sayyid* Aziz, her father, Hubala, Sufyan, and others carrying the wrapped body to Wadi Al-Raha, the Valley of Rest southeast of camp. Rich clouds of frankincense swirled in their wake, enrobing the men carrying shovels and the sobbing and wailing women.

At the site of his grandparents' resting place marked by piles of stones and surrounded by growing shrubs, Jayida took a shovel, and joined in dejected silence in digging into the hard earth. The surface was so dry that it took some time before they made a significant dent. With sweat fast pouring down the side of her brow, her forearms soon ached, the lingering image of the despised bandits fueling her strength to strike into the rock-like land. They might pierce and scatter what seemed like nothing more than endless pebbles, but they would keep going, and lay him to rest in time before the greedy heat decomposed his young body.

Was Nasr watching them now, in a dream-like state the *kahinat* said the departed lingered in before fully crossing over beyond the veil?

Are you there? Her *qareen* silently asked him, hoping he would give some sign. But there was just more digging, and she almost felt silly for even asking. Wiping a tear away, she met her father's encouraging nod and kept going, wanting to do her part well in helping him cross over and find his well-deserved rest.

Everything had happened so fast, and she still couldn't fully make out their last moments together. How long had he known about her, and did he tell anyone else? As far as she could tell, the secret was still between them and her parents. Had he just found out at the very end, when he was in that in-between space that gave some sensitive poets revelations?

At last a deep pit lay before them, and the form wrapped in its cream linen sheet was brought near it. The tribe made its goodbyes, and several came over to touch his embalming garment one last time. Sufyan and Shams each offered a woven bracelet, and her parents lightly ran their hands over his arms, then let Jayida tuck their woven pouch filled with frankincense tears into the crook of his crossed arms.

Sniffling, Warda and Yazida gave their last tearful kisses to his beloved covered face, and tucked into his hands an arrow to signify his warrior-like bravery, and his woven pouch with his idol namesake, the eagle deity. *Sayyid* Aziz finished with a kiss to each cheek, and passed an incense burner sizzling with fresh frankincense over his full form one last time, as they had done at his birth. Then, carefully using ropes and poles, they lowered Nasr into his resting place.

The sight of his shrouded form in the ground coupled with the enrobing sobs pierced Jayida, confirming its sad reality. The man, a handsome *sha'ir* who'd taught and believed in Jonder; the one whom she once thought she might marry, and had even come to know her real name—was now gone, his life senselessly cut short.

Biting her lip, she closed her sore tearful eyes, a gentle breeze perfectly flowing through the loose spaces around her damp legs, neck, and back.

Something like a rustling gasp called her eyes open. The sheet over Nasr's face had swept aside, rolling over his idol pouch and exposing his face. A silence reigned, their breaths collectively stilled. If she was supposed to look away, she couldn't. Though his dark hair and brows sharply contrasted his paleness, he seemed asleep, his chiseled features with a beauty so striking it was as if she saw him for the first time. She already had so much to look back on fondly to remember him, and her heart tugged to add this last unexpected sight to it.

"My beautiful son, visit us often," whispered Warda.

"Find rest, and watch over us, my son," sniffed *sayyid* Aziz. After a moment he lowered his spear into the grave and gently swept the corner of the linen sheet back over his face. With a last nodding glance, he signaled for the grave to be filled.

Warda's sobs painfully redoubled as her son's frame disappeared under mounds of dirt, while her husband and daughter cradled her in their arms. Once done, they each laid their stone upon the grave, creating a tall mound that would command any passing soul's attention.

"Everyone will know what a great soul rests here. Though his life was cut short, he lived it well," said *sayyid* Aziz with a tearful nod, and turned away with his wife in his arm and the tribe following him back to camp.

Jayida hung back, tears threatening again as her father handed her her pouch of favorite stones.

"I'd forgotten—But he was supposed to live *so long*!" she cried, and her parents swept in around her as they'd done her whole life. She'd had no mind for it but in the rush and circumstances, she hoped she could be forgiven not thinking of which stone to use for him. She sniffled and fished out a polished dove grey-blue oval stone, one of her favorites.

"Please watch over us," said Jayida, and added her stone to the pile.

Back at camp, the tribe gathered around *sayyid* Aziz and Warda, and Nasr's white stallion Bariq at their side as a tentative noble substitute for his departed rider. Meanwhile Yazida, Zoraya, and Samira brought out trays of food offerings for the slain victim. Once all settled, they sat dejectedly around the pigeon pies, gruels, and breads intentionally left untouched, as much for respect as lack of appetite in the unhappy circumstances.

Even in her anguish, Warda wasn't unlike her beloved son, restraining herself from tearing at her hair and clawing at her skin, as some women easily did, even under lesser stress. As devastated as she was, such a heartbreaking reaction would do nothing to bring back her son.

Though Nasr had always been calm and poised, sometimes even self-effacing, the opposite of loud and obnoxious, his absence was even more obvious now. If Nasr were there, his verses would fill their souls with delights. But who would be *sha'ir* now? Jayida could hardly imagine Shams taking up as well after him.

With her singing and dancing ability, perhaps Yazida was his natural successor, or would at least succeed where Shams didn't.

Jayida glanced at Yazida across from them, looking more pained by her parents' anguish than her own. The dark clothing was so unlike her vibrant personality and seemed too harsh on her. Warda rocked side to side, tears streaming, and Yazida began humming a low steady tune that despite its dreary air, added life to their surroundings.

How could Warda and her husband ever be healed from such grief and senseless loss? Engulfed in the melodious heartache, her own loss unfolded: how she'd never again ride off with him, or train with him, or run to him with her latest news and achievements. They'd never even kissed, but how could they when—

Once more, the mystery gripped her: how long had he known? And if it'd been a while, why hadn't he said anything? Had there been someone else that he hadn't said anything about, the secret following him in the beyond? Even his sister had kissed a princely poet, and possibly the finest in the land at that. Apart from Imru, their secret moment was between them now—and her own parents. She wondered what Yazida thought of her brother's recommendation for her and Shams, especially if she surely still thought of Imru.

Jayida caught the weight directed at her, and met Shams, whose sad frown drifted to Yazida. Finally, he could have her: Nasr had supported it. Was he satisfied now, able to release some of his competitive fears off of Jonder? She had no wish or need to challenge him, and appreciated his friendship, as different as they were. The truth was obvious more than ever now, that their lives were changing fast. With a hint of selfishness she was glad that he didn't know of the Imru affair. With Nasr gone, she could at least have one memory of his generosity shared with his sister.

Yazida stopped humming and her mother stilled herself, biting her lips to strengthen and poise herself.

"My beloved, perfect son Nasr," Warda began her *rithā'*. "That monster and his *ghilan* were not worthy, and yet, your generous heart gave. All your life you supported your kin, giving your care, time, and knowledge, and blessing us with verses we'll never be as skilled to repeat, yet will never forget. Ask Imru Al-Qays himself, and he will tell you!" she said, to approving nods. "And for this I am glorified to be the mother of blameless *sha'ir* Nasr, son of *sayyid* Aziz of Banu Sa'd," said Warda, finishing her funerary poem.

Yazida wiped a tear and nodded. "No one was ever as blessed to have such a brother," Yazida said, beginning her words of praise. "He loved, protected, and gave without a second thought. Patient, understanding, and a true judge of character," she said, and looked at Jayida. "My blessed brother Nasr, you will never be forgotten."

Sayyid Aziz raised his eyes to the sky. "Nasr ibn Aziz: generous in life, and in death." He closed his eyes and shook his head, his throat locking up.

"My brave cousin Nasr: I will honor you all my days," said Shams.

"Nasr: the skilled hunter and generous giver of *maysir*, who will forever inspire us," said Sufyan and Hubala in unison.

"Nasr ibn Aziz, who cannot be forgotten," began Jayida. "But will you forget *us*? Where do you go with your generosity that defies understanding? You, who rewards your killer." She stopped. "You cannot be gone, when we pay you with our tears and praise, inviting you to be with us often, and tell us where you are taking your gifts." Jayida looked away, aware that it was too soon to expect the hot tears to slow down. Though words would never be enough to express all she felt, there was a soothing effect to it, like naming it gave it new wings to fly on.

"Another skilled tongue; not surprising given your friendship with my son," said *sayyid* Aziz.

"You're too kind *sayyid*, but no one could ever match Nasr's skill, except maybe Yazida," said Jayida, hoping to deflect. That her words pleased and could provide some relief to the tribe was an added balm.

Others followed in sharing loving words and memories through their *rithā'*, each touching verse reminding how Nasr would live on in similar and different ways to different people. Yet the brigands who'd gotten away with robbing Nasr's life would need a miracle to understand the depth of their wrong and undeserved luck.

"What did he say to you?" said Warda, catching her off guard when the tribe started cleaning up for the evening. "I know I shouldn't, I don't mean to—it was between you two," she sniffled.

"Not to be sad," Jayida improvised. "But he was exhausted so he didn't say much." Even if others knew, she wouldn't reveal the details of it, but had renewed gratitude for her friend's words that secured her place. *Jonder is to be trusted*—another knot loosened within her at his last words, proclaimed even after knowing her true name.

"Do you think it was our punishment?" said Warda, wringing her hands as the tears flowed again.

"Punishment? For what?" said Jayida.

"For failing to follow *mubassir* Ayyub's guidance. He's been here from the start, giving us prayers to recite, and advice on things that Yassu would approve of when Nasr was sick. But we didn't—we haven't always followed so well," she said, burying her sobs in her hands.

"How can that be? He was younger and he recovered. This was different," said Jayida, hoping she sounded convincing.

"Maybe it's *al-ilah*'s revenge for not serving him well, and we deserve it," cried Warda.

Jayida frowned. "Any god who would react like this is not one I'd want to worship. At the very least, he could make it clear what he expected so that there's less risk for disappointment," said Jayida, sensing at least one predictable shocked reaction.

"Oh *Allah al-ilah*, take pity on us, you know how grieved we are. We mean no disrespect, punish us not with your wrath," whispered Samira as if to lessen the impact of Jayida's words, while cueing others to do the same.

The showy gesture so annoyed Jayida that she almost told her to stop. Where had they been, the deity Nasr included, when their own beloved Nasr had been hit? What comfort, what reassurance did they give? Jayida had never questioned them like this before, but she saw now how her past worries were mere children's trifles in comparison. If Shams agreed with his mother, he showed no signs of it, though Jayida was reminded of his fear of the spirits as recently as the previous day—during their very last outing with their friend who now lay buried with his grandparents.

Jayida wasn't trying to offend anyone, human or spirit, but until she had some kind of proof, perhaps even from Nasr, then why should she put trust in any of the deities from the long list? At least with Yassu she knew her mother had prayed to Him for a child, and perhaps somewhat contributed to her current existence.

"We are all grieving. As Jonder said, Nasr is with us still, and will not let harm come upon us," said *sayyid* Aziz, his word silencing them.

"In his honor, I offer to pitch tent and watch over him for the next seven days," said Jayida, trying not to sound too challenging, though it might almost prove her point that she didn't expect anyone to join.

"I'll come, too," said Shams, more from duty than inclination.

When the sky darkened and the chill deepened, they took their weapons and the food offering for Nasr, and went back to Wadi Al-Raha. Solemnly they laid the food down and pitched a tent, the tension evident between them but not unpleasant. Even if Shams's reluctance of being there was from his fear of spirits, she shared his discomfort in her own way. What mattered was that they were there, honoring Nasr with gifts for the beyond and making sure no potential wolves or hyenas dug up their friend.

"*Aywa*, you can hurry and come now; it's just us," said Jayida when they finally laid down, their heads propped outside of the tent and lost into the starlit sky. She recalled *mubassir* Ayyub saying something about Keywan, the star of Saturn guiding the Magi to the site of Yassu's birth, which was then named the Cave of Treasures. Was Nasr somewhere over there now, guided by and gliding along the other brightest stars of Suhayl and Al-Shira?

In the torrent of emotions a child-like awe seized her, clouding her vision. Just yesterday she'd thought of planning their next trip to Wadi Al-Qura, which like so much else, would not be. She sniffled, then realized she couldn't tell hers apart from Shams's.

"I know you're *kahin*, but aren't you worried?" said Shams after a while.

"I am, in a way. But what kind of friend is he if he can't even protect us at his grave, and on the same day we dug it for him?" she said, glad to see a smirk emerge on his lips.

Thankfully they weren't adding to the sadness with the olden *baliya* sacrifice tradition, where a she-camel or horse was left to starve to death at their master's grave, to serve as mount in the afterlife and on resurrection day. Yet she shuddered that it likely still happened somewhere.

"I guess if this happens to us soon too, at least he'll be there already," said Shams. Maybe that was all it would ever be from then on: a constant battle between acceptance and defiance.

Amidst dreamless, light dozing, the night passed without trouble, and in the morning they returned to camp, the tribe's long faces brightening at the sight of them.

Finally alone with her parents, Jayida confessed to them the strange behavior she'd seen once before in Nasr, ignored until it resurfaced again just the day before, along with his last words that echoed in her soul: *He watches, always.*

They tried to make sense of his knowledge of her true gender: how if he'd known all along, he'd chosen not to mention it until then. She searched her memories for the times he might've done things that hinted he knew, but came up empty. Perhaps it didn't matter: as his last words proclaimed, it had changed nothing about their friendship.

And then she shivered at the thought, forcing herself to say it: was it an evil *jinni*, the kind that—taking advantage of his weakness—filled him with darkness? Was that who had told Nasr her secret? Spirits often knew things about people others didn't, and could use it to their advantage.

There was some relief in her parents' conclusion that it was likely some lower *jinni* who, in Nasr's sickness, had sadly revisited at intervals his whole life, and could have infected his thoughts in his last moments. It happened that people, right before passing, could be sharp-sighted; that could explain his sudden knowledge of her true gender. As for that most unpleasant training event, it had thankfully only happened once.

It seemed clear to her father that no one else knew, and was probably why Nasr had requested to speak to her alone, keeping the secret between them. But since he had found out, even if they weren't sure how, it could happen again.

Once more she recalled the eternal advice to always be on her guard, and see what might unfold in the coming days. She certainly preferred the most harmless explanation to the dreadful one of an evil *jinni* sweeping over him, aiming to conquer him for itself. The thought that he may be trapped, roaming in pain in the beyond was more than she could bear.

The following nights back at Nasr's grave, she repeated her silent pleas for a sign, any sign that he made it over well. But they were signless, sleepless, dreamless. Nor was her guardian, the Aksumite princesss, anywhere in sight, and a bitter part of her wondered why she hadn't warned her of this life-changing turn. But then, what if she'd had? Would it have been easier to prevent, or been even worse for knowing about it while remaining helpless to change it? Maybe they were wrong and she wasn't *kahin* after all—she'd never named herself so—because she was not making any sense of it.

As for those vile brigands, who still breathed and roamed the land with their camels, she dreaded what they'd say of the Banu Sa'd. Would they call it a tribe so generous, no one would walk away without having been helped—or one that didn't defend itself, so foolishgly giving to the point of self-destruction?

Had the time come to have Nasr's words and poems written down? In her conflicted longing Jayida tried to recall all his short poems, and other memorable words and advice he'd said, but in her tearful frustration she only came up with bits and pieces. There was so much more and for the first time, the sense that it might be lost, or at least incomplete, hurt most.

Visit us, Nasr! Help me remember!

She pleaded, waited for an answer, but there was only empty silence.

Chapter Eighteen

LURKING DANGER

Please don't! Please have mercy!

The young Aksumite woman begged, tears streaming down her copper skin in such agony that it tore Jayida's heart. The woman searched her assailant, afraid, desperate for a trace of understanding—and then, once again, it all vanished in a blur.

Jayida stopped, closed her eyes and eased her grip on the leather strap and blade, pausing her repetitive sharpening outside in the sheep pen. With a long sigh and a glance at the young, bouncy long-eared Hijazi goats, she tried to wash the images away, tired of waking up sweaty and gripped by a sickening mix of shattering sadness and rage that made her want to vomit. When it wasn't this unknown young Aksumite woman, so different from her princess guardian, it was groups of men, women and children, clustered unshakeably in a suffocating cloak of pity, mumbling repeatedly in the deafening rumble. If it wasn't enough that she still mourned Nasr, this new blend of sorrowful images had to join her already full nocturnal list.

Where was Nasr? In over a month he still hadn't shown any sign of himself, least of all given any hint that he was near, watching over them. Sometimes in a moment of peaceful quiet, she thought it was him, drifting by, but dismissed it as her wishful *qareen*. She tried not to think of it, but if her worst fear of him being held prisoner by a *jinni* or *ifreet*—or something else—was the case, there was nothing to show for it either. Perhaps it was best to stop expecting it of him, when he was now of another world, and one she hoped was better.

It just felt even emptier, except for those tormented souls who revealed nothing besides their distress, and maybe even wanted her to wallow in it, too. As if she didn't have enough of it in sixteen winters! Why couldn't they leave her alone, like Nasr, when it seemed there was little either could do for the other?

Worst of all, she was no closer to figuring out who may be watching her, her parents, or the tribe overall. Each day was like walking barefoot on the burning desert floor, anticipating that a lurker might come out and reveal her secret for all to hear and mock. And then, would she proudly stand firm or break down in tearful apology? But what had she done wrong? That she might not be able to give it all up at once—if that were expected—seemed hardest of all.

And what of her father! The thought of him demeaned by the tribe for having lied and deceived—if they dared call it that—shattered her. She tried to think what they'd do next if that was the case, and imagined their trek northeast to her mother's tribe the Banu Taghlib; anything to get away and certainly not to ever crawl back to the Banu Zubayd.

Zubayd!

Was Moharib behind this, somehow? Did he know, and found a way to tell Nasr, maybe even through Khaled? In his times away from the tribe, there was no telling who Nasr could've been seeing. But how could Moharib have found out? And with his boastful ways, why tell only Nasr and not the whole tribe? In her rambling thoughts a concerning realization struck, and she mentally kicked herself for not thinking of it before. What if Nasr had suspected something and sought out Moharib on his own for answers...

He watches, always.

Though she rarely said it aloud, and only to her parents, Jayida hated most that even after all this time, it felt like Moharib's evil eye fixed on her, constantly on her trail. And yet for all his proud strength, he'd never even come to them himself. However she turned it, Moharib was the reason her whole life had been publicly lived as Jonder, and even if she'd rather not tell the whole tribe the vile words he'd said to her father, she couldn't shake her parents' justification for their decision. Surely the tribe would understand?

Forty sunrises turned into sunsets, and Jayida braced herself for the end of the mourning period, but still, nothing happened. Warda's deep, shattering motherly loss hung over them as much as their *sayyid*'s now muted joy. Everyone saw less of each other, secluded in their tents or on lonely distant forays, or trying to both cheer up and escape by passing out on palm wine, like Sufyan. In his sober moments even his cheerful manner was tamed, and he once more pondered if he should finally settle or finally leave for good, as he'd often considered. In Nasr's cruel absence, it seemed that each, in their own way, sought meaning in the temporary life that they led. At least they could take heart in the eternal conclusion that though brief, Nasr's life hadn't been in vain.

The rare times Warda was seen, it was wrapped in her dark robes that Jayida feared she'd never shed, with Yazida at her side like her faithful shadow. Yazida also kept to her dark robes, though Jayida suspected it also helped in postponing talks of marriage to Shams.

Jayida gathered her blades and joined her father in *sayyid* Aziz's quarters, the open space next to him beckoning to her. Even after Nasr's last words, she was touched by his father's continued doting on Jonder, sometimes even making a point of keeping her around past the others. She usually avoided Shams's darting glances like she evaded his mother's, and as much as she missed Nasr in ways she couldn't express, his father's affection offered reassurance, even if momentary.

They'd hardly sat down when Samira appeared in the entrance with Shams at her side.

"Blessed *sayyid*, all praises to you! Will today be the day? Just say the word," said Samira, with a light bow. Next to her, Shams's pained air already seemed to be apologizing for his mother.

"We've gone over this," said *sayyid* Aziz without looking at her.

"*Aywa sayyid*, but your pain is ours! The mourning period had passed and we're free of blame from anything that follows. You know best of all that they *deserve* to be punished," said Samira, restraining a smirk. "It's surely why neither you, Warda, nor Yazida have seen Nasr in any night visions. We also can't bear the thought that his soul isn't at peace, able to roam freely as he should!"

"Samira!" yelled *sayyid* Aziz in a tone Jayida had never heard but fully approved of. Now Samira presumed to know what the spirits were up to, when *kahinat* themselves weren't always right—though few would dare even admit that.

"For the last time: is this what my son said? Is this what Jonder says to do now?" Jayida fixed on the eagle design on the carpet, woven by his mother for Nasr, convinced that he would be as annoyed by this scene as they were.

"It's never too late to change one's mind; we've all been grieving. I just worry that you might be calling wrath to yourself, since you didn't even take any blood money, but instead gave away—"

"*Aywa*; perhaps now Samira can be *sayyida* in my place, is that it?" *Sayyid* Aziz was so angry and his tense legs on the verge of rising that Jayida thought he might slap the disrespect out of her—and was half tempted to do so herself.

"I won't say it again, so you listen well. I will not have my son's name mentioned again in such a way, *ever*! If you cannot bear to be here, you know what to do," he said, and dismissed her with a wave of the hand.

Jayida reined in her raging storm under her metal chest. It wasn't enough that one of their tribe's best souls had been taken from them, along with his gifted verses, but now Samira had to keep fueling the fire with her constant grumbling. Only now was Jayida almost sure that she was possessed of *jinn* of perpetual discontent, who allowed no one any rest. Samira was wrong: *sayyid* Aziz would not be calling wrath on himself, when she was so reminiscent of Shamshun's unfaithful lover Dalilah—among others—whose constant nagging to know the secret of his strength brought about his end. If she had the power, Jayida would make it law that a man could divorce his wife for nagging and earn a worthy payment for his trouble.

Samira frowned in confused disappointment and reluctantly retreated with Shams, who'd surely get on to the tiring work of calming her down. It was but one of many instances where Jayida could almost laugh at women's so-called gentle natures, when it was known that some women's self-righteous revenge often surpassed men's.

Jayida turned to her father and the dejected *sayyid*, who threw back what was unlikely his first full cup of wine of the morning. It'd become a common sight, along with his lost glazed eyes staring off into space, his once chatty demeanor now silenced amidst occasional drunken mumbles. He hadn't even the heart to remove Nasr's tent from its place, and she was glad it was still there. Even Nasr's stallion Bariq and his she-camel seemed sullen from losing their skilled *sha'ir* rider. Jayida prayed that Yazida was coping, and thought about trying to catch her briefly, perhaps when she went to draw some water, or better yet, bringing it to them.

"Is something wrong with my daughter?" said *sayyid* Aziz.

"*Sayyid*?" frowned Jayida.

"I know you were closest to my son. Why did he choose Shams over you?"

Her stomach clenched, and she looked away. "He knows best."

"You're the son of the man who saved my life. And you were born before Shams," said *sayyid* Aziz, glancing at Zahir who wore a sad frown. Wherever he was, she hoped again that Nasr knew how thankful she was for his last words.

"May his soul be at peace. It's good for us to honor his wish," said Jayida, holding back tears.

"You remind me of him. He was my peace, the one who saw calmly, clearly, like nothing could unsettle him. I don't know where he got it; not from me or his mother. And now that's gone. What am I supposed to do?" said *sayyid* Aziz tearfully. "Sometimes I think of renaming the tribe after him, like they did at Najran for their martyr Al-Harith bin Ka'b. But in his humility I'm sure he'd disagree."

Zahir draped his arm around his friend's shoulders, taken over by sobs. Swallowing back her own deluge, Jayida had a consuming gnawing sense that it might periodically relent, but would never really end.

But even on the long, bland days when it seemed time stopped, like another tragic version of the *Ayyam al-Zalam*, life went on. Jayida sought solitude, drifting between Wadi Al-Hamd and camp. Lost in thought with Hania as her silent companion, she searched out bits of useful woods for fuel, and the occasional *karaz* acacia leaves for medicine and bark to dye leather red, or appealing stones to add to her collection. One day, she would work up the courage to go to the last place Nasr had taken them—but not yet.

With Nasr gone, she had to be on guard even more than before, and continued her self-training, recalling what she'd learned with him. She put all her weapons and tools to use, using sand or stone-filled cloth and leather bags tied to her waist and ankles, and ran for long distances—her metal-concealing body fighting against the elements. Up and down rocky hills she went, jumping side to side, dodging falling rocks, brandishing her sword Al-Wasiyah at potential imaginary attackers, and ran until her breath and heartbeat finally adjusted, so that stopping would be the unnatural state.

Some days were like pounding into stone, and nothing was enough to reflect the fullness of her tormented soul. With a shovel she hit and dug, with no goal in sight other than to see and feel it crush under her blows.

"Ahhhhh!" her raw scream scraped out of her, filling the *wadi* as they'd so often done together in happier times. Then when the mood suited her, with all her might she lifted her father's silver shield that had seen battle at Kutha, and tossed it forth, letting it fly as hard and far as she could. But they were just endless motions, no matter how strong and repeated, that seemed always short of the right mark.

One suffocating day she saw a face—so unsettling, she decided it was like Moharib's—smirking with blinding teeth, curving into a beast's.

You cannot escape! It cackled.

"So then I won't!" Jayida spewed out from the pit of her soul, daring it to come straight at her as she stood her ground, the shield on her back, with a spear and Al-Wasiyah in each hand. Her palms raw with pain, the dry skin peeling, her arms ached but she struck hit after hit, her brow drenching but refusing to stop until all her limbs fell off, one by one.

Each moment she waited for it, but kept battling, surprising herself that she was still standing. Then, all of a sudden, she dropped her weapons and fell back into the hole cushioned with sandbags, the dug earth blessing her with shade. Panting, the sky made a floating blue rectangle up above, smaller than she'd ever seen. Dazed, she closed her eyes, imagining the earth opening up in a cross the way it did for Adam's body, as *mubassir* Ayyub recited from the Book of the Cave of Treasures.

"Jonder? Jonder!"

At first Jayida thought she was dreaming, hearing the blended voices of Shem and Melchisedek hovering over her instead of the First Man, and she was so comfortable in that placed fittingly named Skull where Yassu was crucified that she didn't want to stir.

"Please, get up!" The urgency in her mother's voice called her back, and she saw her fretfully stretching her arms down to her. "Come on!" Zoraya cried, her wiggling fingers reaching to pull her up. With a groan Jayida got up, and heavily climbed out, as confused as impressed that she'd dug so deeply without hardly recalling any of it.

Over and over, her mother's hands brushed over her face, her large fearful doe eyes searching her out.

"Jayida," whispered her mother. "What were you doing? I know it's tough with Nasr, but please, don't do this. I won't have the darkness claim you!"

"*Yama*, stop," said Jayida, brushing her off.

"My heart, let's not tempt or call any darkness to us by such things, even if you don't mean it. Oh, I just want you to be well, I pray my curse hasn't touched you," her mother cried.

"Oh, another Samira; just what I need right now! And what can we do anyway, to make everyone around us happy *all* the time, huh? Maybe I am cursed, or the same: not meant to ever marry! Look where our hopes for Nasr went; vanished somewhere, off with him," said Jayida, her arms waving like a wild eagle. "And why are you crying? Did Samira also rob your faith? Enough of tears! I've shed tears and I have to keep being strong, so stop fussing and let me do as I must!" Jayida grabbed the rest of the belongings and ran back to camp.

She left her wares back in their tent and rushed to the *sayyid*'s tent, eager for the company of self-possessed—or at least quieter—men.

"There you are Jonder, I was just asking your father where you were," said *sayyid* Aziz, handing her some bread filled with goat cheese with an air of unexpected intensity. Avoiding her father's gaze, she noted Shams, like Hubala, lost somewhere in the fire.

She bit into the bread, relishing the warm salty taste. "What's wrong?" she said.

"We've gotten news that young twins, a boy and girl from the Banu Ghatafan, have gone missing near Jabal Abyad and the western branch of Wadi Al-Rummah," said *sayyid* Aziz.

"All they found so far are lion tracks and a shred of bloodied clothing," continued Hubala with a frown. "But that's not all: they fear it might be the very same one that attacked long before. It's been so long though that they thought he was dead, and now they say this immortal beast has returned from the north. Everyone's afraid to face him; they say he's huge, like a *ghul*, not just a regular lion."

"That's not so far from here," said Shams with a somber air.

Jayida swallowed the rest of her bread. "When did it happen?" she said.

"Just earlier today. They sent a messenger to share the news, and are welcoming help from anywhere they can get it."

"What's the reward?" Shams said, probably satisfied that his brother Sufyan was likely passed out from milky-sweet palm wine somewhere.

"They didn't say," said *sayyid* Aziz.

What a silly question, when slaying the beast would be reward enough. She expected Shams to speak through the enveloping tension, but was surprised that for once he kept his stillness. Was he deflecting, or was this demon already having its effect?

"Who's gone off to help?" said Jayida.

"So far, no one," said *sayyid* Aziz. "They fear that the more time passes the less likely they'll find them alive. But if it's not handled soon it could potentially be our problem, too. Oh Nasr, please protect us," he sighed.

In the beckoning fire, the images raced. Missing twins, a mythical wild creature. Terrifying fear. There were cries, a blade striking into skin, drawing blood. Torn clothing, running—small, sweaty hands gripping for each other. And the growling, immortal *ghul*, following them. The flames roared, spitting out burning sparks, outlined in the monstrous pitch black that swallowed up the whole desert once outside the light's range. Jayida glimpsed a pair of yellow-brown eyes dotted with green, fixed on her, his inky, molten lava lips curved into a sneering grin.

Gaping lion eyes... her eyes, drawing her in.

Something slithered up her spine. She knew just what she had to do.

CHAPTER NINETEEN
TRACK

Jayida laid patiently in wait until the nightly quiet fell. She wondered if she'd see Shams on her way out, but hoped she wouldn't. In her intense focus, the last thing she wanted was to see anyone, and preferred to be alone with her thoughts, or maybe even with Nasr.

By the glowing light of the moon, she slipped out into the ice cold, her thick headwrap already over her nose. With her palms wrapped in old leather gloves and Al-Wasiyah at her waist, she strapped her leather bags to Hania's saddle, and mounted briskly. For a moment, the lingering stillness strangely amused her. Was no one else going after the *ghul*, or was she already too late? She'd been standoffish the whole night, and had feigned going to bed without a word to her parents, all too satisfied that they'd taken the hint to leave her be. In their absence she'd filled her belt with a few more blades, but relished the thought of not needing them with her preferred bow and sword to take him down.

She cued Hania east towards Khaybar, the moonlight pointing out the dark volcanic earth and its endless shadowy bizarre rock forms. Her breath warmed her face under her headwrap, stifling the distracting airy forms they'd unleash in the chilly night. Curiously, the combination of dark and pearly light also made the surroundings seem harmless, because if some imagined endless lurking monsters, others could also say there was little there to be seen.

With a hidden smirk and click of the tongue, she picked up pace, relishing the freedom of unrestricted movement, as a potent, wild buzz coursed through her, sharpening her senses to the slightest noise, scent, or movement. If the beast prowled these parts, she would spot him in a moment, if Hania's own sharp senses didn't beat her to it.

"Where are you; come out to me, *ghul*! You like to play in the night, and so do I." She whispered to him, wishing he'd appear like the night *jinni* they told about at the campfire to scare children into obeying and keep them from wondering off.

It had to be a famished monster, for it to come this far south. But then again, did a lion, king of animals, need permission to roam where he wanted? That the region's long, ancient underground lava tube caves made a perfect hiding place for it and other predators only worked to its advantage. It might be even worse if he was someone's proud pet bent on twisted revenge for his cruel captivity. She swallowed back a groan thinking of the twins, and hoped they were huddled somewhere safe, away from the killer and biting cold.

Soon the outline of towering date palms and the walls of Khaybar came into view, and she continued past them and their glittering forts lighting the way from the mountaintops. With bittersweet nostalgia, she hoped that *nasi* Musa, his family, and Attab the Shadow, along with everyone else dwelling there, were all well and sound asleep within its confines.

Further south out of view camped the Ghatafan near the Qusaybah Dam. Jayida sensed the clusters of still, lurking eyes widened with fright then closed tightly shut, a collectively held breath trapped in tents, hoping and pleading the hellish lurker would stay far, or at least ignore them.

As Jayida coursed east, the long valley stretched ahead and what they called the land's tallest mountain, the white Jabal Abyad and its sister volcano, Jabal Bayda, grew larger in the distance. She marveled at the contrast of this wide expanse that was still as dry and seemingly empty, as it was bustling when filled with seasonal winter and spring rains that drew wildlife from near and far.

And now the beast wanted to be part of it. In the heart of night Jayida called to him again, gazing to and fro, Hania faithfully obeying and ceding to her quest to track down the creeping danger. She scouted once more for signs of other brave young men, but once again had the impression of being the only person moving across the land.

Jayida lowered her scarf and sniffed the freezing air, almost disappointed at the hunch that he wasn't there. But she hadn't come all this way for nothing, and instead resolved that she was right where she needed to be.

"No matter, we'll find him," she said to Hania, and reached out to pet her head.

Looking for a place to camp, they continued east when she caught the whiff of something rotting. With its stripes and long neck, the dark mass on the desert floor revealed the carcass of a hyena that perished a few days before. She pitied the animal, with its bottom half torn into shreds, and opened jaw fixed into a final cry. Sadness filled her at the odd feeling that it might've not been killed strictly from need, but maybe even as opportunistic surplus killing.

Half hoping it might draw the creature back, Jayida left it and found a smoother area near the rocky base of the towering, all-encompassing white Jabal Abyad mountain. She dismounted, gathered some rocks in a circle, and using her flint stone and steel blade she struck a fire.

With a woolen blanket on her shoulders and her pouch in tow, Jayida finally reclined on a simple woven mat, and laid Al-Wasiyah across her lap. Hania made a protective wall around her as she unpacked her incense burner, lit some frankincense tears, and danced Shamshun's carved lion in the spicy-sweet scent, then set it down to watch over them.

"Our turn now," said Jayida, and repeatedly waved the smoke over her face and chest. "*Shway*, don't blow it out," she chuckled when she brought near Hania's face, who blew lightly at her.

Cozied in her temporary open-air abode, she laid back against Hania and contemplated the white ash mountain whose ancient glory predated any life on the land. It was said to be the highest volcano in the land, with its nearby sister Jabal Bayda slightly shorter. Stories told of their lava so distinct that in some areas one could stand one foot in white ash, and the other on ebony basalt.

Jayida mentally drifted above them and floated in the endless silver-dotted, indigo space, thinking of Nasr, up there somewhere, still reciting poetry among the stars. Could someone who had crossed over still miss those from earth? No matter what he was doing, he would not be inciting revenge, not even then, and it pinched her heart to think that few could say this.

An image came to her of a girl at his side, so beautiful Jayida knew it wasn't anyone she'd ever seen. Had he kept it a secret and lost her now, too; his unfair death tearing him away from everything he loved? Nasr handed the girl a jasmin flower, and she smiled in grateful acceptance. Then there was Yazida and Shams, married and happy with children who had their father's tenacity and their mother's resilient beauty. They all merged and danced around a fire, the cheerful echoing drums matching their airy steps, as the gathering grew around them.

There was Shamshun with his seven braids, showing off his lion skin to children; Maryam praising *al-ilah* with baby Yassu in her arms, and the Praising Woman with her arms up to the sky. Then she noticed a handsome Rûm soldier shyly approaching a *badawi* girl, an Aksumite prince reciting poetry to a captivated *badawi* girl, and an Israelite scribe teaching *badawi* boys how to write. Bit by bit they joined the dance, the loving happiness sparking in their eyes imbuing them with a kind of resemblance, as if from the same tribe.

They all glowed, and while Jayida wondered how she fit in it, if she even fit at all, in that moment it was enough just to feel that undeniable joy whose source she could hardly begin to grasp. She was both outside and within, the prowling lion and the welcomed guest, and she had something like conflicted acceptance of this.

Tears blurred her vision, and though her ideas might be silly, she could do much worse than imagine such lovely stories. At least they kept her company, as wandering verses did its poet. Wrapped in her warm reveries, she slowly dozed off.

You can't hide forever!

The snarl shook Jayida awake, and she found Hania gazing around in the light grey hazy distance in shared concern. Even if it'd only been in her sleep, she knew the sharp cry she'd heard was a fierce lion's growl.

She quickly packed up, secured Al-Wasiyah at her waist, the dove grey sky revealing the vast patches of dark and milky volcanic grounds. With her full quiver on her back and a bow and two arrows in hand, she walked alongside Hania in the eastern direction. Her sense of cluelessness was countered by her pull to follow her inner calling.

Her bow drawn and nostrils flaring, she scanned the flatlands around them, at once impressed and frustrated by his invisible presence. He was there, somewhere, but not even his sudden morphing from thin air to fleshy *ghul* would catch her off guard.

As their crunching steps made the only sound, they entered a milky stretch of land dotted with thorny acacia trees and bushes that Hania cautiously went to.

"*Aywa*; you stay here and feast then," whispered Jayida. She scooped some earth and rubbed her robes with it, concealing at least some of her own scent, and continued her careful scouting.

Jayida came to a large field of dark, thick lava and paused. It was a wild mixture of flatter surfaces frozen in wavy, braid-like patterns, and others rugged, crooked pillars, like a star had crashed on the earth and scattered its contents. Instinctively she crouched as she walked on, her leather boots now silent on the ground.

She kept in this way for a while and made sweeping circles, like an owl with eyes on the back of her head. He could take his time; she would wait all the same. She entered another patch of flatter terrain filled with shrubs, went straight to them, and positioned and concealed herself among them. Ready with her bow and arrows drawn, she waited.

Soon she caught a faint vibrating; a scuffle of something hurrying under-ground, more like human steps than wild.

"Come on, old man," she chuckled low to herself. She glanced behind her, confirming once more its grey emptiness. Her gaze drifted directly ahead again—then locked.

There, in full view, stood the lion, a giant beast whose dark mane went down to his front legs. His massive face turned side to side, revealing the large scar going across his sealed left eye—a monstrous double of Nasr's killer. His blindness in that eye and older age only made him more terrifying, like it only served to sharpen his remaining senses. Jayida sneered, hating from the pit of her soul the man-eating carnage that dared threaten their lives.

The lion bared his teeth then let out a deafening roar, as if specifically warning her that she'd trespassed on his territory. What vanity! She didn't need his permission, and he was about to see who'd leave this place alive.

Fire swept her soul, as deafening, anguished pleas overflowed her ears.

"Here he is, Nasr," she called tearfully in her soul to her friend who'd so bravely faced death.

With hardly a stir, Jayida aimed her two arrows—for her father and mother—and launched them straight into his side. Struck, the *ghul* howled as she came out of the bush, the earth and sky now a molten pitch black lit up by writhing flames blazing all around them. With a deep breath to still her pounding head, the third arrow for Shamshun buried into his neck, the blood pouring out of him calling for revenge. Enraged, the gnarling monster turned to rush at her, and she launched a fourth for the tribe and fifth for Nasr into his chest in one blow. He groaned and dropped into the inky lava then slowly rose again, and she aimed a sixth into his side. With his loudest cry the demon lifted up, swelling like a terrorizing vast cloud, and she launched a final seventh arrow into his throat in honor of the twins.

Jayida paced straight to him in the hellish whirl, the exploding rush of wailing faces, torn children, cut up bits of flesh, cackling men and women making her nauseous. She unsheathed Al-Wasiyah before him, his strong legs scraping against the ground in attempt to pull himself up. Like lightning one of his claws struck out at her and she stepped back, wondering why she'd thought he might show some remorse in his last moments.

Her grip tightened and with all her force Al-Wasiyah pierced deep into his throat, the blood spilling out in a rich, red sea. Something inside her churned, like kneading bread dough squeezing the blood out of her heart.

Please don't! Have mercy! The pleading voice echoed, her vision clouding with desperate, lonely tears—the worst feeling in the world. The beast gave final jolts and with a swift pull she retrieved her sword.

Forcing herself not to shake as her hot tears cascaded, Jayida drew a blade from her belt, and knelt before the vanquished fiend. She lifted his front left paw, and stabbed deeply, repeatedly, carving a line down through the thick flesh, the warm liquid streaming the wider it opened. She reached in to the right side, felt through the mushy organs for the smaller mass until she found the heart, and with a clawing grip she ripped it out. Her dripping, bloody stiff eagle talons clutched it bare, and held it up.

"I'm Jonder, son of Zahir, and now everyone will know that I'm the lion slayer," Jayida said through clenched teeth. She drenched her other hand with blood and smeared her forehead, ears, and face with it, then licked some of the blood, swished it in her mouth and spit it out, ordering this evil to pass over her and her kin. She took the leather pouch from her waist and dropped the heart in, next to her carved Shamshun's lion. She finished by slicing a paw off and splitting its claws into two pairs, and added it to the pouch as protective charms.

Exhausted, she dropped on her back, and stared up at the now bright, spotless blue sky. She panted as she lay, arms spread out and head spinning.

Is it you Nasr, watching me? she whispered.

Her face turned to the side, her blurry wet vision catching only the outlines of two small, connected shapes. For a moment she remained immobile, until gradually her sight cleared.

Slowly she lifted her head, and saw a girl and boy holding hands, smiling shyly at her.

CHAPTER TWENTY

BANU GHATAFAN

A tribe of marveled stares fixed Jayida as she struggled to smile with lowered chin, her inner stillness still reluctant to settle. Anyone's *hilm* would be shaken after such an event, but she would not let on.

She wanted nothing more than to be alone but she tried to focus through her lingering overwhelming discomfort, the blood on her facilitating a commanding, fierce appearance.

"Al-Lat favors Banu Ghatafan today, by returning our children through our new guest. Welcome," gently coaxed the white-haired *sayyid* Hudayfa.

"Jonder." She paused, caught between revealing something of her identity and yet too little at once. "Son of Zahir, who dwells among the Banu Sa'd, led by the noble *sayyid* Aziz," she said.

"*Aywa*; may he be blessed for one of his men coming this way. Their uncle and guardian Badr has been so worried; he was out looking for them as late as he could, and owes his gratitude to you."

Jayida nodded, satisfied to avoid looking at the grim Badr, whose frown seemed more his natural state than the concern the *sayyid* spoke about.

"May your tribe increase. I confess that my heavy heart would lighten a bit if, instead of thanking me, you'd offer some prayers to Nasr," said Jayida. "This son of the nobble *sayyid* Aziz, a fine *sha'ir* and a good friend to me, was as generous in life as he was in his last moments, even to his vile murderer." For a moment she thought tears would burst again, but instead she floated in a swollen cloud of numbness.

Sayyid Hudayfa's gaze deepened. "By Al-Lat, may his soul be at peace and justice be upon the Banu Sa'd. Your humility does not escape me, and we shall do exactly as you say. Hubays!" He motioned to a young man slightly younger than her that she took to be his son, who vanished and quickly returned with a smoking incense burner that he handed his father. The *sayyid* waved it around a few times then passed it to his neighbor who continued the cycle, as low mumbles spread throughout the tribe, along with the sacred aromatic clouds.

"Surely the good *sayyid* Aziz is the same who camped at Khaybar during the *Ayyam al-Zalam*?" said an older voice in the crowd.

"It is," said Jayida.

"And his good friend Zahir, who offered up so many Zahir camels for *maysir*, is your generous father?"

"He is," she nodded, as a low rumble built around her.

"By Allah, I knew it!" said the older voice, whose owner bolted up like a pillar waving his walking stick, and made his way to her through the crowd. "I am Wabara! I met your father oh so long ago; he couldn't have been much older than you when—"

"You met northwest of Tayma where he traded you Kamila for seven of his camels," smiled Jayida.

"*Aywa*!" said Wabara with sparkling eyes, his hand tentatively gripping her elbow in cautious inquiry. She told him that Kamila made a full recovery, and when she trusted the camels were doing just as well, his watering eyes gave her all the touched confirmation she needed.

"Thousand blessings and praise to them both for their wide cloaks! The camels have been nothing but blessings!" said Wabara to *sayyid* Hudayfa's lingering approval.

Other tribesmen clustered, swearing they had an offspring of Wabara's seven gifted camels, and others with one acquired through a friend of a friend who'd been gifted a camel by Zahir, during those dark, uncertain days. Jayida acknowledged each one with an understanding nod, grateful that her father's generosity had the desired effect of being remembered and uplifting hearts. She also called to their memory the rule of Hujr of Kindah, the bravest of Ma'add and father to Imru who'd recently visited them. She praised Imru's venture to *malik* Al-Harith, and *sayyid* Hudayfa instantly requested another call for prayers for the peace of Hujr's soul, and the speedy return of his poetic son, to resonating approval.

The ten-year old twins Najim and Najma huddled next to her, gazing at her with doe eyes. She tried not to think of Badr a few seats behind, whose feigned easy manner only made his leery glances at them more obvious. He could ease up, when she wasn't out for any reward, and least of all from him.

Jayida ached to wrap the gentle children in her arms again, but settled on the potent memory of their ride home to camp. After confirming they were unharmed aside from being famished, they ate her Khaybar dates as she pushed and rolled the lion corpse onto Hania. At last the children mounted, and Jayida walked alongside them, grateful for her mount that faithfully carried the children back to safety as they took turns poking at the corpse sprawled next to them.

Reading their exhaustion through their half-smiles, her heart tugged with the knowledge that at least they'd been together through the ordeal. As twins their bonds were already strong, but at least this would only deepen it. Throngs of more young children surrounded them, their expressions a mixture of contemplative frowns and awe at the lion carcass displayed before them at the center. A young boy of about seven sat on a man's lap, his dazed look drifting past her.

"Jonder ibn Zahir, you have honored our tribe. Let it be known that you and your kin are always welcome here," said *sayyid* Hudayfa. "Likewise may the twins' father and mother, may they rest in peace, protect you as they protect their children," he added to echoing agreement.

Jayida bowed her head, grateful for the tribe's well-meaning gratitude and good wishes that meant more to her than anything.

"May the great Al-Lat protect you," nodded Wabara energetically.

Jayida pinched another smile, reminded that one of the symbols of this goddess of fertility and war was the lion. But why should she, or any other, get the credit when she'd done the work? She might as well say it was Shamshun along with Nasr and her Aksumite princess guardian, and maybe even an elusive shape-shifting goddess named Jayida who'd guided her mission.

"Perhaps Ziyad, along with our *sha'ir* Hubays, will commemorate the day with verses; by the looks of it, he may already be at it," chuckled *sayyid* Hudayfa, eyeing the contemplative young boy she'd noticed.

"My little *nabigha* does little else," chuckled the man she took for his father, especially for referring to the boy as a genius. "I'm sure he hardly regrets the spontaneous visit now. I am Mu'wiya, proud father to this little poet in the making," he beamed.

"If his *qareen* has chosen him so young to honor his tribe the Dhubyan, then it's a blessing to us all," said *sayyid* Hudayfa.

"I'm only grateful that I could be of help. We must not forget what ordeal the children have suffered too, all alone," said Jayida pensively.

The account Najim had shared disturbed her. They had gone with Badr to graze the flocks at Wadi Al-Rummah and in boredom, ran off to play hide-and-find. They ventured into the dark volcanic fields and Najma fell into a crevice. It was a long time before Najim helped her out of the cave, and when they emerged, the sky had darkened and the plain was empty, their uncle and the flocks gone. They determined to make their way home, when they heard the lion's growl. The beast sighted them and came for them, so they had no choice but to return back to the lightless obscure cave, unsure if they would ever come out again. At dawn they'd heard the lion's cries again along with a scuffle and—cautiously—crept out and found Jayida triumphantly covered in the slain beast's blood.

She nearly shuddered to hear her actions described by them, who'd watched her without her knowledge. Did it look heroic, what she'd done? It had felt like a bad dream, her soul consumed by a horrible mix of consuming anguish and anger, urging her to defend life at all costs. But there was also a release, the satisfaction of stabbing into the living flesh, and finally stopping its deadly wrath. Neither was it like four summers before when the leopard had attacked her, and though her triumph was now even more significant, it was also gutwrenchingly painful. It felt like a part of her own heart had been ripped out, requiring she does the same to the monster's to maintain the tormenting balance of power.

"Oh, to see our youth growing their wings to honor their tribes," said *sayyid* Hudayfa, patting her shoulder. "It's much-needed inspiration for the younger ones. I wonder: have you heard about that slave 'Antarah of 'Abs?"

"No," said Jayida, her curiosity surging through her fatigue.

"He's the son of Shaddad and an Aksumite slave. And not only has he shown skill as a poet, but he's making demands to be recognized as his son, freeing him from his slave bonds. He may be overreaching in his bravery, but heroic deeds often come from the most difficult situations. May he succeed," sighed the *sayyid*.

His genuine tone hinted that his reluctance was more aimed at the Banu 'Abs than at his own doubt of the slave poet. And if the 'Abs were as quarrelsome as they sounded, would they still call what she had just achieved heroic, if they knew she was a woman? And why shouldn't 'Antarah be recognized as Shaddad's lawful son, when it had taken a father to sire him! A defiant satisfaction filled her. It was the first time she heard of 'Antarah, but she hoped it wouldn't be the last.

With a sigh, she braced herself for what she had to say next.

"Generous *sayyid*, I humbly thank you for your great hospitality, but I must return home," said Jayida. Had that been Badr's rough shifting in his seat, radiating all the way to her?

"*Esh!* But you must stay; you cannot leave us so soon!" said *sayyid* Hudayfa, his shock echoed by the gathering.

"You've blessed me greatly by your warm welcome, and allowing me to serve you," said Jayida. She avoided looking at the twins, knowing she might tear up again.

"But they'll have you soon enough! Wait—" *Sayyid* Hudayfa wiggled his finger.

"It's just that I left without—"

"A word! Ha! My kinsmen, hear! Jonder left his tribe to come and help us, without a moment's second thought!" beamed the *sayyid*, raising himself and her along with him, as he gestured to some men. The group took the lion carcass and loaded it back on Hania, and repeated their gratitude and well wishes for her safe return home.

Sayyid Hudayfa motioned to Hubays and whispered something in his ear. Chuckling, the *sayyid* returned, set his arms upon her shoulders and kissed her once on each cheek.

"Jonder ibn Zahir, the lion of Sa'd," he said with an affectionate grin.

"You are too kind," said Jayida with a light bow, and turned to the twins. "And may we meet again," she smiled at Najma and Najim, wishing that the next time it would be different and she might even be Jayida.

A hush fell over the crowd as it dispersed, allowing Hubays through, luring a white Arabian stallion.

"A noble steed for a noble deed," nodded *sayyid* Hudayfa. "My grateful gift to you," he said, stroking the striking horse that shone like smooth pearls.

Jayida's jaw dropped. "I cannot," she shook her head, but the *sayyid* raised his palm.

"You must. Now what will you name him?"

All at once, suggestions filled the air like bustling crowds at the annual market. She heard them all, rushing over with food and small gifts, their joy touching and fueling hers, until she glimpsed Badr gripping Najim and quickly slapping him, as if taking the opportunity that no one would see. She didn't care what he might say: there was nothing Najim could've already done in their short time since their return to upset him. As if they hadn't suffered enough already.

And what did he have to be angry about, when she'd asked nothing of him? Unless... Did she dare say it: that he was yet another angry *ghul*! That there was no way the children could've gone that far out by themselves; someone had taken—or forced—them there...

Jayida looked away and moments later Najma and Najim appeared at her side, their demeanors misleadingly subdued. That they'd protected him with their story only made her anger rise up again. Her gaze narrowed. Only now could her satisfaction be complete.

"Adil!" Jayida thundered above the hubbub that promptly turned into silence. "That's what I'll name this most honorable gift, for blessed righteous justice over any situation." She glanced around and smirked at Badr who forced a crooked smile. "And now I'll make a parting gift to the twins, sure to benefit the whole tribe."

Jayida reached for her pouch and took out the two bloody lion's claws, to resounding surprise. She knelt in front of the twins, whose confusion helped to hide Najim's conflicted air. Torment seized her again: she both wanted and dreaded to leave them there. But how could she insinuate wrongdoing from such a short visit and take them from their family? And worst of all, what if she was mistaken, in the lingering torrent of sensations? She reached deep, past her hateful grief, forcing herself the hope that this time it would be different.

"These will protect you," she said, handing them the bloody claws they took a moment to accept in their hands. "And if any other beast tries to come again, you know where to find me," said Jayida, and softly squeezed one of their cheeks. The sight of them holding their trinket close to their heart made her own burst with new maternal emotion.

Jayida mounted and gave a final wave, then trotted off west, keeping the rope stretched to give Adil space to gallop alongside them. She'd hardly gone a short distance when a playful chant surged behind her.

"*Asad Sa'd! Asad Sa'd!*" the laughing, running children cried, the twins waving their trinket in the air. Laughing, Jayida waved back. The lion of Sa'd: she liked the sound of that.

She pulled up her *qamis* robe to her thighs and leaned forward for her water-skin, when something caught her eye.

Red.

Not the lion's blood, spread in wide erratic pools across her loose bottoms, but higher up. A smaller dotted stain between her legs, seeping through her pants.

Her core gave a subtle, distinct churn. She found the water and swallowed it greedily, happily letting it drip over her lips and chin, her head tilting back as the sun blazed her body.

It was said that menstrual blood had the power to chase evil *jinn* and *afarit* away. She'd been right. Her flowing strength had unleashed right on time, and it was shifty creatures like the man-eating lion and Badr who were no match for it.

CHAPTER TWENTY-ONE

EXPLORING BADAWI

WINTER 541 AD - BANU ZUBAYD, TAYMA

Lying on his stomach in his own tent, Khaled sighed pleasantly, his mother's determined fingers burying into his skin, loosening his tight back muscles like dough.

He hadn't thought it possible, and though he still floated in the pleasant memories of his recent travels with Majid, he was happy to be back home. He'd seen much that pleased him during their travels, but there was a solace to the familiar sight of his birthplace.

Or perhaps it was his restless, young *badawi* soul that would always long to move after a while, no matter where he went. He was no poet, but he had the sense that he might now understand something of their constant searching, grasping for new sights to fuel their verses. The sweeping awe of new discoveries overtook him for a while, until the soul beckoned again for more of its endlessness. He found reassurance in that; to realize that even in his typical, redundant days there could be untold pleasant twists of fate.

If little else had changed in these parts, he felt a surging softening towards Ayida whose swollen belly would soon burst out its new life. In her shyness, and perhaps even humility, the slave-girl said nothing of the father, but instead seemed to glow at the prospect of being a mother. Was that enough to make her forget her troubles? At least whoever it was hadn't forced her, when she said nothing of it and drifted in her mysterious undisturbed world he somewhat envied.

"My beautiful brave son, safely returned at last," cooed his mother, full of affection.

"*Yama*, don't tire yourself," said Khaled, turning and flinching as he rotated his body.

"How can you say this? It's been two seasons! Anyway, a mother dotes on her son as she wishes, and curses who she will, like the devil who did this to you," Khamra frowned, glancing at the gash in his shoulder, darker than the rest of his tanned skin.

"What; my lion's mark? It's nothing," he chuckled, as much to convince her as himself.

Though his wound from his time with the Tayyi had healed, his shoulder had never been completely the same. He constantly reassured himself that at least his endurance was not decreased, pushing him to fight longer than he'd thought possible. If his abilities weren't impacted, at least as far as others could physically tell, he dreaded the occasional, yet recurring thought that the strike's effect was permanent in a way he couldn't, and didn't want to explain. Or was it another test of his *hilm*, at which he was currently failing? But he was still Khaled, the eternal, and he would keep going until his last breath.

"So, tell me everything about your journey," said his mother.

Maybe not everything—Khaled thought and propped one cheek on his joined hands, grateful that she wouldn't see his lingering mixed emotions. Thankfully, the happy memories were still fresh, and speaking of them would extend the effect.

"I'll gladly risk a recital for you, blessed mother; and not from my poetic abilities which I lack, but from the places themselves," he chuckled.

"I'm enjoying it already," she smirked.

"So, then. After we left Tayyi, Majid and I went north to visit our kin—"

"The Zubayd the Small," she said, her hurried tone hinting of envy.

"I just wanted to see more of the land, and meet them. I know you'll forgive me for not stopping here on the way—"

"Because you correctly knew you'd be held back at least a little bit."

"*Aywa*. So we coursed further west, passed through Wadi Al-Qura, then Hijr, which really impressed me with its massive outcrops. Somehow I felt different there."

His mother smiled as she smoothed more of the warm olive oil on his back.

"It seems to have that effect on many travelers. Your father once mentioned playing there as a kid, with your *amo* Zahir."

"*Esh?*" His shoulders raised for a moment. "At least that sounds like one nice memory." His mother nodded and he was about to add that his father had never mentioned it to him—but why would that be surprising, when he hardly wanted him seeing his uncle and cousin Jonder. He gripped his gold cross amulet gifted by Hatim and flattened back down.

"So then, we continued and reached the camps of Banu Thalaba and Banu Mudar, those brave *badawi* of the Rûm. They each welcomed us with such generosity that we left with more than we had upon arriving. Some had even heard about us, through their kin ties and dealings with Banu Tayyi. Of course, when I mentioned *amo* Zahir, they filled us in on stories of their march and time in Kutha. We hunted, saw the inscriptions at Jabal Umm Jadhayidh, and basically everyday they treated us to generous feasts; filled with jokes and complaints of the tax-gathering Banu Salih, in service to the Ghassanids and Rûm. Naturally, they also loaded us with tons of dates."

"I'll have to try some of them, seeing as they're kin to the nearby groves gifted by *malik* Abu Karib to *Qaysar* Justinian," said Khamra dreamily.

"*Aywa*, you will," said Khaled. "Then we passed through Ruwwafa, and found its isolated Nabataean and Rûm temple dedicated to *Qaysar* Marcus Aurelius and his co-*Qaysar* Lucius Verus. Even with its torn walls and scattered brick remains, it stood out from the natural outcrops behind it. Majid recalled that a bilingual inscription had been made by a confederation of the Thamud when it had been under Rûm rule, thanking them for restoring peace between feuding groups. Nearby, away from the temple, some rock walls were covered in simpler drawings of goats, camels, and ostriches. It was so quiet and peaceful that we decided to camp by this lonesome temple. Even if sometimes I couldn't be sure what it was or what it meant, it was one of those moments when it made me think about us, and what we're leaving behind," he said pensively.

"You have your whole life ahead of you. Someday you'll marry and leave children behind to recite of your legacy," said his mother.

She finished massaging his back and he sat up to slip his linen shirt on, happy that he'd made a point to bring back great amounts of the treasured olive oil from the famous presses of Al-Sham. His mother filled two cups of fresh sour milk and handed him one.

Khaled sipped and let the thick saltiness refuel him, reluctantly realizing that even as his traveling wasn't in search of a wife, he'd stil yet to find one who spoke to his soul—then caught himself that he could hardly explain what he meant by that.

"And *then*, for the best part of the trip," he smirked, and glimpsed her flash of worry. "We entered the Tabuk area further northeast, and met Ghassanid allies the Banu Bali and Banu Judham, along with miners from the coast of 'Aynuna. Later, we payed our respects to the mountain of almonds Jabal Al-Lawz, and kept north into the phylarchate of *malik* Abu Karib, along Trajan's New Road that led us to Wadi Rum. Its red valleys, sandstone mountains, and arches proudly grazed against the blue sky and called to us from the distance, and once there, it was like we'd slipped into another world. We took some time lingering, before continuing north to Wadi Musa, and unsurprisingly, it was better than any story we'd heard about it.

We ventured through the dark, winding *Al-Siq* passage, the high-walled, tunnel-like space so narrow it was as if the rock had split apart just enough to allow us through. When at last we reached the mausoleum, the glorious towering Nabataean temple carved into the red rock, we just stared, awed at the craftsmanship fit to be the Nabataean King Haritat's IV's burial tomb. As usual Majid filled me in on details, recalling that it was this king's daughter Phasaelis who'd married—then divorced—Herod Antipas, the man who'd tried to kill Yassu as a child and was responsible for the death of Yuhana the Baptist generations ago. The long history breathed all around us, as further beyond to the northwest lay other ruins, with an amphitheater, ancient columns of what they call the Great Temple, a public fountain, a temple of the winged lion filled with mosaics, and so much more."

He paused to catch his breath, as his mother's pleased demeanor urged him on.

"We decided to camp there across the mausoleum-crypt the first day, and after some rigorous climbing that was worth the striking panoramic views, we made multiple scattered campfires, the light reflecting the stones' reddish glow against the ebony, star-studded sky. You know I'm no poet, but with such sights it's easy for me to get carried away and try. We lit much incense and I played the tablah as an offering; it seemed the fitting thing to do," said Khaled with a nostalgic air. He sipped his milk and continued.

"On our way out we considered making pilgrimage to the nearby monastery of Jabal Harun to the west, but chose to leave it for another time. We kept north on Trajan's New Road into the phylarchate of *malik* Al-Harith, dotted with milestones and outposts. I imagined the past Rûm troops that once dwelled there, now replaced with local allies instead, mostly Ghassanid, although some Tanukh, Judham, and others remain in service. We camped briefly with the Tanukh, who faithfully sang the glorious praises of their ancestral Queen Mawiyya. And speaking of marriage; if you could find me a woman like her, who isn't afraid of taking arms and successfully leads troops in times of need, that just may be the woman for me," laughed Khaled.

"Finding one so skilled would not be easy," said Khamra pensively.

"And yet, not impossible. From what I hear of *malik* Al-Harith, he seems to be the kind who may agree to such training for his daughter. Who's to say that a Ghassanid father, or other local, hasn't taken inspiration and trained their own daughters?" Khaled smirked with a far-off gaze.

"Ah, so I'm to envision my son with a Ghassanid warrior-princess, then. I think I can live with that."

"Surely not; they'll want a prince for their princess, and I'm just a simple *badawi*," shrugged Khaled.

"Funny." His mother feigned a frown.

Khaled shook with laughter, and reached for her hand that made her encouraging smile return.

"All the same; everyone spoke highly of *malik* Al-Harith and *malik* Abu Karib; and we had no reason to doubt the Banu Judham and Banu Salih who welcomed us, nor the many other locals we met, some of whom spoke our *'arabi* with light Greek accents. We inquired of our kin, and they helped us track them down in the Lajat. As I glanced over the vast, rugged basalt lava fields that stretched around us, I recalled nearby Daraa and the Namara inscription, along with Daras, that Rûm stronghold much further north. I envisioned *malik* Al-Harith and *Qaysar* Justinian's general Belisarius victoriously fighting in Daras against the Lakhmids, back when we were just boys. At last at the end of our journey, we entered the Hawran region and passed through the capital of Bosra, where I got my new beauty Al-Naji, though I'll probably just hide it for now."

He pointed to his scabbard, trying not to catch his mother's conflicted air.

"Finally, we reached our kin on the southwestern edge of the Lajat, near Zorava. They were so glad to see and host us and lamented how far we were from each other; insisting that we have to see each other more often despite the distance. So be aware that you may have guests in the near future," he grinned.

"And how do they fare? It's true that we hardly hear from each other; there's enough going on here."

"Our kin are brave and strong. As you can imagine, some take well after the Rûm, and many are followers of Yassu, although they also have varied *badawi* neighbors. Many are devoted to the cult of Saint Elyas, while others are as loyal to Saint Sergios as the Ghassanids, who built their own church in his memory in nearby Jabiyah, since the original site at Resafa is a far journey to the northeast. Yet they still try to visit it; they say that after Jerusalem it's the second most important pilgrimage site in the region."

"It seems that's the one thing the one-nature and two-nature Yassu believers can agree on: Sergios's sainthood," said Khamra and sipped her milk.

"*Sah*," sighed Khaled. "I confess that I was as impressed by the many buildings in surrounding regions as I was by the Lajat's hardy terrain. It made me proud to see and think of our kin; both as allies to the Rûm Empire, while just as able to retreat to their rugged, nearly untouchable dwelling. Even if they didn't share streams of stories of past rulers trying in vain to conquer its residents, I would've guessed as much."

"Sounds like the best of both worlds."

"*Aywa*. At Zorava they showed us the former temple replaced by a new majestic martyrium to Saint George. We also saw remains of theaters, colonnades, temples, bathhouses, and inscriptions that seemed to compete with the numerous new homes and churches being constructed. We also went east to Philippopolis named after *Qaysar* Philippus, where they gushed about the famous native who'd risen from soldier in the army to become Rûm *Qaysar* generations ago. Though smaller than Bosra, and left unfinished after his death, we can still enjoy the fruits of his early achievements to transform his native village into a Rûm town, complete with a theater and temples."

"May his memory be eternal," said his mother, echoing his thoughts.

"Back at camp, amidst pigeon pie feasts they told us about the monasteries and dormitories *malik* Al-Harith built and oversaw to welcome travelers. As loyal believers, they support other traveling faithful eager to see the Holy Land. It was tempting; Majid and I joked that perhaps we'd do likewise, but decided once more to save it for another time. They continued into praising song of their vineyards, especially that of Al-Andarin, taverns full of happy customers, grazing grounds full of fine Arabians ripe for racing and battle, and their factories overflowing with quality steel swords. Last but not least, the *malik*'s marble court at Jabiyah welcomes poets from near and far. As you can see, I do believe we momentarily visited Paradise, and I'm certainly not against returning there again someday," Khaled contemplated.

He got up and fetched a basket of her delicious *maamoul* pastries, offered her some that she declined, and gratefully swallowed a few that went perfectly with the sour milk.

It's not that he didn't want to tell her everything, but why worry her? He could always tell her at a later time—like when things got better—that their somewhat hurried departure came in light of alarming news of the plague. It was bad enough that it was ravaging Egypt, and was now spreading to different parts, including ports that serviced markets across the land. With some remorse he hoped it would reach its end or stay confined there.

Worst of all was fighting the consuming fear that he'd already caught it, but wasn't showing signs of it yet. But they'd listened to the advice of wise men saying to wash as often as possible with clear water. This they did, thanks to the scattered winter showers and storms, clenching their jaws in the freezing temperatures while immersing or dousing themselves with water as often as they could, then planting themselves nearly inside the blazing fire until they were all dried through.

Of all the kinds of deaths he might face, that of painful, dark pustules spreading on his body, debilitating him, sounded among the worst. He wasn't sure if the Yassu-loving *Masihi* standing their ground there was admirable or foolish, or even a mixture of both, but part of him envied that strength and conviction that quashed their fears.

"Seems you'll have to take me there, then," said his mother. "And what of the way back?"

"We took the eastern path along *Qaysar* Diocletian's Road, and enjoyed a day at the large fortress and oasis of Qasr Al-Azraq. Then we continued southeast along Wadi Sirhan, and camped at Dumah with some Kalb tribesmen we'd met at Tayyi."

"Dumah, huh. You know they say that ages ago, a boy used to be sacrificed each year and buried underneath an altar there."

"Eesh, *yama*, I hate these stories! All the more reason not to serve their deities," shuddered Khaled as he gripped his amulet again. It was no help that he now could only think of the area in relation to the unfortunate incident at Tayyi connecting his father, the dead Imran, and himself.

"I know. So on another note, I imagine you ventured to castle Marid? And speaking of strong women, I hope you paid your respects to Queen Zenobia. Though she tried and failed to storm it and our very own Tayma, it's sad to think of her capture and exile by *Qaysar* Aurelian to his Rûm Empire," she sighed.

"I did, though I'm sure I didn't do her justice," said Khaled. How could he, when he'd been too busy thinking of the buried Kalb tribesman his father had wronged and whose mysterious death still tore at him. "After that, we were back here before we knew it."

"And how grateful I am for that, my love," said his mother, and kissed his hands. "Now I'm ready for the goods."

Khaled brought over several full leather bags. "Here you are *sayyida*, with more of it yet," bowed Khaled.

Khamra unpacked like a giddy child uncovering treasure.

"Clarified butter, more blessed olive oil, goat cheese, lots of dates, spools of fine wool, steel blades and small knives—and what a beautiful glass lamp!" she said, holding it up for the colorful tesserae to catch a ray of sunlight.

"When I heard it was from Jerash in the Hawran, I knew you'd love it in your collection, along with the bowl," he smirked just as she traded the objects.

"My son has great taste." She carefully set them down and went on to another bag. "And these wines are from?"

"Al-Andarin, Adhri'at, and Wadi Jadar," said Khaled, pointing out each wine-skin from their northern to southernmost source.

"Very nice, and then—oh! More beauty!"

Khamra pulled out the pile of folded clothing, and held up saffron, blue, and green dresses and cloaks embroidered with red and gold floral designs at the sleeves, neck, and hemline. She saved the best one for last, staring at the striking silken dress.

"What a heavenly garment, and so like the royal purple," she said, her fingers delicately grazing the red-purple see-through fabric. "You know, maybe you will have to go back sooner than later," she grinned.

"It might've been luck. On the way back we fell upon a market along the Wadi Sirhan at Dumat Al-Jandal. We proceeded cautiously since it looked like a potential secret market, but from our experience it was all polite and fair."

"More earnings in their pocket that way. It is winter," said his mother.

While Khaled doubted that they were stolen goods from a Fars caravan, every-one knew how they tried to buy all the silk so they'd be the only sellers of it and overcharge the Rûm and everyone else. Not that he condoned the thievery, but for some types it offered an added challenge and defiance to the Fars Empire.

"*Sah*, as for us, we were honest traders, seeking new wares and blessed with fine Zubaydi-Zahir camels in tow, and we got what we needed," nodded Khaled, trying to shake off the mounting thought of his father.

"As always, you did well, my son," beamed Khamra. "And of course I trust you also enjoyed your time at the Banu Tayyi, even if of a different kind."

"Of course. I often think of *sayyid* Abdallah and his kind son, Hatim, who so generously welcomed us and whose amulet gift surely protected us. I would've stayed longer, maybe wouldn't have left at all, if only," he trailed off, catching his mother's saddened air. "I just rarely felt like I could connect with him as a son would like to with his father. Sadly, it wasn't different there."

"He's not an easy man, I hardly need to tell you." She draped the soft silk on her shoulders and sighed.

"I'm sure he didn't say much, and part of me doesn't want to tell you this," he paused, the wine-like garment matching her intensity. "You know I've always stood by him, and I'm not sure what got into him at Tayyi, other than it would've caused a lot of talk. But he wronged another trader, so I offered to rectify it for the man. And I did. But it wasn't enough for *yaba*; seems to him it was even worse. And one night he struck me." Khaled shook his head. It was bad enough to say all this; the rest could wait. "I don't know how others would react, but I'm a man, and I'm not going to just allow him to do that to me. I'm not his slave," he said in his calmest seething manner. "So I distanced myself."

"By going north," nodded his mother. She sniffled and her eyes glistened as she peeled off the silk and folded it carefully.

"And I'm glad I did. As much as he may not like it, I feel like I had to show him where I stand. Like it would get worse if I didn't." His nostrils flared. "I don't think he'll ever know how much I hate to say this, about my own father."

"My love, I can hardly blame you. He knows I support you, and you've surely noticed that we've been distant for years, too. And though I pretend not to hear and no one dares say it to my face, there are whispers that he's the one who got Ayida with child, while others say she's been seen with another since she got here. I just don't know."

"I'm sorry, *yama*. You've been here alone, with this, while I was away, trying to escape," Khaled shook his head.

As difficult as his father was, the man was also the target of endless envy. They could certainly be nothing more than vicious lies meant to tarnish his family's name. But there was also more to his father, that he still didn't know how to tell her. He wanted it from the pit of his core for that day to be a one-time overreaction, one that he never intended to repeat. And he could go with that, and never mention it again like a passing bad night vision. Who in the world didn't ever make mistakes?

"We will get to the bottom of it. It was my hope that he would know, if he didn't yet, that of all people I'm not out to make him look bad or be his enemy. How could I?"

Plus, I came back—he almost said, but didn't.

"He's disappointed, I know, but then again, after all this time, shouldn't he be used to it?" Khaled shrugged.

"Oh, my heart. I pray that someday he honestly, aside from selfish, material gain, proudly boasts of how honored he is to have you as a son. It must be his deep fear of *al-'ayn* that it would only make you more of a target to others, as he fears himself to be. But oh, he's such a closed man; I wish he would say something, and *al-ilah* knows I've tried to get him to let at least some of it out! How unlike anyone he is, when *siddi* Gayas was not such a hard man," she said dejectedly.

"Every man to form himself, I guess," said Khaled. He gulped the rest of his sour milk and perked up. "But by the way; did you hear of Samaw'al lately, or a particularly special guest who came by?"

"No. Why?"

"When we were at Tayyi, Imru Al-Qays passed through to see Hatim and gift him some camels as repayment for Hatim's help. He was in a hurry and on his way here to see Samaw'al, hoping to be connected to meet with *malik* Al-Harith."

"The poetic heir to the house of Ma'add was here and I didn't know it? Perhaps I'll pay a due visit to Qasr Al-Ablaq, in case he's still there."

"I doubt it, since he seems to be staying discreet. But that's hardly the only surprise. The camels he brought were gifted by *amo* Zahir. When we saw him he'd returned from being among them a while before."

His mother appeared shocked. "That is a surprise. But again, not the only one."

"What do you mean?"

"I know how much you've been wanting to see them, and who knows when that will happen, but I try to keep up on the gossip. And the latest is that Jonder rescued a pair of Ghatafan twins from a massive, man-eating lion, one some say attacked before. They say Jonder ripped out the beast's heart and smeared his face with his blood. The children saw it, and even young Ziyad, that *nabigha* poet of Dhubyan, is starting to recite verses about it. The Ghatafan says that they must be protected by Al-Lat, while others say *kahin* Jonder needs only his own *qareen*. They call him *'asada saed*."

"That lion of Sa'd! I must meet this impressive cousin of mine, and hear all about it myself!"

"So gruesome; I admit I wouldn't have expected a son of Zahir's to do such a thing," said Khamra.

"What are you saying? Do you find fault in him now, too? Slaying a lion is hard enough, and a man-eating one at that!" Khaled frowned.

Her mouth dropped. "No, no, it's just that Zahir wasn't unlike *siddi* Gayas in his easier manner. Regardless, every man must unleash his strength when necessary, as you know," she said, and bit into her lower lip.

"I can hardly believe it," Khaled said in a daze.

His mother leaned in and kissed his forehead.

"My trusting, well-meaning son. Just don't forget your own achievements, and how happy we are that you're home. And by we, I include Layla, of course," she added and pinched his cheek.

"Oh *yama*, I'll keep evading her like the plague—" he said before he could stop himself. Apart from occasional boredom, his night visions of her had as good as stopped.

"Not even a little bit interested? Oh, my handsome son, I can't wait to see who wins your heart."

"Who says anyone will? I'm beginning to think I understand a bit more about these cave-dwelling hermits. We peeked quite a few of them up north."

His mother shook her head sadly. "I see you're tired, so I'll let you rest," she said, and took the leather bags away.

Would his mother, would any woman ever understand? He'd barely returned, still basking in his freedom, and here she was referring to Layla and marriage again, when all he could think about was this person; his mysterious cousin whose ostrich eggshell remains graced his collection from when Jonder had made his first kill. *There* was someone he could learn from, who seemed incapable of doing wrong, unlike him.

Khaled rubbed his face and saw his small statues along the tent wall, covered in a thin sheet of dust from his absence. A smirk stretched his lips: only now did he remember he'd forgotten to visit the shrine of Al-Fals at Jabal Aja, though it had to count for something that their travels included a string of other religious sights and visits that Hatim would approve of.

Would Jonder disapprove of his neglect when he might serve Al-Lat and others? Or might Jonder instead praise Khaled's own urge to fly free and follow his own *qareen*, as Jonder also surely did, even if Khaled himself hadn't been aware that he was doing it?

Chapter Twenty-Two

DISCOVERY

Banu Sa'd

My heart.

Zoraya's call traveled along her scuffling steps, ending as a soft touch on Jayida's back.

"*Tsk, tsk*; what would *yaba* say of you allowing people to slip into your tent?" her mother chuckled.

"I know it's you, *yama*. I'd recognize that graceful tip-toeing anywhere," Jayida groaned, shifting from her stomach to her side. "Like I could stop you, or any of my endless handsome suitors anyway," she smirked sleepily. All the same, Al-Wasiyah lay hidden under her bedding at the ready.

Jayida glimpsed the light-like figure of her mother adding another coal to the pile at center. The cozy warmth contrasted the outside chill, inviting her to stay in it forever. A heaviness seemed to pull and chain her to the ground, an immeasurable combination of her continued self-training and the signal of her womanly flow whispering her body into slowed movement.

"*Aywa*. At least anyone who was special enough to be invited would be treated to a worthy sight," said her mother proudly. "Well-pitched waterproof tent of the best camel hair; host to the sacred shrine of *kahin* Jonder, his leopard and lion skins slain by his fine weapons. And of course, not to forget Adil reclining on fine woven rugs made with the loving help of Jonder's parents', along with ostrich earrings for the bride, which she has safely hidden here somewhere." Zoraya leaned into her and poked her sides. "Come on, before everyone catches us and follows us on *our* secret foray."

With a yawn, Jayida rose and matched her mother in wearing one of her lighter-colored robes under her dark woolen cloak. Though Nasr's mourning period had long since passed, it was an added benefit that Jonder's lion feat could inspire the tribe to cheer up a bit and change their attire if they so wished. After a quick greet to Adil in his quarters, Jayida grabbed her weapons and silently followed her mother out into the damp, icy pre-dawn winter darkness.

She breathed in the delicious moist air of recent rains that replenished the earth and confirmed how sturdy their homes were. They quietly set off on their mounts in the northern direction, and Jayida gave a smirking parting glance to the shadowy pole adorned in arrows next to the entrance of her wide tent.

For once, she had to boastfully agree with her mother. Even if she'd wanted to, Jayida hadn't needed to do a thing, when the event quickly circulated with slightly changed details that kept a similar essence.

"At first the Banu Sa'd was confused as to who or what exactly was approaching the camp: an unidentified majestic horse, trailing a camel, but ridden by whom? A man with a lion's face and flashing eyes? Oh! It was Jonder covered in the beast's blood, whose corpse laid lifeless at his side!" beamed her father, who often repeated her favorite, and most trusted version. Zahir suspected that they would never let Jonder live that down, and each confirmation of it refilled her with a proud rush of accomplishment. All the better if anyone who heard of Jonder and his allies would now rethink their harmful intentions, for fear of whom they'd be dealing with.

Her skilled bravery established, she'd agreed with her parents that she was ready for her own tent. Together they'd spent long days piecing together thick, sturdy fabric, using the best waterproof dark wool to secure the roof. Her mother also insisted on new rugs, blankets, and storage bags, woven with their *wasm* of disk, spear, and bow, now with the added pair of Jonder's lion eyes.

Jayida and her father worked on one piece at a slower pace, mixing Jonder's stories into other heroic narratives of Shamshun, Gilgamesh, and Iskandar. Meanwhile, her mother playfully frowned back and forth between them and the fabric she skillfully held taut using all her digits down to her toes, monitoring the playfulness with seriousness. They wove so much that it only seemed natural to make her tent double-layered, as much for added weather protection as privacy.

They pitched the three-room tent north of her parents', and *sayyid* Aziz hosted a feast with camel meat, the first since Nasr's passing. At least it was a change from Warda and Yazida's seclusion, and the *sayyid*, who kept up his drinking, could try to think of it as a good sign. It couldn't be easy for him to put on a cheerful air for his tribe's morale on days when he wasn't feeling it himself.

In the subdued yet enduring air of support, they ate and burned frankincense, and Yazida and Shams sang to Nasr's memory and his friend Jonder's feat. But the sense of emptiness and void lingered with such force that it seemed to become part of them.

As an added gift, *sayyid* Aziz later secretly gave her a stack of four clay demon bowls. At first she'd jokingly refused, swearing she had all the protection she needed living among the Banu Sa'd. But the *sayyid* had so insisted, that she'd half wondered if he'd gone out of his way to get them especially made from the Hawran in Al-Sham or thereabouts.

With the spirals of Aramaic text on one pair and Syriac on another adorning the surfaces, they looked so decorative that at first she hesitated to use them as intended. Why conceal from view the work that had taken so long to achieve?

"What should I do with them?" Jayida asked her father.

"He's protecting you, in his way. You do remind him of his son sometimes."

"I would rather keep them on sight but I don't want to offend him. Or would I be offending Shamshun, Yassu, or Al-Lat, or others? If only they would come forth and make themselves clear," she frowned. What if she didn't need anyone and could just trust herself?

"Then again, would it hurt to just do it, if only to reassure him?" said her father.

She nodded, pleased to bring some solace to the *sayyid*. With all his suffering, it seemed such a little thing she could at least do for him.

One damp early morning Jayida dug around the four corners of her tent and buried the divination bowls upside down. Was she wrong to doubt that it would trap and contain any passing harmful *jinn*, *afarit*, and *ghilan*? Would it make a difference if she knew exactly what the writings said? Did Shams also use them—and if so, surely more than four? Perhaps now was her chance to learn about their effectiveness when she'd never used any, and perhaps might even help with her gruesome night visions. But best of all had been the relief on the *sayyid*'s face when she confirmed the matter done.

They slowed their pace as they entered Wadi Al-Wafra, already green with sprouts of grass, and Jayida kept a distance as she followed her mother. They turned west and reached some rocky hills, revealing an area so undisturbed that she instinctively knew there weren't any large animals around in these parts.

"Up we go," said her mother, and dismounted and took her mount by the reins.

Jayida followed suit, maneuvering slowly up the mounting path. They reached the top and entered a shadowy cave, with a striking view into the valley below.

"At last: the place where you were born and named," said Zoraya with a satisfied air.

"How did you ever find this place?" said Jayida, who could hardly take her eyes away from the wild garden-like scene. Like the sprouts of grass, she'd have to grasp it all while it was there, before it vanished again.

"I didn't; it found me." Her mother chuckled, and set their mounts into a seated position, creating the perfect barrier for the rare chance anyone or anything tried to enter.

"I might not be able to stay away from this place as long as you have," said Jayida, and set about lighting two oil lamps.

"Maybe you won't have to. Now come along."

With oil lamp and woven bag in hand, she followed her mother down a curving path further back and turned slightly east, where lay a long pool with a depth of about half her height, filled with fresh, glistening rainwater.

"*Aywa*; I think I've found my second home," said Jayida. "What more could I need?"

"Believe it or not, I had no idea this was here until recently. I've waited for this day to finally show you this place, and to find this was another confirmation of the happy choices we've made about you," said her mother with emotion.

"Oh *yama*, I know you both did. How could all this have been possible without you two?" said Jayida, and fell in her embrace.

Her mother helped her undress and into the pool.

"Eesh, it's cold!" cried Jayida, crossing her arms over her chest. Before she could stop herself, she dunked herself fully in and sprung back up. She repeated the act, her body's warmth magically clashing then melding with the cold.

"Good. Now lie back, and try to ease into the slowed stillness that this time demands," said her mother, and she obeyed.

Jayida opened her eyes underwater and saw her mother's blurry face hovering above. Water filled her ears, a faint echo resonating, like a low thunder before a storm. For a moment she was a floating statue hidden in a Hijazi cave, who might hear more visitors' confessions if she listened long enough.

Slowly, she lifted her head above the water and regained her hearing, as the incense waved around by her mother drifted over her and their perfectly enclosed space.

"Welcome to your womanhood, my love. It has not been easy, but don't forget how far you've come, and that men themselves already envy your achievements." Zoraya set down the burner, helped her to kneel comfortably, then handed her a cup of herbal tisane filled with leaves, eyeing her expectantly.

"Avoid the *khat* leaves; too much and you could get sick, or even die. For sweet cravings, honey and dates are the best, along with some cinnamon. Bitter aloes—"

"Are purgative," nodded Jayida.

"And dandelion—"

"Helps in digestion and wound healing," said Jayida, and sipped the aromatic drink her mother had made and brought for the occasion.

"For cramps—"

"Olive and sage leaves can be used for tea."

"And as for the delightfully sweet-milky smelling *diflah*—"

"Steer clear of that oleander, as it could be deadly. They're only for decoration, like others we might know," smirked Jayida and finished the tisane with a big gulp. "Happy now?"

"Always," said her mother and took her empty cup.

Submerged to the waist, Jayida draped her free arms over the pool.

"I think about Yazida sometimes; how she seemed so willing to have Imru's child, so soon after her monthly flow and so fast after meeting him," Jayida said with a surging moodiness. "You might not like to hear this but I'm not suddenly filled with longing for children just because I'm a real woman now," she chuckled.

"You're different people, my love. You mentioned that she wished as much, and yet they didn't go through with it. Thank Yassu we're the only ones who know of it, even if we know how forgiving our good *sayyid* is."

"Samira's surely in a hurry for the wedding to secure her dear Shams's place," said Jayida.

"Probably. But Yazida is understandably taking her time in mourning her brother's passing. But if she's also using it to extend the wait and using you as a point of comparison, I can hardly blame her," smirked her mother.

Jayida bit her lip. "She shouldn't and yet, I'm flattered by it. It's his job to prove himself to her, and he may have. It's just, I've often wished I could talk with her as Jayida," she said, a longing surging through her again.

Jayida lowered herself to her neck, with only her head above the water surface as her arms waved like wings or fins. Her weightless hands drifted to her chest and cupped her breasts, then trailed down to her lower stomach, and further down into her dark wooly mound of hair.

"*Yama*—sometimes just the thought of a man touching me repulses me," said Jayida.

Her mother tilted her head and caressed her face.

"I know what you mean. I think it's meant to feel that way, unless you're with the right person. That urge to procreate is a very private and special thing, that's why *al-ilah* is serious about it. And just in case you worry about how long it takes to meet your loved one, they say the wait will only augment the sacred act's success."

"And how do you know if they're the right one?"

"You just do; like I did with your *yaba*. Even if it's with our inherited *kahina* sight, your life has already taught you parts of this."

"Like how sometimes I have feelings about something, and then I see I was right," said Jayida.

"*Sah*; you learn to listen to its faint voice and it guides you."

Jayida brought her knees to her chin. "But what if I never want to?"

Her mother gently drew thick wet strands of hair away from her face, the water turning them into a floating veil.

"Then you don't. We certainly will never force you into an unwanted union; we want you happy. It's just that, as parents, we want you protected, and it would be nice for you to find someone to share your life with after we're gone. I just don't want you to ever feel alone, that's all." Her mother pinched her lips together and barely held back tears.

"And a husband can guarantee you won't feel alone?"

"Not necessarily, but with the right one, you shouldn't."

Jayida rose up slightly. "The blessed Bnat Qyama, the holy Daughters of the Covenant at the monasteries, don't get married, and dedicate themselves to their faith. Some of them even travel, make pilgrimages and go all the way to the Holy Land, constantly traveling without a fixed home. I think it's Melania, whom *mubassir* Ayyub said came generations ago from the edge of the world in Hispania in the western Rûm territories, and built churches at the Mount of Olives," she said, her gaze lost in the water.

"*Na'am*, that's right. Does that appeal to you more?" said Zoraya, a flash of worry crossing her features.

Not that Jayida didn't share her mother's concern of those with morbid lifestyles, filled with accounts of venerating dead bodies and self-imposed starvation and other sufferings as proof of *al-ilah*'s so-called favor.

"I don't know. But in some ways I've sometimes thought that it might not be so different from my life now, if I don't meet anyone."

Her mother frowned. "Oh, my love, it pains me to hear this, but it's because you're unaware of your beauty. Many men would be honored to have you, though I know it doesn't mean you'll want any of them. Please, try not to compare others to Nasr."

"I don't; not that I've been meeting many to begin with. As you know, and may he forgive me for saying this, but even when Nasr was still alive, I wasn't sure I wanted to marry him, should he have asked for me. Did he know this, too? Because though he knew about me, he never did ask, and we'll probably never know how he figured out that I'm a girl. Maybe we're both meant to keep our secrets, to appreciate each other from a distance," shrugged Jayida. She'd even been surprised that *sayyid* Aziz's recent removal of his son's tent was a kind of relief.

Her mother cupped her face in her hands.

"Life is unpredictable, and yet I dare to know that you have more ahead of you. You're my constant proof of it, when I was once told I wouldn't bear children. And look where I am now: mother to a fierce lioness. When the time is right, everyone will know who you are and you'll enjoy the security you bring others. And whether they come flocking to you from afar like pilgrims to Sim'an's pillar, or as suitors that give you the opposite problem of choosing only one, we'll be the proudest parents," said Zoraya, and lavished her face in kisses. "Speaking of matters concerning your lovely form: you've never wanted to touch yourself in a private way?"

"No," said Jayida, raising an eyebrow.

"Now, with your monthly flow and your sight, you may have already noticed that you might have stronger emotions at times. That could include desire and could still be a tempting factor, like it is for many. I wonder—it reminds me of *mubassir* Ayyub, I think reciting from Saint Ephrem and Mar Jacob of Serugh, about holy lust and the sinful women in the *injil*."

"And like Shamshun's? Sometimes I still wonder how he could've been so foolish with women. No wonder some men dread confiding in theirs," said Jayida.

"Seems like his pride got to him. But oh, how I thank Yassu everyday that we are not of those who circumcise their girls and women as a way to control their so-called lust," said Zoraya. "Perhaps it's even true when some say that, like a sword that passes through light, even Yassu's flesh wasn't truly cut at his circumcision."

Jayida grimaced. "I hate that they would do such a thing to women! What about all the poor sacred prostitutes at Mina and other shrines? Are they all cut, too?"

"There must be all kinds, and you can imagine the horror of it for those trained from childhood. Seems like a conveniently selfish way to try to manipulate the gods for one's wishes; may Yassu help them realize the error of their ways."

Jayida stretched out on her back again, her eyes closing to wash away the images of the helpless girls forced into such a vocation. How many submitted to it, accepting the will of the deity to watch over them in exchange for the use of their body? How many fought it, ran away, either to die or live another harsh life elsewhere?

The whirl of images spewed out of a growing, raging cloud of soot and rain at once: the running twins, a knife-holding man pursuing them, the lion. Dug graves with living, breathing bodies forced into it while the victims pleaded for mercy. *Please have mercy.* Laughter echoing, a tormentor turned on by the desperate pleas.

Dig: scrape deeper.

Rough claws gripping her, holding her down, her legs spread wide open, the flashing blade coming nearer. Her bones were stones pulled down into the pool, and Jayida choked as air and water competed for her.

"Jayida! Jayida!" cried her mother.

In a rush Jayida sat up, crying and gasping for air as her mother gripped her. "My love, I'm here, I'm here. What is it?" Her mother stroked her face.

"The lion—the twins," Jayida panted through tears. "When I killed the lion, I heard all these screams, some like before, but others not. Some... were of those he ate! But there's one still alive! Oh, *yama*, tell me he won't do anything. Tell me that I've stopped him!" she pleaded.

"My heart, what are you talking about? Tell me."

"Their guardian, Badr. He—I think he wants to hurt them," cried Jayida. "But now, with what I did—he won't do anything, right? It'll turn him away—it has to!"

"Oh, my love. I pray Yassu hears you! People can change if they really want to, but if they become worse! Oh, my heart; how fearsome and strong you are! But if anyone ever touched a hair on your head, your father and I would become something else, too!" cried her mother, their hot tears mingling. "We can always send someone there to visit and check; perhaps Sufyan, and anyone else he brings."

Her mother helped her out of the pool, wrapped her in soft blankets, and back into her layers of clothes. The mounts dutifully followed them down into the valley, and they arrived back to camp before anyone had arisen, except for Zahir who awaited them with breakfast in their tent. She might have her own space, but frequently eating with one's parents had to be an eternal law written somewhere.

She sat next to her father, whose hint of sadness pinched her heart. That had to be part of it—that mounting emotion her mother and her changing body spoke of. Nothing had changed in appearance, and yet there was a distinct impression of a passing season—that her youthful years as Jonder with her father were more counted than she'd thought. But she wouldn't worry herself or them over it when they weren't over yet, and there was yet to be a prospect for her marriage. It seemed that was the cycle of life: that some things would change and others would always stay the same.

"It's a lovely place where I was born and named in," Jayida said and placed a kiss on the smooth part of his bearded cheek.

In the bleak, dove grey slow winter days of seclusion from the cold, her days floated one into the next, immersed in bonding with and training Adil. Time flew in his quarters, combing and braiding his hair, and brushing his soft coat whose form made a massive block of warm snow.

"You're my favorite ghost," Jayida chuckled, and he nodded up and down the way he liked to do when he approved of what she was doing.

Nasr wasn't a horse, and anyway, how did she know if he was a ghost? The more time passed the more she resolved that he would always be absent from her night visions. She only wished his parents would have some sort of reassurance in their lingering heartbreak, which might help with their loneliness his absence fueled.

"Did you know we would meet? I didn't, and yet you're a nice surprise, given the circumstances," she whispered to Adil.

Eventually Shams visited her tent, his mother's nagging pushing him to the brink of his own beliefs.

"Such a blessed creature he is," said Shams, referring to Adil. "You deserve him. But I still think you should't have done that." He shook his head.

He didn't mean the lion's heart impaled on the seven arrows strapped on the pole outside her tent. That impressive mark of powerful authority made a point to anyone who had working eyes, and maybe even to those who didn't. Shams meant licking the lion's blood, mixing it with her saliva, and spitting it out. As if she'd planned it, when it was more like something else had acted through her. That would probably scare him even more if she told him.

"Aren't I the *kahin* here?" she smirked. "Anyway, I haven't transformed into a beast, have I?"

"Don't joke about this; you know it could be dangerous if you provoke," said Shams, for once controlling his frown.

"Everything's dangerous and potentially provoked; starting with an innocent outing with friends. If my *kahin* sight can't help me tell the difference between do or don't, then what's the point."

From the corner of her eye she caught him pinching his lips and dropping his head. That he was even in her tent was proof that he wasn't sure himself, and tried to see past the fears and noise of what he and others around him thought, as difficult as that often was.

"I know you care for the tribe, so when you're worried, burn incense and think of us all, as I know you already do," said Jayida.

He nodded as if humbled that she would trust him to, and she followed his tentative gaze to the lion skin, almost certain he shared her own ambiguity towards it. Unlike with the leopard skin, all she remembered from skinning it was a nightmarish vision thundering with more atrocious impressions. She'd tried to block it out by floating in a strange trance, and in the end her father had done most of it and burned the carcass outside camp.

By contrast, her memories of that slaying day were so vivid, always close at the back of her head, that she didn't need to have the lion skin or anything else to remember it all. But it was proof and served its purpose, and all the better if it inspired a mix of awed fear, respect, and even protection. Then, there was the selfish part of her that wondered if that's what Shamshun had felt as *al-ilah* filled his body with His holy might... then she released the thought with a growing sense of horrified disappointment.

"Sufyan said he's waited long enough; he wants to honor Nasr's life by going after his goals. He's going to the Sulaym, for the gold mines and a bride. His dowry and our reputation will only help," said Shams with a mix of pride and sadness.

"Thousand blessings to him. He'll miss us, at least," said Jayida.

The days warmed and her father joined her with Kamila and Adil at the camp's training grounds; hers a bouncing restless white stallion next to the elder-like grey mare.

"Respect your elders," Zahir teased Adil. "Look how far she's come! As will you," he said, and swiftly mounted him.

Adil was easy-natured, though like her father always said, it also had to do with the owner. They naturally took to each other, and she loved to imagine Kamila whispering to Adil in her magical way her own story of how she'd come to be with Zahir. Amidst all the weighty sadness, Adil offered a burst of joy, always running and jumping, or even lifting and folding his front legs to show off his upright walk on his hind legs.

"*Aywa*; we're convinced! You practically walk better than us," Jayida laughed.

She trained him to comfortably rock back and lower each knee in a gracefully held bow, and she'd jump on him and grip the reins as he flew off like the immortal winged Bayghasus pursued by her father upon Kamila. Sometimes *sayyid* Aziz, Shams, and Sufyan joined them, and the bittersweet knowing settled over them when at random times, they called to mind the endless battles they'd staged with Nasr. With a pang she contemplated how it had been Nasr's encouragement that had drawn his sister out with them. It was a perfect, vanished moment locked in time, that was only complete and made sense with all of them there in one place to share it.

A gentle morning a while later, Jayida stirred awake, alert to a faint calling.

Ta'al. Come—it whispered in her soul.

She crept to Adil's quarters, and found the beautiful angel facing her, vigorously nodding his head up and down.

"Are you thinking what I'm thinking?" she narrowed her eyes. He stepped to her and she wrapped her arms around him, lost in caressing his face. For a moment it was just her and him alone in the quiet world, his deep ebony eyes blinking knowingly under her touch.

Ta'al—she heard it again.

Jayida dressed and made seven long braids of her hair, then tied and tucked them in the back of her headdress. She was a full woman now, her body able to create life even if she didn't yet care for it. In the rare times she glanced at herself, she was so used to thinking of herself as not fully either that she welcomed the change.

In her own private space, she could soften her serious facial features that everyone knew as Jonder, and enjoy the feeling of her thick, silky dark hair caressing her shoulders like a hidden veil, grazing against her lower back. She'd cup handfuls of her oiled hair and bury and nuzzle her face in it, then brush it in long, slow strokes that relaxed her into sleep. Of course, her mother was right again. She may not have considered her life as a girl much before, but it had its own attractions.

With Al-Wasiyah at her hip, Jayida saddled Adil, tied her Bag of Treasures and spears to him, and led him outside. A quick glance revealed the perpetual early morning peacefulness that she so adored.

"*Aywa*, I guess we're off towards Wadi Al-Qura," she said and rode north, parallel to Wadi Al-Hamd.

They picked up pace as the sky brightened, the sun protectively rising over them as she went further north from the boundaries she'd known all her life.

"This is delightfully new to me," she said, trying to see the area from her parents' eyes when they'd gone to the Banu Sa'd. She sniffled some forming tears as she recalled that Wadi Al-Qura oasis was where her parents had first heard about the massacre at Najran, on their way to their new home.

Before she could say more, Adil took off in a run, swift as an expert racehorse.

"*Aywa*, I'll let you show me what you can do," she said.

Joy and sadness warring in her, Jayida dropped her legs forward and with eyes closed, tilted her head back and spread out her arms, flying on her trusted steed whose body melded with hers.

"Soar high and far like a noble eagle, to where we need to be!"

A new, invigorating longing burst through her: someday she would fly, away from there, to places she'd heard of, and maybe even to some she didn't. If other women, fragile as they were, could do it, then so could she. It was not from ingratitude to her parents or *sayyid* Aziz, and it would only add to her experience. There was just so much calling: Najran and its famous fabrics, the Zafar Cathedral restored by *Negus* Kaleb, King Abraha's Al-Qalis church at San'a, and the markets and the trading port at Aden. Then she might cross over into Aksum, maybe find a princess not unlike her guardian in a monastery somewhere there, her royal form blessed by clouds of frankincense, holy icons, and soothing chanting called forth by a skilled composer.

After, Jayida might continue north in a boat, pass by the pyramid-filled lands of Meroe, and arrive at Eilat. Then she'd travel up, east of Wadi Araba in the Negev desert with its pigeon farms, on to Wadi Rum and Wadi Musa, filled with inscriptions and at least one Praising Woman drawn with her arms to the sky. Then she'd drift west, and see other monasteries and secluded holy men and women in their dwellings, as she coursed deeper into the heart of the Holy Land and the rest of Al-Sham. She would shed tears in Gaza where Shamshun was betrayed and died, and at Yassu's birthplace of Bethlehem that drew the wise Magi from the east, then Jerusalem, where he was crucified. She'd soak in the Jordan River where he was baptized, then marvel at Bosra and its cathedral, and someday, maybe even Hagia Sophia in Constantinople.

The order didn't matter; just the movement did, meeting people and hearing their stories and discovering her own place in the world. With a surge of happy tears, she realized it had to be her own version of what Nasr and her father had mentioned before when they'd cited that sense of endless yearning.

After a while Jayida glimpsed a small pool of water among a trail of shrubs. She thought to pause and give Adil a break, but he bolted to the water and drank his fill so quickly as if in a hurry to keep going.

"Slow down, oh my supernatural steed," Jayida laughed. Perhaps he was as excited as she for new sights—until she caught herself and realized it may well have been a place he'd already been to before becoming hers. "*Sah*; I'll just follow your lead. After all, if I can't trust you, then who can I?"

Adil rushed on, and by the early afternoon the distant hills of Wadi Al-Qura came into view, with a far-off bustling air emanating from that "valley of villages." Some men were surely already deep into the mines and others smithing away tools, objects, and jewelry.

She began wondering what she'd actually gone there for when Adil started drifting west of the approaching scenery.

"*Esh?* Where are we going?" said Jayida, but Adil neighed and kept on. "*Aywa*; it's not like I have a specific destination," she chuckled.

They made a curve and veered further west, drawing away from and parallel to the lively oasis ahead to the northeast. They coursed along a mountain range, and it was so quiet and peacefully deserted that she nearly thanked her mount's silly behavior. Some took their master's clothing or belongings and raced off, while hers took her to a simple place that figured somewhere in his equine memory. Jayida kept her gaze east up to the mountains, contrasting the vast empty space that stretched west of them.

After a while, Adil stopped, scratched a foot along the floor and snorted.

"*Sah*, I can perfectly see that this is my stop," she laughed and slid off him. "Now I'm ready to hear your wonderful story." She arched her back and folded her legs in a welcomed stretch.

Jayida walked on when all of a sudden there was a strong pull at her back. She tried to turn, but instead was dragged up towards the mountain, as Adil held onto her cloak. The unexpected motion combined with his strength so shocked her that for a moment she couldn't speak. Confused, she let him nudge her on until she made out what looked like the entrance to a secluded cave paces away.

"*Esh?* Of all the places, why this one?" she said, half annoyed. What if Shams wasn't totally wrong, and this was a bizarre joke by Al-Lat, or some other *jinni*?

Adil kicked a leg again, and snorted so strongly that it was the closest she'd come to seeing him angry. Jayida crossed her arms and snorted back, waiting, and Adil stepped to her, nudged her face side to side—so gentle he could not mislead her.

"Fine then, I'll be back." She pet his face, and glanced around again at the vacant place. It could be as dark inside as it was bright out, so she lit an oil lamp and grabbed a spear. "Of course, I imagine if anyone were to show up, you'd know just what to do." She eyed him once more then went towards the cave.

An undisturbed thick cloud of hot air swarmed her at the entrance, the trackless ground so even that it had to have been a while since its last visitor. Thankfully, the further Jayida went in, the pleasantly cooler it became. By every appearance it was a simple cave, until she stopped at the sight of some unexpected markings on a wall ahead.

After a moment she drew closer and noted the several drawings of camels and ibexes, and stick-figured men with spears, looking like a possible ancient hunting scene. But largest of all was a figure at center, a man with large frowning eyes and an angry mouth, his wild hair shooting out like sunrays. His arms were tassels that stretched out around him, and the more she tried to follow where they ended the more impossible it seemed.

Jayida stood back and looked them over again, laughing at herself for having been momentarily struck. It would've been enough for some fearful ones to flee already, but something told her that Adil hadn't brought her here just to look at some drawings. Curiously, she mused that if these were recent, the impossibility of telling them apart from ancient ones worked to its advantage.

Tapping the ground with her spear, she continued further in, the spacious cave confirming that it could easily, and comfortably accommodate one or several in need. There were no more drawings, and only a plain cave wall closure ahead, marking the end. Frowning, she drew closer and hovered her lamp over the wall.

Disappointed, she was about to turn when she caught a small black hole at the bottom corner. She knelt and set the lamp down, and carefully fitted the tip of her spear through the space, taking pauses to listen and make sure no horned viper or other dangerous creature appeared. Curiously, the spear easily slipped in, confirming there was indeed more cavernous space behind the wall.

Excitement filled her: surely it had been arranged so for that reason. She carefully pushed it further in, and to her shock the loose, thin wall yielded with a rattle. She rose, lifting the spear along with her, and with continued pressure the wall moved aside, widening the dark gap as it slid aside. When the gap was wide enough for an arm she paused, wiped her brow, then peeked inside with the lamp, revealing only darkness. And yet she had the deepening sense that it had been done so on purpose.

Gathering her strength, she used her body weight and the spear and pushed aside more of the wall until she could pass through. Panting, she lit up the area again with the lamp, and caught a glint to the far opposite side, in a corner nearly out of sight. There, safely tucked away, were stacks upon stacks of bulging leather bags.

Each had a marking on them of a leaf, like *wasm* marking a personal stash.

Her heart pounding, Jayida unsheathed her sword, and lifted a first flap with its edge. Her jaw dropped. Before her shone mountains of various golden coins, and trinkets, precious stones, and jewels, all stashed and stored in this secret, forgotten place. Had she stepped into a thieves' den, who might come upon her at any moment? The nearby mines and the rest of the Hijaz's gold and silver mines drew as much honest, hard-working miners as thieves bent on enriching themselves at any cost. Were all these stolen goods? Or were they someone's proper earnings and belongings, kept there, secure from prying eyes?

After confirming there were no concealed poisonous snakes or scorpions, she sifted through the Rûm gold *solidi*, their clinking sounds amusing her. There were bronze goblets, and gold and silver bracelets, brooches, and earrings studded in precious stones, so striking she marveled that they could've even belonged to a nobleman or high-ranking officer. But why was it there, unclaimed, perhaps even forgotten? It couldn't be Nasr's, when he surely would've said something in their private final moments—and when he'd had another closer place to hide things if he wanted. Did Adil want to reunite it with its owner with her help? Amidst her rushing thoughts, she concluded that the wall had apparently proven quite effective.

But if they were to find the owner and she came forth about it, that could also arouse suspicion. What if *she* was meant to find it—a secret treasure that only Jonder-Jayida could keep, as she'd already been doing all her life? But a gnawing restraint seized her, a reluctance to do anything about it: after all, they weren't her belongings.

Conflict raged. Was she foolish for holding herself back, when others would've gladly pounced on these riches without question? Her fingers dug into the sea of shiny coins, and revealed several with a crowned *Qaysar* and a winged form she couldn't recognize. She took one and slipped it in her pouch, eager to see what her father had to say about it.

Overcome by urgency, she hurriedly pulled the flaps back, ensuring no golden glint would be glimpsed this time. She gathered as many large stones as she could and concealed the leather bags, then pushed the wall back into place—hoping that its ease was due to her excitement as much as to the efficient system of concealment. A final check confirmed that this time no obvious hole remained.

Jayida covered her tracks with her spear, and emerged from the cave to find Adil quietly waiting, his side glance dripping with self-satisfaction.

"Who are you and who sent you?" she said, her brow wrinkling then easing in laughter. She packed up her spear and lamp, and met his inquiring face turned to her with an embrace. "*Aywa*; us and our secrets," she sighed.

They rode home in a blur, the rotating coin in her hand unleashing endless questions. There was the longing again: to reach deep into the unknown, to places she could hardly imagine, at the source of which lay a perfectly peaceful, undisturbed happiness.

Near camp a calm swept through her, whispering that her timely powers were only growing.

CHAPTER TWENTY-THREE

FREEDOM

LATE WINTER 541 AD – BANU 'ABS

Is Shemia weeping
for me? I wish
she'd let me know before
refusing to speak,
entrancing me with
the eyes of an 'Usfan gazelle.
When the staff was thrown
'Ablah towered above me,
a precious idol
swarmed by its priests.
You are my lord and master,
I am yours.
Will you show mercy today?
You forget my prowess
when the battle's in rut
and the sleek mares swarm
Like locusts, sweat-flecked saddles
ridden by hawks,
and my lance driven deep
till the blood spurts.

The chanted poem echoed in 'Antarah's soul, as Shemia and 'Ablah danced teasingly before him since that torturous picnic. Better than nothing. Usually it was Shemia crying, but sometimes even 'Ablah. But always, there was only one idol to worship.

With a long sigh he reluctantly dropped down to earth again, to another same evening on another same day.

"The camels are returned home, their liquid gold renewing their blessed owners' bones," he sang to Shaybub and the flocks.

With a tinge of envy 'Antarah watched the camels pool into their vast camp, a dedicated, protected space he'd yet to have for himself. He circled the fence, tugging and confirming it held, proud and a little sad that they'd always stayed obediently within under his care. With just slight maneuvering of their massive bodies and a small exercising of their independent spirit, they could easily push through if they wanted—and as they'd often done before. Maybe it was habit, convenience, surrender, or an odd combination of all, but 'Antarah liked to think that they also enjoyed his company, even wanted to remind him he wasn't completely alone.

As usual, with Shaybub he milked the lactating females, filled up jar after jar, and let the net-covered bowls of fresh milk for his father and uncle Mutaz cool in the evening breeze, offering the best taste. As much as he enjoyed the predictable, yet important caretaking routine, he dreaded that it was all Fate had in store for him.

Everything around him moved, following in their perfectly designed cycles of newness and burgeoning life. The tribe still gossiped of Khaled and Majid, that beloved duo of the Zubayd cavorting among the Tayyi, and of that fifteen-year-old *sha'ir* of the fierce Taghlib, Amr son of Kulthum, who'd led men with him southwest to Jabal Tayyi in search of the brigands misusing their name. Most shocking of all was Jonder, the lion slayer of Sa'd, and even the seven year-old Ziyad, the budding *nabigha* poet of Dhubyan. Only *al-ilah* knew of Imru Al-Qays, the heir of Ma'add whose name would at least never be forgotten, and whom Hatim of Tayyi, in his generosity, would surely praise, as he did everyone else. A spark struck 'Antarah deep within: in Hatim was at least one other poet whose hospitality he might want, and trust, to experience.

Leaving the camels for the night, he closed the latch, carefully picked up a bowl, and with a familiar frustrated sigh, reflected again that the natural wheel of life turned for everyone—except for him.

How shall he offer himself as the sacrificial lamb? Where shall he hack into—when his flesh had already known so many cuts? They looked at him a bit more gently since their return after the women's picnic two springs before, challenged by their own constant doubt in the face of his unwavering loyalty. But he knew, in his nineteen springs, how the slightest event involving him stirred just as much fear.

He sensed their pestering terror nagging them: What did it mean? What would have to change? Did *anything* have to change? What might they lose from acknowledging him? Like he was their competition instead of one of them. That they leered at each other that way regardless, locked in perpetual distrust of one another, didn't ease the sting for him. What more did he have to do? Because there was more; in the monotony of his grazing life he could at least count on the terrifying—and appealing—magic of that.

'Antarah *wanted*. He always had, and he always would. Even if it was just his *qareen* speaking of poetry, he knew the insatiable longing all too well, the way his fiery soul ignited his bones and blood into bold creation.

But the same *rithā'* funeral ode echoed: poor 'Antarah, who'd done enough and should remember his place; like they ever allowed him to forget. Season after season and still Zabiba's slave son, but also Shaddad's *badawi* seed. He was no wise Israelite King Sulayman to decide for others, but where was he to make the cut on himself and separate between the two? Where exactly to split his body in half and give it to each side, just for the chance that order might be restored?

But they couldn't fool him, as if they knew where the one began and the other ended, when it was just another reason to control him and keep him where they wanted. If they wanted him to choose, he chose none alone, but his own immeasurable—and to them frightening and confusing—mix of both.

At the tent 'Antarah announced himself then slipped in, and set the bowl down before Mutaz, who sat expectantly between Suhayyah and 'Ablah. 'Antarah filled their cups with a ladle and stepped back along the tent wall, should they ask for anything else. At least 'Ablah's brother Waiz wasn't around, away on some tribal affairs.

'Antarah stared at the glowing gold dish on the floor, stolen by some 'Absians, wondering why everything had to be so complicated. Why did he love 'Ablah, when she was so cold; a ghost had more life in itself! At least *shabah* roamed the earth because they still had something to say, some unfinished business that needed attending. 'Ablah said nothing; he unworthy of even hearing. And if she was ever to let a man touch her, would she lie there like a slain lamb, eyes vacant, searching for something else she couldn't find?

He'd saved her life once at the picnic, and hoped he always would, but no, not even dead would she allow him to be acknowledged with the slightest hint! Soon she'd choose a husband, and she'd order him to guard her tent and he would, even when he had to hear all those awful passionate groans that should be half his.

With a curt nod, Mutaz dismissed him, and 'Antarah left his *amo*'s tent, not bothering to add another ignored gaze to the long growing list.

But the worst part was that all that changed nothing. He still wanted her, no matter how often he unpleasantly turned her image over. It was there, stronger than him and by some incomprehensible twist of Fate, he'd been chosen to not only serve, but love her. He would bow down to her, be her ripped carpet, and if he had to wait until her death he'd do it with a patience few since the dawn of man had ever had. Finally, he'd cautiously draw near her bones and graze them with his fingers, then grab them in greedy handfuls and kiss them, lick them, bite into them—her sacred body and blood still blessing his worthless corpse and soul in his desperate version of Yassu's Last Supper tradition.

His.

She was his no matter what others said, no matter who touched her in ways he couldn't and hardly dared imagine, for fear of offending her essence. His mad *qareen*: that was the only truth he knew, the only thing that made sense. The one thing that pushed him on, away but always back to her, no matter what happened. He might not win—and ultimately no one would; a twisted solace—but in the meantime he could at least try to serve as he walked with Fate. He would march to it, grasp it and face it and maybe one day, something would be just a little bit different. Daring, always daring just a little bit more.

He slipped into his father's tent and sat quietly at his side, the weight of the matter palpable between them.

"Blessed *yaba*, you've given me everything, and I know you can give me this, too," 'Antarah said, unrelenting. *What you do to me is a reflection of you*—he had the kindness to hold back, in case his father didn't know. Wasn't it time for the thick marks on his flesh to be replaced with something else?

His father only nodded—contemplating, 'Antarah at first hating then slowly wondering, even pitying, that it might be just as hard on the owner as on the owned. In that moment, it came to him again, but this time with a deeper shattering realization: his father was a slave too, of a different kind. The kind that hid behind harshness, hoping no one would notice.

Strangely, for once 'Antarah had the impression that his father might genuinely fear losing him, and might not be completely wrong in the thought.

"Insha'Allah, if Allah wills it," said Shaddad, repeating what he'd been saying for moons ever since 'Antarah first asked for his freedom. *Insha'Allah*: the timeless way to say that it may never happen, and not to get his hopes up. Freedom from his father, when he could never free himself from her. What was the difference then, between his father's love for his mother, and his own for 'Ablah?

The first time he'd asked for his freedom, he'd braced himself for more blows, when curiously a part of him hadn't feared it, even welcomed it. Maybe it was the resulting numbness from his last whipping, a painful nightmare carved into his skin and memory like a commemorative battle inscription, but at least one that also proved his relentless resolve. Thankfully, none had come, and Shaddad had just listened quietly to the wild beast-man of a son finally worth hearing.

Shemia also seemed different, and whether her nagging stopped from a combination of some sense of appreciation for him or his mother's intimidating eternal poise, he was grateful either way.

Most of all, somehow, 'Antarah loved. How could that be? He already knew he was *majnun—jinn*-possessed—but if others knew how happy his verses made him, they might be even more confused by spirits who brought such bliss.

When once it had struck him that his heart, like those of the entire 'Abs, might also be one of stone, he'd shed a tear at the realization that such a contemplation still involved a degree of emotion. It was almost reassuring, that despite everything he might still have scraps of feelings, no matter how pointless. And how could he escape them, when he'd known flesh-ripping suffering the likes he wouldn't wish on others. In those moments 'Antarah thought he understood a bit more what his blameless *ema* meant, when she said no one has, nor ever would, suffer as Yassu had. Her Iyasus: the only god-man 'Antarah might ever be able to trust, as did the great *Negus* Kaleb, King Abraha of Himyar, and Hatim of Tayyi.

But what was an animal-man to do? Some days were blissful hell, every image, every moment filled with 'Ablah, ravaging his thoughts—and body. He didn't hate his dark, contorting form then, ebony volcanic clay against her milky, silken sand-skin. In his torment he tried to make sense of it. Of course he wanted, could never reject it. But a part of him held back from reaching that high, and summoned all his *hilm* to tame his raging desire. At times he was sure it was his *qareen* just pushing him again, and at others he was sure it couldn't be his doing. Worst of all, he wasn't sure if it was right or wrong to be consumed by these hazy dreams that made him walk on clouds. Anything but the thought of disrespecting her—if only he could have some sign of how to stop it, or at least, control his wild longing.

'Ablah's wraith
appeared in sleep
to her wearied slave.
Losing my grip
I stood and screamed
"She's far away!"
A breath of musk
was her response,

and ambergris.
Blinded by tears
I tried to seize
her flitting shade
with a kiss.
On the soaked sand
I exposed
her sun-bright face
and night became
as hard as day.
Her body a lance,
battle-true,
supple to
the grasp,
hidden in her tent
behind a veil,
lions on guard
with war-tested pales
and tempered swords.
'Ablah, I
am so far gone
because of you
locked in lust
like a camel
in rut. 'Ablah,
my love for you
is my lifeblood
the very breath
in my bones.
Lust is sovereign.
O my friend,
lust is all.
Lust has 'Antarah
in its thrall.

In his unworthiness the poetry somehow made it hurt less; even seemed to offer a kind of distance from his troubles as he recited of them. Perhaps boldest of all, he hoped it'd been chosen for him; his *qareen*'s gift to him to even have such a perfect subject to think of, and if needed, recite of. His heart tore at the idea of some not being able—or allowed—to get lost in their own secret happy worlds, as if their simpler minds, reviled and mocked by some, was prevented by some evil *jinn*. 'Antarah knew then that no one in the world—white, black, red-skinned, or any other mix—loved like he did and transformed his torture into such pure beauty, and that was his triumph no one could take from him.

One perfect spring day he awoke with her ardent kisses all over him, her presence so tangible he'd swore she'd been lying next to him all night, right until he awoke. For a moment he wallowed in it, then bolted up, yearning to look at her physical form which, though elusive, did indeed walk the very camp he dwelled in. It wasn't long before he realized why his mother and Shaybub had passed him heavy glances in the midst of his reverie.

From Mutaz's tent the news spread fast that Umara's arrival was for none other than to ask for 'Ablah's hand. 'Antarah almost laughed. 'Antarah the slave might not be good enough for the coveted princess, but at least he was no soft half-man, who cared more about his combed, oiled hair and flamboyantly bright, embroidered clothing than herding the life-giving flocks and taking up arms.

Amidst the large gathering, he made out Ahmar's hawk nose and hard gaze. They had an even deeper hatred than when 'Antarah had accidentally—yet deservedly—killed his slave four springs ago at the pond. Fire rose up his spine, to think that surely Ahmar knew that his heart burned for 'Ablah, and would therefore assist anyone in preventing him from his goal in delicious revenge. Besides, Mutaz would want Umara as son-in-law, when he would get a rich dowry in exchange.

That evening in Mutaz's tent 'Antarah restrained his inner lion, caught between submission and rampage. His kin sipped their milk in the usual silence and poised 'Ablah held still as ever.

Until.

A fleeting moment—Mutaz and Suhayyah's attention turned elsewhere—and there at the edges of 'Ablah's wings were two tight fists. Two smooth pearls, restraining all the angelic wrath she could muster.

His, his! To gather into himself and restore to the proper order, if such was her word. She might not want him, but she didn't want Umara, either, and that was all he needed to feel better when leaving the tent.

"Something on your mind?" said his father with a barely contained smirk to Shemia back at their tent. Always pushing, and he always yielding.

"When will be the wedding? In case I might—"

"Nothing's settled yet; there's still talks, as you know," said Shaddad.

Was it a generosity, for his father to cut him short with his own reluctance of the match, when it wasn't enough to hide the lingering chance of deceit? Even if his father meant well, the match could be made—and consummated—before any of them knew anything of it.

But 'Antarah would know—by his mother's beloved Iyasus, he would.

"Shall I prepare some verses for their union?" said 'Antarah, knowing he never would.

"You know he would never allow it."

"Not even if you freed me," said 'Antarah flatly.

"Some are harder to convince than others," said Shaddad, staring into space. Here was the man who might soon be eclipsed by his younger brother's wealth, should he marry his daughter off well. Everywhere, dreams coming true, except for themselves. Maybe that's why he had the nagging sense that his father wanted to set his younger brother in place.

Ya Allah, 'Antarah!

'Antarah stifled the sneering reprimands that followed him the next days, as Umara and Ahmar taunted him like unrelenting harpies. They might need convincing but so did he, and when Umara dared tease him about his love po-etry—hinting at exactly the one he didn't deserve—the loud slap 'Antarah served him was better than he'd imagined.

"How dare you! I'll remind you of your place!" spit Umara.

"Why don't you both! I'd love to scar your pretty faces and show who lives according to his word," said 'Antarah, holding up his fists in pent-up excitement. The opportunity was just too good to pass up, and he might crown it with a poem, too.

"*Hadha*, enough; he's not worth it," said Ahmar, his feigned indifference resurfacing. 'Antarah's disappointment was so deep that he struggled to settle down. How typical and pathetic of certain types to rise up others, and then back down before a challenge. Whatever he was, or wasn't, to 'Ablah, he could make his mark on this unworthy suitor, and she would see its effect, whether or not she married him.

Even so, as much as 'Antarah disliked Umara, and though he had no wish to kill the *sayyid*'s son Ahmar—if it ever came to that—he'd want it to be much more than what his slave had suffered.

"What's gotten into you?" yelled his father that night, pacing around him, while Shemia snacked on sweet raisin-filled and cardmamom-spiced flatbread made by his *ema*. Even invisible behind the curtain, he knew his mother and Shaybub stood there, listening. "Are you going to start your old ways again?"

"*Yaba,* he started it. He's been doing it for days, surely encouraged by Ahmar. As usual I ignored it, but today when he insulted my poetry—and 'Ablah—I decided to do something about it. You can imagine how that ended," said 'Antarah. Shemia slowly smacked her lips, savoring the flavors.

"I won't have you embarrassing me all the time!" said Shaddad, waving his fists.

"Embarrassing you? I am not going to let myself be whipped by them, or anyone else, when I already take it from you!" 'Antarah blurted, stepping to him. 'Ablah flashed in his mind—tangled up with him in his sweaty night visions, calling to him. "What if—I've a mind to take her with me and marry her myself if I have to!"

"What did you say?" Shaddad flew at him, gripped his skull-face and dug his fingers into the hollow of his cheeks, a blade hovering near.

Stiff as a spear, 'Antarah stood firm. *What's it going to be now?* 'Antarah's *qareen* called from deep within—when the answer was already there, somewhat surprising that it hadn't happened yet. In a hard swipe, the blade sliced into his left upper lip, releasing warm, metallic liquid.

'Antarah winced back excruciating tears, sensed the shifting all around him, the sad-angry faces wanting to soothe and quell. But not him, the price of his words too worth it.

"You can't stop me, so you might as well figure out a good way to use me," grimaced 'Antarah, tasting his own bloody fountain.

And like that, this time the claw eased, allowing him to rejoin his *ema* and brother.

That night, blessed by his mother's poultice of honey and strong herbs, he stared into the dark. Why had he said that when he wouldn't do it, and yet—he knew he could, even partially burned to do it. Again, his *qareen* had burst out—as if he could always control it. So why not, for once terrorize them with possible unrest, push back, when he was pushed all his life worse than they'd ever been and might ever be.

When sleep found him, 'Antarah expected his night to be as empty as it felt, but it was only more, more, and more. More of 'Ablah, wrapping him up and herself together tightly in her veil, possessing him the way he hardly dared to possess her. One night, then another, and another... A thousand *jinn* latched onto him when he only wanted one. Too much, even for his wildest dreams, so how to explain it!

'Ablah remained secluded, Umara and Ahmar left, and his lip got better, but the wrathful trace remained: a slanted scar, yet another made by his father-owner, now publicly blemishing him. At least it hadn't cut deep enough to impact his speech. But at this rate, his whole body might soon be covered in shameful marks, and what would 'Ablah think then? He chuckled through his senseless wishful tears, and even considered his *ema*'s and Shaybub's continued, well-meaning reluctance. But unlike the Fateful wheel of life, it never lasted.

"There might be one way," his father said one evening while alone. "An impossible mission for an impossible reward." In his mad joy, 'Antarah almost wanted to joke that he was sounding quite poetic, but only nodded and listened. "One thousand Asafir camels."

'Antarah's blood went cold. The coveted breed, owned by none other than the Lakhmid Al-Mundhir, dwelling northeast in service to the Fars *Shah* Khosrow. A *ghul* who sacrificed Yassu-loving women to Al-Uzza's blazing flames, who might do the same to his own blameless believing mother if he could. Even as 'Antarah suspected that the proud *Shah* Khosrow was more tolerant, he'd also executed his older brothers, their offspring, and other conspiring nobles for plotting against him.

"With *sayyid* Zoheir's far-reaching eye, this would only add to the 'Abs's glory, though everyone would know it was your doing. If you agree, I'll grant you your freedom before you go. And on your honorable return let them try to refuse you 'Ablah," said Shaddad.

"May I ask you something?" said 'Antarah.

His father gave a curt nod.

"Was it his idea?"

"It wasn't mine," almost chuckled Shaddad, and in his relief 'Antarah could've embraced him. This man, who could be easy and light one moment and violently impulsive the next, who'd so often deeply hurt not just him, but his *ema* and brother, was trying to help him in his own way.

It was hopeless and possible banishment, but it was something. Not only could he die without ever reaching the court at Al-Hira, but also without even having had the chance to recite at the annual market of 'Ukaz. But he shook off that conern, when his mother preferred he stayed away from that den of unbelievers, surely also disliked by *Negus* Kaleb from his monastery retreat, and King Abraha from his Yassu-loving court at San'a.

And yet—if by some miracle 'Antarah made it and came back, he'd have even more marvelous exploits to recite of then. How hooked they'd be on his words, and who could challenge him then, dripping with jealous incompetence! Maybe that's why his father hadn't said it; that he might also be granted the honor of becoming *sha'ir*, when they both knew that no one could stop him from composing and reciting his own verses, regardless of his real or imagined audience.

To his surprise, his mother instantly favored his mission, and though she'd always been his strongest source of support, she redoubled it in a way that he soon became excited at its wild prospect.

"Don't fear and go boldly. You are on a brave, honest mission and intend harm to no one," she said. Her love was a shield, suggesting he could not fail in honoring his family, and that 'Ablah might finally be his. "People often barely truly live with each other. But when Iyasus calls, you ascend with glory they envy," she went on, circling them with an incense burner, clothing them with the sacred scent. "*Badawi*, Aksumite, Rûm, Fars; there is no separation when Iyasus is the home. That was Najran; may their brave sacrifice, on the year of your birth, never be forgotten."

'Antarah closed his eyes and inhaled the holy smoke like he did her wise words, filled with a power he envied and respected.

"Never forget that Iyasus is the True King who subjected himself to *our* cruelty. So who are we to avoid trials? But if more hearts truly followed Him, how different this world could be!" she said.

"Ameen, ameen," 'Antarah and Shaybub echoed.

Then it was her turn to close her eyes and take a deep breath.

"The words of the blessing of Henok, by which he blessed the elect and righteous, who will be living in the day of tribulation, when all the wicked and godless are to be removed. And he took up his parable and said—Henok a righteous man, whose eyes were opened by God, saw the vision of the Holy One in the heavens, which the angels showed me, and from them I heard everything, and from them I understood as I saw, but not for this generation, but for a remote one which is to come," she said, its ancient power already preparing him for unknown battles.

She did not recite it often, but each time she did, 'Antarah had the delightful shudder all over again. This first line of the sacred Book of Henok, the great-grandfather of Nuh who walked with *al-ilah* then was no more, was said to be the first and oldest sentence written in any human language by Henok himself.

"My blessed crowned princes," said Zabiba pensively.

Glowing with prayer, she temporarily vanished and returned with a woven bag. At her order they obediently shed their headwraps and yielded to her loving care as she lightly applied the pleasant mixture of clarified butter and musky scented oil to their hair. Using sticks to make long curled locks, Zabiba continued with more verses from the Book of Henok and the Garima Gospels. The soothing mix of sacred verses and head stimulation confirmed to 'Antarah once more that his mother might be the most powerful *Masihi* angel in all the land. She then praised King Abraha's new Al-Qalis Church at San'a—proof of the true faith's enduring power—and finished with a *zema* chant from the composer *Abba* Yared of Aksum—adding to the precious bits and pieces that made him yearn to one day see her previous home.

Humility called forth tears. What was his poetry compared to her heavenly prayers heard by Heaven itself? She was a living, breathing pillar of strength that humbled him, and made him grateful for everything, and even made the pain seem less intimidating. Her unshakeable strength was her gift to them, and though he didn't deserve it, he was honored to be her son.

'Antarah agreed to the mission, and his father called for an audience with *sayyid* Zoheir, who reclined with his sons Ahmar and Hashem immediately at each side of him amidst countless eagerly gathered tribesmen. 'Antarah's heart shook with such fear and excitement, that he thought its explosion would settle his earthly Fate right there and then without even having taken a step.

But not even angry Ahmar's shooting glances at him could reach him, when Hashem's smiles beamed gently at him, a welcomed reminder that not everyone there hated him and wanted his death. Even Mutaz seemed cheerful, even if it was from daydreaming of the far-off dowry 'Antarah was to bring back.

"My brother Mutaz and I have agreed," began Shaddad, "that 'Antarah will journey to Al-Hira for a thousand Asafir camels. These are to be his dowry for 'Ablah, whom he will marry upon his return." Shaddad paused, the heavy cloud suspended above them waiting to burst with blessed pouring rain at last.

"For this brave mission, I recognize and proclaim to everyone that as of this day, my son 'Antarah, mothered by Zabiba, is a free man."

Praise *al-ilah* for 'Antarah's big sleeves that hid his hands, because it was a moment before he realized his clenched fists slowly eased. Praise *al-ilah* for his thick scarf wrapped around his neck, a loosened rope that hid his emotional, choked up throat. At last, the words he'd never thought he'd hear from his father had been sprinkled upon the entire tribe like holy water, to fly and spread over the land to other tribes, maybe even the world. He might never come back alive, but now everyone would know that at least he'd died freed by his own father's word.

Later when alone, Shaddad promised to make sure that 'Ablah was not married off before his return, when his father knew all too well that Mutaz couldn't resist choosing the one with the best dowry. More importantly, no one had to say a word for him to know that 'Ablah had not given her consent. It would've spread like wildfire already, and anyway, 'Antarah could not be so easily fooled or deny what he felt in the pit of his soul.

A knot tightened in his stomach at the thought of asking his father to free Shaybub too, but knew the *badawi* would consider it too far, another proof of his insolence. They'd return, triumphant, and then he might grant that request.

"I know it wouldn't be from you, but I must say it before I go. If anything happens to our mother while we're gone, you know what will happen," said 'Antarah.

There was such a relief to saying it lightly yet directly, the pleasant silence betraying the mutual awareness that it was said more as a natural fact than from a place of revenge. That had to be what free men experienced when they spoke and did things; filled with that distinct sense that nothing could stand in the way of their desired outcome.

Another chain released, that he might actually have ample time to succeed, either in life or death. Shaybub could accompany him, so long as he swore before them to release claim to any potential spoils prior to leaving, as it was all to be 'Antarah's to give Shaddad. If both Shaybub and 'Antarah agreed, it was only because 'Antarah would never let his older half-brother go empty-handed when the time came.

As for the journey, they'd each have a new robe and woolen cloak, a few extra spears, and a camel, along with a shared tent with some cooking supplies.

"Take this with you, too," said Shaddad, and 'Antarah recognized one of the thief's swords from the day at the picnic. 'Antarah nodded, wondering if he would ever have his own honorable sword, though it was better than nothing. Azmari—a word like the one for entertainer in his mother's tongue—seemed fitting.

The time approached for their departure, and they gathered around their *ema*, whose loving presence they'd miss most. In weighty silence they sipped her precious *tej* mead, imagining the Aksumite honeyed drink with its shiny-leaf *gesho* stems filling him with protective energy.

"I know you'll use these wisely," said his mother when they finished. She set several heavy satchels before him, filled with gold coins.

"*Ema*, that's too much," said 'Antarah. So caught up in the rush of preparation, he hadn't even thought of payment.

"*Shh*, there's plenty more, especially for my sons," she said brightly, and kissed both his cheeks. "May Iyasus bless your journey beginning on the end of this first month of Dhu-Di'awan. You are my eternal witnessing pillars, like *Negus* Ezana's proud stone first proclaiming his loyalty to Iyasus at Aksum. Use all the scented butter for your locks, and when you return, then you shall braid *my* hair," she beamed.

He carefully split up and buried the coins deep into separate leather bags, marveling again that he was not only going further than he'd ever been, but with more money than he'd ever had.

The final day at camp arrived, and his heart could take it no longer. He waited until Mutaz and Suhayyah were out of the tent, and with Shaybub keeping watch, he quickly sneaked in. He found 'Ablah in her space at the back of the tent, and at the sight of him she gave a start, then looked away.

"Forgive me, 'Ablah. I mean no disrespect," 'Antarah said with a light bow. "I just wanted to give you this before I left."

He set down a knotted bracelet with two cords that could be pulled to adjust the width to fit her as she wished. He waited a moment, hoping, begging she would at least glance at it. She didn't.

"I hope—" he began but stopped when she turned away. Was he that repulsive to her, even though he cast no evil eye on her, and would do all he could to protect her from it? Why did he think it would it be so different just because they were alone?

Another moment stretched around them, wishing... but nothing, except her perfect frame he knew so well and not at all. There was the wraith's perfect image he wanted etched in his soul, in case it was the last time he ever saw her in this life. *Na'am*: he asked for much, when he had much to provide. He swallowed hard.

"May you and your family be blessed." 'Antarah bowed deeply this time, then left.

Perhaps it was best that he hadn't seen her reaction, neither approval nor disapproval, the bracelet taken or ignored. All he could do was his part; for the rest he wouldn't fight how his heart loved. At least he always had his night visions, where she might let it out with him—in rage, in cries, in violence, in lust... in love? It was sweet to think, through all the wrong.

She: the cold marble pillar, untouchable in her perfection that would outlive him and all other humans. She: always dwelling and fixed in her higher place, giving no response to pathetic, lowly visitors' desperate pleas.

Foolish to dream, foolish to risk.

No guarantee.

In such a hurry to crush his body with hers into another world.

Chapter Twenty-Four

Al-Hira

Turn back, you'll never make it!

The tar-blood sky thundered and smoked, suffocating with fire and ash, as sharp shadowy mountains sliced out of the ground. The saffron timeless earth shook with its mighty strength, yearning to swallow or impale any living thing that dared walk on its surface. The dry air greedily sucked up liquid eyes, clay nose, lips, and flesh, working its way within.

Na'am, hurry, before it's too late! Come, and meet your death!

'Antarah sighed as the familiar scenery reluctantly receded, yet lurked from somewhere in the distance.

What was he doing? At last, after living through nineteen springs, he'd finally gotten his wish to be freed. And for what! To walk right into his death towards an unknown land he may never even reach, and worst of all, for a love he may never even get in return.

But even that goal, no matter how hopeless, was worth fighting for. He'd go on being what he'd been all along: a doomed poet, who listened for and memorized his verses as *kahen* did sacred scriptures in their secluded Aksumite mountains. He tried not to think that his father hadn't even given him more spears, let alone new weapons for the journey, but at least he had Shaybub's company and their combined skills that had sustained them so far. Just as important, he didn't need to glance at his sword to know his fiery defense was always there, ready to pounce again in defense of his beloved 'Ablah like it had that perfect picnic day.

In the misty, foggy long stretch of the early morning Wadi Al-Rummah, he had the impression of him and Shaybub being the only men alive in this dead-quiet land. But that couldn't be worse than being surrounded by *ghilan* who wanted his death. At least in the stillness, he could hear any coming sounds, and prepare himself.

Walking with his back straight, he took in the hills, his vision this time shifting their patchy desert grounds to the lush Semien Mountains, with its lobelia palm trees stretching across part of their beloved mother's land. In the winter the mountains would be white with snow, and transformed in spring to heavenly cascading waterfalls that Najdi desert dwellers could only dream of. In the mist he caught a movement, and Shaybub gestured with his chin up a mountain.

An oryx.

Without knowing why, 'Antarah rushed off after it, leaving Shaybub below. The oryx bounced from place to place, as if waiting and amused at his following him. Pacing his breath and monitoring his large steps, 'Antarah realized he was smiling.

And what if?

What if they'd been the ones to make a mistake by sending him away! They expected him not to come back, but there was at least a chance he would. And how could things be the same then! Whether he died or lived, the Banu 'Abs would experience a change, and for the first time, flying up this hill after this dazzling white *jinni*, 'Antarah had the budding conviction that it might be in his favor.

Without realizing it he was almost at the top, darting here and there while the creature at times vanished in the thickening mist, with only its clinking hooves or occasional snort to suggest its location. Panting, 'Antarah reached the top, the thick enrobing clouds momentarily catching him off guard.

At this height, all he could see was the moist ground at his feet, and the cold grey-whiteness shrouding everything else around him. Something powerful, at once intimidating and endearing, in that dense stillness called to him, and he reached out his spear to it, half doubting it would even pierce through it. There was a shuffle nearby, and from the fading sound he knew the oryx was going back down.

But what if he took that invisible step above? Was that how Henok had vanished when *al-ilah* took him away? And then those Aksumite stories of holy men conveyed away on clouds... He was no angelic being, but his *ema* was. Should he test it, see if he'd be gracefully forgiven and whisked away into the peacefulness, the way he'd so often wanted? How many others had done it, and now invited him to meet them?

"Come down from your lofty cloud, oh 'Antarah!"

Shaybub's thundering call shook him out of his reverie. Strange, but it had sounded a lot like his mother and 'Ablah, or maybe it was just the altitude toying with him. He rushed back down, and they coursed on without stopping until nighttime. They camped in a place safely away from the water, each night filled with tormenting thoughts of 'Ablah.

Come back to me, my dark, strong prince, she cooed, coiled around him like a snake he never wanted to be free of.

"The frigid deity and the fiery servant; I don't know which of us is more wrong," he said to Shaybub. It might be a verse he'll weave into a poem someday, or it might be one that remained between them, the fruit of their brave travels. Maybe he was just a man-animal driven by hopeless lust, but at least he was trying.

On the third day they reached the red Thuayrat dunes of the Ad-Dahna, marking the eastern end of Wadi Al-Rummah that disappeared underground. 'Antarah made three pillars of mud to mark their passing, and said some words of thanks to Yassu and any good lingering *jinn*, recalling the stories of underground caves and acquifers that sounded as alluring as frightening.

They coursed on to Wadi Al-Batin, avoiding the Banu Tamim and Rabi'a who camped nearby, yet ready to explain their mission if needed. They bathed in the river, ate their mother's honey pastries and sour spongy injera flatbread made of blessed teff, and joked about it being the last chance to turn around, knowing full well they'd do no such thing.

"So all the *badawi* and royal courts of the south, north, west, and east want to know: what does it feel like to be a free man?" said Shaybub, his tone impersonating an arbiter of poets at the 'Ukaz market.

"Same as before," smiled 'Antarah. He hoped it would ease his brother's pain even as they both feared things may never be so different for them.

To his pleasant surprise, as the days elapsed and the further they went, the more he had the impression of a burden lifting off him. Sometimes they looked over their shoulders, then back at each other and laughed, amused and grateful that no one had followed them, and not to have anyone to answer to but themselves. The danger was still everywhere, but it also wasn't the same.

They ran through vast fields, raced up and down hills, staged mock fights on their mounts, sure they'd make the oddest-funniest sight if anyone happened to be watching them. 'Antarah had the shocking realization that it might be just one of many reasons why some tribesmen kept others close by, bent on controlling their movements, lest they find things—and worst of all a better life—they preferred elsewhere.

At the eastern edge of Wadi Al-Batin they bid goodbye to their known lands with three more pillars, amused to think that they'd remain unscathed, and happily descended into the fertile lands bordering the southern Euphrates. Keeping north, they slipped past the camps of Banu Bakr, rounded a patch of lava fields to the west, and reached the outskirts of Al-Basrah, just in time to catch a small market of Al-Mirbad.

"I can't believe it," said Shaybub. They dismounted and took in all the rich, bustling sights, cacophony of sounds, and spicy and sweet scents that thankfully surpassed those of animal dung. There were all kinds of men there, and even more as dark as themselves than he'd expected. "There's poets here, too; there's your chance!"

A shiver filled 'Antarah, but he shook it off. Every part of him yearned to recite before new audiences and see their pleased, impressed, and touched expressions, but he wasn't yet ready for it.

"Maybe on the way back," said 'Antarah.

"You could improvise." Shaybub gave him a side-eye.

"I know, but I don't want to, especially not for my first public recital." He had to prepare, be sure of exactly what he wanted to say, especially if there was a chance it might be repeated.

They strolled through the market full of flour, spices, butter, seafood, along with woolen and silk clothing, and weapons made by Fars, Indian, and *badawi*, and so much more they could imagine. But he liked most the exotic animal quarters, full of reptiles and furry hyraxes, and sand cats and caracals either napping or eyeing pigeons, doves, quails, or colorful parakeets from Africa, Aksum, and India.

Then, his heart caught in his throat.

In a cage were two lion cubs, huddled into each other in the corner. One lifted his head and opened his small jaw at him, either in a yawn or faint hiss, but he hoped both. His heart pinched. How could he just leave them there?

"I must," said 'Antarah. Not only did he have money for the first time in his life, but it seemed a waste unless he could use it as he saw fit. For the first time he had the rush of wanting something and being able to have it unimpeded.

"If you say so. You saw them; must be a good sign," chuckled Shaybub.

'Antarah took his time haggling with the merchant, feigning indifference to bring the price down. He was about to walk away when the merchant's impatience ceded—better a bargain than no sale in the midst of winter. Containing his joy, 'Antarah paid the merchant with gold *solidi*, then held up the cage, gushing at the cubs who squeaked in demanding greeting.

"Antares the Enemy of War and Al-Shira, the brightest Dog Star: our guides for the journey," grinned 'Antarah.

Thrilled with his first purchase, they browsed a bit more, and coasted along the colorful mountains of spices and dates ranging from gold to ebony. He couldn't resist buying some, along with dried salted *binni* fish from marsh-dwelling *badawi*, and *basturma* dried beef. After some lingering glances, they continued their journey northeast, along the Tigris-Euphrates basin that would lead them to the Euphrates.

With such mud brick homes, churches, temples, and inns that created bustling, guarded towns amidst the garden-like land, 'Antarah contemplated the impressive extent of this ancient rival to the Rûm Empire. He shuddered at the thought of approaching the dwelling lands of Al-Mundhir, but tried to take comfort in recalling that they walked along the path taken by the prophet Ibrahim when he'd left Ur and journeyed through Babylon on his journey to the Promised Land.

At their last stop before reaching Al-Hira, 'Antarah washed his clothes, bathed, tended his hair, and finally put on his full garb, complete with Azmari at his hip.

"That's how you should always be: the princely raven," smiled Shaybub.

"That's how we both should be," said 'Antarah.

"I don't mind, you know, if they think I'm your strong, silent servant," Shaybub said with his understanding air.

"I do, and I'm strong, too," 'Antarah winked.

Shaybub chuckled as he practiced walking leisurely, swaggering like Imru Al-Qays might, both amused and at ease in this dignified air. Maybe there was some truth to the clothing making the man. But that he had to be so far away from their camp to feel safe enough to try it was both emboldening and sad. The thought of 'Ablah seeing him in this way pushed him on.

Four afternoons later they entered a long plain of abundant pastures dotted with dark shapes.

"Do you see this? We may have entered a corner of Paradise," said 'Antarah, holding up Antares to the horizon. There were so many thousands of the prized Asafir camels that 'Antarah could hardly believe his sight. "On second thought: we came to buy some from *Shah* Khosrow, not Al-Mundhir," said 'Antarah, slightly alarmed by and yet grateful for his constant *qareen*.

"Don't worry, as usual I'll let you do the talking. Still, they must think they're invincible, even if they're hiding out," said Shaybub, glancing around with a smirk.

'Antarah took a deep breath, swelling his chest.

"Blessed are you, land of sacred beasts!" shouted 'Antarah, letting his voice resonate across the land to show their harmlessness. They waited a moment, half expecting heads and weapons to rise from different points, but the camels kept grazing, peeking at them every now and then.

They coursed deeper into the striking valley, singing loudly and keeping a distance while they glanced at the dark wooly creatures that roamed freely and lazily in this Eden. It was too good a place for the likes of Al-Mundhir, and 'Antarah mused that he and Shaybub were much worthier of caring for it, if they were ever to be assigned the task.

They were well into the land when the sun came down and had yet to see a soul anywhere. They decided to make camp some distance away, behind a hill that separated them from some of the prized gifts that might earn him his beloved's heart.

"Now who could think we'd mean harm by making our location obvious with a fire?" chuckled Shaybub. They eyed each other as they quietly ate their rationed dried bread and fish, and fed the cubs some dried meat, the stillness only lingering. With the cubs sound asleep in their cage, they reclined and glanced up at the starry skies, bracing themselves for any movement that didn't come...

⚘⚘⚘⚘⚘ ⚘⚘⚘⚘⚘

A harsh grip on his shoulder shook 'Antarah awake, his hand reaching for his sword as the hissing of Antares indicated they weren't alone. 'Antarah glanced at Shaybub, surrounded by two men, as concerned understanding flashed between them.

"What in the Mighty One's name!" yelled 'Antarah in his strongest tone, brandishing Azmari, hoping his reference to Al-Uzza might help somehow.

"*Aywa*; some Aksumite spies who think they're so smart," spat a voice at his side in a drawn-out northeastern accent. "Just what do you think you're doing here?"

'Antarah turned to the young man whose thick headwrap crowned his head, while a fold draped across his shoulders like a shawl, hovering above his sword at his hip. His appearance along with the hint of whining in his tone suggested he couldn't be much younger than himself.

'Antarah eased his shoulders and slightly lowered his sword.

"Kind *sayyid*, did you not hear us singing the praises of your camels all day? As you can see, we mean no harm. We've come from far and would like to meet with *sayyid* Al-Mundhir and request safe passage to *Shah* Khosrow to discuss buying some kin to these fine, blessed camels," said 'Antarah.

He tried to stifle his surprise with cautious admiration: he'd assumed the camels would alert them, but these servants of Al-Mundhir apparently perfected their silent movement—or somehow bewitched them all into submission.

"*Aywa*; that's something *yaba* will love to hear," chuckled the young man. "You're in the presence of his oldest son, Amr," said Amr sternly. "Where do you come from?"

"From the Banu 'Abs. *Sayyid* Zoheir is eagerly awaiting our news," said 'Antarah, trusting the renowned name to do its work.

Amr tilted his head, looked them over, drifted and lingered over the cubs, then glanced back at him. "I shall take you to my father."

"Thousand blessings to you and yours," said 'Antarah with a light bow and sheathed his sword.

They followed Amr and his two companions to a large camp further north, trying not to let the mounting tension overcome him. It had gone well so far but from what they'd heard, Al-Mundhir was not like other men, and he tried not to think of him.

Please protect us: ema, Yassu, and lion-cubs, 'Antarah pleaded for the first time, hating the discomfort consuming him. Focus: his *qareen* would guide him, as it always had.

"Wait here," said Amr near camp and slipped away. Moments later he returned and led them to a guest tent at the center of camp. It might be a sign of hospitality, but it was also a way of keeping close watch over them, and 'Antarah eased his jaw muscles lest they hint at his tense reluctance.

"Rest as you please, and he will see you shortly," said Amr, then disappeared.

"*Sah*; not a chance," whispered Shaybub, echoing his thoughts. Even the huddled cubs seemed quiet and alert as if to counter their discomfort.

The morning and afternoon seemed to stand still, the waiting almost worse than anything else.

"Stalling? Even if he might be busy," said Shaybub.

"North, south, east, west: everywhere on this patch of land the tactics aren't that different," sneered 'Antarah. "But we can't get impatient now." Assuming all went well and Al-Mundhir agreed to help them meet *Shah* Khosrow, it would involve more waiting.

In the late afternoon, the swarming scent of cooking made their stomachs growl.

"Do we trust them?" said Shaybub, reading his mind again.

"Maybe just some bread; we can say we're tired and ate already," said 'Antarah.

With Al-Mundhir's reputation for gruesome killings, 'Antarah tried to find reassurance in the thought that there'd be no point in poisoning them, even if it was a convenient, and cowardly, form of killing. He'd have to make it clear that the tribe awaited them soon, and that whatever befell them would not go unanswered by the expanding Banu 'Abs. Even if that was just his painful wishful thinking about his own tribe, whatever happened, he and Shaybub would not go down without a fight.

They caught the rustling sounds and nodded at each other, and a pair of thick woolen boots stopped at their entrance.

"Al-Uzza has brought us more visitors," said the smirking massive figure whose glance instantly settled on his lip scar, then to the cubs. Al-Mundhir wore so many layers and trinkets of silver jewelry at his neck, wrists, and waist that 'Antarah had the impression he was imitating a leisured version of *Shah* Khosrow's renown cataphracts. At least his son was a more handsome, easier version than him.

"Honored to meet you, *sayyid* Al-Mundhir, and your blessed son Amr," said 'Antarah, and Shaybub followed him in a light bow.

"Welcome," said Al-Mundhir hastily, more from habit than sincerity. "So you've come for some of the Asafir beauties." His evading gaze was as annoyingly dismissive as his rough, nearly accusing tone—was he calling him a liar?

"*Sayyid* Zoheir of the great Banu 'Abs would be honored to eternally praise your generosity, and that of *Shah* Khosrow. There are no finer camels in all the land," said 'Antarah.

"*Sah*. Why not buy from me, then?"

"It has been requested that they come from the *Shah*. As a matter of honor, you understand the importance of keeping my word," said 'Antarah.

"Does he seek to breed them, then?" said Al-Mundhir suspiciously, and looked away.

"It is rather a matter of gifting," said 'Antarah lightly, doubting that anything would ease the man.

"Generous gift indeed. A wedding, then," said Al-Mundhir, his chest rising. "And whose might that be?"

"Mine, *sayyid*," said 'Antarah, his unflinching tone the most confident he'd ever been. "Though I plan to keep none of them myself; I'm only pleased for my tribe to be satisfied, and I to have my treasured bride."

"And you've come all this way for them," said Al-Mundhir with a far-off air.

'Antarah pounced. "We have. And we've had a blessed journey without incident. Al-Uzza even granted us Antares and Al-Shira to protect us in this life and the next," he smiled.

Al-Mundhir's brow twitched, and he gave 'Antarah the darkest, coldest stare he'd ever seen, then looked away. But there was distinct fear in it, just as he'd wanted.

"My son will bring you food, and I'll let *Shah* Khosrow know of your wish to pay your respects, though as you can imagine, it will take some time," said Al-Mundhir.

"Praise your generosity," said 'Antarah, and let out a long breath as Al-Mundhir vanished.

Long days stretched as they had during the *Ayyam al-Zalam*. They took walks with Antares and Al-Shira, and fished carp, barbell, and catfish in the Euphrates, the tribe unusually keeping its distance. There was a curious freedom in that, too, while pondering what Al-Mundhir told them. Though they didn't expect to ever see Al-Mundhir's Yassu-loving wife Hind, they sometimes joked that they might finally peek a glimpse of that aunt of the famed Imru Al-Qays.

From time to time Amr appeared with small news of local tribes, and 'Antarah liked to hear of the cousin tribes the Bakr and Taghlib standing their ground against Al-Mundhir when necessary. Sometimes Amr even accompanied them on their outings, but from his cautious manner 'Antarah suspected that he was not supposed to be with them. They kept their guard up, and there was nothing Amr could spy on them for, so they concluded that he was perhaps as curious as lonely. Most of all, 'Antarah would not reveal his poetic talent until he got to *Shah* Khosrow's court, wanting nothing less than to entertain Al-Mundhir, or worse, praise him with forced, dishonest verses.

Thankfully, amidst his restlessness at night he often saw 'Ablah, her presence as palpable as if she was there with him.

Return to me, she moaned, her hot breath searing his skin with new markings. But being the reason for all this, he hoped she was suffering the way she enjoyed making him suffer, too. The wait was most unbearable then, and the thought that she might be betrothed to someone else in his absence was agonizing. Hurry, they had to hurry.

Seven days passed and 'Antarah could take it no longer.

"We should've heard something by now; it's only two days' ride away," he said. When Amr awkwardly confirmed again that no news had come, 'Antarah had the resurging odd impression that something wasn't right. Quelling his mounting frustration, 'Antarah kindly asked Amr to inform his father that they were planning on leaving in the coming days. Even the cubs were restless and moody, and with their growing energetic forms, it occurred to him that he'd want to gift them to *Shah* Khusrow before they got too big.

Another seven days passed without any signs of Amr, and 'Antarah was about to march in search of his tent when Al-Mundhir reappeared again.

"My guests, why the hurry to leave? Word is bound to come any day now, and you can rest assured he'll be ready to receive you with his letter of approval," said Al-Mundhir.

"You've been kind as it is, but as you know, we must get going. We don't want the ambitious Banu 'Abs marching here now," chuckled 'Antarah. The more he was around Al-Mundhir the more he sensed that he'd rather speak to *Shah* Khosrow than him.

"Trust me; I know well this common frustration. I shall gladly send word again, and make sure it's dispatched with the highest urgency," said Al-Mundhir. But there was nothing 'Antarah trusted about him, and they wanted nothing more than to leave.

A few days later Amr announced that *Shah* Khusrow awaited them. They sighed in relief, and that Amr appeared dejected only touched him more.

"Maybe he wants to come with us," chuckled Shaybub. "I might only stay to live here if Al-Mundhir wasn't here."

'Antarah almost said that as his son, Amr must feel differently about his father, but then realized how wrong he might be. Like any children, Amr might have his own issues with his father, but at least as the eldest he would inherit everything.

They barely slept and were awake before the sunrise, ready for the last part of their journey that would bring them closer to their glorious return home. Next to marrying 'Ablah, creating his own epic-poetic story of their journey—perhaps The Qasidah of the Raven of Sa'd, or something like—to be repeated across time, fed his yearning soul.

They had finished saddling their mounts when Al-Mundhir appeared, his arms swinging heavily at his sides like he'd been bothered from his routine. 'Antarah had half hoped that Amr would come with the letter to *Shah* Khosrow instead, but it was the hospitable custom to say goodbye to one's guests.

"My guests, you'll have to wait a bit longer," said Al-Mundhir. "*Shah* Khosrow has been called away, and won't be at court for a while."

"But he's been informed of our arrival," said 'Antarah, calling on all his self-control to keep an even tone. There *was* something different about being there, when he'd had to yield so often before, but this wasn't home, either, and he was finally a free man.

"The news just came in; leaders are often called away, as you well know," said Al-Mundhir flatly.

"All the same, we will proceed and take our chances and wait there. Al-Uzza knows all you've done for us," said 'Antarah. Every bone in his body begged to just run, grab, and fly anywhere away from him.

"Not at this time," said Al-Mundhir coldly, his hand dropping to his sword handle.

"What do you mean?"

"As I've said, there's no need to hurry, but I'm not granting you leave to go."

"*Granting* leave? We came here without malice, stated our intentions, and now we are to be treated as prisoners?" said 'Antarah. He fixed their host so intently that 'Antarah realized he evaded his gaze, just as Al-Mundhir had from the beginning.

Liar.

He had lied from the beginning, while they'd been there, waiting and wasting time.

"There's nowhere for you to go. Although if as you say, you're protected by Al-Uzza, we shall know soon enough." Al-Mundhir smirked, glanced at the cubs, and let out a cackle.

There was the *ghul* in his full form, hidden in plain sight, and now they'd have to pay for having foolishly trusted him. As if on cue, 'Antarah noted a group of men surrounding them. Did the whole tribe know of his plan?

"You'll be kept to your tent and fed by us. The cubs will grow, as will their hunger, and I'll believe that you're protected by Al-Uzza and let you go if they happen not to maul you," said Al-Mundhir. 'Antarah would've doubted his hearing if it wasn't for that evil glint in his eyes.

In that moment 'Antarah knew what it was to want to kill without a second thought, without any hint of remorse. Al-Mundhir was not just worse than what he'd thought, he was a sick, twisted being who enjoyed his victims' suffering. Though *shaytan*'s minion stood before him in a human form, 'Antarah was not only unafraid, but wanted to stand his ground and fight him.

'Antarah stepped to him. "You don't know what you're playing with," smirked 'Antarah, the tremor of surprise washing over their captor somehow enough to thrill him into satisfaction. 'Antarah glanced at Shaybub and without a word, led their mounts and cubs back inside the tent.

He paced, making circles in the raging chaos. How had he been so confident during all of their exchange, and to say what he did! How would they get out of this when they were in the *ghul*'s lair, and had come to it of their own choice? The more he turned it over the less he saw a chance of a clean escape without bloodshed. Is that what the Lakhmids wanted, and were waiting for 'Antarah to do this work too, when they could, and should be the ones to do it themselves? But it was Al-Mundhir who was the aggressor, and they would defend themselves.

And where did he get the idea that it would be better at *Shah* Khosrow's court? Not only did the Magians lay their deceased in the open air on a ziggurat where they fell prey to birds of prey, but the bones had to be free of flesh to be collected and buried. It was only a few steps above the fate of the *su'luk* poet Ta'abbata Sharran, when 'Antarah had done all he could to avoid that rogue life. What was he to do, when even the fierce Rûm general Crassus, who'd overcome Spartacus's rebelling slaves and had six thousand of them crucified along the Via Appia, found his end at the hands of Parthians in one of Rûm's most crushing defeats!

But they'd come too far to go back empty-handed.

"You know I can do it," said Shaybub.

'Antarah shook his head. "I know, but it's only a worst-case scenario."

Shaybub laughed. "*Aywa*; worse than this?"

"You know what I mean," said 'Antarah, when he himself wasn't sure he did. Their arrows poisoned with *diflah* were one possible option, but as much as part of him wanted to end Al-Mundhir once and for all, they hadn't gone on the mission to kill the Lakhmid vassal of *Shah* Khosrow, and unleash yet another war in the process. 'Antarah didn't know what was worse: that Al-Mundhir's whole tribe feared him or that they supported him enough not to end his tyrannical power. He dared to think that one day there would be someone fitting to do the job, maybe even his biggest enemy—and by default 'Antarah's potential friend—the powerful Ghassanid-Jafnid *malik* Al-Harith himself.

"I wish I could offer you some wiser counsel," said Shaybub, sighing with a cub at each side.

"You always do, just with your presence," said 'Antarah.

For safety, they couldn't act immediately, so they'd feign acceptance and think of something in the meantime. They'd ration their food and wait some more—and though his soul raged against it, demanding justice this instant, everyone got tired in time, and so would their captors. He thought of threatening them with him being *sha'ir* of 'Abs, proud owners of some Hijazi gold mines, who'd come looking for them if they didn't show up soon. But why inflate his vague, wavering sense of pride and say such things, when Al-Mundhir had probably already assumed they were slaves, as anyone could be to the likes of his vile thinking.

At first they paid no mind to Amr when he brought them their food, and 'Antarah hated that he'd even once thought there had been something like budding friendship between them. Surely he'd been in on it from the beginning! And yet, what choice did Amr have?

"Why is he doing this?" 'Antarah asked Amr days later.

Amr tightened his lips and took some time before speaking.

"Your dark skin scares him. He says you shouldn't get married and have children, especially not if it's with a *badawi*, which he assumes it is," said Amr.

"*Aywa*, and that's for him to decide," sneered 'Antarah. "You can tell him that I'm also *badawi* through my father; maybe that'll kill him even more." Just the thought made him smile.

"Don't be afraid," said Amr, gazing at them.

"I'm not. It's the likes of your paranoid father who are," said 'Antarah, once more surprised and pleased at his own strange conviction.

"My mother and I, we believe in Yassu and the afterlife with Him," said Amr. "We try, but we can't talk about it with him, or with most people here. It makes us untrusworthy to the Fars, who'd think we're allies of the Rûm."

"I mean no disrespect to you, but regardless of his faith, I don't think anyone trusts your father, and with good reason, given his past and current actions," said 'Antarah. Part of him cared less now, even if Amr was reporting it to his father. He stood by what he said. "As for others, at least you have some Taghlib and other neighbors in the faith; maybe you should pay them a visit, even if your father has a problem with them."

"Do you really praise Al-Uzza for the cubs' protection?" said Amr.

"No, but if it works to defeat Al-Mundhir, all the better."

"What about Yassu? Do you believe in Him?"

"I would like to, if only for our blameless mother who loves Him. If it wasn't for her, we wouldn't have made it this far," 'Antarah sighed. He wasn't sure why he was confessing this, but he was tired of second-guessing and holding everything in. People everywhere died no matter their faiths, but the truth was their Yassu-loving mother was the only one they'd ever been able to fully trust without a single doubt.

Dazed, sleepless days passed, and he summoned his *qareen* with all his strength to contact their *ema*, yearning for her protection and helpful answers. Though they didn't see Al-Mundhir, they sensed his presence like the all-watching evil eye.

"I hate to say it, but with all the time that's passed, is it worth trying—"

"No. We will not offer him the gold either," said 'Antarah, even as the thought had occurred to him, too. "I'll not give the liar the satisfaction of taking the gold and keeping us here. I'm glad I scare him; I just wish it was enough to release us."

But each day, the thought of risking it and killing whoever they needed was becoming more tempting. To what end? To get a few out of the way and be killed in return, maybe without even taking the life of the one who most deserved to die! Even in the desperation, to live seemed its own kind of triumphant defiance.

"We want to help you," said Amr evenings later.

"How?" said 'Antarah, his spirit already soaring.

"Several men want to leave. So you'll leave with them while our mother makes sure my father and his guards sleep soundly through it. Unlike my father, my mother's informed *Shah* Khusrow at Taysafun about you. For security there's no letter to give you from him, but he will welcome you and you'll get Asafir camels there," Amr said.

No letter for proof, even if he could read, but it was the best plan yet.

"You'd betray your father to help us?" frowned 'Antarah.

"How can it be betrayal? I'm ashamed of what he plans to do—I keep foolishly thinking he's going to change. I was only a little boy when he kidnapped and burnt the poor nuns to Al-Uzza," Amr paused. "He still boasts about that letter that he received from Dhu Nuwas of Himyar when he was at the gathering of Ramla, inviting him to convert to the Israelite faith, and to follow his example and kill the *Masihi* in his midst like he did at Zafar, San'a, and Najran. As though he's some saint for not acting on it, when he'd initially considered doing it for three thousand gold coins," Amr sneered. "I can't stand by while he does more evil things, and I know this would at least scare him, even if it doesn't make him change."

'Antarah glanced at Shaybub, then nodded. "We'll be ready for your plan," said 'Antarah.

In the privacy of their tent, 'Antarah repeated his own version of their mother's last ritual before they left the 'Abs. He burnt incense, repeated as many sacred verses as he could, and oiled their hair, forcing himself to believe that this time it would be for a fruitful meeting with *Shah* Khosrow.

Days later Amr announced that they should be ready in the coming days, though they would've been ready to leave right then and there. The night came and they followed Amr into the darkness, and met up with the group of men stationed to the north. He'd expected a large group, but not one that large.

"The men may split along the way, but from now on you're just riding north along the Euphrates then northeast to Taysafun. May you have a blessed journey," said Amr almost shyly.

"Praise Yassu and your mother for you," said 'Antarah.

"Remember me? As Amr ibn Hind," he frowned.

"As you wish," said 'Antarah, and kissed him on each cheek to hide his emotion at his preference for his matronymic.

In a last parting gesture, Amr touched the faces of Antares and Al-Shira and waved them off with a conflicted smile. With a final nod, 'Antarah thought he might add him and his mother in his *qasidah*, if he ever made it out alive.

In the moonlit chilly night they coursed without stop along the river, not lighting any oil lamps to ease their discreet passage. Whatever their stories, they all shared their deep yearning to get away from Al-Mundhir, and maybe never return so long as he was there. By morning they were already almost halfway through the journey, and some men split to go northwest towards the Taghlib and the easternmost Rûm and Ghassanid borders.

By the second evening they felt safer to slow down a bit, the approaching capital drawing near like a welcomed sanctuary. Even if Al-Mundhir came after them, they'd at least escaped with none of the Asafir camels, even if 'Antarah almost wished they'd taken some just to spite him. As it was, the balance of power was in their court, when he'd betrayed the code of *badawi* generosity with his treacherous, vile test. They decided to camp for the night in a secluded place, and all the better to throw off any potential pursuers.

CHAPTER TWENTY-FIVE

TAYSAFUN

'Antarah and Shaybub rode off the next morning and to their shock, the awe they'd had at the sight of the extensive lush grounds at Al-Hira had its match in the bustling capital of Taysafun that lay east of the Tigris. With the cubs obediently leashed at their side, they breathed a bit easier, hardly believing that after nearly two moons—when it should've been less than half that, at most—they'd finally made it without trouble to this land with such marvelously long history.

To the west was Saliq, founded by Siliochus I, that companion of Iskandar the Great. Awestruck, for a while all they could do was speechlessly take in the imposing buildings and sights of this place that had been the main capital of the Fars Empire for centuries. Cargo ships docked along the river with throngs of sailors and merchants unloading, and the scent of fresh bread and aromatic food already drifted from taverns and homes in anticipation of the day. They craned their necks as they looked over the carved walls of the main façade of Taq Kasra, with its massive archway entrance at the center leading to the audience hall where they'd finally stand before *Shah* Khosrow.

A shiver snaked through him, recalling that this *Shah*, who it was said modeled his city after Antioch, had so recently sacked it and relocated captives from Antioch into their own city nearby.

"Am I imagining things in our happiness to be away from the *ghul*, or is there some feast under way?" said Shaybub.

"You might be right," said 'Antarah. They would certainly welcome it, after the gloomy second half of their journey spent against their will in Al-Mundhir's camp.

They passed beneath the majestic archway and through the smaller doorway into the entrance hall's courtyard. They informed one of the finely armed guards in a coat of mail about *sayyida* Hind's message to *Shah* Khosrow regarding their visit for the Asafir camels. The guard glanced at the cubs with a smirk, nodded and disappeared for a while, then returned with an older, long-bearded man in a flowing robe, whom 'Antarah guessed was the *Shah*'s advisor. He smiled and said something to them that sounded familiar but which they couldn't quite understand.

"Unfortunately we do not speak Ge'ez," said 'Antarah with a small smile. That they should be addressed as envoys coming from their mother's land already made a pleasant difference.

"We shall understand each other regardless," said the man in an accented northern *'arabi*. "Follow me, please."

They floated through wide halls, trying not to stare at all the finely woven carpets and winged horse tapestries. Unable to resist taking inventory for potential poetic imagery, 'Antarah noted the steles carved with ancient writings and images, the stone, silver, and gold statues, more winged horses and lions, and mosaics and panels colored with blue and saffron. They were walking in a dream-like, incense-scented palace of memories, but he couldn't relent and think the nightmare over until he'd settled affairs with the Fars king.

They entered a court of marble, and stood paces away from a silken curtain, beyond which lay a domed canopy and gold couch with a lion carved at each armrest. From the ceiling hung a gold chain that held up the famously heavy Fars crown. The space was so quiet that he was sure no sound could penetrate from outside.

"He shall be with you shortly," said the *Shah*'s advisor, and left them.

"*Aywa*, he can trap us here if he wants," whispered Shaybub when they were sure the man was gone. The space was such vastness of peaceful silence that it was easy to want to stay there. On the other side was a large marble table with flowers and other trinkets 'Antarah wanted to see up close, but decided not to yet.

"Seems they love their new home already," sighed 'Antarah. Antares and Al-Shira, who sat obediently on their hind legs, seemed caught in their own awe of the majestic aura of the place.

Moments later there was a bustle, and a throng of guards emerged to attend to their *Shah*. Through the veil that prevented directed sight of the *Shah*, 'Antarah glimpsed a tall, robust man with kohled eyes and long dark hair and beard. Donned in cream silk garments and a crimson mantle embroidered with gold, for once the clothing didn't need to add to his frame when his form was naturally massive. Even reclined in his shining throne, he was the largest man 'Antarah had ever seen, and his gold, jewel-encrusted crown suspended above his fragranced, oiled head, and matching scabbard at his hip only added to his intimidating authority. Only now did 'Antarah understand the stories of the *Shah*'s image as the ruler at the center of the celestial arrangement. For an instant 'Antarah had the sense of being so small before him, which had to be some of the pleasure nobles enjoyed over their kingdom and other subjects.

'Antarah bowed and Shaybub followed his cue, hoping the *Shah* wouldn't notice the scar at his lip. He might think it unappealing—a bad omen—though 'Antarah could hint he'd gotten it in battle, which wasn't entirely a lie and rather a sign of his strength.

"Good day to have two Aksumites at my court interested in my Asafir camels," said *Shah* Khosrow, his deep accented tone tinged with humor. "You know, I recently had a dream of King Abraha, and here you are. I would've expected him to send word given our diplomatic differences, but some might say he is full of surprises. And yet, it is for civilized men to discuss like men."

At last: confirmation that the message had reached him. 'Antarah could've fallen at his feet, but he had to stop thinking like that.

"Blessed *Shah*, we are not of the court of King Abraha. I am 'Antarah, son of Shaddad of the Banu 'Abs of Najd. We are honored to have reached your great eternal city. Please accept these as an initial gift."

Careful not to stare at the monarch, 'Antarah gestured to Shaybub who gave the lion cubs to a guard to hand them to the monarch. *Shah* Khosrow smirked, then gestured for the guard to bring them closer, and 'Antarah thanked his *qareen* for the cubs obediently and gently going to him as if they already knew him. Chuckling, the *Shah* pet them vigorously as 'Antarah secretly sighed in relief.

"These are fine beasts, well-trained. Even if you've gifted the same to Al-Mundhir," said *Shah* Khosrow, and handed them off to a guard to be taken away. Jealousy, competition, and teasing, all in one.

"Not so. In fact, blessed *Shah*, I wish to be frank with you, if I may, without intending offense?" said 'Antarah, keeping his gaze respectfully somewhere near his beaded shoes.

"Of course," said *Shah* Khosrow with an inviting tone.

"We had hoped to have better dealings with *sayyid* Al-Mundhir, but that did not happen. It was only by the kindness of *sayyida* Hind and yours that we managed to safely leave and arrive here. I humbly ask your protection from him, as we've unfortunately found that he is not a trustworthy man." No matter their differences, the monarch at least knew what he meant.

Shah Khosrow smirked.

"His reputation precedes him, yet you chose to go to him. As a young man in the spring of his youth, I imagine your tribe chose you for your skill, and you were searching for adventure and, most of all, immortality?" The *Shah*'s powerful voice seemed an extension of his all-seeing eye trying to pierce into him.

"I've not thought much of immortality, and it seems vain to even want to try to reach it. But as the *sha'ir* of Banu 'Abs, I do know the power words can have, and sometimes that can feel like immortality," said 'Antarah. "Still, as any words said about a man can also be wrong, now I know the truth about Al-Mundhir."

Once again, his *qareen* had done it, but there was something about the man that made 'Antarah want to present the best of himself—humble, free, poet, yet poised—and while he had the chance.

Shah's Khosrow's serious air returned.

"Your humility impresses me, and might even be a lesson you've learned from our great Gilgamesh. The Egyptians, the Israelites, the Rûm, and others may have old traditions, but we have the oldest written stories," said the *Shah* self-assuredly.

"A most honorable, eternal achievement," 'Antarah nodded and smiled, thinking of his mother, *Negus* Kaleb, and King Abraha who'd boldly disagree and remind him of the book of Henok. But no matter which was oldest, if that could even be certain, they were surely significant in their own way. At least there was an unexpected well-meaning tone to the *Shah*'s natural air of superiority that they'd never find in Al-Mundhir.

Shah Khosrow rose. "As for your request, your tribe wouldn't have sent you unless you were among the best, so I grant you my protection. Come, take a walk with me. Fear not: you may gaze upon me, though surely with caution."

Swallowing his amused surprise, 'Antarah followed from a slight distance, with Shaybub hanging further back still. Their steps were nearly soundless on the ground, except for the swishing of their robes.

"How many camels?" said the *Shah*.

"One thousand," said 'Antarah, and caught a flash of his kohled gaze. "It is known that they are the best, and they are to be an honorable dowry."

"Ah, the things we do for love," sighed the *Shah*. "I know something of it, when I welcome all kinds to my court, whose ancient walls I restored. I've created a court to host the best philosophy, literature, and poetry, and I have the best doctors learning and practicing at the University of Gundeshapur. Let's not forget that I welcomed those lovers of knowledge whose Platonic Academy *Qaysar* Justinian closed, and those two-nature Yassu believers that he considers unbelieving heretics. I am even father to a son of such a Yassu-loving woman, and if my Anoshazad is proving a challenge to me, it is only temporary. As you've heard, I've just made a new city for the Antiochians now among us, run by their own Yassu-serving bishop."

"Weh Antiok Khosrow," nodded 'Antarah, wishing the name *Khosrow-built-this-better-than-Antioch* was a joke. Like the locals, he preferred to call it Rumiya for their Rûm and northwest origin.

"Indeed! How could they want to leave when I keep extending my *kirbag*, these good deeds of providing them with Rûm baths, a circus, and charioteers! They have everything to make them happy, especially with their church headquarters here, while the plague rages there. Perhaps that's rightful retribution for all their *Qaysar*'s greedy expanding to the west," said the *Shah* with a dreamy air, though not enough to conceal envy.

'Antarah's throat clamped. Was Khosrow's feuding—much like his father Kavadh—with *Qaysar* Justinian over the Armenian gold mines not greedy, too? And how typical for a powerful ruler to assume he knew what others wanted, and that he was doing them blessed favors by his actions. Surely at least some would say they'd want to return home, even with the threat of plague. The *Shah* might've given them comforts, even some they'd never had before, but they were still chained captives. 'Antarah wasn't sure what was worse: that powerful men didn't see this wrong or pretended not to.

And yet—what if he was saving their lives in his own twisted way, and at the cost of the prosperity of Antioch? At least living and making families offered the chance of one day returning, no matter how small. 'Antarah tried to take comfort in concluding that Al-Mundhir held captives with intent to harm, while *Shah* Khosrow tried to seduce opponents into collaborative submission. He did think of himself as the King of Kings, after all, which still required other living rulers and people around.

"Your generosity is known far and wide," said 'Antarah. "We're honored to pay with three thousand *solidi*." Though the proud monarch wouldn't comment on it, he surely appreciated this price comparable to horses and offered without haggling.

"Three thousand *solidi* from the other side of the *badawi* desert, hmm," *Shah* Khosrow chuckled, his plans already reaching far into the Hijaz. "Let us not talk of payment today, though I'm beginning to think you may be part of our *xwarah*; what you might call good fortune. You see, I cannot think it accidental that you've arrived on our Nowruz, the blessed reminder of spring's victory over darkness. It adds to my pleasure as much as my newborn son Hormizd's powerful cries. Let us celebrate."

"Many blessings, kind *Shah*, to you and your kin," said 'Antarah and bowed. "I wonder if you would allow me one thing first? I'd very much like to see your table."

"Certainly," said the *Shah* with a hint of surprise.

They came to the massive cream marble table with crimson veining. One side was covered in vases blooming with hyacinth and rose flowers, and bowls of dates, grapes, pomegranates, and other fruits. There were painted eggs and colorful spices, and bowls of water and wine. At the center was propped up a delicate, striking circular dish. The center had the *Shah* carved into clear rock crystal, enthroned on a lavish couch. All around him were rows of rock crystal, garnet, and emerald glass rosettes set in gold, as if representing the *Shah*'s power emanating from him. The *Shah* had reason to boast, when he clearly had the finest artisans to create such unique and costly pieces to honor him.

"You admire the image of my father Kavadh," said the *Shah* sharply.

"I thought it was you," said 'Antarah, relieved to catch the pride in his demeanor. "Surely words will fail to describe such treasured craftsmanship."

"It's my favorite memory of my great father who chose me, his youngest, to rule after him. If only—" He stopped and 'Antarah kept his gaze averted in this unexpected display of evident, if restrained conflicted emotion. There was a deep sound and 'Antarah realized the *Shah* had switched to snickering. "You know, I don't think of them as often as I thought I would. What say you to that?"

'Antarah lifted his gaze directly into the *Shah*'s.

"I say that it was survival, that your good works are evident to all, and that you spared your great empire from brothers who not only scorned your father's wise choice, but invited death by scheming against your life."

For a moment their gazes locked and the *Shah* appeared in genuine contemplation, and most surprising of all, even somewhat relieved.

"How different things might've been if only *Qaysar* Justin and his nephew Justinian had adopted me, as they'd initially intended," said the *Shah*, as if in a daze.

Or not, but that wasn't your fault—'Antarah thought but didn't dare say as he maintained a demure yet strong bearing. He hadn't imagined the monarch would bring up any of this pain he partially shared with him, and concluded it explained some of the *Shah*'s bitterness with the Rûm.

With an inviting hand motion from the *Shah*, 'Antarah moved to the other side of the table, where rested a large oil lamp surrounded by open texts, and two square boards, one of which he guessed was a game of backgammon.

"Is that the Avesta?" said 'Antarah, gazing over the largest book that lay open, propped up on a gold plate.

"It is," said the *Shah*. "It is a new revision that contains all the texts sacred to our Zoroastrian faith."

'Antarah took in the neat Magian script, cementing in his memory this text of Zoroaster.

"And what of these; new poetry?" said 'Antarah, gesturing to the much thinner group of lose pages, surely unfinished yet worthy of display.

"Of a kind. These are the first few pages of an Indian text called The Pan-catantra, currently under translation by my physician Borzuya," beamed the *Shah*.

"Who I'm sure will also record all your *kirbag*," said 'Antarah. A knot formed in him, reminding him that he had to begin working on his own *qasidah*, now that he mused that they were in a safer place. And then, would anyone ever recite, let alone write about him, 'Antarah son of Zabiba and Shaddad?

"It's a lot for him to keep track of, along with all the other work I have him doing. And since you're *sha'ir*, perhaps we may hear some of your poetry, too," said the *Shah*. 'Antarah stared, startled. In the midst of all the monarch's achievements, he was sure the *Shah* hadn't heard him, or just ignored him.

"It would be my honor, although I'll need some time to do you justice," said 'Antarah.

"I'm sure you'll find plenty of inspiration here. Even Iskandar couldn't resist our ways; naturally we also have a translation of the Iskandar Romance," grinned the *Shah*.

With a nod, 'Antarah drifted further to the other side of the table, and stood over the curious square with a black and white checkered surface. On it were sixteen ivory pieces lined up on one side, and sixteen onyx pieces on the other. He tried to make out some shapes in the vague forms, but only recognized two large and smaller thrones, horses, and something with protruding horns that could be elephants.

"This looks like a complicated battle," said 'Antarah.

"That it is. This game of *chatrang* is a new import from India. What you see here are pawns lined up in front of each side. They protect the *Shah* and Advisor behind them at center, along with the Elephants at their sides, then the Knights represented by horses, and the pointy, tower-like Rooks at the outer corners," said the monarch.

"So how is the game played and won?"

"You follow the proper rules of movement for each piece, and you either 'check' the *Shah* so that every move he makes is under attack and blocked, or one resigns the game, meaning surrender. Your goal is to be the one to say *Shah Met*: the King is Dead."

"Something tells me it can take very long for that to happen," said 'Antarah, both impressed and intimidated.

"True; it can even take days. Let me know if you'd like to try it sometime," laughed the *Shah*.

'Antarah pinched a smile. Though he was a little curious, he wasn't sure he wanted to engage in what looked like a game that mixed strategy and luck when he had enough of that in his life. The nobles at court had plenty of time and resources to spare, a harsh reminder of this state he wasn't familiar with, and would probably never be.

"You have an honorable, praiseworthy court, with so much to teach us and the world," said 'Antarah with a deep nod.

For the first time, the *Shah* seemed humbled.

"I'm pleased for you to be this year's first guests to see my Nowruz table. May it be a blessing for you," said the *Shah*, with a sincerity that reassured him.

"For the camels, when shall we—"

Shah Khosrow waved his hand. "We'll come back to that soon enough. Today, we celebrate. Please, do not be in a hurry. Stay as long as you like, and even better if you choose to stay among us. I'm informing my guards of you, should you need their help at any moment. So go, see and enjoy our lands, and I welcome you to return later, to feast on our heavenly *sabzi polo mahi*, and stay in our quarters."

"Good *Shah*, that is too much, we don't want to intrude."

"Impossible! You've come a long way to gift me cubs at my blessed court on Nowruz. I will see you soon."

'Antarah bowed to him and left with Shaybub, both relieved and still tinged with some doubt. He wanted the camels and to return home, but he also wanted to see more.

"It might be crazy, but even with his *majnun* pride, I think we can trust him," said Shaybub when they were back outside amidst the swelling crowds.

"I was thinking the same, not that we have much choice," 'Antarah chuckled.

With the amount of camels he wanted, they'd need the help of his guards to at least safely get past the lands of and around Al-Mundhir's. But the *Shah*'s unexpected light air was beginning to fill him, too. By some miracle, they'd safely escaped Al-Mundhir's grip and could now also count on the *Shah*'s protection. Despite the eternal uncertainty, friends, or at least help, could show up when he least expected it, and he vowed to be grateful and never forget those who genuinely offered it.

The morning elapsed coasting along the Euphrates River and visiting the markets and taverns. Most people wore their best and brightest clothes, and there was a relief to being there, unknown, and sometimes even mistaken for merchants from Aksum or Himyar. Some older women passed out *naan berengi* rice flour cookies and sugar-coated almonds with their children, while some street singers sang praises to the long endurance of the Fars kingdom. They told of Gilgamesh, Cyrus the Great, Cambysses II, and Shapur I, who'd triumphed over *Qaysar* Valerian and *Qaysar* Philippus, and first used the title of *King of Kings to the Fars and non-Fars*. Naturally, the empire's prosperity endured with *Shah* Kavadh and his good son and heir, *Shah* Khosrow.

They drifted across the river that had a pleasant subdued air. After passing by several wealthy Israelites going about their work, they rode southwest and visited the two-nature Yassu believers in Kokhi. Some of the locals, happy to see such distant visitors, eagerly greeted them and shared some of the area's history.

Though *Shah* Khosrow was considered a tolerant ruler, his father Kavadh's reign had been turbulent. In his time, this Veh-Ardashir area had been the site of an Israelite revolt, that had established seven years of independence from Fars rule. Even forty years later, to hear that its Israelite Exilarch Mar-Zutra II had been punished with crucifixion on the Mahoza bridge left them nearly speechless. The Israelites tried to take heart that the son, Mar-Zutra III, born on the day of his father's death, had at least escaped and made it to the Promised Land, where he still lived. It seemed that no matter where they went, there'd be variants of harsh stories, and peoples of all backgrounds trying to live, both separated from and immersed in memories.

'Antarah made a mental note of the ample glassware and incantation bowls for sale in case they'd want to get some, and as the sun set they went back across the bridge to the archway. Light filled the streets as people walked with oil lamps, and some even competed with each other by jumping across scattered fires. More sweets and *halvah* pastries were passed around, along with wine and pomegranate drinks, sometimes both mixed together.

The sound of tambourines and singing drew near, revealing a procession around *Shah* Khosrow. Clad in a facial veil and full cataphract armor, he waved happily to the crowd from atop his black horse also dressed in metal. With all his majestic force and vast empire, no wonder some called him the new Cyrus. People called out to the *Shah*, waving red embroidered cloths or other silken fabrics in a loving frenzy.

For a moment 'Antarah shook with worry, lest Al-Mundhir may be around, hidden in such a large gathering... then he smirked. Even if so, the *ghul* was too late, and would face not only him and Shaybub, but all the *Shah*'s soldiers, who would at least disarm him before he ever reached the *Shah* he reluctantly served.

The procession arrived steps away from them, and 'Antarah's jaw nearly dropped when *Shah* Khosrow saw him, and fixed his wave on them. The *Shah*'s pause drew his guards' attention, and soon even throngs around them were looking at them both and cheering.

'Antarah smiled and bowed with a hand on his heart.

"Are we dreaming?" whispered Shaybub.

"Maybe, and haven't we earned it?" said 'Antarah. To his shock, he realized that the day had elapsed with limited thought of 'Ablah. But that had to be forgivable, amidst all the fear, anger, and excitement that were still part of his tormented, driven love. Even that realization had to count, proof that he always brought her with him, now as a free man in magical Taysafun whose *Shah* not only offered his protection but wanted to hear his verses.

Shah Khosrow passed on and 'Antarah made a double take at Shaybub's fixed air.

"What's wrong?" said 'Antarah.

"Now I know we've died and gone to another place," said Shaybub. He gathered himself and discreetly nodded in an eastern direction.

'Antarah followed his gaze and his heart nearly stopped.

There, not far from them, was a girl in a saffron belted crimson robe and cream silken veil. She looked the perfect copy of 'Ablah, except that she was smiling at him, along with her cheerful friend who also gazed at Shaybub. 'Antarah waited a bit, lest it was some mistaken impression in the bustling night crowd, but as torches of light danced through and around them, the girls lingered, and even gave some delicious flaky *baqlava* pastries to younger boys and girls to bring to them.

All his protection, all his cut flesh, all the sadness, and never once had 'Ablah acknowledged him. Could she even cook and make such things, and *want* to make them for him? Just like that, his erratic hurry vanished with the countless whirling flames, and calm clarity set in.

'Ablah could wait a little bit, and there was a shattering release in thinking she might already be married to someone else without his knowledge. He couldn't decide what it meant that it'd taken this long to admit his denial that the tribe might've just waited a few days for them to be out of sight to finalize the whole thing. And yet, already something told him he'd done the right thing by leaving.

Was that what it felt like for her—to wave around that power to dismiss him without a care? He wasn't sure if he liked it or not, but like his unsung *qasidah*, it was worth thinking about.

"You know what? I think we will take *Shah* Khosrow's invitation and stay a while," said 'Antarah.

CHAPTER TWENTY-SIX

SU'LUK

SPRING 542 AD – BANU SA'D

Get the women... and the men.

Zig, zig, zig—screeched the blade as Jayida ran it widely across the whetstone. Following the steady repeated motion, her torso rocked back and forth, her gaze lampooning a lurking shadowy form.

What would it be like to slice into a man and peel off his skin? The question pestered her soul, teasing, inviting to know. She didn't have blades on her tongue like a lion to lick off the flesh, but it couldn't be much harder than peeling a lion's, when the human layer was so thin, so meaningless, yet so full of evil.

Did they expect her to just lie there, quiet like a fragile dove, and let their wrath fall upon her; cowering and submitting to make them feel strong? Her body shook and to her grateful delight there was the piercing echo of her own laughter.

That would never happen! She'd fight with everything she had—generously giving!—and might even win. Whether right or wrong, she hadn't wanted this, tried to deter it—four demon bowls at each corner!—and still they came and asked for it. Oh, she'd defend her own, until her last breath: *tribesmen hit and get hit together.* The question taunted her: how could the victims at Najran just surrender for Yassu, when some said he was just another man preaching the word of *al-ilah*?

The grinning *ghul* locked on her, teasing her, and she pounced on him again, kicked him down in the dirt where he belonged, squeezing his throat and hovering over his eyes with her blade, her lion sight tearing into him.

If you really want it, you'll get it!

She hadn't said it—or had she? Was he sensible enough to have heard Jonder's silence? But she was Jonder-Jayida, and she'd heard his—and showed him what would happen if he, or anyone else, dared to come in their space.

Hard, hard, hard—she'd become harder than stone, to stop and freeze her forming tears, crying out in disgust and righteous justice. She couldn't let him see it—he'd think she was sad, afraid, when no! It was exploding excitement, the uncoiling satisfaction of rightful release.

Jayida relished the delight that she hadn't even felt it at first; her father's tight grip on her asking her to ease up on the pitiful invader. Like an immortal obelisk, towering to the sky, that even if scattered into pieces would still retain its power from its bits of sacred drawings and writings etched into it.

Those beastly tribeless rogue rejects had dared come to them, driven by accounts of Nasr's death and the rewarded killers, thinking they'd have the same luck. There was the result of what they'd feared most: that their generosity would be taken as weakness, and invite more evil.

So the Sa'd showed them.

The rush blazed through the tribe and they charged on the assaulting, evil-eyed enemy, spears and swords clashing—and overcame the invaders so fast that for a moment she'd been consumed with shocked disappointment. Was that really it, the best they could do; presenting the worst example of how vanity truly blinded those it possessed!

Best—and worst—of all, she'd heard him, that leading demon, and her wrath had come pouring out with such force that she charged and struck at him so hard that she threw him off his mount. She'd pounced down on him, blade in hand, contemplating the possibilities, until her generous father eased her off him. Even Nasr's killers hadn't gone that far with their vile intents.

Reading her unrelenting intensity, her father had taken her aside, at which point she somehow managed to reel in her wrath enough to tell him of their evil intentions of violating the whole tribe. His disgust at once mirrored her own, and he at once informed *sayyid* Aziz of the seriousness of the situation.

The attackers were tied up and kept in a thin tent, which she almost protested as too good for them, when they dared to complain and invoke their status as guests. She asked *sayyid* Aziz's permission to gag them, and with a gleeful smirk, he granted it. It was bad enough to hear them, but the tribe wouldn't risk them scheming up yet another, even if laughably unsuccessful, plan. They would be given blankets for nightfall, proof of their hospitality, after all.

What if their tongues were swollen, or cut off somehow—that still kept them alive, though at that point they might well choose death. In her disgusted rage

Jayida had her double in Shams, who demanded to be the one in charge of the task and making sure the prisoner tent was kept under close guard at all times. He might have Yazida in mind, but just the thought of any harm coming to her own parents was enough to make Jayida a thousand times worse than him—of that she was convinced.

Jayida turned the blade over and continued the steady sharpening process, her favorite part waiting for its turn in her memory like a theater or mosaic scene. With Shams and everyone else aware of her plan, she waited until late night to creep out, spear in hand and her lion skin draped on her like a shroud. Upon seeing her, her fellow tribesmen—veiled up to the nose—glowed with grinning approval and followed as she made her way.

Near the prisoner tent she dropped on all fours, paced around it, shook her second lion-face, and scratched at the fabric here and there, snarling. A small, purposeful lamp outside perfectly reflected her lion-shadow against the tent wall. She continued until muffled groans resonated inside, the rising pitch confirming their mounting fear of what lurked nearby. With a dark grin she stopped, snorted, and her throat rattled with a low growl, surprising even herself at her authentic sound. Just lying there, within, waiting to be let out.

Through the stillness radiated the prisoners' stifled rising breaths, their pungent sweat wading out of them for any hungry animal to find. Restraining a surging laugh, she lingered by the entrance, and after a few moments of perfect dread, she slowly poked her lion-face through the entrance. At the hubbub of whining, muffled pleading, Jayida thrust the face forward and back, side to side, the long wooly lion's mane only adding to his massive size.

Fueled by her cue, her veiled kin swarmed inside the tent. Knives in hand, they yelled, seized, and held down the flesh-demons, ripping off their pants. The prisoners cried out, begging to be spared, the blades coming closer and closer to their pathetic genitals that only shrank amidst so much unkempt hair. Their terrified moans filled the space, and Shams dug his knife so deep into one that she thought he'd go through with it. In the rush, fists and feet dug into their bodies, conveniently feeding their confusion. From their grateful sobs as they receded, she knew its effect, and she doubted they got much sleep that night. No matter their beliefs, they would not forget their stay at the Sa'd, and might never speak of it again, lest they be mocked to death.

The next day *sayyid* Aziz gathered them to decide what should be done with the prisoners.

"Thoughts?" said *sayyid* Aziz, sipping his wine. With wine-loving Sufyan gone to the gold mines, Shams and his father Hubala had been going to Khaybar to keep their *sayyid* well supplied.

"Send them naked into the desert to fend for themselves," spat her father. To her relief, she saw only nodding approval.

"Yet they might say they were not treated well," *sayyid* Aziz smirked.

"They are not guests! They invaded us, intent on harm, and we defended ourselves, as we always will!" said Jayida.

"What about selling them as slaves to the Sulaym mines?" smirked Hubala. "I'm sure Sufyan would gladly make good use of them," he said, eyeing his amused son with a thought for his older departed one.

"And you, my pearl?" *sayyid* Aziz turned to his daughter.

"Any of these sound good to me," said Yazida.

"*Aywa*," said *sayyid* Aziz. He rose and they followed him to the prisoner tent. The attackers were ungagged and untied, and stood there dumbfounded.

"I could send messengers to our vast kin, including Banu Hawazin," said *sayyid* Aziz, feigning contemplation. "*Aywa*; they'd find plenty of use for you all at Mina and other shrines; that might be fitting punishment for your filthy ways."

The leader shook his head. "Please, no. We'll leave, and never come back—we swear," he stammered.

"Hmm. Yet can your word be trusted? Because I assure you, mine can, like the blessed sight of a true *kahin*," said *sayyid* Aziz. The leader lowered his head, as if agreeing but too afraid to say anything else.

"You've heard that I'm generous, and so I am. So be forever grateful that we didn't remove your sorry excuse for living. I've decided to let you go as you came; now hurry and vanish without a trace." *Sayyid* Aziz dismissed them with a thrust of his chin, and the men mounted their camels in clumsy silence. *Sayyid* Aziz went to one of the men and took his bow and quiver. "On second thought, watch your back as you ride off," smirked *sayyid* Aziz. "We might or might not wait until you're far enough out; we'd like to have some fun, too," he added, pleased at their startled faces.

Jayida smiled, certain that Nasr would approve. Their *sayyid* was blameless when he, most of all, had become a different man, his bottomless angry sadness fueling his usually dormant wrath.

The ground thundered and *sayyid* Aziz burst into laughter as they scattered in the distance. He aimed and released a few arrows so far off range that it couldn't be an accident.

"*Aywa*, even if I aimed well, my son is generous in death," he said. "Join me, but don't hit them, or shall I say, I think the lion of Sa'd made his mark already," he winked at her.

Her father handed her bow and quiver, and standing next to him and Shams, with the *sayyid* before them, they aimed and launched off together. Their arrows flew high into the sky, disappearing in another direction. Jayida took aim again, her gaze narrowing, finding, then released one that came close but missed, pleased that she could hit one of them even at this far distance.

And what if she did and let it fall where it may, as it sadly had for Nasr? Could it still be an accident, or on the contrary, the rightful hand of fate? If some wanted to push and provoke, they could hardly blame the consequences. That vile pride again: if only they had asked instead of attacking—though asking was no guarantee of satisfaction, either—how different things could've been.

Jayida stopped sharpening, looked the blade over on each side, then ran it lightly down a palm leaf, satisfied at the perfect nonresistant slice. The attack had been on an afternoon about two moons ago, and though successfully passed, it whirled fresh in her mind as if it'd been the day before. Daily she re-lived the moment, disturbing and soothing—turning the image wheel beyond the veil that would one day claim each of them, to remind the bandits of what she, and the whole tribe of Sa'd, promised if they tried again, or inspired others to it. At least, the rush of fighting the chaos as one had deepened their unshakeable unity and bond as a tribe, and though she knew not everyone was blessed to experience it, it was becoming harder for her to sympathize with ruffians. While some sought to bond by causing chaos, she was proud to be among a tribe that bonded by setting it in its proper place. She hoped that her mother's news that the young *sha'ir* Amr ibn Kulthum, barely in his fifteenth year yet already *sayyid* of the Banu Taghlib, would approve.

Engulfed in the late afternoon warmth of her tent, Jayida stashed away her blades, pleased and a little surprised again that she hadn't even noticed that she'd sharpened all of them. She reached for the coin from her pouch, smiling and deciding again that it couldn't belong to some dishonorable bandit.

Zahir had recognized it as one of *Qaysar* Anastasius's gold *solidi* coins, whose rule dated back to shortly before he was born. It was said this wise emperor—who had one black eye and one blue eye—had ended the fierce gladiatorial contests between men and beasts, built a wall at Constantinople that kept invaders at bay, and finished his reign with a full treasury.

Though she'd already memorized it, she couldn't get enough of looking at the crowned, helmeted, and breastplated emperor, holding a spear over one shoulder, and a shield decorated with a mounted cavalryman on the other. She flipped the coin over to winged Victory facing west, holding a long cross, with a star to the east, reminding her of an angel.

As for the potential treasure-owner, perhaps he'd left it there to return to later, and the thought that he was still alive pushed her to try to find out who it was. But getting more information without rousing suspicion was another matter. For the moment, she didn't mind keeping it quiet, and at times it filled her with a thrill to imagine that someday soon she'd get to the bottom of it.

"I'll be back soon, my shining pearl," she cooed to Adil and gave him a sugar cube treat. With her small gourd at her belt and a spear in hand, she cast a prideful glance at the lion's heart impaled on her outdoor post and walked on to her parent's tent before her evening walk. After all that had happened, she had the urge to scout the grounds more often. Sometimes she went with Shams, but usually alone.

"As always, the fruit of your delicious work strengthens me," said Jayida to her mother as she finished her fill of meat pies. She rose to leave and glimpsed the handspun wool-filled pots of saffron and earthy shades of dye nearby.

"Just a moment," said her mother, and momentarily disappeared and returned with a woven bundle. Zoraya gripped its edges and it unfolded, revealing a long cream woolen cloak with emerald vines and floral motifs at the sleeves and edges, and a saffron lion embroidered on each shoulder. "For my beautiful Jayida," said her mother, and draped it on her shoulders.

"My *yama*, the finest mother-weaver in the land. It almost looks a bit Israelite, eh?" said Jayida, and wrapped her in a tight embrace.

"*Aywa*, it looks great on you."

"I'm taking *her* out for my walk," grinned Jayida, and gripped her spear purposefully for the task.

Jayida slipped away, and headed southeast towards Wadi Al-Raha. The sun-setting shadows engulfed her in a sadness she'd never known before. She dreaded that it was all life would ever be, just variations of unexpected sadness, each worse than the one before. And yet they were still there, not just surviving, but living to learn and tell the tales. That had to be enough, at least on days when she wondered about the purpose of life.

She found Nasr's grave and his grandparents', piled with stones amidst lightly moistened earth from recent rains. Squatting, she carefully retrieved some fresh alyssum flowers from her pouch and laid them upon his grave.

"Some honey fragrance for you," she said. "Oh, Nasr. Maybe you know why sometimes it feels like time is just standing still?" she sighed. The lingering winter cold seemed to hold off the spring, and yet seeing the flowers at Wadi Al-Hamd had been the perfect reminder that the seasons still moved despite appearances.

She closed her eyes and breathed deeply, hoping he was happy wherever he was, and that he watched over them, even if, like her unpredictable, free-roaming Aksumite princess guardian, he didn't say anything. There was a slight rustle behind her; probably a cautious sand-cat eyeing her from a safe distance. It'd been almost a year and still no sign of Nasr, much less of Al-Lat or any other deity, or even lower *jinn* to offer some guiding answers.

A muscle twitched deep within. What kind of friend was she being?

"Forgive me, Nasr, if I drain you and ask too much without realizing it. But I hope you like my new cloak," she said, and laid a hand on the earth in a parting gesture.

Leaning on her spear, she got up and turned—then froze.

Steps away hovered a ghost, clad in sooty black from head to toe. Instinctively, Jayida tightened her grip on her spear and reached in her folds for her knife, and kept her hold there.

Shaded by his hood, the ghost's cryptic grin spread, revealing blinding teeth. She fixed him and he started swaying, hissing a low hum.

"Get up the chests of your camels, and leave," he recited in a near whisper.

"Sons of my mother. I lean to a tribe other than you. Shanfara?" said Jayida, certain that she hadn't mistaken the opening line to his famous *Lamiyyat* poem—and his manner.

"So I *can* still be recognized," said Shanfara as if to himself. "You seemed quite engaged; I guess I'm not the only one he's been calling. Still, I thought Jonder the Lion of Sa'd would hear me coming," he said, and slowly pulled back his hood.

His tall, thin frame was a mere pile of bones covered in clothing, his sunken eyes and cheeks countered by his intense bearing. Contrary to his nickname, his lips were not large, and his dark eyes glistened in amused confirmation, amazing her as much to see the famous *su'luk* brigand-poet as to note his grave condition. He seemed about to go on with his verses when his knees bent and he swayed to sit on the ground, his body begging for rest. In a moment his frighteningly dazed manner had shifted to a pained contemplation.

Still gripping her weapons, she dropped next to him, considering that she was sitting with, and likely about to be hosting, a man who had done his own fair share of devastating forays. But at least he hadn't attacked any of them.

"I'm surprised, but glad. Some said you might not even be alive, and though your *qareen* has done well to bring you here, from the looks of it we better get you treated right away," said Jayida, trying to sound light.

His body rattled, releasing the strangest, gurgling laugh she'd ever heard.

"Don't look so shocked, my lion-eyed friend! You yourself love death, at least a little. Shanfara knows these things."

She frowned, wondering if the *badawi* had half lost his mind. But if his aimless wanderings still yielded him poetry, then he still had at least some sanity.

"So what brought you here?" she said a bit roughly.

"What else? Words brought me here." He paused, and she waited, still as him. "There were brigands who roamed the land, returning at times with plunder, at times without. One day, they came upon three young men riding nearby. The brigand leader aimed his bow and struck straight into an innocent young man riding ahead. The boy's father swore revenge and the leader expected it, was ready to fight and claim what was there, and even if he failed he'd die in chaos, as miserable lawless thieves were want to do. And would it have been strictly his fault, having been rejected by his own tribe?"

Jayida held back, his rhyming flow and sincere air subduing the story's harshness. She'd at least give him the benefit of finishing his narrative, as mixed up and self-serving as the details might be.

"But the biggest shock was the next morning, when the leader, his son though dead, let them go. And not just that, he gifted them what they wanted! Is that not a generous love of death?" said Shanfara, his gaze lost into space.

"A man's word is his life, and I will not have you mock the death of the most honorable Nasr, son to *sayyid* Aziz of the Banu Sa'd, and my dear friend," she shot back.

His face contorted painfully. "I do not mock him. He called me here, and I want to see the man who rewards the one who slays him. What does it mean? Are we to reward every person who kills our own? He's your friend; has he told you?" His brow creased significantly, appearing genuinely conflicted and concerned.

"It was not reward; it was the dying man's wishes, if such demons can even understand the concept of loyalty beyond their selfish greed!" said Jayida. "Man is to forgive sometimes, otherwise it's just constant war and madness. If I remember nothing else from him, I want to remember that. And what do you mean by he called you here?"

"We were good friends; we used to raid together, shared our spoils. Like a brother from another tribe, proud to claim me as his," Shanfara paused. "He called himself Ta'abbata Sharran. He was among the men who attacked your camp that day and killed your friend."

The image of that last bandit who'd looked back at them as they left came to mind. A conscience calling out with guily remorse.

"It changed him, what *sayyid* Aziz did. He was done with that life, he said, and he begged me to go with him, to retreat south in the Sarawat Mountains, this time for a changed life like repenting monks seeking the divine—but I didn't. I roamed alone, meeting bandit after bandit. They say one day he came out and was killed by a band of Hudhayl, in revenge for a past raid. The hyenas, mountain lions, and vultures who tasted his flesh all died, and then they threw his body in a cave, and I only wish I could've been there—" He shook his head. "It fueled my rage, but then, I saw your friend. In my dreams, he said to come here. I tried to ignore it, but he kept coming. And here I am."

"You saw him in your dreams? How do you know it was him and not someone else, or just your imagination?" Jayida glared, trying not to lash out at him.

"It's just... something I know. It's always like this—and though it appears faint it doesn't make it any less real. Sometimes, I think to have grasped it is its own reward," said Shanfara pensively.

She looked away, at once hurt and touched that Nasr should've appeared to him, of all people. What about his parents, sister, and Shams? What about her? Just as odd, if Shanfara was half lying it still didn't make sense.

"In any case, it's not like he's some oracle you can summon at will, as if they even obey," she scoffed, and noted his smirk at her irreverence.

"My life story is to be pursued by *jinn* but saved by my *qareen*-given verses. Who am I to make demands? As for the Sa'd, some would say such stories could attract others, make them test this forgiveness, perhaps even to its limit; I think you know what I mean," said Shanfara, shifting to a taunting air she hated, heavy with experience.

"So then let them come here and see!" yelled Jayida, for once refusing to restrain the raging fire he—and maybe even she—enjoyed stoking. She'd already shown some of them, and she could do it again, as often as needed. "If you haven't heard, some have already learned that one situation is not like the other. Our law may require generosity, and though many are unworthy, we will abide by it, and as *we* see fit."

Leave it to that hidden big-mouthed *su'luk* poet hinted by his nickname to arouse the deep discomfort in her. Yet as disturbing as it was that he vocalized what she'd worried about so often, there was a distinct power in voicing her stance, and to one such as himself. He who'd lived the wayward life had come to the Valley of Rest, of all places, so if he wanted to be a vessel for spreading her and the Sa'd's stance, all the better.

Shanfara let out a small chuckle. "So then, shall we all become like Hatim of Tayyi and deplete ourselves? Many a *badawi* despise the sound of that."

"All we can do is address each situation and act in the moment. We help if we can and deter violence. But if they still want to fight we'll defend ourselves, until it's done. Hatim might be an exception, and even if it's too much, if he wishes to give away all he has, that's his choice, too. Maybe in some way it's freeing, not to be weighed down by all these things, and to have faith that he'll be provided for by Yassu. I'd think even you'd understand parts of that," said Jayida.

Shanfara nodded. "The hazy boundary between generosity and self-destruction. Maybe we're not so different," he mumbled. His head drooped and his weight shifted to the side, as if abruptly drained of strength. His arm folded under him as a pillow but missed, and just before his head could hit the ground, she caught it and let it rest on her leg. He managed a grateful glance before closing his heavy lids. His breath deepening, his sallow skin against her bright new woolen cloak pinched her conflicted heart.

She uncorked her small gourd and tipped some water in his dry, cracked lips, surprised at his weightlessness, like a mere child. Shanfara swallowed slowly, the defiant *su'luk* poet who had inspired so much fear now reduced to a frail man who'd clearly let his life drift away. There was so much about him that she stood against, but rather than be angry, right then she pitied him and the rough life he'd had.

"My father Zahir told me about seeing you at the 'Ukaz market before I was born," she said gently.

Keeping his eyes closed, he smirked. "Oh, to be remembered," said Shanfara, his voice like a quiet lull. "Zahir, son of Gayas of the Banu Zubayd the Great, and surely of the prized camels. Memory is a curious thing, and I remember him."

For a while he was so still that she thought he'd fallen asleep.

His eyes reopened. "All my life I've felt alone, except for poetry. The one beauty that keeps me company, makes me feel that maybe I'm not so bad," he said with emotion. It couldn't be easy for a man like him to admit such a thing, and she was touched that he would confess it.

"Your loyal *qareen*," said Jayida, seeing her smile reflected in his.

"Who's yours?"

"An Aksumite princess." She chuckled and shook her head.

"*Esh?* And she helps you with poetry?" said Shanfara, his surprise energizing him enough to slightly raise his torso.

"No, she's just there. But comes and goes."

"Tell me about it. Some moments it'll just flow, like the gates of Heaven opening up and you're just there to try to catch it all. Other times you have to keep knocking and it seems like the answer will never come. But it does! And when it does, it's the best feeling in the world." He stared into the sky, his vision glinting.

"Why don't you go to the courts? Ghassanid, Lakmid, or Aksumite, you'd be unlike the other poets they'd seen. Even better if you manage to scare Al-Mundhir a bit."

Shanfara shook his head, clicked his tongue, and sat up. "They wouldn't like my poetry. Some people only want to hear what suits them. No matter, I'll keep my own secret court and audience."

"Ah, so there's the big secret: Shanfara is scared." She smirked.

Shanfara frowned. "Heh! A *su'luk* poet, scared!"

Of all the personalities he might take on, this strained act failed him. She held back from smiling at his increasingly guilty manner.

"Are you so sure that they wouldn't like your poetry? How could you or they know if you don't share it? At the very least you'd be offering some variety. And if they don't like it, it doesn't make it less an achievement."

He flicked a small stone in the dirt, lost in thought.

Relief washed over her to note that despite his life's unpleasant choices, at least some of them were exaggerated, as much to protect as to fuel his fierce image. With a hint of amusement it dawned on her that perhaps no one was as fearsome as they wished, or tried, to appear.

"Shanfara the rebel poet. Why don't you try? You'd rather suffer and make it harder on yourself?"

Shanfara sighed, exhaustion claiming him again. "Because I'm fine being alone with my poetry. I think it's always been fine for me, but not others. And then, there's material things and they only satisfy for a bit. And people; they always have to make you feel that you owe them everything, even with the smallest thing they do for you. Price, price, price—what will be the price in exchange for what they do! As if no one had ever done a thing for them. Hospitality; but it's not for me, or for anyone else that they give to. It's for themselves, how others will talk about them, think of them; what they'll get *in return*. For their satisfaction of being able to say they gave to you, so you *owe* them. Like they own you, or a part of you. What if I can't ever repay it back; am I less worthy then? So I let the earth feed me, just the basics, what I can find. I don't want to need anyone, and sometimes I'm rich and sometimes I'm poor. I'm just tired, so tired," said Shanfara.

Jayida had to look away, moved by the biting sharpness of his keen observation. He was right. People could be so cruel when they felt their person or property were threatened, and its proof was constantly all around them. It only revealed the rarity of genuine, selfless generosity, and made it more worthy of praise.

Though she'd never been made to feel as he had, that kind of selfish misleading giving, as opposed to the true, honest kind, would inspire a similar aversion in her. Denigrated, unwanted: that her father had been reduced to his own painful version of that, no matter how different his own situation had been from Shanfara's, made her sympathize with the wayward poet at least a bit more than she'd expected.

"You have to give me your word," said Shanfara, breaking through the silence.

Was she hearing right? The *su'luk* poet who shrank from requests was asking her for something, even if she didn't yet know what it was?

"About what?" She tried not to smile at the hint of his change.

"Give it."

"What is it?"

"So it's your turn to be afraid, now."

"Maybe. I have to know what I'm agreeing to. What if you'd send me off on a raiding mission; I'd automatically have to refuse and claim innocence for your trickery."

"*Aywa*, it is a mission," he chuckled. "If you ever found a dead man, I'd ask that you bury him, no matter how bad he was."

"I think I would anyway, but did you have anyone specific in mind?" That he might have lurking companions that he was warning about filled her with dread.

"Hard to say." Shanfara shrugged.

Jayida sighed, convinced he needed rest. "As for you, you came here, so you can't keep going like this. Whatever we can, we'll give you. No one has to know, in case you're worried about that." Regardless of his faults, she couldn't just let him waste away after he'd found them.

He bit his lip, looked away. "I hope they're in a better place. I wonder what Ta'abbata would say if I told him I made it. Your eyes are just as Nasr said."

"Better than a *jinni*'s," she smirked, alluding to a verse of his Ta'iyya poem that included a beloved woman and another who roamed with *sa'alik*. "It's getting late, I have to get back," she said. He wrapped his arms around his knees and shrank by half. She wanted so much to help him, if he allowed it. "Of course you're welcome to come but I assume you don't want to be seen just yet. So one day at a time."

Taking his silence as confirmation, she offered to return with a leatherbag of goods that would sustain him through the night, until he was ready to meet the *sayyid*.

"Don't trouble yourself," said Shanfara, slowly waving his hand.

"Uff! Shanfara, please; it's no trouble. You must know it; otherwise, why did you come," she grinned and ran off before he could stop her.

Discreetly, Jayida slipped into camp and in and out of her tent with a satchel filled with a woolen blanket, food, and water, and hurried back to him. At the sight of her return Shanfara lowered his chin and turned his head, hiding what she hoped was a shy smile. It struck her to see him so conflicted over the simple suggestion of accepting basic needs for survival.

Don't be ashamed, don't even think of it, she wanted to say, but instead gazed at his profile, his strong handsome features roughed up by years of struggle. Shanfara mumbled what she hoped were some of his happier verses partially to himself and to his invisible audience.

Leaving him into the hands of poetry and Nasr, she left.

CHAPTER TWENTY-SEVEN

REUNITING POETS

"He saw Nasr? He says he saw *my* son, *my* Nasr?" said *sayyid* Aziz, staring at her in her parents' tent. At the mention of Shanfara in their midst, her father had gripped his sword, which she'd promptly stilled by her grateful reassurance. She'd accepted long ago that despite her age his fierce protectiveness would never diminish, and loved him all the more for it. Instead he'd brought over their *sayyid*.

"*Na'am*," said Jayida. For a moment he was still as a stone, then nodded with a growing frown.

"*Sah, sah*, naturally—why wouldn't he; poets tend to meet each other," said *sayyid* Aziz, as if to himself. "And if he puts that in one of his poems, surely it will help redeem him. In any case, he is in safe hands," he said, filling Jayida with relief that he took it that way. Better that than a possible creative lie.

It was agreed that they'd sleep with one eye open just in case, and if as expected all went well, they'd meet him together at dawn, with a gifted camel from the *sayyid* and one from Zahir.

In the undisturbed dove grey early morning, they drifted to Wadi Al-Raha with the two gifted camels, loaded with blankets, clothing, and leatherbags of food and water, as calmly observant as them. The only forms that graced the desolate scene were scattered shrubs and the pile of stones marking Nasr's grave—and her leatherbag nearby, right where she'd left it.

"That restless *su'luk* poet, stolen away already," said *sayyid* Aziz flatly. Glancing past the leatherbag, he marched to his son's grave, and fell to his knees in tearful prayer before it. Sharing Zahir's frown, together they looked all around, the pure stillness countering the lurking fear of a potential set-up. It hadn't even occurred to her that he might leave. Why come all this way, then?

Jayida walked west, glancing at the short clusters of leafy shrubs ahead, watered by the recent rain, any potential footprints washed away by nocturnal winds—or the elusive poet himself. She stopped, lingered and looked up at the surrounding rugged dirt mountains, in case he'd climbed up for a higher location and better view, but with his limited strength wasn't surprised not to see him there. A frustrated sadness filled her. If he'd changed his mind and chosen to leave, why leave the leatherbag behind?

"Where are you, Shanfara? Did you walk to Wadi Al-Hamd? But you had more chance of being seen there," she whispered to herself, and randomly went towards the bushes. "*Aywa,* maybe these called to you." She reached the bushes and crouched to touch the flowering *rejleh* nearly concealed at its base, its tiny yellow purslane flowers hinting at a longer trail.

She pulled, then reached deeper and further back, thinking of the lemony taste it'd add to their soupy meals, when her hand grazed a hard mass. She lowered her face, hovering a mere thread space above the ground.

"Oh!" she gasped. She shot up and bent into the bush. "Shanfara; that's the second time you scare me! How are you still—"

Jayida stopped, struck by his frozen appearance. His body was so folded over, curled up on itself, that she could hardly believe any body would be capable of such contortion. He was so diminished, helpless, that the last thing anyone would think of was of a vicious, lawless brigand poet before them. But it couldn't have been the first time that he'd tried to make himself as small as he could. That he'd succeeded for the last time caused the tears to fall down her cheeks.

Sniffling, she waved her father and *sayyid* Aziz over, and by the time they arrived at her side, they guessed the answer from her watery eyes.

"Shanfara? He looks almost like a child," said *sayyid* Aziz, his own voice breaking as he peered at him. "Couldn't you wait to tell me and answer my questions about my son; not even for an old man?"

Her father drew near and held her shoulder. "I never thought I'd see him like this, so different from that day at 'Ukaz. May he find rest, at last."

Jayida shook her head, anger flaring within. She hated it; hated that draining sadness that enrobed him, in death as it had in life. Why had he exaggerated his image in his poetry to be worse than what it was? Or worse—he'd indeed told the despicable truth, and it was she who didn't want to admit that he really was that heartless cruel man, lurking in the shadows for his next prey, and therefore deserving of all that came to him. The carefree, unbound man roaming the land as he pleased—only to die like this!

But just like with Nasr and Imru Al-Qays, she didn't know how or why these men played with words, and probably never would. Maybe that's just how he'd wanted it to be. She hadn't known him long enough to know anything—if that would even make a difference—but still she clung to the conviction that something in him had changed, no matter how recent, or how small and insignificant it might be to override his past wrongs.

"It's just so sad. I wonder—I shouldn't have left him alone," said Jayida.

"It wasn't your fault," Zahir shot back. "I suspect he knew, and at least I commend his final decision to come here. No vulture will be feasting on his blood now, perpetuating his misery, in case he believed in that."

"He's in good hands now. Nasr will guide him, I know he will," said *sayyid* Aziz, and wiped his face.

"Ugh," she sniffed. "I thought he was exaggerating when he asked me to promise to bury any man I came upon, no matter how bad he may have been. But as you say, Nasr will guide him," nodded Jayida.

They solemnly set about the task and lifted him out of the bush, and laid him in a clean undyed linen sheet that should've been worn in life. Kneeling, she loosened some of the dark fabric of his headdress and covered his greying, bony face. She crossed his arms, his rough sooty hands and blackened fingertips already cold, and pulled the fabric over him.

"Shall we put him near Nasr?" said Jayida, and placed the flowering bunches of purslane on his covered torso. "If he wanted it secret, it can be just for us to know." Simple and unassuming, almost like he hadn't been there at all—she refrained from saying.

"I was thinking that," said *sayyid* Aziz.

While they used their spears to dig a pit some paces away from Nasr, she hurried back to camp and returned with three shovels. Helped by the recently moistened earth, they soon lowered the body in, and added the filled leatherbag she'd made for him. If he wouldn't have gifts publicly displayed, he could have some close to him, out of sight. The bare, patted down earth contrasted Nasr's mountain of stones and alyssum flowers, the thought of her friend's famous generosity softening the moment. If flowers soon appeared on Shanfara's grave, she wouldn't be surprised.

Her father took a deep breath.

"What must be is at hand.

The moon is full,

Mounts and saddle frames secured

For distant crossings," said Zahir, reciting some of the opening verses from his *Lamiyyat* poem, as he once had when he'd left the Banu Zubayd.

For those who shrank from Shanfara's unsettling verses, what was worse? That he dared to say them, or that they revealed the truth of life around them? They were such ugly, sad feelings, that it was enough to make anyone reluctant to think about them, let alone repeat them. Yet she wondered now at the mysterious beauty that somehow it could've eased his pain by simply expressing it, freeing him from some of the burden. That had been his best work: to weave these easily discarded scraps of pain into a full garment, creating in him limitless riches that no matter how senseless and worthless to others, gave him a sense of value and his life some meaning.

"In this land is a refuge for a man
From wrongs,
For one fearing scalding hatred,
A place to withdraw.
I have in place of you other kin:
The wolf, unwearying runner,
The darting sand leopard,
The bristle-necked hyena.
These are my clan. They don't reveal
A secret given in trust,
And they don't abandon a man
For his crimes," finished Zahir, as cautiously as he'd repeated them the past few times in her life. She wondered which of the animals they each might be, witnesses to his last earthly moments: perhaps her father the wolf, *sayyid* Aziz the leopard, and she the hyena.

"May Nasr guide you on your way," said Jayida.

"May you have happier things to recite about soon," said her father.

"It may have been harsh, but you had a kind of honesty that others flinch from, maybe even gratitude. That my son appreciated and called you here is enough for me," said *sayyid* Aziz.

In the enrobing silence, they returned to camp, shadowed by their camels.

"Our secret, at least for the time being," said *sayyid* Aziz, a budding resolve already strengthening him.

Jayida hated to think about how Shanfara's life had spiraled into the worst, the desperation leading to murder—she shuddered at the number. Had he tried to atone for it by letting his own life slip away; striving, even if horribly, to tame himself?

As much as she understood aspects of his dislike for relying on others, she still despised that deep self-destructive pride that wouldn't admit for basic needs. What could be more natural? As he'd said himself, everyone had been given things, or needed help at some point. Was the giver not also given that which he'd come to have? It seemed impossible, and maybe even undesirable, to avoid the cycle of giving and receiving that constantly repeated.

At least he'd mustered the courage to ask to be buried, so then the impulse was in him, when he wanted. And if she couldn't give him as much as she'd wanted, she could at least help soften some of the stories about him. Too many would rejoice to know he'd finally perished, surely poking fun at his less than heroic end. She was grateful that even in the startling circumstances, she might help shape it into something else. Perhaps Nasr would show them, too.

"*Aywa*, perhaps it is time," said *sayyid* Aziz, breaking the silence just short of reaching camp. She met her father's equally enquiring glance. "I've decided. You are each important to me, and you deserve to know. Warda and I—we've tried. It's been twelve moons and we've tried for another child, and nothing. I've pleaded, burned incense, fasted, made offerings, cut my hair, let it grow, and now, this with Shanfara and Nasr... Oh!" He reached for his Hand of Miriam amulet, grasping for something invisble. "I cannot dismiss it. It is a sign. We three will go to the 'Ukaz *aswaq*, and then make the pilgrimage to Arafat and Muzdalifah, and the kabah at Mina, and it will all be made right."

Through his poise, she caught her father's reluctance.

"Are you sure? It's bound to happen when the time is right," said Zahir lightly. She smirked, imagining him saying something similar to her mother, all these seasons ago.

"I think so. In my selfishness I've never made the pilgrimage, and I *pray al-ilah* the most high will be pleased and answer our wish after this," said *sayyid* Aziz. "Perhaps I've neglected my religious duty and it is Nasr himself urging me to go there."

Jayida swallowed back her disagreement. Why would Nasr be behind this when he'd never gone there himself, let alone expressed much interest in going? He'd been happy roaming their grounds, and despite his poetic talent cared little for the crowds promised at such events. Most importantly, if he'd really shown himself to Shanfara, he could also do the same with the very man who sired him.

As for *sayyid* Aziz, if *al-ilah* wasn't happy with him, then there might as well be little luck or hope for anyone else. He was a generous man who gladly ensured the well-being of the tribe while skillfully keeping the peace, and the sacrifice of his son was more than he deserved to pay. What more could he do, short of killing himself, which was hardly a solution either! Whispers of the plague from the north were little motivation either, and even if it was in a different region, she wondered if it might spread more easily with traveling merchants and large crowds.

"I've discussed it with her, of course, and she agreed," said *sayyid* Aziz.

Jayida almost wished she'd been there to see it, because she hardly believed it. *Mubassir* Ayyub—and at least some of Tayyi—would hardly agree to this venture to the heathen and some said, power-hungry owners of that Hijazi kabah, but it didn't stop all kinds from trying things across faiths. Still, even she couldn't deny that she was at least a little curious to see what it was all about, though sadly neither Nasr, Shanfara, nor Imru Al-Qays would be directly breathing their poetry into the 'Ukaz air. And yet, they might honor their memories just by being there.

"Let the preparations begin," said *sayyid* Aziz, with a curious hopefulness.

CHAPTER TWENTY-EIGHT

YATHRIB

Jayida filled pouches with incense tears, playfully avoiding the pouting eyes following her.

"I'll be thinking about you the whole time, *yama*," said Jayida.

"Uff, do you *have* to go?" said her mother, shoving another thick blanket into a leather bag. Her father was hard at work reinforcing arrow after arrow, and guiding blade after blade against a whetstone.

"I think so. With this whole Shanfara affair, it might help *sayyid* Aziz to finally get some answers."

Her mother sighed, a budding frown creasing her smooth skin.

"He's so resolved; how could I decline now?" said Jayida. Not that she didn't understand her concern: it was to be her first and longest time away from her mother. Despite her confusion about Shanfara seeing Nasr, she had a surprisingly growing pull to the place, and was just as curious as their *sayyid* to get some closure.

"One day is a long time, let alone twenty, or more if you end up wanting to stay longer. Your father could join him, and you could stay here with your beloved *yama*, just the two of us," cooed Zoraya with a pinched smile that almost called forth a tear. That on some days Jayida felt unshakeable, while on others the slightest thing could rattle her core was a mystery she loved and sometimes dreaded.

"I know, but I want to go. There's so much to see that I want to absorb it all." Jayida went and wrapped her arms tightly around her mother, caught her heavy sigh, and wallowed in her honey-almond musky scent that no one else would ever have.

"Don't worry. My new beautiful cloak will protect me, and I'm always wearing my Mikha'il amulet and leopard fang. Plus, the lion skin will surely generate so many stories to share when we return," said Jayida.

Her mother looked at her, swept her hands across her cheeks and kissed each.

"*Sah*, my heart; at least I know in whose blessed hands you're in. But it's in a loving mother's nature to want her family near her. Return soon," she said tearfully.

"We're all in the best of hands: you here with the tribe, weapons, and Adil, and us with ours. And anyway, given the importance of the market and this peaceful season some call *Rajab*, everyone will have to be on their best behavior," chuckled Jayida, trying to comfort her as much as herself.

"*Aywa*, yet as I say: always be prepared," said her father to the weapons like it might enhance their effectiveness.

A long day elapsed, spent selecting the three camels to bring along, making pile after pile of breads, and packing dates and leatherskins of water for the long journey ahead. There might be rest stations along the way, but they should never rely on that, and no matter how good the food, it just never compared to the one from home. With a pang Jayida hoped that Shanfara, so recently gone, might watch over them during their journey, along with Nasr.

Early the next morning, Zoraya draped woven *wasm* necklaces of red dyed wool around their necks, and attached some to the camels. Jayida tugged at the bottom knot with fringes, hoping that the sacred markers that put them in the consecrated state of *ihram* would be honored, and keep them inviolable and free to pass across territories during their journey. With fiery pride, she contemplated that the display of her Mikha'il amulet and her lion skin draped behind her on Hania like a carpet would also be extra help.

Ready to depart, Hubala and Shams offered praises and well wishes, and promised to watch closely over everything. Cross-armed and serious, Shams had to be at least a bit proud to stay behind to watch camp, while his father had prime command in the *sayyid*'s absence. Not to mention Yazida to himself, if he could call it that. If Shams was a different kind of man he might try to seduce her in their absence, but he was no Imru Al-Qays. Still, with Yazida's father away for this long, she wondered what Yazida thought of being left in Shams's fiery hands. With a sigh, Jayida concluded that it was best that the women had made their goodbyes inside the tents. She didn't want to think, much less see, their conflicted longing gazes as they rode off.

They followed behind *sayyid* Aziz with his two consecrated camels and, keeping the Khaybar lava fields east of them, they rode leisurely south to the oasis of

Yathrib. The hills rose around them, the path winding them down to their destination. Each time they stopped, they lit incense in honor of Nasr and Shanfara, and for the peace and safety of their loved ones, and all those they came upon during their journey.

On the second day they spotted Jabal Uhud in the eastern distance and the beckoning vast stretch of date palms, engulfed in its own festive air. There were the prosperous mudbrick home dwelling and forts of the Israelite tribes of Nadir, kin of *nasi* Musa, along with Qaynuqa and Qurayza, and the Azd *badawi* branches of Aws and Khazraj. Jayida recalled that as kin to the Ghassanids, the Aws and Khazraj had been helped by *malik* Abu Karib seasons ago while feuding with some local Israelites. Not only were the Aws proud of their kin connection, but one of their men named Ibrahim had been made commander in the Ghassanid army, and had commemorated that honorable service with an inscription at Jabal Usays.

The bustling air of this trade and writing center engulfed her even from the distance. She had the resurging thought of revisiting all that she and the tribe remembered of Nasr's poetry, so that she may return in the near future to have it written down in a prized collection. Then she might hear some of the Israelite poet recitals from those who wouldn't go to 'Ukaz, and maybe even take some writing lessons herself, if only to learn how to write a few things.

They reached the stationed guards, their lock of curls at the side of their bearded faces not unlike some of their kin at Khaybar. *Sayyid* Aziz rode ahead to the leading guard with a golden amulet of an angel at his neck. At the sight of *sayyid* Aziz, the guard, who seemed not much older than her, scrunched up his eyes, set down his quill, then stood and went to him. *Sayyid* Aziz slipped off his mount and met him in a long embrace.

"Long life to you, *sayyid* Aziz abu Nasr. May Nasr's memory endure," said the guard, and kissed him on each cheek.

"Blessed Alyasa, so good to see you, after all this time," sniffed *sayyid* Aziz. "Zahir and his son Jonder are with me," he gestured to them, and Alyasa gave them a friendly nod as they hopped off their mounts.

"*Aywa*, we still have descendants of the blessed camels branded with the *wasm* of spear and sun," beamed Alyasa as he embraced her father.

"It's our honor," said Zahir.

Jayida pinched a smile, aware that it went back at least to the time her father had seen Shanfara at the *aswaq*—something she never would.

"And what a sight that is," said Alyasa, eyeing the lion skin. "The lion of Sa'd in the flesh?" he smirked.

"That's what some say," said Jayida, and embraced him, the smoky-citrus scent of his fumigated robes almost as pleasant as hers.

"The fruit of his piercing eye," said *sayyid* Aziz, discreetly hinting at her *kahin* sight.

Alyasa nodded. "Perfect timing then! Join us for some of our Pesach celebrating. Welcome, welcome," said Alyasa, ushering them in.

"By *al-ilah,* what a good omen," said *sayyid* Aziz, and their host pointed them to their designated area.

They led their flock to the troughs, where they eagerly lapped up the glistening freshwater, then found a shaded place to camp for the day. All around were scattered clusters of travelers who came and went, their hubbub still quieter than the drumming celebrating radiating from the distance.

A while later an elder Israelite man approached them, with a staff in one hand and basket in the other, and she guessed from his dignified bearing and wise air that it was *nasi* Ibrahim of the Banu Qurayza. Informed by Alyasa of their arrival, he welcomed them with a kiss on each cheek, praises to Nasr's eternal memory, and some treats. With his tasseled cloak tucked into his belt and his staff at his side, he sat with them as they shared the crispy unleavened flatbread pastries and dates. Taking their time, they emptied the leaf-decorated bronze teapot of its aromatic, cooling mint tea that irrigation made abundantly possible.

"So why now?" said *nasi* Ibrahim, glancing at their *wasm* with a tentative air of lightness.

"Maybe *al-ilah* has a message for me. Have to meet the divine halfway, *sah?*" shrugged *sayyid* Aziz.

"May He guide your path and Nasr's," said *nasi* Ibrahim.

It occurred to her that *nasi* Ibrahim, and *nasi* Musa at Khaybar—whose tribes were said to descend from Harun—had likely tried in the past to convert *sayyid* Aziz to the Israelite faith, like many at Yathrib and elsewhere had done. But he hadn't, and she wondered again what it took to change, and keep, men's hearts. It had to be something so deep, so unshakeable, that one knew without a doubt that it was the one and only answer. It was a loyalty she both envied and sometimes doubted actually existed.

It was just as confusing that some Israelites felt more kinship with the Fars than the Rûm, when their holy *injil* recorded their capture at Babylon for generations. Amidst all the historical feuding between empires, was it that simple to choose one over the other? Or was it simply a matter of convenience?

A burst of cheerful singing and clapping radiated over, making *nasi* Ibrahim chuckle.

"Ah, youth. While our Passover is always a reason to celebrate our survival in the face of ancient Egyptian, and other, trials, I'm among those few who chooses to honor the Pesach in a quieter way. Some say we even outdo *badawi* with our noise, and I don't always disagree," said *nasi* Ibrahim.

"I think I know the feeling," said *sayyid* Aziz soberly.

Jayida listened dutifully as *sayyid* Aziz cautiously shared more details of his son's senseless death, the wound always bleeding anew. It was a balm of sorts that *nasi* Ibrahim had heard the news from *nasi* Musa and others, but each time the grief took hold, it demanded to release something, similar or new, to each listener, who added to the tapestry with their own mark of sympathy.

Nasi Ibrahim's face hardened, and his offering to pray again for Nasr before *sayyid* Aziz even asked was worth expressing the unrelenting pain. Strangely, there was more to the story with Shanfara, though that part remained only between them.

"No matter what happens, He is the Lord who brought us out of Ur of the Chaldees," said *nasi* Ibrahim.

He shared some recitals from the holy book of Exodus, when God had passed over the blood-soaked doorframes of the Israelites at the end of the ten plagues, and spared their homes when He struck down the Egyptians by taking their firstborn son. Her father held *sayyid* Aziz's shoulder as he shook with tearful grief over Nasr, and a shattering wailing echoed in her soul, reminding her of her lion slaying. Her jaw clenched and swallowed back her own torrent, pleading, hoping that the twins Najma and Najim were safe and well.

Nasi Ibrahim also recalled the camels Zahir had gifted him long ago and lived on through others, and the gloomy Pesach they'd celebrated during the *Ayyam al-Zalam*, softened by prayers and poetry. Even after six springs when it first began, Jayida sometimes feared it might come back again, as devastatingly unannounced as it was then. She hoped it would stay away, along with the plague they said was quickly killing large amounts of the Rûm population in Constantinople.

Jayida pushed through the discomfort, reminding herself that even in those uncertain times life had gone on, adding to their growing list of tales. Maybe that's what life was: one story flowing into the next, and there was something reassuring in thinking of it that way.

There were recent whispers that—aside from those Israelites who favored alliances with the Fars if only for their shared common enemy in the Rûm—some Fars came all the way from the Fars capital of Taysafun near Al-Hira to partake in the nearby silver mines.

"We'll have to keep an eye on *Shah* Khosrow and his restless vassal Al-Mundhir, casting their long gazes out here," said *nasi* Ibrahim.

Were some Fars miners around as they spoke? She could hardly imagine journeying so far for such cruel work, but then again, men often traveled great distances for just a chance to find treasures. A hint of joy filled her, for even though her discovered treasure wasn't her own, it seemed an unexpected miracle.

A while later a young girl about her age approached, clad in layers of cream silk with golden belt at her waist, the veil barely hiding her lovely large eyes and full lips. *Nasi* Ibrahim introduced her as his daughter Adinah, who immediately asked about the lion skin she'd seen on Hania. *Nasi* Ibrahim told her of Jonder's brave feat, and the Mikha'il amulet he'd gotten from *nasi* Musa during the *Ayyam al-Zalam*, and though out of respect for her modesty Jayida nodded and evaded her gaze, she felt it all the same.

"What a timely sign from Shamshun and other Israelites beloved by *al-ilah*. It's worthy of poetry," said Adinah shrewdly, reading her mind. *Nasi* Ibrahim cast his daughter a playful frown, and something told Jayida that he was more approvingly amused than displeased by his daughter's boldness.

"Who was the lion skin dedicated to?" said *nasi* Ibrahim with raised eyebrow.

"No one," said Jayida. So long as no one came forth to claim it as theirs, so it would remain. Or maybe she'd actually gone along on this journey to start her own cult of Jonder-Jayida near the pilgrimage sites.

"Not even Allah?" said *nasi* Ibrahim.

"No. If anything, I'd dedicate it to Nasr and the Ghatafan twins who set me after the beast," said Jayida. And the countless other slain spirits who'd swarmed her vision since childhood, but she also kept that to herself. Jayida maintained her poise despite Adinah's distinct excitement that their host couldn't miss.

"If you don't mind, might we take the skin around for a while? For Nasr's memory, and Jonder's brave achievement in defense of righteous life," said *nasi* Ibrahim.

"It would be our honor," said her father, as she tried not to blush. Even if it was more to please Adinah, it was more than Jayida could've expected. Zahir handed them the skin and their host excused himself to attend to some business, and if she'd had any doubts, Adinah's discreet glances back to her confirmed it.

What was Adinah looking at—Jonder or something else? Where was she going, and would Jayida see her again? That Jonder could incite a beautiful girl's interest wasn't without appeal to her pride and growing sense of power. She was the lion slayer, maybe even protected by Shamshun himself, as undeserving as she was.

Though she never forgot that the Israelite scripture condemned women dressing in men's clothing, the Yassu-lovers had plenty of stories where that happened. So which was it? Jayida had the sense of a bold suggestion emerging. Could it be that women, first created out of Adam, were allowed to dress as men to control their weaker natures, but not the other way around? It could be one way to explain her successes so far, if in her feminine wrong she'd been—at least to some—practically destined to fail from the start.

Nasi Ibrahim had wine sent to them, from both his Qurayza and kin-tribe the Nadir, and *sayyid* Aziz lit incense in praise of these two blessed *al-kahinani*, or priestly tribes, and everyone who helped made this place so welcoming. In the pleasant winding atmosphere they decided to spend a night there, and while *sayyid* Aziz napped in the afternoon, she took a walk to the date palms with her father.

They veered away from the forts and mudrick homes, glimpsed some far-off flocks that included some Zahir camels, surely along with their kin Sulaym camels, sheep, and horses, among others from near and far. They came to the peaceful groves, even fuller than those at Khaybar. She looked up to the giants who grazed Heaven as singing tambourines echoed faintly.

"Someday soon we'll travel all three of us; no leaving her behind," said Jayida.

"I know," said her father, and looked away.

"Do you know anything about Adinah?"

"No, not more than you. And don't be getting any ideas, *Jonder*," he smirked.

"Is it me getting ideas, or her?" she grinned.

In the morning *nasi* Ibrahim and Adinah bid them goodbye with baskets of bread and pastries, inviting them to return soon. Jayida postponed the look until the very end, then met Adinah's smiling, searching doe eyes. It was just as she'd imagined: a warm, pleasant feeling, full of longing of so much to say, yet still somehow satisfied not to say a word. One quiet moment enough to relay the boundless, well-meaning intention.

It was another beautiful memory to add to the list, and there was a solace to contemplating again how so much depended on blessed remembrance.

CHAPTER TWENTY-NINE
'UKAZ

With Yathrib behind them, their journey continued south along the mountainous Hijaz, and coursed through the dusty stations of the ancient trade route. They passed through the lava fields of Quran, whose mines were run by the Banu Faran. They sent some blessing thoughts to their larger kin the Banu Sulaym and Sufyan, who was in the midst of their coveted Cradle of Gold to the east.

On their way south they glimpsed some of the Banu Aws and Khazraj making their own pilgrimage west to the shrine of Manat at Qudayd, near Jiddah. Most days were of perfectly cool weather, and in their alternating chatty and silent trekking, Jayida wished it could last forever, and if only her mother were there with them. At different times she'd ask herself what she was doing at that moment: probably weaving or baking, or passing time with Warda and Yazida, missing them as they missed her.

About six days later they reached the arid campgrounds of the Banu Hawazin and other branches of the Banu Sulaym, those tough lords of the nearby gold mines. They coursed on and on the eighth day they came upon those of yet another common kin, the Banu Qays Aylan. Though out of their path, Jayida recalled that to the east lay the Samallagi Dam, built to catch the rainwater that caused fearful flash floods.

Like the territories of other nearby markets of Majana and Dhu Al-Majaz, the land was usually free of permanent residents year-round, until the seasonal markets drew tribesmen from all over for moons at a time. Despite being on the camping grounds of the Hawazin, Sulaym, and Qays Aylan, management of the *aswaq* was granted to Tamim to split and minimize control as the peaceful occasion required.

Her stomach pinched at the sight of so many tents dotting the land. In her curious excitement, she'd given little thought to the sheer number of visitors there would be. The endless scattered camps already surpassed what she'd ever seen, with more to come. The resumed feuding between *Shah* Khosrow and *Qaysar* Justinian that disrupted the flow of trade was only another push to make business at the 'Ukaz market. She took a deep breath and released a light shrug. She'd wanted to come and there was so much to be seen, after all.

Before them, the market stretched out in a vast sea of plain draped stands, and countless varied, colorful tents that confirmed visiting tribes come from near and far to catch up on news, settle debts, conduct trade, and enjoy the poetry contests. A constant, low rumbling radiated and pleasantly hung over the whole place.

They fell into the long line of visitors, heading towards the wall-like gathering of armored Tamimi guards who stood by the entrance, collecting the small entrance fee and monitoring the throngs. With many wearing their best clothing to show off their tribe's skilfull weaving and prosperity, sometimes it was easy to guess how some would pay, based on how they were dressed. Those in thick, brightly dyed fabrics and silks often had coins and choice beasts, while most others paid with food, rough leather clothing, and smaller animals like doves or sand cats.

Jayida straightened her spine, proud to show off her mother's skillful motifs of saffron lions and emerald vines and florals adorning her cloak. Some visitors, noticing her lion skin, wondered if they were there to sell it, but her father and *sayyid* Aziz instantly chimed in to clarify that it was the proof of Jonder's proud feat. It was easier to have others speak of it for her, and to see the impressed and approving nods were constant touching confirmation.

Through the smelly bustle was a playful air of excitement, and she breathed easier to recall the law of laying down arms, forbidding violence at the market. Just as telling, women wore their veils lazily and sometimes not at all, as if unafraid or certain that the effects of *al-'ayn* might be lessened in this time. Though surely difficult to achieve, the prospect of everyone leaving the 'Ukaz market happy and satisfied was an honorable one to aspire to, and a giddiness invaded her for being there to witness some of it.

Sayyid Aziz paid their fee with some silver *dinar* and once in, she was overtaken by a delicious cloud of grilled spiced meat. Right timing indeed: if there was one place to indulge in her impending monthly feminine ravenous hunger, that was it.

"Perfect place to start," said *sayyid* Aziz, echoing her thoughts and dismounting a short space away from the stands. *Sayyid* Aziz handed the cook some *dinar* for three servings of spiced meat and mint tea, and they each took their portion. "To our first meal in this place. May Nasr hear us and honor our visit," he said.

She dug into the meat, the aromatic tender flesh spiced with tamarind transporting her away.

"Everything is calling to be tasted," said Jayida, trying to decide what to have next.

"Time for your first purchasing," said her father. He gave her a pouch of copper, silver, and gold coins, and reminded her to haggle. Though she could pay for most things with the copper and silver coins, she wondered if she'd find anything interesting enough to make her use the coveted gold. Either way, like her father she'd rather use up the coins at the market than part with one of their precious camels.

Wide-eyed as a curious child, Jayida glided from stall to stall, and returned with two types of meatballs, one sweet and another spicy, and they playfully agreed that while tasty, they were still not as good as those *yama* and Warda made. Jayida returned to a stall with an Aksumite man and woman, their saffron dresses embroidered with bronze thread and complimenting jewelry reminding her of her Aksumite princess guardian. With her father and *sayyid*, she shared grilled parrotfish from the Red Sea, a serving of thick spicy stew, and injera flatbread fresh off the sun-shaped hot plates that pleasantly filled her up.

"Kebabs, pigeon pies, lentil and fenugreek stew and teas, more soups and fresh breads and pastries; there's so much more but I think we'll save it for later," she said, looking around with a delightfully conflicted air.

"Good idea, otherwise I'll also be here all day," said *sayyid* Aziz, and pat his round belly. Surprisingly he hadn't had wine yet, but the day had just begun.

"Don't worry, it'll still be there; they're well prepared, even if most have been impacted one way or another by the *Ayyam al-Zalam*," said Zahir.

"*Sah*. On that note, some desserts to take along the way," said Jayida, and whisked away.

She strolled through the mountains of dates, from golden to the darkest varieties, even the stone-like hard ones that softened in water.

At the merchant from the Asir region in the south, she had to narrow down her choices from all his lush produce. She got some of his wheat and barley grains, alfalfa, grapes, dates, olives, lemons, and pomegranates. Then appeared the Hudhayl merchant with his proud display of bee-filled honeycombs, and she added a few of their honey jars, along with some of their famous honey pies with almonds and nuts to her purchase. Beaming with goods, she returned to her kin and treated their camels to some of the pomegranates, who inhaled them happily as they continued on their way.

In the rising heat, they strolled leisurely through the shaded market, their flock obediently following along with the thickening crowds streaming around them. Pleasant sights, scents, melodies—everything called to Jayida at once, but she would at least try to take it all in first, and be sure before touching anything, even if she hoped no one would dare to play tricks there.

"Come to *yaba*," said Zahir, drawn to the stands covered in weapons.

Everywhere were sturdy bows and arrows, spears, and straight and curved swords of quality steel from Bosra to India. Others were simpler, with handles wrapped in leather and others decorated with gold ornamental engravings and precious stones, fit for princes. She decided that someday she wouldn't mind having one of each for different occasions. The place swarmed with men and boys of all ages, even a few women, examining and bargaining over different weapons.

"Be like Belasares; that brave Rûm general to *Qaysar* Justinian, or the brave Jafnid-Ghassanid *malik* Al-Harith! Or perhaps Al-Mundhir, fierce ally to *Shah* Khosrow!" yelled a merchant with an amusing accent to entice the crowds to his swords, shields, helmets, and facial and bodily coats of mail. Jayida almost protested that *malik* Al-Harith was most worthy of praise, but decided not to, lest she start an argument. Word further spread as her lion skin caught attention, earning her new showers of congratulations and praise.

As if on cue, voices lowered and heads turned to a figure appearing through the crowd.

"What do we say; overcompensating?" said *sayyid* Aziz, muttering under his breath and gesturing with a discreet head tilt. "Reminds me of a walking Lakhmid or Fars cataphract."

Discreetly she looked at the tall robust young man wearing breastplate armor, his hands heavy with golden rings encrusted in precious emerald and jasper stones. His long wavy dark hair was smoothed with oil, and he flashed two frowning kohled eyes that countered the modesty of the dark veil concealing his jaw. He paced around with folded arms, his snide air as if rising above the gaze of the other, more simply dressed tribesmen in his midst. Not even Imru Al-Qays strutted his own envied poetic flair that way, and she doubted that he ever had to that extent.

A knot tightened in her stomach. Could that be Khaled? She hadn't even thought that he could be there at this very moment, along with his father. And all the better if it was: who'd want to see his face? But with relief she caught herself:

he could hardly be handsome enough to warrant wearing a veil, if this man was even handsome at all himself.

Her father chuckled. "Seems more like he's trying to attract *al-'ayn* than repel it," he whispered.

"*Sah*, and maybe even do some of his own evil-eyeing! Though hopefully it won't have its desired effect," said *sayyid* Aziz, and led them away.

Next to the area were equally striking garments—quality wools for the biting cold and light, breathable linen for the heat, even cotton from Egypt and India—along with jewels, and rugs for those interested—and able—to create the perfectly rich, welcoming setting anywhere.

They went straight to the Najran textiles, where her father eyed some blankets and garments, and began haggling over some of them in exchange for *solidi* coins. Soon they happily settled on ten long-sleeved robes and some woven blankets with floral motifs.

"Young man! The finest garments for the fiercest lion!" said a short, stout merchant. He nearly startled her as he rushed over with an indigo woolen mantle floating like a *jinni* from his fingertips. "Be as majestic in your garb as you are in battle," he said, stopping just as her father stepped between them, towering over him.

"My good friend, it's a worthy garment indeed. But just before we do potential business, I make it clear that neither my son nor I partake in *mulamasa* or *munabadha* trading," said Zahir. That she did not touch things to avoid potential misunderstandings seemed almost countered by the option of purchasing by casting pebbles or stones. "We won't agree to anything unless we've fully inspected it with your express permission and supervision," said her father in his most direct, yet polite manner.

The merchant draped the robe on one arm and raised his free palm.

"I give my word. But if my *qareen* is right, I think he won't be able to resist this beauty," winked the merchant.

He was right: she couldn't pull her eyes away from the alluring dark blue shade. "I'll try it," smiled Jayida.

"*Tayyib!* Come, come! Inspect this and other fine specimens I have," said the merchant, inviting them towards his spacious stall.

"Any silks for women?" said *sayyid* Aziz.

The merchant handed her the garment and she slipped the mantle on top of her outfit, while he helped *sayyid* Aziz with silken robes for Warda and Yazida. Jayida glimpsed her reflection in the propped up disk-shaped mirror framed in gold, enamored of the effect. Something about the color made her look at once as trustworthy as commanding.

"It suits you," said Zahir, returning her pleased nod.

"There's also the Tyrian purple, for the most noble effect. It's quite popular, especially in this ongoing wedding season," said the merchant, gesturing to a row of red-purple cloaks and robes.

Her father's sobering air complemented her own amusement. While striking, it just didn't have the same effect on her as the indigo and other shades she'd seen. Not only was the Tyrian purple dye-making process famously demanding of tons of sea snails, but it left its makers reeking of a nasty fishy stench. Its rarity and cost that usually only nobles could afford, along with its laborers who often weren't paid their rightful dues, left her much more sad and dismissive than yearning for it. Unsurprisingly, it inspired a range of imitation shades, and for once she couldn't blame the merchant for referring to them as if they were the real thing. If Jayida ever wanted to wear the color, she wouldn't mind the flatter, muddier shades that satisfied others, too, and at an affordable fraction of the cost.

Jayida then tried a full plain black ensemble, necessary for more solemn occasions, and as if to lighten the mood, the merchant offered another matching cloak with some gold embroidery. At the sight of the contrast, an unexpected rush filled her, and she understood a bit more why some women liked to play with clothes and beautify themselves. Something about the intensity of the dark color made her at once stand out and disappear in it. She decided on the dark pieces and the indigo outfit, with matching headwraps, and helped her father also with some cream silken robes for her mother and herself, even if it may be some time before she wore them. She was so delighted in her newfound interest in playing with clothing that she didn't mind parting with more of their gold for it.

With their goods in tow, they came upon glittering stands of precious stones: raw emeralds from Aksum, and jewelry made from gold, silver, and copper from the nearby mountains. Onyx, agate, chalcedony, and cornelian greeted them from San'a, and coral and pearl from the Gulf of Aden from even further south. While the variety of beaded necklaces, dangling earrings that went past the shoulders, and gold, silver, and jasper bracelets adorned in stones were striking, Jayida decided that she wasn't the type to wear these, and especially not as heavily as some enjoyed doing. And yet, she lit up at the sight of thicker, finger armor-like bronze rings and headdresses with jingling coins, regretting that she couldn't try them on. There were a few delicate earrings made of ostrich eggshell, and she smirked at the memory of her own first proud achievement.

In the rising afternoon heat, they led the camels to water troughs and decided to take a break in a designated space amidst the market. They reclined and shared their desserts, relishing the pastries and the fresh sour milk they summoned from the young servers who went around. There were so many different kinds of people that for a while she had the pleasant impression of being in another, unknown land. Rich, poor, young, old, light, dark, local, foreign—they had all come for their varied reasons, seeking solace, amusement, and prosperity, or at least to finally glimpse so much of what they'd imagined in that one, special location. Though aside from the poetry she'd hardly had expectations, so far it was better than she'd anticipated. With humor she wondered how many unattached men and women found love there and followed it to new places.

While some napped and others relaxed and chatted, at intervals people greeted them. Her heart pinched when some parents or even the children themselves asked if they could touch the lion skin, the youngsters a mix of daring and cautious personalities that walked away a bit prouder of themselves for their bravery. Despite the attention on them, it was an opportunity to praise Nasr and the Ghatafan twins.

Once rested, their stroll continued, lured by the heavenly scent. They entered a precious carpeted space whose varieties of incense and perfumed unguents welcomed her, their warm, musky essence hinting at frankincense and myrrh from the south. Resting on tables blanketed with embroidered tapestries, small and large incense burners of bronze, copper, or gold blew off a range of beloved clouds, some smelling of roses and others of citrus, amber, or aloes.

"Any divine help that you need, we have the finest collections here," said an elder merchant with a toothy grin. "Will you honor Al-Lat with a new statue of limestone or marble? Or Sekhmet, in black granite or bronze? Perhaps both?" He gestured towards his collection connected to lions. Another young man, likely his son, drifted around, protective of their coveted merchandise yet attentive to customer needs.

"Large sanctuary indeed," said Jayida. If she wasn't sure she had use for one of them, it wouldn't be two.

Though there seemed to be enough to cover, or at least help with a range of health concerns, the tables overflowed with various charms and amulets for stomach and fertility issues. From the Holy Rider carved in hematite, khnoubis in jasper or clear chalcedony, Heracles womb amulets in red jasper or carnelian, and Annunciation cameos with Maryam and the angel Jibril in sardonyx, there were ample combinations of powers to call upon for help.

Jayida mused that she'd be more interested in amulets with Psalm verses, demon-repelling Sulayman seals, or even cameos of a Rûm *Qaysar* and Fars *Shah* fighting each other, and other various important historical scenes. Eventually she might even consider some of the displayed feminine rings and necklaces made of varied metals or precious stones.

"Maybe it's a good thing we didn't bring your mother," she overheard a man whispering to his son who browsed nearby.

With loving thoughts to her own mother, Jayida discreetly glanced at the plethora of eye-catching—plain or decorated—containers of kohl, perfumes, herbs, and oil mixtures for beauty and healing regimens. Most coveted of all was the ostrich oil said to have been used by the Queen of Sheba and Cleopatra to maintain their beauty. Out of reach yet present, some funerary masks, prayer sheets, a few books, and demon bowls rested on displays behind the stands, both for respectful distance and handling, as to avoid potential stealing. It pleased her that she didn't see any parchments dyed in wine shades with holy *injil* verses in imitation of imperial manuscript texts.

Yet the largest displays were of carved wooden, clay, and limestone idols, smooth or roughly shaped and of multiple sizes. Jayida assumed a trio of female-like forms to be Al-Lat, Manat, and Al-Uzza. Browsing the collection of faces with hollow eyes and gaping mouths, she marveled that the vague forms could leave her as indifferent as some of the angrier ones repelled her. If she was supposed to be frightened into serving them, it made the opposite effect. Besides, with her reluctance to rely on the merchant's word on their exact identity, she'd rather just make her own if necessary. In that case, at least she'd know where it'd come from, and wouldn't have that draining sense of desperation that seemed to hang over the place.

Jayida much preferred the display of carved animals, and was equally awed by the bronze and alabaster camels, ibexes, and horses. Just as striking was an older bronze bull, possibly honoring the southern deity Almaqah, whose colors had turned a bright blue-green. She hoped that passing time might pleasantly shift her own colors, too.

"A fine one for you, to preserve your manly strength and fertility," said the merchant.

"Perhaps this one," said Jayida, lingering over a limestone eagle that she meant to show *sayyid* Aziz.

"I'll take that one, and your best frankincense," said *sayyid* Aziz, quickly sweeping at her side. She sensed his fidgeting to avoid his emotion at the sight of the figurine that also made her think of Nasr.

"And we'll also take some frankincense, and three ornamented kohls for my wife," said her father who gently nudged her.

They went on and came upon a large gathering, surrounding a mock temple made of propped up poles on which hung bright fabrics. At the center was a large bronze vessel in which burned a fire, and a man in a white headdress and belted white robes, holding a book in one hand and what looked like a bundle of twigs in the other.

"Looks like the *Yasna* ritual is just about to start," said her father. Another man emerged on the scene and stood nearby, announcing with a northeastern accent that he would be translating.

"Remind me what that is," said Jayida.

"If I recall correctly, it's the ritual that a Magian priest performs to benefit the positive energies that they believe constantly counter the dark forces," said Zahir. "They believe Ahura Mazda created the world, and dwells in the spiritual world of light. By reciting the Avesta, the sacred texts that include those of their first human spiritual leader, Zarathustra, they contribute to the cosmic struggle, and increase good fortune. The light of good is represented by the fire, which he'll keep alive for the ceremony."

"Yet another reason why I love having you around; I wouldn't remember all that," said *sayyid* Aziz.

"Guess I was a bit more curious about it than you when we were at Kutha," laughed Zahir.

"I'm still hoping their *Shah* Khosrow disposes of that hellish Al-Mundhir someday. Perhaps this *yasna* will help in bringing it about," said *sayyid* Aziz, to which they nodded in sober agreement.

"Is he holding a bundle of twigs?" said Jayida, fixing the priest's left hand.

"*Sah*, it's a barsom, made of sacred pomegranate twigs, to represent plant creation," said Zahir.

The priest opened his book and began reciting in Farsi, his tone smooth and even, pausing while the tribesmen translated for them. Jayida sensed a hubbub nearby, and found some of the listeners in the crowd, their bejeweled clothing and slippers covered in pearls confirming their Fars origin. Some whispered amongst each other, frowning and displeased. Sensing her chest flush and stomach churn, Jayida drank some water, hoping to still her rising discomfort.

"This is blasphemy! *Yasna* should only be performed in one of our temples!" a man exclaimed. "And this translation is wanting at best!"

"Didn't you hear him earlier? He's doing it as an exception, given the alarming state of our world," said another.

"Is he even a Fars, or another convert?" said the first, generating more retorts.

"Some people are never satisfied. How else can people learn about your so-called light, when unbelievers are not allowed in your temples?" came yet another mocking tone.

"And don't forget what the ruling *Shah*'s father Kavadh did to the reformer *mobed* Mazdak, who was a Magian!" yelled an elder.

"Who cares about Mazdak? No one—not Magians, Israelites, *Masihi*, or followers of Mani agreed with his excessive views of wealth and property sharing," spat a young man.

"Now what does sound increasingly inviting is a pilgrimage to King Abraha's new magnificent Al-Qalis Church at San'a," chimed in an opulently dressed man.

"What's wrong?" said her father, gazing at her.

"Just hot, I guess," said Jayida, wiping her brow and praying for the queasiness to pass.

"I don't mind taking that as our cue to hear something else," said *sayyid* Aziz, leading the way through the crowd.

They came to another assembly around three speakers in dark clothing standing distance apart, the onlookers' contemplative and worried airs adding to her unease. An Israelite clad in dark robes, with curls at the sides of his face spoke heatedly.

"What more proof do you need? Our God, the one true God of the Israelites, is finally unleashing his rightful calamity upon the Rûm Empire! This plague is fast ravaging their lands, and yet as His chosen people, He will guide us back to our holy Jerusalem! Centuries of Israelite-Rûm wars, destroying our temples and scattering us, and yet with endurance, we have remained. Repent, join our faith, and study the holy Tanakh to prove yourselves worthy, for He remembers us! Our time has come and we will at last return to our promised land!" said the rabbi with a raised fist.

"Surely you're not suggesting that simply being Israelite would protect you from catching the plague? If it's as bad as they say, quickly overtaking the body and covering it in sores, followed by a slow and painful death, then everyone is at risk regardless of faith," said an Aksumite trader with a southern accent.

"God is Almighty! Study and obey the holy Tanakh and you will be protected!" said the rabbi, causing rising whispers and protests.

"I've just gotten several amulets and evil eye charms, so that will help," said a woman to her nodding friends.

"Bah! Why stir the fear? It can't be worse than the *Ayyam al-Zalam*. It won't reach us here. And if it does, the remedy is death," said another, his ill humor causing laughter even as it added to the tension.

A hubbub followed, and the man at center raised his hands in gesture to settle down.

"Dear friends, do not fear, for salvation is at hand in Yassu *al-Masih*," calmly said the grey-haired man. Clad in dark embroidered clothes, he sat on a camel as though on a pulpit, and spoke with a slight southern accent that hinted at his Najran origin. "You see, Yassu is the promised messiah of the Tanakh, whose life is told in the *injil*. Out of love for us, God sent Him, his Son, to us, to bear our sins, and in our cruelty He was crucified; as was foretold in the Israelite *injil*. And yet, He was resurrected in three days, triumphing over death in the way only *He* can!" The man raised a hand, his fixed gaze piercing the audience, and for a moment all was silent. "Salvation is at hand in Him, so repent, and seek Him! He will teach you to turn the other cheek when necessary, and to love your enemies, instead of taking an eye for an eye, in a hellish cycle that never ends! He is our bridge, our way of ascending higher. Do not forget His One divine nature, and seek Him!" said the *mubassir*.

The conviction in his tone blazed through her like fire, reminding her of *mubassir* Ayyub and the shattering Najran massacre that they'd both surely often spoken on. Whether recited in animated or serene fashion, it reminded her of the different ways the same story could be told, and the different emotions they inspired. Best of all, each could be effective in its own way, and that there was little chance of predicting its impact was part of its mystery. Like the gently firm *mubassir* Ayyub, this *mubassir* also stood unafraid, ready for battle at any moment.

"Now, dear listeners, take caution from the *mubassir* who ignores Yassu's human nature," began the youngest man to the right, speaking with a northeastern accent. "We two-nature believers know better than to aspire to lofty ideals, well-meaning as they may be. Yassu was in a human body, and died in a human body, so we must not forget that he was a great God-inspired man, but a man nonetheless!" said the young *mubassir*.

The Najranite *mubassir* at center shook his head. "That's exactly why some say that the plague is ravaging the Rûm lands, because while even you and the Rûm disagree, both of your two-nature creeds are displeasing to Him!" he said.

Jayida shared a sigh with her father and *sayyid* Aziz. The stories she'd heard of the debates over Yassu's nature that turned to violent bloodshed sounded just as bad as those of volatile tribesmen feuding over minor disagreements. In some ways this seemed even worse, because this was about holy Yassu, and while she might not be qualified to comment on these complicated, learned and spiritual subjects, she still didn't think Yassu would approve of such interactions in his name.

Others chimed in, clamoring that Buddha was the way in such unpredictable times, while others said it was Mani who was the final prophet, after Zoroaster, Buddha, and Yassu. Still others said that it was simply blue-throated Shiva, the third god of the Hindu triumvirate of Brahma and Vishnu, doing his destructive part in order to recreate the world.

"*Sah*; since that's one whose end we may never see in our lifetimes, we'll let that sink in along with other things," said *sayyid* Aziz.

In the pleasantly cooling late afternoon they reached the wine stands, conveniently located near the closed poets' red leather tent. They each bought multiple skins of wine, then found a good spot and reclined. Hania's back covered in the lion-skin made both the perfect noticeable display and comfortable lean-on as they awaited the recitals.

Jayida playfully tried to keep her cup away from *sayyid* Aziz, who often refilled it before she could stop him. Out of caution she tempered the dark red with water, but soon she settled into a floating ease that only the *jinni* of wine could provide. As tribesmen of all kinds gradually clustered around them, she was sure that soon several were also either hovering above the ground or communing with their own wine spirits.

"Jonder, the lion of Sa'd!" exclaimed a high-pitched voice, and she turned to find its young source approaching her.

"Ziyad ibn Muawiyah!" she said, amused that her tipsiness made her more happy than emotional to see this poetic Dhubyan boy and his obliging father. "Blessing to see you both," she said. She embraced his father Muawiyah on each cheek and passed him over to her own father. "Muawiyah, meet my father Zahir. And of course, our honorable *sayyid* Aziz who needs no introduction."

"Long time, my extended kin! Of course, this is often said, but not always meant; not in this case though," laughed Muawiyah who heartily leaned into *sayyid* Aziz, and settled down with them.

"Ziyad often talks of your lion slaying; it's one of his favorite stories," said Muawiyah, and cast glances at the skin draped behind her.

Warmth pulsated her cheeks and she hoped he wouldn't notice.

"I'm honored. He's growing so fast, and I'm sure he wanted to be here just for the poets. Let me guess: you want to travel to the royal courts?" said Jayida to his enthusiastic nodding. He scuffled out of his father's lap and sat next to her, then gently touched the skin, his captivated air as dreamy as her own.

"Sometimes I think he's been thinking of nothing else since he was born. What's a father to do but submit?" chuckled Muawiyah.

At last a tribesman who announced himself as Sawad of Banu Tamim emerged in front of the red tent, his authoritative air confirming he would be the arbiter of the poetry recitals. A group of young Tamimi men joined his side, formed a close circle around him, talked then disbanded, each to different areas of the fast growing crowd.

Sawad gestured with a wave of his arm, and three tribesmen, their faces covered except for the eyes, walked to him and stood facing the crowd. A rush filled the excited audience, who tried to guess the identity of each. Jayida guessed that they were closer to her age than her father's, and she was most caught by the intensity of one on the left side, with dark robes and a tall, proud bearing. These poets from the first round would battle out for the prize of *solidi* gold coins.

"As we get settled, dear tribesmen, I'll remind you of the rules: in this special time known to some as *Rajab*, you will keep your arms to yourselves, and no blood will be shed over any displeasing verses! With the precious spring blooming season upon us, now is the time for settling feuds; there's the rest of the year to stir new ones," said Sawad with a playful warning finger. "But as I'm sure I'm among like-minded souls who enjoy beautiful language as much as I do, you'll be pleased and appreciate the work these poets have labored over, coming from great distances just to share them! So let us enjoy, and be light. And if you needed an excuse, there's also the beloved wine to help you loosen up, although I'm guessing many of you are already there," Sawad smirked to resounding laughter.

"Hopefully not too deep in though; even if drunken repetition and interpretation of poetry might be hilarious to hear," said Zahir.

Jayida hadn't even considered that and it now seemed even more questionable to rely on others' memories of poems, and made her respect the poet's dedicated art even more.

"Now, for the first round of *qasidah* in line for the gold prize," said Sawad. "The criteria of excellence of these odes will be as such: each composition will have at least twenty lines of couplets or quatrains; maybe both. The poem may follow an identical rhyme, or offer a significant variety of meters. The poem may—or may not—include the segments of *nasib, rahil,* and *fakhr,* and may—or may not—be in order. Now let us begin!" Sawad clapped his hands and stood aside.

The intense young man stepped forward and began with a wine song, his strong voice emanating her mother's northeastern accent. He paced himself, taking pauses to allow the spread out criers to repeat the verses to the audiences in the back.

"A Taghlib?" Jayida smiled at her father.

"Could be. He could also be using it for performance."

The poet then followed with the *nasib* and *rahil* segments, laying sharp verse upon verse that hinted at the Banu Bakr whom the Taghlib had fought in the forty-year-long Basus War. Just when she thought he would close with a boast of the Taghlib, his *fakhr* shifted and eased up with playful praise for their cousin the Bakr, with whom they'd finally made peace at nearby Dhu Al-Majaz before the *Ayyam al-Zalam*. Though every young man made it his duty to know his tribe's history, his passionate reciting and proud manner hinted at the personal nature of the composition.

The poet's closing passage was one she'd be sure to remember.

"They feed with their fair hands our noble-born horses, and say to us: 'You are not our husbands, unless you protect us from the enemy';

Na'am, if we fail to defend them, we keep no valuable possessions after their loss, nor do we even think life worth living;

But nothing can afford our sweet maidens as sure a protection as the strokes of our swords, which send men's arms flying off like harmless arrows;

We seem, when our drawn swords are displayed, to protect mankind, as fathers protect their children;

When a tyrant oppresses and insults our nation or kin, we despise to degrade ourselves by submitting to his will;

We have been called injurious, although we have injured none; but if any persists in defaming us, we will unleash the fire of our *jahl*;

As soon as a child of our tribe is weaned, the loftiest *sayyidun* of other clans bend the knee to him in reverence."

The first poet stepped back, and the second poet in light robes followed, lashing out at the restless Lakhmid Al-Mundhir who'd surely inspired *Shah* Khosrow to attack Antioch and breach their Eternal Peace agreement with the blameless *malik* Al-Harith. Amidst the plague, the poet praised Al-Harith and his brother Abu Karib, whom he insinuated would surely be victorious someday in their enduring enmity. Jayida suspected a Yassu follower from an allied tribe, possibly from Kalb or 'Udhrah.

"You think Al-Mundhir will try to venture out here and attack us, or tax us to death, if he gets wind of this? Though part of me thinks it might be worth it," said Muawiyah. Back on his father's lap, Ziyad was quiet and slightly frowning in concentration, listening and thinking as if trying to memorize all the verses.

"I think he's got enough to deal with, but we'll be ready if he tries," said *sayyid* Aziz.

The third, and likely oldest, poet in faded robes began his invective of an unnamed man, soon to be forgotten. It didn't matter that the nameless came from an ancient southern royal tribe, as ironically branches of that tribe had assisted in the Najran massacre that had so impacted tribal and empire relations. How ironic, he mocked, that soon after the Kindah had disbanded into clans across the land, when the Aksumite *Negus* Kaleb invaded and overthrew a self-confessed Israelite ruler.

As he continued his invective, it was clear he was targeting Kindah's famous princely-wandering poet, Imru Al-Qays, blaming him for everything and therefore unworthy of praise, and even inserted a sneering question, wondering where the nameless hedonist poet had been of late? There was collective shock, for no matter one's view of the pleasure-seeker, he was still thought of as the finest poet in all the land. If he'd still been alive and inclined to poetry, she'd half think it was Imru's father in a perpetually displeased frenzy. To counter his bitter recital, she sent thoughts to Imru, hoping he was staying safe.

The recitals complete, Sawad reappeared before them, enthusiastically rubbing his palms.

"So then, which was your favorite? Wave your *wasm*; we'll count," said Sawad. Though they each had merit and command of language, she preferred the first, as did her father. *Sayyid* Aziz, Muawiyah, and Ziyad favored the second, and she suspected that they weren't the only ones who didn't care much for the third.

Sawad pointed to each poet, causing such a stir each time that she thought it nearly impossible to determine the winner. After a few minutes the criers gathered around Sawad and combined their counts.

"And the winner is... the first! Blessings to you who's *majnun* enough to be a poet! You have moved the crowds! Please, honor us with your name," said Sawad, shaking the beckoning pouch of jingling gold *solidi*. The young poet pulled off his headwrap in a swift motion, and revealed a fiercely handsome face. It struck her, for despite his tall bearing, he now appeared even younger than she'd expected.

"I'm honored that I, Amr ibn Kulthum, *sayyid* of the glorious Banu Taghlib, pleased you with my skill," he grinned.

Her jaw dropped. She'd been just as shocked as her parents when they'd recently heard the news of the Taghlib having elected a fifteen-year-old as new young *sayyid*. Though two springs younger than her, he'd clearly stepped fully into his important role, and had the right bearing for it. This timely appearance and recital would only add to his name and establish him as a skilled poet.

"Ha! That explains it!" said her father, who rose and called out to him. "Now we'll all meet this fearsome kin of ours!"

As Amr made his way to them, the two other poets' identities were revealed: the second was Samad of 'Udhrah, and the third was Abid ibn Al-Abras of Asad, that sworn enemy of Imru Al-Qays whom he'd mentioned during his visit. He looked as glum as his poem had been, and he had that pathetic air of aiming to overcome the invective Imru had rightfully launched on him at 'Ukaz seasons ago, in revenge for his role in stirring rebellion against his father Hujr that had led to his murder. Judging from what she'd heard, he had a long way to go before he came near Imru's skill level. Perhaps he also hung around the region to avoid the far-reaching hand of 'Abs, to whom his tribe now paid tribute.

At last Amr was before them, leading a group of older Taghlib men, his dark eyes gleaming with pride and playfulness.

"Honorable Amr, what a blessing to meet you on this glorious day. I'm Zahir ibn Gayas, father of Jonder. His mother is Zoraya of the Taghlib, whose father died fighting alongside—"

"My *siddi* Al-Muhalhil, of course," said Amr, leaning forward in hearty embrace.

"Jonder; good to know I have lion-eyed kin," said Amr and kissed each cheek. "Your *Umm* Jarida often told me of her daughter Rania—may she be at peace—who bravely died to give life to your mother. It has inspired me," he said, his hand on his heart tugging at her own.

"Bless you, Amr. What a great honor to finally meet you, and I hope someday also the rest of our Taghlib kin," said Jayida.

"*Aywa*; speaking of which, you are overdue for a visit!" nodded Amr.

"We've been blessed to be with *sayyid* Aziz of the Banu Sa'd," said her father, gesturing to the *sayyid*.

"Ah, to be young, *sayyid* and *sha'ir*! Honored to meet you," said *sayyid* Aziz, drawing out his embrace to hide his emotion, and her heart pinched again at what he must've been thinking. There was life and much promise around them, but his own son was removed from it. Jayida looked away for a moment, wishing that Nasr could be with them, maybe even reciting his own poem to the eager crowds.

Ziyad tugged shyly at his father's sleeve, and glanced back and forth between him and Amr.

"I'm Muawiyah of the Banu Dhubyan. My poetic son Ziyad is eager to meet the best," said Muawiyah, and gently urged his son forward.

"The youngest fans are the most loyal," said Amr. He leaned down to the boy, grabbed his chin, kissed each cheek, then affectionately pinched them. "Maybe someday we'll share our poetry at the courts together," he said.

"Please, join us," said *sayyid* Aziz, and Amr accepted and laid his sword across his lap. He introduced his group of companions, all men older than him whose counsel he respected and needed.

"Honorable token of your work," said Amr, smirking at her lion skin. "Is your cousin with you?" he said, and gave a few glances around.

"Cousin?" said Jayida, stifling her surprise.

"Khaled, of course. I met him last summer when he was at Tayyi, though unfortunately it involved a scuffle," said Amr. She shot a glance at father. "But not to worry, I'm sure he bravely recovered. He spoke of you, and that he hadn't met you yet. All in due time, surely," he added, and she had the welcomed impression that he was discreetly dropping the subject.

There was a shuffle in the front and another group of poets gathered around the arbiter Sawad.

"Any *sa'alik* poets here? I was hoping for Shanfara, but it seems no one has seen him," said Amr.

"You like his poetry?" Jayida perked up.

"*Na'am*. It's the edge, like he has another kind of resilience; I could learn from this. May he be well, no matter where he is," said Amr.

"May it be as you say," said Zahir.

"You are a generous soul," sighed *sayyid* Aziz.

"As you say," she echoed in a near whisper.

"For the time being I try to keep Ziyad away from such verses, although I can't totally prevent it," said Muawiyah, while Ziyad's attention lingered on the poet's tent.

A weight fell on her, and Jayida had the strange impression of someone watching her. She shifted, casually glanced about her, seeking eyes in the crowd. It was hard to know who might be looking, when Amr drew enough attention himself. For the second time that day, she wondered if Khaled might be there among them, but realized again that she had no idea what to look for, or if she even wanted to.

And then, something she hadn't considered: would her father go to Moharib if he saw him—when it should be the other way around? What would she herself do, and in the midst of such a large audience? Or was it someone else entirely, whom she hadn't even met, but knew her doing—the elusive owner of the secret treasure she'd found! She searched again, as the gaggle of merriment, accents, praises, both sincere and exaggerated, enrobed them, and she resolved that it must've been a reasonable mistaken impression.

The hubbub quieted down and Sawad announced the start of the next round of noncompetitive poets, and the criers returned to their scattered posts. The first poet, seemingly slightly older than her, had a subdued yet commanding air that reminded her a bit of Nasr, without her friend's striking handsomeness. Reciting in an even rhyming tone, he cooed verse upon verse on the wickedness of war, comparing it to a millstone that grinds those who turn it, and praised the virtues of peace and brotherhood. Though he did not name any specific tribal feuds, it added to the air of mystery, while allowing a larger audience to identify with them without the weight of identity.

"That might be Zuhayr bin Abi Sulma," said Muawiyah with a contemplative air. A smirk crossed Amr's lips, whose poetry had shown he could be as playful as fiery, contrasting the moralist tone of Zuhayr's composition. "I knew it; he's from Banu Muzaynah but recently joined the Ghatafan," said Muawiyah when his identity was confirmed. With his quieter, restrained manner, she wondered what Zuhayr thought of her lion feat that earned her one of the Ghatafan horses.

Zuhayr stepped back and another man in a grey beard and saffron robe came forth and introduced himself as Jabra. With the brown and black designs of embroidered bees and honeycombs on his ensemble, she knew that he had to be of Banu Hudhayl. In his deep voice his poem praised the simplicity of his tribe's ways, citing the motifs of walking and running rather than horse riding, and using spears and bows rather than steel swords, shields, and other weapons used by empires near and far. She pinched an emotional smile, recalling the images that Nasr had woven into his poetry when she'd first slain the leopard that now seemed so long ago. Enthralling them into his world, Jabra sang on of their onager hunts along the strip of Hijaz mountains, and raging thunderstorms, so different from the flatter and drier central Najd deserts.

Most of all, there was their bee-keeping that sweetened their lives with their famous honey—and which they could, of course, amply buy during the fair they'd traveled to from near and far. Jabra finished with a smiling bow and gestured to an older man with a jovial look who stepped before them from the side as if he'd just arrived on the scene and decided to recite some poetry.

Sawad came forth again, barely containing his own excitement.

"And now, for that most generous of all who came down his mountain of Jabal Aja to grace us with his verses," said Sawad to resounding shouts of praise.

"Oh, Hatim made it! Finally, we'll get to speak with him," Jayida exclaimed, hoping that Imru's camels had reached him.

A hush fell and Hatim stepped forth. He wore a simple yet crisp cream robe and clasped his hands, his smiling demeanor radiating like pure sunlight.

"I call this shorter poem 'On Greed,'" said Hatim.

"How frail are riches and their joys!
Morning builds the heap which evening destroys;
Yet can they leave one sure delight—
The thought that we've employed them right.

What bliss can wealth afford to me,
When life's last solemn hour I see?—
When Mawiyah's sympathising sighs
Will but increase my agonies?

Can hoarded gold dispel the gloom
That death must shed around his tomb?
Or cheer the ghost which hovers there,
And fills with shrieks the desert air?

What does it matter, Mawiyah, in the grave,
Whether I loved to waste or save?
The hand that millions now can grasp
In death no more than mine will clasp.

Were I ambitious to behold
Increasing stores of treasured gold,
Each tribe that roves the desert knows
I might be wealthy, if I chose.

But other joys can gold impart;
Far other wishes warm my heart;—
Never may I strive to swell the heap
Till want and sorrow have ceased to weep.

With brow unaltered I can see
The hour of wealth or poverty:
I've drunk from both the cups of Fate,
Nor this could sink, nor that elate.

With fortune blessed, I never was found
To look with scorn on those around;
Nor for the loss of meager ore,
Shall Hatim seem to Hatim poor."

Zahir bolted up before the roaring of elated praise could overtake the poet. "Hatim!" he yelled at the top of his lungs, and waved him over. Hatim caught his call with a happy wave, and they kept eye contact until the poet reached them through the crowd.

"Blessed Hatim, what an honor! I'm Zahir ibn Gayas, father of Jonder, and blessed friend of *sayyid* Aziz of Banu Sa'd. We hope that the camels reached you with Imru," said her father. Hatim embraced him on each cheek, then did the same with her.

"Good Zahir, they did indeed reach me, my good brother-in-generosity."

"Please join us, even for a few moments," said *sayyid* Aziz, and greeted the poet, then introduced Amr, Muawiyah and young Ziyad, and happily reclined together.

"Your composition is unforgettable," said Amr. "Ziyad and I, as *sha'ir* or *sha'ir*-in-training, may obsess a bit over your skill; in your generosity you will forgive us."

"There's nothing to forgive," chuckled Hatim. "My only advice is to listen to your deep inner voice and practice, practice, practice, though from what I've heard earlier, I see you're on the right path," said Hatim.

"It's an honor to hear it from you," blushed Amr.

Hatim turned to Zahir again. "You know, I've also had the pleasure of meeting your nephew Khaled, who was there when Imru arrived."

"Khaled? What happy news," said Zahir, trying not to look too surprised.

"*Aywa*; he was there quite a while, and Moharib came a while after, too. But as you know; youth can never stay in place, so eventually Khaled left for more traveling," said Hatim.

Jayida had the distinct feeling that, like Amr, he was politely restraining himself, and ironically the one time she'd want to hear the gossip it would likely not come from such a kind soul as his. *Sayyid* Aziz shifted, the presence of different generations of *sha'ir* surely calling to mind his own lost son.

Hatim fixed on her. "Khaled was most curious about you when Imru praised you, so I can only hope that perhaps someday you'll also meet."

Hatim, Imru, Amr. Somehow Khaled had managed to meet all these poets and others in his travels, except them, and she wasn't sure how to feel about that, though Khaled seemed vocal enough to share his curiosity about Jonder.

"It's an honor to meet you and hear your poetry in person. Forgive my boldness, but since I'm in the presence of such skilled poets, I wonder if I may ask, when you have a moment, to remember the memory of Nasr, *sayyid* Aziz's son, and my good friend," said Jayida.

"By Yassu, what happened to him?" said Amr intensely.

Sayyid Aziz and she took turns telling the sad story to Hatim and Amr.

"May you and your son's generosity be rewarded, and the vile act not go unpunished," said Muawiyah, whose frown radiated to Ziyad.

"He will be in my prayers, just as I'm sure he watches over you from the beyond," said Hatim, and that it came from him brought reassurance.

"May he, and you get the justice you deserve," said Amr darkly, his sharp tone as piercing as the fatal arrow had been.

That sense of coiled wrathful revenge might've repulsed her in another time, but there was something in the way that it mysteriously enrobed and subtly displayed in Amr that she liked and respected. He might be a young *sayyid*, but he was no fragile boy, and she had the near conviction that he didn't get to his honorable position without aptly proving himself. The fiery thought rekindled in her the pride of her Taghlib heritage inherited from her beloved mother.

Amr called for wine to be brought over to them, and they drank to Nasr's memory, Imru's wandering, and even roaming or fallen *sa'alik* poets. As visitors eager to pull Hatim and Amr away from them hovered near and offered praises, some even pleaded for any other potential verses. Hatim and Amr improvised, eager to cheer their spirits, as their own *qareen* granted. In exchange, Hatim joked that if anyone saw his Tamimi wife around, to kindly bring her so that they could pretend to meet again for the first time.

"Although, without the excuse of our son Adiyy being here, too young as he is, she might not be as interested to see me," Hatim winked.

Gradually the glow of the wine and poetry eased the smothering effect of the large crowds that seemed drawn to them, like moths to a flame, and gratitude filled her for Amr's strong personality that added to her own confidence. It was bound to happen when she'd have to face such large gatherings, and she realized she couldn't have prepared for it even if she'd wanted to: she just had to do it and face it in the moment, and it delighted her that she was enjoying herself.

In the chaos the impression of being watched overcame her once more, and she discreetly glanced around for the potential source of it, but found none. She'd been so absorbed that she'd hardly noticed the sky was now a deep indigo, the air only slightly beginning to cool. She washed it away with another sip of undiluted sweet wine from Najran.

"Speaking of poets; anymore news about 'Antarah of 'Abs?" said Jayida, recalling it'd already been a spring ago since she'd first heard of him at the Ghatafan.

"I've heard whispers that his father has granted him freedom, and he's gone on a mission to prove himself worthy of his freeborn beloved's hand," said Hatim.

"May Yassu give him strength. My sources spoke of a nearby group of fugitives from Al-Mundhir's camp, with two Aksumites among them. May he succeed if he's been sent to deal with Al-Hira," said Amr with a hint of dislike for both Al-Mundhir and the 'Abs.

"And then Bosra? And San'a?" said Ziyad with excitement.

"Maybe, though I could only hope it would be as adventurous and rewarding as you're imagining," Muawiyah forced a smile for his son. "I'll say it now that I'm almost sure that what I've heard must be slander. It goes: As big as a harelipped elephant, as dark as the night, dumb as a mule with flashing, beastly eyes," he said, as Hatim shook his head.

"May the son, wherever he goes, return safely to his father," said *sayyid* Aziz, and raised his cup to his reddened face.

They shared this last drink, then Muawiyah took his leave with Ziyad, kindly wishing them a pleasant visit and hoping to see them again before they left, to which they heartily agreed and bid them goodnight.

"As for me, dear kin, I'm honored to have seen you all and shared this pleasant time. You must visit with us tonight. Only please, find me a bit later; there are Fars-serving *badawi* who've been looking my way all night. I'll gladly send them away in favor of hosting you all. We're just beyond," said Amr, pointing east behind the poets' tent.

"We shall find you," said *sayyid* Aziz.

Amr went to her, gazed at her lion skin and ran his hands over it. After a moment he tilted his head, inviting her to draw closer to him in an intimate gesture.

"With those magic eyes of yours enough to lure whoever you want, just a word of caution *there*. When I might've once joined you at the women's lair, now that I'm a happily married man, I have eyes for none other than my beauty," whispered Amr with a smirk.

"I hadn't even thought of it," said Jayida, her mind dancing with wine. Amr grabbed the lion skin and draped it on her shoulders, and merged the dark wooly mane with her headdress's layers.

"It catches us all off guard," Amr said, pat her shoulders and retreated with a grin.

"Fifteen and married; well good for him," chuckled Jayida, crowned with the lion skin and floating along her father and *sayyid* Aziz. That his wife was a slightly older beauty from another tribe, if she recalled correctly, surely only added to his prestige.

"I guess it's about that time," said *sayyid* Aziz, with a tired and contemplative air.

Zahir slowed his pace, letting *sayyid* Aziz march ahead with the camels.

"We're making a stop at the *mumisat*'s lair," said her father almost under his breath. "If you'd like to hold back, look around, while I keep an eye on him."

She shrugged, something like annoyance at his manner oddly sweeping over her.

"The lion of Sa'd can have his look, too," she shimmied to emphasize the lion and walked on, not waiting for his reaction.

The sky had turned ebony when they came upon the dim lamp-lit quarters, swarming with incense and low echoes of music. Closed tents dyed of intense bright red and draped with decorative fabrics—genuine and imitation silk—clustered intimately together. Jayida tried to find a pattern in the visitors, but the men were as varied as the prostitutes themselves. Attractive women, young and old, clad in alluring red, white, and gold robes and jewelry sought their attention with their seductive smiles. A few dogs and cats strolled leisurely by, disappearing freely in and out of tents.

"It won't be long, so don't go far. And if we don't find you here after, I'll assume you went back to the poets' area," said her father, for once looking more uncomfortable than her. Discussing payment for the next day's sacrifice might not be pleasant, and after a long day, she was glad not be involved all the same. As for the woman herself, she'd see *sayyid* Aziz's selection to conduct the *woquf* to address the deity the next morning.

As Jayida lingered in the dark, smokey maze of tents, humming whispers echoed around her, followed by giggles. A group of young women, about her age, hung around, smiling and laughing to each other and glancing her way.

"I'll venture these lion eyes see everything in the dark; what a gift," said a slightly older, tanned woman in a red low-cut flowing robe that lay loosely on her shapely form. Her naked shoulder revealed a sun tattoo on her arm and a barely concealed left breast.

Jayida stopped, lingered and looked her up and down. Not only was she a striking beauty, but she had a captivating sweet fragrance that could make anyone think they'd encountered an angel. Not even at the incense stand had she encountered such a blend, confirming that it couldn't be duplicated and had to be the result of her own essence combined with whatever she applied on herself. Even if this beauty was rare among them, no wonder some would travel far just for the chance of seeing and being with her. Jayida restrained a laugh: maybe she wasn't so different from men, at least sometimes.

"Surely a man can only crumble at your feet," said Jayida, and pulled the lion skin over herself to give the effect of it bowing to her.

"And a noble poet, too," said the woman with raised eyebrow, the hint of gratitude only adding to her immeasurable allure.

"May I know your name?" said Jayida.

"Noor," she said, her teeth like pearls between her full, fragrant lips.

"Noor, you are too good for this place; don't let them forget it," said Jayida.

Noor grinned, and pulled down the rest of her top, exposing the fullness of her smooth breasts in playful thanks.

"I'm afraid if you keep doing that I'm never going to leave," said Jayida, to resounding laughter. Even in the darkness Noor seemed to blush, and Jayida gave another slight bow and left.

Her blood pulsing in her throat, Jayida strode along, drifting towards a shadowy path between pitched tents. She didn't care who the woman had dedicated herself to—if it'd even been her choice at all. Part of her wanted to take the woman away, tell her that she only wanted to look at her, observe all the details of her beauty. Without distraction, all for herself. And then, ask her questions whose answers she both wanted and feared to hear. What was her story; why was she there, of all places? Was she happy? It slithered in her mind, ripping her gut: in another life, would she have been there herself?

A grip closed on her arm and Jayida suddenly found herself yanked inside a tent, with a claw-hand smelling of charcoal pressed on her mouth from behind. In a swift movement, Jayida felt the lion skin slip off, and herself forced into a seated position, the culprit maneuvering heavily in front of her, straddling her.

"At last, the lion has come to my lair," said the older woman, running her hands over Jayida's hard torso and shoulders, and once again Jayida was grateful for her protective layer of mail. "I know you want to. Every man wants the best, and I am the best; they all come to know it, sooner or later."

In the musty, poorly-lit tent, Jayida made out her smeared kohl on her droopy eyelids, and her pungent smell of fragranced oil mixed with sweat, like she hadn't bothered to freshen up throughout the day. There was a grim hardness to the woman's thin lips that was just as off-putting.

"*Sayyida*, please," said Jayida, calling on her inner *hilm* not to push her off from herself.

The woman's pitiful bed was but a few mats covered in strips of red silk-like fabric, accompanied by a low table to the side holding an incense burner, trinkets, and jars of different sizes.

"Shh," the woman said, pinning her arms back and bringing her face so close to Jayida's that she held her breath to keep from breathing her in. "I've been watching you. So young, so brave, so promising. We can give each other what we need. Come, tell *kahina* Sahira what you desire." Sahira started gyrating on her, and Jayida had the overbearing sensation of being unable to move.

Amidst piles of stones, Jayida glimpsed pieces of uneven cut red obsidian stones, making an odd effect with their strip of flesh appearance, while others were wrapped in knotted strings. But some also had two eyes and hard straight lines for lips carved on it that fueled her disgust. She grimaced, hating that most stones were given to men to rub their genitals to purify themselves after their relations with her as a shrine *mumis*, and others still for harmful divination purposes.

"Please, stop," said Jayida, shuffling her torso. Sahira's rough, stone-like hands went down to her waist and thighs, digging, scraping flesh.

"Oh, you're a tough one," said Sahira, her eyes rolling back as if to turn her on. Jayida winced, and in an instant she pushed her off, gladly causing Sahira's backside to hit the floor.

"*Aywa*; that I am," said Jayida. She got up, picked up her lion skin, and straightened her robes. "It might run counter to your nature, but a woman pathetically forcing things is quite repulsive."

"How dare you!" spat Sahira, her crouching position making her look more feral than human in the obscure light. "They all come to me, after trying everyone and everything else; they always do because I'm the best! You think you're so different?"

"You tell me."

Sahira released a sinister laugh. "Oh, I will. I know plenty. I know things people would do anything to hide, and pay great sums to keep secret. I even know some of yours," she sneered.

Jayida's gaze narrowed. "*Aywa*? So then let's hear it."

"Oh, I know. I know you're not what you seem, what you want everyone to think."

"No one is." For the second time Jayida held back from laughing. The crook would have to do better than that.

"Hmm. But you, you have *al-'ayn* on you. Yet I can lift it," smirked Sahira, now rocking back and forth on all fours suggestively.

"Don't we all," said Jayida. "I'm still waiting."

"Oh, yours is tenacious. Tsk, tsk, sad," cackled Sahira, her threat swelling like a suffocating toxic cloud in their midst.

"Oh? What's a poor beast to do, then? So tell us, what else do you see?" said Jayida, and dropped on all fours, too.

Sahira frowned, tried to back away but froze as Jayida brought the lion face over her own, merging with it. Her head spun with wine, smoke, and a strange entrancing power she was beginning to know. Tilting her head side to side, Jayida's breath deepened as she sniffed high and low, then let out a low, purring growl. Sahira's lightless eyes widened as Jayida brought her face so close to hers, and searched her murky pit, confirming what she already knew. It was more pathetic than she could've imagined.

"Well, if you can't say, then who can?" said Jayida and rose, towering over her.

"That's nothing! Just because I don't know everything doesn't mean I don't know other things! No one refuses Sahira! If I wanted I could tell them that you forced me and that would be the end of it!"

Jayida lunged at her and slapped her so hard she rolled over.

"*I* forced you? Like you forced those babies out of their mothers with your evil potions, putting them in jars to reflect on your so-called talents? Your shrine to the dead to look at when you're bored—or maybe a rejuvenating drink for you? Shall you have some now?"

Jayida hovered over her with a jar, contemplating pouring one down her throat, but set it down in respect to the innocent soul.

"Or what about your robbing of visitors, that you think your lies cover up? *Aywa*; there's plenty for the Tamim arbiters of the market, and everyone else to know!" Jayida spit at her. "Now, you've been the one doing all the forcing and threatening, so you're going to let me be, or you'll be worse off than you are now."

"How dare you! I help people!" said Sahira, holding a hand to her red face.

"You help no one but yourself, and it's your kind who are even worse than men. Consider yourself lucky to have been put in place by me," said Jayida, and left the tent with the lion's head covering hers.

Her head painfully pounding, Jayida strode back to the better lit entrance area, searching for her father and *sayyid* Aziz amidst the lingering friendly, welcoming glances. She walked up and down along the path and seeing neither, decided to go back towards the poets' area, bent on washing away the unpleasant event with some more wine. Stifling her short, flaring breaths, she'd almost reached the last of the tents when a voice stopped her short.

A girl's voice.

Jayida slowed her gait and went towards it, bringing her to an open tent. From the multiple oil lamps inside, she made out two older men and a young boy and girl, holding hands.

Her jaw locked. It could not be.

"To become a servant of Allah at your age is a great honor. Remember this, Najma," said Badr, with his condescending tone she'd hated from the first time she'd heard it at Banu Ghatafan.

"A great honor indeed. You'll be well provided for, and Najim as well," said the other man. Her chin down, Najma stole glances at her brother, looking as uncomfortable and afraid as her brother stood defiant.

"I'm not leaving her," said Najim. "Can't you use me instead? I know there are men who'd pay—" He stopped, the little he said enough to relay the horrifying truth of it: an evil she'd vaguely sensed but hoped had been her motherly protective zealousness. Badr glanced at the other man, a sick sigh pregnant with contemplation passing between them.

Bile rose in Jayida's throat, forcing her to look away, her lion paw-covered hand automatically falling on her stomach to magically still it. Her heart raced as all her disgusted rage pierced her soul and body like a thousand enflamed *jinn* from the pit of hell. She closed her eyes and took a deep breath, trying to reel it all in, considering if she should barge in there like the lion she'd slain and break the seasonal law of no violence to finish what the beast—or she—should've then. But she had to find her father and *sayyid* Aziz quickly, and rushed on to the poets' area. Snapping in and out of distraction, she eventually realized some nearby crunching steps weren't hers.

"There you are," said her father, frowning at her obvious distress as he came up behind her with *sayyid* Aziz, who appeared distraught himself. "What's wrong?"

Jayida waved her arm to urge them along, until they paused a distance away. "There's plenty wrong in this place. Just now—" she gulped. "I saw Badr presenting Najma and Najim for service to Allah," she said, struggling to keep from breaking into tears.

"Shameful! Like the favor of Al-Lat wasn't enough for him after what you've done for them," sneered *sayyid* Aziz. "Come."

They found Amr's tent beyond the poets' area, which was already empty of his visitors, and of a wineskin.

"You have perfect timing, my kin," smiled Amr.

Their mounts settled outside like faithful guards as he welcomed them in his vast cozy space. He freed her of the lion skin's weight by laying it on their prepared bedding for the night.

"Eat to your heart's content," said Amr, and they reclined alongside him, surrounded by crimson and cream woven separators and rugs. To be in a Taghlib tent, made and traveled all the way from the land of her mother's birth made her suddenly want to hold her mother and never let her go.

Amr offered them wine and they thanked him for his generosity, but neither of them could do much more than a few bites of fresh bread and sips of buttery milk. At times Amr gazed at her, and when she managed to meet him, she could only force a crooked smirk.

"I sense something is troubling you, and I'd like to be of help," said Amr. For once, the impression that he could read her mind wasn't entirely unpleasant.

But the conflict tore her. It wasn't her place to meddle in others' affairs, and yet she couldn't just do nothing, least of all when she'd saved the twins' life in her greatest feat yet. *Mubassir* Ayyub said that Yassu said to love one's enemy, but there was nothing she could even *like* about Badr, not even if he finally let them go and never saw them again. Life, as wretched as it could be, was too good a gift for him.

"You know how Jonder rescued the twins of Ghatafan," said *sayyid* Aziz, his chin gesturing to the lion skin.

"I just saw their guardian Badr presenting them as servants of Allah. Hardly eleven years old." Jayida shook her head, though she'd never feel better about it no matter the age. "The worst of it is that I don't think they'd be safer back at home, with him." That was it, as close as she would say it without bursting in unrestrained pain and rage.

"That vile, greedy vulture," sneered Amr. "So what do you propose?" His poised calmness somewhat confused her.

Her nostrils flared. "That they be removed from Badr's guardianship and that he never come near them again. But I imagine he may not give them up easily," she said, her throat tightening. Just the thought of what they might've endured with him made her hate him as much as she marveled at their young strength and bravery.

Amr nodded. "It's been a long day, and up until these news, a pleasant one. Perhaps with some rest, we'll see more clearly in the morning. I will leave you to it." With a nod, Amr rose and disappeared into his own quarters, leaving them in silence.

They set the lamps to a far corner of the tent, and reclined into their sleeping positions, with ample cushions at their sides for extra comfort. But how would she ever truly rest again after what she'd just seen? The lion slaying—all the blood, the pulsing heart, the paws she'd left them as charms of protection.

All for nothing.

All for them to still have their innocence taken from them. And now, countless men lining up to use Najma's young reproductive body for the chance to contact the deity, or even work something else with Najim in secret. All while Badr and the temple owner enriched themselves. No matter how Jayida turned it, the less she saw a way out, and couldn't decide whether it was better for them to die or live just for the chance of eventually freeing themselves from their horrible grip.

But this is the best place to die! Instant access to us, who welcome all with open arms!

Jayida seethed, hating this passing vile suggestion given her by a *ghul*.

How naïve and foolish she had been, how arrogant.

And yet, the eternal beckoning whisper from the depths: it didn't have to be so hard—did it?

After what seemed like a long time, her father and *sayyid* Aziz's sleepy breaths pierced rhythmically through the stillness. These were twins she knew and had rescued, but there were others, too, being sold to horrible fates in this place she wished could only be a market of delicious foods, clothing, incense, and poets. How could she have been so wrong?

She buried her face in her cushion, and smothered her soul-crushing sobs.

CHAPTER THIRTY

WOQUF

Jayida sat staring into space as if she hadn't slept a moment. She drifted in the most desolate space she'd seen yet, drained as a dry well. The familiar ghostly torrent of images shrieked in her soul, and she shuddered to think of how the twins had slept all this time—with one eye open or too exhausted to try to fight it?

She peeked outside, but even the dove-grey predawn she so loved reeked of dull gloominess there. When they stirred, her father and *sayyid* Aziz didn't look much better either, and she sensed they shared her feeling of wanting to get the pilgrimage over with and promptly return to the Banu Sa'd.

Though she'd hardly considered spending extended time at the *aswaq*, any possibility of that had been dashed since the previous night. She reached for some scrap of solace at the fact that at least she'd seen the twins in time and might be able to help, while hating that it would've still happened without her knowledge otherwise.

"We'll have to get going soon," said *sayyid* Aziz as if to himself. It was just as well he had to fast for the ceremony because she was sure neither of them had much appetite. A growing hum of voices resonated from beyond, indicating Amr's approach.

"*Sabah el-kheir*," cheered Amr from behind the separator in momentary wait.

"Good morning, Amr." *Sayyid* Aziz's gruff tone cued the Taghlib's tall, lean frame to emerge.

"I hope you are rested," smirked Amr, forcing her own small smile. With his smooth, oiled hair and crisp linen robes, he looked so refreshed that she almost felt bad at their lingering dejected airs.

"We did, and we can't thank you enough," said *sayyid* Aziz, echoed by Zahir.

Amr nodded, his hands resting on his hips. "I'm pleased to share there are good news. The twins are taken care of."

"Oh? Bless you for reaching a favorable agreement," said *sayyid* Aziz.

A wave of relief washed over her. She'd hoped something would happen, had even considered taking the twins with them if there was no other option, as impulsive as it sounded.

Amr chuckled. "*Aywa.* Things have a way of unfolding sometimes. Curious, really. In any case, who knows what happened to Badr, but no one will ever have to see his living face again." His smirk drifted to each of them. Was that a twinkle in his eyes? Yet even she couldn't deny that it was satisfying to hear that, and maybe especially from him.

"What happened?" said *sayyid* Aziz.

"It is said that," Amr paused and glanced at them, as if relishing the playful teasing. "He was found with his severed private organs in his mouth. Now, that's quite telling of his vile crimes, and curiously, no one seems to know a thing about the source of it. May his despicable kind decrease and, as usual, Tamim has already handled the body as they see fit," Amr waved an arm. "Best of all, Muawiyah has agreed to take them in. So Ghatafan will be compensated for their loss, Dhubyan gets the twin survivors of the man-eating lion slain by Jonder, and now we can rest knowing they'll be well taken care of. Perhaps little Ziyad, that little *nabigha* of Dhubyan, will remember us in verse someday. But even if not, well, *we* lived it, didn't we," said Amr, and looked at her.

"We hardly know what to say," said *sayyid* Aziz.

"They are better news than I could've hoped for," said Jayida without hesitation.

"What a blessed turnout for the twins. May they get peace at last," said her father.

"Glad to see we are in agreement. I don't think I'm alone in this feeling, but even if I am, I stand by it: there's nothing to mourn here. I may not be the most devout or the best servant of Yassu, but even I know evil when I see it. You don't harm children, and now it can be a reminder to whoever needs it, *aswaq* or no *aswaq*," said Amr, his strong stance adding to his handsomeness.

Jayida imagined that was the unshakeable poise he took when difficult matters came up, and of which he'd already known many. He turned away with a grunting sigh, the powerful bonding energy palpable between them.

"Sometimes I imagine my blameless mother Layla as a swaddled newborn, left out to the bitter cold, the searing heat, and wild animals. Until—by some miracle—her father, my *siddi* Muhalhil, changed his mind. I used to be so angry that he'd even had that terrible thought. Until Yassu made me grateful that at least he realized his wrong, when others don't! Later a *kahina* told her she would birth me. My father Kulthum, may he rest in peace, married her, and here we are. Can you imagine how different things could've been? Might any of us be here?" said Amr, turning back to them with controlled, intense emotion.

Her heart rose to her throat. In the little time she'd spent with him she'd instantly noticed his tough, direct manner, and to hear these intimate details directly from him touched her in more ways than she wanted to admit even to herself. The fiery urge to defend his life was in him, perhaps put there by his mother, just as it had been partly with her own.

Every girl Jayida met made her put herself in their place, and to see him do the same with his own mother forced her to hold back tears. She often thought that she could trust no one but her own parents and a few in the Banu Sa'd—but even that could change someday, once they found out the truth about her. Yet despite their limited time together, to see Amr, so young and already experienced with so much difficulty, confess his raw emotions comforted her that there were other good kin souls around, even if it was sometimes hard to see them, or they seemed too far away.

"Praise your mother and father for you," said Zahir.

"Most noble hearts, may their names and yours live on," said *sayyid* Aziz.

Amr straightened himself. "As we signed the peace treaty with Bakr at Dhu Al-Majaz when I was just about the twins' age, ending the Basus War, so we settle this matter."

There was such confident authority in his manner that it was hard to disagree, had they wanted to. Still, even with the Taghlib's fierce reputation, his potential involvement could still put him at risk for retaliation. Given the ongoing market, when tribesmen laid down their arms and swore off fighting, it would at least earn a postponement of clashes, but nothing could ever be sure. Yet as she was learning herself, so little in life seemed sure that sometimes action just had to be taken in the moment. Though there was no telling what came next, it wasn't a reason never to act, especially in the face of wrong. Like a gamble, life was a spinning wheel of wins and losses, and his *sha'ir* role guided him in poetically weaving his flowing verses to honor his tribe's story.

"We thank you for everything, noble Amr. You'll be in our thoughts, though now we must get going for the pilgrimage," said *sayyid* Aziz. "Would you please extend our blessings to Muawiyah and the twins? With all that's happened, we trust to leave it in your good hands."

As much as Jayida wanted to see the twins, it was best this way, because she didn't think she could prevent herself from crumbling into a heap of tears in front of them.

"I'm tempted to hold you back, but I understand, and of course, you can count on me. May your son Nasr be at peace, and your prayers be heard. And anything I can ever provide, you have but to look for me and I'll be honored to assist," said Amr.

He embraced them all and she tried to cheer herself with the thought of the good things from their visit, like the delicious food, the poetry, their new merchandise, and meeting him.

"Please keep the pair of our consecrated camels; one to take back with you to Taghlib, and another for the twins," said her father. That meant parting with their two extra camels for the journey, and she only wished that this heartfelt gift could've been made in happier circumstances.

"It would be my honor," said Amr with a hand on his heart.

Sayyid Aziz took a deep breath. "As another token of our gratitude, we'd like to tell you something about a fellow poet. We'd just ask that you keep it secret for the time being, though I imagine you all have a way of communicating," said *sayyid* Aziz emotionally, and glanced at her.

"Of course," said Amr with a concentrated frown.

"Shanfara is also no longer of this world. Perhaps someday when you visit us, we can show you where he's buried," said Jayida.

For the first time Amr appeared caught off guard.

"May the most gifted *su'luk* be at peace. I would've liked to meet him, but perhaps in another life," he said with a pained air, and was silent for a moment. He looked up at them and sighed. "Bless you for the confidence, and I reluctantly release you then, until we meet again." With their shared silence as full as any words of parting, Amr followed them out like a benevolent shadow, then left with the camels.

As the sky turned grey-white, they headed west towards Jabal Arafa and Muzdalifah, the outlines of the mountain and other pilgrims gradually growing larger in the distance. *Sayyid* Aziz rode ahead, and from his contemplative air Jayida imagined he was offering prayers for Nasr to be there and witness him, of all days.

Her father, astride Sabah, drew close.

"There's no easy way to say this, but here it is," said Zahir in a low tone. "The woman he chose won't just be addressing Allah."

Her eyes widened then turned into an uncomfortable frown.

"I'd never imagined—And here I thought he was just picky about which woman to see her character, and ensure the effectiveness of his offering," Jayida huffed, shocked at the extent Aziz was willing to go for it. "I don't care what he or anyone says, I know Warda doesn't want this. He probably doesn't, either. And least of all Nasr."

"I tried gently to dissuade him. He's known since we met that I don't put faith in these things. But we talk, listen to each other, without forcing. How can faith in anything be forced? It should be your own choice. Anyway, he hasn't said much about it since we got here, granted 'Ukaz has offered plenty of distractions."

"Sleeping with a shrine *mumis* won't guarantee anything. So what's the point?" she shrugged. "Does Yazida know?"

"I don't know. Perhaps her mother told her."

"Uff; I'll definitely be keeping my distance, then," said Jayida.

"*Aywa,* I'll be right behind you," he said, echoing her reluctance.

Jayida shook her head. "It just... feels even more sad," she said. The Tayyi, Taghlib, Kalb, and others' refusal to honor the sanctuary somehow started to make more sense, even if cults varied across the land. She folded up her lion skin and stuffed it in a bag, not wanting it to draw endless undue attention and demands for blessings that she couldn't, and wasn't sure she wanted to, offer.

With the sun burning over them, they descended the rugged terrain, and the peak of Jabal Arafa came into view, with strips of coiling smoke rising up from the mountain into the clear brightening sky. A handful of cattle stood on the edge, facing them, and though she liked the idea of being greeted by them as they passed by, she had the urge to push them safely back. A frown contorted her face at the sound of a far-off plaintive chant that sounded more eerie than anything she'd ever heard while awake.

"Don't," said her father, and came so close to her that their mounts bumped into each other.

"Don't what—"

In an instant, the cattle jumped, kicking and bellowing in agony as their burning tails flapped in vain effort to kill the flames eating their flesh. In a chaotic roar, they sought escape, but the surrounding frantic forms that shouted commands and wildly waved their arms ensured they had only the mountain cliff. Jayida's throat closed at the sight of their chosen unblemished bodies dropping into the valley below, their flesh splatting on the floor like huge heavy stones. Panting, she looked away, trying to stifle the sickening resounding cries of the few that hadn't died on impact, the life draining slowly and painfully out of them as their owners continued imploring divine mercy like whining children.

Her punched gut squeezed out burning tears. The stories of *sola*, full of toxic, sticky white sap, and other succulent plants tied to animals' tails, then lit on fire to stampede to their deaths into the abyss to emulate lightning and call forth rain had always disgusted her, but she knew then that witnessing it made all the difference. Just the thought of all the other practices she'd gladly ignored before made her want to drench their so-called holy dead grounds in her vomit.

"I think I'm going to be sick," she said, acid rising in her throat. Wishing she could be anywhere else, she reached for her water and took small wincing sips to still the mounting queasiness. At least they weren't going further south to Al-Uzza's shrine with her acacia trees at Nakhla or even Al-Lat's at the southeast walled dwelling of Wajj.

Zahir grimaced. "I didn't want you to see this."

"Hence why we don't come down here?" Jayida was starting to think she should've stayed with Amr.

He nodded. "Do you want to walk a bit?"

"No, not yet."

Her father reached for Hania's reigns and picked up pace, luring her along, and they veered towards Muzdalifah slightly further north. At the site, *sayyid* Aziz dismounted to gather the seven stones, and she noted a woman glimpsing at them from a nearby tent. Jayida's lips parted in surprise.

"I guess it's convenient that the woman also ressembles Warda. Surely that's almost like being with your own wife," she frowned, her father sighing with his own understanding frustration.

They proceeded north to Mina, whose three pillars and sporadic tents immersed in circumambulating crowds came into view. She had the sudden unsettling impression of being encased. Its dejected plain terrain amidst rugged hills with only the nearby Zamzam well for its chaotic crowds added to its suffocating fatalistic air. Why so many willingly put themselves through the long, multi-step process in such a place disgusted and almost enraged her in a way she couldn't explain. Demeaning and pathetic—and she wasn't sure which was worse.

Unrelenting defiance filled her like a blazing fire, and she offered a thought to Shanfara, recalling the stories about him having killed a man amidst the attending throng. Even if it was an exaggerated motif for added *su'luk* effect, she was starting to understand the feeling, and that even she might be prone to something of the kind if she lingered there too long. If others came from near and far to expiate and justify themselves of their endless good and bad deeds, hers was to stand firm while she was there by not participating, and probably never coming back again.

Sayyid Aziz slowed down, turning his face to call them over to each of his sides.

"My friends, you've loyally accompanied me this far. For one last time before I do this, I ask for your honest opinion. What do you say? Do, don't, or wait?" said *sayyid* Aziz, staring into the distance.

"Aziz, you're my truest friend. You've welcomed us, and I've been blessed to raise my son among your tribe. And though he is my only one, I would trade him or have him replaced by nothing else, just as with you and yours. In his time Nasr achieved more than others do in a lifetime, and all that while maintaining a pureness of purpose. He will never be forgotten. I've never lied to you and I won't now. I don't see the necessity for this. I say don't," said her father, warming her heart.

Sayyid Aziz nodded, and tilted his head in her direction. "And you? You may know best since you're a *kahin*."

Was she a *kahin*? Because if she was, she wanted nothing to do with what she'd seen since they'd left the Banu Sa'd. But in her defiance she recalled that it didn't mean that she wasn't one, and that she didn't have to be like others to be one brought its own comfort.

"I feel the same. Your question shows that you're already having doubts, and especially if it was from Nasr, I would've expected unshaken conviction. That's clearly a don't," said Jayida.

It might've been a wait, too, but one which would reveal answers that linked to don't, so she settled on them being almost the same. It remained that her father had married her mother knowing she might not have children, and as he said, even if she was the only one, she was there. Quality, not quantity, in its own timing.

"Praise you, my friends. We've come a long way and to have you here is priceless. It is said that this sacrifice will wash me of my sins, buy me back to the deities and purify me. So now I will go, and I suppose you may watch me from as near or far as you wish," said *sayyid* Aziz, struggling to keep an even tone. He dismounted and sad desperation filled her, even seemed heavier there, and she wished they would hurry and leave its draining effect behind.

"We'll be right here," nodded Zahir.

Looking more fragile than she'd ever seen him, *sayyid* Aziz walked off with his sacrificial camel towards a large tent. He stopped in front of it and moments later a man emerged, inspected the sacrificial *hady* for flaws, and she smirked when the man noted that, of course, it was none but the perfectly requisite unblemished, fat, five-year-old she-camel. The guardian draped a red cloth on her neck, marking approval for sacrifice. He then gestured to *sayyid* Aziz's clothing, the pillars of Isaf and Naila, and the two nearby hills of Marwa and Safa, instructing him to follow the stream of circumambulating naked crowds making the *tawaf*. *Sayyid*

Aziz shook his head, and after some more words and gesturing hands, he handed the guardian some coins. Leaving the camel with the man, *sayyid* Aziz walked towards the pillars, and they drew closer to follow him from a distance.

Jayida kept her gaze elevated to the unknown faces, revealing a range of ages and troubled expressions. She hated to think of their *sayyid*'s once cheerful demeanor caught among them, paying and begging for something that probably wouldn't even come. She half wished that he'd drop the whole thing at any moment, no matter if it angered any elusive *jinn* for her to think it in their midst.

"Seems he's chosen to pay the tax; can't say I blame him," smirked her father..

"Neither do I, and he'll be easier to follow as the rare clothed one," said Jayida.

"He can always resort to it if the divine urge suddenly seizes him," said Zahir, catching her side-eye.

Sayyid Aziz merged into the crowd making the *tawaf*, and went to the first pillar to cast his stones to release his sins, at least three of them hitting its target. He continued to the pillar of Isaf, touched its black rock, and followed the flow of repeating circular movement from east to west. Finally he reached the pillar of Na'ila and placed a hand on her.

Though Jayida had once found amusement in its legend, she wondered what made some follow its cult. The legend went that Isaf and Na'ila were a man and woman whose tribe the Banu Jurhum hailed from Himyar before migrating north to the area. Enflamed by passion, they yielded to it in the temple itself and were changed to stone in the middle of their affair. It was similar to the other tale of a man who, noticing a beautiful naked woman, approached her and tried to touch her, causing their members to stick together as right punishment for their profanation. Either way, little about it could feel romantic or even endearing, if that's what it'd ever even been at all. Noting *sayyid* Aziz keeping his distance from the crowd, Jayida hoped Nasr was watching his father and guiding him.

The cycle then led him to the small hills of Marwa and Safa, and after circulating seven times in honor of the planets, he went back to the guardian who awaited with the camel. They stepped aside to a designated vacant space dotted with sacred trees, said to be sites of manifestation of a certain power or deity. Some trees were honored with clothes, weapons, and offerings of flour and ostrich eggs hanging on them. The shrine guardians surely had more such prized gifts piled elsewhere, for themselves or sold to others for their gain, profiting on people's suffering.

Hence why most were decorated in simple woven *wasm*, about half of them cream and faded grey-black, and the other crimson and saffron shades. Simplest of all were those made of human hair. It was no glittering shrine at San'a, Bosra, or

Al-Hira, with the undyed strips and varied brightness confessing to the visitors' often modest means. But she was touched, and a little torn, by those who at least tried from the goodness of their hearts, and searched and gathered, offering what little they could in hopes of making themselves worthy of being heard by someone—anyone.

The guardian withdrew his long knife and, keeping his free hand on the creature, swiftly struck the knife in the hollow part above its neck, the quick death and minimum blood loss fulfilling the sacrifice requirement. A group of poor pilgrims clustered nearby, eyeing the slain camel in hopes of acquiring some of its sacrificial meat. Of all the things that could bring solace in such a desolate place, the dried meat, purified by the sunlight, to feed the needy was the most satisfying.

Sayyid Aziz came back towards them in the last, and most important stage at Muzdalifah. He walked by them without looking up, and they followed silently along, sympathizing with his internal struggle. The *woquf* had that effect: anyone about to "stand before" Allah or any other deity, either through words or physical relations to address their pleading worries, had to be filled with raging thoughts. Whether the previous steps had sufficiently prepared him for it, the moment was at hand to face the woman he'd chosen that looked like his wife.

"Let this be the quickest of all," Jayida whispered to herself, looking away and not wanting to think about a single moment of it. She crouched on the dirt and pulled her headdress over her face, trying to drown out the echo of endless voices.

Discreetly she glimpsed families with their children, lined up outside the tent of *kahinat* to have their futures read based on their appearance. What would they have said to her mother? *You're going to have a daughter; but you can end that now and try again after.* Or directly to her? *Those unusual eyes, could be a target for al-'ayn; but we can pluck them out. If it's a sign of favor the deity will protect her, maybe even make her kahina.* But also: *there's always Al-Uzza to whom you can offer your burning flesh in exchange for protection; such a sacrifice would surely bring great honor.* Jayida's nostrils flared: if that was honor, she wanted none of it.

On yet another side some prayed in the direction of the kabah, while a group of visitors listened to a *kahin* who instructed them how to repel a *ghul* by repeating a formula. Jayida shook her head, suspecting it had no effect, or maybe even served to call them forth in a cruel twist to have *kahinat* always in demand.

Her breath deepened under her layers, dying to scream out her growing hate. Why did people so easily listen to others, just for the illusion of security? Desperation, laziness, greed, or a childish attempt to avoid—and place— blame? Maybe a terrible mix, along with other things. Though she knew the longing for security all too well, she doubted there were other girls disguised as boys in these parts, and at least, none with her reputation so far.

"*Esh?* He must've forgotten something," said her father. She turned to the sight of *sayyid* Aziz hurrying back to them. He came to a stop, and then began pacing back and forth.

"What's wrong?" said Zahir.

"It's done. I can't, I've told her I can't. I'll offer another *hady* sacrifice at the kabah, and we're finished here," said *sayyid* Aziz, shaking his head and searching the ground.

"As you wish," her father said soothingly, and for the second time that day she sighed in relief.

"Nasr forgive me. I may have called divine wrath upon me for this, but then again, who am I to expect anything else," said *sayyid* Aziz, with an emotional kind of acceptance she hadn't expected.

"Now *that* is blasphemy. You've done no such thing, and if you have, then we're all in the same place," said Zahir, and wrapped his arm around his friend. *Sayyid* Aziz broke into a tearful smile, and despite the emotional toll, there was some consolation, too.

They went on west of Mina, dotted with more trees decorated with varied *wasm. Sayyid* Aziz gave his second consecrated camel to be sacrificed to Allah, and circled the large roofless square kabah seven times. Believed to be one of the sanctuaries of the ancient water and fertility religion, she remembered vaguely that the kabah was also said to be aligned with the cycles of the moon and the rising of Suhayl, second in brightness only to Al-Shira, the Dog Star. With over three hundred idols said to be inside of it, she wasn't sure if the endless stream of pleas were bound to reach the ears of at least one deity among them, or if they were all gathered in decorative, but equal uselessness.

Just as concerning was the revered black stone. She didn't care where it came from or what secret powers it might have: she would never rub her body, let alone her private parts against it to help her fertility. How could anyone be sure, or even trusting, that it was truly sacred and not just stories that people repeated? The same went for men who rubbed stones against their private areas, and the more she wondered the worse it all became. At least her parents hadn't gotten their idea to raise her as a boy from anyone there.

With so many deities in one place, who had come up with the rules and how many times had they changed across time? What if no one chose to come at all? It had to be fear and desperation that pushed at least some to try anything. She wasn't trying to be blasphemous, but if she was, then as her father said they all were, for who had given her her ability to think, maybe even put these thoughts in her—and while there—to begin with?

Sayyid Aziz finished by drinking the sacred, healing water of the Zamzam well, and hurried back to them.

"The closing ceremony demands that we leave the terrain fast, something I think we can all agree on," said *sayyid* Aziz, and blazed off north in direction of home.

"*Aywa*," chuckled her father.

For a moment she'd thought of looking behind her, or even climbing a hill to look south toward the imagined sight of the Asir that stretched beyond the Hijaz. In the blessed Asir region that fed all the land, there were the Sarawat Mountains, where Shanfara's poet-*su'luk* friend Ta'abbata Sharran had hidden out before his demise. Nearby south was Najran, and further south still, San'a, and Zafar in King Abraha's realm. But a thrill coursed through her to realize that she could climb and envision it from anywhere, and already had.

A warm confidence filled Jayida. She wouldn't be like Lut's wife in the Israelite Tanakh, who hadn't listened to the angels as they fled, turning back as if she was losing something precious only to be turned into a pillar of salt for her disobedience. She would look ahead and keep going, and follow Nasr as he safely led them back home.

CHAPTER THIRTY-ONE

TIME HAS COME

BANU ZUBAYD - TAYMA

"Good morning," said Khaled as he swooped inside his parents' tent. He went straight to his mother and planted a kiss on each of her cheeks.

"*Sabaho*," she cooed back as he held her for a moment. Emotion seized him, at this woman who had birthed him, too good for his father. But at least he would keep protecting her, keep these repulsive images he knew from her.

He sniffed roughly and took her hands. "Tell me *yama*, it occurred to me this morning that I haven't seen Ayida in days. Has she been sick?" said Khaled.

"I wondered the same, but your father just said not to worry about it. You know how he prefers to keep her away from our space; doesn't want to soil it with her presence," said Khamra in her usual genuine concern.

Sah, and yet if the great Moharib was so worried about Ayida's inconvenient effect, he could've just made sure she'd never come in or near it in the first place. Khaled seethed again at these raging mounting thoughts he wouldn't say, or at least, hadn't yet. When would be the day? The glorious day that he unleashed it all on him in perfect revenge? That he might finally get the satisfaction of purging it out of him, never to enter again, was the best reward he could imagine.

But despite his restraint, he was just as concerned as his mother, for it would not leave him alone. It was there, when he fought in the tents with Majid, when they rode off to hunt, or into the ruins of Qasr Al-Hamra, or to the pyramid mound of Tuwayyil Sa'if. Ayida's sad-angry eyes, with words and questions she never said but wore like a shroud. He'd reach into his robes throughout the day, and take out the messy salt-carved form of an oryx, the companion to go with the camel he'd made for newborn Liya. He'd rub and press its surface, hoping he was somehow transferring a part of himself into it. A bit of protection, no matter how wanting.

He let a few days pass then he could wait no more.

"How are Ayida and Liya? I haven't seen them," said Khaled nonchalantly one bright morning while his mother still lay asleep.

His father continued gathering his *khat* leaves as though he hadn't heard him. He took his time, then selected some leaves and stuffed them in his cheek, the unsightly bulge half as big as an ostrich egg.

"She wanted to leave, so she left," said his father after a few moments.

"*Esh?* When?" said Khaled. "How could you just let her leave?"

"Should I have forced her to stay?" said Moharib.

Na'am; like he forced him, his son to stay when everyday he contemplated doing like Shanfara and other *sa'alik* and never coming back. Worst of all, maybe he was going *majnun*, too, because something new, unusual, was in his voice. Amusement.

"Where did she go?" said Khaled, so tired of having to control himself. Soon, let it be soon.

"She left with a caravan heading somewhere north. And as much as she might like it, you're not to go after her like her rescuing prince. She knows where we are," said Moharib, with annoying sucking noises.

With coiled disgust, Khaled wished the *khat* would offer him no escape, pleasure, or relief. Let him stuff his big mouth over and over, sucking the land dry of it and realize that nothing would ever satisfy him. That he might already know it felt fitting, too.

"May *al-ilah* watch over them," said Khaled with a nod, and left before he could be held back.

He rushed to his tent and closed it before anyone could interrupt him, wracked with a frustrated angry sadness he couldn't, and didn't want to, explain. So often he'd wanted nothing more than to leave himself, but couldn't she at least say goodbye? He took out the oryx, tears cascading down his grimacing face and onto the glassy-white surface. It would've been a companion to the first camel he'd made, but then again, maybe Ayida didn't care for it to begin with. How vain was he that it had taken him so long to realize it! Maybe Ayida wanted no reminder from Khaled, just like she wanted none from Moharib.

Clutching the form, he wiped his face with his free hand, comforting himself with her bravery. He couldn't pretend to know her full story, and part of him dreaded to know it, but at least she'd been bold enough to leave this place, even if it hadn't been the way he'd wanted. How could he blame her?

He already knew that no amount of *khat*, or wine, or anything else would ever get the image out of his head. That night he'd gone to Ayida's tent to check on her and Liya, only to hear grunts and an unmistakeable gruff voice. Without a second thought, Khaled had swooped in, only to find his father panting over Ayida, her torn robes exposing her smooth dark brown skin. Khaled had left them there, his lips sealed shut like her own mouth and eyes on a conflicted face that modestly turned away towards sleeping Liya steps away.

"No more need for pretenses, then," Moharib had later said. "At least your mother doesn't know."

Moharib's little drop of consideration, even if he was wrong. It might be a blessing that she hadn't seen what Khaled had seen, but it was no less painful for his mother to endure the whispering gossip. And then, the question that had lingered ever since: was Liya his father's, and therefore, his half-sister? Through all the rumors, no one had ever concluded—or dared say—who the father was. If it was his, how could his father be so indifferent, even if Liya wasn't the usual oh-so-wished-for boy, or of the same race?

All the same to him: Khaled would watch over her, might even train her like he did the other children, even in secret if he had to. He wasn't sure whether to feel better or worse that as the potential half-brother, he had the sense of caring more about Ayida and her child than his own father, who owned them.

Though he'd been so removed from them and his father, living in his own world, so filled with Majid and fighting and thinking of when to finally visit *amo* Zahir and Jonder, he knew that something had changed in him since that day of seeing them in bed together. A mix of brotherly, fatherly, and kin concern erupted in him in a way that both shocked and pleased him. If he'd had doubts before, he knew then that no one could ever dictate to him his level of care, not even his perfect, blameless father. He might not be the ideal son Moharib wanted, but at least he knew this and would cling to it.

Khaled lit some incense and danced the oryx in the spiraling smoke, wishing them safe and protected as the refrain not to go after them echoed in his soul. And he wouldn't, especially not if it might be too soon and exactly what Moharib might suspect him to do—so he'd wait. Wait, wait, wait; as he'd done all his life with his *amo* and cousin. But even as long as it'd been, he had the deepening conviction that someday soon the wait would end, as Imru Al-Qays liked to remind that all things did.

One late night Khaled returned to his tent with his spears, sweaty and happily exhausted after a long day of training the camp's younger children, when his jaw clenched at the sound of his father's cough emanating from inside. He would've slowed his step, but he had the damning sense that it would make no difference, just like his own healed shoulder injury was no remedy for the fact that it had happened.

"There's Khaled, returned from war," said his father with a hint of mockery that pierced through his languidness.

Khaled set his spears down. "Forgive me father, but I may fall asleep at any moment," he said, wishing it would happen sooner than later. From the looks of it his father might too, sedated as he looked.

"Not until I say so. Tonight, I want my son to chew *khat* with me. It will ease you," slurred Moharib.

"Some other time, please. I'm exhausted," said Khaled, trying to stall as his frustration rose again.

The man had the worst timing! From the one time he'd tried the leaves with Majid, the so-called pleasant effect had been too brief and unimpressive for him to be interested in repeating it. Stranger still were the odd visions and impressions that came after, though from what he heard of others, it was nothing compared to the worrying side effects of paranoia, depression, and insomnia. He didn't need a plant to worsen such already naturally-occuring effects.

"*Na'am*, you can," said Moharib flatly.

It was this constant pushing and manipulating that boiled Khaled's blood. It could not go on, it had to stop. He dropped next to his father and watched him produce a bundle of carefully rolled up leaves from his clay jar, and set two clusters of leaves for each of them. Moharib stuffed the leaves into his cheek while Khaled pretended to gather them and looked over the seemingly harmless green leaves. Might they show him what he needed to see? But it's the person they came from that made the final decision.

"Have this, too," said Khaled, and gestured the leaves towards him, praising his restraint from saying that he'd already had enough.

Moharib stopped chewing. "You're rejecting what I give you?"

"No, just that it's best left for another day," said Khaled.

All of a sudden his father seized his wrist and clenched it with a grip like iron chains. But time had changed Khaled too, and in an instant his free hand closed on his father's gripping wrist, ultimately forcing his hold off of him.

"Ungrateful, disoybeying, betrayer, just like Zahir," sneered Moharib.

"What were you going to do, *yaba*? And what does he have to do with any of this?"

All at once, this new scene looked more predictable than Khaled cared to admit. A new variation of the same coiled wrath, but he was done.

"After everything that I do! This is how you show your gratitude!" yelled Moharib.

"*Esh!* What! *What* do you want? Everyone obeys you as it is, isn't that enough?" retorted Khaled, not caring if anyone heard them. For all he knew the whole tribe was tired of his father's oppressive manner, as carefully controlled as it may be. "You want to shove the *khat* down my throat for your own twisted pleasure, and want me to praise you for it?"

"Shame! What kind of son are you? Shall I make Majid inherit everything?" spat his father.

"It's not for me to say, is it?" said Khaled, relishing his own defiance. In the unrecognizable contorted muscles and reddened eyes before him, there flashed what he had so long sensed and tried to ignore, but could no longer deny.

Hate, undiluted hate.

"Shame! Shame!" yelled Moharib, his face swelling like a pulsing red disk. He leaned forward and tried to grab Khaled again, but he was too fast out of his reach.

"What are you going to do? You still haven't answered," said Khaled. A moment later, Moharib rolled back, racked with coughing again.

Khaled stood back, remembering how some *kahin* would interpret this as a clear sign of the presence of spirits. *Jinn* indeed, when the person before him was someone he could hardly recognize, and maybe never even knew at all. Who was he to stop it, when he and his mother had so often tried and been rejected? So let him cough it all out, and all the better if it made him be quiet and stop trying to hurt his son once again.

Khaled waited a few moments for it to pass, but the racket kept going, and he drew closer again when his father began rapping at his throat and chest.

"*Yaba? Shway,* slowly; it must've gone down the wrong side," said Khaled, and knelt at his side. He was about to grab his back and help him eject the lodged culprit, when his father grimaced even more grotesquely, and summoned some unearthly strength to push him away with a grunt.

"I'm trying to help you!" said Khaled. He reached forward again, and Moharib's hand flew up, the strength of his frozen arm impressing and scaring him at once.

Was he imagining it, or on the contrary, seeing so clearly that even amidst his ailing struggle, his father somehow still found strength enough to be violent? Was there no ounce left of gentleness in him? Khaled wished he would wake up from this unbelievably worst nightmare he'd ever had, but Moharib gurgled some more, and huffed so violently that Khaled thought he was trying to talk. His father rolled out of his grasp, laid on his back and convulsed some more, then went still, his frown gradually yielding to a red-eyed vacant air.

"*Yaba? Yaba*, wake up."

Khaled hung suspended in the silence, caught somewhere between shock, confusion… and relief. He went to his father, lifted his arms, then shook him, and though it'd been just moments before, already the difference was final.

Blinking fast, Khaled swallowed hard, his nostrils flaring and heart pounding.

"Is that it? Won't you do something! You must still be here, watching everything with your angry eyes, open into death itself with so much to say!" Khaled sniffled.

He lit some frankincense, waved the smoke over his massive frame and waited, but there was just emptiness. No sounds, no signs, nothing; not even, or maybe especially not for him. When the incense tears burnt out, he slowly reached out his hand over his father's face, and closed his red eyes.

Khaled went to his mother's tent and informed her that he'd never be in his own again, because his father *sayyid* Moharib had left this world in it. He told her everything that happened, and she fell at his feet and buried her sobs in the bottom edge of his cloak, so gentle that if Moharib was still there watching, he'd have to approve of her unfussy manner that he'd so often claimed to want from her. Such a sight told him again that he could've only gotten his own self-control from his blameless mother, who kept so much within without wanting to burden the world with it.

Then he quietly fetched *sha'ir* Hakim and they shared the news, and together they wrapped Moharib in new crisp linen sheets.

"Now it's your time to rule," said *sha'ir* Hakim with his usual caring tone his father lacked.

"Is it? Maybe—"

"It's what he would've wanted," said *sha'ir* Hakim firmly. As an elder who went back to the time of their *siddi* Gayas, the *sha'ir* had always had a commanding manner that outstripped even his father's, and even in the circumstances, there was comfort in it. Surely the elder would be a better leader until Khaled was ready—until he shockingly realized that no one might ever be ready the way they wanted to be for anything in life. Sometimes things happened and one just went through it as best they could.

"I trust your word, faithful *sha'ir*," said Khaled, and bowed.

In the cold grey dawn, the tribe arose to the news shared by *sha'ir* Hakim. With Al-Fatih at his waist, Khaled, along with the *sha'ir*, Abjar, and Majid, carried the mat with the body and their offerings, followed by the clusters of ebony forms who wailed their way to the outskirts of camp.

At the burial site, the grave, dug in the early morning by *sha'ir* Hakim and Abjar, already laid open in wait. They set the body in it and gathered around to look upon it.

"We praise you for watching over us, in life and in the beyond," said his mother, her congested voice revealing her grief even as her full-length black veil concealed her own conflicted emotions.

With a stiffled sigh, Khaled mustered the memory of that fleeting instant of unspoken care from that day at Tayyi when he'd told his father he was going away. So much time and yet, what a difference words, or even a gesture, could've made. His soul tore between wanting to cling to it and releasing it with him.

It might've been more of his wishful thinking, but under the collective mourning ritual he also thought there was a shared composure, an unspoken reassurance that they trusted in him and his counsel, and might even be more confident than him that all would be well. Moharib's death may have been unexpected, but it was far from catastrophic.

You think it's gonna be that easy!

This sneer—could it be?

Aywa, anything will be easier with you gone; I feel it already, Khaled responded in his thoughts. Maybe if he taunted his father it would make him come out, say what he had to say at last.

The worst part—or was it the best?—was that Khaled didn't care if he'd be punished for thinking so, as he looked down below on his father's linen-wrapped corpse.

"Your tribe will always remember you," said Khaled, and bent to lay down his hyena pelt on top of him. The first horrible memory of his father could stay there with him, covered in the first attacking beast he'd slain in self-defense.

I had to be sure you were ready to join the men—Moharib had said that freezing morning after.

And are you ready to join the beast, and others, beyond? said Khaled. His own boldness shocked him, but it was almost like it wasn't entirely, or only, his. It was a valid question, after all.

He tried to search out some meaning in the last moments they'd had. Would it have been better if he'd just yielded and chewed the *khat* with him? That he'd mentioned *amo* Zahir of all people showed that it had been in his mind, despite his feigned indifference across time.

What did you do to Zahir? That's the thing with bringing things up; it can make you look like the guilty one. And what about Imran of Kalb, and Ayida and Liya, those others you were so indifferent about, and who knows who else?

Had he gone too far this time? And yet there was satisfaction in pushing back to the person who'd always pushed first. And if Khaled couldn't say it then, at his fresh grave, where his soul navigated between the veils, then when and where? Because he could no longer deny that the doubt had always been there, somewhere so far he couldn't reach it, and out of respect, and fear, and disappointment, could hardly allow himself to even think it. But like a thief the time had come at last.

I didn't come to bring peace, but a sword. For I have come to turn a man against his father, a daughter against her mother...

He'd heard that from a Yassu-loving *mubassir* while he was north at Al-Sham and it had danced in his soul, on and off, wishing he could ask Hatim about it. Only now did he dare to think it was beginning to make sense. And how perfectly timely for this ghostly whisper to soothe his torment, that despite being an unworthy son, he might even be justified for defending his life... as he was first assigned to do when he was only a shivering frightened boy of ten, left alone on the other side of that same, vast ancient graveyard. It might've well been the *sayyid* of Tayma himself who'd forced, and even enjoyed, chaos and divisions around him.

Khaled looked around, in case some fiery sign—or backlash—might magically appear from the ever-powerful Moharib now dominating from the beyond.

Shall we add a statue to you in our tent-sanctuary, cementing your name and memory?

But there was nothing.

At first he thought that, as usual, his father wanted it all for himself only, down to his own death, until it dawned on him that instead he was no longer able to control and decide how everything would go.

Death has a way of changing things; sah? Khaled taunted again. He was starting to think he shouldn't expect anything other than silence; at least a welcomed change from the lifelong complaining.

Khaled took Al-Fatih and laid it first into the grave. "The best he gave me goes with him," said Khaled, relishing the double meaning it had.

The grave filled up with more gifts and dirt, and they went back to camp, burnt Khaled's tent his father had died in in offering, and cooked and sat around uneaten meals, as the incense-scented *rithā'* chants wrapped them like fresh robes.

"May Moharib meet his father Gayas and kin in the beyond," said *sha'ir* Hakim.

"All that we have is because of him, we shall not forget it," said Khamra, her low voice already stronger than earlier. *Yama.* His blameless, saint-like *yama*, whose deep, quiet strength others could jealously covet, but never deny. It was etched on her person like a new woven cloak, and to know that the tribe still looked to her as a respected *sayyida* despite her husband's passing was added reassurance of their enduring bonds.

"He was also a great teacher," nodded Khaled, thankful that the full weight of his few words would not be lost on the tribe. At the very least, he'd learned a lot about how not to do things from this man who'd sired him.

Khaled caught Majid's gaze, his contemplative frown reflecting his own. Majid would make a great leader, perhaps an even better one than himself—he had often said as much to him. His father Abjar had taught him well, and he'd often envied their closeness; this fatherly bond that other sons seemed blessed with except himself.

"He shall never be forgotten," said Abjar, to a low rumble of agreement.

"Praise to him for his generous son Khaled," said Majid.

Generous.

Sayyid Moharib had used the term so often that he wasn't sure he wanted it applied to himself. The *sayyid* did love to boast of his generosity, and yet he'd also inherited all he had from their ancestors. If Moharib had done so much to make some yearn to be away from him, perhaps his desire to be needed—no matter how mistaken, at least when it came to his son—and have an audience had been stronger still to temper at least some of his off-putting impulses.

With a mix of frustration and sadness, Khaled realized that his father had probably never been close to anyone, though he surely had been at one point with *amo* Zahir. Had Moharib, in his disappointment in his own son, tried to secure more offspring with Ayida? Or had it just been some self-fulfilling pleasurable flings to satisfy his lust? And while Khaled understood a man's needs, he could not blame his mother for keeping her own distance from her harsh husband. What of her own needs? She did not look for other men like some women did, and instead directed all her devotion to them. If only his father could've just shared what he'd wanted to say, but something told Khaled even that would look too much like weakness to him.

At night he pitched camp with Majid near the grave for the traditional seven day vigil.

"And what if I just let him be dug up by hyenas or whatever else, just like he left me alone in the graveyard," said Khaled, and pinched back angry tears. There was solace in looking at the blanket of stars, especially when he doubted he was there among them. He made an oryx-like image in the sky and happily imagined that Ayida and Liya may be looking up at the same stars at that very moment.

"You're not him," said Majid.

"How do you know?"

"I just do."

"Majid the *kahin* and Khaled, *sayyid* of the Banu Zubayd," sighed Khaled.

To be *sayyid*: wasn't that the very definition of stepping in his father's shoes, when he wanted nothing more than to walk away from them? The vigil passed, and he returned to his parents' tent, though thankfully he saw again how the absence made a distinct difference.

"It's like a relief, but my doubt comes and goes," said Khaled, stopping himself from adding his suspicion that it was his father's reach across the veil. His eternal reward. And he'd yet to work up the nerve to tell her about his reason for wanting to look for Ayida and Liya.

"That's natural, my heart. No man can be confident all the time," said his mother.

"But I wish I didn't feel like we're cut from different cloths. Why am I his son?" he pleaded to his mother with a dread that always caused her tears. How the woman had any left in her was a miracle itself, a magic well that never dried.

"To show us what's possible," said Khamra, molding his anger into humility in the way only she could.

The next day the tribe gathered again, their bright colored robes under their dark cloaks reflecting their varied spirits.

"With the tribe's unanimous agreement, we praise Khaled as our *sayyid*." *Sha'ir* Hakim stepped forth and placed his *siddi* Gayas's carefully preserved cloak on his shoulders, to a hubbub of praise.

His mother's tender, reddened eyes pierced straight into his heart. They could not ever be alone in the world so long as they had each other. And if no sign had come to change his inheritance of the title, and they'd still chosen him amongst others, knowing his honest, more relaxed manner with everyone from slave to prince, why should he reject it? Khaled would honor them by accepting, grateful to have other skilled men alongside him.

It might not have happened the way he, or anyone else, expected, but he would take his rightful place, and henceforth assert his kind authority. Though his weakened shoulder still sometimes affected his confidence, Majid faithfully reminded him that his skill still surpassed the average fighter's.

"I'm not worthy of this cloak, but I'm grateful for the honor of your trust," said Khaled and bowed. "If you agree, I would have *sha'ir* Hakim and Abjar as main managers of the caravans, along with the black rock alum mining, and metal alloying, with the earnings split equally between us. Majid and I will also handle the hosting tents with their wise guidance, and that of our poetic friend Samaw'al's too."

To his relief, the men agreed and he hoped he wasn't imagining the genuine air of surprised gratitude washing over them. It's not that he wanted to outdo his father in increasing their earnings. It had simply been the right thing all along and if it had taken this long, he hoped the changes would soon be felt in a better way.

They sacrificed a camel and feasted, praising Gayas, Moharib, and Khaled who kept on the proud line of honorable sons of Zubayd. It wasn't until late at night that Khaled finally went back inside the tent, hoping it wasn't just the precious wine's calming effect that felt like a weight had wonderfully lifted off of him.

Shame! Guilty! sneered an all-watching eye in the dimly-lit space.

Sah, guilty.

For one reason or another, they'd always be guilty.

Khaled fell back, his mind surprisingly alert even as his body gradually dozed. He was nineteen and *sayyid* now, and had important news to share right away.

Chapter Thirty-Two

YAZIDA

Banu Sa'd

Fss, fss, fss.

"Nasr?"

Jayida jerked up, and in her momentary disorientation realized it was her first predawn morning back in her own tent after their long trip. Her gaze shot to the entrance's tightly knotted flaps, even as an unsettling feeling swept over her. She sat up and listened, but only silence lingered.

Hania, surely happy to be home, was away from her tent with the flocks. Then, a stomping sound, coming from Adil's quarters.

"Adil," she moaned, and shoved her sheets off. For a moment she considered taking Al-Wasiyah from under her mat, then reached up to her Mikha'il amulet at her neck, and shook her head in drained frustration.

It had to be exhaustion. She hadn't slept well all the way back from 'Ukaz and the pilgrimage, and she had to remind herself it'd be a while before she got over the sight of Najma and Najim at the market and everything else unpleasant she'd seen during their trip. It had ended well, but the thought didn't bring more comfort in this instant.

Jayida rubbed her face, trying to wipe off that lingering, oppressive feeling of something—or someone—watching her. It couldn't be Nasr because it wouldn't feel like this. She quickly dressed in full, clean garb, and went to Adil.

He fixed her with alert eyes, his tail whipping and front leg stomping.

"Easy, Adil. I know you missed me but I'm back now," said Jayida and wrapped her arms around his head. It had been the first time she'd left him this long but she couldn't make sense of his fussiness that seemed worse with her than anyone else. She pet him gently and he lowered his head submissively to her frame, until he suddenly came up again and pushed her with his nose, rougher than ever before. For an instant his bared teeth made her afraid that he'd meant to bite her.

"Adil, what's wrong with you!" she stood back and frowned, then circled him again.

He didn't seem to have any bites or bleeding anywhere, and as usual he'd been well fed and his trough was full of fresh water. She stood at his side when he stomped a foot again, shoved his massive nose towards her once more, then unleashed a roar so deep and guttural it remided her of a lion.

"Stop this! I don't know what's gotten into you, but we're going to get to the bottom of it."

She put on his bridle and led him rustling and skipping to her parents' tent, half expecting the whole tribe to be awake with the noise he'd already made. Her father peeked out of the tent just as she arrived.

"I'm leaving him here for a while," she said. "Maybe you and Kamila will cheer him up."

Zahir nodded. "Still acting *majnun* hmm?"

"*Na'am*. But why are you awake so early?"

"Not sure; couldn't sleep I guess," said Zahir and exchanged a knowing glance.

Pacing back to her tent, her mind hovered somewhere high above her as it looked down below. In a dazed whirl, she lit some incense and set it on the ground, then gathered all her and Adil's belongings—satchels, pouches, statues, jars, weapons, clothing, blankets, mats, cushions, bedding, leopard and lion pelts—and set them in a pile near her tent's perimeter. Leaving the tent skeleton, the smoking incense burner inside, and the lion heart pole outside, she removed the tent dividers and added them to the pile.

With wafts of citrus smoke dancing around, she stood back and looked at it, a smirk curving her hard lips. Even with the occasional bittersweet tinge attached to the sight of the nearly empty tent—the vacant space made by leaving a temporary home that the poets so loved to recite of—there was always something freeing about seeing her belongings gathered this way, minimal compared to some pampered women, yet no less precious. But there was also that sense of being in control, that she would put these objects to use as she saw fit, and not the other way around.

"What is it, what is it?" whispered Jayida, her thoughts racing, searching for something unwanted in her midst.

With the incense in hand she went to her pile, and examined each item one by one for anything she might've missed. There was nothing, and while each confirmed item—swept over the incense for further purification—fueled her relief, she couldn't shake off the lingering impression of something wrong. With a grunt, she laid back flat on the ground, her vision filled with one eternal grey-blue, spotless sky. Something hard pressed into her from the lower side, and she reached down under herself to shove away the bothersome stone. But it wasn't there, and with annoyed confusion she realized that the hard form came from within her own cloak.

She sat up, reached deep in and took out a sticky piece of jagged red stone wrapped in a web of knotted string. Disgusted, she shook the flesh-like roped-stone off her hand and flung it to the ground.

Sahira.

It could be no one else, since she was the only person who'd come close enough to her to slip it inside her cloak without her knowledge. As uncomfortable as it'd made her and Adil, if Sahira thought this was enough to harm her, she was wrong yet again. Baring all her teeth, Jayida searched her folds for any potential others, and thankfully found nothing more.

She went back to her parents and called her father outside, who gazed at her inquisitively.

"I'm putting something in your robe; don't look at it. Now follow me to see Adil; I'll go in first, then you follow after," said Jayida.

At the sight of her Adil shook his head up and down and she nearly cried tears of joy as he nuzzled her like his old self again. Her father then appeared and at the sight of him, Adil tensed and stood back, stomped a front leg and swished his tail angrily.

"*Shway, shway,*" said Jayida. Petting her beloved mount, she motioned to her father to stay and wait where he was.

"What's all this noise?" said her mother, just waking up.

"We've found the culprit to Adil's discomfort, and my own, too," said Jayida. She reached out her hand to her father, who took out the roped-stone from his cloak, so small in his large, strong palm.

"Vile reminder from Sahira. That's what Adil was trying to tell me by shoving me and trying to bite my robe. I hate to say it but she knew just where to put it to avoid quick detection," said Jayida.

"As witches do," frowned her father, and smothered the stone in his palm. "It was a long trip, and though we're obviously still catching up from it, it will be done."

"Thankfully, knowing what it is takes at least some of its power away," said Jayida.

"Eh! If that witch ever again tries to harm my child, I'll go after her myself, and no stones, knotted ropes, spells, or anything else will help her," said Zoraya. She swept her hands over Jayida's face several times, then kissed each cheek.

"That makes two of us," echoed Zahir, his rock fist stifling the witch from this distance.

"And to think, I almost felt sorry for her. Now I know why on our way back I was starting to think it was a mistake going there at all, like something clung to us all forever," Jayida said.

Her father sighed. "Your mother and I had our concerns. That's why many, especially those more sensitive, will avoid 'Ukaz. But given the situation and your relative excitement, we resolved that at least you'd see some good from it."

Like with Najma and Najim—how she'd hated what she'd seen, but hated even more what might've been if she hadn't.

"Must be what Hatim meant by not having his son Adiyy accompany him there yet. I'm just glad none of us were hurt," said Jayida, and went to her stallion.

"*Shway*, slowly; I know, please forgive me. I'll never doubt you again, though I am still learning your language," cooed Jayida. She hugged him then turned back to her father.

"I'll get it ready for the fire tonight," smirked Jayida, her father only reluctantly ceding it back to her.

"*Aywa*, yet another good reason to celebrate your glorious, safe return laden with treasure," beamed her mother.

Back at her tent, Jayida lit more incense, and dropped Sahira's roped-stone in her jar that held a glass vial filled with the lion's blood, and the pouch that had temporarily contained the lion heart. Then she refilled the tent with her things as they were, her own simpler version of her parents' tent set up. The entrance faced north, with the public area as the first room, decorated with the leopard skin hanging west towards Wadi Al-Hamd, and the lion skin hanging east towards Khaybar and Wadi Al-Rummah. She added some of the new famous woven blankets from Najran, its saffron and wine decorative flowers, and green leaves and vines on the milky wool surface adding a softer garden-like effect.

Next was the usual women's private area, serving as Adil's quarters and fitting added protection for her. Behind it was her sleeping area, with the bathing area next to it. In her most private sleeping area, her statue collection and the head of her bedding laid north, while the rest of her weapons and belongings gathered south and out of easy reach from strangers.

Satisfied, she took a small pouch-like cloth, stuffed it with straw until it looked like a breasted, feminine form, and sealed it loosely with a thin strand of rope.

She got the glass vial, and carefully dropped a few drops of the lion's blood to bind this witch's form. Smirking, Jayida went outside to the lion heart pole, and impaled the witch's form on top of the lion heart pierced with arrows.

If it didn't make a difference, it at least made a striking visual. Because it remained that the divination bowls *sayyid* Aziz had gifted her obviously didn't work, when not a single one had helped to keep the dark *jinni* away from her space. Or was Sahira's power stronger than the bowls', hence the outcome? A cruel thought emerged: what if somehow the bowls had been what allowed, or maybe even drew it there, especially if they'd been made by one or more who practiced the dark arts? But she decided against it, when she'd never felt uncomfortable until her encounter with Sahira. Jayida contemplated digging them out and using them as decorations, or even selling them for a little fortune. But then again, if they didn't work, leaving them there made no difference. She'd never really believed in them, and though their ineffectiveness now only fueled her doubt, she preferred to remember them as a well-intentioned gift from their *sayyid* in memory of Nasr.

Jayida fumigated her space some more, paced around the rooms of her tent from east to west seven times with the incense, and repeated the motion outside of it. Finally pleased, she took her lion jar to her parents' tent, grateful that her appetite was returning in anticipation of her mother's missed delicious cooking under way.

At the evening fire, Hubala looked on, pleased to have them back again, as Shams took cautious glances at her jar.

"How dare she! She clearly has no idea who she's dealing with," said *sayyid* Aziz, shaking his head. "And what if I'd sought help from another of her kind?" He shuddered.

"You'd probably be the one helping them, with your generous heart," said Zahir.

"Thankfully they're not all alike," said Shams, looking more worried than convincing.

When the sky turned black and everyone gathered around the fire, she took out the roped-stone and held it in her open palm.

"May Mikha'il bind you and protect the Banu Sa'd," she said, and cast it in the fire. A roar of ululation and clapping erupted in a happy rush, and their stories of their journey circulated again, this time with *kahin* Jonder's vanquishing of the foolish witch. Maybe that's what it meant to be *kahin*: to act naturally, genuinely in the moment from the heart, and praying that it would be heard by good spirits, because anything more than that seemed too much like wanting to control fire.

As usual, she lingered with her father and *sayyid* Aziz around the fire long past everyone had left, and she decided to leave Adil with her parents for one undisturbed night of rest. Hania still seemed nowhere in sight, and she chuckled at the thought that her beloved mount would always appear right when she needed her.

She'd barely put out the fire and lit the small oil lamp in her public area, when the sound of approaching footsteps made her sit up. Would she never have a moment of peace alone again?

"Jonder, it's me, Yazida," she whispered.

Frowning, Jayida went to the entrance and untied the straps.

"Yazida? What's wrong?" Yazida wore a dark veil she hadn't seen before and in the darkness made it difficult to tell if it belonged to man or woman.

"Nothing. I made you these," said Yazida, and held up a tray of pastries whose sweet scent were no match for those at 'Ukaz.

"You just might lure all the dead here with your honorable libation," chuckled Jayida, before she could stop herself. She didn't want to scare her at this hour, but to her surprise, there was playfulness in Yazida's curious eyes that wanted to be allowed in—hardly appropriate at this time, even for Jonder. But she could hardly refuse her generous offering.

"By *al-ilah*, that's so generous of you. May you rest well, it's late and I wouldn't want—"

"Everyone's asleep. And more importantly, everyone knows I'm safe with you," said Yazida, and slipped so swiftly into her tent that Jayida was caught off guard. She wasn't sure what surprised her most: for Yazida to be there of her own choice or that it may even be shrugged off by her parents and the tribe if they knew.

Jayida set the tray down on a mat and watched her glide to and beam at the Najran blankets, her demeanor shifting as she went from the leopard to the lion skin. Yazida drew her head close to the form, as if it might reveal something more.

Jayida tried to see it from her perspective, and though the lion pelt hung with its arms spread out and its dark-maned head drooped backwards, its frozen grimace of bared jaws and glassy eyes made it no less intimidating. She wondered if she would ever get over her own surprise that she'd actually killed it.

"That must've been so terrible," said Yazida, and clasped her hands.

"It was," said Jayida, and looked away to hide a surging frown.

"So brave. Seeing you covered in all that blood, it was..." Yazida trailed off.

The memory of the wailing visions of the burning Najran martyrs, the buried girls, the circumcised girls in whirling chaos engulfed Jayida anew, as if it'd just been that very day. By now she'd given up thinking they would ever truly vanish.

"What matters is where he is now," said Jayida, harsher than she intended.

"What was going through your head?" said Yazida, turning to her and approaching.

"Survival. In those moments, that's all it is, and fighting with all the life you have, until the last breath if necessary. Though I hope you'd never need to, if it does happen, I can only advise you do the same."

"Like Nasr did, in his last moments," said Yazida almost to herself.

Jayida nodded. "Oh, how your brother is missed," she sighed. At least they were back and closer to his grave again.

"I think about it every day, as I'm sure you do, too. I try, but sometimes it still doesn't make sense; why he had to go. Or why he chose the way he did. And I know you respect his wishes. But all this time, without closure or answers, and now *yaba* with the pilgrimage—" Yazida paused, and Jayida hoped she wouldn't cry. "Maybe I shouldn't but I just wanted to be sure before it's done."

"What do you mean?"

"I don't want to marry Shams without being sure: was there never a place for me in your heart?"

Her jaw clenching, Jayida drew close and towered over her, thought about touching her smooth skin with the side of her finger.

"*Na'am*, and there will always be. I've always cared for you, as a sister. So it must be as your brother said."

"As a sister," nodded Yazida and looked away as she bit her inner lip. "You're being kind, and cautious with your words. I know; perhaps I ruined it with that night with Imru." She'd surely grabbed the ebony veil to blend in the darkness, but it also gave the sad effect of her being in mourning.

"No, you didn't. I thought that was understood," said Jayida.

"Still, I know I'm nothing like those women you saw *there*," frowned Yazida.

"Of course not! I would tell you to go see yourself, but I don't want you to see," Jayida tried not to yell in disgust.

"So what is it then? I still want to know. What am I doing wrong, that I don't inspire this feeling in you? I know; it's your life to be away, and you seem so out of reach sometimes, in another world, just like Nasr. That must've been part of why you were so close," said Yazida, her tearful emotion threatening to unleash Jayida's own.

Jayida's chest rose under the weight of her coat of mail, both hating and trying to appreciate what was happening, as difficult as it was.

"Yazida, you haven't done anything wrong." Almost the opposite—she refrained from saying. "There are many things in life that don't make sense, but I hope someday when I'll explain, you'll understand."

"Someday? Why not now? Hasn't enough time already passed? Or let me guess: it's not the right time?" Yazida flapped her arms like the loveliest *jinni* she'd ever seen.

"It's not. And speaking of which: am I to take it that your feelings for Imru have already vanished, then?" At the very least, Yazida couldn't say she didn't have some options, when it was more than others ever had. She'd had Nasr, and he was gone, and that might be it for her forever.

"I don't know if he'll ever come back!" said Yazida, her cheeks coloring in the darkness. "You're *kahin*; maybe you know what's happening with him but you won't tell me."

"You think I'd do this to you? The moment I know I'd tell you, and I do wish he'd come back and do this thing right, for once."

Yazida's jaw twitched, betraying the conflicted pained love. "He's probably forgotten me; maybe that's why I'm so restless."

"But you haven't forgotten him, and despite our knowledge of his ways—or at least their rumors—it didn't stop you from liking him. Isn't it worth waiting some more then, if only to confirm? Imagine him returning and finding his loyalty repaid with you marrying someone else," said Jayida.

"He's already been married; why shouldn't I be, too?" said Yazida, and crossed her arms.

Jayida shook her head. "*Aywa*, so it's about petty revenge. That's a great way to make such important decisions. But why not; have as many husbands as you'd like, and hopefully at least one of them will make you happy."

"Men and their secrets; you all protect each other! If you would just say what it is, then I wouldn't be left here becoming *majnun* trying to figure it out," Yazida said.

"And if that's true, are women any different? You claim to trust me, so why can't you just trust what I say? Is that what it means to be a woman: to doubt everything that others tell you, all the time, because you like thinking you always know better? Do you like this pain, of imagining things and then spreading it everywhere, until your paranoia has made them true? And maybe just for the childish chance to say 'I told you so'? As we've told you before, you don't know how dangerous it can be out there. So then at least trust us, pray for us, have faith in us—*that's* your priceless gift to give, as your husband should do for you and you are to do for each other, forever! Otherwise it's just poisonous noise that no men are interested in," scowled Jayida and dismissively waved her hand.

Silence fell, and though her impassioned statement had flown out in an unrestrained stream, she gratefully noted Yazida's attentive, compassionate air. Indeed, some men were as impulsive as women, lashing out with their anger at any moment, while others kept it buried inside, until it either exploded and burst on others or themselves in the cold, empty night. By now even she knew neither was restricted entirely to one gender: the variations existed in both.

Jayida closed her eyes and rubbed them, and felt arms close around her neck. Yazida's face reached up to her, and pressed her lips against hers. For a moment Jayida froze, unsure what was happening. Should she push Yazida away? By the time she decided to wrap her arms around Yazida's waist, Yazida had shed her cloak and veil to reveal her long hair, and the neckline of her dress was untied and loose enough to expose her breasts.

How could she be so bold, so... giving? Then again, there had been Imru before... maybe even Shams.

"Forgive me, I'm selfish. I just wanted this before I marry," said Yazida, her tearful kisses imbued with heat.

There was a sweetness to kissing her soft lips, but it was more out of Jayida's stunned, dazed curiosity and to accommodate her visitor than from her own desire, which despite her guest's undeniable beauty was surprisingly lacking. Jayida's hands glided up her back, found her shoulders and gently pushed her back, as Yazida's dreamy gaze pleaded silently to her.

Standing slightly back, Jayida admired her soft tanned skin, ample breasts and curvy waist, and ran her hand through her glorious, thick dark hair, and brought it down the front to cascade over the perky mounds on her chest. She tried not to smile at the thought that Shams and Imru would be jealous if they knew about this. And what of Nasr? Was he shocked, laughing, maybe both?

For a moment she had the impression that she was looking at the ideal version of herself, then realized she'd yet to fully look at herself, alone.

"You're perfect, Yazida. Don't be surprised if men don't know what to do sometimes." Jayida embraced her again, caressed her skin, and lifted the top of her dress back up. She took her veil and cloak off the ground and draped them on her, as Yazida's stare followed her.

"*Sha'ir* or *kahin*; always elsewhere," said Yazida, and Jayida noted something in her air that she'd never seen before.

Jayida grabbed her waist and in a swift motion turned her around, and wrapped Yazida's hands with her own as she buried her face in her spicy-sweet, fragrant hair.

"Nothing has to change between us," Jayida breathed into her ear. There was just another name to add to her concealed feminine shape that would finally bridge the gap of their unusual friendship.

Yazida's hands loosened from hers.

"You're right. Maybe nothing's wrong with me, after all," said Yazida, and let go.

Jayida followed her receding shadow, the sweet pies the only proof of the visiting spirit.

In the morning Jayida knew she'd drifted fast into a deep pleasant sleep, because she awoke in the cool dawn, refreshed and grateful to be home. Even her Aksumite guardian had graced her sleep with a visit to welcome her back.

She got Sahira's now charred red stone and some ashes from the firepit and put them in a pouch hanging at her belt. Then she got Adil from her parents' tent, and fed and brushed him back at her quarters. She braided seven braids into his mane in honor of Shamshun, his soothed demeanor confirming that any intended harm had gone.

With her beloved stallion Adil and Al-Wasiyah, bow, and spear in tow, she took him for a ride to Wadi Al-Hamd, relishing that early morning peace she so loved, when nature gently stirred awake. She located a deep crevice and tossed the pouch into it, then added some frankincense tears to seal it in as it transformed again into the earth.

Adil grazed and Yazida whirled in her thoughts like a hair-waving dancing girl encouraging warriors to victory, as she'd done during Imru's visit. In her dreaminess, Jayida hoped Yazida could hang on, both for Imru and for her to explain, but realized she didn't know exactly when either of them would do so. Despite the awkward situation, she was flattered by Yazida's interest, even if it was just a fleeting moment of curiosity from one or both of them. It was an unfortunate misunderstanding that stood between their sisterhood, but one that would someday eventually end.

But as tempting as that was, the recurring sinking feeling brought the same concerns: what of the rest? The comfort she'd built for herself wasn't so easy to give up, especially not without a husband to quieten gossip and share her life with. For the first time Jayida pondered about the kind of man who might want her. Everyone seemed to have at least one person they were set on, and the closest she'd come was Nasr. All the same she couldn't, and refused to force her feelings. She preferred being alone forever rather than have that kind of dishonesty, or even well-meaning pity, even if it was true that feelings naturally changed over time. She had a deep conviction that she knew what she felt and would not ignore it, and she came back to the same conclusion that she just hadn't yet met that special person. And if she was to stay alone, at least she was starting to become used to the idea.

Chuckling at her budding tears, she marveled at the meaning of the surging emotion tinged with confused sadness. A motion in the sky caught her, the sight of an eagle nearly stopping her heart.

"Nasr!" she cried, smiling through tears as she raised her arms to it. "Where are you going and why not take us with you?" She followed his swaying path and closed her eyes, letting herself move along with it. When she opened them again it was already a nearly invisible black dot in the north, and she let it go.

She went southeast to Wadi Al-Raha, found the graves and thanked Nasr and Shanfara for watching over them during their trip, as bittersweet as it had been.

"Please help your sister, and everyone, to understand," she pleaded to Nasr, and buried some frankincense tears at each of their graves.

She left them just as the sun appeared high in the sky, promising another beautiful, conflicted day.

"What's it going to be today, my Adil?" she cooed as she walked next to her glistening cream horse with seven braids. They came to the end of Wadi Al-Raha that opened up into the vast plain of their camp. Adil turned to look at her, and she glanced past him to the north.

She squinted, stared.

Some camels, one with a *hawdaj* and another with a rider, were approaching.

Chapter Thirty-Three

MEETING

"Ready for this one?" said Zahir, waiting outside her tent on her return.

"It's them," said Jayida, somewhere between asking and telling.

He nodded, and rubbed his bearded chin. "From what Aziz and Shams said, it seems to be just Khamra and Khaled."

She looked at Adil, whose amused stillness almost surprised her.

"That doesn't sound too bad then," she said, before she could stop herself. She had a warring sense of relief and erratic annoyance. A cacophony of cries shot up her spine, and she arched her back and stretched out her arms to shake it off. They'd barely returned from an exhausting trip to the Hijaz, cast off a witch's evil eye, and now this. Perhaps it might be as she hoped, even if she couldn't bring herself to say, or even fully believe it just yet.

"Your mother will be with Warda to welcome Khamra at their tent, and I'll have Khaled in ours, in case you'd like to join us at some point. No hurry, though," said her father. He pat her shoulder with a weighty air and left her to prepare.

She led Adil to his quarters and unsaddled him.

"That should be interesting, hmm?" she said, Adil's eyes glistening in mute understanding.

Jayida picked up the bristle brush, and took deep breaths as it swept across Adil's shining, smooth white coat. She might've preferred a break in between, but there was yet another opportunity for her to challenge her *hilm* unlike ever before, and make herself an even stronger, unbreachable fortress. Though five springs had passed since *sha'ir* Hakim had seen her young form soaked in the leopard's blood, it seemed much longer, and almost like child's play in comparison to what had happened since. So what could be simpler? They'd meet, exchange some cordial words, let them gossip and enjoy their visit, then return home.

After a short while of straightening and gathering herself, she walked to her parents' nearby open tent and entered. She directed her light gaze to *sayyid* Aziz and her father before turning to the dark massive figure next to him. Khaled rose to meet her while she kept her direct, hard stare. Khaled towered over her, his deep-set ebony eyes oozing of something like playfulness, even excitement that contrasted his crisp, somber robes.

"At last, blessed cousin Jonder, it is my honor to meet you," said Khaled, and stepped to her.

"Praise *al-ilah* that you made it safely," said Jayida, trying not to think if her tone had been sarcastic.

At once he gripped her shoulders and kissed each cheek, making her proud that he'd notice that she was a hard mass too, even if it was her coat of mail.

"I'm so glad—" said Khaled, his brow twitching. Was she dreaming or was he nervous, even emotional? At least he smelled nice, too, even if it might be to hide something of his unpleasant traits. *Sayyid* Aziz smirked and gestured for them to recline for this long overdue meeting. "I hope you'll enjoy your aunt's *maamoul*," said Khaled, pointing to the large tray of pastries before them.

Jayida smirked with a curt nod, and for a moment they lingered, silently scrutinizing each other like well-trained, cautious enemies. His aquiline nose protruded and curved down like an eagle's, and a trimmed, thin trail of beard outlined his strong jawline. The layers of draping linen added to his robust frame, easily making him among the largest young men she'd ever seen. She was almost surprised at her ease in maintaining her focus, refusing to be shaken by something as simple as appearance, even if she was pleasantly struck by his. But handsomeness be damned; a man of such looks had to be aware of his own impact and might surely use it to his own advantage. Most importantly, she wanted to finally hear it.

"There are some news," said her father solemnly.

Khaled nodded. "My father, your uncle Moharib, has passed."

"May he find peace," Jayida said flatly, yet still kinder than the way Moharib had often said things about others.

Khaled tightened his lips. "Since long before either of us were born, your father can attest to his nature: a proud man, who'll have no one see any weakness in him. He's been coughing for seasons, and over time he'd started taking more and more *khat*. Until he reached his limit," said Khaled, his invisible sneer lurking. Like he might've enjoyed it, and even wanted Jonder to see it.

"May his memory live on," said her father, and she wished he didn't look so dejected. If he was reminiscing on their few happier memories, he seemed to be the only one.

Khaled clasped his hands. "It was important that I pay my respects to my *amo* Zahir, and to you and your mother. I'm sorry we've not come sooner, and despite the news, I'm glad to say he can no longer protest against our reunion."

At last, the confirmation they'd suspected.

"My kind *amo*: I apologize for my father, and that you felt you had to leave your tribe, but I hope you may get to know me and know that I'm at your service, however I can be. And of course, if you'd like, you could return with us."

Jayida searched his face and tone for hints of deceit—discomfort, overacting, plaintive whining—but found none. Could the son really be so different from the father? Either he was sincere or an expert liar, and she hated to think he'd learned from the best. He had his own prosperity now, all inherited from Moharib. But her father's presence, no matter where he went, also had a way of adding security and comforting others like his blessed well-bred camels that roamed across the land.

"How noble you are Khaled; that was long ago, and not your fault," said Zahir. "It's true that sometimes I imagined I might see him once more, that we'd talk happily, like we did as children. But it seems it was not meant to be." Her father laid his hand on Khaled's shoulder in understanding, while the other stretched a tearful eye.

"I thank you for welcoming me, and if you haven't decided within our three nights, you're still always welcome to join us after, of course," said Khaled with a contemplative air.

While the invitation to return was kind, he could hardly be surprised at their decline when the Banu Sa'd had been their home for slightly over seventeen springs. If her father had hoped to see Moharib again most of all, what was there for him now? Khaled's offer was right, but that it should've been Moharib's left a lingering, unpleasant weight on them, and her most of all. Like his evil eye might be turned on them even more now, through his son, whether or not he knew of it or wanted it...

But she had not lived all this time as Jonder to let that happen.

"Despite the circumstances, we're happy to see you. Good timing too, since we just returned from 'Ukaz," said her father.

"How was it?" said Khaled, perking up like a child called to a better subject.

Surprisingly, his demeanor only took on the brooding tone she would've expected him to have from the start when her father shared Nasr's passing that inspired *sayyid* Aziz's desire to go. Thankfully, it could at least explain some of Jonder's desire to keep her emotional distance from him, at least for the time being.

"May he be at peace. I couldn't imagine losing my dear friend Majid," said Khaled, looking genuinely distraught. His sad tone even suggested he needed the prized friendship in light of potential fatherly trouble.

Khaled then told of their travels up north to Al-Sham, yielding the image of two happy, trouble-free friends enjoying each other's company tinged with hints of fear and danger amidst bravery and friendship. A curious thought emerged: might she ever travel with him? Attentive and willing as Khaled was, it reminded her of a lonely child eager to be liked. Overcompensating—but he seemed so genuine that she decided the poetic impulse of acting found in gifted poets like Imru Al-Qays and Amr ibn Kulthum, and sometimes even Nasr, wasn't present in him.

"I might be *sayyid* now, but my good friend Majid is a natural-born *sha'ir*," said Khaled, confirming her impressions when they talked of the poets they'd seen at the market.

He spoke mostly nostalgically of his time with the Tayyi, meeting Hatim, Imru Al-Qays, and Amr ibn Kulthum. But his mention of their scuffle yielded the Sa'd's own vile version of attackers, and she sensed that something about it still hung over him. *Sayyid* Aziz left the harsher, more personal parts of their visit to southern Hijaz unsaid in favor of showing him around the camp.

Word was already fast spreading that Khaled, now *sayyid* of Banu Zubayd the Great was visiting. Tribesmen gathered to express sympathy and bless his prosperity, praising him to keep hosting the famous beloved fighting tents. Shams proudly announced that their guest tent was pitched near the *sayyid*'s, hinting at his own role in setting it up. Jayida had to suppress a laugh at Shams's child-like awed enthusiasm over their visitor, even if she couldn't deny Khaled's unexpected effect. Still, she wasn't sure if it was Shams or she herself who was most bothered by the thought of Khaled being so close to Yazida. That it might be a test, including for night-venturing Yazida, made her want to laugh again.

Just as comical were some curious mothers fawning over his bravery heard from Tayyi stories, while their younger daughters stole shy glances at him from under their veils or from behind their tents. Jayida didn't have to hear them say it to know what they were thinking: that he was surely the most handsome young man they'd ever seen.

In *sayyid* Aziz's tent they rejoined Zoraya along with Warda, Samira, and a graceful, plump woman from whose dark eyes and tanned handsome features Jayida now recognized as Khaled's mother.

"Khamra, meet our son Jonder," said Zoraya, gesturing Jayida over.

Khamra raised her soft hands up to Jayida, who offered her cheeks to be kissed.

"Oh, what a happy day, to see you two finally around each other! Khaled has wanted it for so long," said Khamra whose sad eyes diffused a gentleness that drew her sympathy. Jayida instantly had the overwhelming urge to cry and scrunched her nose distractedly, pretending something had gotten in her eye.

"What a good omen that you finally feast with us, and so soon after our return," said *sayyid* Aziz, and pinched Khaled's cheeks with a grin. Jayida smiled, wanting him to be right.

The festivity engulfed the camp as if they had another beloved poet in their midst. They slayed one of her father's young camels for the feast, and the tribe gathered, eager to converse with and hear Khaled's stories. Yazida and Samira helped set the trays of food and wine all over, then sat close by across the Zubaydi guest and his mother. Jayida happily dug into the tender meat with added *aqit*, the hardened dried curd of buttermilk with its beloved metallic taste nothing less than a heavenly gift after a long day of barely any eating.

"Excellent meal, but that's common knowledge, thanks to my *amo*'s fine flocks," nodded Khaled.

"Surely you still have some of the forty he left behind," said *sayyid* Aziz, already cheered with wine.

"*Sah*, we do, and my beloved Sadiqa is one of them," said Khaled.

He cast a loving glance at his mother who smiled shyly yet happily, their palpable bond a shield against Moharib. Two against one; a concept she knew all too well.

"May we hear some of your travel stories? We're eager for more after those of my father, Zahir, and Jonder from their 'Ukaz journey," said Yazida, and Jayida was both pleased and surprised at her boldness. Yazida's gaze glued on Khaled like honey, and seemed so unconcerned about her obvious attention to him that she had to be doing it on purpose. Once again: if not one, then the next.

"I'd be glad to, though I warn you I'm no poet. But before that, I must ask something of my hosts that I've wanted to ask for so long: will you please share your stories of Kutha and how your friendship came to be?" said Khaled.

For a moment her father's eyes widened and *sayyid* Aziz let out a knowing chuckle. As usual, Moharib had probably never spoken of it, and even Samaw'al, whom she'd met six summers ago at Khaybar, and who resided in his castle so close to Khaled had probably limited his own sharing out of respect.

Zahir shared how he'd felt called to go, and would've liked Moharib to join. But he'd protested the decision, while *siddi* Gayas had approved of his venture, in shared dislike of the encroaching Fars through their Lakhmid allies. Either way, change seemed inevitable, as some wondered how this foray from the boldly Yassu-loving Ma'dikarib Ya'fur might change relations between empires and tribes. In the midst of fighting for their lives, the adventure had yielded his deepened friendship with Samaw'al and a new one in *sayyid* Aziz, and best of all, the love of his life in Zoraya. Jayida thought Khaled seemed to perk up at the fact that their wedding had at least happened at Tayma, and yet, it'd also been the source of their departure. Questions, so many questions he surely longed to ask, but the burning one was too soon to be asked—and answered.

"A story of true friendship and loyalty," said Khaled with a hint of envy.

She dared to think that he hated just as much as she did that his father was on the bad end of it. And yet, if her parents had stayed, she could've grown up near him, as Jayida. Would she have liked him, played then trained with him, or avoided him like she did Moharib? Or maybe it wouldn't have made a difference, lost as he was in his time and forays with Majid.

"*Aywa*, guess it's my turn now," Khaled smiled, but not enough to hide his conflicted air.

With a resolved air and a deep tone, he spun story after story—beginning with a hellish night in a cemetery when a boy killed his first striped hyena, earning him his first sword Al-Fatih. Then came wolves the boy fended off with his friend, protecting passing caravans that passed through Tayma, carrying far-off treasures, sometimes even women and children. There were the cold, dark days of *Ayyam al-Zalam*, of stone hearts unmoved by suffering, as some grew poorer and others richer—a sure sign of divine favor. There were exploits in the red hills and mountains of Tayyi, where Hatim's generosity called to all from his mountain peak, and journeys to Al-Sham along the old trade routes, evading the mysterious deadly plague as Ghassanid troops kept the Fars at bay across invisible yet real frontiers.

Khaled's gaze met his audience as he spoke, constantly turning back to her, as if she were the main recipient and everyone else happened to listen in. She casually observed to see if he ever returned Yazida's lingering attention, and drew a selfish delight that he didn't.

Through all the stories, said Khaled, the boy often thought of his *amo* and cousin whom he wanted to see but wasn't allowed to until the right time. So as a dutiful son he listened, even if every day he thought of disobeying. At first she thought he was reciting as a way to apologize to his dead father—whose *qareen* might know Khaled was now among the Banu Sa'd—but then realized he was apologizing to them. He had not a word of insult, but neither praise for Moharib, letting it pass like the wind, and all at once she knew that all of Zubayd the Great breathed easier from Moharib's passing.

Though it wasn't a recital in any particular form or even one that rhymed, she couldn't be the only one thinking that it reminded her of a nicer version of a *su'luk* composition. That he would reveal so much so soon in his recital was either foolish, trusting, or simply unworried about what the Banu Sa'd might say. But then again, he was *sayyid* now, and freer to do as he liked.

But her doubt kicked in again, recalling Imru. Why did Khaled have to be so easily *likeable*? And if he really was that good person that she wanted him to be, why did it feel so messy, chaotic, annoying, yet fun and even joyful at the same time? Was that what Yazida enjoyed from it all, the thrill of the impossible that a man's love called forth? And why did Jayida suddenly feel the urge to push Yazida away from Khaled, and place herself there instead?

CHAPTER THIRTY-FOUR

DISCERNING

With her Aksumite princess guardian floating in her head, Jayida looked once more around her tent, confirming that everything was arranged. Not that it needed to be, but she noted that Khaled's impending visit already felt different from Yazida's a few nights before, even if it was early morning. And to think, just the day before she wasn't sure she'd want him around at all! Strangely amused, she tried to let herself enjoy the new budding urge to make her space more inviting.

She rose and went to the sound of heavy footsteps approaching, and stood behind the closed entrance.

"All praises to the good lion slayer! It is I, Khaled, who approaches. May I pay a visit to the shrine of my cousin Jonder?" he said.

Smiling, Jayida lifted the tent flap and pinned it back, casting him a smirking glance and taking her time barring the entrance. If he could take this long to visit, he could wait as long as she deemed fit.

"Are you always this dramatic?" said Jayida, trying not to laugh at what appeared to be his distance from the pole with the impaled heart and witch's form.

"Do I have to remove my boots or anything? I know you're *kahin* so I wouldn't want to offend." That he seemed honestly concerned only made him frustratingly more handsome.

"Too late," she grinned, and tied the last knot. "*Aywa*, now it's safe to enter. I trust you had a pleasant first night among us," she said, gesturing to the display of her mother's pastries and fresh milk. Perhaps someday soon she would practice and make her own, even if it wouldn't be as good as her mother's.

"Perfect rest," grinned Khaled. He scanned the place, a hunter marking the terrain. Perhaps even his cream robe under his dark cloak was a good omen. "And who is that impaled outside?" he squinted playfully.

"What else? A witch bent on harm. I trust she got my response," she said.

Khaled gave a curt nod and drifted to her lion skin hanging east. He stared and released a low whistle.

"I'm not even sure I could've taken him," he said with admiration.

"Oh, you could. We do all kinds of things when we have to," said Jayida, his father's sudden shadow forcing her serious tone. If only his son knew, though he eventually would.

Khaled grew pensive. "I'm sure you're proud of what you've done to earn your sword, as you should be. But I never was, not in the way I wanted to be. It's like it was always all for him. He probably noticed that I wanted little to do with Al-Fatih. I got my second sword Al-Naji while at Bosra, and never told him about it. So now Al-Fatih rests with him, where it belongs."

"We talk and recite verses of these feats as if they're easy, but they're not," said Jayida.

"How right you are. So whose cult do you follow? Al-Lat's?"

"No. I wouldn't say I follow any, though I do sometimes pray to Mikha'il and Yassu, as my parents do."

"Forgive my asking, but does it work?" said Khaled, fixing her.

"I think so. It gives a sense of peace. *Nasi* Musa from Khaybar gave me this amulet of Mikha'il when we stayed there during the *Ayyam al-Zalam*, and I like to keep it on. I bound the witch I just mentioned in his name, too, and I think that did the trick."

Khaled drew close to her, filling the space with his massive enveloping presence.

"I also like to wear this cross amulet Hatim kindly gifted me," he said, revealing the gold jewelry around his thick neck. "I'd like to have faith like him and you, if you'll teach me."

She smiled invitingly and they sat down.

"I'm not sure it can be taught, other than you go within, into yourself," said Jayida. And try to listen without knowing, then see horrible things, because it's not just lush gardens and overflowing treasures—she thought of adding but didn't. She was beginning to think he wasn't the kind to have four demon bowls under his tent, and might even think her a bit *majnun* for having them, even if it had been a gift to the *kahin*.

"I suppose as a *kahin* that's your added advantage," said Khaled, with a hint of disappointment.

"I don't call myself *kahin*. It's Nasr who called me that, and it seems it's stuck since." She wasn't sure why she'd said it, but it didn't have to be a big deal when it was true all the same.

"But you see things, and know things sometimes?" said Khaled, his frown searching deep into her. Why did he have to be invasive, and worst of all, why did she have to like it?

"*Na'am*, I guess." Though she hadn't known he was coming. Unless she'd had, faintly, caught in the distracting net of Sahira's and Badr's evil ways.

"As *sha'ir*, maybe that's how Nasr recognized it in you," said Khaled. She'd considered it before, especially after Nasr had said her true name, and for some odd reason she liked hearing it from him. At this rate, maybe Khaled was *kahin*, too, though she hoped maybe not as sharp as her. "So which idols do you have?" he said.

"Idols? None. I have some statues that my father made, even from the Tayma rock salt, and others that I made myself. But I don't venerate them. They're more like representations of nice ideas and feelings, and decorations I like to keep."

"Like your ostrich egg I have in my collection," said Khaled.

"*Esh?* You do?" said Jayida, hoping she sounded more playful than surprised.

"*Aywa*; the one *sha'ir* Hakim brought back from the day of your leopard triumph. I see that unlike others you don't show off your proud collection in the men's quarters," Khaled smirked.

"I wasn't thinking there was anyone to show it to. But in a way I also thought it best kept closest to me," she said, referring to her sleeping quarters. "So what about you? Any particular goddesses you're fawning over?"

"No. I don't know. I want that conviction that Hatim seems to have. Majid is into his head too, a bit like you. I think you'd like each other."

"Surely your father had his own beliefs, too," she said lightly.

"*Sah*, but I don't want his kind. *Yama* mentioned that yours prayed to Yassu for you, so that sounded good to me."

Jayida stared, touched at his confession. Who had Moharib prayed to, or even thanked, for his son who now sat in her tent, without his father's blessing?

"At least you have one guardian," said Jayida.

"Do I?"

"Everyone has at least one. Haven't you seen yours?"

"If I have, I don't know, which sounds very sad if you ask me," he shrugged. "Who's yours?"

"An Aksumite princess."

"And you're certain of that because?"

"I've seen her since I was a child," she smiled.

Khaled nodded. "I've had no such thing. I didn't even—"

Jayida waited, not wanting to push. Khaled sighed deeply.

"You've lost your closest friend, so you know what that's like. But maybe at least as a *kahin*, you've had some closure. I haven't. Maybe I shouldn't even be asking," he said. He looked away, hiding lurking conflicted tears. She'd prepared to have so much dislike for him but in that moment she felt only compassion.

"I haven't had the closure I wanted, either," she said. "I keep hoping it will come soon, though." He looked back at her, and in the coiled intensity was the flicker of grateful reassurance. Moharib and Nasr were a world apart though, but at least she was beginning to see more that Khaled was not like his father after all.

"Maybe you could make me something," said Khaled.

"Why not. Just say which you want," she said, concealing her surprise.

"Yassu, to honor our great Tayyi kin and Hatim."

"*Sah*. If you're still worthy of it in the coming days, I'll make you one," she grinned as a rustle came from the side. "Looks like it's time for a walk."

She rose and went to Adil's quarters, swept aside the separator and revealed her beloved stallion.

"Striking creature," said Khaled, and went to him. Her jaw tensed as Adil walked straight to Khaled, but then again, he was surely smelling his own horse on him, and maybe even a snack.

"Meet Adil, my honorable Ghatafan gift for my lion-slaying," Jayida smirked.

"*Aywa*, what a pair you make," Khaled cooed to her stallion, petting Adil's face and neck gently. Adil closed his eyes and there was such an air of closeness between the two that a yet deeper annoyance surged in her. Was Adil already betraying her to *him*? Adil snorted, and Khaled reached in his folds for a pouch and retrieved a date that disappeared in an instant.

"I think we'll get along just fine," said Khaled, his large hands rhythmically sweeping Adil's silken skin. Jayida grabbed the saddle and gladly stepped between them.

"*Sah*, though it's easy for people to look nice at first glance. Thankfully, that's one thing I've always loved about animals: the way they won't fake their impressions," she said, pulling on the straps and adjusting the saddle as needed.

"Very true," said Khaled. "I like to think they're great judges of character."

She secured her Bag of Treasures over her mount, filled with her bow and quiver.

"We'll get Kamila for you and venture around and to Wadi Al-Hamd," she said. As the elder mare, Kamila might have a different reaction to Khaled.

Jayida got Kamila from her parents' tent, packed her father's bow and quiver for Khaled to use, informed them of their whereabouts, and left to their amused glances.

"Blessings, Kamila," said Khaled, and to her surprise, the mare also went straight to him, buried her face and nuzzled him like she'd known him forever. It had to be the rest of the dates that worked their charm on the resilient mare.

With a mount at each side, they walked southeast, their comfortable silence giving it an air of pilgrimage. She'd only shared that kind of pleasant stillness with Nasr, confusing and pleasing her at once that she should also have it so soon with this unknown kin. So much about him was different than she'd anticipated, and it was another favorable trait that he didn't need to fill every moment of stillness with words or noise.

They came upon the shadowy Valley of Rest, where Nasr's pile of stones stood out with those of his grandparents, along with clusters of alyssum flowers. She almost gasped out loud when she looked further down near it. More small white flowers sprouted in the unmarked place where Shanfara's body secretly laid.

"Welcome to our Wadi Al-Raha. This is where Nasr's body rests." She fixed Khaled, trying not to laugh in delight.

His black eyes widened and he seemed caught off guard, as if awakened from some reverie and bracing for some hidden danger. Just as quickly, he eased up, an inquisitive frown taking him over.

"I wouldn't have expected it to be so peaceful. They must have something to do with it," said Khaled. He kneeled, untied his pouch, and set it among the stones. "Praise your generosity and accept some rock salt from Tayma," said Khaled almost in a whisper.

Jayida froze and took a moment to realize she'd been holding her breath. He couldn't be pretending. He was too... *natural*. Too uncalculated. Despite its danger and foolishness if shown to everyone, she saw again that it might be his way, perhaps stronger than him, and even endearing. She yearned to ask about the graveyard he'd mentioned the night before but vacillated. So why had he mentioned it at all, then, if he didn't want it known and brought up, despite the risk of mockery?

"You're blessed, you know. I wish I could've grown up knowing you two," said Khaled, staring at the multicolored stones. "And I understand that you don't like to call my father your *amo*—you always say 'your father', or 'him'—but I hope to show you that I'm not like him, or at least, I hope not like his worse traits."

Aywa: If Nasr had decided for his grave to become a revered place of confession, she would indulge him. Just as well, it was further confirmation for the unnecessity of going all the way to Mina, Wajj, Nakhla, or any other shrines in the Hijaz.

"Khaled, you've been forthcoming, so I'll gladly return the favor. I don't call him my uncle because I've never *felt* related to him. I mean no disrespect to you, but I try myself to understand how my own father, such a great, loving man as you see him, could be related to yours. And though it's a common enough story, your father with his seventeen summers of silence, has also given me little reason to see him as such. Now so far, I'm glad that you've come, I really am. But what does that change in terms of him? Calling him so now feels a bit pointless, seeing as he's gone. So it seems whatever comes will have to be from us," said Jayida. It might be done for his father, but not for her yet.

"I understand," said Khaled. "As difficult as it is to talk about, I'm glad that at least we can talk openly; we both know how others would've held grudges over lesser things and for much longer."

Starting with his father, of course.

"*Sah.* I'm only part Taghlib, so I might split my forty-year grudges to smaller portions," she said, and returned his emerging smirk.

"Why though? Not dedicated enough? Does Amr ibn Kulthum know of this?" said Khaled with a side-eye.

She rolled her eyes playfully. "It's exhausting, and I've no wish to add more of that to my life."

Khaled chuckled. "If only more people saw like us, how different things could be."

Jayida invited him to keep going west to Wadi Al-Hamd. The pleasant occasional quiet between them expanded even more, releasing the years of built-up tension.

"So this is where you come to escape," said Khaled, taking in the long valley.

"As much as you can call grazing the flocks escaping," she chuckled. "What's yours like?"

"He didn't want me grazing; said it was low work for slaves to do," said Khaled as she returned his frown. She had to stop hoping she'd hear something pleasing about this bitter entity. "I snuck out sometimes to go with them, but in time I took to the fighting tents. At first it was in part to escape him, but I've grown to love them; watching the boys grow in their skills, the bonds that form. Makes me think sometimes of doing that with my own children, but who knows when that will be."

"Troubled heart, eh," she smirked. Handsome as he was he must've had endless girls and women fawning over him, and probably more than that. "Everything in its time."

Khaled seemed relieved. "Glad you agree with Majid. I know maybe for others it looks like it's all easy for me. But sometimes I don't feel that way. Though my shoulder was hit while at Tayyi and has since healed, still sometimes I feel like something's changed, like it's taken a part of me away with it."

Why was he telling Jonder this? Looking for sympathy to override his father's ways? And what about the chance of their own friendship and connection; could it genuinely exist, separate from that lurking shadow to constantly cast doubt over it? He knew how such information could be quickly spread to others' advantage. Once again it seemed that he was either too trusting or didn't care anymore, and she wasn't sure which was worse.

"Maybe you have a remedy for it?" said Khaled, and his inky eyes pierced so deep into her that she had the startling thought that he knew who she was. Jonder-Jayida. Had Nasr brought him here, too? She waited, almost expecting Khaled to say her names.

"Stronger than Hatim's prayers?" she tried to cheer up. "I'm sure he'd agree with *mubassir* Ayyub of Al-Sham that some fasting, incense burning, and time alone with *al-ilah* to clear your thoughts might also help."

"What if your thoughts are what scare you?"

"No one has only nice thoughts all the time," she said. Better not tell him all her lifelong nightmarish visions, though his unspoken curiosity somehow whispered to her, asking to know.

"As a token of my not complete hatred, let's make our bows sing," she smirked.

Armed with a bow and quiver, they let the horses graze nearby, and selected a distant dry bush as their target to face side by side.

"Today *sayyid* Khaled proclaims peace regained with his *amo* Zahir and cousin Jonder," said Khaled, and shot off an arrow into the bush.

"Bold assumption, but it's a start," Jayida smiled and let hers fly.

They took turns improvising lines on their achievements amidst their tribes, and each time he mentioned the Zubayd she imagined it from her father's conflicted perspective. Khaled might know the feeling, if she said it aloud that Zahir had never felt truly happy until after he'd left. Even now, she doubted her father would want to return to the Zubayd. The gap had widened, filled with Moharib's palpable silence that not even Khaled could, or even should, fill. As they playfully unleashed teasing line after line, at least she could allow that there was something nice with Khaled, a not so unpleasant tie, maybe even worth keeping.

"Seems we have company," said Khaled a while later.

They turned and waved to the approaching band of *sayyid* Aziz, her father, Shams, and the veiled figure that could be none other than Yazida upon her brother's white stallion Bariq. Jayida struggled not to frown. Was that appropriate for her to come? At least in the past Nasr was there. For once, Jayida wondered if it was she or Shams who was more eager to get Khaled's attention away from Yazida.

The group reached them, a mixture of cheerful camel and horse riders.

"What do you say Khaled, up for a hunt?" said Shams, sitting proudly atop his father's grey stallion, his bow emerging from his back.

"If you'd like," said Khaled, then turned to her. "Will Jonder join us?"

"Not this time," said Jayida. Let him prove himself, or at least entertain.

Khaled nodded, and in a swift movement he jumped upon Kamila, his imposing massive frame contrasting his gentle maneuvering of the graceful creature. They coursed north along sunny Wadi Al-Hamd, a pleasant easiness beckoning to them despite her tension. Jayida discreetly stole glances at Yazida, her veil more like a wedding decoration than attempt to conceal her focused attention on Khaled. If Khaled noticed he gave no indication of it, but Shams did, and kept near Yazida, often blocking her view with his own figure. Jayida caught her father's lightning-fast wink, and even *sayyid* Aziz seemed his old playful self again.

They'd ridden quietly for a while, not wanting to disturb any potential wildlife, when they spotted a group of gazelle in the distance. Their horned, sand-colored bodies blended into the background as they lingered near the water's edge.

They stopped, and Khaled turned to her again.

"So, my blessed cousin Jonder. To slay, or not to slay?" he cooed, his controlled tone merging with the stillness.

"Not to slay," said Jayida. It might be an easy way out, but strangely she had no wish to see him shed blood, and so near their camp.

He gave a curt nod and Shams lit up with satisfaction, as if already imagining his trophy. If all their famous visitors yielded to his hunting conquests, he clearly had no problem with it. *Sayyid* Aziz waved his hand in blessing, and Jayida was certain Yazida had been on the verge of doing the same.

Khaled and Shams exchanged a knowing glance and Shams held back, granting their guest open terrain. Khaled quietly proceeded ahead, at times leaning forward into Kamila's face, her ears pointing back to his secret whisperings. Keeping the pace slow and cautioned, he maneuvered his bow and arrows and drifted ever closer to their target. Jayida read Shams's challenged confusion as her own. Why had he asked her if he was going to shoot anyway? Shams frowned in deeper concentration, lest it be one of Khaled's tricks.

Khaled had just stopped when a gazelle looked up suspiciously at him, and after a moment, darted off, cueing the others along. In response, Khaled tugged on Kamila's reigns and flew off. Jayida's heart pounded as he reached the herd, leaping nimbly from point to point, blocking and cornering a galloping gazelle's path at every turn, reflecting her motions like a double. Everything seemed to slow down, like a perfect mirage.

Khaled's poised, yet fluid form merged with the mare, his bow and arrow drawn in unfailing victory. What was he waiting for, then? In the rush, he wore the deepest concentrated frown she'd yet seen, surely part of his focusing tactics.

The gazelle suddenly turned back, prancing in the opposite direction, and Kamila twirled on her heels to catch up to it. They coursed parallel to each other, so close that Kamila might trample the runaway prey. In a swift motion, Khaled passed the bow and arrow to his left hand, and reached out his right palm to the gazelle, his hand caressing across the sandy skin as he let the creature slide by him.

"Oh!" Yazida blurted as if to herself, though they were all thinking it.

Shams instantly bolted off after it, raised his bow and arrow, and struck straight into a front knee, the legs buckling and body dropping to the ground in rushed finality. He unleashed other blows, the quicker to end the pain.

Jayida pinched her lips together, and tried to slow her heart with even breathing. Had she imagined it or had Khaled and Kamila been nearly as one? But the mare had been rescued and trained by her father, so it was at least partially her father's skillful doing. So why the new, undeniable unease she couldn't name? She'd only dreamt that a hunting scene could look like such a gentle dance so tensely close to death, but now she'd witnessed it in person. A conflicted sadness tore through her, wishing she could have a similar effect if she ever needed to hunt. She may have thought they didn't have much in common, but they'd both been pushed to violent slayings for different reasons.

The hunters rode back to them, each wearing his own cloak of silent pride.

"Well done, the both of you," said *sayyid* Aziz.

"It was a joy to watch, I know Nasr would be proud," said Yazida, even if she might've preferred one over the other.

Khaled nodded humbly and Shams grinned in acceptance, the boon draped across his grey stallion's short, smooth back. Perhaps in time he'd convince Yazida to recite on the event like her brother used to.

Jayida's night visions danced with the fireside stories of Khaled and Shams's generosities, each needed at different times. Giving and taking; such was the eternal cycle of life. And a blessed, gentle gazelle of all creatures! It had to be Khaled's *qareen* or whatever magic followed him from Tayma. To most it was obvious: as the new *sayyid*, the creatures were all flocking to him, offering themselves as willing sacrifice, a sure omen of his prosperous rule.

Even in her dozing off, Jayida knew it couldn't be her own imagination's doing when she beheld the Aksumite princess guardian. Beaming, her open palm stretched out to her with a pair of glowing golden rings.

CHAPTER THIRTY-FIVE

DECISION

Early the next day, Jayida stifled her frustration with time, buzzing like a bee who had little need of sleep. It couldn't be... could it? What was the Aksumite princess saying? And if she was saying it, why wasn't Nasr coming forth and saying it, too? Was it too much to ask for some confirmation? Khaled had finally come to their camp, in Nasr's old stomping grounds, and had even left a gift at his grave. She brushed Adil, her rushing thoughts like a gathering of competing *sha'ir*.

"And what do you say, huh? Surely you know more about—" Jayida dropped the brush, buried her face in her hands, and moaned piteously. "Is that what *love* is? That fast? And why is it so—annoying, but also... *nice*, I guess?" Cautiously she glanced at Adil, but for once he looked as amusedly clueless as she. "Are we hopeless?" she laughed, wondering how she'd say all this to her perfect parents, and when she could catch her mother away from Warda and Khamra. But in the meantime, let her venture out with Khaled alone some more.

Jayida took him further north in Wadi Al-Hamd, and he followed obediently though slightly suspiciously as they turned west at the diverging north and west paths. Though it'd been about a year since she'd been there with Nasr and Shams, she found it without trouble, and hoped Nasr's guidance played its part in it. With Shams's concern over the stones, she doubted he would've visited either on his own or with others, and from the looks of it, the place was just as they'd left it.

"*Aywa*, I'm ready to hear about this special place," said Khaled.

They reclined against their mounts, with Khaled's massive form taking up its own considerable space. He wiped his brow with his dark headdress then pulled it off, his long wavy ebony locks falling down past his shoulders. He shed his black cloak, and tugged at his cream robe to make air flow into his strong chest and limbs. She smirked, amused at the two Shamshuns in Nasr's cave, one a large and long-haired *sayyid*, and the other *kahin* and lion-slaying.

"What?" said Khaled.

"Just surprised you let your hair grow so long. Trying to rival the women? Or just greedy by withholding your offering?" she said.

"Maybe both," he chuckled. "Really it's just easier to let it grow. As you can see I'm not one for doing much with it."

"Not even braiding?"

He shrugged. "You can, if you want."

"*Aywa*, let's tame that mess," she said.

"And I'll listen attentively."

Jayida crouched behind him, gathered his thick cluster of hair, and ran her fingers gently through it to loosen damp knots. He smelled of musky sweat and a sweet tanginess from scented oil. His neck and shoulders, along with the rest of him, were so bulky that he looked older than his age, which would serve him well as *sayyid*. With a thought to Nasr to guide her storytelling, she made seven different clusters, and began braiding the first.

In sign of attentiveness, Khaled turned his profile to her, and she told him of the place being the last they visited with Nasr, on that day they were followed and attacked. They'd spoken of poetry, and who and what would be remembered, and how she'd been thinking about having Nasr's poetry written down. Even if they couldn't read it, someone someday would delightfully enjoy it and maybe even share it with others. Khaled's gaze lowered in contemplation when she spoke of 'Ukaz and the poets, wishing that Nasr had been there, even though he'd never seemed too interested.

"Do you think he regrets it?" said Khaled.

"I don't. He had a certainty about himself," she sighed.

She finished the last braid, gathered them together in a bun, and secured it with a piece of leather string. He shifted and she glimpsed a dark purple gash in his right shoulder. Her breath stilled—wanting to touch it, graze her fingers against the scar, maybe slowly dig her fingers into it. Had one of the girls of Zubayd, maybe his betrothed, put a healing honey ointment on it... and thought of licking it off like she did? He was just the perfect, rock-hard body any woman would love to get lost in. He was so naturally masculine, but there was also a surprising softness to him that she wanted to mold out of him like dough.

"Any news on Shanfara? Or 'Antarah of 'Abs, for that matter?" said Khaled, and turned back to her.

She shared that, per Amr, 'Antarah likely passed through Al-Hira and made it to Taysafun.

"You think he'll make it back? I hope he does," said Khaled.

"So do I."

Tilting his head, his chin lifted while he looked at her in that exceedingly piercing, alluring way of his. Why did he have to be so handsome? Yet so was she. "Does that mean Shanfara didn't?"

"*Esh?* Why would you even say that?" she frowned. "Do you *want* him dead?"

"No, but it's like you're hesitating. Are you defending him? Is he here?" said Khaled with a flash of teasing excitement she almost didn't want to crush.

"*Aywa*; the *sayyid* of Zubayd knows my ways so well. So if you already know then what needs to be said?"

He grew somber. "What happened?"

She shook her head and sighed. "Later." One secret at a time.

She called his attention to the stones, made him turn them over, and he guessed, chuckling at their rough forms that could so easily be taken for different things.

"So what's the first thing you'll do when you get back?" said Jayida, not really sure why. He hadn't mentioned any pending marriage, but as wealthy *sayyid* that would soon change.

"Settle you in and celebrate your return, of course," he smiled. And the worst was that he reeked of honesty.

Jayida raised a playful eyebrow. "Aside from that?"

A stillness weighed between them, full of his disappointment. Even if he was the blessed *badawi* who'd often gotten his way, this time it wasn't against him, and maybe not even his father. Sometimes, there had to be something better elsewhere to call you away from one home to the next.

Khaled glanced into his hands. "I'm looking for two people," he said, visibly uncomfortable. "Maybe you might know? An Aksumite slave named Ayida and her daughter Liya."

Jayida's nose crinkled. "Your father's, of course."

He nodded. "She left without a word, and he said they headed north. I know she wasn't happy, but I just want to make sure they're safe. You haven't heard or seen anything by any chance?"

"No."

"I still have the oryx that I carved for Liya; nothing special, but I wanted to give it to her," he said, his frown wrought with conflict. He scrunched his nose and looked away.

His father... his half sister? A jolt shook through her; how bad it must've been for Ayida to want to leave. Another reminder that only few wanted to be around Moharib of the Zubayd.

"May you get the answers you seek soon," said Jayida.

After a while they leisurely returned towards camp, and took precautions in case they might be followed. Thankfully she felt safe with him, and despite the sad memory she released the morbid thought that it might repeat itself each time she came.

They went back to Wadi Al-Raha, where she stood by the cluster of lone alyssum flowers and told him of Shanfara's appearance, who'd said Nasr had summoned him there. Then how she'd left him with supplies, only to find him the next morning curled up in a bush surrounded by purslane sprouts, his previous plea to her to bury an unworthy man making final sad sense.

"And now Nasr has shared his alyssum flowers with him, too," said Khaled. She thought of replying, but maybe she would let herself get used to him often finishing her thought.

Back at camp they followed the hubbub buzzing around a new large tent near the *sayyid*'s, and spotted him waving to them.

"You're just on time! Blessed Khaled, ours won't compare to yours, but allow us to indulge you," said *sayyid* Aziz, and gestured to the temporary fighting tent already filled with a range of eager participants.

"I'll be right back," said Jayida, and lured Kamila and Adil away. She'd almost wished they'd stayed away longer because the last thing on her mind was fighting, and to her shock, she didn't even particularly want to fight him. It now seemed so pointless, like boys' games she'd indulged in too long. But curiosity called to her, and after returning the horses to their quarters, she returned to where she'd left them.

"There you are. So, will you fight him?" said Shams, appearing abruptly at her side paces away from the tent.

"No," she shrugged, putting on her best indifferent air.

"All the glory for me, again? Because I'm more than ready to," frowned Shams. He disappeared into a mass of fighting boys and men nearby, but not before Jayida caught his angry glance set in Khaled's direction.

Khaled stood steps away outside the tent, talking with Yazida who was surprisingly close to him, smiling under her cascading veil. Tall as he was, he had to lean forward, allowing Yazida to whisper into his ear. If that wasn't enough, her hand constantly grazed his arm. As if aware of her being watched, at that moment Yazida glanced in her direction, paused, and let a coy smile creep on her lips.

Jayida stifled a grunt. If the girl wasted no time, she might do the same. At once Jayida marched in their direction, happy to disrupt that scene.

"Jonder! Now that you're back, we can begin," said Khaled, straightening up.

"*Aywa*," said Jayida, and turned to Yazida. "Though I don't blame your interest, careful not to get too attached, Yazida; Khaled has a lot of men to tend to," she grinned as Khaled returned her amusement. Already he seemed disinterested in Nasr's beautiful sister.

"May the best warrior win," said Yazida, her hand once more falling upon Khaled's bulging bicep. It lingered there for a moment, and he seemed at a loss for words, nodding shyly as he looked away.

Jayida almost burst out laughing. If that's how easy it was for a woman to unsettle a man, what did she have to fear?

"We'll see you at dinner," smiled Jayida to the roaming night dancer who'd pressed her feverish lips against hers just a few nights before. Just the thought that she might try the same with Khaled made Jayida ready to remind her of Nasr's last wish for her union with Shams. Yazida nodded, glimpsed back at Khaled who smiled politely at her, and she finally vanished.

Khaled cleared his throat. "Yazida says she's been conflicted over who to marry. I'll say cousin, I'm a bit surprised you haven't remedied that," said Khaled lightly.

"Nasr thought otherwise, and I agree with him."

"Not even a little bit interested?" said Khaled with raised eyebrow.

"Are you marriage advisor to the *kahin* now?" she said. He hadn't mentioned any girl himself, and as curious as she was, it'd have to wait.

They slipped inside the tent and joined the crowded fighters who cheered at Khaled's entrance.

"As you can see, no matter what you do, our loving tribe will cheer for you," chuckled Jayida, as her father made his way to them through the crowd.

"That's reassuring, in case I get repeatedly defeated. Will you be my first opponent?" said Khaled, curiosity and reluctance in one. Her double, this time.

"Perhaps not today. I yield the honor to the others, for there'll always be another day for me to humiliate you," she said, narrowing her eyes.

"Oh! Bold! And to think, I've been deprived of this rare breed of honesty all this time," he said, pretending he was pulling out an arrow from his heart.

"Perhaps you weren't ready for it. You know; baby steps." She cocked her head, self-satisfied.

Khaled laughed heartily, lighting up his handsome face. "True. So long as you cheer for me today, then. I'm but a humble servant to your whims," he said with an exaggerated bow.

"Well said. Maybe there's some poetic merit for you after all, but let's not get carried away and stay humble," she grinned, and with amusement he rejoined the cheering men in the center.

"Good to see you and your cousin getting along great," said her father with a pat to her shoulder.

"He wanted it; he's getting it," said Jayida.

Affection glowed in her father's gentle eyes, hinting at his envious understanding of their separation since Khaled's arrival. She was still figuring things out, but she'd yet to tell him and her mother of her own changing feelings. And then—it dawned on her that surely they already knew, and were only waiting for her to bring it up. She stared into the loud swarm, full of its chaotic raised voices and fists, marveling that even it might be less frightening than romantic feelings. But to her surprise, in her mind's eye she saw herself step in it, joined by Khaled, standing before her, each free of weapons, with no audience but each other. For the first time, whatever it was—yes or no—she wanted to know.

Boys and men lined up and one by one Khaled fought them, younger men first to warm up, the chants echoing each time he won. Sometimes he let himself be overcome, cheerful as he taught them better maneuvers to protect themselves in the future. After Khaled tired a bit, his brow covered in sweat, Shams approached with a dominating frown.

"So, which one are we for," smirked her father, already knowing the answer.

"Is it that obvious," she laughed.

My brother and I against our cousin, my cousin and I against the stranger. Poor Shams. Though she'd grown up with him, this time she'd have to go against the proverb and side with Khaled against him. Was that loyalty, love, or just common sense? If Shams would have Yazida, Jayida would have Khaled. In their flustered states, only now was she starting to understand Shams's struggle with Yazida; how hard and complicated it could be to find someone who stirred feelings that might not be easily washed away, and worse, may not be returned to the same extent. To her delightful surprise, if Yazida wanted to play games, and test the different men who visited, she could have them all... except Khaled.

In the cacophony of sweaty, hot breaths, Jayida realized she was reaching her own end amongst them, easing her male burden. The truth presented itself, asking to be let out at last.

Shams and Khaled agreed on the softer, weapon-free pankration, like an Iskandar and Heracles duo ready to face-off. Even if they'd never revert to the original brutal practice of allowing everything except biting, facial gouging, and targeting the genitals, the excited tension, and even a hint of dread, swelled with unknown possibilities.

They faced each other, paced at a short distance then closed the space, aiming for each other's shoulders, and as expected, Shams struck out his fist first. Khaled ducked in avoidance and in lightning fast motion, wrapped his arms around Shams's waist, lifted him and threw him down. In an instant, they were both on the ground, and though Khaled's massive form stretched over him to pin him down, Shams squirmed, as slippery as butter.

"Khaled! Khaled! Shams! Shams!" the shouts resounded as their bodies rolled over and over on the mats like entwined vines, each taking turns for control. Jayida's throat closed, and though Shams's strength and determination impressed her, she still expected Khaled to win. Khaled wasn't showing any signs of weakness from his wounded shoulder, but then again, she wasn't the one fighting him. In a flash, Shams was atop Khaled again, had his arm and shoulder in a lock and his knee buried in his back, his flustered grimace already lighting up with triumph. Time stood still as she waited for Khaled to hurl him off and get the upper hand again, but he winced and tapped the ground fast in surrender.

In the swarming praise, a mix of relief and disappointment filled her. But when Khaled fought a few other fighters, and curiously won them all, she decided he'd let Shams win. If Khaled wanted to pacify him and let him know he wasn't a threat, the feeling was all too familiar. And yet, he didn't have to either, when their history was nothing like hers and Shams's, and to top it off, he was the honored guest. The afternoon heat swelled in the tent, and Khaled respectfully called it an end. He embraced Shams in congratulations and walked over to them, right into her father's open arms.

"Time for a well-deserved rest before dinner," said Zahir, his tone already nostalgic. They parted ways, leaving her consumed by the bittersweet feeling that at least she wasn't the only one already thinking she was going to miss him.

A while later she awoke from her nap with her brow and chest covered in nauseous sweat, leaving her more drained than refreshed. A woman's familiar voice echoed in her soul, but the more she tried to focus on the vision the blurrier it became. Jayida rinsed her face with cool water and refreshed herself for this last night with their handsomest visitor. How could she deny it? Everyday she would be thinking of him now—what he was doing, who he was with? Was he thinking of Jonder... when it should be Jayida? Before Khaled she would've never thought it would take only a few days for her world to not only turn upside down, but for the hidden part of herself to beg to finally come out.

At the campfire, she floated pensively as she listened to his recital of his love of their surroundings. Khaled praised everything: his host's generosity, Nasr's memory, his *amo*'s and cousin's friendship, and Shams's skill. He understood why they enjoyed living there, in communal harmony, and hoped to come back soon while inviting them all to Zubayd as well. It might be their final night of their first visit there, but surely not the last.

Maybe it was all the death they'd talked about earlier in the day, but she had the impression that he was trying to cheer her up. It worked in a way, and with Shams keeping close to Yazida, who surprisingly didn't seem to mind, and even returned some of his attention, Jayida relished the impression of having Khaled to herself. They could hardly be blamed for being a distant pair in the last few days, when it was a long overdue family reunion after all.

Their bellies full of fresh bread, sour buttermilk, sweet pies, and wine, they reclined when Khamra announced that Samira, Yazida, and Khaled had a surprise for them. Jayida's heart almost lodged in her throat at the sound of that, and thankfully Shams was more obvious with his angry shock, probably because his own mother was part of the plot without his knowledge. Khaled disappeared and returned with a tablah, and soon Samira and Yazida stood by him in their embroidered saffron-red dancing dresses.

Jayida summoned all her strength to quench down her frustration. Who had planned this? What else had they kept secret? But it was surely only a dance and music show in honor of their last night among them. So why did she suddenly have this pressing, unbearable need to hurry?

Samira began singing in her plaintive tone, offset by Yazida's softer pleasant sound, and the drum followed, swaying their bodies like weightless angels. Jayida's heart matched the thumping, louder and louder, and though she tried not to look she couldn't resist.

At last, in the camp she'd grown up in, there was the sight she'd often imagined but had always remained unspoken and faceless, until that moment. Of all people, it was Khaled, sitting, his skillful large hands masterfully playing the tablah drum secured between his thick thighs. There, the sight she'd never wanted to express to anyone, keeping it all to herself. Her heart exploding, she knew that this tablah player was the one to win her heart.

Intoxicated, she let herself be drawn by the undeniable pull, demanding she release her control. And she knew then that her nights were forever changed.

In some unknown late time she finally returned to her dimly-lit tent, caught between hating and wanting to be alone. Khaled had lingered so long with them around the fire that she thought he might stay up all night with them, until they sleepily said their goodnights and went their own ways.

Feverish frustration filled her and, eager for the cooling night chill, she left the front flaps of the men's quarters hanging untied and slightly open, at once grateful and conflicted by the privacy of her precious space. No one would come to her tent, and certainly not Yazida. With a rush, she defiantly tore off her headdress and tossed it aside, her messy bun of seven braids begging for caring attention. Suddenly, she mused that Khaled might've tried to help turn Yazida's attention to Shams with his defeat. She smiled dreamily at the thought of that.

Drunken love consumed her, though she'd hardly had any wine. She lit some incense to calm herself down, and set it before the entrance, the sacred scent protecting her inner sanctuary from the outside world. But it only seemed to bring him closer, the musky richness so similar to his own fumigated robes and oiled flesh...

She took off her belt and let her cloak fall down, then pulled off her *qamis* robe, coat of mail, and under layers. Finally she dropped her pants, her heart thumping under her skin and bones. Following her whim, she walked in slow circles in the room, surrounded by the leopard and lion skin, allowing herself the lightness of her weightless, uncovered flesh—exposed, yet powerful in a way she'd never considered before. All this time she'd had her own tent, and only now did she walk in it as she was born, Jayida in her full form.

Easy in her newfound pleasure, she got her scented oil and worked her way up, rubbing her legs, hips, arms, and breasts with the musky sweet blend. Then, she loosened her braids and ran her bristle brush through her long locks, over and over. She closed her eyes and slowly swayed her head, making her thick silky black hair graze against her lower back. How had she not done this before? Maybe she could be a tamer dancing girl, who instead of violently twirling her hair in the air to stir men's passion, touched and waved it gently, setting the right, reluctant yet willing heart on fire.

Her core delightfully firing, Jayida glided to the thick smoke dancing with the shy breeze, her moist naked limbs pricking up, longing for ghostly caresses. She turned a few times, inhaled the intoxicating air, then stood a few paces away from the entrance, her body facing inside.

And if someone were to appear, then and there? She'd laugh—say they'd entered the *jinniyeh* Jayida's tent, whose obviously closed sanctuary they were trespassing! And yet, an exception could be made, based on the visitor. She almost said his name but held back—in that moment, her thought sounded louder than anything she could ever say.

Jayida closed her eyes again, heard the tent walls shaking lightly, allowing an icy chill to graze her thigh like a cold blade. Lost in the vision, for a moment she thought there was a rustling just outside. She stilled, listened. Would she dare to peek, then step out, in the fullness of her fiery nakedness? She turned around and crept silently to the untied entrance. With an eye searching through the narrow glimpse of night, she held a palm up against the woolen fabric, the lioness waiting to leap out. But there was only stillness, another lonely breeze brushing against her tent, nothing else. After a few moments of painful waiting, she drowned a sigh and double tied the flaps.

With her clothes in hand she rushed to her sleeping quarters, and fell dazedly into her blankets. Burying herself with them, her searching hands kneaded into herself, her deepening breath caught between struggled silence and sound, freedom and confinement. Self-controlled, always restraining herself... But why should she, when he was everywhere, impossible to forget, imposing himself. If he wanted to visit and stand before the deity, would she refuse?

In the darkness, a heavy guttural groan approached, somewhere near her feet. It paced, rotated its weight, claws scraping against her legs, thighs, stomach, arms, breasts—so gently it hurt. She raised her legs, letting it, wanting the massive strong force to merge with hers. Gradually a steady rhythm settled over her, rattling out of her core, faster and faster.

Stifling her panting moan, Jayida finally exploded with him and saw, in the vastness of his dark innocent eyes, their melded, tormented yearning for something they'd both hardly hoped existed.

CHAPTER THIRTY-SIX

CONFESSION

In her parents' tent, Jayida chipped away at her woodblock, gradually forming into Yassu as a good shepherd. Why would Khaled want this? It would never be good enough compared to how she imagined it. Should she really betray the source of her strength, when Shamshun had suffered greatly after revealing his?

"How do people do this? Maybe it's just better to leave it as is," said Jayida, avoiding her parents' weighty, knowing gazes. How many times she'd visited them this early before, but never for this reason.

Was she expecting too much? They were the perfect combination of supportive collaboration: the wife consulted in important matters, irreplaceable in the care of the home and children, outspoken when needed, gentle yet strong in her loving care. It had seemed almost impossible before, but now that Khaled was there, Jayida could see herself sharing her own version of that with him. She might be unusual, but her manly skills would be helpful to them regardless.

Nor did she want to submit to him, or him to submit to her—or was it that they would take turns, as in the hunt? She liked his company, they enjoyed an unexpected bond, liked similar things, and a burgeoning excitement filled her to realize that a resolution she'd hardly imagined did exist, offering the person she could do it with.

At least her parents' distinct expressions of happiness reflected her own: her mother shone behind her praying hands pressed on her lips, while her father wore an emotional smile.

"I feel like I don't know what to say. And yet you both always said when it happened, I'd know," said Jayida. She stopped carving, let the knife drop.

"Oh, I hate this—this restlessness! I must be in love, because ever since he arrived I keep being emotional; especially when I think of him leaving—without knowing," she frowned, and pinched away tiny tears from the corners of her eyes.

Her mother flew at her side and wrapped her in her arms.

"Oh my beauty, we suspected as much!" said Zoraya, who gripped her face and covered it in kisses. "At last it's happened, and how fitting! Don't fear; it's natural all that you're feeling. It's just all so new to you but you'll see how beautiful it is," she said, her eager strokes soothing her.

"We're so happy for you, and to turn this story around," said her father. "Khaled has also impressed us. But why do you fret so? You've been getting on so well that I'm sure it will all be fine."

"*Sah*, even I've been surprised by his earnestness. But I know there could already be someone he's set to marry from Zubayd, though I haven't wanted to ask."

"And he hasn't hurried to mention it," Zoraya grinned.

Jayida bit her lip and cast a shy glance at them. "That's a good sign, *sah*? Oh, I feel like my heart is going to explode." She shook her head and buried her face in her hands.

"Don't torture yourself so. I know he won't be able to refuse you once he sees you, at last graced with all your feminine beauty concealed behind honorable manly skill. As I've said; you just don't know your own beauty, my love; not surprising given your situation. He'll be impressed too, once he realizes all that you've been through. Finally, it will be revealed and made clear," said her mother, looking even younger in her excitement.

"So what now?" said Jayida.

"Go on your last walk with him as Jonder, and on your return, I'll speak with his mother. You can hear it all while you're hidden behind the separator, while *yaba* keeps Khaled away," Zoraya gushed like she'd planned for this exact moment. "Oh, I just know that she'll be so pleased at the news that she'll be as honored as excited to inform Khaled and finally resolve all this."

Jayida grew somber again. "*Yaba*? Are you sure? Is it wrong; am I betraying you by falling for the son of the man who's caused you so much unhappiness?"

"Oh, my little *asad*, no. This is all long passed now, and we know Khaled didn't have anything to do with it. We both want you happy, and though we hardly expected it to be with him, it's obvious that he's a fine match for you."

"We're all surprised; he'll be surprised too, once you tell him," chuckled Jayida and took a deep breath. "And then, what will the tribe think?"

"Don't worry about that. There's a good reason for it, and remember how you've honored everyone here. So enjoy your last moments as Jonder, and your father and I will take care of the rest," said Zoraya.

"Even if we have to leave?" said Jayida before she could stop herself.

"I doubt it'll come to that, but of course, no matter what happens, we're always together," said her father.

"Don't underestimate yourself!" said her mother. "You're a success story. Oh I can't wait to tell Khamra, and they'll joyfully rush home, full of the preparations to be made for your blessed union. It'll be a big wedding, full of guests, celebration, not to forget all the verses that will be said! Your name will be greatly respected and remembered far and wide!"

Jayida wrapped the form of Yassu in a piece of undyed linen and slipped her knife in her belt.

"*Aywa*, time for my walk. Pray that I keep my nerves, and I'll see you later, then," said Jayida, and slipped out.

The sky was just beginning to lighten and she intended to walk to Nasr's grave and seek his guidance before seeing Khaled, but a knot formed in her stomach when she saw him coming her way. How could she look at him the same now, after last's night pleasurable outburst? Part of her wanted to repeat it while the other settled on guilty gratitude for having tasted its pleasure once. Her weak shame fought against what she wished, and hoped, was her version of selfish holy lust. Perhaps he even knew, and was ready to blurt it all out right then and there—just one of the many scenarios that whirled in her soul, ready to catch her off guard.

"*Sabah el-kheir!* Does the lion slayer never sleep?" Khaled said with distinct surprise. Was it her imagination or was he staring at her more than he'd done before?

"Good morning to you too, and only when necessary," she said lightly. Hopefully he was also up because he wanted to make the most of his last moments there.

"May I join you on your walk?" said Khaled.

"Sure." What else could she say? "In fact, here's your gift," said Jayida, and handed him the small bundle. Averting his gaze, she fixed on his large hands peeling off the covering, observing, rubbing, turning it in his strong hand. Too real, it was just too real.

"I'm grateful that you would devote your time to this, in the midst of everything," he said with a playful glint in his eye.

"Seems my *qareen* visited and decided I couldn't let you return home without some protection," she smirked and picked up pace, and he fell right in step.

"Mmm, if only I could've seen that." His chin lowered coyly.

"Something amusing you?" said Jayida with arched brow. They'd been walking so fast that already Nasr's grave beckoned from the distance.

"I guess I failed you, cousin. I thought I'd earned your trust, that you'd confide in me," he shrugged. "I realize that it will take time. I'm just genuinely curious who she is, that's all." He paced with his hand still clasped around Yassu, his glance to the floor like some contemplative *mubassir*.

Her frown deepened. "What are you talking about?"

"Last night I came by your tent and—I didn't mean to, but I saw someone. I must say, I envy you," he said with an air of embarrassment.

She stopped walking. "Envy me?"

So it hadn't been her imagination: he *had* seen her! Her blood throbbed in her throat, and she was sure her heart would finally burst through her chest, to explode and splatter all over him, as well it should after all these years of mounting stress. He'd stopped, too, but stood a few paces away.

"Who wouldn't? For you to possess such a beautiful woman in your tent. Although I'll admit I'm surprised that you haven't mentioned it at all. But I keep forgetting that you still see me as a stranger. If you're to be wed, I wish you all the blessings and happiness," he said almost shyly.

She wanted to scream, the whirl caught in her chest threatening to shatter through the veil of her indifferent air. She wasn't sure if she was relieved or even more frustrated that he still hadn't come to the truth.

"No wedding," she said flatly, and resumed her fast pace. "And what were you coming by my tent for, anyway?" she added with feigned lightness. He might not be very experienced with women, but it didn't mean he had unnatural interests... Just the thought was another stab in her poor, erratic heart.

"To talk, in case you weren't tired, and to thank you overall," he said, now closer to her and looking at her. His gaze bore into her, and her body boiled all over again, recalling the allure of his consuming essence in her passionate rush.

They came closer to Nasr's grave, and she silently thanked him for his help in keeping her demeanor fixed in self-control. An odd relief washed over her, thinking of Khaled's departure. As much as she'd enjoyed his visit, she was tired of the misunderstandings.

"Please, don't be mad. I didn't mean to pry; I respect you and your woman's honor and privacy. I swear I'm no peeping Imru! If it's any reassurance, I didn't see her face," he said with a sincere hint of regret. He was so genuinely remorseful that there was no doubting him. He'd seen her, and yet he hadn't.

She shook her head, and her shoulders relaxed.

"I'm not mad." She might've kept a step ahead of him, but now they were both at a loss. Absurd, it was all just so absurd—and a little hilarious.

"Seems like sleep eluded us both," sighed Khaled, and he looked so relieved that she struggled not to jump on him and lavish him with kisses of forgiveness.

"Let's just forget it," said Jayida, and turned her attention to Nasr's grave. "May he guide you on a safe journey home," she said.

"And with this, I know we will be," said Khaled, and added the form of Yassu into his waist pouch.

"Which reminds me: my father mentioned a *solidus* coin that he'd had as a child growing up with your father. He hasn't had it in years and it's probably lost somewhere, but I wanted to check if you or perhaps your mother might've seen it?"

"Wish I had; I would've gladly brought it along otherwise. But I'll check and ask my mother and others, just in case," said Khaled.

Jayida nodded and considered showing him the *solidus* from the anonymous treasure of Wadi Al-Qura, but decided against it. There was enough happening as it was, and even if it was base selfishness, she wished to keep it for herself a little longer. The perfect stillness that needed no words or explanation overcame them again, and her heart ached, yearning to reach out and touch him.

"Maybe you can keep me in your thoughts and prayers, as wicked as I am. I know, you probably already know, but confessing is its own release," said Khaled. His tone had changed now, cold and distant, and she almost flinched, hating to think it was his father's influence. She stood still, not wanting to break the moment.

"I had no remorse—it still surprises me. No, it was a release when he died, and I challenged him! But the worst of it is that he didn't even... react. No sign, no appearance, nothing! How can that be? I half expected him to return a moment later, stomping in a new body, animal, human, or spirit, snarling, *Did you think it would be that easy*? And I hear it sometimes, but I don't know if it's my imagination, him, or something else. *Majnun*, eh?" he chuckled, but there was only sadness in it.

"You're mourning. It'll be a while," said Jayida.

"I'm trying to recall his good qualities. I know life's not easy, but men like your father and *sayyid* Aziz are different. Sometimes I try to tell myself that he was being cruel out of protectiveness, but it's no excuse for how he treated your father, and us. Like he couldn't tell friend from enemy. It's just one of the many reasons that makes me think I'll never forgive him. At least—do you think he's at finally at peace?" said Khaled.

Jayida looked away, sensing his yearning for answers. She didn't see how death would automatically transform a personality. It seemed too easy a way out, and there was a satisfaction to imagining that beyond the veil people might be the same, or maybe even slightly amplified in their leanings, good or bad. She disliked Moharib, even in death, as she did the likes of Badr and Al-Mundhir, but thankfully, even miraculously, these feelings were not transferred to his son. On the contrary, the intensity that each of them stirred were opposites, and though Khaled was still a new acquaintance and she couldn't quite explain it, there was relief to silently confessing it before her childhood friend's grave. Not unlike Khaled with his father, she now half hoped Nasr would emerge on the spot and reveal the truth she was scared to admit herself, even as she doubted it would happen. It only deepened her budding love for Khaled, to see him struggle to understand and forgive his father, despite everything.

"I don't know if he's at peace, and I'm glad that it's not in our hands," said Jayida, and saw him nod from the corner of her eye.

"*Kahin* Jonder, I will always count on you to tell the truth," said Khaled.

Except now it would be as *kahina* Jayida, she mused as they returned quietly to camp. Her father met them upon their return, and lured Khaled away to the *sayyid*'s tent. She snuck into her parents' dwelling, where her mother hurried her to the back to change into a heavenly scented dress from Najran with matching headdress. Her mother brushed her hair and set a thick cluster of it at each side of her face.

"Come, come!" said Zoraya, and urged her up. "You are a vision!" she cooed, and smothered her face in kisses.

How lightly Jayida moved in such few layers! How her headdress stretched around her like a pair of wings! Even her soft thick hair seemed to bounce happily with each movement, ready to prove her worthy femininity. Her mother dabbed some more scented oil on her earlobes, nose, and wrists, and stood back, smiling and tearful at once.

"Just perfect. Now I'm off to get her, so just wait here."

Jayida nodded and sat down. Then rose. Moments passed like days and she paced back and forth, wringing her hands. She might be a vision indeed, but she wouldn't be reassured until she heard Khaled's answer. She took a deep breath. What was there to fear? Her father would explain it all to *sayyid* Aziz after Khaled saw her as Jayida, and the proposal was done. Why shouldn't it be as simple as it sounded, when she was the same person, even if she was really a woman. What was taking so long? If only her mother and Khamra would hurry back already.

A few moments later, warm gentle voices resounded, confirming their return. Jayida's heart shook and she forced herself into feigned stillness by sitting close to the separator. Sitting with her knees tucked under her, she closed her eyes, willing herself to release all her fears. It would all go well. She was Jayida, known as Jonder, honorable daughter of Zahir and Zoraya.

As her mother poured fresh buttermilk into two cups, Jayida sent her floods of gratitude for her saintly patience in leading this unusual conversation.

"Blessed Khamra, before you return home, I must tell you again how your visit has brought us great joy, and what a blessing it is to have rekindled our friendship."

Cautiously, Jayida peeked through a space in the woven separator. Their feminine shapes wrapped in undyed linen robes made a disarming scene, like beholding two gazelles gently grazing in a peaceful green field.

Khamra smiled, the creases at the corner of her eyes stretching. Though she was still an undeniable beauty, her sadness had aged her. A protective tenderness emerged at this impression of the woman who'd borne Khaled, whose husband had so impacted her, and whose son Jayida now loved. But with his departure all the pieces were coming together for this strangely delightful meeting.

"*Aywa*, the same for us. I can hardly believe how long it's been, and how grown they are. Oh, the times Khaled wanted to be here," said Khamra, shaking her head.

"We're thankful Khaled took the initiative to bring you both here, after all this time."

"I was so worried you might be upset, with the way Moharib could be and his long absence," paused Khamra. "Are you sure you don't want to come back with us? I've always seen you as a sister, so I can tell you freely that I don't miss him; *al-ilah* forgive me if I say it's even a relief," sighed Khamra. "I'd be less lonely with you there."

Zoraya pinched a smile in pained understanding, and reached out her hand to Khamra's. "You'll always have my friendship, and Khaled's generous soul will always protect and take care of you. The rest already feels long forgotten. In fact, I'd like to share with you some good news, which I'm sure will make you so happy, as well as your son."

"Tell me," said Khamra.

"*Aywa*, there is here the perfect woman for him. In fact, the one most deserving of him, out of all the women in the land," said Zoraya.

Jayida froze, felt her heart rise to her throat. That's what it felt like to say goodbye.

"*Esh?* And who might this be?" said Khamra, her cautious enthusiasm lighting her up.

Zoraya leaned towards Khamra, full of unwavering strength. "My blessed sister in spirit, it's none other than our daughter Jayida."

There was such complete stillness that for a moment Jayida was sure she was dreaming and would awaken at any moment.

Khamra stared. "Your daughter? How can this be? Why have we not met her yet?"

Jayida's nostrils flared, trying not to take that as a hint of accusation in her tone.

"Unfortunately, the source is none other than your husband," said her mother, and Khamra appeared thunderstruck, a guilty gazelle caught off guard. "Did he ever tell you why we left?"

Khamra's shoulders slightly rose and fell. "Only that you were ungrateful, which I never understood or agreed with," she quickly added.

Zoraya chuckled. "You see, Moharib made the ultimate insult on the man least worthy of it. He threatened his future by suggesting Zahir may never have any sons. After everything else, Zahir had had enough of Moharib's evil eyeing. He was so concerned when we left, but he didn't know of the pregnancy until after our departure. I'd had signs of it before, but I wanted to wait. I myself didn't mind the idea of starting anew somewhere else, so I waited until then to tell him."

Jayida's jaw clenched, recalling the details that led to that most fateful decision that had dictated her life so far.

"It was his wise idea that if we had a daughter we'd raise her as a boy, for her safety and glory. So you have met her, for the person you know as Jonder is actually our daughter Jayida," said Zoraya with her loveliest proud smile.

Khamra's doe eyes widened. "But how? I've seen Jonder—although briefly, since he and Khaled have been gone—and he looks like any able fighter and tribesman, even if he is smaller than Khaled."

"*Sah*, and most men are smaller than Khaled, regardless," laughed her mother. "But words are meaningless if not supported by truth. So please, you have only to see for yourself."

"*Aywa.* By *al-ilah*; all this time? And all these stories, these brave achievements? Some will say it's unnatural, but in the circumstances, only more impressive. How strong—it must've not been easy for her," said Khamra on the verge of tears.

Oddly, Jayida had the sense that she'd been as wrong about Khaled as she'd been about his mother.

Khamra gripped Zoraya's hands. "So then, may I meet Jayida?"

"Of course. It's our hope and wish for you to report on all her endearing qualities to Khaled, some of which they already share," said Zoraya. "Jayida, please come and join us."

Her whole body throbbing, Jayida rose, passed her hands over her dress, hair, and veil in final adjustment. There was no turning back now, and with a deep breath, she stepped from behind the curtain.

Her mother beamed as she glanced back and forth between her daughter and Khamra. Any lingering doubts Jayida had now dissipated as she saw the truth of her mother's words in Khamra's marveled gaze. Without a word, Khamra rose and approached her, circling around and looking at her up and down in fascination.

"By *al-ilah*! I've seen many young beauties, and Khaled is rather picky. And yet, now, with such combination—" said Khamra.

Jayida bit her lip, a shyness overcoming her, unused to such blatant scrutiny of her now openly feminine qualities.

"Jayida it is! Certainly slimmer, with a striking face and fine shape without all the layers of clothing and armor," nodded Khamra. "With such beauty and skill, Khaled will be the most honored of all men in the land to have you for his wife. Praise *al-ilah* we are both blessed with such children," Khamra smiled at them both.

"*Sah*; we did well with what we were given," grinned her mother.

"There's no time to waste, I'll tell him right away," said Khamra, beaming with hope. "Finally, a fine match to be made, and we'll be a family again."

Khamra made for the exit, glanced back at them again then left, her gentle steps rushing to Khaled the way Jayida longed to do.

CHAPTER THIRTY-SEVEN

SLIGHTED

Back alone in the guest tent, Khaled gazed at the oryx and Yassu forms in his hands, wondering where Jonder had gone. He'd reluctantly excused himself from his *amo* Zahir to have a few moments alone, lest he break down and beg him to just come with them for an overdue reunion, after which he could then return to the Sa'd—if he still wanted to. For his plan was that they'd be so touched by his genuine care that they'd just decide to stay. Time alone didn't dissolve family bonds, did it?

Khaled packed away the forms and glimpsed at their packed belongings in bittersweet conflict. Despite the feeling of being at home in many places, it sometimes didn't feel any easier to leave. But even without his family's return, their bond had been rekindled, and he certainly had much to share with Majid and the tribe.

"Khaled, Khaled, Khaled!" his mother's panting broke through his contemplation, and she appeared at the entrance, nearly out of breath.

"What is it?" he said, as confused as amused by her elation.

"Oh, my son! I have the most marvelous news for you," she said, rushing to his side. "Khaled, the jewel of my eye: I have found you your wife!" she said with a dreaminess he'd never seen.

"Oh, *yama*, no need to make up stories just to extend your stay," he laughed.

"No, no; you say that now, but it's only because you haven't seen her yet," said Khamra, pressing his cheeks over and over. "And the best part—do you want to know the best part?" Her eyes playfully narrowed. What had gotten into her? She hadn't seemed this happy since he'd returned from trekking north. His brow creased in amused confusion, waiting for her elaboration.

"It's your uncle Zahir's daughter, Jayida!" she blurted, her hands locking at his wrists.

"*Esh?* Zahir's *daughter*? What are you talking about?" he chuckled.

"Trust me, my heart! At last here's the chance for you to be so happy! And you already know her! For your cousin whom you know as Jonder is actually Jayida! What an accomplishment! I know how you've been enjoying your time with him, I mean her, and by *al-ilah*, you must believe me when I say she's the most beautiful young woman I've ever seen! Come, you must see for yourself!" she said, pulling at him. She was so insistent that for a moment he almost didn't recognize her. Was she so blinded by her wish for him to marry that she couldn't see that none of what she said made sense?

"So you're saying that—no. It can't be," Khaled shook his head. "I've spent all this time with Jonder, and he's a man. A handsome man, but a man. He's self-controlled, with a distant manner and serious air—sometimes I thought too serious, even more than Majid—but that's surely part of being *kahin* and his mastery of *hilm*."

His mother shook her head.

"Khaled, my love, listen to me: these are the best news you could have! You have a beautiful woman who loves you, who's skilled in manly arts, has a great reputation, and is from a good family—what more could you ask for? It's your dream come true!"

"My dream come true? It's *your* dream come true, and everyone else's, and I'm tired of hearing about it!" he yelled. He couldn't tell if he was more shocked or annoyed by the news. "This is madness! Some *jinni* must have gotten into them! My uncle had a daughter and raised her as a boy? Let me guess: for the glory of his name, surely! And all this time since we've been here, they've lied to us? And to everyone else, unless they're in on it, too? I know; you say you saw her. But what exactly did you see?" said Khaled.

"Her, in her woman's attire; it makes all the difference, come—" she pleaded.

"Oh *yama*, is that it? Is it really that easy? My kind mother, how could you be so easily fooled? I mean no judgment by this, but now—I suspect she must have some defect they've hidden well, maybe even several," he said, and pinched the bridge of his nose.

He hadn't given it much thought, but it suddenly made more sense. That had to be why she hadn't hunted with them or fought him in the fighter tent. Here he'd been, opening up to Jonder, when all along she was keeping her own secrets. He couldn't help but second-guess their time together, and all the heroic stories. How was he to know what was real, when she'd been so easily lying to his face?

Marriage—ha! He'd finally been released from his father's stifling rule, only to be lured to this other form of bondage with this deceiving two-faced person who claimed to love him. And he was supposed to pretend and go along with it, risk all he had when just the previous night she'd had at least one other woman in her tent? The flatness of her response when he'd asked her about it the next day; indifferent, but without qualms about putting others' services to her unnatural use... A deep disgust unlike any he'd ever known filled him, when it looked like more of women's manipulative wiles he wanted nothing to do with.

"Khaled, please, just come with me," said his mother, her persistent tugging of his hands nearly breaking his heart.

"*Yama*, please stop," he said, holding her shoulders as she stared. "That's enough. I've come here to find honest friendship and bond with my cousin, and now there's this silly charade. I'm *sayyid* now; I'd expect her to understand that most of all. I'm sure she's just having passing feelings, and at least all this will be forgotten soon enough. As for me, I'm going home right this moment. Tell them what you want, even that I'd forgotten some urgent business and I had to go. I'll slow down once camp is out of sight and wait for you," said Khaled.

He gathered his bundles and without another glance, left the tent.

❧❧❧❧❧❧ ❧❧❧❧❧❧

"What's taking so long?" said Jayida, wishing she could stop pacing. "It doesn't take that long to reveal the news!"

"My heart, I'm sure it's coming to it," said her mother. There was a rustle and they held their breath as her father entered.

"She's coming," he said, and Jayida had the unnerving impression that he wanted to say something else. He stood aside and moments later, Khamra appeared.

"There you are," smiled Zoraya. "Where's Khaled?"

Khamra bit her lip, wrung her hands. "Beautiful Jayida, I'm sorry. Just give him some time."

Her mother's brow twitched. "All the same, surely he should see her before leaving," said Zoraya with controlled confusion.

"That is... he left," said Khamra, looking downcast. Zahir winced, and passed a hand through his beard.

Jayida's eyes narrowed. "He *left*? Without even a word?"

"But why?" echoed her shocked mother.

451

"Oh, my blessed beauty," said Khamra, approaching Jayida. "You know men; let him come around, surely he'll realize his error. He must," she said, as Jayida looked away. "I'm so sorry. Jayida, please know I won't stop praising you to him. I thank you for your hospitality, and must get home. I hope we will see you again, soon," said Khamra, glancing sadly back and forth at her parents.

None of it made sense, and Jayida had the gnawing impression of being at a standstill. But the arrow was cast and so much had not been stirred up only to remain without closure. Her mother silently handed Khamra wrapped bundles of food, and with a last parting conflicted glance, Khamra left.

"I'd hoped I was wrong, but that confirms it was him I saw riding off. Regardless, if he's so stupid, then he doesn't deserve you," said her father, opening his arms to her. She fell into his embrace, and caught her mother's upset air.

"He'll have a lot to answer for, the next time we see him," said Zoraya.

"I feel like I did something wrong and I don't even know what it is," said Jayida.

"You did nothing wrong," said her father. "I don't understand it. If he'd only come he would've reacted differently. Now, I haven't yet told *sayyid* Aziz or anyone, although since the guests quickly left, I suppose I will soon. What do you think?"

"Can they be trusted? Can anyone in that family be trusted?" sneered Jayida. "I would rather it comes from you than they hear it from anyone else, as though we're ashamed. As for these clothes, they can wait a bit longer yet."

Jayida disappeared behind the separator and quickly discarded her new dress for Jonder's clothing, welcoming the chainmail's protective weight. She tied her hair in a long bun, and tucked it in her headdress, as if in a daze, hardly aware of her movements but knowing exactly what she was doing.

With her parents' unwavering supporting airs, she slipped back to her tent, trying to gather herself in her blur of emotions. How could he refuse her? Where had she gone wrong, when his eagerness for Jonder's friendship was more than she could've imagined?

Unnatural.

If he thought that of Jayida, what was she to think of him, with his world filled strictly with men except for his mother? At least for her case it had all been a response to his father's perpetual evil-eyeing. What was his explanation, except his own escapist selfishness?

And then it hit her.

In his ignorance he might've not been fully aware of his own doing, but the end was the same. It was too much; she'd initially thought so herself. Too much emotion, confessing, opening up, too much to be genuine. It was an act, meant to trap her into doing the same, so that *al-'ayn*, inherited from his father, could discover her weakness and put an end to her strength.

How could she have been so foolish? She kept giving people chances, as she had with Badr, and they kept revealing who they truly were, so different from their appearance and what she wished them to be. She had two names, and yet she was more honest than so many others in existence who hid behind one.

She buried her hammering head in her hands. Suffocating darkness clouded her thoughts, unearthing memories from 'Ukaz and the pilgrimage.

I beg you, have mercy!

She'd heard the wail long before, and again just the previous day! So why hadn't she paid attention? Wrong, how wrong she'd been! Ignoring it and for what? For him?! But she would make him pay. She fell to her knees at the sickening desperation, her clasped hands begging for forgiveness.

There was a *jinni*, maybe more, and whether it was Moharib's, Badr's, Sahira's, Khaled's or any other deceitful combination, it didn't really matter. And if he was repulsed, filled with contempt enough to disrespect her, leaving without a word of explanation—after all his own streams of unexpected, emotional confessions, and *he* was the man!—what did that make him? Letting his mother do the work for him! Too afraid to face her: a mere woman, too!

I beg you, have mercy!

The deafening cry consumed her, and she doubled over in sobbing pain.

"Forgive me for not hearing!" Jayida cried out in her soul, hating the ugly truth. She rocked back and forth, the torrent coming and going.

Guilty, guilty!

The audacity of his disrespect, when he was no better than his father; a mere little boy claiming to evade his shadow, when his merged right with it.

The day elapsed in a blur, and when she eventually stirred, she had no appetite and thought of nothing else but to shift the situation back in her favor. A tiny, nearly invisible spark struck in the unlit, pitch-black tent, reviving her.

"My heart, won't you come eat with us? You need to maintain your strength. We've told them you're not feeling well, so no one will be barging in."

Her mother's concern broke through her thoughts, checking on her in the evening.

"Don't worry, *yama*, I've never felt better. No fear, everything is as it should be," said Jayida, lost in a trance.

Though Jayida evaded the inquiring gaze, through it she sensed both her parents' well wishes that always covered her like wings. Zoraya lit fresh incense and retreated like an all-knowing angel, leaving the sizzling smoke to bless and restore her aching soul.

Alone again, Jayida gathered weapons and satchels, and changed into her new raven robes from 'Ukaz. In the pitch night, she'd sneak out with Al-Wasiyah at her waist, and take one of her father's unbranded, consecrated camels for the journey north to Tayma.

If Khaled thought that he could just run away, and go on with life as though nothing had happened—as if he had the final say—she would show him.

CHAPTER THIRTY-EIGHT

TAYMA

BANU ZUBAYD - TAYMA

Hovering in the stone grey dawn, Jayida fixed darkly on the horizon, the wall surrounding Tayma beckoning to her through her ebony face covering. A shadowy, patchy light and dark castle rose to the west, none other than Samaw'al's. Perhaps after it was done, she'd pay a visit to the half-Israelite warrior-poet and recite of her own achievement in regards to Khaled. Amidst all the other accounts he'd surely hear, at least that would be the one straight from her own lips.

Sah, I'm in your land now. But it was never just yours!

She smirked, the undying flame firing through her all over again as she trotted ahead.

Time had passed like a whirling night vision since she'd left the Banu Sa'd, her restlessness shunning sleep to push on right past runaway Khaled and his mother. With young and obedient Asifa, they'd flown right through Wadi Al-Qura, that valley of villages with its lion tombs protectively looking down at her from the cliffs.

At Hijr, the massive elephant shape of Jabal Al-Fil had welcomed her like one of *Negus* Kaleb's mammoth mounts storming into Zafar, San'a, and Najran to avenge the Yassu-loving slain at the hands of Dhu Nuwas. Then, she'd bolted straight to the largest nearby form, and glanced up at the unfinished yet proud towering tomb, reminding herself, Nasr, and the past and present *jinn* that it was where her mother had revealed her pregnancy to her father. Though the tomb was linked to the one good memory her father had of Moharib, now it would be part of her story with Khaled too. She'd never imagined her first visit would be alone and under such wrongful circumstances, but the unshakeable strength fueled by the valley's palpable silence left little room for lamenting.

They'd continued, riding nearly nonstop without light and only making a small fire in secluded places, and evaded the camps of Banu Mudar and Thalaba. Not even two days had passed, and now they could rest at camp until unsuspecting Khaled arrived.

A lot of death here, but it's you who's always been most afraid!

She sneered at Moharib, despising his jealous fear of their success that had kept him at bay. Did he even know now who was approaching, when Jonder-Jayida's face had been covered the whole way? Had his sight sharpened somehow in the beyond, or was he still trapped and blinded by his hate?

Pride swelled her chest, satisfied that if anyone had glimpsed her on the way, they'd be as curious as hesitant about the mysterious rider—just as she planned. But they'd have to wait for it, and now the new *sayyid* would get a taste of it, too.

Her hot breath radiated all over her covered face, drawing the dark fabric of her headdress on and off against her lips. And if his whole tribe was like him? But who was to say she wasn't strong enough to convert them to her side, when the wrong was his!

She summoned her *qareen*, stretched and draped its shape like a veil over the oasis, making it circumambulate from east to west around it seven times. Then she launched imaginary arrows at the Zubaydi tribesmen, catching them off guard and daring them to come charging at her. Let them underestimate this strange concealed rider—soon they'd know him as the one who sees through dark and light when too few could properly do either one.

Jayida reached camp and dismounted, Al-Wasiyah concealed in a different scabbard at her hip. At once she sensed the curious glances, lingering with a mix of surprised confusion and challenge. Some even stood back, as a young guard did a double-take at her, trying in vain to find her gaze through her veil. It was just as pleasing if she might look like a *jinni* made of Khaybar tar come to life or a Holy Rider from the holy *injil*.

The guard cleared his throat. "Where do you come from?" he said, trying to sound tough.

"From *al-ilah*, of course," said Jayida, feigning a deeper tone. The guard's brow twitched in a frown, more nervous than amused. "I've heard there's a new *sayyid*, and I'd like to pay my respects and witness his great fighting." She slightly lowered her head in respect, but apparently no matter what she did would look odd—yet another welcomed benefit.

"*Sah.* Just a moment."

He vanished and returned with an older white-bearded man at his side, tall and thin, and wrapped in his timeless air of wisdom.

"Welcome, traveler," said *sha'ir* Hakim, fixing somewhere around her eyes. He who'd lived through so much; would he recognize her?

"Bless the journey that brought me to your generous camp," she said. It'd been five springs since she'd seen him, but he looked the same sturdy pillar, though maybe even better with Moharib's absence.

"Come with me," said *sha'ir* Hakim.

They walked through camp and passed the Haddaj well, as *sha'ir* Hakim took occasional side glances at her, his bright eyes lit with cautious curiosity. All the better. If she could have that effect on someone she knew, even if barely, she couldn't wait to see the impact on others.

"We hope this tent will satisfy you. The fighting tents are near, and we are at your service," he said.

"Bless your kindness, and I look forward to meeting the *sayyid*," said Jayida.

Sha'ir Hakim pinched a smile and left her, his silence on Khaled hint enough of his absence, even if she didn't already know of his whereabouts. She reclined inside with Asifa, her smaller body posing no trouble amidst the large, high-pitched tent. The weight of exhausted relief overtook Jayida, and she allowed herself a well-earned rejuvenating nap.

I beg you, have mercy!

Jayida awoke in the late afternoon, draining voices painfully crying out in her soul. She wondered how anyone could sleep there, and she comforted herself that she only had to wait a bit for Khaled to reappear. Only let all this horror strengthen her when needed!

She went to the fighting tents, engulfed in the echoing shouts emanating from around the fighters at the center. Reeking of sweat, this smaller version of a market made her grateful for her own pleasant odor. Attendees and fighters young and old circulated and filled the space, from tribes near and far.

Eyes turned to her, dark and light following her, whispering, frowning, trying to gage her faceless and compact frame hidden in black clothing. Some feigned indifference, stroking their beards, crossing their arms even as they straightened themselves to reinforce their taller, stouter statures.

Overgrown babies, that's what they were. Except maybe a few, and though she sensed one such gaze on her, hidden in the crowd, she did not seek it out.

"My five-year old brother can do better than this!" a shout resonated.

"Is this all you've got? Still, lucky for you to be learning here!" laughed another.

"Say, mysterious one, why don't you step in?" said a man, and she turned to the weighty source. The contender was a short, stout man wrapped in faded clothing, with gaps in his teeth, and given how exhausted he looked, she nearly asked if he was joking.

"*Aywa*, you asked for it," said Jayida huskily, to communal amusement. She stepped into the center, and faced the man holding up his fists, amused at his wide protruding stomach that rivaled a camel's.

"I'll snap you in half!" he sneered, offended.

"So then do it! As for you, can we play drums on that thing you call a stomach? I think I'll try," she said, to resounding laughter. They paced around each other, and Jayida let him throw the first punch, and easily avoided the blow. He kept up the same predictable tactic and he grew so frustrated that she let him strike her, barely grazing her lower back.

"My hand!" he said, shaking his fist after the impact. "What sorcery is this, with your covered flesh!"

"Oh, just some things called skill and the right armor!" she laughed. Though he had a strong punch, his panting suggested he didn't have much energy left. She taunted him, punching him in the protruding gut each time he reached for her and missed. In his tired eagerness he lunged forward so abruptly he lost his balance, and she helped along by tripping him. He fell flat down and she swooped on him from behind and held him in a chokehold, until he quickly tapped out in surrender.

"Nice warm up. So, who's next?" said Jayida.

Fiery stares set on her, and contenders stepped up. One after the other she defeated them: tall, short, skinny, fat, muscular, young, old, and even the one who claimed he was the best after Majid and Khaled. Though the fight was the longest by far, she finished by knocking the wind out of him.

She was surprised and almost disappointed that he seemed to be moving so slowly—until she realized it had to be her long pent up, constrained power bursting out in the midst of fighting. Just like holding off on the sacred act of creating life only made it more likely to succeed—and even as she'd been wrong to think she'd want to do it with Khaled—she relished this guided release of zealous vitality.

Her clothes melded into her flesh as sweat poured down her hidden face, and she paced herself, sucking in all the swarming living breath into herself. An endless burst of power blasted through her, and she realized that she might never get enough, not even after she faced Khaled. If this was what she had to deal with, it was laughable at best.

"But how can this be? It's like he knows what their next move will be!" someone marveled.

"Half human," chuckled another, too concerned to complete the disturbing thought.

The space around her widened with emptiness, fighters standing back and second guessing. Clustered men whispered, spreading the word that this unusual veiled fighter—possibly Hijazi, Fars, Himyarite, or maybe even Indian or from far-off China—was defeating everyone.

"*Esh*; is there no one else willing?" laughed Jayida. She looked around, and saw some turn away to limit contact, until she finally found the one lingering on her. The bearded, serious robust man with his arms crossed had to be Majid. He stared at her as if lost in thought, and she recalled Khaled's guess that they would get along.

"If he can endure that long and still stand, he deserves his praise," one whispered.

"How hasty you are! Our Khaled will surely defeat him in a second," loudly huffed another.

"*Aywa*, where is he, then?" said Jayida.

But to her shock, Majid reminded them that it was already very late, so he invited them to retire for the night until the next day. Some feigned reluctance to leave, but she was the last one there, reeling in her unrelenting thirst for justice for later use. If some were relieved by the excuse of night, surely others worried, leaving them sleepless with the stranger in their midst. Either way, it all worked to her advantage. She spent most of the night lighting incense and calling on Nasr, Mikha'il, Yassu, Shamshun, and her princess guardian to help her punish the wrong, and free her father's name from blame.

The next afternoon a boy announced himself at her tent.

"Brave soldier, Khaled wishes the honor to fight you," he said.

"I'll see him there," said Jayida, restraining a sneer. Three days to make him face her, because she wasn't about to wait seventeen years or more for permission.

At the fighting tent monitored by Majid, and with all eyes glued on them, even *sha'ir* Hakim's, Khaled wore that same feigned light playfulness that she couldn't wait to slap off his face. It wouldn't work this time, and finally everyone, maybe even any of his foolish fawning girls, would see, or at least hear of him going down.

Khaled glanced at her with an intense, searching glint in his eyes, and looked away as if thinking of what to say. Without a word he tossed his cloak aside. Poised in full *hilm*, she would not just lunge at him, as much as he deserved it. If he wouldn't inquire of her identity and welcome her, everyone would know it soon enough, and then he'd hate himself for the rest of his life for having brought about this situation.

Jayida followed his silent lead and they laid their swords aside and positioned themselves. His massive body crouched and he began to pace, as she mirrored his movements. He came close and struck first, lazily, and she ducked, slapping him so fast that his face turned aside and a loud gasp swept through the crowd.

"Like lightning!" said someone.

Khaled bit his lower lip, the odd look on his face like he'd enjoyed it. Fine with her.

All of a sudden, Khaled lunged at her and they fell to the ground, and she squirmed and kicked wildly to keep her side exposed, anything to avoid being overcome by his large frame. His hands searched for her wrists, aiming to pin them down. For a moment she could hardly breathe and all she saw was a dark, ghoulish mass—grotesque vulture eyes, mouth drooling with black lava, his wings stretching, burying, suffocating—and she thrashed so violently that she thought her rattling bones would break against him and the hard carpeted floor. With her free hand she punched his side repeatedly, her jerking knee finally reaching into his groin, sending him rolling over in pain.

She fell on him in a chokehold, his nostrils flaring and face turning red.

You see: now I have you both! Her soul screamed, as much to Moharib as to his offspring. Enraged triumph intoxicated her, until he swiftly reached over and threw her aside, the cycle of domination repeating over and over. She grunted, as confused as annoyed by his ease of manner that hinted he wasn't using all his force.

How dare he! If he thought he needed to go easy on her, she was far from done. She wouldn't fall for this, surely one of his tricks to endear himself to his opponent. Wasn't he embarrassed, to try to get by with only doing the minimum? The memory of Shams defeating him urged her on, and she redoubled her efforts, punching, smacking, pushing, kicking, taking her own hits in turn. She was an endless well, drawing forth on the insatiable power of *jahl* she'd first unleashed the previous day. Only his surrender would end it! But to her mounting frustration, she soon had to admit that defeating him wouldn't be as easy as she'd expected.

To break up their deadlock, Majid called for a break and suggested they switch to sword fighting, recharging the air with eager excitement. Jayida grinned in her sweaty darkness, when she couldn't have asked for better. While she could've aimed for his shoulder much earlier, she'd no need to resort to cheap tricks and possibly betray herself in the process. This story would live on, and at least with multiple witnesses to the event.

In their pause the young boy returned to her with a water skin, and handed it to her in respectful amazement. His eyes widened as she shook her head. She wouldn't drink until it was over, and when she declined again and he finally confusedly relented, the awestruck gazes that came her way were all the refueling she needed.

At last they retrieved their swords and instantly struck at each other, each swipe and pass hitting air or slicing layers of clothing, but missing the flesh. The more time passed and they matched in skill, with neither gaining ground, the quieter the audience became and the tribe's concern mounted.

How was it that Khaled was so matched by someone else?—the whispers and frowns questioned, praise and shocked confusion competing.

As Khaled panted and adjusted his gait, Jayida caught his deep conflicted sadness, revealing a hidden turmoil so unlike his light manner. Enough with the moping, especially from the little boy who ran from her and marriage! He loved fighting, so then let him be a man and fight!—her soul commanded him. But she realized that to him and the tribe, such was their beloved *sayyid*'s way, a spectacle never seen from Moharib—but a spectacle no less. Amidst the constant fighting, Khaled was unmistakably tiring, but even she had to concede that he wasn't relenting.

They hovered, suspended in time, as if waiting to see how things would magically change. In the crowd she found the attentive, handsome young man about her age, whose resemblance to Samaw'al suggested his son Hassan. In contrast, a draining, invasive weight seemed to tug at her, and she caught an almond-eyed beauty clad in a red-purple dress, smirking at her in teasing curiosity. That had to be one of the most calculating, cruel Zubaydi beauties vying for Khaled, whose ensnaring manipulations hovered around her like shadowy tentacles. Perhaps that was the type he should marry, and was only avoiding glancing at her and drawing from her dark charms because he didn't want to look embarrassed in front of this mysterious fighter.

Disgust sickened Jayida at the thought of being trapped in that endless tunnel of deception with him, with little variation of lies and suffering. His father was gone, and she'd made her point, even if it wasn't as she'd wanted. Either way, she was done living with these ghosts.

In the stirring commotion, Majid came forth and announced that no clear winner could be determined, sending the whispers spreading like wildfire.

She cast Khaled a last glance as he wiped his brow in a contemplative air, resolved that if she couldn't defeat him, the perplexed looks and the doubt stirred among the tribe were enough to do the rest.

Jayida rushed to her tent, raging to flee the place at once.

Moments later she heard an approaching step, revealing *sha'ir* Hakim with a subdued air.

"What shall you eat, brave one?" he said from the entrance.

"Nothing, my time here is done," said Jayida, and urged young Asifa out.

"*Esh?* Why leave? Please, stay; you haven't eaten nor had a drop of water since you began," he said, his genuine manner not unlike her father he'd once lived with.

"*Sah*, and so you have all the proof of the kind of person I am."

"Might we not have the honor of your name?" said *sha'ir* Hakim, the emotion in his widened eyes unnerving.

She turned her face to him. "Eventually you will. Be blessed for your kindness, and I know you're one of the few who'll tell the truth. May you and the tribe prosper." She quickly mounted and rushed off in southwest direction.

Caught between satisfaction and restlessness, the draining pain of nostalgia and loss lurked, something her father surely often thought about. Great civilizations and names had passed through Tayma, and though she didn't compare, now she'd also added her story to its long, eternally growing collection.

If Khaled wouldn't risk knowing who had bravely fought him, he could live with the shame that such a person not only existed, but that too many others had witnessed it for it to not only be real, but to tell the tale. In some ways, staying anonymous made it even more unsettling, and it was his task to remedy it if he wanted to.

In her contemplation she noted a dark mass like a short obelisk on the desert floor. The closer she got the form appeared to stand still, gazing around and waiting for something. When a curved beak and brown plumage revealed an eagle, she slipped off Asifa and went cautiously towards the creature. She crept closer on the uneven dirt ground, until she was about two arms' length away from him. He turned around and fixed on her, his serious glance hinting of affection. Through her veil they locked eyes, a sob caught in her throat—and then she knew.

Do it.

I can't.

Do it—or go with her.

She shook her head, cheeks swimming in tears, pleading.

That cold, unwavering presence.

I beg you, have mercy!

Overflowing tears burned Jayida's eyes shut, and she laid her hand on the dirt in silent prayer for Ayida and Liya, lying below. It shook her to the core that they should be so close yet so conveniently forgotten.

"But he won't escape what he's done, he won't!" sniffled Jayida and pounded a fist on the floor. How could someone hate their own flesh so? The torrent of her anguish poured, searching for solace in the fact that at least they'd died together. Sobbing, she pressed on her headwrap that glued to her face like a second skin to breathe through. When she finally opened her sore eyes and wiped her face, the eagle was gone.

"Thank you, Nasr," said Jayida, eager to hurry home.

She dusted and gathered herself then mounted Asifa, ignoring the bustle approaching from behind.

"Wait, wait!" yelled Khaled, racing to her on Sadiqa.

This pathetic being and his timing. Jayida trotted on lightly and he hurried his pace and reached her.

"Noble warrior, forgive me; I've no wish to disturb you, as I see you're on your way," said Khaled. "Yet up to now I've failed in courtesy towards you, and now I beg you, would you please tell me who you are and to which honorable tribe you belong? The truth is, I've never met your equal among brave tribesmen, and it'd be my honor to know."

Jayida stared ahead, considering if she should even reply at all. Why should she, when he hadn't even bothered himself to see Jayida? She looked at him, turning her face side to side in an exaggerated manner, relishing the cryptic effect she made.

"I know, you're thinking you don't owe me an explanation, and you're right," he said, looking into his hands.

"Oh, shut up, Khaled," Jayida stopped him before he continued in his innocent manner again. "Of course I'm right; and some might say you deserve to be kept in the dark—you know; like your father. But you see, you already know my name, and apparently, upon learning it, you had such a reaction that you ran away."

She reached up and with a strong grip she pulled off her scarf. Her bundle of seven braids poured out, and with a single swift grip she pulled off the hair ties and shook her head, letting her thick locks loosen like wild tassels or prayer ropes.

Khaled stared, wide-eyed.

"One thing you're right about: there is none equal to me—perhaps you knew that when you saw that girl in my tent; me of course. But as events keep showing me, I have to stop thinking of you as brighter than you are. At least, it seems our disgust is mutual. It'll be quick for me, when I let myself have feelings for the son of a *ghul* who buried alive his slave and baby girl." She let the words sink in, savoring the enraged frown that morphed his face.

"*Hadha!* I understand your anger Jayida, but you go too far," said Khaled.

She tilted her head back and let out a screaming laugh.

"*Aywa*, Khaled understands! Oh, imagine my surprise! You're almost there, Khaled. Your search for Ayida and Liya is just steps away!" she said, waving her hands wildly.

"Have you gone mad? I heard you haven't eaten or drank—"

"And if I have, what are you and your wretched family!" yelled Jayida, and pulled Asifa so close to Sadiqa that he swerved and hopped off Sadiqa to avoid falling off his mount. "Poor Khaled, will you do it? You're already in it, you know; you're practically *in* their grave, your feet reach down to them like roots," she said, and pointed to the uneven ground nearby.

"What are you talking about?" He looked around him quickly.

"Why don't you finally ask him? Like he was going to tell you what he did to them, and to so many others—but the thing is you can't decide if your offspring will be girls or boys, and he sure tried for other boys. Don't believe me? Dig! Dig, and find the robes worn by bones; then you could finally add your oryx to the camel you made wrapped in her folds, and say an overdue proper *rithā'* for them! But also now; don't forget to confirm it all with your mother!"

Her eyes burned into him and with a click of the tongue she rushed off south, drunk with this final blow that struck deeper than any weapon.

CHAPTER THIRTY-NINE

MISTAKES

Aghast, Khaled spun around, and rubbed a large palm over his face, his mind and heart raging at Jayida's vanishing frame. How could he begin to make sense of this?

He contemplated racing after her but stopped himself: there was no need to spark further fretful questions from the tribe, and when he'd just barely returned. So far, of the Zubayd only his mother knew what had happened with Jonder-Jayida and thankfully, no one had been around for this, either.

It was enough that for the past day this unknown warrior had frustrated as much as impressed him and everyone else. Just when he'd thought he could be welcomed back and forget all about this Jonder affair, she'd been one step ahead.

He groaned, awed by the strength and self-control she'd had to ride hard to arrive to Tayma before him.

Could it be? Reluctantly he glimpsed at the disturbed earth, half thinking he would start digging right then and there, just to prove her wrong. But as much as she'd amazed him, it didn't mean he'd start jumping at her every word. A *sayyid* had to take his time, gather information and think before acting on anything, especially given Jonder's whole deceitful identity.

He mounted Sadiqa, lost in recollections as he hurried back to camp. How could he have thought she'd be too masculine or repelling? It seemed no matter what disguise she took on, she'd made a striking sight. Hiding her eyes was especially perceptive, because he would've recognized them anywhere. And to think, he'd struck at her hard, metal-covered body, even as she lashed out her own ferocity, confirming her years of fruitful training.

As their fighting went on, he'd hoped to disarm and tire the visitor. But his seemingly endless strength had unsettled Khaled, and he'd had an increasing fear that he might not be able to stop him. Surely in her anger, she'd wanted his humiliation—his impacted shoulder inspiring her persistence while he agonized in creeping, silent pain. And yet she hadn't hit there—was it pity or a trace of care? Even without a clear winner, he tried to reassure himself with the fact that he'd stood his ground while being pushed further than he'd been since the scuffle happened.

Her endurance was as commendable as it was concerning, and no matter how he tried to turn it, it was another strike to his wavering self-confidence. He let out a long shudder at the realization that he was both stronger and weaker than he'd thought.

And yet, even with all of this, it wasn't all unpleasant. The image of her flushed face crowned by her wild ebony hair flooded his soul, a nameless beauty he hadn't known could exist. How could he—when he hadn't been sure what he was looking for, let alone that even he could feel that frightening yet alluring fiery rush some called love? How peculiar, that in a moment this same person could seem so different. Only now did the term *jinniyeh* make sense, when he could hardly disagree with her shapeshifting traits.

Then it hit him again: that had to be the source of the problem. While he realized how wrong he'd been on the physical part, whatever confusing relief he felt over her true identity was overshadowed by her last words. She'd proven how skilled she was, but she'd also led a life full of twisting and misleading behavior for her benefit. Even as *kahin*, or *kahina*, it could've still been her raw anger talking.

An onslaught of doubt surfaced. He could try to sympathize with years of hurt from his father's behavior and distance, but that was no excuse for the accusation she now so daringly hurled at him. Moharib was no soft man, but extreme though he often was, his wrath was kept to other men. It was clear that, no matter how much Khaled wanted to, he couldn't just take her word for it, especially not when he suspected it could be a powerful product of her feminine revenge.

Resolved, at camp he quenched the fire by informing that the fighter had left, wishing to remain anonymous for the time being, and in Khaled's own desire to oblige, he'd relented. As such, the visitor's true identity would remain secret, at least until they revealed themselves, and no one would guess a thing, let alone that it was a woman behind it.

Khaled cast off the surging concern at the tribe's potentially changing opinion should they discover it was a woman whom he hadn't defeated. But in the meantime, if anyone expressed concern on this undefeated stranger, he could always joke that he'd gone easy on him as his guest. Also, the success of all this depended on Jayida and her parents not spreading the word on it—at least just yet—and given the way things had turned out, he liked to think they weren't in a hurry to.

The evening passed just as he'd planned and they feasted to welcome their *sayyid* home, though all he longed for was to speak to his mother alone. He assured the tribe that their visit with Zahir and Jonder had gone well and that their bond had been rekindled. Was it less of a lie if it was still a wishful thought? After years of being away, he could hardly expect them to want to return right away, but at least the offer had been personally extended. A few times he thought he'd glimpsed *sha'ir* Hakim looking pensive, but then again he was always that way, and was surely more concerned about the so-called unknown fighter than Zahir whom he hadn't seen in years.

With difficulty Khaled tried to steer away Majid's confusion and perceptive questions, discreetly hinting at his suspicion that his friend might know more than he let on. Hating the reluctance stirred by the whole mess, and wishing his friend could read his mind, Khaled sent silent thoughts to Majid to only wait a bit more until he told him everything.

At last when evening set in and the whole camp retired, he rejoined his mother for the dreaded but necessary talk. Somehow, even she seemed a bit different now, sitting and brushing her hair in her nightdress in their cozy cushion-filled surroundings.

"Would you like to guess the unknown fighter?" said Khaled, and tore off his headdress with a hard grip. Would he ever erase that heart-pounding image from his soul? And why was he suddenly unsure that he'd ever want to?

"What do you mean? My only guess would be someone from Tayyi or your travels, someone you've already fought with," said Khamra. She cast him a side glance and set down her brush. "Oh, if you know, tell me!"

"You know better than me who it is," said Khaled, and locked his hands around his neck.

Instantly her face brightened.

"Jonder!" Her voice was a whisper of secret awe and marvel that she'd come all this way without their knowledge. "And where is she now?" Her sad eyes pleaded for this most mysterious of daughters, and he thought he was beginning to understand that.

He took a deep breath. "I'm torn, *yama*. I have this new, consuming sense of something very wrong that needs to be made right. But I can't say what it is, or maybe I do, and I'm afraid to say it," he shook his head. "Part of me feels wrong for asking, and yet, you're my blessed mother, to whom I've always felt I could say and ask anything. So I must ask and beg you: *yama*, is there something I'm missing or misunderstanding? I wanted so much for this reunion to go well, and instead it made it worse!"

His mother lowered her gaze, bound her own fingers like a bundle of twigs.

"My love, my Khaled. It's been a long time and now, I must ask your forgiveness, too," she said, her shifting tone filling him with uneasiness. "You well know how your father has always been an impulsive, hard man, despising competition, needing to always be the best, to be first. But something changed when your *siddi* Gayas died. It's like he didn't want anything more to do with Zahir. He tried in his way to hide it, but I could see through it—our gift as wives. And gently, I pried it out of him." Khamra paused with visible emotion, as a thick, warm current seemed to fill and drown his ears. "You see, Zahir is not actually your uncle."

"*Esh?*" said Khaled, his jaw hanging open.

"Your *siddi* Gayas adopted him. I remind you that at the time, *Qaysar* Anastasius made an agreement with the Kindah settled there and the Ghassanids that made them into imperial allies who served as *foederati*. Soon after, in the early rule of Al-Mundhir, there was famine and flood in their territory. When *Qaysar* Anastasius refused to help, *Shah* Kavadh—not unlike his currently ruling son *Shah* Khosrow—tried to take money by force, and relaunched a series of feuds that had laid dormant for generations."

"And continue on and off to this day," sneered Khaled.

His mother nodded.

"So when your grandparents awaited their second child, Gayas had little interest in venturing away... until the baby boy was stillborn. Your *sitti* Rumayma, wracked with grief, stayed in her tent, refusing to see anyone and admit the child's death. *I know he's out there; find him and bring him back to me*, she pressed Gayas over and over again, until finally he rode away. He didn't know where he was going; he just trekked until he ended up north, like his *qareen* had pulled him there. He followed the reports of the battles and tried to steer clear of them. But one day, on the outskirts of Bosra, he came upon a deserted mercenary camp along the Rûm-Fars frontier. The silence and devastation told him what he suspected even before he came upon it: they had all been slain. All, except a concealed newborn boy, who whimpered softly, then cried out just as he was about to ride away." She paused to catch the sob in her throat, wiped a forming tear, and continued. "He suspected it was likely done by Lakhmids or *badawi* in service to the Fars, attacking enemy Ghassanid territory at any chance, near and far. Your father was still barely an infant himself, so they named the boy Zahir and kept it a secret. They raised them as brothers, until Gayas revealed it to Moharib on his deathbed. As you can imagine, that only added to his already difficult attitude that only further drew them apart."

Khaled's jaw clenched. He saw his father: enraged that *siddi* Gayas would not only take in another child, but pass him as his brother, as though it were that simple.

"Zahir, of course, never knew any of that, nor the true reason for Moharib's behavior towards him—after all Moharib had been cruel to him even before he'd discovered this. It was just another detail to unleash Moharib's wrath," said Khamra. "Though your father mentioned the basics, I got the details from *sitti* Rumayma before she passed away."

"*Yama*, I wish you had said something, if only for you not to carry this burden alone," said Khaled. For the first time, his clenched fists tried to reel in his annoyance at his mother. All this time, without a word. And maybe worst of all: what if that wouldn't have changed anything?

She tightened her lips. "If that wasn't bad enough, at least our visit to the Banu Sa'd finally revealed to me the cause of their departure."

He took it all in like another slap, hating the familiarity of his father's ill-treatment to uncle Zahir, insinuating—perhaps even *willing* with the dark help of *al-'ayn*—that he might never have any sons. Other men would've killed for that—and it made him despise his father even more that he might've intentionally provoked Zahir to the act if only as an excuse to take Zahir down. Each time Khaled thought he'd seen his father sink low enough, it went lower still.

"That's what I tried to tell you when I wanted you to see Jayida, but it all happened so fast," said his mother.

"*Aywa*, it did," said Khaled. Then he froze, even as the past formed before him into full form again. "The stillborn boy—was he named Salim?"

"*Na'am*. But how do you know this? They never mentioned that name again," said Khamra with a sad frown.

Khaled pinched the bridge of his nose like it might release built-up tension.

"That night he left me at the graveyard. I thought it was my fear or *qareen* when I thought I'd dreamt and heard a boy named Salim saying he'd protect me. Maybe he did, especially since I'll assume he was secretly buried there?" He searched his mother's face and her pained nod confirmed it.

He sighed and clasped his hands.

"There's one more thing, something Jayida said about Ayida and Liya. She says they're dead and buried outside camp, and showed me where. I beg you *yama*, what do you know of it?"

Her face dropped. "*Esh?* I know nothing of it. I had my suspicions, as did everyone, about him and Ayida. And why would he—"

There was no need to finish, when the horror of it was too great.

"Oh, please forgive me, my love, for not saying anything. It's just that you had enough to deal with yourself," she looked away, sniffled, then looked up again. "After you came I once told him I'd like a daughter, and he got so enraged that I never mentioned it again. And after years of marriage to him and being so grateful for having you, I was less than a willing wife. Sons, sons, sons—that's all he wanted. Before you were born he even sometimes commented on you—if you'd turn out a girl instead of a boy. I did all I could to change that thinking of his, and thankfully you were born a beautiful boy. But if you'd been a girl, I don't know what would've happened, or where I would even be now, because I would not have just submitted—as I've tried to do for so many other things, to make things easier," she cried, nearly cracking her knuckles. "Forgive me! I only wanted to protect you from his constant anger. But I was so scared of what he might do, and if I told you and you chose to confront him about it. Oh! It hurt to think of it and to have to say it, but the truth is stronger; I know it now!"

He reached out to her and drew her in his embrace, and let her cry into his sore shoulder.

"Oh, I hope Ayida and Liya are safe. Please don't think me a bad wife when I say that I wasn't angry when Ayida eventually joined us, and even when she was with child. I even foolishly hoped that maybe it would calm him. I've asked about her several times and he always dismissed it."

"As he did with me," Khaled seethed. It seemed that if there was one thing he could say about his father, it was that he'd deceived them all.

She looked up at him with searching eyes. "Do you see? Even with this, it makes me more grateful for my treasured, miracle son."

He rubbed her shoulder and closed his arms tighter around her, all the better to hide his angry tears. Of all the million things he felt, the only "miracle" seemed the sheer weight of the pressing self-hate his father had passed on to him, seeking to brand him for life. Why hadn't they, his own wife and son, been enough for Moharib? When would he ever have enough?

At dawn Khaled shook Majid out of his sleep.

"Take a shovel and come with me," said Khaled.

In the chilly silence they walked to the spot where he'd last seen Jayida, and he asked his friend to help him dig into the uneven earth.

"What are we looking for?" said Majid.

"We'll see."

Their clanging shovels struck and lifted like rhythmic swords, the earth proudly fighting back and welcoming their challenge with its endlessness. There was so much of it, cascading down the sides that he dared to think there might be nothing other than some slaughtered creature, or maybe even some ancient trinkets left there by a visitor...

Then, in the brown earth, a patch of cream.

They paused, looked at each other, and kept going carefully, the strip of undyed clothing growing wider, longer. Faster they dug, trying to look only at the outline, below the waist, until finally the full picture lay before them. A woman, with her bundled child in her arms.

His pounding heart flooding his vision with tears, Khaled fell to his knees.

"Is that—" Majid croaked, as reluctant as himself to believe it.

Clenching his jaw, Khaled reached out to the corpse. He patted around the waist until a hard form stopped him. He reached in, and took out the camel—the one he'd made, and that he realized he hadn't mentioned to Jonder, so embarrassed was he to think, let alone say aloud, that he might've been rejected by them. And yet, she'd known of it.

He let his tears rain on Ayida's dusty dress, a long overdue sorry token of his grief for them. How? How had Moharib done it—made the pit and then forced them in it, then tossed the earth over them, indifferent to their heartbreaking cries? How long had it taken for the painful end—and how could he live with himself? A cry sliced out of Khaled's throat, and it was only when he felt a strong grip on his shoulders that he realized it was Majid holding him together. His friend offered him his own pained expression as he patiently awaited his orders.

"We're moving them to the cemetery. Then you and I are going back north. I've got things to tell you," said Khaled.

CHAPTER FORTY

PERSISTENT AL-'AYN

BANU SA'D

Jayida sighed as she glimpsed the jagged hills in the horizon, confirming she was almost home. Since shedding her dark clothing at Hijr for her usual cream ensemble, she felt better, even smug with satisfaction.

The more she reflected the more she realized that Khaled had been right on one count: she had jumped to conclusions in her feelings for him and let her fancy run wild. Just because he wasn't what she'd expected didn't mean that he was the one for her. It'd been a new moment of careless wishful thinking, making her act contrary to her self-controlled nature, and in her shameful weakness, she'd let her flesh be deceived with lust for him. The love-ridden poems were a pleasure to hear, but for their skillful composition and mastery of language, not for the chaotic, misleading feelings themselves.

As for whether Khaled would reveal her identity to the tribe, she suspected that in his pride, he'd be even more ashamed of admitting he'd been so publicly challenged by a woman. At the very least, she had some time before he finally worked up the courage to reveal it—if he ever would.

A short distance from camp, she caught a small caravan coming her way. Curious at this sight of one coming so close to camp, she picked up pace to meet it. Soon she reached a lone, middle-aged merchant, who walked between the two camels that each carried a *hawdaj*.

"Greetings, traveler. I'm Jonder, son of Zahir. May I be of assistance?" she said, and slipped off Asifa in a swift motion.

"Greetings, Jonder ibn Zahir. I'm Wadd, son of Ghadar. Praise your generosity, but we're almost to our destination," he said. His thick southern accented hinted he hailed from there, or might've lived there long enough to take it on. With his ashy beard and eyes that squinted under matching bushy eyebrows, she had the impression that he evaded her gaze.

"Where are you headed?" said Jayida.

"To the great Moharib ibn Gayas of Tayma," said Wadd. "I don't want to keep him waiting; I'm sure you understand."

A blade of ice shot up her spine. That vile name, infiltratiing her space again.

"So you've not heard, then," she said lightly, and slowly drifted to the closest *hawdaj*.

Wadd frowned, and cocked his head.

"Moharib is no more of this world, so you don't have to worry on that account," she said.

Wadd wrung his hands, appeared even more confused, and when he still didn't offer some wishes for the rest of his soul, she realized it was because he wasn't sure he could believe it himself.

Just then, a painful moan resounded from inside a *hawdaj*.

"What did I just hear?" said Jayida, still controlling her playful tone.

"Oh, probably just one of the girls awakening; it's been a long journey," Wadd said awkwardly, and a muffled shriek followed.

In an instant Jayida stepped forth and swept aside the *hawdaj*'s covering drapes. This time blades sliced her throat.

There lay three young women—two *badawi* and one Aksumite—sprawled on each other; their lavish embroidered and bejeweled robes contrasting their horrifyingly frail bodies on the verge of emaciation. They were surely singing girls, worth a lot more than the average slaves—more property for Moharib to use as he wished. Peering at her with drooping lids, one of the *badawi* girls raised her hand, shaking as she pointed, pleading with utter exhaustion—for water, food, help, life!

Jayida tried not to think of how many days they'd gone without food, and even worse, without water in the sweltering heat. As she stared, a deep chasm widened in her.

Without a word she went to the next *hawdaj* and found an older full-formed woman, reclining on her side and staring back at her blankly, the invisible *sayyida* watching the whole scene from the comfort of her private space.

"Greetings, *sayyida*?"

"Nuha," said the woman haughtily. Nuha waved her wicker fan steadily, the golden amulet at her neck probably that of an Israelite demon.

"Of course; how fitting. You shine just like the sun goddess. And praise it be that at least you're not plagued by strange sickness," said Jayida with a light bow, feigning dumb confusion. "Brave travelers, you must all be so exhausted. I insist you take a rest with us; the Banu Sa'd is just ahead," she said with a sweep of her hand.

Wadd glanced at Nuha, whose fixed empty smile reminded her of a lifeless statue she wanted to deface.

"Perhaps that may help. I don't know what's come over them. Moharib likes to receive them thin, and he's instructed not to overfeed them, as they would be taken care of once there," said Wadd, awkwardly rubbing his neck.

Jayida couldn't decide what was most absurd. Could the fool not tell the difference between light eating and starving? The worst of it was that he looked every bit the genuinely simple-minded man, manipulated by none other than Nuha who surely didn't mind keeping the bulk of the food, and earnings, for themselves.

"*Aywa*, I can see you're a faithful, loyal man." Jayida paused, noting the air of relief washing over him. "I know this rest will do you good, and then you can get on to your business in Tayma."

He contemplated for a moment, then his features relaxed. "We shall accept, then," said Wadd.

Jayida led them on in alluring silence, moderating her quiet distance with reassuring smiles that diffused her respectful reluctance to pry into their personal affairs. Her soul invisibly churning, she wallowed in the looming situation. Even with Moharib gone, how could she let them go there, to be possibly sold off elsewhere if Khaled didn't keep them himself? And if they wanted to stay with the Sa'd, what price would he request for their release?

"Here we are," said Jayida gratefully, and picked up pace.

In the distance was the tall silhouette of her father, and her bouncing mother waving as she raced to them. As the travelers dallied behind her, Jayida dismounted and fell into her father's embrace.

"Welcome back," said Zahir. "And don't worry; it's still as is," he whispered in her ear just as the travelers arrived. He released her and her mother stepped forth, bathing her cheeks in searching kisses.

Her jaw tight, Jayida nodded. "*Yaba*, our traveling guests need rest; three of them are ill," she said, meeting her mother's concerned glance. Somehow she'd kept her sneer to herself, when only the singing girls made worthy guests.

"Of course. Right this way," said Zahir. He showed them the location of the guest tent, where Nuha disappeared like a pampered princess.

While her mother set about gathering her herbal ingredients and ointments, Jayida helped her father and Wadd move the ailing girls to the women's area in their tent, frighteningly eased by their frail states. Carrying the Aksumite girl in her arms, Jayida suspected that the girl was about her age, though her state made her look much younger. Light as a feather, Jayida set her down next to the two other girls—and for a moment the image fleeted in her mind that she would recover, her striking garment stretching like wings that flew away into the bright blue, endless distance.

"We'll keep close watch on them. Now let me take you to our *sayyid*," said Zahir, who glanced at her, then led Wadd away.

Jayida knelt at the side of the Aksumite girl, dipped a cloth into the clay water bowl full of coriander seeds, dandelion flowers, and sage leaves, and dabbed her forehead and neck. In the sadness she willed the soothing herbs to seep through their skin to soak their root-veins and pulse their bodies back to life.

"Here," cooed her mother, and handed her a cup of honeyed herbal tea with a wooden spoon. "May it help."

Jayida took it and cautiously tipped the spoonful of tea into her lips, her barely twitching throat muscles as if reluctant to strain their little remaining strength. She kept going, from one to the other, until their eyelids closed heavily and their breaths deepened in united sleep. Even in their exhaustion and thinned forms, they were like a trio of angels whose sight defied speech.

She wondered if they'd become friends on their long journey, and a glance at the similar knotted bracelet they each had at their wrist mercifully hinted that they had. The neck of the Aksumite beauty was covered in coral from the Red Sea coast, an emerald-eyed gem traveled far only to end up in their midst, her youthful strength cruelly put to the test. Jayida huffed, seething that once again, it just had to be connected to Moharib, when she would've hated it enough without it. But miraculously, in her musings, it was like a cloud formed to push him off, casting him away for his unworthiness to be in their presence—a thought she welcomed.

Jayida imagined the Aksumite girl awakening later, smiling and radiant, not so unlike her Aksumite princess guardian she'd seen all her life. With a heavy sigh, Jayida called on her guardian to protect and help them recover.

"*Yama*, why are people the way they are?" said Jayida, hardly recognizing her own grating voice.

"I don't know," Zoraya sighed. "I do know there's no excuse for such cruel neglect. It will rightfully come back to them."

"Like I did with pathetic Khaled, even if this is about Moharib," Jayida sneered on the verge of tears, as her mother's lips opened in awe.

"Oh! What happened?"

"He's taken care of. But his father's stories just keep adding up. Wadd said that Moharib wants them thin, likes to fatten them up—" She couldn't finish it, couldn't even say the words as a question rather than a statement, asking, *Is that what he did?* When she already knew that he enjoyed making others his objects. What a long lost soul, caught in his pit of hell, and he could stay there for as long as necessary.

"*Aywa*. They say miracles happen, right? So they will heal. It's what we do; we're better than them. And maybe, when it's long passed and a less painful memory, one day they might speak of it, too," said Jayida.

"May Yassu hear you," said her mother. "I'll light some incense."

With the pleasant smoke wafting all around them, Jayida closed her eyes and rocked side to side, calling also on Nasr, Yassu, and Shamshun to heal them. In a trance she let herself be pulled, up and away, in a noiseless place she wanted to always be in. There was no time there and she floated, unconcerned. Then, a faint buzzing, like that of a blossoming spring garden. Gradually Jayida became aware of her head slightly spinning, and when a hand settled on her shoulder, she realized she'd no idea how long it'd been since she'd drifted.

"Time to eat, that's an order," whispered Zoraya.

Jayida blinked, took a moment to readjust herself, and followed her mother to the adjacent men's quarters. Her appetite slowly returned with each bite of fresh bread and buttermilk. How easily she could forget to nourish herself, and how good it felt to partake in it again.

"As your father says, no one's very keen on these travelers."

"Good. It's always nice to know when the tribe covers you," Jayida chuckled.

Her mother laid a hand on her arm.

"Of course it does. That's why we had to temper concerns by telling them you had some matters to handle with Khaled, in the light of his quick departure. So when you're ready, I'm ready."

Jayida shared all that happened: from her choosing Asifa, to arriving to their old home at Tayma, to seeing the aged *sha'ir* Hakim, his closest friend Majid, and Hassan, and maybe even his future wife, down to their long, anonymous fighting that ended in a draw. Just as she'd thought she'd just disappear as quickly as she'd come, the eagle on the outskirts of camp showed her where Ayida and Liya lay buried.

At her mother's astounded confusion, Jayida confessed that she'd seen them in past night visions, but it wasn't until after Khaled left that she understood who they were. She was paying her respects when Khaled finally summoned a drop of courage to come after the fighter, and at last Jayida revealed only to him who she really was—along with the truth about his father, in case he had anymore doubts. Even if Khaled did spread the story, it was another kind of victory that he may be laughed at in disbelief of the gender.

Zoraya gave a sad frown. "My heart. I'm happy if you're happy, but I wonder what this means? It's hardly how I imagined it'd all turn out."

"It means we don't need them, just as we never have," said Jayida. "As for me, for once I did what many inexperienced girls my age do: I assumed Khaled was someone he isn't. Guess we're even then, though I still say I'm the real winner," she smirked.

"In a way I'm glad we didn't know that about Moharib, but then my soul aches that you had to see it. But do you really think Khaled knows of it?"

"I don't know. I didn't think he did, but now I'm not so sure. He could know and pretend he doesn't. That would be the easier thing to do, which unfortunately sounds more like him by the moment."

Zoraya sighed with a conflicted smile. "I'm not sure what to say but that it hardly sounds... finished."

"Looking at his father's history, I'll hardly hold my breath for anything else," said Jayida.

They finished eating and draped a blanket on their shoulders to rejoin the camp fire in the deepening night chill. Before leaving the tent she went to the girls and knelt by them, the sense of peacefulness stirring her emotion anew. She pulled the woolen blanket a bit higher over them, when an unexpected brush stopped her.

It couldn't be.

Jayida reached again and touched hands, arms, and faces. All cold. Lifeless.

"*Yama!*" she called out before the sob closed her throat. A moment later her mother towered over her.

"Earlier, I thought—" Jayida mumbled. She looked at them, then rose and turned away. Pacing, her breath deepened, something breaking and rattling through her at increased speed.

"Yassu, please take them," said her mother and stood close to her. "They had to be too far gone, for their hearts to give way like this. Still, it's—it's like they all wanted to go at once, together?" said Zoraya in a mixture of sadness and awe.

"And it just had to be here. They, and others just conveniently find me so they can die, is that it?"

"Not to die, no. Maybe for you to help them cross over," said her mother, her hands reaching out to her.

"Cross over? Cross over *to what*? I don't know a thing of it myself! Maybe no one else does either, living or dead!" yelled Jayida, and backed out of her reach.

"It's hard, I know. Maybe it's time to visit *Umm* Jarida; she'll surely explain it better to you."

"What would that do? It doesn't make sense! All my life I've seen things, but how can I tell them apart; what's real, what's imaginary? It's like they're in a pact together to fool you, with the help of countless demons, and who knows what else! And all this cruel death—I'm so tired of it!"

Jayida stormed out of the tent, and marched straight for the bustle around the camp fire, her mother's rushing steps following paces away. The lashing flames flickering in the distance gave the impression that it was bigger than usual, its shadowy arms growing into the skyline and reaching into her heart. At last she came to it, the tribe's eager welcome bolstering her spirit as she gathered her strength.

"Ah, you join us at last. How are they doing?" said Wadd, holding his posture proudly with a hand on each knee. Jayida stopped and glanced at him and his vain, crooked-nosed companion Nuha, seated next to annoyed Zahir and *sayyid* Aziz. Recalling her mother's words, she didn't have to look to his side to guess that Warda, Yazida, and Shams wore similar displeased frowns. Even with her mother's appearance at her side, there was no easy way to say it.

"They are no longer of this world," said Jayida flatly.

"*Esh?* But they still had so much life in them; you saw it," said Wadd with an odd chuckle.

"In the great expanse of time, I saw only a moment of what you saw, given your long travels together," said Jayida, struggling to keep an even tone.

Wadd raised his palms, feigning lightness. "I'm sure we can work something out for you to make it up," he said.

"Make it up?" said Jayida, her brow twitching.

"Only the usual reparations for this loss," said Wadd.

"We trust you," Nuha chimed in. "And that's why we came, but surely you realize that we don't know what happened. What if they were poisoned? In your generosity it's not the case here, but things like this do happen," said Nuha nonchalantly. With sickening disgust Jayida realized she'd likely done the exact thing herself.

"*Sah*, because it would make no sense," chuckled Jayida. "Generous as we are, why would we soil our camp with death, in possible addition to, as you just said, agreement on terms that would then leave us short one way or another? And that's not including the funeral rations."

Her blood pumped so fast and hard in her throat that she marveled at her ability to speak. If anything, maybe that had been their plan; aware of the girls' sickness they could then try to get out of the burial burden by leaving it on others. How could the Sa'd trust them with any kind of bounty now that she saw their selfishness and scheming? They might as well hand these criminals directly to Khaled and let him settle the final matter of their fate. Yet simply spreading word of their wretched ways didn't seem like enough. In her internal chaos Jayida wondered how to maintain a straight face. And for the first time it dawned on her that no matter her reaction—wild with the fury of *jahl* or coolly composed with *hilm*—either one could look *majnun* in the face of such evil.

"Now, Wadd and Nuha," said *sayyid* Aziz with a raised hand. "As upsetting as these news are, there'll be no casting doubt on Jonder, who kindly invited you here to tend to your girls. I know that he and his mother did all they could, as they, along with Zahir, always do."

Distress washed over Wadd and Nuha, as Jayida wavered between repulsion and delight at the sight of two such conniving *ghilan* in their midst.

"Let's get on to the funeral feast then," said Jayida. "We've just the right beasts for the occasion; won't you come and see them."

Jayida cued the vile travelers up, relishing the tribe's intent focus on her. They rose lethargically and Jayida swept between them, and placed a friendly arm on each of their shoulders as they drew closer to the large fire pit.

"You know, there is something that might bring even more fortune to this situation," said Jayida.

"Oh? What's that?" said Wadd.

"Living sacrifice, of course!" Jayida grinned.

"I confess it's always made me squeamish, I'd rather not see it," Wadd said.

"And which might be your offering?" said Nuha, looking around them with a condescending frown.

Through the flames Jayida caught the surrounding glassy eyes and widening grins, awaiting only her command.

"Oh Nuha, what could be more fitting than *you two*?" Jayida laughed, and swiftly wrapped her hands around their throats, forcing them on their knees as they curved backwards over the fire. They gasped in horror and uselessly gripped at her unshakeable hold as the flames licked their backs.

A thundering roar resounded, engulfing Jayida with heat, and she grinned her lion grin, eating the light that gushed out around her from all angles.

"But why fear, fearless travelers? Surely it'll be as painless as losing your three singers!" said Jayida.

"Please, please don't hurt us," croaked Wadd, drool dripping out of his mouth.

"Me hurt you? What power do I have? Perhaps you should plead to fire-loving Al-Uzza instead, or that angel at Nuha's neck," said Jayida, as Nuha's eyes rolled in the back of her head.

In the blinding flames was her father, a pillar of calm understanding.

"You know what enrages me? You didn't have to listen to Moharib, unless of course, you agreed with him. So then, here's your chance to join him!" cackled Jayida.

Something about their pitiful manners—tearful, selfish cowering faces—fueled her wrathful disgust for them. She was not just seeing them, but endless variants of them; their evil actions protruding out of their purple-blue flesh the harder she squeezed, their skillfully concealed ugliness surfacing like buried masks. Were they even human? Some might be naïve and no less harmful for their ignorance, but Wadd and Nuha knew what they were doing—greedy, watching the life slip out of the girls without remorse. Lawless and shameless at any chance, just to suit their own whims; relishing their filth and calling it pride and power, spreading darkness and death wherever they went.

Jayida was always digging, reaching, scraping, and gathering up together a sorry mass of the slightest morsel of good in others, to deter her aversion—and all for what? They'd come upon her path in the perfect time, so who was to say it wasn't an offering for her to do something about it, and deter Moharib's evil eye yet again? He would keep trying, pushing—and so would she, with one more timely deed to ensure her security! Addicting, stronger than her, the intoxicating rush of power filled her body that was its vessel.

"So what shall it be then?" Jayida yelled, and scanned around, her limbs stiff as steel. In the echoing rumble the tribe's intense, pleased gazes waited on her, allowing her the decision. It was just as well because she doubted that they could stop her even if they wanted.

Her father rose, and his soft air yielded to a sharp frown. The scent of burning fabric wafted, and she noted a flame catching the edge of Nuha's robes. Why not? It's what she deserved, so why should she pull away? It only made sense for them to stay there a while, see what happened.

"You see, Nuha and Wadd? Isn't it glorious! Don't you feel the fortune of your secured future already coming to you!" said Jayida.

Just then, something tugged at her knees, pulling her back insistently.

"Jonder, please," and she knew before she looked down that it was Yazida who lingered near her.

For a moment Jayida remained locked, transfixed, reluctant to let go yet wanting it to finally stop. She tried to move but couldn't, only her eyes somehow widened in terrified fear. Who was she and what had she done?

Jayida summoned all her strength and with a grunt she tried again, and pulled back so hard that she tossed the bodies aside like mere sacks of grain. Panting, Wadd rushed to Nuha, groaning as he tapped her cheeks back to consciousness. He was so insistent that she finally opened her sleepy eyes, and shrieked upon seeing where she still was, then gripped each other like small frightened, cornered prey.

Jayida pointed two fingers at them like horns, satisfied at the alarm that rattled them all over again.

"You'll remember this day as the one when a woman of Sa'd saved you," said Jayida, and vanished into the beckoning pitch darkness.

CHAPTER FORTY-ONE

SECLUSION

Who am I? Where am I going?

The questions ceaselessly taunted Jayida, like vultures tearing into a fresh carcass. With Al-Wasiyah as her sole companion, she'd ended up in Wadi Al-Wafra, in the valley of her birth, with no sense of time other than night had passed. But even this place seemed different now.

Shrouded in a haziness that left little in sight but a vast, dusty space that barely concealed a sea of looming sooty clouds, she might as well have been on another planet. Sitting cross-legged and rocking back and forth, Al-Wasiyah's concealed blade pressed against her stomach as it lay across her lap, submerged in her layers of clothing.

Blades, blades—everywhere she turned, blades! The hard desert floor itself protruded through her bones: no matter how she shifted, it would soon hurt again. But slowly, even that sensation was fading. Engulfed, Jayida kept swaying, cloaked in her disheveled headwrap, staring into nothingness; this lethal void that permeated every part of her being, down to the very dry air that filled her nostrils, suffocating as it scraped its way through her lungs.

At least there she could be blissfully alone, and just in case this time—the one time more than any other when she wished to be left alone, so that she almost expected it to be disturbed—if a sad soul should come upon her, she would be such a frightening sight that it might well be the end of their life. And not because she was the one who wanted it, but because someone else, inside her, did. Because there was no more denying it: she was possessed.

When had it begun its entry into her? Was it at 'Ukaz with Sahira and all the blood sacrifices of the Hijaz pilgrimage sites? Or was it when she'd captured the attackers, ready to castrate them for their evil intentions? Or when she'd slain the lion, his blood swished in her mouth seeping into her gums, blood, and very marrow? Or surely it was the *Ayyam al-Zalam*, whose seasons of darkness had opened a wide passage to the earth to all the greedy evil spirits! No, it had to be earlier than that still, when Moharib had hurled his hateful words to her father even before her birth. There was no more excusing it: there had always been people like him, who enjoyed conflict and death, killing whatever didn't please them, and there would always be, going back to the times of Yassu, Shamshun, Nuh, and Adam, that very first man.

And now she, too, had been targeted to become one of them, and it'd taken seventeen springs for her to realize it. So much for *kahin*. Maybe it was already too late, for them and herself, and not only might she have cursed herself, but done it right in front of the whole tribe.

A blade of fire slashed her soul. And what if, shockingly, it was just as it should be? The *injil* said that Mikha'il fought *shaytan*, and that the devil wasn't strong enough and was cast down to earth with his followers. Why hadn't *mubassir* Ayyub said it? He'd been too afraid of uttering it—that the place where he'd fallen was the very stretch of land on which they dwelt, where everyone constantly fought and thirsted for the next prey!

That's why it was the same cycle, repeated everywhere: tortured, torn bodies, buried wailing innocent babies, scraped skin, burning flesh, oozing fat, gut-wrenching pleading, the suffering feeding the sadistic grins—all blurring into one endless, revolting hellish scene. Sickening smoke, justified by selfish *asking, asking, asking*!

Poor Hatim, up at Jabal Aja, fighting the endless stream of demons who hated his kind heart, as he made secret verses like protective amulets—the true cost of poetry that few knew!

A deep grunt whistled through her throat, rattling her neck like an angry animal. How pathetic and useless could they all be then, fearing hell with offerings of more blood and flesh, when they were already *in* it! And still, some hurried to cross over, hoping to see and search the other side in faint hope of something better!

And yet there had to be, otherwise it made no sense and everything was meaningless and pointless, and for some odd reason the earth still hadn't opened up and swallowed them all up...

But until Jayida found such a better place, if she ever would, there was just death and blood and killing, and head-exploding screaming—and she'd defend herself because she would *not* just submit! They were coming for her, as they had her whole life, and finally she laughed at the craziness of it! What had she been thinking? She'd once been afraid that she couldn't kill if she had to, but now she knew that not only she could, but that there may not be enough in all the land to exhaust her! Endless vile monsters, rushing, hurling themselves at her, but she would catch them all—shed their pungent blood until it was all finished once and for all. Even when her own life was forced out of her in neverending revenge, she would cling and fight back, maybe even come back in another shape, and pursue and continue into miserable revengeful eternity.

A consuming delight burned through her, as the holy stories of the lives of the saints told by *mubassir* Ayyub resurfaced. If that's what they meant by their gruesome deaths, finally she understood them!

She would be like the Fars noble convert Anahid who picked up her breasts ripped off by ropes and gave them in defiant offering, ready to slice off any other of her limbs for the greedy Magian's banquet. Or she might talk back to a tyrant demanding her submission, who'd kill her and make her mother drink her blood, as had been done to Ruhm of Najran with her own granddaughter during the massacres in the south. Whether stripped, slapped, or scourged to the bones, she'd defy them with every breath, and scattering her limbs and blood would only grant her more territorial points of contact. There was no *ending* her, when no matter where she was, the stories of her fight would live on, cementing their shame and foolishness across time!

A sound of clashing swords and cymbals echoed in her soul, and she doubled over, covering her ears to drown out the noise. And what about *al-ilah*! People always cried about themselves, but no one ever asked how *He* felt! To see His human creation become even more beasts than beasts themselves; no wonder He'd only had Nuh and his kin and the animals to fill His ark, then sent His divine flood to wipe the earth from such filth!

And ever since, He'd retreated far into His divine territory that few could ever reach! How could Jayida blame Him, when men sickened her to death, and it was He who'd given them everything they needed, only for them to choose destruction instead! A shattering sadness deeper than any she'd ever known filled her to consider what it felt like for Him, when he'd seen it constantly since the dawn of creation. But she was no deity to give others endless chances only to be destroyed by them!

Nauseous and exhausted, Jayida became aware of her panting, and took long breaths to adjust herself. Her mouth stung and her tongue flicked her cracking lips. Oh, why did Khaled have to come and set her life in shambles—but there was no point to that. It was done and he would no longer be granted the advantage of having had this effect on her.

Alone! Alone! Alone!

Stones dropped in her core, punching out hot, streaming angry tears. She had the frustrating impression of crying for everything and nothing at once. Why cry when it didn't matter? It would pass as everything else passed anyway. But where oh where was Nasr? Lost in the chaotic lies, how could she know what was right or wrong? She shrank even from the thought that for the first time, she wasn't sure which way to go. All these seventeen springs of her life and there she was, still as clueless as a newborn into this cursed, barren desert land.

She buried her face in her knees, holding herself together and sobbing into oblivion, begging for strength to hang on. The lurking, pitch black void consumed her again. What if she wasn't strong enough, she who'd skinned a lion in her sixteenth year, securing her reputation? Someday, even her beloved parents would be gone... and what then? Her tears redoubled at the thought of her blessed father, who'd once also felt so alone, and had done all he could to protect her. Let everyone defame her—maybe part of her even deserved it—but that her parents might suffer insults because of her shattered her heart most of all.

Her stomach clenching, she begged for one of *al-ilah*'s servants to hear her cry, reveal himself and just tell her *what* to do! She was no better than anyone else to ask, but how could she know without trying? She'd never called on anyone before, and she'd never been so lost before, either. Recalling her mother praying to Yassu, as great-grandmother Jarida said to do, she pleaded that He hurry before it was too late, terrified that she might go the wrong way.

In her torment she realized that she didn't need to die to find out what came next. Because if some doubted the existence of Paradise, hell was certain—and she knew what hell was, because it was everywhere. There was no escape, and soon she'd have to go back to the tribe, and face what everyone had to say. She'd have to be prepared when they shunned her, despite her achievements: their shock at her father's deception, the shame of her true feminine identity overshadowed by years of unnatural male activity, and Khaled's rejection—even if they might succeed at also suppressing this information for a while. How much dishonor could a tribe take?—she could already hear the grumbling. But she'd be ready, and would do as her father had done eighteen winters ago, before he'd even known of his impending fatherhood.

My brother and I against my cousin, my cousin and I against the stranger.

Except: Herself against the world—that's what it would be now.

Banished, she would leave, roam the deserted wastelands, scraping by for survival at any cost, aware that at any moment she might have to become the one thing she hated most of all: a thieving, murdering criminal. Alone in the world, maybe Shanfara would remember and visit her sometimes, and she sniffled hard at the redoubling tears.

A dab fell on her leg, then another on her shoulder. She wiped her face, opened her heavy eyelids, and looked up into the dark grey sky. To the west was the cave she'd been born in, discreetly hovering above the *wadi* stretched out all around her like a thirsty garden. The drops continued, slow, then faster, until a persistent silvery stream dabbed her clothing to a resounding gentle hiss.

The ground darkened everywhere as the earth drank, and the low buzz turned to an enveloping rumble. Jayida blinked fast, marveling at the sight of so much rain. Had she fallen asleep and awakened in a dream? But when such rare rain came in the summer, it was too marvelous to question. Soon the grasses would protrude through the surface, lighting the valley in pure green. In the eastern distance a thunder echoed, calling forth and unleashing thick veils of rain. She laid on her back, her arms stretched out and eyes closed, the pebble-like drops dancing on her face.

Let it come, let it wash over her, and she focused, committing every sound and impression to her memory. For a while she let herself merge with the earth, as her clothes drenched for the first time with precious heavy rainfall.

She became aware of a strong light as if concealed behind the clouds. At the sound of laughter she sat up then stood as it approached, and saw in the distance a young boy and girl clad in white robes. They seemed to float, then turned to her and smiled, joining hands as they drifted towards her. They grew larger and slightly older as they neared, their forms merging as a single person.

For a moment she lost sight of the boy, who seemed retreated behind the girl, and who now looked about her age. Jayida had never seen her before, but her glowing face and gentle doe eyes felt familiar even as her striking beauty left her amazed. The boy then emerged and stood by her side, his angelic demeanor lit up with pure joy. A sob caught in her throat—but thankfully not of sadness—as she stared at youthful, healthy Nasr, whose smiling eyes shone with loving understanding. He held up the girl's hand, and she understood then that he was presenting her his wife.

They circled around Jayida, and she smiled at them through tearful eyes, overwhelmed with warm, happy emotion. Nasr and his wife merged together again, their glowing love filling her with a reassurance she couldn't explain. It was a few moments before she realized they'd vanished from view, though their presence somehow lingered.

A stronger presence emerged ahead, with powerful heat engulfing her, like a wool blanket had been wrapped around her. Jayida walked towards it, and the more she looked, the more she became convinced it was a white light she'd never seen before. Though she saw no one, she couldn't shake off that overpowering sense that she wasn't alone, like her every action was known. She stopped and waited to see if anyone would appear. Eventually she glimpsed something like an earthy mound on the ground and, squinting, she realized they were a pair of bare tanned feet with a hole at the center of each.

Suddenly, blood gushed out of them, pouring like red roots down the feet and into the earth. Then the growing fountain shot up high like bright crimson palm trees or angel wings. A terrible anguish, close to her earlier torment, engulfed her, but it yielded to a surging, mysterious strength as the blood became clear as fresh water. She realized that presence was the source of heat, matched with its unshakeable strong air of authority. Jayida tried to look up, but could not: so blinded by that glow which only grew stronger the more she tried to seek the man's face.

And yet, despite her averted glance, gradually, she had an idea of what he looked like: cloaked in white linen, a bearded man with dark wavy hair, a protruding nose and piercing, yet gentle eyes. He was beyond description, and she knew then that no poetry would ever do Him justice, though He would welcome every attempt. For the first time, that she would try, and fail, filled her with grateful humility. More than a mere human, she had the impression that He looked at her as though He knew everything she'd ever thought, felt, and experienced, and not only understood, but could help her.

In speechless awe, she stared at his feet, not daring to speak, although she was free to.

There is more, the commanding voice thundered, and she knew then that she wanted to be a servant of that consuming flame.

Jayida looked up again and basked in the stillness, wondering how she could ever express what she'd just seen of Nasr and, to her lingering and humbling shock, Yassu *al-Masih*.

The clouds were already scattering, leaving only the calm after a storm, the freshly blooming garden its own magic proof of its passing.

Chapter Forty-Two

RENEWAL

Her vision blurry, Jayida stood at the entrance of the cave of her birth, looking down into the lush valley below. She took a deep breath, and lifted her arms up to the sky.

"Thank you Yassu and Nasr," she whispered, and sniffled away small tears. A sense of childishness swept through her, making her feel wonderfully small. All this time, that's what Nasr had meant in his last moments, and in her fear she'd thought of Moharib or one of his minions.

She caught herself, touched that even now Khaled's name didn't feel right to put in that list. Was that proof that whatever she still felt for him, no matter how small or silly, and despite everything, was real?

There was a soft swishing behind her, and she turned to the sand cat and her kitten curled up against the wall inside the cave. She'd found them there when she'd come about thirty days ago after the spring storm, and made rough markings on the wall to commemorate her stay. To her surprise, they hadn't rushed off but stayed, and they'd shared the space in a kind of vague, yet mutual trust ever since.

"*Aywa*; take good care of the place while I'm gone," said Jayida.

With a final parting glance, she descended into the valley, her hand resting on Al-Wasiyah at her hip. Her body as weightless as her heart was full, she tried not to step on the yellowing grasses called forth by the storm, still struck that though everything looked the same, everything felt different, and that Yassu had to be the one behind it.

A shyness mixed with loving gratitude filled her each time she thought of Him. She couldn't believe that she had been so bold and vain and yet, in her selfishness she didn't want to part with that lingering trace of pride. After all these years she hadn't expected any deity to reveal themselves, and yet Yassu had come, glowing with the greatest powerful essence that made her feel both grateful and unworthy of it; enough to make any man recoil in shame. Yet, He seemed to beckon, to welcome her to Him, inviting her to search for and latch onto His dazzling source—dare she say so that she might partake in it too? Somehow, she saw how unworthy she was of it, but the one thing she knew without a doubt was that she could not deny it.

Reluctantly she recalled her shattering anguish, and realized it had to be His perfect timing, as only the Almighty can have. He'd seen her on the edge of a precipice, and pitied her enough to come and comfort her by saying *There was more*, even if she wasn't sure what that meant. Though she still had a lot more to understand, her desperation was replaced by a calm she'd never known, and the one she realized Nasr had come to know through his own struggles.

"Oh, *sha'ir* Nasr, whose sight surpassed ours," cooed Jayida, as she came out of the valley and entered the camp's vast plain he'd lived in with them.

She continued southeast to Wadi Al-Raha, breathing in the early morning air. Nasr could've told them and yet he had to have his reasons. Was it his selfishness that made him want to keep Yassu for himself? If so she couldn't blame him, when she felt it already, too: this conflict between wanting to share and keeping it all to herself. It was her experience to do with as she saw fit, and no one else's! All the same, Yassu had come to him, offering a refuge, and revealed to him Jonder's true identity, whose secret he kept. Thankfully, it was another kind of proof that life went on after his death, providing her answers she'd wanted for so long.

Her concerns on how she'd reveal what had happened fell away, when she knew the reality of what she saw. It was not her imagination, nor her wishful thinking—Yassu would know better than anyone how often she'd wished to see Nasr, or just anyone, in her yearning for signs, and nothing had happened.

Until it did.

Her heart soared that Nasr not only looked happy, but had even been granted a partner whose beauty would leave anyone speechless. It was comforting to think that even if she never met hers in her human life, it would come later. A surge of tears invaded her, because no matter how *majnun* it sounded, at least she'd have a nice story to tell his sister and parents.

She reached Nasr and Shanfara's graves, and noted the three new stone piles across from them.

"You're probably guiding them already," said Jayida, and sniffled away tears for the three singing girls. For a moment she wished it could've been Nuha and Wadd in their place, but then again, life could be its own punishment. Best of all, Yassu knew just what to do with them.

Jayida reached in her pouch, retrieved incense tears and a stone she'd found for each, and laid them on the graves. She tried not to focus on losing them but on the gift of having known them, no matter how brief, and offering a moment of commemoration.

She sat down, crossed her legs, and closed her eyes. Her stomach fluttered and she sighed at the surging thought of Khaled. Apparently it was stronger than her, when she still wondered what he was doing, if she might even cross his mind. With a sad gratitude it dawned on her that she might always think about him, even as they went their separate ways.

She loosened the fabric around her neck, recalling the way his whole expression had changed as she'd finally shown her uncovered face. She'd been satisfied then, to just leave him there dumbfounded, so why did it still feel so... incomplete? A part of her hoped it was just the lingering pull of unexpected outcomes that would soon wear off.

But with a secret pleasure that she could at least keep to herself, she couldn't deny that, as much as there were things about him that disappointed, there were others she liked. Just as curious, it had taken time for her to realize that as much as she'd needed to make her point, getting her revenge hadn't exactly felt how she'd thought it would. Something like a meaningless void filled her, limiting any satisfying true sense of accomplishment. Though she didn't regret it, the alternative of doing nothing carried its own sadness. At least it was done, and she'd never again pursue anyone. She prayed that with Yassu's help, in time she would learn to better use her sight and to tell the truth apart from tempting, chaotic lies.

A faint, graceful shuffle approached, and Jayida gently opened her eyes. At last, the moment she'd so often thought of had arrived, and to her surprise, there was no fear or even worry. She rose and turned, just as the steps came to a halt nearby.

"You're back," said Yazida with a shy laugh, looking timidly back and forth between her and the basket balanced on her hip. She radiated such a lovely olive glow in her cream robes and headdress, and Jayida hoped it was partly from practicing her singing and dancing. Jayida opened her arms, touched as much by her beauty as by her friend's lingering curiosity.

It was over. Finally, the secret was out.

Yazida dropped the basket and bolted into her arms, her cloud of musky sweetness like a gift after being so long away. After a moment Yazida reached up, and pushed aside Jayida's headdress, brought out fistfuls of her hair, then passed her hands over her face, neck, and chest as they both erupted in laughter. Then, like lightning, Yazida planted a quick kiss on her lips, the *jinniyeh* testing what she could get away with.

"And what would Nasr say of his sister being the singing-dancing-kisser of Sa'd?" chuckled Jayida.

"He knows," smirked Yazida. "Oh, Jayida. I can't believe it; all this time," she said with a searching gaze. "I've been hoping to see you and though I haven't, I liked to think you enjoyed the food that I was all too glad to refill."

Jayida grabbed her face and kissed her forehead. "*Aywa*, I'm grateful."

"I'm glad," said Yazida, gesturing invitingly to the basket.

They reclined paces away from the graves, and Yazida eagerly set out the date pies and fresh milk, and watched her eat in silence.

"You're as gifted a cook as you are singer and dancer," said Jayida to her beaming friend.

Jayida wallowed in the sense of playful understanding that hung between them, and dared to think that Nasr might not be so far away.

"So then, now you understand that it was never you," said Jayida, breaking the silence.

Yazida nodded, looked down into her hands on her lap.

"Sometimes I still can't believe I didn't know, but it's not like there was anything in particular to give it away," she chuckled. "And yet, in some ways, it doesn't seem to change much," said Yazida with a contemplative air.

"I've thought that, too. One of life's mysteries; the way that things can seem so unchanging, and then, also full of unexpected shifts," sighed Jayida. "There's something else, and it's going to sound *majnun*, but it's true: I saw Nasr. With his wife. And Yassu."

Yazida froze. "*Esh?* How? When?"

"Right after I left. I don't mean to frighten or confuse you, but I didn't imagine it. The vision was real: it was him and his beautiful wife, looking happy and at peace in their dwelling with Yassu. And I believe he was trying to tell us, in his own way, that he became a *Masihi* before his death," said Jayida, already relieved by saying the words.

Yazida frowned, bit her lip and looked away. "I saw him, too," she said, her voice shaking. "It was a few days ago. I didn't know what it meant, and I could only think of telling you, but you were away. He did seem so happy, so I thought maybe it was my own wishful thinking." She wiped her tearful cheeks and straightened herself. "So is that how Nasr found out about you?"

"That's what I assume. But when he revealed it on his deathbed while we were alone, it made no sense, so you can imagine how much that worried me, thinking someone knew and would expose it at any moment. But that moment never came," said Jayida, noting the air of understanding softening her face. "So, does the tribe hate me now, with this revelation of being an angry man-woman ready to feed merchants to the fire?"

"Hate you? How could you ever be hated? After all your father, mother, and you, have done! They admire you, and we're amazed at your parents for how they've raised you, how you turned out—your strength! Oh, Jayida, we're all honored," said Yazida, her hand tightening on hers. "And don't worry, the demonic merchants left, empty-handed this time."

"Should be glad they left at all, though Khaled can host them now," frowned Jayida. She sighed and folded Yazida's hands in hers. "I have to thank you for stopping me. I've been thinking about it, and if it hadn't been for you, who knows—" said Jayida through gritted teeth.

Yazida nodded. "I knew it was just your anger, though you know we probably wouldn't have stopped you. We trust you."

"Maybe that's what I'm afraid of," said Jayida, and looked over her shoulder to the graves. "I never thought this place would fill up so soon."

"At least they're together, and with my brother."

"*Aywa*," said Jayida. "So, any other news since I've been gone?"

Yazida's brow flickered.

"Don't worry; you can say it," said Jayida.

"Oh, no. Did you see that, too? That's too cruel; I don't think I could take it, even if your *kahin* sight is a gift."

"I didn't see it, but it's the natural next step. So out with it."

"News are there's been a big wedding at the Banu Zubayd; one of their hired poets raved about this Layla's supposed beauty, whom I don't need to see to know doesn't compare to yours," said Yazida, rolling her eyes.

Jayida tried not to breathe and stiffened herself, as if it might keep the words from getting into her, and sinking deep down into her empty, punched gut. That's where the real cruelty lay: in that constant lurking sadness, always ready to strike her unexpectedly.

"I wish them happiness," said Jayida.

"Oh, he's the biggest fool on earth, you know it's true! I'm so glad you went and showed him. That's no man for you; you deserve better, and you *will* have it," said Yazida, gripping her hand.

"And what about you; have you decided?" said Jayida, eager to change the subject.

Yazida sighed. "Maybe you'll think me fickle, but I'm getting tired of waiting, especially when I don't think Imru's coming back. I think I've always known about Shams, but I wanted to be sure. He's been patient and forgiving, and I think we can make each other happy," Yazida said with a dreamy air she'd never seen.

"I can say without a doubt that Shams has cared for you your whole life, and would fight for you til death—and maybe even after. And now he no longer has to worry about me. Oh, how he used to get so jealous! To think of the hard time you both gave me," said Jayida, and they laughed, emotion claiming them again. "Now go on, before they worry and search for you everywhere," she said, hoping her friend wouldn't notice she wanted to be alone again.

"When will you return?" said Yazida.

"I'm not sure. Maybe even later today, but I'm here; if you'd like to reassure my parents."

"You know I would anyway. But I'll keep bringing food until you're back," grinned Yazida.

Jayida nodded, their lingering locked gazes confirming the understanding of their deepened bond.

"Don't be long," said Yazida.

Jayida pinched a smile, grateful that her friend didn't see her torrent of tears as her light steps retreated. At least this was one friendship that hadn't been lost over this whole ordeal. Jayida turned and walked off in the opposite direction, trying to bury the violence of her sobs in her rough hands. So what if she still cried over Khaled? No one had to know but her and Yassu. She sniffled, feeling silly and yet relieved to let it out, one long last time before she returned to camp as Jayida. She was only crying because the pain was still recent, but eventually it would fade, and one day she would even be amused at this old memory, part of her unique, brave story.

She wiped her face and looked up to the sky as she paced, grateful that the Banu Sa'd was still her home, its arms ever open to her as it'd been to so many others. She made long circles with her steps, reminding herself that if she'd been pleasantly surprised by Khaled once, it could happen again. It's not that she expected or even wanted it, but the thought that men might rush to her with marriage proposals was as comical as it was a little off-putting.

Though it would be some time before it spread, there would be little controlling what was said. While some would be surprised and praising of her story, there would always be those with other ideas. Jayida had the resurging nagging feeling of wanting to get away, somewhere where no one would recognize her or know her names... So would she take on yet another?

Maybe she'd finally seek out and settle on that island of Soqotra off the southern coast, and watch the trading ships make port at midpoint between Egypt and

India. Then she'd roam the land whose dragon blood trees shed red sap, and other trees looked like fat silver or copper stumps with short roots and flowers sprouting out of its narrow tips like spiky hair. There she'd find some waterhole by the sea, and swim with bonefish that shone like pearls. She'd catch crawling crabs that camouflaged into the rocks, hunt calamari, and gather horse mackerel washed up on the sea, and bring some to the monastery of Yassu-believers. And sometimes, when thick fog blanketed the coast, she'd wander through the surrounding mountains like a ghost, unknown or at least forgotten by the world—and at peace.

Jayida stopped and faced the sun, soaking it in like Yassu's consuming blinding light. Who knew when she would fall in love again, but life would go on and she would not be miserable until then. She lifted her arms, and cupped her hands in offering, letting the weight fly off and evaporate in thin air. Her whole life she'd always tried to stay a step ahead, anticipate what was next, and though that had its advantages, she couldn't control it all, and trying to do so was exhausting.

It would take time, but she would learn to release the draining weight she'd come to know too well, whether at Banu Sa'd, or elsewhere.

CHAPTER FORTY-THREE

RETURN

Yassu, please help me.

Sitting astride Sadiqa, Khaled tried to ease his hard grip on the form of Yassu that Jonder-Jayida had made him. The gathering, with its single *hawdaj* at center, surrounded him like a wall, at once protective in valiant conquest and suffocating in shameful public defeat.

Sah, she might hate him, but whatever happened, it would be well—he repeated to himself, his heart pounding at the sight of the looming Banu Sa'd camp. He grimaced a sigh, realizing he probably looked more angry than inviting. He closed his eyes, at once happy and tormented over this person who made him nervous. Would he ever get this right? Now was not the time to give conflicting signs!

He opened them again, and met Majid's knowing gaze. A day had been like a thousand years away from her, filled with Layla's impatience that had already tried him enough. But Jayida was no Layla, praise Yassu.

Khaled let the impatient smile-frown overtake him. People still asked him about the identity of the veiled fighter, confused by the elusive, dreamy-eyed response he'd give them. If nothing else, at least he would have that story from her, so *majnun* as to be unbelievable, but whose perfect truth they secretly shared and no one could take from them. At last, the final step was at hand, his last chance to prove to her his sincere intent. He tried to console himself that if he should go down in eternity as the sorriest rejected suitor, at least his far-reaching committed effort would've demonstrated his loyal dedication.

As much for her worthiness and to humble himself, Khaled had contacted and gathered as many people as he could in what had to be record time in the history of horse-riding messengers—whether Rûm, Fars, Ghassanid, Himyarite, Aksumite, or otherwise. Aside from his mother and Majid, he'd brought along

Samaw'al, and the *sayyidun* of Taghlib and Ghatafan, Hatim of Tayyi, and even *mubassir* Ayyub, all the way from Al-Sham. In the miraculous event that she agreed, the *mubassir* would properly unite them, but regardless, this story would be made right once and for all, and if nothing else he would surprise her with these unexpected well-meaning visitors. He gave a quick nod to Majid, and raced off into the quiet, early morning Banu Sa'd camp, letting his companions trail him into his hopeful new life and not his well-deserved downfall.

Khaled made directly for his uncle's tent, put the form of Yassu back into his pouch, and slipped off Sadiqa. He brushed his shaking hands across his robes and bearded face in attempt to straighten himself, his galloping heart now a beating drum rattling through his veins. He took a deep breath and let it out.

"*Amo* Zahir, it is Khaled returned to see you," he said, grateful for his even tone. There was a momentary rustling and Zahir appeared at the entrance.

"Khaled?" said Zahir a bit sternly. "What a pleasure to see you again." Zahir stepped to him, kissed him on each cheek, and invited him inside. Khaled entered, and greeted Zoraya with a smiling nod, concluding from her soft gaze that she guessed his conflicted air.

"We pray all's well," said Zahir inquisitively, and gestured him to some fresh bread and milk. Khaled shook his head, leaned forward and took Zahir's hands in his. Thankfully, his sharp, widened eyes were followed by a controlled smirk, so unlike the paternal anger he'd known all his life.

"Honorable *amo* and *a'mah*, please accept my deepest apology for my rushed departure," said Khaled. "I've come on an important mission, and there's much I need to say."

"What might that be," said Zahir, and he sensed Zoraya's glance on him like a thousand flying blades.

"I wish to marry your daughter Jayida," said Khaled with a firm nod.

"Is there a Jayida here?" said Zahir, crossing his arms with such undisturbed poise that Khaled was momentarily left dumbstruck.

Khaled cleared his throat.

"Honorable kin, I humbly beg: please forgive me. The shameful fault is mine. I've been made aware of the circumstances of her upbringing, and sadly the role my father played in that. You see, I've returned, as I have important things I must say to her and to you both, which I hope will help explain some things. I've much respect for you and your family, and wish for Jayida to be my wife." The torrent in his ears so contrasted Zahir's deep, silent stare, that Khaled was sure his uncle could hear it and make out the extent of his unworthy foolishness with it.

Zahir cocked his head. "And yet, that's not the impression that you gave before. That could be enough for anyone to consider the matter settled."

"You're right *amo*, and I'm a fool for this. It's taken some time, but I seek to make it right. That is why I came, along with the others waiting and ready for the next steps." Khaled noted the flicker of his brow, hinting at his uncle's surprise.

"I'm afraid no more can be said about it from us. I admit, Khaled: I like you; we all like you. I was very happy to meet you and see what kind of man you've become. In many ways I already see you as a son, despite my own troubles with your father. But as you should know, perhaps especially after what happened, who Jayida marries is up to her," said Zahir, and exchanged a glance with Zoraya, whose gentle yet firm stance mirrored her husband's.

Khaled nodded. "Of course, and I accept her decision, no matter what it is. Where can I find her?"

"Yazida's just returned and saw her at the cemetery. That would be a place to start," said Zahir.

"Right," said Khaled, a bit confused by what looked like amusement on his uncle's face.

"Good luck," smirked Zahir, and pat his shoulder.

Leaving his companions to quietly camp and await his orders, Khaled paced hard southeast to the burial place of Nasr and Shanfara, his anger and disgust threatening to unleash at the sight of the three fresh mounds. At least they'd come here, he tried to tell himself.

At last, he found Jayida sitting with her back to him, her scarf draping down her back like a veil. He thought he heard her talking and paused to listen, then realized she was gesturing to some creature he couldn't see.

"Go back! What are you doing here," Jayida teased, and for a moment Khaled thought she was talking to him, like a *kahin* preferring to keep her distance from the lowly. But there was something playful in her tone and the way she moved her arm. Then magically a small furry head appeared from her side, followed by another, and he thought he might cry at the sight of a sand cat and her young studying him from afar.

Aywa; enough waiting! Get over there now! Khaled berated himself and cautiously stepped on, not wanting to startle anyone. He hoped that she would turn around, but caught only glimpses of her dark hair under her headdress. But at least he was there, in the midst of the one who was meant for him, and she hadn't yet chased him away from her inviolable sacred space.

"You can pay your respects to the dancing girls there," said Jayida, and waved to their direction without turning to him.

Pinching a smile, Khaled crouched down next to her, her striking eyes hidden from his sight, somewhere far from him. He glanced at the judgmental cat hovering protectively over her kitten, and implored her to help him, too.

"Jayida, forgive me for disturbing you. But I've come to tell you some things." How could he have so much to say and be so at a loss for the right words?

"Khaled: your father consumed enough of our time, and I'd like to think that's finished, even if by some ill-luck more of his dark dealings may still show up. If you're here to gather congratulations for your wedding to Layla, you have them, so do as you please, and we'll each return to our peace," she said flatly. Or was that a wishful tremor in her voice, hiding her own emotion?

"My wedding?" Before he could think twice, Khaled erupted in laughter, his glimpse of her frown only making him happier. "Oh Jayida, I'm so sorry. I know I don't deserve it, but may I please explain?"

"Now, after all this time, you want to explain? I won't be just more fodder for jokes for you," said Jayida, finally flashing him her flaming eyes, and it took all his strength not to seize her in his arms right then and there.

"Of course not; you never were and never will be. But *na'am* I must explain; seems there's more than either of us knew. I—there's so much to say," said Khaled, his hand rising to the bridge of his nose. "Everything got so confused. But first, let me make it clear: I am not married. Layla did indeed get married, and has been paying many a willing, so-called poets and others to go around spreading those stories of her glorious union to a gold mining tribesman of Sulaym. She tried to blackmail me with spreading rumors about the strange fighter, in exchange for camels, and even hinted she'd come here to test your generosity over mine. That she's still among the Zubayd is proof enough of mine, though I wish she'd leave sooner rather than later," said Khaled.

Jayida stared blankly at him, her perfectly smooth, carved stone-like face as controlled as her father's. For a moment he took in her features, trying to decipher the ways in which he could've realized before that she was a woman. With her long thin nose and sharp cheekbones, she was a striking beauty, even more so with her untamed wild locks surely ready to lash out at him. Her presence still commanded respect, radiating an inner wisdom that invited trusting loyalty, from both human and wild creatures. Her small yet full lips clung tightly together, but the main striking difference was her relaxed appearance, missing its previous frown, that gave her a renewed, alluring air of unshakeable resolve. Her unique amber eyes dotted with green spoke an ancient, unknown language, and though he'd yet to learn it, he was ready to dedicate his life to it.

"Jayida, I'm sorry, so sorry that I refused you. I didn't know what I was doing; it wasn't my true intention," he continued quickly. "I mean, it was at first, but I didn't—" He stopped at her surging frown.

"*Sah*, so thank you for confirming what I already knew," said Jayida with a wave of the hand. "What is this about? Did you come here to humiliate me more, like once wasn't enough?"

"That's a bit much from someone who also tried to do so with me, and quite publicly, and successfully, at that," said Khaled, fighting his rising turmoil even as he rejoiced to see her softening face. "But I had it coming," he sighed, reached for her hand, and breathed a little easier to see that though reluctant, she did not retreat it.

He looked at her, letting his aching heart fill in the outlines of her curves concealed under her dusty, milky robe, grazing her wide hips and small, firm breasts. Her sculpted arms carried her gentle feminine hands roughened by loving masculine toiling in sharpening tools and hunting. His direct gaze drifted up to hers, refusing to relent, begging that it wasn't just his imagination that she was allowing him.

"Lion eyes," said Khaled. "Lion eyes, like your grandfather."

Jayida rolled her eyes. "You're going to have to do better than that, poet. Everyone knows that *siddi* Gayas didn't have them."

Khaled looked down at his hand holding hers, and gave it a gentle squeeze.

"Jayida, I want to say that I came here with one intention, but that's not true: I came here with two."

She shifted uncomfortably, but continued to listen.

"You see, our fathers weren't actually blood brothers. Your father was adopted by *siddi* Gayas; he found your father orphaned after a Lakhmid raid up north, and brought him back to his Zubayd camp and raised him as his son. After losing her second child to stillbirth, this was a blessing to *sitti* Rumayma, so they kept the secret. Moharib learned this truth on *siddi* Gayas's deathbed, which in part explains the senseless, yet mounting competition he felt against your father. So you see, your family is actually from there."

He paused, taking her shocked subdued air as cue to go on.

"I would've come sooner, but I wanted to confirm things and bring it back to you and help make it right. When my mother revealed all this, it reminded me of someone I'd seen when I went to Al-Sham, so I went back to piece it together. As I said, I'd visited our Zubayd kin there, and I recalled our quick visit through Bosra. When we stopped to drink at a fountain, there was a healer, a blind man with a crown of white hair who walked with a cane and smiled right at me, saying I'd be back someday. It was like an arrow hit me; like he'd seen through me and that I didn't really want to return home, but of course I had to. As you can imagine, I didn't know what he meant, and assumed he was just being hospitable. I'd think of him from time to time, but after what my mother shared, I just knew I had to go back and speak to him. When I returned, I found the man named Eliyas, and he seemed even more distraught than me. He kept saying that I had 'lion eyes around me,' and I assumed he meant somehow that I'd recently seen you, which I confirmed. Before I could even tell him why I'd come, he told me about a beloved man who'd lived at the time of *Qaysar* Anastasius. The man had lion eyes, hence his name Ayan, the watchful. He was a brave Ghassanid warrior from Bosra who fought alongside *malik* Al-Harith's father Jabalah. He loved to travel, and often visited the holy Yassu sites throughout the land, but he, along with his wife Wafa and others, were killed during a raid while stationed further east, likely by troops serving the Lakhmids. Some say it was Al-Mundhir himself, his conceit inflated by the fresh start of his rule." Khaled stopped, his heart aching as tears cascaded down her cheeks.

She bit her lip and nodded for him to go on.

"But yet another mystery, said Eliyas, was that Ayan had an infant son named Harith, whose body was never found. As time passed they suspected that either the baby had died, or had been taken by the brigands to be raised in their renegade lifestyle. Either way, they considered him lost, never to be seen again. Before leaving, Eliyas took me to their grave near the great domed Bosra Cathedral, and it's then that he tearfully confessed that Ayan was his son, and that he still had hope of seeing Harith again. So you see, you still have family there, and as you now know, that child named Harith is your father, called Zahir by *siddi* Gayas," said Khaled.

Jayida shook her head, disgust pouring out of her.

"It *was* al-Mundhir. Anywhere there's destruction and death, he isn't far behind. Oh! Now my pride can burst out of my chest even stronger, glorifying that my father faced him at Kutha; a perfect immortal ghost returned to balance the scales!"

Khaled nodded, eager to finish and ease her torment.

"Once again, I must ask your forgiveness, as I can now also confirm the case of Ayida and Liya," he said, with his head bowed.

"*Aywa*, the one time I'd hoped to be wrong," said Jayida and retreated her hand.

"Jayida, I'm so sorry for what you had to go through. Still, I'm grateful you didn't have to know him. You know best the good you and your parents made from it; how far you've come. You're strong, and I'm honored to do my part so that everyone knows that this was your brave doing, that he couldn't stand against it!" said Khaled, struggling to keep his even tone.

"But I *did* know him, and I see traces of him everywhere, in others like, and even worse than him!" she yelled, her hands drawn into fists. He held his breath, bracing himself for what he feared most—that she'd say he was just like him, too.

"We both do! I know it's hard, and despite being his son, I'm begging that you trust me and don't count me among that crowd, because I'm not like him in his dark ways."

The slicing silence hovered and though he wanted to fill the space that hung between them, he stayed in place. He would not let her walk away so easily this time. He reached in his pouch, grazing the figure of Yassu, and found the hard, round form.

"Moharib's hidden it too long, but at last; here's the coin your father's been looking for. He was found with it tucked in his folds as a blessed amulet left by your grandparents," said Khaled, the gold shining in his tanned hand.

Without a word Jayida took it, absorbed its familiar engraving of the black and blue-eyed *Qaysar* Anastasius in his battle attire.

"There's another bit to the story, probably made up, but since it's part of your family stories, you should know," he said. "It goes that during his travels, Ayan acquired much treasure and decided to stash it in a cave in the Hijaz, to come back to at some point. It was quite a large one, and therefore he told few, but of course Eliyas knew. As a cautious, wise man, it was Ayan's way of ensuring it wouldn't be preyed upon by brigands. And he may have succeeded because of course, no one knows where it is. Still, Eliyas insists that it's in some cave, containing several satchels branded with an eye *wasm* and full of coins and trinkets. You should've seen how insistent he was describing it, practically urging me to go after it," Khaled chuckled. "Not surprising to see why they love hearing that tale, though if you ask me, I know who should be the one to find it."

"Hidden treasure," Jayida smirked. "At least there's a good thing from all this: I don't share blood with your father after all. Not that it means much sometimes, considering people's ways."

"But that's the part I hope we can change, at least in terms of us both," said Khaled. He reached out to her and her avoidance nearly broke his heart.

"Can we? I used to fear time, but now I know I don't have to. I never thought it would happen, but finally I profess Yassu and only Yassu now, as unworthy as I am, and with all the work I have to do. But I'm not casting away one beast and welcoming another. The beast will walk into hell of his own doing," she said, her dreamy vision lost somewhere beyond him.

Khaled restrained a grunt, his soul tearing him to pieces even as he fought to keep himself unshakably whole.

"Jayida, please, answer me this: can you honestly tell me that you ever thought I was like him? Did you? Could you have had feelings, any at all, for me if you'd really thought that? Especially as *kahin*?" He crouched near her, his massive form threatening to fold over in begging position. Never before would he have done it, but he'd known nothing before, and would do it if only it would change her mind.

Jayida closed her eyes and shook her head, and as tears cascaded he knew that he would always be there in her heart, in one way or another, despite all his wrong. He slid over to her and took each of her hands, like it might somehow stop her from slipping away.

"Jayida, will you do me the honor of being my wife?" he said, searching her anguished, flooded eyes. "You possess all the qualities I've ever wanted, and even the ones I never imagined I would. I know, all your life you thought you had to keep yourself safe from us, but for me it was the opposite. All my life I just wanted to come here, to see *you*, if only to know why my uncle left and have you as a companion! And now that I have, I can't be the same. If you will have me, please don't ever doubt that I'll protect you and take care of you with all I can, as I'm sure you will of me. I know—I know you don't need me. But *I* do. And that's what scares me most," he said, his voice cracking with emotion. "Is it so impossible to revive that love, despite what I've done? Or has it all gone? And still, though every part of me would protest, I would never force you," he said, unable and unwilling to restrain his own tears from flowing.

How could it be the best and most painful feeling all at once? But he would get an answer from her, even if it was the one he would never fully accept.

"Anyone would be blessed to have you, but I need that to be me. And that's what I want: to live up to that challenge of being with you, and live this life together, side by side, and growing into better people, together. Will you please say something?" he croaked with a smile. "Do you accept?"

"Of course I do!" Jayida exclaimed. "If I could forget you that fast, it's that it wasn't real. Or maybe it's the new manly beard, too," she chuckled through her tears. "Oh, what a sight we are, though part of me thinks Nasr, his kin, and Shanfara are smiling over us."

"Oh, my heart, you make me the happiest of men," he stammered, then caught his breath and drew her into his arms. "Thank *Yassu*, those who've come with me will be so happy to hear this," he said, burying his face in her musky hair.

"Those with you?" She looked up at him.

"Many good people, with more to come."

"Many people?" Her vision narrowed. "To publicly tell them that I like you? On second thought—"

Khaled lifted her chin and drew her into a blazing kiss before she could change her mind.

Chapter Forty-Four

WEDDING

There's more.

Jayida smiled dreamily as she wallowed in the pleasant echo. New name. New family. New home. In her wildest dreams, she couldn't have imagined that they would come together so quickly—and easily. There was a faint shuffle near her, and her mother's embrace enveloped her in her parents' beloved tent.

"The blessed day has arrived," whispered her mother into her ear, and covered her face in kisses.

Lulled by her mother's gentle stroking of her hair, a flutter radiated from deep in her core, stretching her lips. Khaled had better be awake at that same moment, caught in a million similar happy and nervous emotions! With a chuckle Jayida buried her face in her clove and honey-scented hands decorated with saffron-brown henna florals, bidding goodbye to her last morning as an unmarried girl. She may not have cared much for time-keeping before, but she'd never forget this most beautiful and important day that blended late spring and early summer.

"Come along," cooed Zoraya.

Jayida joined her parents in the men's area, the soft-sweet aroma of fresh honey mead nearly calling forth tears. Ever since Khaled had returned two weeks before, every detail, every moment took a new importance to be sealed in her memory, as they led up to their ultimate union. But none was as important as her father's quiet pinched smile, a mix of happy acceptance and sadness that added to her own whirlwind emotions. Dressed in his freshest fumigated full attire, with his hair and beard full of fragrant oil and Al-Khalisa across his lap, he pat the space next to him. She sat, and stilled the tightness in her throat as she caught the gleam in his eyes.

"To our new names, and more to come," said her father, and took a sip of his drink, hinting at their future children.

Overcome by gratitude and humility, Jayida nodded, and took cautious sips of her drink. She gazed into the fermented gold liquid, merging her beloved happy Aksumite princess guardian with Ayida, Liya, and the singing girls who'd died in their camp. She drank as much for her and Khaled's new beginnings as for theirs, and even if the seeds Khaled had put on all their graves never took, it was enough to know they were there.

She sensed her father drifting somewhere else. Zahir Al-Harith: son of Ayan of Ghassan, and son of Gayas of Zubayd. It didn't have a bad ring, but behind his usual composure Jayida knew as well as her mother that it had a different effect on him. Unlike her own dual names she'd always known, this one had been hidden from him, and partially from the supposed brother he'd been loyal to as much as he could. Like it wasn't bad enough for Moharib to know that Zahir's parents were killed: instead, Moharib had to sap any other joy from his life by tormenting him with more feelings of inferiority. *Cursed without sons*—he'd tried yet failed when all of it had finally come full-circle. That's where the true triumph lay, when she sensed in herself a subtle, yet distinct change, a reduced urge to lash out that did not in the least diminish the power of her stance. The truth existed somewhere in peaceful stillness: her father, in his generous, calm nature, could never be cursed; instead, it was those who were never satisfied and constantly stirred wrath who cursed themselves.

Gradually, their shared initial shock was followed by disappointment that gravitated to *sha'ir* Hakim, who'd known the longest. Even Khamra's long silence had surprised Zoraya, when some women were so inclined to gossip, though it was true Khamra's nature thankfully shrank from it. No matter how Jayida turned it over, about how it could've been revealed sooner, it all came back to fear. A fear that, though she was grateful she'd never been directly around, had consumed her all the same, no matter how much in her pride she liked to think otherwise. Jayida could try to find fault with them, with how they could've done things differently, but she could not blame their concerns over disloyalty, disobedience, harm, maybe even death—that made them wait until after Moharib's unexpected death to finally visit them.

Jayida took a big gulp and let the Hudhayl honey sweetness remind her that at least it had finally come out, and worked out better than she could've imagined. She'd proven herself, and *al-'ayn* had failed and vanished, ensuring her security.

"I shall say it now and release it at last," said her father, and looked at them both at each side of him. "Sometimes I think I could be angry forever. But as I've always said, it's good to forgive. Otherwise we're just repeating the same never-ending cycle. There's always things to be angry about and old feuds to bring up. But how far back do we go? I've had enough: that was decided when we left the Zubayd. So now, learning we have Ghassanid blood, who are *Masihi* and follow the teachings of Yassu, it feels even more important not to hold grudges, or let the past hold us back." Zahir paused and turned to her. "Which is why I'm honored to give you both my blessing,"

He leaned into her and kissed her forehead, each of them feeling the pinch of resurging happy tears.

"And now, I leave you, my beautiful *kahinat*, to do your magic." With another loving gaze, he left the tent.

Jayida followed her mother to the prepared women's area, shed her night dress, and stepped into the low water-filled clay basin made especially for the occasion.

"So, with the thousands upon thousands of things, what are you thinking of most right now?" Zoraya gently ran a washcloth across her skin, her smooth legs still tender from the previous day's honey-lemon waxing. Despite the pain Jayida was sure men would hardly endure, she had to admit that the effect, along with her now sculpted eyebrows, was worth it.

"Right now; the crowd. I still can't believe all the people here," said Jayida.

"*Aywa*; it will be the talk for a while," beamed her mother.

A few moments later they knew that the determined steps sweeping through the tent were none other than *Umm* Jarida's. The elderly stout Tayyi woman swept around them with her air of ancient knowledge, as much from age as from being wife to a renown Taghlib fighter in the Basus War.

"The perfect woman, through and through," said *Umm* Jarida with her unique blend of Tayyi and Taghlib accent, as she approvingly looked her over. "Just let anyone make doubting jokes, I'll embarrass them to death with the truth!"

Jayida blushed, touched to be truly seen for herself by the great-grandmother who'd raised her mother and who, recently widowed as she was, would now stay with them. Though they'd yet to say much to each other, there was that beloved feminine intimate sense of understanding that needed no words to express it. Often they looked at each other with sparkling eyes, hinting that they could also converse through their shared, deepest *kahinat* thoughts. That her renowned Taghlib kin would only support her unusual story was another necessary balm in her changing midsts. Her mother handed her a long sheet to dry off, then disappeared with *Umm* Jarida behind the tent divider.

Like so many others, their kin hadn't come alone, but with their young *sha'ir-sayyid* Amr ibn Kulthum and over a dozen men. The growing gathering now included *sayyid* Aziz's invitation to their kin the *sayyid* Safwan of Banu Hawazin, whom Jayida and others were meeting for the first time. He'd come all the way from near Wajj, and together made at least three additional *sayyidun* in attendance. There was also Muawiyah of Dhubyan with his young *nabigha* poet son Ziyad, and just the thought of his adopted twins Najma and Najim of Ghatafan to witness her day was enough to get her emotional again. There were others and more guests than she could count, sure to keep spreading their unique story far and wide.

All would be well—what more proof did she need? Her bursting respect for *sayyid* Aziz and the whole tribe expanded with every passing moment. By the time she'd finally reappeared to the tribe, and—most surprising of all—with Khaled at her side, the welcomed return had been overflowing with mutual awe and recognition. It was then that she knew that she'd never lose their loyalty, despite the secret kept for seventeen summers. Instead of the criticisms she'd feared her father might face, there was a support and pride for Zahir's choice to raise their child among them, adding to their glorious legacy. Not unlike her father, *sayyid* Aziz's eyes had filled with laughing tears, as he'd pieced together his son's curious last words.

Her timely confession that she had seen Nasr in the afterlife with his wife and Yassu urged Yazida's own revelation to them—until even Warda, and *sayyid* Aziz himself confessed to having seen him, too. She'd never forget how, at this development, their wide-eyed confusion yielded to life-changing joyful tears that fast spread through camp. Shams had been silently upset and envious until his own humbled confession followed days after—confirming that their long walk in darkness, filled with unanswered questions, at last made more sense. As the *injil* said, if madness was its name, then apparently they gladly shared it.

"I also thought I was just imagining," said *sayyid* Aziz. "But it felt so real, so reassuring! Even with all my desperate yearning, I'd never imagined it would be like this, and why would I make myself wait so long to see it, if it was me doing it and I could make it up in a moment?" He shook his head, now full of long wavy hair. "It reminded me of us at the end of my pilgrimage at Mina; how I thought that I'd called divine wrath upon myself. Even if I deserve it, I still accept it, but it just feels different now," said *sayyid* Aziz with an air of relief that touched her heart.

Oh, how she would miss the Banu Sa'd! From the moment she and Khaled had confessed their love to each other, the unavoidable question of relocation tugged at her from all angles, until the answer appeared clear as day and had to be let out.

"Khaled, you know how much I want to be with you, as your faithful wife. But I can't deny this longing I've had ever since you told us about our heritage. I feel now that I've always had it, but it didn't make sense before—and now it does. I want to go to Al-Sham: I want to meet our *baba* Eliyas, and see and be in the land of our family. It just feels right," said Jayida.

She hardly expected him to leave his tribe or even be pleased with her wish, but their union had to begin with honesty. Even if they had to spend some time apart, split between camps, it was too tempting not to try.

"I've considered as much, and I'm not surprised," said Khaled, and for a moment she thought she'd misheard him. "I loved the region when I visited and even with lurking concerns over the raging plague, it was hard for me to leave. The Zubayd the Small at Philippopolis is just north of Bosra, and they'd love to see us and have us close by. We'll have to discuss with *sha'ir* Hakim, Abjar, Majid, and the others on splitting duties, but we'll make it work regardless. Isn't that why we're getting married?" he'd smiled, melting her heart again to doughy lava.

It had happened all over again when she'd taken him to the cave with *siddi* Ayan's hidden treasure. With emotional solemnity they'd slid aside the wall, approached the treasure with lingering awe, and decided to keep the secret between them and their parents. Though another perfect story to add to her unusual legacy, not everything had to be revealed at once, or even at all. She'd been shocked again by their perfect agreement, as if they were already fast fusing into one mind, and if that's how she already felt, she could only imagine how much it'd deepen after their vows.

The warm-sweet scent greeted her as *Umm* Jarida reappeared with a fuming bronze incense burner in each hand and settled them at opposite sides of the room. Behind came her mother, holding her layers of sleeveless white linen robe, her immaculate white dress with gold embroidery at the neck, cuffs, and hem, and a matching gold satin belt. Beaming with pride, they both helped her into the precious clothes for the blessed day that she hadn't dreamed would come so soon.

"Your happiest day is at hand!" came Yazida's singing voice from the tent entrance, followed by a bustle of cheerful noises. "May we come in?"

"You may," said Zoraya.

Yazida instantly spilled in, followed by Warda and Khamra in crisp new embroidered robes, and armfuls of baskets filled with wrapped packages.

"By *al-ilah*, you're such a natural beauty that you could forego the embellishments," said Khamra, her clapped hands resting on her chin.

"*Sah*, but a woman marries for the first time only once, so she will have everything," *Umm* Jarida chuckled and winked at her.

Yazida flew to her side. "How are you feeling?" she said, gripping her shoulders.

"Mostly under control, though I want it over already, too," Jayida chuckled.

"What a lucky man; he has no mere delicate flower in his hands," said Warda. "And though you've shown him already, he'll see the full extent of his prized choice."

"Let's get to it, then," said her mother.

Jayida looked on, curious and a little worried, as her mother brought out the new long carved wooden chest. She set about gathering the pots of animal fat and powder jars with *Umm* Jarida, while Warda laid out some small sticks with bits of wool tied to its ends with thread.

"We've brought you gifts," said Yazida, and handed her some of the small packages, revealing an abundance of woven knotted bracelets dyed in saffron, red, and purple with black accents in varied patterns.

"And here are mine, for the daughter I've always wanted," said Khamra with emotion, the blue-grey shades drawing Jayida's attention.

"They're beautiful," said Jayida, extending her arms to let them slip them on her wrists. "Now they're all together, side by side, as they should be," she said, caressing the soft dyed threads they took dedicated time to make.

"Now close your eyes," said her mother. Jayida obeyed and felt a sticky substance followed by gentle dabs on her lids. "And hold still for this." Carefully she slid the stick above her lashes to thicken the line of kohl across each lid, and past the corner of her eyes. "Now open up."

Jayida obeyed and blinked, and saw her mother standing back with a satisfied grin, along with more approving, fascinated stares.

"*Aywa,* now your lion eyes have wings," nodded *Umm* Jarida.

"A heavenly sight," grinned Yazida.

"My blessed son," said Khamra, on the verge of tears.

"Can I see?" said Jayida.

"Almost," said her mother. Zoraya grabbed an alabaster jar and rubbed a musky-sweet cream on her face, then grabbed another jar and dabbed red powder to her lips, as *Umm* Jarida vigorously spread the red ochre on her cheeks, its striking hue slightly alarming Jayida. At least her perfect ebony hair wasn't colored using dyes extracted from leeches left to rot in wine for forty days.

"Now, then?" said Jayida, and her mother handed her a heavy wrapped package.

"It's from your beloved," smiled Khamra.

Jayida unwrapped it, and her jaw dropped at the polished bronze, hand-held mirror that reflected a striking portrait. For a moment she could only stare, wide-eyed like a noblewoman eternally etched in a mosaic in her lavish home. There was the reflection of a delicate, feminine woman, her amber feline eyes enhanced by the contrasting sooty smoke and pair of wings, with the red cheeks and lips adding a fieriness she loved. She'd never imagined that she could look like this, and would not only like it, but feel right at home in it. It was soft and a bit dangerous, just as she wanted it.

"*Aywa*, I'll agree that I'm a sight to behold," Jayida chuckled, turning her face to catch herself from different angles.

"Don't sound so surprised," laughed Yazida, and they exchanged a knowing smile.

"And last but not least, the jewelry," said Warda.

Her mother brought over an open box and presented it to her. "Remember this?" she grinned.

"Are those?" said Jayida wide-eyed.

"They are; earrings from the ostrich eggs you brought back," beamed her mother.

"They're beautiful, and with the patterns you drew on them! Queen Mawiyya would approve," said Jayida.

"I think so, too," said her mother. She slipped the metal hooks into her newly-pierced earlobes, and though large, they sat delicately in place.

Khamra brought over another carved chest, and opened it to reveal it full of so many different gold and other jewelry pieces that it reminded her of *siddi* Ayan's treasure.

"I like this style of bracelet with the grapevine pattern. And these copper and bronze pieces are surely from the Tayma mines," smirked Jayida.

"*Na'am*," said Khamra. "Khaled wanted you to have some pieces from there, and concluded you might like the variety."

"*Sah*," chuckled Jayida. "But I can't, it's all too much."

"Not at all. You deserve it, especially today," said Khamra, echoed by everyone else. Grinning, they each took a piece and offered it invitingly, as Jayida surrendered in humble acceptance and let her neck, wrists, and ankles be decorated in the delicate jewelry.

"See; suits you perfectly," said her mother, who slipped two wide, armor-like rings across her fingers engraved with flowers and leaves.

Jayida held out and looked over her ornamented hennaed hands and sandaled feet, relishing the new sight of the reddened nails, amber drawings, and golden colors blending on her skin. Everything on her seemed to burst with elaborate, time-consuming embellishment born out of a pleasant feminine stillness that wanted more of her attention.

"It's funny how I can be wearing so much of this and feel a little naked without my coat of mail and Al-Wasiyah. But I could go for more of these rings," chuckled Jayida.

"*Aywa*; it's already working its magic and seducing you," said *Umm* Jarida, reading her mind.

"Now time to reveal this other pleasant surprise to your husband," said her mother, who disappeared again with *Umm* Jarida, and returned with her multi-layered white headdress and veil.

Jayida chuckled as they set the thick crown on her head, full of jingling golden coins, and topped it with the white silk cascading down the sides of her face.

Umm Jarida's grip settled on her shoulders. "We're so proud of you, as is my recently passed Amir, and your *sitti* Rania and *siddi* Ghanam," she said, and kissed each cheek.

Jayida nodded, biting her lower lip to hold back the happy nervous tears, and with one last round of her mother's kisses and a confirming look, her mother lowered the sheer silk veil over her face.

They stepped out and walked on, with her mother and *Umm* Jarida guiding her at each side, while Yazida, Warda, and Khamra followed behind. Jayida took deep breaths, grateful for the veil that sheltered her flickering brow and pinching lips. A dark veil had helped her at Tayma, but this eggshell silk that danced and shifted with the sunrays was no less powerfully effective. She caught the scent of roasting seasoned meats and pastries, humbled by the nearly countless food already in preparation, and to Nasr for being invisibly there to see and protect their most important day.

Her heart pounding to the tune of jingling coins, she imagined all the unseen people who were there, gloriously stretching the Banu Sa'd's camp parameters. Feeding the lot of them for several days would've worried her, if it wasn't for their combined resources that made it possible.

They reached her father who waited ahead, and *Umm* Jarida and her mother gave her hand to him. He took it and held it protectively as they walked on solemnly. His twitching fingers made her tear up all over again, and she sent him silent thoughts not to fear that he was losing her. It was a transition for all of them, but not a separation.

At last they came upon Khaled standing at the left side, with *mubassir* Ayyub before them, his hands folded over his small leatherbound book with a silver cover plaque decorated with a cross. With an emotional smile and quick nod, her father released her hand and stood a few paces away.

Jayida straightened next to Khaled and quickly met his kohled gaze, matched by his stiffened jawline and serious air. That he was as nervous as she and trying hard to control it made him even more handsome in his crisp white and gold embroidered attire, and Al-Naji at his waist.

Two young boys and a girl appeared: one holding a fuming bronze incense burner, another a goblet of wine, and the third a small pouch. She took in deep breaths of the heavenly scent, and with emotion she realized that it was Ziyad and the twins Najim and Najma who joined the *mubassir*'s side like dutiful angelic helpers.

Quiet awe descended upon the audience at the sight of the far-traveled *mubassir*, whose *malik* Al-Harith now seemed a closer kin by association. *Mubassir* Ayyub looked back and forth between them, his sparkling eyes and grey beard amidst his wrinkled skin adding to his timeless air. Her throat pinched, touched that this man who'd cared for Nasr had now come all this way again for them. Sometimes she had the impression that her forehead still gently pulsated right where he'd anointed them with oil a few days before, after their renunciation of Shaytan to serve Yassu, required by their baptism in preparation for their lifelong union.

The figure has passed and the truth has come, with oil you have been sealed, in baptism you have been perfected, you have been mixed in the flock, from His body you are nourished... the words of Saint Ephrem recited by *mubassir* Ayyub echoed in her soul.

Mubassir Ayyub nodded to Khaled and she turned to her beloved, his hands reaching out to her to cautiously lift up her veil. She gazed up at him, his striking love deepening the red on her cheeks to the low hum of communal approval. They both turned back to the *mubassir*, a sense of giddy reassurance already sweeping through her.

Mubassir Ayyub lifted his hands, one clasping the holy *injil*, the other with his palm facing them.

"We thank Yassu *al-Masih* for this day in the rule of the brave *malik* Al-Harith, and *sayyid* Aziz of the Banu Sa'd. We are gathered here to witness the union of your children Khaled and Jayida. In His holy name, we witness today that they are no longer two, but one flesh, just as He is of One divine, undivided nature." *Mubassir* Ayyub turned to Najma, who held up a small embroidered pouch from which he retrieved two gold rings.

"What our savior Yassu *al-Masih* has joined together, let no one separate," said *mubassir* Ayyub. He took the first ring and slipped it on Khaled's left ring finger, then did the same with hers. Then he turned to Ziyad who handed him the goblet of wine.

"May He seal the sacrament of your union with His blood," said mubassir Ayyub, and gave the sweet wine for Khaled and her to drink. "In Yassu's name, I now pronounce you husband and wife," smirked the *mubassir*.

Happy shouts rang out as she beheld her husband who instantly wrapped her in his arms, his fiery passion piercing her like a spear as if he'd practiced to put as much of himself as he could in that brief public moment. In the blurry rush she looked away shyly, before she dared to repeat it again in her eagerness.

"Generous Banu Sa'd and guests, I proclaim before you today what has been growing in my heart and known to a closest few," said Khaled, turning to the crowd. "All that I have is now also my wife Jayida's, with full ownership rights and authority to speak on my behalf. To her father I also grant two thousand camels, not because it can fully reflect his famous generosity or his daughter's value, but as a token of gratitude for all that he's already selflessly done for us, and others. And should my life end before my wife's, she and my mother are to fully inherit their even share of all that I have, as agreed upon."

Jayida swallowed back tears at the meaningful number of camels so close to that her father had donated during the *Ayyam al-Zalam*, and read gratitude in her father's own demeanor.

"Praise Yassu, and blessings to Khaled and Jayida and their kin!" shouted *sayyid* Aziz, catching her off guard as much as *mubassir* Ayyub who chuckled in agreement.

All at once rainbows of flowers showered upon them, as deep ululating and clapping echoed, led by Yazida, waving her tambourine. She twirled around like a graceful bird, but not fast enough to hide the playful gaze she passed to Majid. Jayida chuckled at the sight of him looking away in meek respect, and as if on cue, he turned and made his way to them.

"I'm honored to see my closest friend united with the best woman for him," said Majid with a light bow. "It was hard to believe, but I will never tire of telling everyone how wrong I was."

"I'm grateful for your presence," said Jayida. His air of austerity did not detract from his handsomeness, and she'd already joked with Khaled that perhaps Yazida might stir his heart—if Shams allowed it.

In the happy assembly and swaying rush of her parents, Warda, and Khamra, she noted Samira, smiling shyly at her as she scattered flowers and made her way over, for once looking even more apologetic than her son.

"I'm moved by your continued success. I hope you can forgive that I haven't always given that impression," said Samira who for the first time in her life appeared on the verge of humbled tears.

"Praise Yassu it's a bright new day," said Jayida, hoping that it might be the start of an overdue change. At least the thought that Yazida would have none of her envious nagging was also satisfying.

"And we also offer you our blessings, since it will soon be Shams's and Yazida's turn," said Khaled.

Jayida smiled in agreement and glanced at Shams, who appeared distraught. Ever since she'd returned to camp, she hadn't seen much of him, and suspected he still felt embarrassed.

"Jayida, I know we've had our troubles. I feel so silly now and I hope you won't remember me that way. I wish you both all the happiness; you deserve it," said Shams, his emotion visible through his frown.

"Oh Shams, it's all in the past. We've all had to figure things out," said Jayida, and playfully cupped his chin. "I know you'll take good care of Yazida, too, so all is well," she smirked, and caught the glint in his eyes as he nodded and smiled.

"Time for wine!" said *sayyid* Aziz, bursting upon them. "I could use your help," he said to Shams and Samira, who followed him.

From the approaching alluring voice and tambourine, they knew Yazida was upon them again, trailed by the twins, Ziyad, and other children who quickly surrounded them and made a wide circle. With Najma and Ziyad at his side, Najim stood proudly before them in a small circle, and took out his lion claw from under his robes.

"See; I still wear it," said Najim.

"I'm so happy to see you again," said Jayida with controlled emotion as she touched his cheek. No matter how much time passed, she always wished she could just peel off that evil chapter from his life. "I'm glad that you keep it, though I don't think it's any help."

"I think it is, because you were there, right on time," said Najim. She glanced at Khaled, then back at the twins and the young poet Ziyad.

"My father told us," said Ziyad, and from his serious tone she knew that it was not in vain when the three had already formed an unbreakable bond.

"The twins and their poet," said Khaled. "Something tells me we'll be hearing more of you."

Fighting her tears, Jayida wrapped the twins in her arms, and squeezed hard as if to bind an invisible and flexible knotted-rope bracelet around them. She marveled at the strength of her love for them despite not being her own children, but then realized, perhaps in a way they were. Sniffling back tears, she made them swear that they would take time to remember and get to know Yassu. All the better if the lion might be His, and not Shamshun's.

"Coming through; one Taghlib making his way to another," echoed a deep voice through the crowd, revealing Amr ibn Kulthum with a cup in each hand. "To our happiest, most unique couple; may our tribes increase," he said, handing one to each of them. "This is the potion which diverts the anxious lover from his passion; and as soon as he tastes it, he is perfectly composed."

Jayida returned his grin, recognizing one of his verses.

"And before you say anything: *na'am*, my dress is perfectly overdone, though I do look better in it than a pearl-loving Fars. And why not? It's not every day that I attend Jonder-Jayida's wedding! I'm proud to be your kin, and as I've said before, I'm at your service. Let this be the day that I say: some I eliminate, and others I praise beyond the grave," said Amr, inviting them to sip their drink.

"We thank you for coming all this way and bringing *Umm* Jarida. It means everything," said Jayida tearfully. She tried to gather herself and glanced at the twins, laughing and singing as if it was all just a bad dream. Surely it was possible to move on, no matter how long it took.

"And you'll *have* to visit us at Bosra, and grace *malik* Al-Harith's court with your verses, sooner rather than later. Though preferably in Taghlib attire, for the *malik*'s sake," smirked Khaled.

"My sweet Zaynab of Kalb would like that. And it would be a good chance to restock on wines of Wadi Jadar, Adhri'at, and Al-Andarin," said Amr. Just then, a striking slightly older woman, adorned in a red and gold embroidered ensemble, came up behind him. With her arm draped on his shoulder holding his wine cup and the other holding their young boy on her wide hip, Jayida loved that they made a headstrong couple. "And here's our fierce Kulthum," said Amr, and scooped up his son in his arms, named after his grandfather.

"The handsome picture of his parents," said Khaled, whom she knew was thinking of their own future children, too.

In the crowd they spotted Samaw'al and Hatim making their way over.

"At last we reach you! Now I have full proof that the Banu Sa'd makes as strong a wall as my Qasr Al-Ablaq," said Samaw'al. He winked at her and kissed Khaled on each cheek. "A thousand blessings on you and yours, into eternity. Jayida, my

Rashel and Hassan have not stopped asking about you since they heard the news, and can't wait to meet you," said Samaw'al with a hint of lingering curiosity.

"I'm looking forward to it," nodded Jayida, amused that Hassan must've told him about her as the anonymous rider fighting Khaled at Tayma.

"Likewise for my Adiyy," said Hatim, presenting his son who held something covered in a cloth. "May Yassu watch over you, and over us all, always."

"It's a blessing to hear it from you, and to see my previous student-in-arms," said Khaled, reminding her of the happy and conflicted time he'd spent among them.

"As has been said, you were a sight already with those eyes. Either way, it's great inspiration for new poetry," Hatim said with a twinkle in his eye.

"Poetry, for me? Perhaps if you leave the names out?" Jayida chuckled.

"Khaled is incomplete without Jonder-Jayida. The names will out," grinned Samaw'al, fueling her smile.

"Please accept this humble gift of ours," said the sage-looking Adiyy, and handed her the covered item that revealed a birdcage with two white doves in it.

"Oh! They're beautiful and perfect!" said Jayida, trying not to tear up at the thought of bringing this living piece of them with her to their new northern home.

"May we add them to your honorable gifts?" said Adiyy. "And see your skins?"

"Of course," said Jayida and glanced at their tent, where people streamed in and out with praises and offerings. Even the lurking sand cat and her kitten—whom she'd named Ramila and Ramiya—had now become part of her flock, along with quails and some of Yazida's pigeons. Her heart fluttered again, not because she and Khaled already had more than enough, and could survive on much less, but because so many had come from near and far to add to their happiness in their own special way.

Moments later, Shams reappeared with his brother Sufyan and his friendly Sulaym bethrothed named Tala. Sufyan took them aside, saying he was gifting them gold he'd sweated and bled for himself.

"Gold! No, Sufyan; that's too much," said Jayida. "It's enough that you were able to come."

"*Esh?* It's the *wedding* of Jonder-Jayida, who's actually a woman who grew up among the Sa'd! It must be the most marvelous story in all the land. Anyway, you can always show the gold to *malik* Al-Harith; remind him we have quality metals, too. You know; in case he ever wants to do business, even if he has his own happy mines at Al-Sham," said Sufyan.

"If my wife hesitates, I'll gladly take it," grinned Khaled, and she gently elbowed him as they laughed.

"And look who else just arrived this morning!" chanted *sayyid* Aziz, returned and surrounded by her parents and more familiar faces.

"*Nasi* Musa, Dawud, and Attab! And *nasi* Ibrahim and Adinah! How kind of you to come!" said Jayida, nearly speechless. For a moment her stomach coiled, dreading to find hints of disapproval, but found only cheerful demeanors.

"How could we miss the wedding of Jonder the *kahin* of the *Ayyam al-Za-lam?*" said *nasi* Musa. "Plus, it was the only thing that could get Attab out of Khaybar for once."

"*Aywa*. As soon as Adinah heard about the lion-slayer who'd visited us at Yathrib, she wouldn't relent until I agreed," said *nasi* Ibrahim, whose glance darted between her and his bright-eyed daughter.

"It's also a perfect opportunity to restock you on Khaybar wine, which might be the second best after our Yathrib vines," said Adinah, whose daring cheerfulness hadn't diminished since they'd first met.

"It's an honor to finally meet you all," said Khaled and called for them all to recline and enjoy the feast.

They settled around the campfire, and the food came piling in on glistening gold and silver trays etched with grapevines and geometric designs.

"What will you have first?" said her father.

"I can't decide, so a bit of everything?" chuckled Jayida.

"As you wish," said her mother.

Her heart full, she savored small portions of buttered *tharida* soup, black Hijazi goat stew seasoned in saffron, fat-tailed Awassi sheep stew, and tender young camel meat. There was even slow-cooked lamb braised in wine for their Israelite guests, and gamey, crispy pigeon pies—surely from Yazida—along with meatballs with crushed nuts, Zubaidi truffles, fresh goat cheese, lentil and *rejleh* stews, and buttermilk endlessly going around.

The day elapsed into long feasting, filled with pyramid mountains of gold, copper, and bronze dates, and desserts of rosewater and nut-filled sugar cubes, with pies glistening with Hudhayl honey in so many variations from different tribes that none tasted exactly alike. Wine flowed, and there was more gifting from and to guests, as some discussed their concerns and sought help. As usual her father gifted camels to those who needed it, causing happy tears from souls touched by his famous genuine generosity.

In the late afternoon they let their horses out for some light racing. *Sayyid* Aziz rode his ebony stallion Al-Nabith while Yazida gladly paraded their white stallion Bariq, that precious happy memory of her brother Nasr. When Zahir brought out Kamila and Adil, Jayida's free-spirited stallion first dashed straight to his previous owner *sayyid* Hudayfa of Ghatafan, and the two pairs of mounts he'd brought as gifts for the newlyweds. From his own suggestion, that his fine horses—and even descendants—might serve *malik* Al-Harith during his forays against Al-Mundhir and the Fars was an opportunity he wouldn't pass up. Jayida named the new cream pair Luluwa and Al-Asal, and Khaled named the gray pair Al-Makhmal and Sababa.

"And now, up!" said Khaled, and swooped her up onto Adil.

"Be easy now, my prince! I can only ride side-saddle in this dress," teased Jayida.

"Somehow I think you'll be fine," smirked Khaled. He hopped onto Kamila, just as their father came upon them and handed them their bows and her banner.

They trotted off and merged in the throng of Ghatafan and Dhubyan horses, the sole happy riders surrounded by clapping praise and happy snorts. She spotted Muawiyah's horse Al-Raed who, true to his name, thundered freely, and tearfully imagined him accompanying the twins and Ziyad the young poet on their future adventures.

Brandishing her banner adorned with the wine-colored eagle that brought so many memories, Jayida wallowed in their guest's echoing cheerful praises. Her heart pinched at the sight of her leopard and lion skins hovering above ground, happily carried by rows of excited children, and even Yazida and Adinah among them. They sang to her, calling her Jonder the *kahin*-lion of Sa'd, Jonder-Jayida friend of Nasr, Jayida ibn Zahir of the two fathers Harith and Gayas, and other combinations, but her favorite was Jayida, Khaled's *kahina* lion-slaying wife.

"So, since we're going to Bosra, does that mean we'll be unflinching Green supporters from now on?" said Khaled.

"That might please *malik* Al-Harith and the Believing Queen Theodora," said Jayida. "But I've no plan to become as *majnun* as some of them are. There will always be conflicts, but right now, I just want to be your wife," she smiled.

"Just right now?" said Khaled with narrowed eyes.

"One day at a time," sighed Jayida, and tried not to laugh as she tried to hide her face behind the banner. Best of all, she didn't have to look to know that Khaled's gaze longingly burned through her layers, as she did his.

They rejoined the gathered *sayyidun* and tribesmen with their bow in hand, and once lined up together, they raised their bows and let arrow after arrow fly like doves in the endless blue sky. Women circulated with incense, cheered, and sang praises to each present tribe, as the children rushed to gather the fallen arrows to begin the cycle again. As the arrows soared, they sang of the lavish gifts from near and far: Ghatafan horses, woven garments and items, cloths and clothing from local and foreign merchants, with wines from Al-Sham, Yathrib, and Khaybar, a range of bronze dishes, and even dark camels that Amr boasted Al-Mundhir had gotten from their Taghlib kin. The humbling spirit of heartfelt giving filled her again and she had the growing sense that it was the root and perpetuator of all life.

Before she knew it, Khaled had a tablah in his hands, and she knew that the longed-for moment had come. Yazida began singing along with Adinah, and when Shams, Sufyan, Majid, Amr, Hatim, and Samaw'al joined in, cueing everyone else, she decided that they had all planned it somehow and didn't mind it one bit. Khaled's drumming swept her up, filling her heart with such happiness that joyful tears matched her endless flushed grin. Free to be a bursting noticeable young woman on this of all days, she danced with inviting Yazida and Adinah, floating and twirling in that secure space of women and men who shared a similar vision of life.

In the evening they drifted back to the fire and sat around *mubassir* Ayyub, where they took turns honoring Khaled and Jayida's parents full of generous deeds, and those of *sayyid* Aziz. *Mubassir* Ayyub praised Jayida's Ghassanid ancestors, and urged her and her parents to go boldly in that new path that called them back to Yassu.

"I, too, wish to confess to you the rest of the story about my Nasr," said *sayyid* Aziz.

He unleashed what so far had remained secret between them: that he and others in the tribe had seen Nasr in dreams, convincing them not only that his soul lived on in the beyond, but that Yassu was real, too.

"And I'm more moved than I can say, more aware of our unworthiness, because," *sayyid* Aziz paused, all choked up. "My beloved Warda is now with child!" There was a sweeping rise of voices, and he shook his head and hand to still it. "I would've done anything—" he paused. "And though I may never be a good enough servant to Yassu, I know that it's too important and I can't ignore it. Not after all this."

"What a blessing to hear you say this," said *mubassir* Ayyub with a touched air. For a moment she wondered if *nasi* Musa and *nasi* Ibrahim might disapprove and protest, but at least Yassu was also Israelite.

"It's always a balm when I see others' hearts touched by Yassu," nodded Hatim.

"Like Nuh, Ayyub, Ibrahim, Moshe, Dawud, and Sulayman, he's an Israelite whose teachings I value," said Samaw'al, his gold menorah and cross medallions reminding any observer of his dual-faith upbringing.

Jayida smiled through her blurry vision, as Khaled closed his hand on hers. To know that their decision at Mina had been right, and that Yazida would be a sister again was a welcomed strengthening of all their confidence.

The beloved evening serenity settled upon them, as the incense accompanied Samaw'al's poetic memories of their shared march to Kutha and her parents' wedding at Tayma, followed by more of his, Hatim's, and Amr's improvised verses of love. Hatim opened with a thought for the prince-poet Imru, then *sayyid* Hudayfa of Ghatafan said some words about Imru's father Hujr, honoring his brief rule over the Ghatafan. Hatim continued by praising the generous beauty of selfless true love, and Samaw'al and Amr praised and teased Khaled and Jayida's combined strength that would surely yield strong children, and finished with the mysterious ways of their wives from other tribes.

Muawiyah then introduced Ziyad, who sang of brotherly love to the twins saved by Jonder-Jayida. In turn Jayida, along with Yazida and Shams, recited parts of Nasr's poetry. Touched that Nasr had woven some Hudhayl elements into his poetry, *sayyid* Safwan of Banu Hawazin shared some that he recalled from his Hudhayl neighbors near 'Ukaz and Wajj. Surprisingly, Majid, probably with some help from wine served by striking Yazida, offered himself and Khaled to improvise some—first warning that they were not meant to be memorized, but should at least be remembered for making them laugh.

Nasi Ibrahim then offered to recite from the Tanakh about Shamshun, and after a while Adinah took over without a trace of shyness or remorse for knowing and reciting these sacred verses usually part of men's education. Dawud, who'd once shown her and Nasr how to shoot from the top of a Khaybar fort, recited on his namesake who'd defeated the giant Goliath with a sling and a stone. His father *nasi* Musa closed with memories of her father's indulgence at Khaybar during the tense *Ayyam al-Zalam*.

In the midst of the tipsy lull, Jayida caught her mother discreetly motioning to her to step away, and followed her to an area away from the fire.

"My heart, your new tent is set up just northwest. It's been a long day, and my heart rejoices for you to grow in your blessed marriage love," said her mother. "It's normal to be nervous, but you will see what a blessing it is, one no one can know but you two." Zoraya took her face into her hands and kissed her cheeks and forehead.

"*Na'am, yama*," said Jayida. Warmth stirred deep in her as it had that last night he'd been with them. She'd been nervous ever since that day, but she was also ready to finally be alone with him. He'd already seen her, after all. "I'll be waiting."

Her mother nodded and drew the veil over her face, leaving Jayida to walk on in a fast pace as the camp's hubbub of voices faded to a pleasant low hum.

In the glittering, star-lit night stood the new, large pitched tent with its black roof. She slipped inside, the scattered oil lamps revealing a warm, inviting men's area. Smiling, Jayida removed her sandals and melodic crown of silk and jingling coins and left them there, then went to the women's space and shed her jewelry.

At last, their sleeping area was a perfect combination of Khaled's belongings with a now more feminine touch of red draped silks and fabrics, an alluring touch of her own with her mother's guidance. Their swords lay dutifully at each side of their straw-stuffed bedding, beckoning to them with their crimson cushions, crisp new bedsheets, and soft woolen blankets.

With a deep breath she slipped out of her dress and set her Mikha'il amulet on it, the angelic form outlining her new role as wife. She stood naked, except for the florals that danced on her hands and feet. They would fade like spring blossoms in a few days, unlike her heart-pounding memories.

The rustling nearby hinted at the entrance being closed, and she refrained from covering herself as the footsteps approached and finally stood behind her. Slowly she turned, imagining her silken hair not unlike ostrich feathers grazing her soft, oiled skin. His wavy hair draped his naked shoulders, having shed everything too, his rippling torso and arms demanding to be scratched, pounded, and molded into new life.

"Are you going to stay and watch this time? Or run away?" said Jayida, his eyes flashing with mutual hunger.

"I'm thinking something else," said Khaled.

"Big plans?"

Slowly she drifted to him, his eyes taking her in as he dropped his pants. She reached up to slow his chiseled chest's rhythmic breathing, and kept her hand a thread's distance away from his skin, gliding up his neck. Her fingertips grazed his oiled beard and smooth lips, and like lightning she swung back her hand, until he stilled it with his grip. Keeping hold of her wrist, Khaled drew close to her, his *hilm* maintaining a wall of torturous space.

Jayida smirked. "Strange. For once I didn't even really want to do it."

"That's what love does; it changes things," said Khaled, his raw manliness launching a thousand arrows into every part of her.

"Hmm. Are you sure?"

He cupped her chin and pressed their flesh into each other's with a consuming fiery kiss, dissolving them into their passionate red sea.

CHAPTER FORTY-FIVE

NOBLE DOWRY

EARLY SUMMER 542 AD – TAYSAFUN

"Blade-thin, war-spent
    he shocked 'Ablah
    with sinewy hands
    and matted hair
    in a year's grime
    and coat of mail
    its battered iron
    so long worn
    he had turned to rust
    and looked a wreck.
    'You're worthless,'
    'Ablah said
    shocking me
    by the laugh she got
    from gathered friends
    as she cast
    a scant glance
    at this glorious warrior
    this brave lion
    famed for largesse.
    Look me in the eye, 'Ablah.
    Don't leave—
    I've had better flirts than you
    and far prettier, too.

I've had my way
and then roamed free.
Get that into your head.
My soul has been mired
in battlemurk—
the blade's glister
would make you forget
all your henna
and your kohl.
Who cares if I'm thin?
I've been hard at it,
dodging spears.
I've floored many a warrior
like your precious lord
posh lumps of flesh in the saddle
sprawled in dirt
mid wounded soldiers
and unhorsed riders
while we, mounted
or dismounted,
fought on to the kill,
our spears bloodied
black to the haft
our swords reaping
skulls like gourds."

'Antarah stopped at Shaybub's horrified gaze. It was in such moments that he thought he could get used to being within four walls that enclosed their intimacy uninterrupted.

"Impressive, as usual. But you can't recite them that; that's for us," said Shaybub, his bulging crossed arms as if larger than usual.

"I know," sighed 'Antarah, and clasped his hands behind his neck. He paced about the large living area, with draped tapestries on the wall and woven pomegranate and vines at his feet gracing his way. "What do I say, and what do I not say: that's always the problem."

He wanted, needed to appear the strong, conquering 'Antarah of his imagination, who had his tribe's respect, if only before the *Shah*. Even with the gold, he couldn't have him thinking it was stolen and second-guess his need of the Asafir camels. But every day in this lavish land with its flowing Tigris, sweet rose-scented water and pastries, and thick walls that kept them from the burning heat, he walked the fiery sands, fearing he would give himself away. But like his poetry, he wouldn't always be able to avoid it. At some point, something in his verses could give him away, or worse, be twisted and used that way by others.

"Or at least, I have to be lighter about it," said 'Antarah. "But how could I be light about what rages in my heart? To recite a *qasidah* requires that I fixate on it, refusing to let go." He shook his head.

Shaybub smiled. "Wine?"

"And let it intrude, too?" 'Antarah chuckled. "The truth is, if I'm too angry then I'm the bitter slave, unworthy of his freeborn beloved. And if I'm passionate and sing her the most glorious verses ever uttered, they'll be curious, wonder who she is, and then wonder who I am—who am I to deserve her? And I don't," 'Antarah shrugged.

"*Aywa*, you do," said Shaybub. "Who else do we know who's gone that far on such a *majnun* quest? That alone is a memorable story for them to boast about, that one of theirs was at *Shah* Khosrow's court. More importantly, I know your *qareen* is faithful, and it won't stop just because we're here."

Shaybub was right. Something about being in Taysafun both eased and fired him up in ways he could've never imagined. For one, they'd been given fine quarters near the palace, removing the strain of pitching and upkeeping a tent, and worrying about cold or crawling animals, attacking hordes, and least of all, food. In those nearly three moons since their arrival, they'd had so much mahi, pupfish, caviar, *masgouf,* and honeyed cardamom tea and rose-scented pastries that he almost worried he was starting to give off these odors.

At first he'd resisted this tentative languor, as if he wasn't doing enough, or Al-Mundhir, the Banu 'Abs, or the whole world itself would come falling on him all at once. Until he replayed their heroic escape and meeting with the *Shah*, and realized that if he was to die at any moment, he could at least enjoy a few things on the way. They were the ones who'd sent him there, after all.

They roamed freely and undisturbed in the five cities called Al-Mada'in by some *badawi*, and visited the races, sometimes even cheered for charioteers. They'd even been invited for an evening at the *Shah*'s court, where they were treated to some of the moral tales from the Pancatantra, with The Hare that Outwitted the Lion and How The Lion's Servants Got the Camel Killed as his favorites. When the *Shah* suggested him to share some of his verses, without a second thought he shared what he'd first said of 'Ablah at the picnic, changing a few details and replacing her name with Anahid's that made a pleasant effect.

At the baths they took private quarters where only Shaybub attended to him, keeping his scarred back concealed to the best of his ability. He'd bask in the steamy bath with thoughts of Anahid, the beautiful girl who resembled 'Ablah, yet welcomed his presence. Anahid was the perfect, soft-spoken vision, from a farmer family whose added generous gifts were full of tasty dishes, sweet halva pastries, pomegranates, and family stories. On her father's side, her ancestors had been Magians who'd converted to Yassu's teachings, while her mother's Armenian ancestors prided themselves on being descendants of the first Yassu-loving kingdom.

Then, her eyes had shone with a light that reminded him of his bursts of poetry when she told him that she was named after the noble martyr who'd been cruelly killed for converting to Yassu's teachings. Somehow, the horrifying tale had lit a familiar fire in his soul akin to his love for 'Ablah.

During the trial of Anahid, daughter of *mobed* Adurhormizd, they tried to convince her to reject Yassu, and that her nobility could save her from death if only she admitted her mistake and married a worthy Magian. But she refused, and then his jaw clenched so tightly he thought they'd remain that way. 'Antarah struggled to hold back his enraged floods when she was scourged until the flesh of her back and thighs was cut into from every side, reaching the bones, making rivers of blood.

Still, the martyr kept praying, and the next day the guards were shocked that all her wounds had healed, and that her body was without a scar. But it wasn't enough for them, so they tortured her by ripping off her breasts, then smeared her body with honey and left her stretched out on a mountain, amazed and hating that she kept on with supernatural strength, lest it might inspire others over to her faith. At the end of her recital, his heart was pounding like a deafening drum all the way to 'Ablah. Doomed, his love seemed to others, but still, refusing to die, like one chosen by *al-ilah*. It was so ugly and beautiful at the same time, like his own life.

I want my scars removed, too, he'd wanted to but didn't dare say, not wanting to disappoint Anahid's eagerness. As the son of an Aksumite mother, she'd assumed he was of faith too, and seemed to look deep into him, as if seeing and encouraging something that though possibly there, might never reach her level. It was endearing, and he was fascinated by that source of strength she seemed to so naturally have and want to share with him.

But there was something too distant, too removed about the place, a dread he couldn't and didn't want to name, and though he often thought it had to be his anguish over 'Ablah, it was also something he couldn't quite express. It was enough to know his mother would disapprove of their practices of diminishing Yassu's divinity in favor of his humanity, even if others like Anahid seemed to share a faith similar to that of his Aksumite mother.

Anahid had invited them to church and introduced them to Patriarch Mar Aba, who went tirelessly to remote areas to settle disputes and reunite the conflicting church.

"Always good to see others from the far-off flock," Aba had said, his gaze as bright as his long white beard. 'Antarah had only smiled and humbly lowered his chin, his whispering mother reminding them of their confessional differences. "The longer you stay with us, the more I can show you and teach you, if you'd like," the Patriarch had kindly offered.

It was tempting, not least of all when, after Anahid, Mar Aba was the second most trustworthy person around them. Himself a convert from the Magian faith, she shared that he was no less a target from Magians who disliked his betraying apostasy and his active sharing of Yassu's teachings. When she was sure they were alone, Anahid confessed that she suspected that they were pressuring *Shah* Khosrow to act against him, and might be secretly keeping close watch of him. Was the *Shah* doing the same thing with them? 'Antarah wondered and dreaded to know.

Yet nothing discouraged the tireless Mar Aba, who told them about all the important texts of Theodore of Antioch and Nestorius he was translating from Greek into Syriac. In just a day of visiting with him at the Taysafun school he'd founded on the right bank of the Tigris, 'Antarah longed to hear more of what this wise scholarly man had to say.

"In a way, you remind me of my good traveler-pupil Cosmas. He's traveled far for his merchant business; and you for your verses," said Mar Aba. "And to think, you must've been a newborn when he was at Adulis while *Negus* Kaleb was preparing his expedition to Himyar."

'Antarah wished he could've met the Greek traveler and ask him more about that event, Aksum's great history, and the Greek Yassu worshippers from Soqotra, along with all his travels to India and Ceylon, and see the maps he'd drawn. It was out of his depth, but he also wanted to know how he'd come to the conclusion that the world was flat and modeled on Musa's Tabernacle made during the Israelite Exodus from Egypt. Shouldn't it have been modeled on Yassu's cross instead? More importantly, if he stayed longer perhaps Mar Aba could even teach him to read and write or, as Anahid had suggested, help him have some of his verses written down.

"I would swear on my life to preserve the texts myself," Anahid had smiled at him, stirring the shaking tremor in him, making him wonder if it was, after all, love.

Would that finally be his chance of becoming someone whose name would be remembered? But to what end? Even after he brought back the Asafir camels to the Banu 'Abs and was once more ignored by 'Ablah, would he really return with his mother and Shaybub to be with Anahid? He wanted to tell her how much her kind friendship meant to him, a poor slave who had no one else besides his mother and brother to talk to, but he couldn't confess all that. Maybe with her gentle perception she'd already guessed as much, and there was reassurance in that, too. Nor would he have minded being a farmer with her, when he'd never be a priest or noble of Magian society.

Most importantly, with each encounter, it always came back to the same thing: it was different. Try as he might, he could not cast 'Ablah from his thoughts, though there was everything there to help him with it. With his night visions filled with her consuming fiery breath all over him, he didn't need to visit any taverns with their tell-tale flag if he'd even wanted to. His love simply was, and he'd accepted long ago that no one would ever understand or accept it but him.

He might've looked more cursed than blessed with love to Shaybub as they discussed it, but the truth was that as much as he was drawn to Anahid's caring and humble ways, she didn't need him the way 'Ablah did. It was the emptiness he couldn't take, that despairing void he couldn't bear to imagine 'Ablah trapped in. He wanted to be the person to make 'Ablah glow with her own version of loving reassurance that Anahid already had. And if he had to die for it, he would ask to be 'Ablah's invisible guardian, protecting her from the beyond, even without her knowledge. He knew too well the shattering possibility that he was just imagining her. But if his *qareen* had chosen him to use poetry to see the best in her and the world, was that really wrong? To get his answer, he had to go back and try it with everything he had.

But there'd been another surprise, too. That of wanting some of this time to himself, to wallow in all the new sights and the world of his poetry, and just be with it without the constant burden of tasks of watching, grooming, and milking flocks, scrubbing pots and washing clothes, or tending to one person or another as he had to all his life. Maybe it was the free time, the food, the kind and even unkind people, and the learning, but that restless boldness in his soul had pushed something like the beginning of a *qasidah* out of him.

"*Aywa*, I have something else then," said 'Antarah, and Shaybub nodded invitingly.

"Did poetry die in its war with the poets?
Is this where 'Ablah walked? Think!
The ruins were deaf—refused to reply,
Then shouted out in a foreign tongue.
My camel tried to withdraw—
I couldn't move,
ranting at the charred stones.
'Speak. Live. Prosper.
Here in Al-Jiwa 'Ablah dwelled,
A timid gazelle, doe eyes,
Sweet smile, soft neck.'
I reined in my camel, big as a fort—
I needed to weep, needed the shame..."

He went on, weaving a rough, unfinished passage of his mount and a battle scene with grotesque imagery, ending with the symbolic images of hyenas and vultures as the arrival of death.

"*Tayyib*; that's more like it, even if I'm not sure it's about 'Ablah at all, though it starts that way," said Shaybub.

"*Sah*. Exactly what I wanted; it could be, but it's more about death, that lurking certainty," said 'Antarah with satisfaction. At least it was a start, and even if for whatever reason he never got the camels they traveled all this way for, he would have his visions and his unique composed words, the one thing that had ever truly been his own.

He'd held it in until 'Ablah released it out of him, and like that his restless urge to return home also resurged. As much as he was grateful for their visit, a gnawing sense of wrong consumed him again. Was he letting himself be seduced by false gods? The monotony of endless plains of dry, hard mud filled him with a sense of despair. Strangely he recalled a myth of the Egyptian god Khonsu, whose miniature image had been sent as a demon-expeller by Pharaoh Rameses II to nearby Babylon when his kingdom had stretched out that far, then after a while suddenly spirited back to his home. The newer story they'd heard of the hero Rostam who unknowingly killed his leopard-skinned son Sohrab only added to his confusion.

It had to be a test, when despite all their enjoyment, the pleasure didn't seem to last. Or most shockingly, it dawned on him that it was that way everywhere, like nothing was permanent, not even in ancient places that inscribed things on stone and paper. Curiously, that only brought out the permanence of his verses and his hopeless pining for 'Ablah. The gifts he hoped to bring back were for the tribe, but if none of it was his, he was returning with more of his poetry, possibly to share, but probably for his kin and himself.

With the end of their stay approaching, he confessed to Anahid his plan, and she beamed at him with tears in her eyes. Was it innocence, envy, or even both? But surely the place was already making him forget himself, when it was probably just pity.

"I'm honored to have met you, and pray Yassu leads your way," said Anahid, and gave him baskets of pomegranates and bundles of food for the long journey home. He'd thought of touching her hand, maybe even embracing her and holding her in his arms, but if it would've been most wrong to her purity, or 'Ablah's, he couldn't say.

A few days later they were packed and ready to see the *Shah* and finally return home.

"I'm too nervous. We should say some words to Yassu," said 'Antarah. They closed their eyes and lowered their chin as 'Antarah recited a plea to be protected on the last part of their quest. "It's almost over, we can do this," said 'Antarah, and off they went to the palace, as agitated as they'd been the first time.

They had to wait to finally see *Shah* Khosrow, which only added to his restlessness. Finally, the *Shah* appeared and took his time sitting on his throne.

"You want to leave? But why? You have everything here," said the *Shah*, his frown evident through his sheer veil.

"*Na'am*, most honorable *Shah*, and we're grateful to have enjoyed your hospitality even longer than planned. As much as I'd love to stay, I will also enjoy reciting to them of your generosity and leadership that will faithfully keep their hearts turned your way," said 'Antarah.

"Ah, let us hear it," said *Shah* Khosrow with a hint of challenge.

'Antarah hid his tremor of shock with a small smile, and improvised and elaborated on the small poem he'd begun for him. In a way there was little need to force it when the *Shah* had been nothing but the best of hosts, so that his verses were less boasts than simple, if nearly unbelievable, truths for simple slaves like themselves.

Then, before he could stop it, a thrill seized him as he went into a segment about the great kingdoms of Aksum and Himyar, led by Yassu-loving rulers. He softened the pride in his mother's faith by citing the similarities with the Magian faith that also believed in the importance of doing good and its triumph over evil. He concluded with a friendly reminder that King Abraha had recently built the Al-Qalis Church at the new capital of San'a, crowning his list of brave achievements in assisting *Negus* Kaleb at Najran, then defeating the two expeditions that failed to strip his power. Surely the king and the Shah's gifted independent spirits would result in a diplomatic friendship in due time.

His heart pounding, 'Antarah had a flash of doubt at what he'd done, then banished it in favor of this ever-mysterious poetic strength. After all, if he wanted to make a lasting honorable impression, what better way than to defend his inheritance and stand firm with skilled, memorable verses—no matter the cost.

After a moment, the *Shah*'s flat demeanor yielded to deepening satisfaction, and 'Antarah knew once more that he could trust his *qareen* when he needed it most.

"You cannot leave yet; I want the court to hear it," said the *Shah*.

'Antarah swallowed hard. "Kind *Shah*, you do me great honor, but it's nothing compared to your court's poets," said 'Antarah with a bow.

"What is the point of a poem if not to be shared? At least let my wife hear it; a wife never forgets such things," said the *Shah*, and leaned forward.

"It is but a humble poem that does not match its inspiration. In your kindness you will forgive my limitations," said 'Antarah, wondering how his voice wasn't shaking. He tried to think of anything but the creeping discomfort of Al-Mundhir's ill-willed stalling. "As the Banu 'Abs already thinks highly of you, the sight of the Asafir camels will surpass their wildest dreams. I would hate to deprive them even longer of this opportunity to boast of you and your blessing for eternity."

Shah Khosrow sighed, cocked his head, and 'Antarah secretly breathed a bit easier. Of course the *Shah* would favor even wider praise from gold-mining connected *badawi* tribes in the heart of Najd over one of his little poems in a stream of thousands.

The *Shah* rose and looked him over. "Come along, then."

They followed him to the fields where thousands of guarded Asafir camels grazed in the lush, irrigated valley. If they'd intended to steal them like mere thieves they couldn't have done it without killing several men on the way, and he thanked his mother again for the honorable payment.

"Here they are. Always here, always grazing. Today, tomorrow, moons from now," said *Shah* Khosrow.

'Antarah nodded with a pinched smile, discreetly looked around, fighting every urge to look over his shoulder and at Shaybub. Was there anywhere on earth he could go without having to fear being trapped?

"You know you could always come back after," said the *Shah*.

"After?" said 'Antarah.

"After your holy visit to Jerusalem. Perhaps that's where you're headed like that traveling Aksumite in your *injil*, and don't want to say."

"Perhaps someday, but honoring your name first is most important," said 'Antarah, hoping his mother and Yassu would forgive him for all the blasphemies he was saying to this nonbelieving ruler. When he'd once thought he'd never leave his tribe, it now seemed just as hard to go back.

"And what else do you want?" said *Shah* Khosrow.

'Antarah blinked. "I'm not sure I follow."

"The camels for your tribe, *sah*? What do *you* want?"

To go home alive. To marry 'Ablah and finally have happiness with her, if only for a few moments.

"To keep my word," said 'Antarah, and a flash of surprise swept over the *Shah*. 'Antarah got the loaded leather satchels and handed over their mother's gold.

Shah Khosrow opened them, looked in, then looked back up at him and Shaybub as if he was missing something. A moment later he walked off and 'Antarah tried to ignore his whispers to his guards, who soon dispersed in different directions.

"My guards will accompany you just past Al-Hira," said the *Shah*, as he glanced over at his flocks one last time.

"It has been an honor to meet and be hosted by you," said 'Antarah, and at least there it wasn't a lie.

Even if this *majnun* king came after them like wavering Pharaoh after Musa, and they were killed in the fray, he'd seek out a *jinni*'s help from the beyond. For if his unburied body was left forgotten, his *qareen* would call out and cite the *Shah*'s Magian faith and duty to lay his body on a ziggurat in the open air to birds of prey. Then, when all bones were free of flesh, they'd be collected for his overdue burial. 'Antarah tried not to think that sadly, even this might be more than his own tribe might do for him.

After what seemed a long while, the guards gathered with the flocks and awaited the *Shah*'s orders.

"'Antarah and Shaybub of the Banu 'Abs. I declare that I, *Shah* Khosrow, and Antares and Al-Shira will remember you," said the *Shah* with a light frown. 'Antarah bowed, grateful for these words that had to be as difficult as rare for him to say.

They rode south, the impressive flock of dark camels in single file following their unspoken, strict order. They veered east of Al-Hira, and soon, the *Shah*'s guards helped them count the flocks, ensuring none had strayed or been lost along the way.

"But what's this? This isn't ours," said 'Antarah, noting some bulging satchels attached to a few strong males.

"It is if the *Shah* commands it," said the guard, and with final kind wishes, they each went their own way.

When 'Antarah finally worked up the nerve to look inside, they found they were filled with wine skins, floral engraved bronze plates, and containers. There were also amber precious stones, and heaps of gold, silver, and copper necklaces, bracelets, and jeweled rings.

"Why would he do this? More reasons to boast?" said 'Antarah.

"Probably surprised you didn't ask for anything for yourself. That might be the kindest *majnun* ruler in existence," chuckled Shaybub.

"Maybe there's some truth to calling him *dādgar*," said 'Antarah, recalling his epithet of "the Just."

Despite their large caravan, the further they went the more the burden lifted, and not even the extreme heat that made some of the flock pee themselves to keep cool distracted him. He floated in a forming misty cloud not unlike the one he'd seen up on the hill after following the oryx on their first day on their own. Had it really happened? Had he really achieved his mission?

They kept southeast along the Euphrates and 'Antarah, strangely unconcerned about the attention they'd draw, decided they'd return to the market of Al-Mirbad near Basrah. He was prepared to fend off prying eyes with a claim of being in service to the *Shah*, but for once he was glad to have foolishly underestimated the creatures' power. By a combination of their dark coats and sheer numbers, they announced their importance without either one of them needing to say a word. Curious, awed expressions followed them, wondering, yet quickly able to see that these two wealthy Aksumites weren't there to part from them. For the first time in their life, the crowds kept a respectful distance, as if wanting to partake in the miraculous sight while aware of their unworthiness. 'Antarah basked in the moment, wondering if that was the effect of riches or something else he couldn't quite express.

They drew such attention that a few respectefully asked for news of Aksum and Himyar and 'Antarah skillfully deflected by inviting them to share their latest news of the region, which seemed to please and flatter them. Soon, an eager young boy approached and put himself at their service, and begged to know their names and where they were going. Touched by the boy's genuine manner, 'Antarah told him and had him fetch a clothing merchant. The boy returned with an older man, with whom 'Antarah traded some jewelry for a cream silk dress for their mother, and a genuine purple-red dress all the way from Tyre for 'Ablah.

He gave the boy a gold coin, and after a short pause, he packed the goods carefully on his mount. As they continued on their dreamy way, sometimes he reached in to touch the purple dress. He might never see 'Ablah in it, but maybe she'd feel the lingering presence of his fingertips if he touched the fabric long enough.

They reached Wadi Al-Batin, then entered Wadi Al-Rummah, where they found 'Antarah's three mud pillars still intact. Taking it as a good omen, they made camp and rose early in the mornings, and wallowed and stayed up late to elongate the remaining free days. At night he stared up at the sky, and spotted Antares's bright red glow, wondering at this inexplicable change that filled him. Had he left himself behind somewhere along the long journey, and switched to another *jinni*, maybe even a Magian fire-loving one, trading lives? How else could so much still look the same but feel so different?

"At least by now so many others know your name," said Shaybub with a long stare.

"To think, after everything, I have to brace myself for more of the same. Anyone else would've run, or at least taken longer. But they have to see it, and I want them to see it, otherwise they'll say it never happened," 'Antarah sighed.

More importantly, he had to see her, if only one last time. Because as much as he dreaded to say it, he dared to think that something had stretched around him like wings, a mysterious but now magically more reachable space of once only wishful possibility. Not only had they faced the treacherous Al-Mundhir and escaped his grip, but they'd been hosted and given enviable gifts by one of the most powerful kings in the world. Having fulfilled his part of the bargain, 'Antarah had to know if he'd finally turned Fate in his favor.

At sunset, gazes found them before they even reached camp, following their every movement. But still 'Antarah walked in his cloud, praying that he would never be taken out of it. They could have their camels and gifts; he just wanted his space with 'Ablah in it, and if not, for him and his faithful *qareen*.

Shaddad met them at the edge of camp, his smirk full of satisfaction.

"By Allah, you've done it," said Shaddad. 'Antarah didn't even think to flinch when the man suddenly seized his shoulders and embraced him, and kissed each of his cheeks. Even with the man's rough, unfamiliar affection, anything was better than his whip marks on his back, or the scar at his lip that he hoped would keep fading.

"*Ya Aba*, we're blessed and honored to be back. The camels and the gifts from *Shah* Khosrow are yours," said 'Antarah with lowered chin.

Shaddad fixed him, until a tremor made him break contact.

"I have something for you, too," said Shaddad with a tone he'd never heard before. He swept aside the fold of his cloak and loosened a scabbard. "This is yours."

'Antarah froze. Was he imaginig it or were the vine embellishments from one of the Ghassanid weapon factories? Most of all, had his father trusted he would return, if only to give him this first and most prized gift of a sword, no matter how full or empty-handed he was? 'Antarah scrambled for the right words to say, but nothing came, and when Shaddad invitingly gestured the sword towards him again, all he could do was accept with a deep nod.

"What will you name it?" said Shaddad.

"Azzami," said 'Antarah. Like a lion, for better or worse.

Shaddad nodded thoughtfully "Come, rest and tell us all about it, my son."

Curiously, the widened space still lingered as they went to the beckoning fire. Even blind he would've known all the eyes that followed: confused, shocked, inquiring. But always, one pair that cast them all off: his mother's watery, beaming gaze, always so certain he could never fail. Zabiba stood alone at the fire, waiting for him and Shaybub to rejoin her, and this time he relished the reverential space that appeared between her and the speechlessly awed others.

"Bless your return on this early sixth month of Dhu-Qiyazan," his mother whispered, and kissed his forehead and cheeks.

'Antarah sat with her and his father at each side of him, as the tribe fell around him, impatiently waiting for his every word. He nodded to *sayyid* Zoheir, with smug Ahmar at one side and pleased Hashem at the other. 'Antarah gave a quick nod to his uncle Mutaz, his awestruck wife Suhayyah and son Waiz, wondering if his sister lurked somewhere, too, unseen like his *qareen*. Turning his attention into the fire, he withheld a smile at the sight of Anahid and 'Ablah dancing with each other in the flames, teasing him with all he could have...

With Azzami across his lap, he took his time, speaking slowly of their journey, knowing at least this part would be told as he wanted. They descended into Al-Hira with the cubs Antares and Al-Shira, who so impressed—or rather, frightened, though he would not say it—Al-Mundhir that he kindly hosted them. Soon he was forced to admit lacking sufficient Asafir camels for 'Antarah's need, so he informed *Shah* Khosrow of their visit. He went on about the trusted *Shah*'s unmatched protection, and his beautiful Taysafun, full of festivities, trade, races, baths, churches, temples, and schools.

'Antarah told them of the arched entrance of Taq Kasra and the palace with its great hall, host to Magian poetry by Zoroaster, and stories and poetry on Gilgamesh, Iskandar, and the new board game of *shatranj*. He didn't tell them about Rostam and Sohrab, or the Pancatantra and his favorite stories from it, when they were already getting far more than they deserved. He praised the *Shah*'s generosity for their lavish, tapestry-decorated quarters that were filled each day with wine and mahi and other seafood dishes. There were the *Shah*'s heavily armored cataphract guards at their sides, and the market of Al-Mirbad and the travelers who saw and praised their honorable flocks. And last but not least, he shared the cream silk dress for his mother, and the Tyrian purple dress for 'Ablah—to resounding gasps.

Through the echoing praise and surprise, 'Antarah caught the snorts of doubt, and he quenched it by inviting them to review all the trinkets the good *Shah* had gifted them. Then the dark frowns turned to grimacing envy and jealousy. Who was this low slave to reap so many benefits, when he wasn't even supposed to survive the journey long enough to arrive, let alone return with gifts! Beneath it all, his *qareen* saw that the sneering reeked of demands for their share of his glory. And they could have it all!

But it still wouldn't change a thing, when it was too late now, and everyone knew that it had all been his and Shaybub's labor. Let them find out that Al-Mundhir had almost killed them, when he had an ally in Queen Hind and her son Amr, and maybe even the *Shah* himself. All the same, it would require Al-Mundhir admitting that he had failed in his vile plans, as much with them as with the other runaways who had their own stories to spread.

Of course Anahid would also be his secret, another kind of love they wouldn't believe, let alone understand even if he ever chose to tell them. Only then, in the throes of his flowing words speaking of his triumphant return, did it occur to him that no matter what happened, he might see Anahid again someday.

"Praise the Banu 'Abs that you've returned safely," said *sayyid* Zoheir, and nodded to him. 'Antarah pinched a relieved smile.

"Praise the 'Abs indeed," smirked Ahmar. "As it turns out, you're not the only one who's been having all the fun. There's been strangely surprising news here, too."

'Antarah's stomach contracted, cementing his fear. Not only could he hardly enjoy his glorious moment, but he was too late—what else could he have expected.

"My brother is simply referring to a recent wedding of the Banu Zubayd," said Hashem with a hint of lightness and amusement that somehow brought down the tension. His heart starting to race, 'Antarah wondered how that could possibly match his own achievement.

"You see," said Mutaz, "What's most unusual is that Jonder of the Banu Sa'd, that lion slayer, is none other than a woman named Jayida! And now she's *sayyid* Khaled's wife!"

"I wouldn't believe it myself, except everyone from Tayyi, to Taghlib, to Ghatafan, Dhubyan, Hawazin, and Sulaym are talking about it," said Waiz with annoyance.

Shaddad chuckled dismissively.

"An amusing, silly story! Thankfully, by now others have also seen that 'Antarah is an honorable, *real* man of his word. By Allah, his story and dowry surpasses it all, not to mention all the poetry his *qareen* has granted him during his journey," said Shaddad with a twinkle in his eye.

'Antarah's heart pounded, grateful that his father was on his side. But even that his father wouldn't get out of him just yet. He would recite his *qasidah* on the day of his wedding to 'Ablah—or never at all. They could ignore his achievement all they wanted; he hadn't done it for their hateful, dishonest praise. But now it was Mutaz's turn to keep his word and pronounce that 'Ablah was finally his.

He spent his first night back sleepless, with his mother between them holding each of their hands against her heart.

"He heard me. I begged and I begged, and Iyasus heard me and brought you back safe," said Zabiba in a tearful whisper.

'Antarah thanked her and told her everything else, all the details he hadn't shared around the fire, his throat nearly closing at their entrapment and survival, and what it could mean for the future. Options; he had to convince himself there were always options, no matter what happened.

"If you don't already know it, it means you're loved. And sometimes, you'll be surprised where it comes from. But that's the thing: you have to hold on and go, you have to *live* to *see*," she said, squeezing his hand so tightly they merged together like dough.

The next day Mutaz visited Shaddad's tent and announced that 'Ablah was honored to be his, and that they would begin preparations for the wedding to be held in a few days, starting with the day's first celebration of his return. Before he could ask if he could see 'Ablah, Mutaz said that she was moved and accepted everything. 'Antarah almost protested but somehow restrained himself. If she agreed, why couldn't he at least see her to offer his respects and confirm it himself? Was it 'Ablah's genuine shyness or Mutaz's last attempt at keeping his daughter to himself—or even both?

'Antarah tried to enjoy himself during the feast, but he couldn't shake the consuming need to see and speak to 'Ablah. What was he celebrating when frustration, filled with unanswered questions, taunted him? As much as his heart ached for her, he needed to hear from her that she wanted to be his, and was not just obeying, or worse, pining for someone else while with him. He might be too vain and giving her the easy way out, when he'd gone so far for her, but he was also realizing that some of it had been for himself, too. She would come to him of her own choice, or not at all. Nothing was worse to him than the thought of forcing her, or any other woman.

Shaddad roamed the camp with a constant grin on his face, reciting of this son of his whom he'd always known would make something of himself. Even Shemia boasted that their daughter Waha would gladly spread the news among her husband's vast tribe of Tamim further southeast. His *ema*, glowing with her everlasting consuming love, gave him some warm sweet wine, and he sipped it, thinking of an Aksumite communion service honoring Yassu. He took only a few bites of the tender camel meat, and to his surprise, the wine flowed enough to intoxicate almost everyone around him as they reclined around the fire.

"Now visitors will come to us from near and far, just to hear about and meet 'Antarah, son of the great Shaddad and Zabiba," said Hashem with a dreamy air.

"*Sah*, though nothing is over until it's over," said Ahmar with an odd smirk.

"I hate to say it, but as brave as 'Antarah's achievement is, there *is* one thing that would add even more honor to it," said Waiz with a shake of the head.

A ghostly flash of pain shot up 'Antarah's spine, and he instantly regretted not having drunk enough wine to soften yet another blow. He stared straight into space, fearing to catch his father's gaze. Perhaps he was still tired from their long journey and had misheard 'Ablah's brother.

"Ah, women and their demands. And who are we but to oblige, especially when love is in the balance?" said Ahmar with a long, exaggerated shrug. Hashem frowned and glanced at Mutaz, as 'Antarah turned himself to stone.

"'Ablah has demanded for Jayida to hold her bridle on your wedding day," said Mutaz flatly. Like it was the most natural, planned thing.

"I can just imagine: our undefeated hero, whose praises will only keep spreading through the land, going to capture her to make it happen," grinned Waiz.

"*Aywa*; me, too," nodded Ahmar.

"Of course, Khaled won't just hand over his witch of a wife, who has him bewitched the way she does any creature necessary," said Waiz.

"But your glorious success will only elevate your father's name, and your own," shrugged Ahmar.

"If that is 'Ablah's wish," said 'Antarah with feigned lightness, and met his father's hard stare.

How could he have been so blind, so foolish? That couldn't be 'Ablah's doing, even less if she didn't want him. After returning to this thankless tribe, 'Antarah had the final, shattering proof that they would always find another way to avoid fulfilling their promises, anything to push him away, and maybe even more so now that his father was not part of their scheming. Raging lava boiled deep down in his core, and he had the strange impression of sensing his own strength and weakness battling each other in his blood. It would never end—unless he ended it first.

For the second night in a row, sleep eluded him, as this time he paced with his father in their tent.

"Which words am I supposed to believe? He said one thing, and now he says another. Imagine I succeed with Khaled and Jayida, doubtful in itself, then what? You, my father, set me free but they'll always judge me unworthy. So why should I do it again? For all I know, 'Ablah doesn't even want me, so why would she make such requests? I might love her but I'm not stupid," gritted 'Antarah through his teeth, hating the mad irony. "I just want to *know*."

"I did not know about it," said Shaddad, and 'Antarah roughly sniffled back tears at the one thing he'd guessed correctly.

"Can't you convince him to change his mind?"

"I know him. His calculated waiting to reveal it like this tells me that he's set on it."

"He's a liar," said 'Antarah. "Though at least I hope he's never dared to do it to you."

"He tried with your mother, *once*," said his father, his hard stop doing more intense explaining than words.

That it might be another reason for Mutaz to be against Shaddad filled 'Antarah with an urge to both prove him wrong and release his daughter from his domineering hold.

"Maybe it's time for me to leave once and for all. At least I kept my word, and 'Ablah has proof that I could provide for her, even if she rejects it." He might also leave a few pomegranate seeds somewhere nearby, and pray that it'd grow into a tree, whose fruity juice 'Ablah would drink like his blood.

His father sighed. "It's not just you, though of course now they envy you even more. Khaled and Jayida's story is so unusual, and with their consuming greed, now they see a way to add even more to their name."

"*Sah*; through unprovoked violence! They keep dumping their endless greed and envy on me, hoping that I die in the process! And like I should be grateful for it? If they're as great as they want others to think, why don't they do it themselves?

Perhaps I do deserve a crown of glory after all, because it's me doing it, even if I do it for you and *ema*. They can't always take others' greatness for themselves; they have to do their part, too. And so far I owe it all to you and *ema*, not them," said 'Antarah. He almost added Yassu, but something held him back.

"I wish I could tell you, for once, exactly how it's going to go. But one thing I can say: though I hate their tactics, there will surely never be another story like this in your time," said Shaddad. "You're the poet; you and your mother are worthy of yet another honorable story."

'Antarah didn't know what shocked him most: that for the first time there was sincere sadness in his tone, or that it had unmistakable faith in him.

'Antarah laid awake, hating how they had so easily suggested he capture Jayida, thinking it weak to just simply invite them to come. The more he thought of it the less he could see how they would agree to come along, especially after what they must've heard of the 'Abs across time, and when they had to be in the blissful throes of their new union.

But his own curiosity made him want to see them, if only to lay eyes on the unusual woman whom Khaled had chosen to marry. Surely her father had his reasons for that decision, and it couldn't have been easy for Jonder to live that way, let alone bravely kill a man-eating lion. With Khaled's own wealth from Tayma, he couldn't have done it only for Jayida's lesser, though still worthy fortunes. In his contemplation he realized he was set on one thing, though he'd hardly dared to say it. He would not make another move without speaking to 'Ablah first.

Some time in the late night, he stepped out for some cool air, his gaze lost again in the stars and begging Yassu for some guidance. In the stillness he caught a soft rustling behind him, and turned to see a dark form slip inside their tent.

Gripping his short blade, he went in and the dark form suddenly turned around and revealed her face in the dimly lit space.

"'Ablah! Is something wrong? How can I help?" said 'Antarah, trying to keep a low, even tone.

"You can't; I thought you would've seen this by now," spat 'Ablah.

He tucked away his blade and straightened himself, trying not to flatter himself that she had come to him in the middle of the dead night, like she knew exactly when he slept or didn't.

"I meant to speak with you. I thought the camels and gifts would please you, as requested for your dowry. I've also composed a *qasidah* that I wanted to save for our wedding day, though I wouldn't be against saying it only to you."

He pinched a smile, but in the shadows her blank dark eyes and spear-like arms made him think of an oryx contemplating how to best impale him. He looked away, then looked up again.

"'Ablah, I must know if you do not wish to marry me."

"Wish? What does it matter what I wish?" Her arms waved angrily and he both wanted to let them fly free and soothe them into stillness. "Should I marry someone who's as stupid as you are?"

The punch struck every part of him.

"Will you at least say what it is about me you so despise? I at least deserve that much."

"Deserve? What's wrong you, thinking you deserve anything!" The shadows hid her face, but the tremor in her voice shook so strongly he feared the tent might rattle, fall, and expose them.

Somehow, he forced the heartbreaking words out.

"So I will release you, then."

Why had he said it and given her the easy way out? How could he take the words back, keep them bottled the way he'd bottled up so much all his draining life?

"Don't you see?" 'Ablah hissed, and he suddenly realized she was stifling her crying. "Why do you have to force me to say these things? It can never be! I tried to tell you in dreams! You're a poet; I know I don't have to tell you the rest. But at least there—that's the only way I can love you; where no one else can intrude and we can just *be*, just us two!"

His heart thumping, 'Antarah stepped to her and seized her arm, and in the quickness of the motion felt a hard dent in her skin. He shoved her sleeve back and there was the bracelet he'd made her, wound tightly and safely away from the wrist around her thin arm. Knot after knot, tying them together through a purple mark in her suffering, bruised flesh. In an instant, he drew her in his arms, fearing he might suffocate her with his clumsy eagerness.

"'Ablah, oh, my 'Ablah! I wasn't just foolishly imagining then!" He nearly cried, wanting to drown in all her sweet muskiness.

"You should've stayed away; find happiness with someone else! Like I never could," sobbed 'Ablah. She tried to bury her face in his arms but he caught her chin and held it up.

"Never. No substitute; there is no substitute for you!" said 'Antarah, anger and happiness shaking him up. "We don't have to stay here. We can leave, together! Tell me, is Yassu real or not? What do you think?"

"If you believe so, then I hope so," she sniffled through her tears.

"Then it's us two against everyone else. Hasn't it always been?"

"*Na'am*, but can I leave my mother with Waiz? Though on some days I feel myself start to care less, when they think most of themselves."

"And do you want Jayida to hold your bridle on your wedding day?" said 'Antarah.

She shook her head. "I didn't ask for this. I just want to be with you but they won't; they just won't let us be," she cried, her small fist weakly pounding his chest. "I've even thought—"

"No, don't say it. Don't *ever* think of it!" said 'Antarah, rage and fear battling in him. "I will kill them all before you hurt yourself!"

"I'm so tired," sniffed 'Ablah. "But I feel stronger with you."

"As I do, with you," said 'Antarah. "You don't know how you have calmed my heart. So for now I'll play along, go to the Banu Sa'd, and we'll keep praying for a miracle."

He held her a bit longer, then reluctantly released her. It wasn't until he was sure she was gone that he sobbed like a little boy, catching his breath through his newfound fragile happiness.

Nothing could possibly stand in his way now! At last, the gates of Heaven had opened, and confirmed to him what he'd known all along. It had all been worth it, and just like that, he had to reel in his renewed bursting strength lest he betray his joy, as his wise mother had often reminded him.

He wallowed in his secret surging bliss of confidence, baptized by the guarantee of 'Ablah's love. He would've thought himself in a dream except for the memory of her small form still pressed against him.

In his gratitude to her confession, he would do this one more thing for the greedy father who had raised her. Once more, his blameless mother would bless him with prayers and incense, all the way there and back.

Only this time he'd be truly triumphant, because if he had to slay friend or foe to get her, he would. Nothing could be easier for an unfeeling, heartless beast loved by 'Ablah.

CHAPTER FORTY-SIX

DEPARTURE

BANU SA'D

In the perfect, early stillness of their marriage tent, Jayida slowly opened her eyes. Khaled's sleeping fiery warmth wrapped her up as much as his protective strong arms around her hips. Slowly she kicked off the boiling woolen blankets, and turned to him to press her dreamy, satisfied smirk onto his.

Gently, her hands swept over him, softly stroking his arms, chest, face, and long hair, trying not to wake him while playfully wanting him to. He let out a low acknowledging snort, then his deep breath continued undisturbed, and she stifled a laugh at his exhausted appearance.

Jayida closed her eyes and inhaled his perfect manly scent, wallowing in their safe married nest. Where could she begin? Everything was more perfect than she could've ever imagined. The intensity, present from the first moment, would only keep growing: she was certain of this now. In her innocence she'd expected a wild chaos, but instead it was a softer, yet deeper intensity, a kind of all-encompassing, unshakeable gentleness that surpassed the familiar, yet deceiving raging too many mistook as strength. Already she had the sense that she would never have enough of him, and that as consuming as their love was, nothing they did would compare to what she felt deep within. It had bothered, and even scared her the first few days after they'd made their vows. But gradually, assured of her safety, she'd surrendered to the sweet, mysterious thrill of her love and desire, whose sweet joy banished all horrors and fears.

She pinched back happy tears, grateful that even the longed-for Aksumite princess's visit the previous night granted the final approval of her new path. Like her vision of Yassu that dwelled vividly in her soul, she had the humbling sense of being unworthy of such love, and yet ready and willing to keep nurturing and serving it all her life.

Khaled shifted, and squeezed her thigh.

"Blessed day, my wife," he said, and pressed his lips against hers.

"Good morning, my husband," she said, smiling and stroking his chin.

"Is that a nice dream I see shining in your lion eyes?"

"*Aywa*. She's finally come and approved of us, so now our lives can go on," grinned Jayida.

"Perfect timing, too. But from now on, I demand to be the main person in your dreams; that's an order," said Khaled, and drew her into another consuming kiss.

"I'll see what I can do, but also, what you can do about that," she smirked, and jumped up out of his reach before he could pull her back down.

"And to think, I have my whole life to watch my beautiful naked wife get dressed, and better yet, undressed," smirked Khaled.

"Who said I'm getting dressed? I'm Jayida-Jonder; I've proven not only my manly skill but womanly virtue, and since I'm married now I can basically do as I like."

She swiftly grabbed Al-Wasiyah and Al-Naji, and laid her sword across her breasts and his across her hips. Keeping the weapons in place, she shimmied her shoulders and gyrated in a silly dance, and burst in laughter as Khaled's gaze narrowed jealously.

It had to be his perfect love that made her feel so surprisingly feminine. Even with the tribe's support, the blood-stained bedsheet, collected by her mother the morning after, had been the final proof of her true feminine, pure untouched nature. Of course, her parents hadn't repeated her secret jokes to them that after their long passionate night, the blood might've not strictly been hers. But as with so much else since that moment, the amusing thought made her smile. Nor would it have been so difficult to achieve the effect, even if she hadn't bled, but it was another confirmation that despite everything, her mysterious body somehow fulfilled its expectations.

"Let anyone try to talk now; it's all envy, I could almost pity them. And anyway, I'm the only one who has to care about this the most, as you with me," Khaled had said haughtily. After everything she would've never imagined him to be so possessive, but she loved every new side of him that emerged.

She lowered herself to the ground, laid down the swords as she hid behind her knees, and reached for her nearby dress and slipped it over herself.

"Guess I'm just full of surprises! I just realized that if all else fails, I can just be a dancing girl," said Jayida, then jumped up, and pulled him to her by his arms.

"Sah, *my* dancing girl," said Khaled, and spanked her. As he turned to dress she spanked him back, and finished her own new routine.

Although there was a playful ease to her more feminine attire, with her long seven braids coiled with colorful dyed cloths under her veil, and even some occasional necklaces and smeared eyeshadow and kohl on her lids, cautious Jonder was never far behind. Her blades and small knives remained secured in her belt, mantle folds, and leather boots, ready to serve their purpose.

When finally alone, Khaled would draw her to him, nearly ripping off her clothes.

"My perfect wife. I decree that anyone else who touches you, dies," he'd say, his hot breath setting her body and soul on fire.

With playful nostalgia, they packed their few belongings from the tent, with the bulk of it being ready with her parents. They'd even dug up the demon bowls and decided to take them along. At least fourteen days had already passed, hosting and then gradually bidding goodbye to all the guests. Banding together for their journeys, *nasi* Ibrahim and Adinah had gone back to Yathrib with *sayyid* Safwan of Banu Hawazin, as he continued south to his camp in Wajj, east of 'Ukaz. In a similar way, *nasi* Musa and his guests had left back to Khaybar, with *sayyid* Hudayfa of Ghatafan heading further south, to rejoin his camp near the Qusaybah Dam.

Unsurprisingly, the closest kin were set on leaving with them, and with Amr, Samaw'al, Hatim, *mubassir* Ayyub, Muawiyah and their kin, they would make quite a caravan at least part of the way north before splitting ways. Only Sufyan and his Sulaym wife-to-be Tala would remain with the Sa'd, as much to introduce his beloved as prepare for his own and Shams's impending marriage to Yazida, who insisted on being sure they arrived safely to Bosra before proceeding.

It was still early when they went off for a last walk, with Khaled carrying the incense and her the trinkets. Emotions surged as they made their pilgrimage-like walk west to say goodbye to Wadi Al-Hamd, then northeast to her birthplace of Wadi Al-Wafra, then southeast to lay dried flower gifts for the last time at the graves of Nasr, Shanfara, and the three singing girls. Thankfully, that was different, too. Their bones laid there, but as she'd been shown at least with Nasr, his soul dwelled elsewhere with Yassu, as she hoped they all would in time, too.

Their new life awaited, and her heart had yearned for it longer than she'd dared to say. She knew from her father's contemplative manner that he had a similar, yet distinct longing, and at least this second tribal move didn't have an evil *al-'ayn* attached to it. Gratitude washed over her, confirming that this new journey would bring closure and new joys for them all.

They returned to camp to the sight of the gathered loaded camels, and the travelers wearing that combination of flexible ease and alertness common to all travels. Her father, Majid, Samaw'al, Hatim, and Amr along with their tribesmen made additional handsome bodyguards around *mubassir* Ayyub, while her mother, *Umm* Jarida, and Khamra made a beautiful, emotional ring with Warda and Yazida. Jayida discreetly glanced back and forth between her and Majid, wondering if Shams had finally lost her, but decided that since neither Yazida nor Majid had said anything about each other, that there was nothing to it. It amused her to see her poised stallion Adil bearing the caged doves, and in another Ramila and her kitten Ramiya, that added to the perfect scene of a happy caravan ready for Bosra by way of Tayma.

Only *sayyid* Aziz and Shams shared a melancholic mood.

"The lovebirds are flying with Yassu," crooned Hatim, as much to them as to his son Adiyy.

"*Aywa*, we'll sing often of your memorable wedding here," said Amr with an unexpected sigh. How lucky she was to see that so many who visited the Banu Sa'd left with good memories of it.

"The verses are yours, because we hardly have words," said her father, glancing at *sayyid* Aziz.

"For once I'm not sure if the bigger loss is yours or mine," said *sayyid* Aziz, trying to smile.

There was a shuffle and Muawiyah appeared.

"Has anyone seen Ziyad and the twins? I've told them to be ready and here early," frowned Muawiyah, and seeing only shaking heads, went off again.

"If that's an excuse to make you stay longer, I'll make one up, too," said *sayyid* Aziz. He took his time embracing them so tightly and shedding such tears that he left not a dry eye in sight.

When it came the turn of Yazida, for a while the only sounds between them were their sniffling and repeated kisses and blessings of Yassu's protection. Then Yazida took her arm and lured her a bit to the side.

"Will you do me a favor? When you arrive to Bosra, will you find out about Imru and send us a messenger?" whispered Yazida. "I just want to know, then I'll finally be able to get married."

"Of course," said Jayida. Seeing her friend still longing for him almost made her wish he'd just made her his wife and taken her with him.

"And *na'am*, just so you know, I've told this to Shams," said Yazida.

"You did," said Jayida flatly.

"I think he deserves to know as much. But you know the best part?"

"He doesn't mind?" said Jayida.

"*Sah*. Ironic; makes me love him even more. But I want to be sure first," nodded Yazida.

Jayida opened and squeezed her arms around her. "Oh, Yazida. May you be loved as you wish to be. And maybe sing a few nice things about me sometimes, too, after Nasr, of course," chuckled Jayida, her tears transforming the striking girl into her brother.

"Always," sniffled Yazida into her ear as she squeezed her back.

"Jayida! Jayida!" Ziyad's cry echoed over to them from the distance.

"There you are, I've been looking all over for you!" said Muawiyah, joining them just as his son came running, nearly out of breath.

"Jayida," Ziyad panted, the twins coming up at his heels. "We saw two *badawi* heading this way from the east, so I went to inspect. It's 'Antarah ibn Shaddad, with his brother Shaybub, and he says—" he paused, his brow creasing in a frown. "He says that he won't leave without you."

Jayida caught her father's darkened eye, *mubassir* Ayyub made a sweeping sign of the cross with his hand, and Khaled stepped forth, his manner suddenly transformed.

"I may still be glowing from our happy union, but what kind of twisted, cryptic poetry is this?" said Khaled.

Muawiyah went to the children and gathered them to himself.

"*Sah*, especially with their reputation, which, let's be honest, makes us all doubt those latest rumors," said Muawiyah.

"*Aywa*; let's see if it's true then; that these are the two Aksumites who escaped Al-Mundhir's to Taysafun, and returned with great bounty," frowned Amr.

"But just them two?" said Majid, somewhere between concern and mockery.

"Unless—" said Samaw'al, his hand naturally gliding to his sword handle as he glanced somewhere in the eastern space.

"He's been tormented all his life. Surely he will explain himself, and doesn't mean to attack when he could've come charging with his companions," said Hatim.

"He'd better explain himself fast, and not hide behind words, poetic or not," said Khaled, pacing back and forth.

"It must be a misunderstanding," said Jayida, surprised at her own lightness. At least she couldn't be the only one curious to finally see the poet of 'Abs they'd heard so much about. And what could he possibly want with her, especially now that she was married?

"I pray that you are right and this resolves quickly. Perhaps these *badawi*, out in the middle of the scorched Najd, have yet to be blessed with clear language," said *mubassir* Ayyub.

"I'm not taking any chances," said *sayyid* Aziz. "I want everyone armed and ready, now!" he shouted, and word spread fast as Sufyan and Shams alerted all tribesmen, who returned to form protective rings around them.

"If he wants to invite Jayida, for whatever reason, then we'll *all* go, obviously," said Zahir, trying to lighten the mood.

"*Sah*; tribesmen hit and get hit together! And if it's war the Banu 'Abs want, we'll give it to them. People should know who they go against, or learn in the process," chuckled Amr with his infectious confidence.

"At least we know I'll be their favorite guest, when I convince them to give much of what they have away," Hatim smiled at his son Adiyy.

Samaw'al cleared his throat. "In the slight chance that you do go with Khaled, I offer myself as the devoted, unfailing guardian of your kin and goods until your prompt, safe return."

"And you already know you have my arm," said Amr ibn Kulthum.

"And mine, with my prayers," said Hatim.

"And anything I can do," said Muawiyah.

"May Yassu hear our prayers," said *mubassir* Ayyub.

"A thousand blessings on you all," said Zahir with a deep sigh.

Moments later the visiting forms emerged, one taller than the other, and a tense silence thickened the air until they hovered before them on their lean camels, far from the Asafir beauties. Shaybub lingered slightly behind while the leaner, stiff-backed 'Antarah scanned them, as if silently greeting them even as he tried to gage them. For a moment she wallowed in his subdued, even soft appearance that seemed pleasantly familiar, confirming what she'd suspected.

As big as a harelipped elephant, as dark as the night, dumb as a mule with flashing, beastly eyes—he looked none of these things, even if, like all men, he surely changed in the midst of angry fighting. Wrapped in his cream robes, he looked about Khaled's height in a slimmer, *badawi*-Aksumite form. He had chiseled, Pharaonic facial features, with deep, contemplative eyes. Even with the slight scar at his full lip, he was what they would never dare say: he was handsome, and surely wanted by throngs of women. Like any vile, self-serving gossip, they'd twisted the truth into lies, created an intimidating image that even used Shaybub's stouter body, to project the image of 'Antarah that best suited their purpose. Despite Shaybub's bulkiness, he contrasted 'Antarah's proud bearing that instantly commanded attention.

Jayida restrained a smile, caught in his rugged handsomeness. With the wall of eyes and weapons around them, she met Khaled's gaze, and despite his lingering frown, found a glimmer of approving reassurance even as he maintained his cautious stance.

"'Antarah ibn Shaddad, and Shaybub, welcome to the Banu 'Abs," said *sayyid* Aziz.

'Antarah nodded. "Too kind, and quite a gathering you have here," said 'Antarah, his gaze floating across them.

"*Aywa*," came a thundering reply from their crowd that made her heart soar again.

"Our fellow guest poets greet you: Samaw'al of Tayma, Hatim of Tayyi, and Amr ibn Kulthum of Taghlib," said *sayyid* Aziz, as each nodded at the sound of his name, though Amr looked the sternest.

"It's unfortunate that you couldn't come sooner to celebrate our happy news, but at last, we are happy to meet you. How may we help you?" said Khaled. A flash of surprise flickered in 'Antarah's eyes, as if caught off guard.

"Thousand blessings, Khaled ibn Moharib," said 'Antarah with a slight nod. "And Jayida bint Zahir," he turned to her, smirking. "It is a great time of celebration, even when one's father passes away."

Khaled's jaw clenched, and she caught the veiled sarcasm in his tone. Like that struggle was something they had in common.

"Will you recite something for us?" Ziyad blurted as he stepped forth, and Muawiyah immediately nudged him back into silence, to 'Antarah's widening grin.

"With your far-reaching reputation, 'Antarah, you have fans old and young. Meet Ziyad, the little *nabigha* of Dhubyan, hardly eight summers and already learning the art you're so blessed with, as was my departed son, Nasr," said *sayyid* Aziz.

"May his soul be at peace. Perhaps it's he who called me here? Or even Shanfara? He's been in my head all morning," said 'Antarah with a sad frown, and seeing only silent hard stares, grew serious again. "*Aywa*; perhaps we'll meet someday. But until then, I dare to say that I'm not the only one making a name for myself."

"We trust your affairs are prospering, and congratulate your success," said Khaled, his stiffening shoulders hinting at his rising impatience.

"They are indeed," said 'Antarah dreamily. Then his lingering gaze turned to her again, and Khaled's nostrils flared so wildly she thought they might release fire.

"A most unique wife you have; the likes of which they don't make every day. Although, not quite just a wife, is she," smirked 'Antarah, his playfulness surprising her.

She would've almost returned the gesture, lest it be taken the wrong way in such public display. But how could she tell them what they both saw: his bleeding heart aching for the impossible; him and 'Ablah dwelling in a place not unlike Nasr's.

"And how grateful the coveted 'Ablah must be to have you defend her honor," said Khaled coyly.

"So how can we help you, 'Antarah?" said Jayida, breaking her silence with a smile.

"That's a good question; I'm not used to it sounding so sincere," said 'Antarah with a contemplative pause. "It's said that *sayyid* Aziz keeps to his word, perhaps even foolishly to his own downfall. Is that true of everyone here, I wonder?"

"Taysafun is a distance away. With all your exciting, honorable achievement, perhaps you haven't heard what happened here since then," said *sayyid* Aziz in a serious tone. He was being kind, when they all knew it was less a matter of 'Antarah hearing than actually being told by his own tribe.

"*Aywa*; like the part when we nearly castrated attackers, but instead sent these fools who thought similarly and dared to test us scattering naked into the desert," said Zahir, the memory striking her all over again. Amr looked so angry she thought he might dart off in the distance and declare war on the 'Abs at any moment.

"Nearly? Even then you took pity," said 'Antarah, as if to himself.

"We may have showered them with arrows, for some excitement," said *sayyid* Aziz.

"Such shame might explain why we haven't heard from them again," said Khaled.

"Surely a blessed man as yourself knows that we've no shortage of ideas, though we're almost sure we won't need to use them all," said *sayyid* Aziz.

'Antarah tilted his head and sighed.

"You or them? By whom should I prefer to be killed, when Yassu knows my torment at their hands has been constant? But that is where she dwells, and so where my heart leans," said 'Antarah. He was quiet for a moment and looked at them hard. "Still, I could've marched on you with any number of bandits, or deceived you with their false invitation, but I'm not this man. I've been tasked to capture Jayida to hold the bridle of 'Ablah's camel on our wedding day, and so, here I am," he said, eerily calm.

"*Esh?* Like all that you've done for them wasn't enough?" said her father.

There was a pause, the heavy, suffocating air battling to invade her as she and the tribe held their breath.

"*Aywa,* and like we're just going to let that happen," scoffed Khaled and stepped forward, creating a boundary between 'Antarah and herself. "All I need to know about Al-Mundhir and *Shah* Khosrow is that we're not them."

Amusement lightly swept over 'Antarah's face.

"I'd be lying if I said I expected anything less from you," said 'Antarah, lingering on Khaled until the sadness crept again, almost pleading. "As you might've guessed, it wasn't my decision." His smooth profile turned away. Somehow his restrained, nonthreatening manner only made the situation more alarming. It was as though he knew that whatever he said would happen, simply would. But if he could do this, why couldn't she? 'Antarah turned back to Khaled. "But I think we both know, as men, how true love can make us do things we'd never imagined."

A chuckle resounded. "*Sah;* and to be clear, your plan was to accomplish this with just the two of you," said Amr, who stepped up and stood next to Khaled.

'Antarah turned to him, his features hardening for the first time.

"We've always been outnumbered; maybe we'll always be. And yet, that hasn't stopped us before," said 'Antarah.

"So what are you saying then? Be clear now, with no space for doubt," said Amr.

'Antarah's gaze drifted back and forth between her and Khaled.

"As I told you: Jayida is to hold the bridle of 'Ablah's camel on our wedding day. I can only speak for myself that I'd much rather you came willingly, as my guests, and receive my gift to you before the whole of 'Abs," he said with a dash of conflicted pride. She might've been *majnun* with love for her husband, but something about 'Antarah made her believe him.

"With all due respect, you could've brought your gift here," said her father.

"And risk you not coming?" chuckled 'Antarah, and she knew they all agreed with him on that. Even if it had been a usual, customary invitation, it was still a detour from their new home.

"'Antarah, and Shaybub: we don't doubt your abilities. But as you know, there's no capturing happening here," said Khaled with a lightness that couldn't conceal his disbelief. "For your wedding, we're honored to offer some of our camels to add to your great flocks, and come to witness your hard-earned union. Yassu knows we've applauded your growing success, especially Jayida. With your history I'll guess that it was yet another unfair challenge put upon you."

"*Sah*, but do you think I've come so far to stop now? Of all people, I'd think you'd know most of all," said 'Antarah and looked past Khaled and Amr's shoulders to her.

Was Nasr in their midst again? She wanted to wallow in that beckoning space, so calm that nothing could disturb her peace. There was no anger firing through her blood, turning her hands to rock-hard fists, no rattling core about to burst, or impulse to reach for Al-Wasiyah and charge at them. Instead, there was a pulling curiosity, and even desire to just go. It was all a misunderstanding.

"I'll go," said Jayida, as 'Antarah glowed with a mix of mirth and surprise.

Khaled looked at her. Her brow flickered confidently and they exchanged an invisible nod.

"If my wife goes, we'll go," said Khaled. "We have no quarrel with you or the Banu 'Abs, and if any of you harm us and we should strike, everyone here is our witness that we did not start the strife."

"*Aywa*, we witness!" said *sayyid* Aziz, his call echoed by the whole tribe.

'Antarah gave a knowing nod and they left him and Shaybub surrounded by the armed tribesmen as they discussed and prepared. They decided that her mother, *Umm* Jarida, Khamra, and Amr's wife Zaynab with their son and some Taghlib tribesmen would ride to Tayma with Samaw'al and *mubassir* Ayyub.

As added precaution, the rest would ride part of the way with them and gather some help from their respective kin, in the guise of a journey towards the Banu 'Abs at Al-Jiwa, if only to limit the spread of gossip on this unexpected affair. First, Muawiyah, Ziyad and the twins would branch off southeast of Khaybar and inform *sayyid* Hudayfa of Ghatafan before returning to nearby Banu Dhubyan. They'd pass the Khaybar lava fields on the way east, and once closer to the destination, Hatim, with his son Adiyy and their men, would track a nearby smaller Tayyi camp north of Al-Jiwa. Her father, Majid, and Amr and the rest of his Taghlib companions would follow them the furthest, and wait for them closer to the 'Abs camp. Finally, she and Khaled would continue east, keeping north of Wadi Al-Rummah to the 'Abs at Al-Jiwa.

"I'll be waiting for quick good news, or I'll go after them myself," said her father, his dark tone worrying her.

"*Aywa*; we'll be right behind you, just like Amr," said Hatim.

"The swords of Taghlib are always ready, my good fellow *sha'ir*," said Amr.

"I hate to see you all go like this, but we'll be standing by, too," said *sayyid* Aziz, and embraced them tightly once more.

Then her mother swept over her at one side, and *Umm* Jarida closed the ring from the other.

"My heart, I pray Yassu resolves this misunderstanding," said Zoraya, her arms tightening around her like strong rope.

"Me, too," said Jayida. "But try not to worry; at least we all know who I have with me," she smiled, more to reassure them than her own easy self.

As agreed, Khaled accepted Samaw'al's offer to protect everyone and manage their belongings in his absence. They selected some camels as gifts to 'Antarah, then saddled their mounts with satchels packed with their concealed swords and food. After a parting glance to *mubassir* Ayyub's blessing and so many beloved faces around them, they followed 'Antarah and Shaybub east.

Their caravan of nearly forty people left behind the Banu Sa'd's campgrounds and entered the vast Khaybar lava fields. Keeping to their strict set pace, they coursed directly for the Qusaybah Dam south of *nasi* Musa and the Khaybar oasis fortresses.

Riding at center with her father, and Majid directly behind them and the rest rounding out the group, she met Khaled's insistent gaze from her side, searching her out with constant dedication. She blew him a kiss, amused and even a little excited at their first unplanned trip together. Thankfully the lingering silence of their trek felt more natural than forced or even awkward.

Propping her veil up like a mini tent around her head, she tried to understand the difficult circumstances of 'Antarah's situation. They'd all acquired reputations that spanned far and wide, and now her own had come back to her at the most unexpected time. Strangely, if they'd left earlier he would've missed them—or would he have come after them and caught up anyway? At least they were going there before the fall and winter rains flooded the long valley. There was a magic-like order to their shared timing, and amidst her whirling emotions over relocating, she was curious to see that unknown side of the region where he came from, and maybe even his beloved 'Ablah. As with the twins, it pained her to imagine what he'd been subjected to, and she pinched back tears at her sincere wish for him to finally earn the one he'd fought so hard for.

At least by coming freely as his guests offering gifts—and when none had been offered to them by the 'Abs—it ensured that threats and violence would be quelled, while hopefully catching them off guard. The desert law of hospitality still held—and some would say especially in their harsh summer season. And with that, any lingering dissatisfaction or backlash from the Banu 'Abs would be their self-inflicted end, especially with so many alerted witnesses who were preparing reinforcements. She breathed deeply, welcoming the sense of Nasr's presence that reminded her to have faith that all would be well.

As they approached the dam surrounded by date trees, Ziyad began singing and reciting verses about her lion feat, as Najim and Najma followed along with him. As the melody enrobed them, Hatim, Adiyy, and Amr joined in with verses on Khaled, though at times Amr's tone bordered on veiled threats to the Banu 'Abs. Touched by their emotion and support, Jayida wondered if 'Antarah would ever recite about her, or at least about Khaled, then caught her selfishness when she wondered if anyone, starting with his own tribe, would ever speak proudly of him.

Suddenly her heart sank. What guarantee did 'Antarah have that his wish would finally be granted, when it seemed they did all they could to keep him from it while enriching themselves on the way? Perhaps at some point along their long trek, they would even tell him about Ayidah and Liya—Khaled's half-sister—her heart still struggling between their wrongful death and Ayidah's loving loyalty to her child.

In the early afternoon they paused at the Qusaybah Dam for a water break, and bid goodbye to Muawiyah, Ziyad, and the twins.

"Come here, you," said Jayida, and wrapped the twins tightly in her arms in a parting embrace. When she finally opened her eyes, she knew it was useless to stop the tears. "You're a blessing of a brother, to protect your sister as you do. And you protect him, too," Jayida sniffled, trying to end on a happier note.

"You'll still remember us, when you're living in beautiful Bosra?" said Najma.

"Of course we will. And we hope someday you'll visit, with Ziyad, too," said Jayida.

"Maybe 'Antarah too, when he's married to 'Ablah?" said Ziyad.

"We'd like that," said Jayida, and she caught 'Antarah's touched expression dart humbly to the ground.

After more intense well wishes and Amr's own emotional goodbye to the twins, they watched their first group of friends ride south towards Banu Ghatafan, hoping that it was all for precaution than necessity. They rode on the rest of the day to Fadak, and made camp for the night at this kin oasis east of Khaybar.

They tried to dissipate some of the lingering tension with their playful lightness and, noticing 'Antarah and Shaybub's distance, her father invited them to join and eat with them.

"'Antarah of 'Abs, Amr of Taghlib, and Hatim of Tayyi together under the fiery night glow of Antares. Shall we say some words to commemorate our first night?" said Hatim, though she suspected none were in the mood for it, least of all Amr.

'Antarah stared, seemed pensive, but declined with his silent shake of the head. When she finally laid down, she fell asleep with 'Antarah's back facing them, and by the time morning came, it was as if she'd barely shut her eyes.

While their flocks gorged themselves in the early morning, they refilled their waterskins, then left behind the Khaybar lava fields for the open, flat terrain of the Najd desert. It seemed so vast and lonely that she imagined all the past caravans and travelers filling up the long Wadi Al-Rummah that ran just south and parallel to them, which itself flooded the region during the winter rains. Soon the monotony of their long riding was filled with Amr's boastful singing of the Taghlib. Hatim joined in with praises for Tayyi, while his pensive son Adiyy, the youngest among them, humbly observed them like a promising double of his good beloved father. Hatim then once again gently coaxed 'Antarah to join in, but instead Majid and Khaled offered silly verses that made them all laugh.

"And what does Jayida wish to say?" smiled her father. Though she'd never thought about it since she didn't have her own verses, she realized he wanted 'Antarah to see her poetic appreciation and memory, too.

"We're at least certain that it'll be better than Khaled and Majid's," winked Amr.

Jayida smiled. "*Aywa*, this is for Nasr," said Jayida.

She took a deep breath and with her eyes closed, she sang what she could remember of Nasr's verses, hoping once again that he was with them and would also inspire 'Antarah. When she finished and opened her eyes again, she nearly blushed at the thrill of their approval, complete with praises for her melodic, soothing reciting voice.

Impressed by Nasr's mixing of motifs from the Najd and Hijaz regions, 'Antarah gradually asked more questions about him. And before she knew it they were telling him his whole life story, from the lifelong sickness, to the poetry and training, to the attack and his nonrevengeful end caused by those tribal rejects, even as it'd done its part in inspiring the *su'luk* poet Ta'abbata Sharran, friend of Shanfara, who'd been among them. Most of all was her vision of him with Yassu in the beyond, and to her surprise, 'Antarah didn't seem shocked or even dismissive when she said it. It was soothing to speak of Nasr and remember all these painful events, reminding her that things might not always be as they seemed.

After an easier second night, they continued in the eastern direction, the long plain trek making her both glad and slightly dreading that their journey was almost at an end. The ease her father had wished for from the beginning seemed to settle in, so that on this third and last night altogether there was almost an air of melancholy to it, even from Amr. 'Antarah and Shaybub ate with them, and with his brother keeping his usual quiet, 'Antarah shared some of his stories from their journey, surprising her with his praise of *Shah* Khosrow and near silence on Al-Mundhir. But nothing escaped Amr's sharp ears, and he got them to confess that they were among those who'd escaped Al-Mundhir.

"All thanks to Queen Hind and her good son Amr, who rightly calls himself in the matronymic," said 'Antarah, and Amr smirked in approval of their shared name.

"Good note to keep in mind for future potential dealings," said Amr.

"Sounds like you had a better time at Taysafun; I'll note that, too," said Khaled.

"I've even been working on a *qasidah*," said 'Antarah cautiously.

"Thousand blessings with it," said Hatim, echoed by Adiyy.

"*Aywa*. Perhaps someday we'll see you at 'Ukaz to recite it," said Amr with a serious nod.

'Antarah pinched a grateful smile, his Adam's apple rolling in his throat.

"Would you like to hear some of it?" said 'Antarah.

"*Aywa*," they echoed in pleasant surprise.

'Antarah nodded, and with his back held stiff, he began.

"Did poetry die in its war with the poets?
Is this where 'Ablah walked? Think!
The ruins were deaf—refused to reply,
Then shouted out in a foreign tongue.
My camel tried to withdraw—
I couldn't move,
ranting at the charred stones.
'Speak. Live. Prosper.
Here in Al-Jiwa 'Ablah dwelled,
A timid gazelle, doe eyes,
Sweet smile, soft neck.'
I reined in my camel, big as a fort—
I needed to weep, needed the shame.
Rise, desolate traces, from dust
Now that 'Ablah's gone
too far for a lover's visit.
The pursuit's too hard, Bint Suhayyah
By chance we came together
As I battled your tribe.
By *al-ilah*, this is no idle boast.
You seized my heart

Make no mistake
About my love—
Did you decide to leave?
The night was black, your camels
readied. I shuddered at the sight
of pack camels by the tents,
chewing khimkhim, and forty-two
dark milk camels,
Their coats' sheen like a raven's wing.
Then a sudden light, a flash
of teeth sweet to mouth and tongue.
I'm caught—the thought
of this young fawn and her tender stare,
her scent wafting before her smile,
sprung from a merchant's musk pouch
or strong Adhri'at wine
which foreign kings like to age
or from rain-soaked fields of flowers
known to few beasts of the wild
where showers have been kind
and pools glint like silver coins
in downpours from the clouds.
By day and dark she lies on her pillow.
My nights I pass in the saddle
of a black horse, bridled,
its leg strong, flank round, girth lean.
Can I reach her on an 'Absian camel,
her teats snipped, cursed to be dry?
She's a high-stepper, tail still twitching
after a long night's ride,
feet like mallets as though
I were smashing stones and hills..."

'Antarah went on, describing his longed-for black horse, then boasting of
his generosity and wine drinking. The battle scene had monstrous imagery that
reminded her of some of her tormenting visions, and ended with death's arrival
in the symbolic images of vultures and hyenas. He stopped, and though he'd
probably condensed it, it didn't lessen its impact.

"So fierce, so bold. I look forward to hearing the whole thing," said Amr with a glint in his eye.

"May it end on a happier note," said Hatim, his hopeful tone countering his guess that it wouldn't.

"Since our camp is closer to you, maybe you'll share it with us first before going to 'Ukaz," said Adiyy longingly.

'Antarah glanced at Hatim as if seeking permission, which was readily given with an approving smile.

"I would be honored," said 'Antarah with lowered gaze.

"Your tribe must not know what they're in for," chuckled Khaled.

"'Ablah will love it, if only for all your references to her," said Jayida.

"Definitely striking; unlike anything I've ever heard," said her father, and she knew from 'Antarah's smile that it was the best compliment he could've gotten.

As they stayed up late into the night, talking, laughing, singing, and shimmying their shoulders to Khaled's tablah playing, she welcomed the warmth of the distinct sense of friendship that seemed to wrap them all up in its embrace. She thought of asking him why he didn't sleep on his back, or about the scar on his lip, but hated even more that she could guess without asking.

In the early dark dawn, Hatim, Adiyy and their men bid them goodbye and headed to the Tayyi camp that lay north of the Banu 'Abs, while they proceeded on the remaining long day's ride towards Al-Jiwa. She thought of Imru Al-Qays who'd cited the area in some of his poetry, and some of the Thamud tribe that had once dwelled in the region, whose carved rocks remained scattered in a few places nearby.

"Can you take us to some of these Thamud sites; since we're here?" said her father.

'Antarah agreed, and they decided to split the last long day's ride in two—with one longer and the last shorter ride—by camping at Al-Rass south of Wadi Al-Rummah. It was an added benefit that it also granted Hatim more time to reach their kin while allowing her father to delay parting from them. She even dared to think that 'Antarah and Shaybub were enjoying themselves and their company, and didn't mind delaying their own return.

In the late afternoon they finally reached the many hills of Al-Rass. True to its name, there were scattered old wells, and several high mountains had dark stones with sketches of camels, cows, and ancient writings, some in shades of saffron, crimson, and blue. Her father and Amr burnt some incense and passed it around, then they settled away from the grounds with the inscriptions for the night. At first she hoped that Amr and 'Antarah might recite during their last night altogether, but then realized they were all exhausted and fell fast asleep in this valley of ancient dreams.

At dawn they crossed north of Wadi Al-Rummah, and a short while after, her father, Majid, and Amr reluctantly embraced her and Khaled, assuring them that they'd slowly head north to meet with Hatim while waiting for them.

"We know you'll take good care of them," said Zahir to 'Antarah, his tone somewhere between gentle request and command.

Despite the previous days' progress, the dreaded tension seemed to resurface, pushing the four of them harder in the blistering heat and towards the area's scattered ponds to get this unplanned visit over with. Their flock sent lizards scattering across rocks offering rare shade, and soon, in the early afternoon, the Banu 'Abs's tents came into view. Shaybub rushed ahead, and they'd hardly dismounted when tribesmen and women clustered yet stood careful paces away, wearing alternating expressions of shock and confusion. Wide-eyed or stone-faced women looked her up and down. Some bolder ones even sneered, clearly hoping she'd take offense, while casting flirty glances at her husband.

Khaled drew close to her, and when his lightning fast pinch on her leg made her annoyingly turn to him, he mouthed the word "jealous" and winked. While she hadn't thought much about what to expect as a woman, she realized that she hadn't expected so many women's invasive, rude stares. With her chin raised, she looked defiantly around, trying not to grin at the many startled expressions that evaded her lion eyes like *ghilan*. She wondered which of these mothered the beloved 'Ablah. Or perhaps she, too, was secluded in her tent, waiting for the strange Jayida to be brought over to her for the pampered, bored princess's entertainment.

Suddenly, a figure in the crowd caught Jayida's attention, and her brow flickered, trying to focus and catch the receding form again. Without a doubt, there was that familiar face; one she'd known so long, she couldn't trace the exact origin. In the palpable silence Jayida fixed on her target and stepped to it with Khaled at her heels, until she came to a stop in front of the person.

All these years the Aksumite princess guardian had been a sure figure dwelling in her dreams. But it was stronger than her, and Jayida swallowed back a sob, realizing how wrong she'd been when that very woman now stood before her, slightly distraught and trying to look away. Though her simple cream attire was no match for her royal silken robes, and gold, pearl, and coral jewelry, her striking beauty crowned with long braids could leave anyone speechless. Jayida's heart swiftly raged at the kind of hateful envy she had to deal with in this camp.

At last the woman looked directly at Jayida, frowning in feigned annoyance even as her gentle, understanding eyes searched hers. Like her sons, her honesty crowned her, and Jayida didn't have to see the whole tribe to guess that they shared in that mysterious, yet distinct quality that made them stand out from the rest of the Banu 'Abs.

"It's our honor to meet you, Zerafina, noble mother of Shaybub and 'Antarah," said Jayida with her hand on her heart and lowered chin, as Zerafina's graceful features struggled to remain fixed. Jayida wondered how she knew the name, then realized she'd unconsciously known it for a while.

"What in Allah's name is Jayida doing?" a mocking laugh resounded.

"Greeting a slave before anyone else; now I really have seen everything, even if it is the wrong name!" said another.

Staring at Zerafina, Jayida smiled, pleased that their sneers only confirmed their mounting jealous concern.

"What is this? Do you mean to mock me?" said 'Antarah, more agitated than she'd ever seen him.

"Blessed 'Antarah, why would I do such a thing? I've paid my respects; the rest is between you," said Jayida, as 'Antarah's frown lingered.

In the rush a path cleared as an older, imposing stern man approached, and Zerafina and her sons took that chance to vanish.

"Khaled and Jayida, what an honor that you've come to us. I'm Shaddad, 'Antarah's father. Welcome and forgive our surprise; we didn't expect you so soon. One might say you're as fast as *jinn* on a quest," he said with a hint of unease. "*Sayyid* Zoheir and my brother Mutaz, 'Ablah's father, are unavailable at this time."

So this was the hard man who'd often struck 'Antarah, yet now reeked of apologetic embarrassment. To her growing surprise, it wasn't that he didn't want them there, but as if he was just as surprised that they'd not only come, but in eager, record time.

"Thousand blessings to you and your tribe. Please accept these Zahir camels as gifts for 'Antarah's wedding, which we're honored to witness as lifelong friends," smiled Khaled, and presented the flock.

Shaddad stared at him for a moment, then nodded a grunt.

"Like a true Tayyi kin, your generosity is evident," said Shaddad. He ordered a young boy over and had him take the camels away. "You must rest now; you must be tired after your long days riding."

It could've been the heat combined with her sudden sleepiness, but she had the impression that he was avoiding speaking with them.

"Kind of you. 'Antarah clearly deserves all the praise he's getting, starting with the honorable parents he has. I admit, though I've only recently been blessed with marriage, having a *kahina* wife is already full of surprises," said Khaled, his gaze burying into Shaddad's with satisfaction. All the better that his tone had been loud for the tribe to hear, freeing her from the need to speak when they were of one mind.

Shaddad grunted again. "It's most happy news that you're here. I'll leave you to rest now, and will see you again soon." With a final nod, Shaddad retreated and was swallowed up in the clustering crowd.

Without a word, an older man with a curved back leaning on his walking stick led them to a small tent with worn carpets and cushions. They brought in their saddles and satchels and, leaving their mounts just outside, finally piled in to share their first moment of privacy in days.

"Some hospitality. And no greeting *sayyid*; Amr would start a war over much less," whispered Jayida.

"*Sah.* Still, if they want to test our patience and see us crack, they won't," said Khaled, reluctantly sitting down on an old mat and rubbing his face.

Jayida got her straw fan and a waterskin, and downed nearly all its cooling water to counter the stifling late afternoon heat.

"And that shock on their faces; to see us here, with not a battle fought with 'Antarah, and even what we hope to be a lasting friendship. And Zerafina; how will they ever live that down," said Khaled.

The waving fan pushed hot air around them.

"I know," said Jayida. "I didn't have time to tell you, but right before I said I'd come, I had the strange consuming urge to agree. It didn't make sense, but now I know it was to make that important discovery. All my life, the Aksumite princess was right here, 'Antarah's mother in the heart of Najd. And I bet—"

"Only Shaddad knows," said Khaled, finishing her thought. "Her sons sure looked shocked."

"I wouldn't be surprised if she didn't tell them. So many women have suffered and kept things secret, for one reason or another, perhaps hoping to have an easier life. Maybe she just wanted to keep that part of her life to herself. I think I would, too." Khaled scooted close to her, and drew her tightly into his arms. "At least that's one good thing I'll take from this place," Jayida yawned. "Oh, this dry heat has me so exhausted all of a sudden, not that I've been sleeping much at night anyway."

"Rest then, my dreaming *kahina*," said Khaled, and as her eyes closed she almost protested his odd tone.

"If anything—" she gripped him tighter.

"Shh, I'm here. I'll wake you, of course, but hopefully by then all this will be cleared up," said Khaled, his full lips on her forehead the last thing she felt.

CHAPTER FORTY-SEVEN

BANU 'ABS

In their tent, 'Antarah paced stiffly as Shaybub stood still with arms crossed, watching their mother wipe her cascading tears away.

"*Ema*, I'm sorry for this. The heat got to her and she's mistaken; I'll talk to her and clear it all up," said 'Antarah.

Her wet bright eyes set on him.

"Oh, my blessed sons, she's not," said his mother, and through her sniffling it took him a moment to realize that she was chuckling through her emotion. Like a graceful angel she settled on the floor, wiped her eyes, looked up to them with a new glow, and lifted her hands out to them in invitation. His heart pounding, they each settled at her side.

"Oh, it's been so long I thought I'd never speak of it again, but it pleases Iyasus that the time has come," said Zerafina. "My father Saizana—your grandfather, may his soul be at peace—was the younger brother of *Negus* Kaleb. As you know, *Negus* Kaleb long yearned to regain his Himyar territory across the Red Sea, so Saizana was sent to Najran to reinforce the Aksumite presence for the *Negus* through diplomatic relations. I was born in Aksum and was still young when we all moved, with my parents and older sister Nura. I grew up knowing mostly Najran, though I never forgot the memories and stories your grandmother Maryam recited about Aksum, and which I told you. Over time, trouble worsened in Himyar with the Israelites and Iyasus believers—themselves feuding amongst each other—all vying for power. Division was everywhere, with few or no one to trust. *Negus* Kaleb launched an expedition and so began the time of his chosen client monarch, Ma'dikarib Ya'fur. One day, an Israelite rabble stormed into our home, seized my parents and Nura and killed them by slicing their throats. Like madmen they sneered that it was well-deserved retaliation, so with prayers on my lips, I waited for them to do the same to me, until—" she paused, her tears redoubling again and calling forth Shaybub's own. "Until one said that he could have some use for me. He took me away and I tried everything to deter his attention, proclaiming my faith in Iyasus as the divine God incarnate, not just a mere man, and that my unshakeable faith would change his blood and convert him if he stayed too long around me or touched me. It worked for a short while, and I tried all I could until he finally forced himself on me. I got pregnant for the first time."

She paused and squeezed Shaybub's arm tighter, banishing any separation.

"I thought I'd been unworthy of dying for Him; why else was I still alive? So I expected that my life would be endless misery. But even with all this, I had a dream I never forgot, one so real it could only be sent from Iyasus to comfort me. It showed that I would someday have a son fathered by a *badawi*, who would be a famous poet. Until then, Iyasus took my pain and gave me you, Shaybub, who look nothing in body or soul like the one who was part of shedding our blessed royal family's blood. I wouldn't have believed it myself, but I was granted more strength than I could imagine. I wouldn't let him win! And that couldn't be my doing because if it was from me, I would've wasted away or been killed for my own murderous vengeance. The best gift was that it made me forget my pain, to focus on your precious life and watch you grow big and strong. My captor kept me as his, hidden north of Najran, and I'd steal away with you and the flocks in the fields, your giggling summoning the angels like *Abba* Yared with his holy Zema chants. I thought we were alone, just the two of us, and it felt like it for a while, watched by an invisible presence keeping us safe and sound. Until I saw him. Shaddad: so far from home on trading business for *sayyid* Zoheir, watching me with his pleading doe eyes while I, the hunter, stood my ground, because there wouldn't be a second time. Somehow, I knew he needed me, and that I could finally get away from there, anywhere. So he did what he does, and he removed the obstacle and took me away," said Zerafina.

"Why didn't you tell us? When were you going to tell us, if Jayida hadn't—" 'Antarah stopped, struggling to control his raging thoughts.

"I meant to, at some point. But how could I say it? To remember it all, and tell you that, only to know how much our circumstances differed... When we heard of the Najran massacres my heart broke a second time. I knew a part of me would always be there, mourning with the believing martyrs. Then *Negus* Kaleb launched his even larger and blessed expedition against that evil Dhu Nuwas, and in my vanity I dared to think that it was in part to avenge us, too. I cried hot tears of sadness and joy to him in my soul, hoping he heard them across the wide deserts and ocean between us. But even time doesn't erase cruelty, so I tried not to think of it, because I didn't want to pass the shock to you. I never told anyone my real name, and until today I hadn't heard it since my parents' last cries to me on that terrible day," she said, tearfully shaking her head.

"And Shaddad in all this? Can you really say it's been better here?" said 'Antarah, trying not to sneer.

"I know it sounds *majnun*, 'Antarah. He knows that I belong only to Iyasus and that I'm the purest love he's ever had, even though he doesn't always show or deserve it. It's my burden to bear, and it took me a while to accept it and realize life truly was a gift, but I learned it when you both came. At least I can say that he never forced me."

Just when 'Antarah thought nothing could surprise him anymore, he felt a weight lift off him.

"And even with all of this, probably nothing will change. They will still be the same way, like I'm some burden," said 'Antarah.

"Maybe, but not your father, and hopefully in time, there will be others, too. At least now they know and their hold on you is finally gone. It's been long and slow, but you can see that he's changing. I've tried to quell his cruelty towards you whenever I could, and with all you've accomplished, I know he realizes his wrong, is proud of you, and wants to be better!" said his mother, unleashing the wishful thought he hesitated to say. "Oh, how hard I prayed that you'd come back safe, and Iyasus heard me; I know you know this now!"

Her hands fell around each of their necks, and pressed their faces against hers.

"Never forget, my sons: though we walk in hell, we shall fear no evil for He's with us! *That's* what nonbelievers can't stand and envy, because they're so closed off in their rage that they don't see! Sometimes I pity them, and sometimes I think they deserve their torment; maybe we all do, if at least it makes us remember Him. Even then, some do want to try, and that's doing the work of Iyasus, too. It's the hardest thing, and after the torrential hard test passes, it's a blessing to know that we live because of Him, only! When you understand that and what that really means, it changes everything," she said, and for a moment they rocked in a tight emotional embrace.

"There is something that I managed to keep." She fished in the pouch at her waist, and retrieved three gold coins. Each side was similar, showing the profile of a crowned king, flanked by two wheat stalks in a beaded inner circle. All around it were letters and crosses. "From *Negus* Kaleb's rule, one for each of us," said Zerafina.

"*Aywa*, we know what that means, then," said 'Antarah, and glanced at them both with a mischievous smile. Suddenly, all his boldness didn't seem so crazy, if it had something to do with their royal heritage.

"*Esh?*" said Shaybub.

"One day we'll have to seek out *Negus* Kaleb at his monastery and tell him his niece survived," said 'Antarah.

"And maybe even meet his ruling son Wa'zeb, my cousin," said Zerafina with a modest smile.

"*Sah,* and perhaps also inform King Abraha who, despite his initial rebelliousness, has become more cooperative and now pays tribute to *Negus* Wa'zeb," said 'Antarah.

"You think—" Shaybub's face dropped.

"Maybe they're already thinking it," chuckled 'Antarah. "But this time I'll only do it *after* we're married and with her at my side, because they keep breaking their word."

Even his frustration felt different now, because he could no longer be dismissed or manipulated so easily, not with the envied combination of his skills, gifts, poetry, and as it turned out, princely heritage. He had even more options now, and this time, they would be the ones to bend to him.

"With Khaled and Jayida here on good terms, may your wedding happen soon, and our new guests leave here as lifelong friends," sighed their mother. "I'm grateful for their visit; a reminder to never lose faith, especially not with how far you've come."

"I'll try, *ema*. I want nothing more than for them to finally be satisfied with my achievements, and for 'Ablah to become my wife." 'Antarah paused, shaking his head with a sigh. The pained look on her soft features brought out the protective beast in him, and he wasn't sure which of them was more conflicted. "I'm grateful for how far I've come, and that's why I won't give up. No matter what, I'll do what I have to, for you, and 'Ablah. You always were, and always will be an angelic queen who's too good for this world," said 'Antarah, hot tears burning his eyes as he kissed her hands.

How long they had tried to keep him down, make him feel like an unworthy beast, but each time he came back and proved them wrong beyond their expectations, and sometimes even his own. In the darkness a small flame ignited straight ahead, lighting the way: that's how it would always be, no matter how often they, or others, tried. They would live or die in their raging *jahl* to see him succeed, but he would not relent. A flash of lightning: he might even outlive them all, just as his poetry would, in ways he could hardly imagine, and maybe wasn't even for him to worry about. All he had was that moment, to extend for as long as he could.

"Pray for us, *ema*, that all goes well; I know He hears you," said 'Antarah.

He kissed her on the forehead and left with Shaybub.

Chapter Forty-Eight

FATAL QASIDAH

With a start Jayida awoke from her nap, disoriented and trying to make out the whispers from a far corner of the tent. Annoyed, she wiped her drenched brow, sat up, and saw 'Antarah and Khaled sitting nearby, both silently glancing back at her over their shoulder. They drew closer to her, wallowing in an air of contemplation.

"I must apologize for my earlier rashness; there were things we had to discuss," said 'Antarah with a thoughtful air. "You knew things I myself didn't, even if you didn't know who she was, or if she was even real."

Though he'd just learned the secret details of his mother's life story, he recited it as if he'd always known it, with melancholy and a natural, poetic rhyming flow, as he had his developing *qasidah* a few days before.

In their unique way, they'd had their own unrelenting longing for answers that might finally explain their distinct thorny paths. Jayida realized that the longing was the answer, calling out to be found, even as it coursed through their veins until finally, the containing skin sliced open like a fresh wound, revealing the bright, life-giving blood source.

"Jayida's had her own recent revelation, which I'm honored to have helped resolve, after my father played his vile part in concealing it," said Khaled. 'Antarah's intent gaze deepened, and an air of intimacy enrobed them as Khaled summarized the discovery of her father's Ghassanid heritage. "Seems we all have new lives calling to us," said Khaled, urging a small dreamy smile on 'Antarah's lips.

Jayida reached for her waterskin, wondering if it ever cooled down in these parts.

"'Antarah; whatever we can offer, we're honored to give you, although your impressive bounty may well outdo ours by now," Khaled chuckled. "There's no enmity between us; there doesn't need to be. Rather, this can be the start of a great alliance, although none of these new developments were needed for us to feel that way and extend our friendship to you," said Khaled.

'Antarah nodded, caught somewhere she hoped was a good place.

"That's what I came to tell you. It must be done; I'll speak with them and finally resolve all this," said 'Antarah. He rose and glanced at them. "And thousand blessings again, Jayida, for agreeing to come. I know it wasn't the best of invitations, and only Yassu knows when I would've learned this if it wasn't for you." With a hand on his heart, he gave a light nod, and left them.

Khaled's gaze lingered after him, his handsome features covered in sweat.

"How long have I been dozing?" said Jayida.

"A good while. You should eat something," he said. He handed her a pouch full of sundried raisins, salted almonds, and nuts.

"Eat with me," she said, and he accepted by snacking with her.

"Seen 'Ablah by any chance? Or at least figured out where they're hiding her?" smirked Jayida.

"No sightings, but her tent is located next to Shaddad's, just paces north of here," said Khaled. She cocked her head and raised an eyebrow. "*Esh?* I noticed 'Antarah kept staring there. Plus it's next to his father's, unsurprisingly the largest and most lavish of all. And also in case you want to peek later," he grinned, and poked her stomach.

A short while later a thump resounded somewhere, followed by muffled raised voices that seemed to grow louder and closer. From what she'd seen, she hardly expected anyone in such a boisterous tribe to discuss things quietly.

All of a sudden, the entrance flap flew up and 'Antarah reemerged inside without announcement. Without a nod or word, he paced around, one hand on his hip and the other around his neck.

"What is it?" said Khaled.

"I've tried—I've tried everything. I'm sorry Khaled," said 'Antarah, his features caught between anger and reluctant resolve.

"Sorry? 'Antarah, what do you mean?" said Jayida. They both stared at him, blood pumping faster in confusion.

"They won't relent. Ahmar, that unforgiving son of *sayyid* Zoheir, says the request was to have a victorious fight between us. Of course they said no such thing. But all the same, now they're demanding that I fight Khaled," said 'Antarah, the words as sickening as poison. All at once, the treachery seized her, slapping them all in the face. "When—when will it ever be enough?" 'Antarah said as if to himself.

"Never; it will never be enough for some types," said Jayida, their averted gazes confirming their silent agreement. Boiling disgust simmered beneath her skin for being in this suffocating, treacherous place. "We know that between us, none of us want this. But by Yassu, I know my husband," said Jayida, hoping that she was talking to the entire Banu 'Abs through 'Antarah.

If they wanted to fight, despite their constant attempt to avoid it with gifts and sincere offers of friendship, they would get it. Khaled would show them, even as she had no wish for 'Antarah to be hurt, let alone die. Khaled would not, could not fall: it was as much a fact as her undying love for him from the first moment she'd set eyes on him. She knew his skill as much as endless others did, and if the conniving Banu 'Abs wanted to use that fact to have their own brave 'Antarah killed, at least Khaled would do all he could to avoid being lethal. And if 'Antarah died, inciting his tribe to further revengeful violence, they'd be ready for it and put an end to their instigating, greedy thirst for blood once and for all. She looked proudly at Khaled, and cloaked him with all her own *kahina* spirit-power to strengthen him for the task.

"Please, believe me and forgive me: I don't want this any more than you do. You'll be called when it's to be done," said 'Antarah dejectedly, and left.

"Khaled," said Jayida, stepping to him as he kept turning away, his hands rubbing over his face. He finally stopped, and she reached up to him, took his face in her hands. "What's this? How could you forget who you are, now of all times? You *will* defeat him; I *know* you will! I hate to say it but we both know you've had worse odds," she frowned, hating the flash of fear in his eyes as much as her own unintended sharpness.

Then it was his turn to clutch her face with his large, strong hands she loved.

"Jayida: listen to me. Are you listening?" said Khaled, in a severe low tone she'd never heard. "If anything—anything happens to me, you run, you hear me? You *run*! Don't stay here; run fast, as far as you can, all the way to Tayma, then Bosra if you can. Now repeat it!"

"*Na'am*, but why would you say even say such a thing? He's not as experienced!" She only wanted to soothe his creeping fears of his weaknesses, but somehow stating the fact wasn't as comforting as she'd expected.

"Swear it, Jayida!" Khaled gritted through his teeth, his hot breath rattling through her.

"I swear I'll run. But it won't come to that," she frowned.

"May Yassu hear us. We must both trust and have faith; that's our life now," said Khaled, and he kissed her so hard that she wished their skin would just meld together, fused as one eternal clay form in Yassu's pierced hand.

"*Ya Allah!*" a shout resounded outside, marking the time. With a hard glance Khaled stepped out, and she quickly followed at his heels, pulling herself together as they followed the old man who'd presented them their tent.

They joined the large crowd gathered in a circle around 'Antarah, as Shaybub, Shaddad, and another man who resembled him stood at his side. It was telling enough that Mutaz wore a crisp new robe and jewelry while 'Antarah wore no trace of his own glorious bounty. Another tall man with an air of authority stood there, surely *sayyid* Zoheir, with a hard-faced youth whom she guessed had to be Ahmar. The vacant coldness in his eyes revealed it was him who was behind it all, and though he wanted 'Antarah's blood most of all, that he didn't mind harming her husband along the way challenged her own wrath.

"Khaled ibn Moharib, you honor us with your presence. Your reputation is known far and wide, and this day will live on through time. If you didn't know, the terms were for 'Antarah to be given 'Ablah's hand *after* a successful fight, clearly required to capture Jayida so that she may hold 'Ablah's bridle on their wedding day. Since this hasn't yet happened, do you now agree to do it here, before us? In the event of a draw, we'll determine the winner," said *sayyid* Zoheir.

Jayida's jaw locked, and a flash of doubt shook her up. Had 'Antarah known this and lured them anyway, feigning ignorance? But she dismissed it, disgusted by *sayyid* Zoheir. If he was just going to repeat his son's lies, perhaps he should just let him take over already. Even with their persistent deceit and sad wish to see 'Antarah fall, she didn't trust them to honor and respect her husband much more, and realized that their offer of friendship would likely only be for 'Antarah, Shaybub and their mother alone.

Khaled turned to them. "*Sayyid* Zoheir, Shaddad, and 'Antarah. I state once more that we have no wish to fight or harm anyone. As 'Antarah came peacefully to us, we came here as friends offering gifts, without violent intent, counting on your hospitality to allow us to witness their union peacefully. Our many brave kin know of our whereabouts, and eagerly await our prompt, safe return, including some who are but a short distance from here. Whatever hostilities, if any, that may ensue from this will be on your hands."

Mutaz shifted, his dry lips curving into a smirk.

"Men must prove themselves; you know all about that yourself. May the best man win," *sayyid* Zoheir said with a dismissive wave of the hand.

Khaled and 'Antarah positioned themselves and began striking their fists at each other, each evading the other. The boisterous crowd cheered, and she had the conflicting impression that they expected Khaled to win. She'd once thought that the Rûm were barbaric for watching men fight to the death in colosseums for entertainment, yet there she was, watching a Banu ʿAbs version that had forced her own husband into it.

How could she blame ʿAntarah? Even after everything he'd done for his tribe, in this crucial moment they still reviled him, and wanted him gone. She could feel it with every glance, every word, every misleading gesture: they were burning with envious rage that they couldn't just be rid of him, and instead he came back stronger and wealthier each time. Surely it was *ghilan* at his call, but oh, if only they could do the same and bring such fortune to themselves! A storm thundered in her soul. They might gladly take Khaled in exchange for ʿAntarah, but after this her husband would never accept their parasitic self-serving praise or anything else from them.

Half holding her breath to control her tormented heart, she cheered Khaled with each blow, assuming it would be a long, drawn out fight in hopes of tiring ʿAntarah and striking him down at the right moment. If only her parents, *sayyid* Aziz, and everyone else could see this! If she was the only one at his side, as they vowed to each other, she would forever cheer him on, and inspire his victory, praising him everywhere, most of all in the midst of these snakes that Amr ibn Kulthum would love to charge upon the moment he heard of this deceitful turn. She relished the thought that ʿAntarah scared them enough that they hadn't the resolve to do their dirty job themselves. Instead they had to find ways and constantly make demands of him, while proclaiming their innocence.

Turn by turn, they struck at each other, and her heart soared each time Khaled pinned ʿAntarah down, his smaller frame gyrating under her husband. But it was short-lived, and their constant switched upper-hands soon showed that he was among the better fighters either of them had seen. But as she knew herself from experience, Khaled's strength was unwavering.

As the fight went on, the suffocating communal weight of frustration accelerated, her heart swelling with love for her husband's dedication to fight for her. The shattering memory of her angry march after him enveloped her, and she saw a shadow of herself riding, shrouded in black, the flash in her fiery eyes distorting her true appearance. As Khaled and ʿAntarah rolled on the floor, locked into and grimacing at each other through continued punches, she saw how she'd struck at him with unearthly force, willing him to surrender. How could she have ever wanted that, when she'd always loved him? Just the thought of it flooded her vision with tears of unfathomable love, and because after everything he forgave her, even as she'd wanted, in that terrible moment, for him to fall. And the worst was that he'd known it, even if at the time he hadn't known exactly who it was from.

Everything seemed to slow down, and for a moment she wasn't sure what was happening—awake or dreaming? Past or present? She stared at Khaled's pinned down, jolting form, his eyes widening and jaw flapping, as 'Antarah slowly withdrew his fist from his neck to reveal a short blade covered in blood. 'Antarah peeled off Khaled's stilling, then motionless body and stood up, his bloody palms clutching the blade tearing open his tunic down to the waist. He reached in a pocket, and with the blade in one hand and what she realized was a red pomegranate in the other, 'Antarah slowly turned, revealing his scarred back in the form of a large, recent cross carved out of raised bumps. Every 'Absian eye locked on him, caught in a trance of awe-full fear like an unknown deity appeared in their midst.

"'Antarah! What have you done? What have you *done*!" shouted Shaddad who stepped forward, horrifed.

"'Antarah, son of Zerafina and Shaddad stands true to his word! Now stand back, his blood is poisoned; I made sure of that!" shouted 'Antarah, as wild shrieks retreated in self-preserving frenzy. "*Mawai temawe meskal!* Victory through the cross! And now, hear my *qasidah*, my gift to you all!"

His opening verses and the tribe's cheers were blotted out by her screams, as she shook and fell to her knees. Agonizing, she rocked back and forth, releasing wails she didn't even know she could make. Endless scattering feet rushed past her, sneering, laughing, shoving, as her fists repeatedly pounded into the hard dead ground, her burning knuckles scraping up dirt and dust from so many other lost souls.

"With quick thrust of my pliant blade
I felled a decent man
his jugular hissing, split like a harelip,
spurting 'andam resin red
'Ablah, Daughter of Mutaz, ask
the riders if you want to hear
how I live in my horse's saddle,
swimming through troops
exposed to spear thrusts
wound after wound
charging the great harvest of bows.
The riders will tell you—
I enter the fray
then decline the spoils
For my victory is through the cross."

Her throat clamped, hearing this terrible part he hadn't shared. How could she have been so blind? He had it all planned and was just waiting for the right bait! She gasped, deserved to suffocate from her stabbing cries, when she'd foolishly thought she'd done right and trusted 'Antarah. But that deceitful Timely Fate had waited patiently for the perfect moment, punishing her for her own darkness. Pain—what was any of her past pain compared to what she felt now? There was no comparison. Like Dalilah who'd betrayed Shamshun, she'd meant to hurt Khaled at Tayma, and had failed him again by bringing him to this place, believing in her own sight and strength.

In her painful struggle to breathe through her endless sobs, she kept her eyes firmly shut when her headdress was yanked off, and the pulling at her hair persisted, until it finally gave way, and they tossed her long shorn hair before her to cement her widowed grief.

"That didn't last long," laughed someone.

"Glory to the Banu 'Abs! Glory to the Banu 'Abs!" the chants echoed.

"Give him to me! Give him back to me!" Jayida screamed, as she felt herself being lifted and dragged away from the only man she had ever, and would ever love.

CHAPTER FORTY-NINE

GRIEF

Alone in her tent, Jayida sat hunched over, rocking back and forth as the nightmare replayed over and over in her mind like a crushing wheel. 'Antarah stabbing Khaled, her beloved's blood drenching his hands and seeping into the thirsty earth. But if only it were that! She'd done this, when her revengeful foray to Tayma had cemented others' doubts of Khaled's skill, leading up to this very moment! Each time she thought she had no tears left to cry, streams of gut-wrenching visions set her gushing fresh floods of wailing.

Folded over like a misshapen monster, her hands tore at her short hair. She winced at her own vileness that was there, and everywhere, as it'd always been, waiting for the perfect, cruelest moment to give her what she'd wanted. Cruel, how cruel she'd been, when like lustful, violent Dalilah she'd tried to use his weaknesses against him. It was all true what they said of women's revenge—she was proof of it. And the worst of it was that he'd known it, still loved her, and even accepted to come along, all to defend her.

But she'd changed her mind about him, and loved and married him, despite being the son of Moharib! Didn't they know this? Why pay attention to one of her fleeting wishes more than the others? Where was Khaled now? Where was Nasr and Shanfara to help in her isolation? How would she alert her father—and did she deserve to live through this?

Surely she deserved to be forgotten and forever alone, never to feel his burning skin and heartbeat against hers again. She summoned every memory of him—his sweaty, musky scent, his thick, long ebony hair, his playful dark eyes and hooked eagle nose hovering above his warm smile, asking her forgiveness and to be his wife—refusing to let him go. Too soon, it was too soon.

Panting, her raw fists dug into her eye sockets, though not even ripping them out would ever erase the horrible sight from her mind. Her short hair glued to her cheeks, she summoned some strength to lift her head and catch some air, amidst the cackles and cheering still echoing outside in the heat of celebration. 'Antarah had played the game and she'd fallen for it. How could she forget deceiving was part of what some poets did? But try as she might, she still couldn't see him like the rest of them. As different as they were, better that Khaled die at his hand than anyone else's.

She tried to take a deep breath, but stopped. She could kill everyone, and be left the only person on earth, but there was no escaping herself—that unceasing whirl of insatiable thirst, demanding constant satisfaction. Her heart pounded so hard that she thought she might go right then and rejoin him—it sounded more tempting by the passing moment. It only added to the list of blows that life seemed just a long buildup full of longing, only for the finally acquired desired things to be taken away just as quickly.

Somehow, gradually her sobs quieted down, plunging her into a blank space.

Run fast, as far as you can!

But how could she, and add to her shame, as if she was afraid of them? With so many at least aware of their location, and especially if in the tribe's drunken vanity they already boasted of the news, they should expect to be charged on at any moment. Perhaps her father, Majid, Amr, and Hatim would barge in shortly and avenge her and Khaled, cementing his heroic legend into eternity. Through her hellish anger a flash of light burst: would the same be done for 'Antarah, even as she hated his role in her guilty misery?

Run fast, as far as you can—the command echoed, and with conflicted resignation she knew that it was exactly what she would do. She owed him that much. The strip of light peeking in from the entrance vanished, announcing the end of this most horrible day of her life. Come nighttime, she would leave this cursed place.

Then, for the first time since witnessing her beloved's last breath, a tiny smirk crept on her lips. Mustering her self-control, she banished it and remained a subdued, depleted woman reduced to tears and weakness—curled over, help-less—exactly the kind of person she'd vowed never to become.

It couldn't be—could it?

Hania and Sadiqa were gone, they wouldn't have...

Jayida slowly turned her head, looked up at her nearby satchel. Silent as a sand cat, she crawled to it. She slipped her hand in, found their waterskins, food pack-ages, their bundles of thick clothes... and wrapped deep in them, their scabbards.

Al-Wasiyah and Al-Naji lay quietly waiting, and whatever the reasons for not having been taken away—failing to check, or even find them, not wanting to touch the witch's things, or just dismissing Jayida in the throes of their glory—it didn't matter.

Let them think her weak, one whose false strength had long gone. Her grief ceding to anticipation, she didn't move or eat, but laid in the tent, a mere mass on the floor, defeated, and feigned sleep as gradually the voices died down. She waited even longer than she needed, savoring the delicious last moments leading up to the hunt. She relished the miraculous clarity that came after the storm: she only had to strike at the one crucial place to affect the whole.

As she promised Khaled, she would make her escape—right after she paid a most important visit.

Chapter Fifty

REVENGE

In the raven stillness Jayida donned one of Khaled's dark robes with cloak and matching headdress. Through blurred vision, she folded and adjusted the ample layers that had so recently covered his beloved massive form now turned into another elusive shadow. But he *was* there—he had to be!—and would protect her and help her escape. She closed her eyes and swallowed back her tears in exchange for some thick air. Just a little more, and everything would be right again.

Using their old cushions, she stuffed her cream robe and laid it down on the floor, a lifeless, curled up sleeping form to fool, or at least delay, them all. She fought and released the chaotic urge to go after and take all his belongings with her: she had to hurry and more importantly, no object of his could ever compare to him. Whatever of his she'd ever wanted and loved, was in her—that's what she would always carry, and no one could take that away from her, even if they killed her.

Let them try to use his remaining belongings and make up all kinds of stories about him: she would hear none of it, and if she did, she would deny it. She knew his story, when she was part of it and no one else would control it, with or without items. Even in her torment, though she didn't know when or how, she took solace that somehow, someday, the truth would come out and set everything in its proper place, as their own lives had shown them.

Her one satchel in hand, she peeked out into the camp cursed not to know the contrasting pleasure of evening chills. There was not a sound, except for some crickets in the distance.

Jayida prowled in the northern direction, Khaled's words drumming in her soul like his tablah. A range of snores whirled in and out, demons too drunk with

577

vain glory to know that someone else's death was in their midst—and the worst was that they'd probably celebrate that, too.

She had the impression of flying to her destination, and she frowned as she approached, when who but none other than Hania sat before the tent, as if marking the way—or knowing they would meet there. Hania turned her head her way, and Jayida smirked, imagining her mount evading and threatening any 'Abs who tried to have their way with her.

My perfect mount, said Jayida to her in conflicted, yet grateful thought. Khaled was right; even in the darkness it was easily the second largest tent, overcome in size only by Shaddad's.

At last she would see if 'Ablah was pleased this night, caught in happy dreams of love—maybe even with someone else—or in fickle, selfish indifference like greedy Mutaz.

Jayida reached Hania, draped her satchel on her neck, and paused at distinct, muffled sounds. For a moment silence reigned, when again it pitched through the night. Her stomach jolted pleasurably: her target left no room for doubt. Her throbbing bruised hand reached for the entrance, and she slipped in like a flash of lightning.

Behind the empty public area lay her stone-cold parents, Mutaz snoring so loudly she wondered how anyone could sleep. She quickly glanced around, and found the pathetic granite square stone with a blank face representing Al-Uzza. She wondered how much of the woven red, white, and black carpets, silken fabrics and other embroidered items, silver trays, and bronze cups and jugs were from raiding, fair trading, or 'Antarah's brave achievements. She stifled a grunt. It was its own delightful punishment that they had more than others and remained perpetually dissatisfied.

Jayida continued to the back of the tent, beckoned by the distinct sobbing that seemed indifferent to being heard. Without a sound, Jayida stepped through and hovered near the small 'Ablah. She sat hunched over, her face concealed by her long veil entwined with her hair, crying into her folded knees.

What was she crying for? What had *she* lost, when she had everything, and it was Khaled, her husband, who now lay dead! Even if it was true when 'Antarah said that it wasn't 'Ablah who'd asked for her to be there for their wedding, someone had to pay! 'Antarah might've tricked them, too, for his own means, and even if by some small chance she was innocent, then so was Khaled, most all. The enraging thought made her hands curl into fists, tearing at her knuckles all over again.

Jayida's flooding, wrathful gaze swept over 'Ablah like a storm, and slowly 'Ablah looked up, her red, sorry eyes pleading as though she'd expected her to be standing there all along. But it was too late, and not even her ruddy face that betrayed her long crying would soften Jayida's heart. She would've never expected it, but it had to be why she'd waited so long to deter her violence towards a deserving person, finally creating the maximum impact for this one painful desired outcome of her life. There were not tears enough to shed for Khaled, and she wanted nothing more than to end them.

Quieting herself, 'Ablah rose slowly, her open arms pleading to be filled. She was as small as she was a sight, a fragile young woman whose striking beauty made men go mad just for the chance to make their dream a reality. But at some point she also had to give, so it it was only too fitting for 'Ablah to sacrifice and to even the scales again.

Did she even love 'Antarah? Did she even understand what that really meant—to love with such fervor that every action, beginning with her every breath, was no longer her own? And if she did, then what better proof than to show it with her own life, as he'd so often done with his for her! After Khaled and Jayida's, theirs would be the second story from this warring land to survive across the ages, two destined souls taken too early from each other due to others' endless greed!

To her disgust, 'Ablah's eyes painfully contorted with something like sincere grief; an unspoken apology. Like that would undo everything, bring Khaled back from the dead.

Jayida went to her and 'Ablah's face buried into her chest, her gentle sobbing rattling her fragile frame. As 'Ablah's small hands clung to her, Jayida stroked her head, over and over, then glided down to her face, wiping and caressing her burning cheeks.

Then, her aching hands wrapped around her delicate throat, and 'Ablah's head tilted back, her wet eyes obediently closing. No, 'Ablah didn't, couldn't know her pain when 'Antarah still lived. An eye for an eye—the ancient law had never seemed so wise and necessary to her before. A long, pleasurable drawn-out bloodless slaying... Or should she make it fast, one last mercy to pass between them?

"Stop crying," sneered Jayida, her tightening grip unleashing another flow of 'Ablah's silent, submissive tears. Wasn't she even going to fight back? How could Jayida resist, with the creature offering herself? At least her blood wouldn't shed, unlike her blameless, nonrevengeful husband's. Locked, her hands were chains that wouldn't let go until it was done.

Run fast, as far as you can!

Khaled trumpeted amidst her turmoil, as 'Ablah already seemed to shrink in her hand, consumed with deepening remorse. So much life-draining sadness it almost looked sincere, but how could she tell anymore? Everyone lied, and this time it wasn't only she alone but Khaled punished for wanting to see the best in others and believing them. 'Ablah's time had come, and like Shamshun Jayida would bring down the temple with this ultimate strike.

No one is to avenge me!

Run fast, as far as you can!

Why—why did she have to be so weak, and think so much in such a moment that called for action? But somehow, in her exhausting torment even that didn't seem to matter anymore.

Holding her breath, Jayida loosened her grip and cupped 'Ablah's face, as the girl clung onto her wrists, bringing their foreheads together in a silent embrace.

In the emerging stillness, Jayida pulled away and vanished.

CHAPTER FIFTY-ONE

VANISH

Her heart thumping, Jayida raced west of Al-Jiwa's ponds, praying she'd soon run into her lurking kin and the Tayyi's nearby camp. In the silence, she constantly looked around for signs of anyone coming after or bent on slowing her down. She hoped that 'Ablah wouldn't say anything about her escape, and somehow trusted that she wouldn't. At least the moonlight helped her decision not to light a torch and potentially give herself away.

Jayida rode hard, and almost cried out when soon she saw signs of a familiar camp marked by what had to be Hatim's discreet oil lamp, and thanked Hania and her *qareen* for guiding her to their kin.

Wondering where her father and Sabah had gone, she slipped off Hania and made her way through the vast area of sleeping bodies in the open air to wake the robust Majid.

"By Yassu, Jayida! And where—" Majid sat up, just as she realized it would be the first time she would have to say it. She shook her head, her tears streaming.

"Don't make me say it, I can't," said Jayida.

"*Esh?* What!" scowled Majid, and bolted up.

"Did my ears fail me, for once?" croaked Hatim nearby, his hand on his heart.

"Those demons will be drained! Let's go!" said Amr, kicking off his blanket.

"Wait. And where—Oh no," said Majid. He looked around and wiped his stretching, perplexed face. "Your father; he was getting worried. Seems he left us to search for you."

"Unfortunate that you didn't see him on your way," said Amr, grabbing his things.

"No! Oh, no! Why did he do this? Please, Yassu, watch over him! I can't—I can't lose him, too!" Jayida cried, and finally fell to her knees from the shattering weight, as they each caught a side of her.

"What happened?" said Amr.

"Oh, I still keep wishing I'm in a nightmare that'll soon end," said Jayida, and related the painful details. "Everything; it was so fast! Oh, his body!" she gasped. "How could I leave it there? But he told me to run, to leave, and that's all I could think of! But we can't leave him there; his bones are too good for them! I must have them!" she sobbed.

"Of course, we'll get him back," said Majid. I never thought—" He stopped, glanced at her husband's dark attire on her. "It suits you, of course," he said, and sniffed to hold back angry tears.

"What *ghul* has possessed the 'Abs to do such a thing," said Hatim, shaking his head.

"Please, bring them back," said Jayida.

"We won't come back until we do," said Majid.

"You'll take my men," said Hatim to Majid. "In the meantime, I'll stay with Jayida and we'll ride on to our kin's nearby camp."

Majid nodded. "Wait there, but if we're not back by dawn, ride on to Tayyi and by Almighty Yassu, we'll catch up with you as soon as we can."

They solemnly split ways and rode on, and soon they rejoined the small Tayyi camp, grateful to be safe and among welcoming souls again. She fidgeted, her grief and worry for her father pouring out constantly, and try as she might to stay awake, she had to lie down, her exhausted body screaming for rest.

Curled up like a child, she sobbed herself to sleep, submitting to this new routine. Just a bit longer and she would finally be with her family at Bosra, where her grandparents had lived and died, where Khaled had walked, and returned to help her piece together their own silenced history. Just a bit longer and she could wallow in her eternal love for him, even if his body was gone, and continue to honor his memory forever. She thought of Nasr and his beloved united in the beyond, the stabbing fear unleashing fresh tears at the thought that Khaled might do the same with someone else. Miraculously, she chuckled at this sorrowful exaggeration. It may have been short, but it was enough for a lifetime—there was comfort in that, at least.

Eventually she drifted and floated, realizing that she might never see Zerafina again.

Jayida!

A man's voice. But not just any voice.

Jayida!

And this time she knew for sure that she'd lost her mind, because without a doubt the voice was Khaled's.

Relentless was their love, their refusal to let go of each other. Such was her life henceforth, and she let it drift before her, envelop her with its immeasurable strength, demanding every last tear out of her. There would be endless imagined scenarios of their reunion, all of them sealed by their undying love.

Despite her heartache, she beamed at the sight of the handsomest man she'd ever seen. In this version of Khaled's holy hagiography, there he was, with Majid and Amr at each side of him. He sat on Sadiqa, his neck and chest stained red, giving her a strained, tired smile, then looked down in distress.

A mass laid across his mount, and her face contorted in horror as he came towards her, revealing her wounded father.

CHAPTER FIFTY-TWO

BOSRA

SPRING 543 AD – BOSRA

Jayida opened her eyes, and laid still on her side for a moment in the peaceful darkness of her sleeping room. All around her, the thick basalt walls shut out all sounds and the nighttime cold. Not even the doves or sand cats stirred.

Quietly she rose and dressed like a nun for early Qurobo service, and glided into the living room lit by a single small oil lamp. She cast a tearful smile at the beautiful table covered in a gold-embroidered tablecloth displaying her small statues nearby, most of them carved by her father, and the sprouting pots of purslane and baskets full of rose bouquets next to them.

It didn't matter how often she stopped and looked at it all over again: she was sure it would always feel like a shrine of not only her, but her family's life. Highest above it on the wall hung a cross with flaring arms. Under it, her father's sword Al-Khalisa lay horiztonally over his shield and the two coats of mail, those blessed pieces both her father and herself had worn without knowing they'd belonged to *siddi* Ayan. At each side of them hovered two demon bowls as decorations. Most unexpected was her ostrich egg decoration saved by Khaled, now painted with floral motifs and holy verses in Syriac and *'arabi*.

Under the table, almost concealed by the tablecloth, was a closed chest containing her leopard and lion skins, along with her banner, lion jar, and Sahira doll seasoned with frankincense tears, sage leaves, and dried flowers for proper storage. On top of it were her sword Al-Wasiyah and her bow, awaiting her moment of need.

Stifling a sob, Jayida laid a hand on her necklace, hosting the trio of her Mikha'il amulet, leopard fang, and her father's Anastasius gold *solidus* coin.

With a deep breath she grabbed some bouquets of roses and slipped out into the dark stillness. She headed west away from the domed Bosra Cathedral that proudly grazed the sky. Her steps as silent as the early hour, she found the mausoleum named after Saint Eliyas and slipped inside the large gated garden.

Jayida lowered her watery gaze in reverence, and walked to the beckoning inscriptions emerging out of the lush, honey-scented garden. Like her *baba* Eliyas who'd spent years watching over and caring for the graves, she would've known the path and the inscriptions with eyes closed, marked with three lines of sharply-shaped Greek letters, and wave-like Syriac, and *'arabi* writing. She laid some flowers on the graves of *siddi* Ayan and *sitti* Wafa, then knelt at her father's next to them and added some bouquets to his. Pinching her twitching lips together, she closed her eyes, both wanting and dreading the precious memory.

"Yaba, tell me who did it!" she pleaded, struggling to keep calm.

"I don't know, it doesn't matter," said her father, looking almost pleasantly sleepy.

"How can you say this?" she croaked.

"Jayida," he said, his heavy breath still pulsating with authority. "No one escapes their wrong. I know this now, and you should remember it." Somehow it eased the creeping sting.

"But it's too soon!" she shook her head.

"Is it ever too soon to rejoin those with whom we belong?"

"But I want you here! I wanted you to be here to see our children!" she cried.

"But I am, and I already do, my little lion," said Zahir, his rough hand reaching out and grazing her cheek, causing another onslaught of cascading tears. Then he took her hand and Khaled's and wrapped them in his. "For to which of the angels did God ever say, 'You are my Son; today I have become your Father?'"

Even with all the torrential emotions surging through her that would never fully cease, none of it made her think of lurking hyenas, *jinn,* or anything frightening. She would never forget Wadi Al-Raha, that Valley of Rest she'd known so well, but his soothing resting place with its dewy emerald grasses, sweet alyssum shrubs, jasmine flowers, and multi-colored roses, irises, tulips, and chrysanthemums surpassed anything she could've imagined. No place was more fitting for her father, she thought tearfully again, grateful that she couldn't quite call it sadness. It was more an overwhelming burst of emotions: of unworthiness, of love, of happiness, even a vague but distinct sense of trusting faith for all that had happened and all that would still come, rendering her fears insignificant.

There was a faint rustle behind her and she turned her head to the towering presence.

"May I join? I don't want to interrupt," said *malik* Al-Harith. With his dejected air, slight Syriac accent, and self-effacing ebony robes as dark as his facial hair, he could've easily passed for a striking wondering ascetic.

"It's no interruption," said Jayida. She smiled through her tears, touched that the great Jafnid leader who'd fought great battles, including alongside General Belisarius, and who inspired so many would be so meek as to ask her permission.

Malik Al-Harith sat next to her, across the tombstone marked with his missing son's name. Even hidden under his robes, his intensity was such that she wasn't sure if it was entirely his, his son Al-Numan's, or a mix of both. Their silence lingered for a while, as if not wanting to intrude on the other even as they mutually welcomed, and even needed, the blossoming friendship.

"Jayida," said *malik* Al-Harith gently. "I know how hard it must be to lose your father, especially one as yours, who decided, with your mother, to raise you as he did. And yet—" His nose scrunched. "It's better for a child to bury his parent; that's how it should be. No parent should have to lose theirs, especially not—" He stopped, and she laid a hand on his arm, not daring to imagine his pain, yet grateful to know it could only be soothed by the One greater than them.

"Sometimes, I think it's best his bones aren't here. And sometimes I rage because they should be. I know it's for a reason, but if Al-Mundhir thought this would stop me with his evil, he is wrong. My beautiful, blameless son, chosen to appeal to his unworthy *ghul*-soul by his martyrdom! And to think: I could've captured his own two sons, too—but I didn't! And yet, I could—I *could* forgive him even this, if he actually finally understood, believed, and repented! But I was wrong. I tried. I pushed myself to love; named my third son Al-Mundhir after our victory at Daras, both to celebrate and to help me see that name in a different, better way. All this, for that demon to capture my second-born while he tended the flocks, and give his pure, blameless flesh to Al-Uzza's flames—knowing it would be the worst offense!" he croaked, making a large fist. "Now, his blood calls to me, and his sword, Shahid Al-Numan, will be at my hip with my own Intisar Al-Masih, waiting for the moment. Until then, I will keep praying and begging. And if it's His will, when the time is right He will give me justice, and I shall build a *martyrion* where my son will be commemorated with the sword in his place," he said with a tearful, curt nod.

"May Yassu hear you," said Jayida, and offered some of her tears in turn.

"Maybe I would've made less mistakes if I'd been blessed as a *kahin*, too," croaked *malik* Al-Harith.

"But you are, *malik*. Everyone has it, but especially you, with all the lives you serve and the tough decisions you often must make. We each have to learn to work with our skills to best serve Yassu," Jayida said, a bit sad that he'd forgotten it.

Malik Al-Harith nodded, then took a deep breath and in his deep tone, recited.

"When he opened the fifth seal, I saw under the altar the souls of those who had been slain because of the word of God and the testimony that they maintained. They called out in a loud voice, 'How long, Sovereign Lord, holy and true, until you judge the inhabitants of the earth and avenge our blood?' Then each of them was given a white robe, and they were told to wait a little longer, until the number of their fellow servants and brothers who were to be killed as they had been was completed. From the sixth book of Revelation," he said, and a wave of relief seemed to wash over him.

She would cling to his kind offer to teach her and her family more about the holy *injil*, along with the other sacred books of their faith, because her heart yearned to know them as well as he and *mubassir* Ayyub did.

Malik Al-Harith set his piercing gaze on her. "These are hard times, but I'm glad that you are here, and reunited with your honorable family who served my good father in the time of *Qaysar* Anastasius, who shared our faith. I want us, all of us here, to be at peace, and live happily in this garden in His service. I've often asked myself why He chose us, but I want to keep defending it, to the best of my ability," he said.

"I'd like that, too," said Jayida. "And I'm honored that my father shared your name, even if he was known as Zahir most of his life."

Malik Al-Harith gave a nodding smile, his contemplative green eyes glistening like emeralds.

"I worry about Halima; I don't want her to be afraid," said *malik* Al-Harith. "Your story reminds that women can and should be taught, but some things are best left to men, as Yassu intends. I wonder; might you like to train her? She's just turned ten, and I'd like an experienced older sister to inspire her, besides her brothers."

"If you'd like, though my training isn't anywhere near that of your brave fighters," said Jayida wide-eyed.

"*Tsk*;" he clicked his tongue. "I don't believe it. But I do believe it'll be a joy for us all to learn from each other."

"We'd be honored," smiled Jayida, half wondering if she'd already forgotten everything, when it all felt so different.

"Come to think it, it'll also be a great story to share in our court at Jabiyah someday. I've begun work on a book I might name *Akhbar Muluk Ghassan*. This would be a worthy chapter to add to our Annals of the Ghassanids, our great kin," said *malik* Al-Harith.

Jayida thanked the early morning darkness that hopefully hid her blush.

"I feel like I'd have much more to say about others than myself, especially certain poets," she said.

"All in time. As always for those of faith, may Yassu guide the path. We'll see you later at church, then," said *malik* Al-Harith, and they parted ways, gracefully reinvigorated.

Jayida returned to their spacious home with four rooms decorated with crosses, incense burners, and candles, and slid in beside Khaled, amused by the sneaky thrill of having gone and possibly returned unheard.

"Had a nice visit?" groaned Khaled, his eyes closed and body motionless, as his thick arm hastily draped over her.

"*Na'am,*" she said, and they merged in a warm, blissful kiss.

It was too much sometimes; just to look at him, as she ran her hands across his bearded face and through his wavy hair now once again shorter than hers. At times she could still hardly believe all that had happened, especially when they all knew that things could've turned out very differently. Khaled had more than proven himself, and she vowed that she'd do her best never to hold a grudge against him. She would not be that deceitful, revengeful wife.

After everything, she learned that her fear and desperation had limits when at last she understood that she would never be alone. If she'd ever doubted what they called miracles, she believed in them after the impossible had happened. The fact was that she'd met Khaled, loved him and lost him twice—or so she thought.

At first Jayida wondered if it was wrong to feel this happy, but dismissed it when she learned that an *injil* verse urged believers not to be anxious and to rejoice in the Lord always, among other similar and different passages she still had to commit to memory. Each day since her flight from the Banu 'Abs, she became more aware that some wallowed too much in pain, perhaps because they thought they had nothing else left, or because others even liked it, and wanted to drag others down with them, too. But the truth was that she had the only real security and so much to be grateful for, and it was all because of Yassu.

"Careful with the thoughts," said Khaled, and cupped her tearful face.

"I know. I'm sorry. Forgive me, and I hope to prove to you that I'm eternally grateful," she said.

"You can thank me by being my listening, trusting wife, as I'm grateful you did," said Khaled, and wiped her tears away.

"So tell me again," said Jayida, her cheek nestled into his scarless neck. She wanted them to always be like this, wrapped into each other as one under Yassu's wide shining cloak. His breath deepened, as it did each time he shared this worst—and best—story of their life.

"While you napped in the tent at the Banu 'Abs, 'Antarah and I talked. As he'd been from the beginning, he was honest and now wanted to open his heart, so that despite the circumstances of our meeting, we knew we had an understanding and budding friendship. Thankfully, the last push out of his cautious reluctance had been your recognition of their beloved Yassu-serving mother. He cited again his horrible ordeal with Al-Mundhir, and what could've easily been their cruel end if it hadn't been for their mother's loyal faith and timely, good-natured help. He'd vowed that he'd never stand by and allow that to happen to other innocents if he could prevent it. His journey and glorious return from Taysafun had changed him, and at his return he told his mother that he wanted to show it, beginning with his skin. Without a sound or grimace he sat as his mother cut into the skin of his scarred back with a blade, and filled the bloody round gashes with ash to create a series of raised bumps in the mark of a cross. He might be a long way from his mother's heavenly faith, but as he inhaled the incense swirling around them, and tested his strength like the straight-faced youths who refused to show or admit pain, he thought it was a fitting start," said Khaled.

Jayida squeezed him tighter, remembering 'Antarah's stiff back and side-sleeping, dutifully waiting for the scars to heal as he wanted. He might've never expected to show it to anyone else except maybe 'Ablah, but from the 'Abs's shocked horror that she'd never forget, she knew that it had worked as he'd intended and made its powerful memorable impact.

"Then," continued Khaled, "All too experienced with his own tribe's ways, it was his idea that if things should take a dark turn—as he sadly knew all too much about—he proposed that I should feign defeat, as he stood alone and took responsibility for killing me. I'll never forget his pained air when he said that even if it didn't finally succeed for him, not even with such a hard strike before the tribe, then at least I'd be alive and it would put this matter to rest from our side. Still, it had to look believable, requiring some sign of bloodshed, so 'Antarah vowed to be careful, but only feign a scratch at my neck, while a pouch of Awassi lamb's blood—prepared by his mother—and concealed in his clothing would provide the desired effect. The added lying claim of poison would predictably keep the 'Abs at bay, and ensure that 'Antarah handle all aspects of my falsely slain body. To remove the tedious and costly concern of burial, along with potential supernatural revenge at my death, 'Antarah offered to shroud my body and have it returned to our family. That way, any risk was all on him, and the helpers in the matter were none other than Shaybub, their mother, and *sayyid* Zoheir's son Hashem who, unlike his older brother Ahmar, had always been friendly to him.

Right after you'd escaped, 'Ablah found 'Antarah and told only him about you, unaware herself of my real situation. This early notice allowed 'Antarah to alert me and gather my belongings. Some of his last words to me were: *Now they'll know that things have changed for good. And maybe when the time is right, we'll see each other again*, said 'Antarah, and when we embraced one last time, I sent a thought to Ayida and Liya, too, whom I'd told him about. Shaybub made sure I got far enough with no one suspecting a thing, let alone tracking me."

Jayida always took a deep breath at this point, as if it could somehow make the next part easier to hear.

"I'd barely left the 'Abs when I met Majid, Amr, and their men, who'd found your good father wounded by a roaming small band of 'Abs just west of where I'd trailed. Without knowing it—or probably from his natural, loving guidance—your blessed father's encounter had likely deterred attention from Shaybub and I," said Khaled, his voice cracking.

"Why was he there?" Jayida sniffled, trying to sound as cheerful as her selfless father would want them to be.

"'I couldn't let my daughter and son face such danger alone,' your father said, and for the first time in my life I knew I had a real father in him," said Khaled, as a tear wet his cheek.

Jayida cleared her throat and took over.

"My blessed father's arrow wound at the side of his chest, dangerously near his heart, had practically knocked him out for the next days, all the way to our meeting that I was sure marked my insanity." She paused, let a smirk creep over her lips. "But there was someone as unnerved as I was, in his own way."

Khaled nodded. "I told blessed Amr and Hatim that we'd never forget what they've done for us. But that this must stay between us, and we must never forget that 'Antarah is not our enemy, even if his conniving tribe keeps instigating. As expected, Amr protested that such a tale should go untold, while allowing them this horrid and underved glory that they're most unworthy of."

"But we reminded him that it had to be so, at least for the time being. We know the truth, and are grateful to live to share it with them," said Jayida, recalling his words from 'Ukaz. "So we pushed on north to Tayyi, with an eye on our back to any pursuit, which never came. We bid goodbye to Hatim and continued northwest to Tayma, praying *yaba* would recover or at least hang on until Bosra. *Yama* pulled her hair at the sight of him, and with *Umm* Jarida they clung to his side, while your mother thanked Heaven incessantly for your safety. Samaw'al also seethed with disbelief, half-joking that they had all the means at their disposal to wipe out the Banu 'Abs—if only they were those kinds of men themselves. But the noble are always few, as his verse said, and the decree not to avenge, shared by Nasr and *yaba*, was stronger than all of us, especially when the more time passed it was clear that they weren't coming after all. We paid our renewed respects to *siddi* Gayas and *sitti* Rumayma in saving and protecting *yaba*'s life, and made our preparations," said Jayida.

"With some reluctance," continued Khaled, "*Sha'ir* Hakim, Abjar, and Majid finally accepted my handing over and separation from Tayma's duties, even as they all professed their loyalty by managing my shares and keeping me informed of developments, considering it would always be my rightful home. I didn't need to tell them that either my father will be proud of my new life, or he'll stay far away."

Jayida nodded. "As for Amr, he insisted on coming with us all the way to Bosra to ensure our safety, and reward us with Wadi Jadar, Al-Andarin, and local Adhri'at wines. And so, we all tearfully witnessed *yaba*'s last moments, from meeting *baba* Eliyas to taking his last breath in the place of his birth," sighed Jayida.

"Back home at last, back to where you began," said Khaled and took her hands in his. "Not a day will pass that I don't thank Yassu for you. He knows how I called on him with all my unworthy soul, heart, and guts that you would listen to what I said. I don't care what people think or say about us: we know who we serve. He brought me to you, who've given my life more meaning than I could've imagined. You have to know how you inspired, and keep inspiring me, too. You risked much, we both have. Let some simple minds think it's weak, but if anyone wants to test us, they have only to come find us, and see what kind of deathless ghosts we are. Now let's begin another blessed day in our piece of earthly paradise."

"*Aywa,* my wise husband," she said and sealed it with a kiss.

They rose and began their morning routine of washing in their water room with irrigated water delivered right to their metal faucet decorated with a cross. They donned simple robes, fed the doves Azraq and Azraqa, and their mother-daughter cat friends Ramila and Ramiya, then ate their first meal of bread and local cheese topped with smooth olive oil, along with buttermilk. On a nearby table were bowls full of pomegranates, and grapes and dates covered in nets.

Part of the marriage bond had to include being in each other's heads, and though she once questioned it, she ultimately knew how wise his decision had been. It had been out of the question to tell her of the plan; it had to look believable after all, and nothing convinced as much as a wailing woman in love—a remark that earned him pinches as much as it filled her with constantly renewed gratitude. That he had taken such care to create a convincingly heartbreaking tale proved as much his commitment to her as to effective storytelling. Neither had he been as worried about being wounded, as he was that they'd be discovered and that she might suffer for it, yet another mark of his generous love.

As much as she'd never tire of hearing the story, the alarming aspect always resurfaced, cementing the lesson in her mind: how easy it could've been for her to do something she'd later regret, and would've been unnecessary—like killing 'Ablah, 'Antarah, or anyone else from the tribe, no matter how much it seemed to make sense and be justified at the time. She thanked Yassu for having made her hear that stillness dwelling deep within; that inner knowing that had insisted she just *keep going*. And keep going they would, with her as his proudly supporting wife, who would one day forget what it even meant or felt like to want to be against him.

She followed Khaled outside to their large plot of rich volcanic land split into two parts for their camels and horses to graze in, along with their Awassi sheep, long-eared Hijazi goats, and chicken, quail, and pigeon pens. Khaled's pigeon-blue Ghassanid mare Aminah hurried over to the fence, along with her white stallion Adil, and his kin the cream pair Luluwa and Al-Asal, and the grey pair Al-Makhmal and Sababa, gifted by *sayyid* Hudayfa of Ghatafan at their wedding. Only the first of the seven was missing.

"I miss Kamila, too," sighed Jayida, as she stretched her arm out and pet them all.

The day that her father passed away, the mare was nowhere to be seen. They searched high and low, and with her kind father as the one who'd rescued her, Jayida suspected that she'd gone out into the desert to seek her own rest alone.

They filled baskets with eggs and went back in and washed up. They changed into crisp cream robes and headdresses made of cotton from Jericho, embellished by their mother's skillfully woven belts. For the final touch they dabbed themselves in rose-scented water, ready to attend the holy cathedral.

They came out just as her mother appeared from her home paces away across from them. Zoraya led *baba* Eliyas by one arm as his other waved his cane in perceptive greeting, his cheerfulness strong enough to enliven the whole region. *Umm* Jarida and Khamra arrived moments later, their light robes matching their own gentle glow.

Jayida's heart pinched again to know that this new living arrangement suited them all. With her mother as the most recent widow, the women had a deepened bond in each other and caring for their blind elder, who loved the company since his own wife Zahriyy had long since passed. Despite his blindness *baba* Eliyas had an unceasing happiness about him, ready to shower them with endless stories at any moment, which *Umm* Jarida often filled in with her own Taghlib tales. There was happiness in that simple joy and gratefulness for the gift of life, however it came, and the safety it provided added to their wish to grow their family.

Together they walked in pairs east towards the cathedral, its dome glistening in the sunlight making her think of the great Hagia Sophia in Constantinople after which it was modeled. Dedicated to the saints Sergios, Bakchos, and Leontios, three Rûm soldiers who'd suffered martyrdom for their faith in Yassu, the circular cathedral enclosed in a square shape was made of solid basalt, like most of the surrounding buildings.

The heavenly incense fragrance swept over them as soon as they entered the church, adorned with columns, and carved with crosses, grape vines, leaves, and niches into the walls. Khaled took over guiding *baba* Eliyas, and they followed behind him down the aisle lined with benches. The blessed smoke wafted across the mosaics adorning the walls, depicting scenes of Yassu's life—the baptism at the Jordan River, walking on water at nearby Tabariyya—that seat of Israelite religious learning—the feeding of the five thousand, the crucifixion at Golgotha, and the ascension to Heaven from the Mount of Olives.

As they approached the altar, Khaled and *baba* Eliyas turned west to sit behind *malik* Al-Harith and his sons Jabalah and Al-Mundhir, while Jayida and the rest of their female kin sat across from them on the other side, behind his wife Mawiyah and daughter Halima.

Each time, as the seats quickly filled, Jayida took in the details anew, marveling at how they'd come to live in this place full of marvelous history and holiness. The altar had a pulpit hosting an open, thick leatherbound Bible, whose silver plaque cover had a long cross and a saint standing at each side of it. The crisp pages covered in ink encompassed the Peshitta, and a copy of the recent version by Philoxenus of Mabbug, adding five missing holy books to the Peshitta. Next to it was a gilded silver chalice with a gold cross, and a silver plate with a cross flanked by an angel at each side of it.

In front of the pulpit was a marble table hosting simmering gold incense burners designed with grape vines. High above on the wall, a large carved cross and, under it, the similar faces of Sergios, Bakchos, and Leontios looked down upon them like angels.

Mubassir Ayyub appeared before them, his demeanor bright as he made the sign of the cross over them.

"Let us give thanks to Yassu for another glorious day," said *mubassir* Ayyub. "Our blessed *malik* has several news he wishes to share with us all."

At once, *malik* Al-Harith stood and joined him, as all eyes followed him. With his crisp dark robes, jeweled scabbard and belt, and serious air tinged with pride that some would mistake for hardness or anger, he was a more poised version of what she'd seen of him earlier at the graves.

"We give thanks for this day and for your faithful presence here. Since there are both sad and good news, I'll begin with the first." Frowning, *malik* Al-Harith cleared his throat, then went on. "It is with a heavy heart that I share that the talented poet Imru Al-Qays of Kindah has left us. The Lord has called His creation to his most important journey back to Him. So let us implore Yassu and Saint Sergios and his companions to keep watch over us all. We pray for his soul's peace, and we shall always treasure our memories of him and his gift of poetry that we all enjoyed so recently."

Jayida's jaw dropped, as echoes of shock resounded all around her. His pause said it all, how Al-Numan had been alive then too, to enjoy this poet's verses, and whose ancient namesake inscription carved into basalt lay just east of them in Namara from the time of *Qaysar* Constantine. In an instant she heeded his first poetic line and wept for him, for his family and daughter Hind, for his constant struggles, and for these hard news that she'd also have to give Yazida. Her mother gripped her hand, and she took comfort in thinking that the wandering king might finally find rest in the only eternal kingdom. She sighed, and a flash of light filled her mind's eye: perhaps 'Antarah would step in to add his own slave-princely-poetic legacy to the land, born out of Aksumite-Himyarite and Hijazi-Najdi struggles.

"May Yassu have mercy on his soul," said *mubassir* Ayyub.

"Please join us in reciting and contemplating this passage of the thirty-ninth book of Job, in honor of all our recent losses and to remind us of His greatness," said *malik* Al-Harith.

"Do you give the horse his strength or clothe his neck with a flowing mane? Do you make him leap like a locust, striking terror with his proud snorting? He paws fiercely, rejoicing in his strength, and charges into the fray. He laughs at fear, afraid of nothing; he does not shy away from the sword. The quiver rattles against his side, along with the flashing spear and lance. In frenzied excitement he eats up the ground; he cannot stand still when the trumpet sounds. At the blast of the trumpet he snorts, 'Aha!' He catches the scent of battle from afar, the shout of commanders and the battle cry!" said *malik* Al-Harith, his eyes fiering with equal parts zeal and sadness.

With *Umm* Jarida and her mother gripping her hands at each side, this time her emotion flowed for her kind father who would always be there, when she tended the animals and plants, pounded the bread dough, or pulled back her bowstring, his protective wings grazing her cheek and whispering in her ear. Faint as a breeze, it would be all she needed to know that they weren't alone and all was well.

"Now, for some good news," said *malik* Al-Harith, his smile brightening his appealing face. "It is with great happiness that I announce that *Qaysar* Justinian has vanquished the plague and healed! We send continued prayers to his health, and for the success of his new Nea Church in Jerusalem, which is fast approaching its completion. May his recovery and achievements inspire us all," he said with praying hands. "Just as importantly, today we also praise his wife, the Believing Queen Empress Theodora for her undying support of our shared faith. It is thanks to her that our chosen *Abba* Jacob Baradeus has been consecrated as Bishop at Constantinople."

A wave of cheerful approval swept through the crowd.

"Let us pray to Yassu to bring them back safely to our shores to continue in their work of sharing and spreading our unwavering faith in His single, divine nature. We thank Him for this time of fruitful change and growth for our church according to His will, and which we trust King Abraha is doing his part in enforcing."

He shone with humbled pride at these good news, proving his commitment to his church's expansion, including further south and possibly even as far as Wadi Al-Qura and beyond. The next time she'd visit the Banu Sa'd, there might be some new churches along the way.

As they recited the Lord's Prayer, it occurred to Jayida that something about his striking appearance and bearing had to be connected to his deep faith. It was more than just honoring his father Jabalah's one-nature creed and service to *Qaysar* Anastasius; it was like a certainty and unshakeable confidence that she herself wanted to grow in. When he spoke with such fervor and conviction of the single, divine nature of Yassu, it reminded her of some of the debates they'd seen at 'Ukaz. She would've easily bet that *malik* Al-Harith could override all the competing debates on religions at 'Ukaz, or anywhere else, and perhaps even win some converts if he tried. With all of their community's differences and similarities, it was reassuring to be among them and keep learning about her forgotten kin's ways.

"We should also use this day as one of remembrance, for those of our cousin tribe in Najran who bravely died for their faith twenty years ago this year. As our father Jabalah helped the Najranites seeking his help, so I pray to offer equal assistance to those faithful in need," said *malik* Al-Harith. "I'm also honored to add that we've begun work on translating the Bible texts to *'arabi*, for the great benefit of our growing community," he nodded and glanced in her direction, then Khaled's. It moved her that they were growing in their faith just as *malik* Al-Harith's church was set to expand.

Mubassir Ayyub stepped forth and, holding the glistening chalice, he raised it above them and made a sweeping sign of the cross with it.

"The holy blood of Christ, the divine physician," he said. "As the martyred Rhum was made to drink her granddaughter's blood at Najran, so we drink His pure, spotless life-giving blood." He turned to *malik* Al-Harith at his side. The *malik* bowed his head to him, and drank from the chalice handed to him.

Mawiyah leaned into Halima and whispered in her ear, and with a nod, Halima stood and got the liturgical plate, her saffron dress and matching headdress making her the picture of a bright spring blossom. With a subdued yet wilfull demeanor, Halima stood meekly next to the *mubassir,* the bits of bread that represented the flesh of Christ surely also reminding her of her recently slain brother Al-Numan. Much as her name intended, Halima diffused a graceful self-control that reminded Jayida a bit of herself at that young age.

As they stood and followed the forming line to the *mubassir,* Jayida steadily breathed away her gentle conflict, relieved by the reality of her ongoing changes. Like the violent hagiographies of holy men and women, the flashing images of gruesome deaths and endless wailing used to shake her to the core, threatening to unleash her rage. Though she might never fully love these details, she was beginning to understand when *mubassir* Ayyub said that it was meant to show the miraculous, boundary-breaking power of faith, and that their deaths served a higher purpose, beckoning men out of darkness and into Yassu's everlasting light.

Still, she'd come to know that it would always be a lurking challenge, ready to erupt if she fed it; this fiery urge to unleash her wrath and annihilate any potential threat. The darkness within tortured and taunted her at every moment to regress, suggesting that she would not always react the restrained way she had at Banu 'Abs. There was a time this knowledge had frightened her and torn her soul, but that already felt like long ago. Because recognizing it was the first step, and each day, Jayida was learning and deepening her faith, rooted in the conviction that there was a deeper meaning, that things didn't just revolve around one, or even a few, persons seeking to indulge in that sense of petty justice so common to some men.

Even after everything, it was a weight lifted to know that she might not even truly hate anyone, but rather their darkness that they fed, changing them in the process into something unholy, herself included. Each time she'd thought she was being strong when filled with the revengeful impulse to kill, she'd instead been made aware to cede and flee from her wrathful evil. It wasn't until later that she realized she was in part being shown a way to love more deeply, something some sadly mistook for weakness.

It had taken eighteen springs, but finally she was beginning to understand that the security she'd sought her whole life could only come from Him. The principles of *muruwa*—with its bravery, patient self-control, strength in the face of attack, hospitality, respect of women and honor, and protection of the weak and orphans—had guided her, but now took on deeper importance in His service. With her new peace came a release of her fears, confirming He'd always been there even when she didn't know it. She could never repay it, and still, there was a joy to knowing she would never stop trying, just as she would never stop loving Khaled. They were two flames that made one unceasing fire in Yassu.

When her turn came, Jayida eagerly sipped the sweet local Adhri'at wine, contrasting the plain unleavened bread, and said a prayer of thanks for *siddi* Ayan's treasure that had been returned to its rightful home. *Malik* Al-Harith had been shocked that they'd been willing to offer the whole treasure to the church, as much to prove their kin ties as to thank him for welcoming them. Instead, they'd mutually settled on a few gold and silver pieces remaining in the cathedral as votive gifts to his memory, while some of the other pieces found their places in their homes, or was stored away for safekeeping. In a way, it also reminded her of that day five springs earlier when, amidst their training, they'd seen the passing caravan carrying holy relics of the slain of Najran.

"Now, please join us in enjoying some hymns. We've chosen some by Saint Ephrem the Syrian, in honor of Jacob Baradeus who appreciates him as we do, and some by Romanos the Melodist, whose chants grace the great Hagia Sophia," said *malik* Al-Harith.

He sat down, while his children went to *mubassir* Ayyub who handed them each some sheets, then stood next to him in a row by order of age. Jabalah stood west, with Al-Mundhir at center, and Halima to the east. They glanced at their parents and after a moment, began.

"Come, let us make our love the great censer of the community, and offer on it as incense our hymns and our prayers to Him who made His cross a censer for the Divinity, and offered from it on behalf of us all. He that was above stooped down to those who were beneath, to distribute His treasures to them," they recited from Saint Ephrem's Homily on Our Lord.

Their melodious voices recited as one in Syriac, while Jayida imagined the heavenly-scented Yassu speaking in a similar way, as they transitioned to one of Ephrem's Hymns on Paradise.
"The Lord of all
is the treasure store of all things:
upon each according to his capacity
He bestows a glimpse
of the beauty of His hiddenness,
of the splendor of His majesty.
He is the radiance who, in His love,
makes everyone shine
— the small, with flashes of light from Him,
the perfect, with rays more intense,
but only His child is sufficient
for the might of His glory.
Accordingly as each here on earth
purifies his eye for Him,
so does he become more able to behold
His incomparable glory;
accordingly as each here on earth
opens his ear to Him,
so does he become more able to grasp
His wisdom;
accordingly as each here on earth
prepares a recepticle for Him,
so is he enabled to carry
a small portion of His Riches.
The Lord who is beyond measure
measures out nourishment to all,
adapting to our eyes the sight of Himself,
to our hearing His voice,
His blessing to our appetite,
His wisdom to our tongue.
At His gift
blessings swarm,
for this is always new in its savor,
wonderfully fragrant,
adaptable in strength,

resplendent in its colors."

They went on to Romanos the Melodist's hymn on baptism, their voices raising such harmony that she had the impression of being among angels. How could she have understood, let alone believed the unexplainable before? It was only after hearing them for the first time, such soothing, indescribably celestial sounds that she understood how it could be so praised. It was like this loving light bursting from deep within, never to be put out.

When the service finished, they followed the procession outside, and walked around the church three times, the spotless blue veil of sky as if beaming over them. The assembly gradually parted ways, as some gathered to hand out or collect grains and weapons, while they drifted through the colonnaded surrounding areas. Soon the nearly month-long Bosra market would be bustling with merchants from near and far, smaller yet no less important than 'Ukaz.

"We're going back to prepare a meal; don't be too long," said her mother, and left them to walk around and wallow in their mixed thoughts.

"I can't believe we won't see him again; no Kindah revival through Imru," sighed Jayida.

"Me, either." Khaled shook his head. "So then, what's next?"

"Let's see," she said.

They strolled north of the cathedral to the basilica built in the time of the first Imru Al-Qays and *Qaysar* Constantine. As they reached the façade of the basilica, she imagined a younger *baba* Eliyas, and *siddi* Ayan and *sitti* Wafa gazing at the same Latin inscription about Legio III Cyrenaica. As *malik* Al-Harith had said, this legion established by Marc Antony had been stationed in Egypt, until *Qaysar* Hadrian relocated it to Bosra. Inside, the niches had seashell motifs built into the curving roof, a remnant of its Rûm pre-Yassu-loving past.

They continued southwest along the colonnaded main street, holding hands like the children in love that they were, floating along ancient basalt Nabataean and Rûm nymphaeum, kalybe, and triumphal arches. She recalled that one of these arches was dedicated to Cornelius Palma, the Rûm governor of the region who'd managed the annexation of Bosra and became its first governor in the time of *Qaysar* Trajan.

They reached the theater, and once more admired the mosaics of camel caravans, hunting, date harvesting, and pigeon breeding, amusing Jayida that it could easily be themselves doing these things. With the thousands of colored stones and time needed to create the images, even some that looked like interwoven rope bracelets, they made a strikingly detailed contrast from the cave drawings Nasr had shown her in their last outing. She recalled the Hand-Up Woman who'd fascinated her most, and could've been a goddess, a cheerful patron, a dancer, pulling her hair, or even carrying wood on her head.

"You know that Hand-Up Woman? I never thought of it before but now I'd like to think she was praising the One true God. So from now on, she's the Praising Woman," said Jayida, returning Khaled's smile.

They drifted to the courtyard from which they imagined the actors entering the stage, and glanced at the Latin inscription *malik* Al-Harith said bore the name of *Qaysar* Marcus Aurelius. At least here it wasn't as lonely a commemoration as the one made to him at the isolated Ruwwafa temple.

Jayida pulled Khaled out onto the stage, and for a moment they stood side by side, facing the vast, empty half moon of ascending seats that could fit at least ten thousand spectators. When she'd first seen it, she'd been startled by the thought that she might've only been pretending her whole life without realizing it, and if she would always remain so, like some shifty *jinniyeh* who wouldn't ever progress to something better. But as she tilted her head back, with gilded columns behind her and the blue open space ahead, she knew it couldn't have been the same when it'd been for her survival. Amidst all the hard lessons, she'd come to know that the author of her life was the first and most important one for whom she had to act and be seen. Perhaps the raw reality of such conflicted moments had been part of pushing Imru and 'Antarah to their verses, seeking to draw out that elusive parallel realm to help them better face life's challenges.

"Yazida would like this," said Jayida with a hint of bittersweetness. "Come on, fighter," she smirked, and he followed her up the long steps, all the way to the top. Even from this distance they had a good view of the shrunken stage, and she wondered about all those who'd sat there before them and those who would still come. Despite the differences, to imagine that part of her family had been there made everything more familiar, less intimidating.

"The climb is always worth it," said Khaled, after a moment of catching their breath and taking it all in.

The breathtaking view stretched panoramically all around them, with their home to the west, and the Bosra Cathedral and several cistern pools to the east. Further north beyond them stretched the valley, full of *malik* Al-Harith's precious camels and horse reserves—ready as much for battle as for racing—as well as weapon factories and dormitories for pilgrims passing to and from the Holy Land. Her heart pinched to know that their Zahir camels were now part of serving the *malik*, too.

"So what does my lovely wife order, after quietly laying low?" smirked Khaled.

"Traveling, of course; there's still so much to see! There's your kin at Philippopolis, rightly named after *Qaysar* Philippus, and nearby Jabiyah with *malik* Al-Harith's court and the monastery of Saint Sergios crowning the hill. Then Imru's inscription at Namara, and the inscription honoring the death of Queen Mawiyya at Anasartha. While in that region we should also see Saint Sim'an the Stylite's pillar west of Aleppo."

"*Aywa*, you've been busy planning—" Khaled stopped as she made the hand sign for him to wait.

"Then we might veer back down to Tabariyya where Yassu walked on water—and glimpse that seat of Israelite religious learning, while we're at it—then on to His baptism at the Jordan River, then Bethlehem and Jerusalem. Chief among them the Mount of Olives where He ascended, and where Pelagia of Antioch lived disguised as a monk in her cell, her identity concealed until her death. Not to mention there must be some Shamshun mosaic at some synagogue in Gaza; it's worth a hunt. On the way back we'll visit churches decorated with tesserae at nearby Jerash, and possibly finish with that overdue pilgrimage to Jabal Harun monastery."

"Set firmly on doing all this in a day, huh? My conquering *kahin*-general, and with a plague in our midst," chuckled Khaled.

"Only a few days... or months. And anyway, there'll always be something happening, though it is comforting to know one can survive it." She clasped her hands. "I just thought we'd do some now, carefully, of course. You know, before our child gets here and it gets a bit busier," said Jayida, her gaze narrowing.

Khaled stared, his face contorting unlike she'd ever seen. His brow and lip twitched, as if forgetting their functions.

"*Eh-esh?*" he said.

"*Na'am*," she laughed.

He jumped up, lifted her in his arms and kissed her, then settled his strong palms around her stomach, at once protective and fearing his own strength.

"Blessed Yassu," his voice cracked, and he shook his happy tears away. "I know it's *majnun*, but after everything, I almost feel like we're invincible."

"I know. Every day I grow more amazed by what He does," said Jayida, and they sat for a moment in awed silence.

"So what do you say? Are they together yet?" said Khaled after a while.

"I hope so. Either way I hope we'll see him again someday," she sighed.

Jayida let the pleasant image of 'Antarah fill her vision, the one she'd so often told Khaled about. One day, on another as beautiful as this one, they'd be promenading in the Bosra market, their children leading their prized Zahir camels for potential trade. She wouldn't be worried, and even amused by the mixed reports that might spread about her and her husband Khaled. *Had they, or had they not been seen at Bosra and other parts of Al-Sham?* With the sound of skilled verses leading them on, they'd float through the crowd to its source, and meet 'Antarah's welcoming smiling gaze in kindred acknowledgement. From the way he spoke, everyone would assume that he was *sha'ir* of his lucky tribe, but his triumph was in knowing that he'd always been so even if he wasn't granted the official title. Sometimes, 'Ablah was there at his side, glowing as one from their blissful union, and sometimes Shaybub was with him, also freed at last. Often it was just him, walking with one foot here and one in the beyond, like Nasr had done. But always, his love for 'Ablah permeated, all-encompassing, wiping out all obstacles. And it was in those moments that Jayida knew that, like Imru, his story would always live on, no matter if and how his verses and life story might be praised, criticized, altered, buried, and forgotten, then unearthed again across the sands of time. As his angelic mother Zerafina had shown them, there might always be a lurking evil eye thirsting for lives to come clashing against each other, but most importantly, there was also Yassu, the only one stronger than that.

"I've been thinking about that passage," said Jayida with melancholy creeping over them. "How I once hated it, caught between wanting to forget and remember it—as much for when it happened as what I thought it meant. But now, it sounds like it was about himself, and I hope not a premonition."

In her wild grief she hadn't considered that 'Antarah's timely choice for reciting poetry might hint that there'd be no wedding for them to attend, or that he was just making the most poetic and explosive impact out of every moment, as his difficult life had taught him.

Khaled took a deep breath and let 'Antarah's words flow.

"With quick thrust of my pliant blade
I felled a decent man
his jugular hissing, split like a harelip,
spurting 'andam resin red.
'Ablah, Daughter of Mutaz, ask
the riders if you want to hear
how I live in my horse's saddle,
swimming through troops
exposed to spear thrusts
wound after wound
charging the great harvest of bows.
The riders will tell you—

I enter the fray
then decline the spoils
For my victory is through the cross."

The fatality was almost too much to bear, but she had to remind herself that though a masterfully crafted poem, it was still just a poem, and didn't have to forever seal fates, or only mean one thing. That had to be part of its magic, whose true meaning Yassu helped understand.

Was it true that what was not remembered was lost? And would a story be forgotten by not being talked about? Jayida had often pondered over it while they foraged in Wadi Al-Wafra, and sometimes even dreaded the answer. But at last she realized that it would always be there, waiting for the right timing and words to be shared all over again.

Only He knew when she'd be ready to tell their story, and when someone would hear her faint, and at times chaotic whispering *qareen* enough to set it down in a new language, just as she was in the process of learning Syriac and the mysterious spiritual language of Yassu. What was certain was that after all this time, she knew she had much more life inside her than she'd ever thought possible. Yassu himself was proof that there was more, and there would always be. Like poetry, love was a miraculous fire that flourished with its constant fuel of right words and actions molded into something better.

If ever they dreaded that, in time, poetry would die in its war with the poets, or that they'd endlessly weep at the memory of many a beloved—as suggested by the opening lines of the princely 'Antarah and Imru's *qasidah*—the fear would vanish in the joyful peace gifted by Yassu's eternal, deathless love.

AUTHOR'S NOTE

'Antarah ibn Shaddad was a sixth-century poet of the Banu 'Abs, of whom little is known other than he had an "Arab" (itself a debatable term) father and a Black mother. In the Middle Ages, and as was popular across cultures at the time, his life story was woven into a long epic known as *Sīrat 'Antar*. One segment of it is the story of Khaled and Jaida (her name entailing various spellings and variations). When I first encountered that story in a college literature class, I was instantly hooked into wanting to recreate it from a larger—and more accurate—historical context, primarily through Jayida's experience.

While my story is centered around the three main characters of Jayida, Khaled, and 'Antarah, from my knowledge it is 'Antarah who figures—no matter how in/accurately—in the historical record. It goes without saying that after years of toiling, all three—along with the others—have come to feel very real to me. The majority of the other characters are also based on historical people, such as Al-Harith ibn Jabalah and Abu Karib, Shah Khosrow, Negus Kaleb, and King Abraha, to name a few. Though the poets' factual existence may be debateable, it was a necessary opportunity to also involve the following: Imru Al-Qays (Kindah), Hatim (Tayyi), Amr ibn Kulthum (Taghlib), Samaw'al ibn Adiya, and a young Ziyad ibn Muawiyah, known as Al-Nabigha (Dhubyan).

From the inception of this work, my gut feeling has been and remains that the authenticity of pre-Islamic poetry is nonexistent at worst, and highly questionable at best. That in my early research I soon found this sentiment echoed by Mu'allaqat *The Seven Odes* British translator A.J. Arberry was bittersweet to say the least. Even earlier sources of doubt include Egyptian author Dr. Taha Hussein in his controversial *On Pre-Islamic Poetry* published in 1926, and David Samuel Margoliouth's *The Origins of Arabic Poetry* in 1925.

And yet, neither was it conceivable for me to write this book without having any poetry—a component that was at least possibly important in an oral-based society—or for me to make up lengthy verses based on complex parameters and linguistic requirements. This was only further enhanced by my impression that *Sīrat 'Antar*, written as longer fictionalized epics about the poet's life, did not seem to ever include his famed *qasidah*, or ode poem. Instead, it often figures in the equally mysterious and debateable collection called the Mu'allaqat, supposedly named in reference to having been hung in the Kabah at Makka. It's as if these literary genres—distinct as they are—were persistently condemned to live separate, fragmented "lives" apart. Interestingly, as a lover of history and facts to ensure accuracy, I've also been reminded that "imagination" may not exclude tapping into some truths, too—and for which, as a Christian, I would always thank His guidance. As such, it felt increasingly necessary for me to weave the story of 'Antarah's early life and how poetry and his burgeoning *qasidah* might've come about.

Therefore, instead of reinventing the wheel, I thought there had to be ways to rehash aspects of the existing poetry (which are valuable achievements in their own right). The more I worked with my story, the clearer it became which pre-Islamic poets were meaningfully joining the ride. The lingering question of the potential "biographical" nature of poems also helped to shape the characters themselves, even if their poetry might not be in the story. The result is a mixture of translated sources that rings true to the scenes and characters, with less concern for exhaustive poetry inclusion. If nothing else, I like to think that the variety of sources reflect the enduring multicultural and multilingual interest in the pre-Islamic poets, along with the historical person of 'Antarah, and *Sīrat 'Antar* across time.

As noted in the following sources page, the bulk of the poetry I selected for 'Antarah's longer passages are from NYU Press's *War Songs*, translated by James E. Montgomery. A relatively late discovery in my research, not only does this more recent collection differ from older translations, but it has a variety of pieces that were a perfect, timely fit for the 'Antarah I envisioned. It seemed like another fitting cue that the book is dedicated to Peter Heath—author of *The Thirsty Sword* and one of the most important sources I used for context on 'Antarah. With that said, my decision to add some Christian element to 'Antarah's poetry was a combination of listening to music while contemplating the powerful role that Aksumite monarchs played in championing their Christian faith. It also hints at my disagreement with some arguments that "pre-Islamic poetry was not the medium for religious imagery." As I pleasantly found, Christian Syriac writings may often be deemed poetry, too, and could suggest some genre crossovers between religious and secular poetry.

For the other emblematic poet of the sixth century, Imru Al-Qays, I used the 18th century British philologist William Jones's Mu'allaqat translation. I also used him for Amr ibn Kulthum, and adjusted some archaic tones and terms when fitting. (Of note that this collection also includes 'Antarah's poem.) As for the su'luk poet Shanfara, I'm grateful to have found and been allowed to use some of the translation from Michael A. Sells's *Desert Tracings*.

Most of the cited events are also based on historical fact and/or oral traditions. The volcanic winter of 536 has been called "the worst year to be alive" and has been recorded across the world. It may well have played its part in the Justinian plague, too. Overall, one of the most challenging parts of researching for this book has been working with various and at times incomplete and/or contradicting accounts that don't make timelines obvious. As such, any potential date deviances or errors will likely be a mix of my intuitive creative choices and/or the scholarly findings I chose to use.

Over years of research, I've read and consulted numerous books, articles, and media, so while my mentions are far from exhaustive, some titles have certainly stood out for my endeavor. Chief among them is Peter Webb's *Imagining the Arabs*, for an overdue insightful exploration of the construction of pre- and post-Islamic history. Robert G. Hoyland's *Arabia and The Arabs* also deserves a mention for his useful if brief overview of pre-Islamic Arabia, and for being the first book in my collection for this dear project. Peter Heath's *The Thirsty Sword* gives a thorough view into the evolution of *Sīrat 'Antar*, with a summary of this long epic that includes the segment of Khaled and Jaida.

I wish to add a note of appreciation to multi-talented French archeologist and epigraphist Christian Julien Robin, specialist in pre-Islamic Arabia. As recently as October 2021 (in the midst of the paralyzing pandemic), he and his team discovered dozens of inscriptions in Hima, northeast of Najran. I find such dedication to answering the call of work inspiring and telling in different ways.

Some other noteworthy entities from a variety of fields that helped breathe life into my tale include: M.C.A. Macdonald, Werner Daum, Stuart Munro-Hay, Michael Lecker, Jérémie Schiettecatte, Yasmine Zahran, Irfan Shahid, Peter Brown, Susan Ashbrook Harvey, Sebastian Brock, Zbigniew T. Fiema, Pauline Piraud-Fournet, Rugare Rukuni, Sidney Smith, Sidney H. Griffith, Philip Wood, and Rémy Cottevieille-Giraudet.

I recommend all of the books and authors cited here and in the sources page, and am grateful to the skilled translated work that I was able to use. I like to think that the poets in question are grateful for it and their inclusion, no matter the (unavoidable?) passing effects of time.

As has been rightly said, a story never really ends: the writer just chooses where to stop.

For some subsequent historical events, it is satisfying to know that Al-Harith did go on to have some justice, namely in the Battle of Yawm Halima in 554 AD. The battle is named after his daughter Halima, during which the Lakhmid Al-Mundhir was killed, though at the cost of his oldest son Jabalah's life. It's also said that Halima was also betrothed then. Once more, I enjoy imagining that Jayida and Khaled, among others, may have played their part in that, too. Given the potentially dubious nature of accounts, determining what came next for 'Antarah is more of a challenge—or forgiving—but may have involved another long feud sparked by a contest of horses known as the War of Dahis and Ghabra, between 'Abs and Dhubyan (the poet Al-Nabigha's tribe).

Somewhat ironically, it is Al-Harith's son Al-Mundhir who succeeded him, and curiously carried the very name of his bitterest Lakhmid-Nasrid enemy. Like his father, the Ghassanid-Jafnid Al-Mundhir had great military successes, and arguably even higher titles than his father. But as a staunch Miaphysite, his relations with Chalcedonian Constantinople grew increasingly tense, and he was eventually exiled to Sicily.

Despite their oft-ignored and/or downplayed significant contributions, in part fueled by biased accounts from both Middle Eastern and Eastern Roman sources, Al-Harith and Al-Mundhir have left a legacy that endures to this day. Al-Harith was the longest reigning Christian "Arab" ruler, while Al-Mundhir was considered the last important Ghassanid ruler. It is the disintegration of the Byzantine-Ghassanid alliance that is often seen as at least partially facilitating the subsequent Persian and Muslim invasions in the region.

Last but definitely not least, I'm grateful for this initially intimidating work that first inspired me to become a historical fiction writer. Through my inexperience, I think I unconsciously sensed the work that was ahead of me, and partially for that reason I self-published three other works in the meantime. The most striking aspect of this significant "delay" centers around my shifting identity as a Christian and writer, which would've yielded a very different book, and one which I'm sure I wouldn't be nearly as satisfied with had it been completed much sooner. I'm not excluding that it might've also been the influence of that famous "Arab time"... and which still conveniently led me to conclude the book 1500 years after the 523 events of Najran.

SOURCES

Information on sources used are as follows:

*EPHREM THE SYRIAN
P. 15. *"There are two sides..."* to *"created all, different."* This quote is my combination of selections from two different Rhythm passages.
Morris, John Brande. *Selected works of S. Ephrem the Syrian : translated out of the original Syriac, with notes and indices* [Oxford : John Henry Parker, 1847]. Pp. 412-413, #16 and p. 285, #1. https://archive.org/details/selectedworksofs00ephrrich/page/412/mode/2up
https://archive.org/details/selectedworksofs00ephrrich/page/284/mode/2up

P. 44. *"The fool makes"* to *"for his soul."* Nisibene Hymn 40, #6.
Schaff, P. (ed.), 1898, 'Nicene and post-Nicene fathers', series 2, vol. XIII. Part II. Gregory the Great, Ephraim Syrus, Aphrahat. P. 203, #6 Nisibene hymns, 40. https://archive.org/details/cu31924092898653/page/n215/mode/2up

P. 196. *"In every place"* to *"fountain of mysteries."*
Morris, John Brande. *Selected works of S. Ephrem the Syrian*, p. 117, #4. https://archive.org/details/selectedworksse01ephrgoog/page/n142/mode/2up

P. 512. *"The figure has passed"* to *"nourished."*
Schaff, P. (ed.), 1898, 'Nicene and post-Nicene fathers', series 2, vol. XIII. Part II. P. 270, #17. https://archive.org/details/cu31924092898653/page/n283/mode/2up

P. 597. *"Come, let us make"* to *"to them."*
Schaff, P. (ed.), 1898, 'Nicene and post-Nicene fathers', series 2, vol. XIII. Part II. Pp. 308-309, #9. https://archive.org/details/cu31924092898653/page/n321/mode/2up

Pp. 598-599. *"The Lord of all"* to *"resplendent in its colors."*
Reproduced by permission from St. Vladimir's Seminary Press, *St. Ephrem the Syrian: Hymns on Paradise*, trans. Sebastian Brock (Crestwood, NY: Copyright © 1990), pp. 145-146, Hymn 9:25-27. All rights reserved.

*'ANTARAH
P. 135. *"I saw a white girl"* to *"her servant."* My adaptation from French.
Antar : poème héroïque arabe / d'après la traduction de Marcel Devic ; illustrations en couleurs de E. Dinet. H. Piazza et Cie (Paris), 1898, p. 11. https://gallica.bnf.fr/ark:/12148/bpt6k852296c/f33.item.texteImage

Pp. 141-142 and 148. *"A beautiful virgin"* to *"lovesick lovers."* My adaptation from French.
Antar : poème héroïque arabe / d'après la traduction de Marcel Devic ; illustrations en couleurs de E. Dinet. H. Piazza et Cie (Paris), 1898, pp. 11-12. https://gallica.bnf.fr/ark:/12148/bpt6k852296c/f33.item.texteImage and https://gallica.bnf.fr/ark:/12148/bpt6k852296c/f34.item.texteImage

Pp. 285, 289-290, 522-523, 528, 555-556, 572, and 602-603.
Reproduced by permission from NYU Press, *War Songs*, edited and translated by James E. Montgomery, Copyright © 2018. All rights reserved.

P. 295. *"The words of the blessing"* to *"to come."*
Charles, R.H. *The Book of Enoch*, 1917. My adaptation of Chapter 1, #1. At sacred-texts.com. https://www.sacred-texts.com/bib/boe/boe004.htm

*IMRU
P. 172. *"Oh, though I've"* to *"the Sa'd."*
P. 177. *"Imru chirps"* to *"Banu Sa'd,"* and *"Stay, and"* to *"twisted sand."* My adaptation from William Jones.
Jones, William. *The Moallakát: Or Seven Arabian Poems, Which Were Suspended on the Temple at Mecca* (London: Elmsly, 1782), p. 5, #8; p. 14 #74; p. 5, #1-2. https://books.google.co.uk/books?id=qbBCAAAAcAAJ

P. 185. *"If any of my traits"* to *"new skin."* My adaptation from French.
Les Suspendues – Al Mu'allaqât, trad. Heidi TOELLE © Éditions Flammarion, Paris, 2009. Reproduced by Permission.

*SHANFARA
P. 331. *"Get up"* to *"leave"* and *"Sons"* to *"than you."*
P. 340-341: *"What must"* to *"distant crossings"* and p. 340: *"In this land"* to *"his crimes."*
Page 24 from *Desert Tracings* © 1989 by Michael Sells. Published by Wesleyan University Press. Used by permission.

*AMR IBN KULTHUM
P. 364. *"They feed"* to *"in reverence."*
P. 515. *"This is the potion"* to *"composed."* My adaptation from William Jones.
Jones, William. *The Moallakát: Or Seven Arabian Poems, Which Were Suspended on the Temple at Mecca* (London: Elmsly, 1782). P. 87, #98-101 and p. 88, #104-106. And p. 75, #3. https://books.google.co.uk/books?id=qbBCAA AAcAAJ

*HATIM
Pp. 369-370. My adaptation of On Avarice by Hatem Tai.
Clouston, W.A. *Arabian Poetry*, Glasgow, 1881. At sacred-texts.com. https://www.sacred-texts.com/isl/arp/arp028.htm

ABOUT THE AUTHOR

Born in Brussels, Belgium, Natacha Pavlov is a bilingual Christian writer of German, Russian, and Christian Palestinian heritage. A lifelong book and storytelling enthusiast, her novel *Jayida* (2023) is the fruit of years of research and the project that first made her want to write historical fiction. She is also the author of the historical fiction novel *The Well-Loved Demon* (2022) on the 18th century French King Louis XV, the novella *Nicola's Leg* (2017), and the short story collection *Twisted Reflections* (2015).

She is currently at work on more historical fiction.

Visit her at www.natachapavlov.com.